TEXAS FURY
—
TEXAS SUNRISE

TEXAS FURY

—

TEXAS SUNRISE

TWO NOVELS

FERN MICHAELS

BALLANTINE BOOKS TRADE PAPERBACKS • NEW YORK

2012 Ballantine Books Trade Paperback Edition

Published in the United States by Ballantine Books,
an imprint of The Random House Publishing Group,
a division of Random House, Inc., New York.

BALLANTINE and colophon are registered trademarks
of Random House, Inc.

Texas Fury and *Texas Sunrise* were originally published
in the United States by Ballantine Books,
an imprint of The Random House Publishing Group,
a division of Random House, Inc., in 1989 and 1993.

ISBN 978-0-345-53301-2

Printed in the United States of America

www.ballantinebooks.com

TEXAS FURY

For Albert Phillip Koval, my pappy, and for my sisters, Louise Crisostomo and Doris Ferensic; lost to me, but not forgotten.

Dink
July 23, 1987

I want to thank Dr. Edwin Baker, my cousin, my friend, my confidant. Your wisdom, your unselfishness, your warmth and caring, as well as your daily tell-it-like-it-is pep talks, will always be remembered. My humble thanks, Juney; you're one of a kind.

{{{{{{{{{ CHAPTER ONE }}}}}}}}}

It wasn't your ordinary dime store synthetic satin ground-
breaking ribbon. This was real French satin ribbon, specially
ordered by Amelia Coleman Assante and trimmed with a half
inch of Spanish lace. Yards of the opulent ribbon festooned
the sequined pylons that were manned by a pair of handsome
guards wearing well-fitted cobalt-blue uniforms. The shears,
while not overly large for such a momentous occasion, were
solid gold. "Nothing but the best for this opening," Amelia
cooed to her husband. "The crowd expects it. Smile, darling.
We're going live." Cary Assante looked up at the tiny figure
standing on top of Assante Towers. He watched as one of the
cameramen signalled to the commentator who waited on top
of the building.

"This is Dave Harrison of KBT Eyewitness News reporting
to you live from atop Assante Towers in downtown Austin.
All you armchair viewers should be glad you're viewing this
dedication in your warm living rooms. Today's temperature is
well below the freezing mark. A record breaker, ladies and
gentlemen, but a nice way to start off the Christmas season.
I'll be switching you to Neal Tyler, my associate, in just a
minute, but first I want to tell you a little bit about today's
groundbreaking ceremonies. Cary Assante, the creator of this
architectural immensity, this city-within-a-city known as Miranda, will be cutting the ribbon shortly. I was told before
airtime that a large crowd was not expected due to this record-
breaking cold, but there must be a thousand people down
there. Cary Assante is married to Amelia Coleman, and here
in Texas, anything the Colemans are involved in is major
news. This affair today, ladies and gentlemen, takes the spot-
light away from the oil crisis that's paralyzed our state for so
long.

"The governor and the lieutenant governor are here, as well
as the newly appointed mayor of Miranda. Yes, Miranda will

{1}

have its own mayor, and even its own zip code. Senator Thad Kingsley of Vermont is in attendance with his beautiful wife Billie, who was once married to Moss Coleman. Two of our own congressmen are here, and every socialite in the register is down there, all wearing their best furs. The Crystal City Band is down there, too, as well as the fire department and rescue squad.

"This is a wonderful turnout for Cary Assante, who worked more than ten years to complete this magnificent city within a city. KBT News will be taking you inside Assante Towers tonight for the gala opening in the grand ballroom. The color scheme for tonight's festivities is red and silver, with over fifty thousand poinsettia plants flown here from San Diego. Special heaters were required for the planes and the trucks that transported the plants. It's obvious that no expense was spared for this momentous occasion. And the crowd down below is loving it. This is Dave Harrison, reporting live from Miranda. Back to you, Neal."

The Crystal City marching band swung into its third lusty rendition of "Deep in the Heart of Texas" as Cary Assante and local dignitaries mounted the beribboned dedication platform outside the Miranda Tourist and Information Center. The new mayor of Miranda drew himself up to his full six foot four inches. Thin streams of vapor escaped his pursed lips. He tried valiantly not to shiver in the record-breaking cold, but was failing miserably. His teeth chattered as he made his short speech, which was amplified by an echoing sound system.

"Ladies and gentlemen, this is indeed a proud day for all of us. This marvelous state-of-the-art complex that has taken ten years and billions of dollars to build is your inner city. You who are privileged to live here will never have to stray outside these boundaries. The creators of this masterpiece have thought of everything. But I won't keep you out in this cold or in suspense any longer—I suggest Mr. Assante cut the ribbon right now! I look forward to seeing you all this evening for the gala in Assante Towers. And now," the mayor shouted, "the creator of Miranda, Mr. Cary Assante."

Cary stepped forward, Amelia at his side. Her smile was brilliant and full of pride as she handed her husband the gold shears. "This is your moment, darling. Your dream is officially a reality."

"*Our* dream, babe," Cary whispered. His hand trembled as he cut the shimmering ribbon. He felt light-headed. All about him was a babble of congratulatory voices. The band members made a valiant effort to render still another chorus of "Deep in the Heart of Texas."

Amelia stepped back. This was Cary's time, and he deserved all the accolades. All she wanted was to find Billie and Thad and get inside, where it was warm.

Amelia Coleman Assante possessed the kind of beauty that comes only with maturity and being at peace with oneself. She was tall, but not as tall as her handsome husband. She carried her height with dignity and dressed to that dignity with carefully chosen designer clothes that masked a thinness that spoke of past health problems. Her soft gray eyes were almost translucent, a perfect complement to her hair, which was more silver now than chestnut. The fine lines around her eyes and the deeper creases alongside her nose spoke more of character than age, as did the light brown spots unsuccessfully covered with makeup. Perfectly white capped teeth, slightly yellowed now from medication and too much tea, nibbled on a thin lower lip to stop it from trembling with the cold. To those standing in the crowd who knew her, she was every bit as striking and commanding as she'd been in her earlier days.

Billie Coleman Kingsley hugged her sister-in-law. "He really did it, Amelia. I'm so proud. You must be about ready to burst!"

"I am. There were times, Billie, when I thought this was nothing more than a nightmare, but Cary can do whatever he sets his mind to."

"What do you think, Senator Kingsley?"

Thad laughed. "What I think is, I'm glad I invested in this project."

"That makes two of us," said Amelia, smiling. "Without you we'd have run out of money years ago. By the way, where is Mr. Hasegawa? I want to thank him for coming all the way from Japan. He really isn't well enough to be traveling. We also have to thank him for his investment. We really did it, thanks to the two of you."

"Mr. Hasegawa is with Sawyer," Billie said. "I thinks he's taking him back to Sunbridge. He's very tired after his long flight, and he isn't feeling well. But he'll be back tonight for the festivities." Billie paused a moment, and when she spoke again, her voice was full of awe. "Amelia, I've never seen anything like this, and Thad and I have been all over the world."

{3}

"You look tired, Amelia," Thad said, his brow furrowing, his voice full of concern.

Amelia smiled. "Now, I don't want to be fussed over," she said. "I'm fine. The doctor says I'm fully recovered from the surgery. I just hate being cold. And before you can say it, I'm going upstairs and rest for tonight's gala. I really am excited about the library dedication. It was Cary's idea, you know, to dedicate it to Mam. The Jessica Coleman Library. What are you going to do?" Amelia asked Billie as she bussed her on the cheek.

"Corral the family and take the tour, like everyone else." Billie watched as Amelia headed toward the gleaming bank of elevators.

"I'll meet you by the jitney," Thad called over his shoulder.

Instead of moving off through the crowds, Billie remained where she was, her thoughts on Amelia. She didn't look well, and it was more than simple fatigue. Regardless of what she said, it was obvious that the heart bypass surgery had taken its toll. A brief, sharp spasm of worry overcame Billie. She and Amelia were more than sisters-in-law; they'd been intimate friends for over forty years.

Billie'd been so young when she met Amelia for the first time, only eighteen, and so very much in love with Amelia's brother, Moss. She'd been scared, too, of Moss and Amelia's father, Seth. What a tyrant he was. Amelia had confided in her, and in turn, she'd shared her life with Amelia. They were more like sisters than sisters-in-law, drawing together out of need, giving and accepting one another's friendship, sharing triumphs and disappointments.

Forty years of memories leapfrogged through Billie's mind. Accompanying Amelia to a back-street abortionist while she herself was secretly pregnant. Seth's hatred of Amelia because she'd had the audacity to be born a female. Amelia consoling her when Seth treated her like a brood mare, demanding that she produce a son—an heir.

While the war raged in England and Amelia couldn't return to the States in time for her mother's funeral, Billie had stood in her place and prayed for Jessica, just as Amelia would have done.

And it was Amelia who encouraged her, after Moss's death, to become a designer. Thanks to Amelia's support and confidence, she'd started her own successful business, Billie

{4}

Ltd., an enterprise that had netted her a seven-figure yearly income.

Until Amelia's marriage to Cary Assante, Billie had felt she was the only one who truly understood Amelia. Amelia had survived her father's hatred of her. She'd survived his bluster and his boasts that he had the United States government by the balls and someday they'd make him a very rich man. How she'd hated those boasts. She'd survived war-torn England, and although she lost her husband in that war, she gained a stepson and raised the boy at Sunbridge. Rand—who was now Billie's son-in-law. How close the bonds were. How long the connection. Forty years!

Forty years was half their life. If she had it to do over again, she wouldn't change a thing—all the tragedies, the sorrows, the happiness that had brought them to this moment.

Thad exited the glass-enclosed elevator. Instead of heading for the jitney, he retraced his steps to the main concourse, where he'd left Billie. He knew she'd still be there. Thinking. How beautiful she was, so serene and gentle. His heart swelled with love. Every day of his life he thanked God for giving him the patience to wait for this woman—this wonderful woman who had been his best friend's wife. Billie was his life. Not the navy, not Congress, and not the Senate. Billie. His partner, his wife, his love. In another year he'd retire from the Senate, and then it would be just the two of them, back in Vermont. Remembering Amelia's recent illness, he prayed silently that nothing would happen to change their wonderful plans.

He knew scores of people, particularly on the Hill, couples who stayed together for political reasons, never letting their mutual disaffection show in public. That was what he despised about Washington—all the blowhards, all the phoniness, the crap you had to wade through, only to find more crap. He was grateful to Billie for refusing to allow the fishbowl life to infringe on their private lives. Everyone on the Hill knew what he stood for, and there was envy in the lot of them, or so Billie said, and he had no reason to doubt her. Every time he heard tales of his colleagues' misconduct he'd shake his head and thank God again for Billie. The woman hadn't yet been born who could make him take a second look.

Billie was every bit as attractive as her sister-in-law, but with a very different kind of beauty. Hers came with sparkling eyes and vivid color, something she was known for in the fashion world. There was a mellowness, a happiness to Billie that shimmered about her like a giant halo. She was half a head shorter than Amelia and only a few pounds heavier. She glowed with good health, and when she smiled the world seemed lighter, brighter somehow. Billie was truly a happy woman, and it showed. High cheekbones lightly dusted with color and her perfectly shaped nose complemented warm hazel eyes that were her best feature. Today she wore a brilliant scarlet scarf with a sapphire fringe, a Billie original. She looked vibrant, vital.

Soon enough Billie would feel his eyes on her and turn, he thought. And the next moment she proved his thoughts were on target, as he used to say in the navy. Billie turned, her eyes searching the crowd. When she spotted him her face broke into a wide, lovely smile. He mouthed the command: "Hold that smile." He could sense her laughter as he shouldered his way through the crowd.

"I knew you'd still be here," Thad said gently.

"I know you knew. That's why I'm still here. I didn't want you to have to search for me and perhaps miss the tour jitney I was on. We want to do this together." He watched as a worried look shadowed her features. "Oh, Thad, I should have come down here more often to see Amelia instead of relying on phone calls and letters. She looks—" she hesitated, seeking the right word, "—unwell."

"Darling, Amelia hates to be fussed over, unless it's by Cary. Don't take any blame. This last week had to be exhausting for her. She'll take a few days off now and she'll recoup." He felt her begin to tense. "No, Billie, I'm not just saying that to make you feel better," he said, reading her mind. "I'm not discounting the seriousness of her surgery or her recovery, but I'm sure Cary, or Amelia herself, would have said something to us if things weren't . . . up to par. A cup of herb tea and a nap will perk her right up."

"You don't believe that any more than I do," Billie said.

"We have to believe it, Billie."

Billie clutched his arm tightly, her eyes growing moist. "I know, Thad. We've lost so many old friends, and now Mr. Hasegawa so ill . . . and Amelia."

There weren't any words, and Thad didn't try to search for them. He circled her shoulders with his free arm and hugged her tight.

Billie took a long, deep breath and came back to the present. "Let's round up the family, if they haven't already taken their own tour!"

"Now, that's an offer I can't refuse. I can't wait to see this place we helped build. I have trouble, darling, comprehending Cary's vision of this complex. I mean, I saw the plans and then the buildings as they were going up, but nothing prepared me for this glass and steel marvel."

"A city inside a city," Billie said. "So self-contained. The outside world could seem like an alien planet if one wanted to live and die here. I don't know if that's good, Thad."

"Choices. Options. They're available. I think it's wonderful for the elderly."

"If they could afford to live here. Do you know what the rent is in Assante Towers? Five thousand a month, and it's got an eighty-five percent occupancy as of today."

Arm in arm, Thad and Billie climbed the broad steps of the center. At the top they stopped to peer into the crowd below.

"Here we are, but I don't see any sign of Cole or Riley. I thought I saw Maggie a moment ago, but she's disappeared." Thad turned to look into his wife's eyes, a conspiratorial smile on his lips.

"What say, pretty lady, that you and I take this little trip all by ourselves? And I'll hold your hand so you don't get nervous."

A tour guide, commandeered by Cary from Disney World, spoke cheerfully as he shepherded the first tour group into the building. Thad and Billie melted into it.

"Let me start off by thanking you all for coming to this wonderful opening of ACH Enterprises," the guide was saying. "For those of you who don't know what ACH stands for, it's Assante, Coleman, and Hasegawa. Mr. Cary Assante is the man who built Miranda, with the help of the Coleman and Hasegawa corporations. I don't think I need to tell any of you from Texas just who the Colemans are!" Most of the crowd tittered knowingly. "For those of you who don't know who Mr. Hasegawa is," the guide continued, "he's the grandfather of Riley Coleman and the owner of a Japanese publishing conglomerate called Rising Sun.

"From the time Miranda first appeared on paper till this day, it has taken ten years and several billion dollars. This," he said, waving expansively at an immense display table strategically positioned in the middle of the vast Miranda City Planning Room, "is the result."

On the twenty-foot-square table, gilded by sunshine from a skylight high above, was an exquisitely detailed miniature rendering of the magnificent city. Thad and Billie smiled as the group shared a delighted sigh.

The guide, with the aid of a long pointer, began his description by indicating an emerald-green park exactly in the middle of the display. "This central area is Grace Park, a seventy-acre wooded and landscaped oval. It was designed and constructed by the renowned Japanese landscape artist, Hing Takinara. In it, among other things, are a zoo, three fine restaurants, cycling and walking trails, an aviary, meditation pools, a slow tramway for older or disabled visitors—or lazier ones." Everyone laughed at this. "Underneath Grace Park is Miranda's ultramodern metro system, a quiet and comfortable one-stop or express ride from the center part of the city to several destinations in each direction. The one stop is the exact middle of the park, where the Jessica Coleman Library and the Lotus Fountain are situated."

Pointing to the street surrounding the park, the guide continued. "This is our Grand Concourse. As you can see, from this street you can go everywhere: Saks, Neiman-Marcus, Martha's. For all you food aficionados, the New Fulton area has fresh produce shipped in daily from all points of the globe. This is where our head chefs from The New Maxim's, La Tut Suite III, and our other fine restaurants buy their food.

"As you know," he continued, pointing to another impressive building at the park's south curve, "Donald Trump managed to grab this prime corner, where he has duplicated his New York effort. Ours is called New Trump's.

"Miranda boasts one each of every well-established bank and large national corporation.

"To your left is Assante Towers, one floor shy of the Sears high rise in Chicago. As you can see, it's a marvel of steel and glass. The ten top floors are residences owned by some of the wealthiest men in the world. There are three penthouse apartments, one owned by Mr. and Mrs. Assante, the second by the Coleman family, and the third by the Rising Sun Corporation. But we're wasting time here—let's go and see the real thing!"

Outside in the clear, cold daylight, everyone clambered

into the sleek new jitney. The tour guide picked up his mike, tapped it once to see if it was on, and continued his spiel. Billie and Thad huddled closer and tuned him out as the jitney moved slowly forward toward the main thoroughfare of Miranda.

In five minutes, the real thing, looming up ahead, took everyone's breath away. From the south curve and Main Street they proceeded onto the Grand Concourse. As far as they could see to their left was a combination of Rodeo Drive and Fifth Avenue, an international shoppers' paradise, with gold-braided and festooned entrance porticoes, parked Rolls-Royces, and liveried doormen. On their right the park beckoned, velvety green and majestically jeweled with flowering entrances and graceful, generously sized park benches.

The jitney came to a halt in front of the Assante Towers building. The guide directed his enthralled charges to its entrance, shepherding them like schoolchildren to the first-floor mezzanine. All eyes were drawn upward to the first five floors, dense with trees and hanging plants, elegant food emporiums, and boutiques of all types. Shining green-tinted glass enclosed it all. Sea-green wrought-iron filigreed causeways and balconies laced the structure, and the sound of gently falling water filled the air. The guide signaled the group to divide into two as he led them to the egg-shaped, glass-enclosed elevators, framed in black wrought iron. Under ceilings sectioned with Tiffany glass, they were slowly carried to the fifth floor.

After giving them a few moments to absorb the wondrous sight below, the guide ushered them toward large iron gates draped in ivy and flowering wisteria.

"This is the Cardinal's Nest restaurant," he announced. "We bring everyone here for coffee early in the tour because the Cardinal's Nest affords the finest bird's-eye view of the entire heart of Miranda."

The guide pointed to New Trump's, directly across the park. "Sparkling and majestic, the entire one-hundred-and-twenty-five-floor building is at once there and not there. It is enclosed in a special mirrored glass that reflects everything around it. This feat is most strikingly apparent when one realizes that the last fifty or so floors reflect the sky and the clouds back to the viewer. . . ."

Billie and Thad couldn't listen anymore. All they could do

was squeeze each other's hands and try not to howl like coon dogs.

"Are you used to the apartment yet, babe?" Cary asked with a smile on his face.

"Darling, I could live in a shack as long as you're with me," Amelia laughed back. "To answer your question, yes, I love it. And we're going to need all eight rooms and three baths. It's amazing what you builders can do. Here we are living high in the sky in an apartment that's bigger than most people's houses."

"It's all for you, Amelia. I had it down on paper right to the last nail. I know you wanted a state-of-the-art kitchen. I kind of like the sunken Jacuzzi myself." He leered at her.

"I know you do." Amelia leered back. "You know what I like best, Cary? The balcony. It's as big as the patio at Sunbridge. The first thing I did was set out my sundial. It fits perfectly on the pedestal. Cary, I just love it. I know I'm going to spend a lot of time out there when the weather is good."

"We can sit out there all year-round. Did you forget about the special heater I installed? The canopy and the sides are insulated. We'll be as snug as two bugs in a rug."

"I did forget, Cary. There are times when living in an apartment, no matter how big it is, gets to you. The need to walk outside, to touch something green, makes all the difference. Thank you, Cary."

They walked hand in hand through the apartment. Each time they did it they noticed something different—an object with a memory, a special gift, something they'd bought together because it pleased them, the colors they'd chosen after months of looking at fabric and paint samples, a cushion with a petit point cover. All the little things that made up their new home in Assante Towers. In Miranda.

"We're going to be happy here, babe."

"Not going to be happy, Cary. We are happy. I'm so proud of you and all this."

"Couldn't have done it without you," Cary said.

Amelia knew he meant every word. Cary was probably the most honest person she'd ever met. "I love you, Cary."

"And I love you, more than life itself. And because I love you, I am going to carry you to that large sofa we bought so we could snuggle into it together. If I remember your words correctly, you said we could get lost in it."

"A nap sounds good to me. What are you going to do?"

"Not a damn thing except reflect on Miranda. I might go out to the balcony and try out that heater."

Amelia smiled at her husband as he settled her in the softness of the sofa. He propped bright orange pillows behind her head and covered her with one of her mother's afghans that had seen far too many washings. "Warmer than cashmere," Amelia whispered as she drifted into sleep.

Cary watched the tour bus from the heated balcony of his penthouse apartment. He straightened his shoulders and threw out his chest. He wasn't going to burst, he was going to bust . . . with pride. He'd created it all, lived it all, 365 days a year for ten long years. For a moment he felt like God surveying His creation. God had created the world out of nothing. He, Cary Assante, had taken his imagination, his own money, his wife, Amelia's, faith in him, and had gone to work. Five years into his project, he'd run out of money. Unable to let his dream slip into obscurity, he'd solicited the aid of the Colemans and the Hasegawas. They'd all invested—in him, they said. From that point on he'd doubled his workday, arriving at the building site before first light and returning home long past midnight. Amelia should have divorced him for his neglect; instead, she encouraged him to keep on. He was glad now that he'd listened. He hadn't lied to the Colemans, to Thad Kingsley, and to Shadaharu Hasegawa when he told them their investment would be returned tenfold. Their belief in him made him deliver; it was that simple.

Cary felt like singing. Lyrics bubbled forth. *Come fly with me.* . . . He wished he could remember the rest of the words to the song. He hummed the melody as he leaned on the railing of his balcony. Down below . . . his blood, his sweat, and his tears.

Nothing in his life had prepared Cary for this moment, this day. This was the bubbly. He'd earned this moment—a moment of aloneness to savor his creation. For a little while, until the dedication, Miranda had belonged to him. Now it would belong to the world.

Come fly with me. . . . It sounded right. If only he could take wing and fly over his creation. . . . If only. . . . He wished he could keep forever this wonderful, intoxicating feeling that was transfusing his body.

This was his dream. Dreams were something the Colemans understood. Moss, Amelia's brother and Billie's first husband, had had a dream, too, but leukemia claimed his life before his revolutionary slant-winged aircraft—his dream—could be brought to reality. After Moss's death, Billie forged ahead, with the family's help, to make the dream a reality. She'd faltered just as he had, but she'd righted herself, just as he had. And with the aid of Shadaharu Hasegawa, Moss Coleman's slant-winged plane took wing before the entire world.

Cary shivered, but not from the cold, even though the temperature was biting and well below the freezing mark. It was a shiver of elation and pride. He imagined he could see Moss Coleman standing on some fluffy cloud giving him his cocky thumbs-up salute and saying, "I couldn't have done it better!"

There was no doubt in his mind that he now belonged.

His feeling of pride stayed with him. Yes, he'd faltered, and yes, the Japanese side of the family had come to the rescue again—to his rescue. He'd never negate the monetary help he received or forget the confidence the Colemans had in him and in his ability.

Cary's step was jaunty, his grin in place. Not bad for a boy raised on the charity of a New York City orphanage. From runny-nosed, barefoot, bare-assed orphan to this.

He belonged now. He proved to *himself* that he was finally worthy of being one of *them*.

Come fly with me....

The cold November wind buffeted him, pushing him back against the sliding doors. He should go inside, where it was warm and cozy. Inside with Amelia.

"If you'd take those clumsy clodhoppers off, you might be able to walk normally. How many times do I have to tell you to leave those work boots by the back door—you almost broke my figurines!" Tess Buckalew shrilled.

Coots Buckalew was in a fighting mood. Nothing had gone the way he'd planned today, and this shindig at Miranda had him twisted in knots. Tess had signed a lease and told him afterward that he'd forked out sixty grand in rent for a suite of rooms at Assante Towers for a year. Rent he couldn't afford. He'd wring her skinny neck, but then he'd go to prison, and there was no way in hell he was going to spend his remaining years in jail because of Tess.

The voice he aimed over his shoulder was a thick mixture of gravel and molasses. "Shut up, Tess. You got me into this, and I don't want to hear a goddamn word out of you. I haven't forgotten that little trick with the Towers. We can't afford sixty grand. When are you going to get it through that pea brain of yours that we have to cut back? I mean, way back. And you better not tell me you and the girls bought new clothes for this thing tonight."

"Damn right, I'm going to tell you that!" Tess shouted. Coots barely kept himself from jumping. He hadn't seen her creep up behind him. Tess was two feet away from him and, judging from her pulsing temples and bulging eyes, fighting mad. The thought that Coots would even try to get in her way now meant war. "Do you want us shamed? Of course you do, I can see it in your eyes. You're a hateful man, Coots Bucka-lew. We were specially invited, so that means something. We have to look our best." Tess poked her clawlike finger into his chest. "That means new clothes." Each word was accompa-nied by a jab of the claw.

Coots began to strip down on the spot, in the middle of her bedroom. He knew it would aggravate her, just as he also knew using her shower would set her into a tizzy. Not that he made half the mess she did. Cold air from the marble floor swirled around his ankles and up his legs. His erection died instantly. Tess laughed.

"It wasn't for you," Coots grumbled.

"A piss hard," Tess mocked. "Don't you-all worry, Coots honey, I'm not interested in that little, and I do mean little, joystick of yours. It's seen the inside of too many whores for me to be the least bit interested—which is why you sleep down the hall."

Coots laughed. He was far from beaten. "At least I get to sleep. Those damn bones of yours don't attack me in all the wrong places." He was just getting warmed up. This was the fun part, because this tack never failed. He turned on the faucets. "You look like a scarecrow," he bellowed over the sound of the running water. "How much do you weigh in at this week, eighty-five pounds? Bones with skin plastered over them, that's all you are." He adjusted the water temperature. "No titties, no ass," he shouted, "no goddamn anything. Ugly, too. Your hair looks like a bird's nest." He howled with laughter before he added, "Without the birds!" Coots stepped into the shower, still howling.

Tess stormed about the bedroom on her three-inch spike heels. If she'd known where the main hot water valve was, she'd have turned it off in a second and locked the shower door. Let him freeze his fat ass off, for all she cared. Then the thought of scalding his fat ass brightened her thoughts.

Fifteen minutes later, Coots walked through the bedroom wrapped in a bath sheet. He stopped in midstride and stared at his wife, sitting at her pink velvet and white satin ribbon-festooned vanity. And then he doubled over laughing.

"I've seen everything now. Rubber bands to pull back the wrinkles—so that's why your hair looks like a bird's nest!" He was laughing so hard he began to slap his thighs, struggling to speak. "You're going to be one pretty mess if those rubber bands snap in the cold weather."

Tess ignored him. She hated what she was doing, but the advertisement had looked so promising—at least ten years of wrinkles gone in minutes. She'd sent her twelve dollars airmail the same day she'd read it. It was unfortunate, but she'd been cursed with her mother's skin. No elasticity. When Coots was in a really foul mood he'd torment her by saying her wrinkles were trenches and if he dropped seeds in them, he was sure they would sprout. She wondered if the rubber bands would really snap with the cold. Damn.

"Coots honey, I need some help here," she called sweetly. "Zip me up and I'll tie your tie. I think we should put our differences aside for tonight. We're going out in high society, and neither one of us need shame the other. We are a family and have to present a united front. Agreed?" Coots grumbled something that sounded like agreement. But he couldn't resist one last dig as he yanked up her zipper.

"You buying your underwear at the sports center these days? Padded brazeers and padded underpants."

Tess had the last jab. "Not at all, Coots honey. My bra and panties came from Neiman-Marcus and cost eighty-five dollars. Chew on that for a while, sweetie."

Buckalew Big Wells, Oakes and Tess Buckalew's personalized version of Tara, got its name from the oil gushers that had enabled the Buckalews to build Tess's dream house in the first place. It sat, curious and sprawling, at the end of the three-mile driveway on the northeast corner of their property. With no recognizable architectural form, its many wings and added-on rooms stretched like tentacles in every direction.

In the early years, at the onset of its construction, Tess had fought with every architect she engaged. Not one, it seemed, wanted to put his name to the monstrosity she wanted to create. In the end she'd hired local contractors, at least a dozen of them to add the cupolas, the Tudor trim, and the widow's walk she insisted upon. The stained-glass arched windows, trimmed in jutting Belgian block, had been Austin's sole topic of discussion for weeks, with the glazier and mason refusing to comment other than to say they were well paid.

In the days when money was no object, Oakes, better known as "Coots," had given Tess free rein, never dreaming Buckalew Big Wells would turn out to be known all over the state of Texas, and probably the eastern seaboard, as a nightmare of architectural misdesign.

Coots, away working in the oil fields, had left the construction to Tess. If he'd been riding a horse when he returned from the fields six months later, he'd have fallen off. As it was, the pickup truck he was driving ground to a halt in the blaze of light emanating from a dozen or so floodlights Tess had ordered installed to emphasize the house's crazily unique exterior. Nothing in his hardworking life had prepared him for the pretentious monstrosity that was to be his home for the rest of his life.

Although Coots hadn't had much fancy schooling, he was a man driven to achieve through hard work. His parlor manners, such as they were, had been learned late, and he only used them when he happened to be in the mood. Tess, on the other hand, garnered most of her education from magazines and movies. Her sole aim in life was to fit her family into what she thought was high society—the Colemans' kind of society.

Among the oilmen Coots did business with, the consensus was that he was an okay guy but his wife was off her rocker. The womenfolk were more astute in their understanding of Tess; they knew she was hell-bent on breaking into Austin's formidable social circle. It was no wonder she never succeeded. The snobbery and pecking order of that elite circle carefully managed, over the years, to allow Tess Buckalew only just so much access, cutting her off when the truly important functions came up. That same elite circle made no bones about accepting her healthy donations to their causes. Tess sighed and glanced at her watch under the rosy glow of the pink-shaded lamp on her dressing table. Coots had stomped on out of the room, and the silence was a blessing. But she couldn't get the past out of her mind. Maybe because tonight was a landmark.

Tess had always known that Coots had no great dreams or aspirations. He had never had any. All he wanted from life was to be able to work the oil wells and perhaps, if God was willing and kind, get another gusher. Right now, though, she knew, all he wanted was to survive the oil crisis. The hell with the gusher and everyone else. . . . At the moment, survival was the name of Coots's game.

Tess thought about her own dream. She knew she'd give up every fur and every jewel she owned if she could be half as important as one of *them*. The Colemans. Revered, wealthy, and accepted. So far the dream had eluded her. Things will change, she told herself. Circumstances changed on a minute-to-minute basis, didn't they? Her daughter Lacey just might be her salvation, if she could just get Riley Coleman to marry her. Lacey had lost out with Cole Tanner; now, at her father's insistence, she'd set her cap for Riley, the Colemans' Japanese-American grandson. With their union in the bag, Tess would be one of the Colemans, one of *them*. Then she would be called upon for her opinions as well as her donations. Tess daydreamed about what she'd wear and what she'd say, how she'd arrive at every luncheon, every tea, and every social function. She'd be automatically invited to all of them, not just the down-home barbecues Texas was famous for. Getting invited to tonight's bash, even though it was only because of Lacey and Riley's romance, was just the beginning.

Tess could hear Coots stomping about the master suite. She wondered for the thousandth time why she'd ever married him, and, why she'd stayed married all these years. He'd been virile and she'd been lusty. He'd been six four and she'd been tiny, a little under five feet. He'd been her protector and she'd been his adoring clinging vine. Coots had come to the marriage with only his bare hands and the promise that he would give her whatever she wanted, sooner or later. She'd had seventy thousand dollars, a legacy from her parents that still remained intact in the bank. No matter how rough things were in the beginning, Coots had never asked for a dime and she'd never offered. What was hers was hers. What was Coots's was theirs. Never once had she allowed Coots to forget his promise to her. Everything she wanted. And by God, she wanted.

The children had come along—first Lacey and then Ivy. That's probably where the marriage started to sour. Coots hated squalling kids and a messy kitchen and a tired wife. Tess had come to hate his dirty body and his dirtier clothes and the fact that his promise looked like it would never be fulfilled.

Coots started seeing other women; Tess took to reading pulp magazines by the pound and planning her dream house.

Now, when everything was almost within her grasp, the cussed oil business looked like it was going to go belly-up. She wished she'd paid more attention to what was going on. Knowing only little bits and pieces about things was dangerous. She knew Coots had been planning to buy the Jarvis ranch, but then Adam Jarvis moved back to Texas with his stepson and decided not to sell. Or said he'd sell but not give up the oil leases. Whatever it was, Coots had lost out. He'd closed off his strippers against Riley Coleman's advice, saying just because Riley went to college didn't mean he knew everything. He'd wanted Riley to pick up some of his oil leases. At first Riley had refused, explaining that the Coleman coffers were empty and he couldn't justify the buy to the family. Tess wasn't certain, but she thought he'd changed his mind. Maybe because of Lacey, Tess thought.

Tess's mail-order course in astrology indicated that Lacey's marriage to Riley was almost a certainty. At first it bothered her that she would have a son-in-law who was half Japanese, but when she weighed the positives against the negatives, she knew she could come to love Riley. Riley could be her ticket into Austin society.

Tess checked her watch again. It was too quiet. Where *was* everybody?

"We're ready, Mama," Lacey said at the bedroom door.

"Now, don't you look pretty. Twirl around and let me see. Just as pretty as a summer flower."

"In the dead of winter," Ivy growled behind her.

Tess's voice dropped an octave. "Let me see what you're wearing, Ivy. Lord, child, where did you get that outfit?" Tess's face was full of horror. "You march back into your room and change your clothes. That might be all right for Lacey to wear, but not you. Where did you get it?"

"Lacey lent it to me. What would you have me change into, Mother?" Ivy asked coolly.

"Something. Anything. Bare backs and low necklines are

not for you. You're too big to wear such things. Lacey, help your sister or we're going to be late."

Lacey grimaced. "Mother, haven't you heard? It's fashionable to be late."

"Not for something this important. Fix her up and do it now!" There was a ring of steel in Tess's voice that made both girls scurry off to do her bidding.

Lacey didn't bother to hide her anger as she stomped her way to Ivy's Spartan bedroom. Out of the corner of her eye she could see Ivy stripping down to her underwear. The scowl on Ivy's face mirrored her own.

Someday, when Ivy got her act together, she would be a knockout. Right now, though, she had the face of a cherub and bulged in all the wrong places. The loss of fifteen pounds would do it. Lacey felt a momentary pang of jealousy when she visualized what Ivy would look like when she pulled herself together. She had a winning smile, with teeth so perfect she could pose for toothpaste ads, the kind of smile that made you forget the pudginess and bulges; the kind of smile that said Ivy would be your friend. She had mysterious eyes with a slight cast to them, and when the chubbiness left her cheeks, her whole face would be in perspective. She wasn't a knockout . . . yet. Until she was, her sense of humor and her views on life would have to carry her along.

"Why don't I just stay home and Mama will feel better? I don't have anything glitzy to wear, and if I did, I'd look like a clown. I'm sorry, Lacey," she mumbled.

Lacey's freshly manicured nails picked at the clothing in Ivy's closet. "It's my fault. I knew better. It's . . . Mama wants both of us . . . Where *are* your clothes?" How was it possible that Ivy had so few things while her own closet bulged to overflowing, necessitating the use of two hall closets for her more costly garments?

Ivy rose to the challenge in Lacey's voice. "When was the last time you heard Mama ask me if I needed anything? When was the last time you heard her offer to buy me something? Whatever you see in there is what I bought myself. I never asked for anything and I'm not going to start now. I'm not you, Lacey," she said tightly.

"What's that supposed to mean? That I'm a grabber, that I take all I can get? Maybe you should try it. Everyone knows you get more flies with sugar than vinegar."

"You said it, I didn't. Well, what have you decided on?" Ivy snapped.

"I guess it's this brown dress. God, where in the hell did you get this? I know your taste runs to casual comfort, but this . . . is . . . Maybe we can dress it up or something."

"Or something," Ivy muttered as she pulled the dress over her head.

"Pearls, a scarf, a different belt," Lacey said desperately.

"Do you really think they'll help? Look, if you're embarrassed to be seen with me, get out of here. I'll wear Grandma's pearls if it will make you feel better," Ivy capitulated.

Lacey stared at Ivy. She wouldn't be caught dead in the mustard-brown dress, not even to take out the trash. She nodded to show she was in agreement about the pearls. Her eyes filled with envy at the lustrous strand. She'd wanted them, even tried to snitch them after her grandmother's will had been settled. Her own bequest had been a cameo broach that she'd tossed in a drawer and forgotten. It galled her that Ivy kept the pearls hidden and refused to lend them to her for special occasions. This was the first time she'd seen her sister wear them.

"Look in the mirror, Ivy. They make your complexion positively glow," Lacey said.

"Then eat your heart out, because they'll never find their way around your neck," Ivy said irritably. The sincerity in Lacey's voice had to be some kind of trick. Lacey never said nice things to her. She still wanted the pearls; it was that simple.

Ivy stared at her sister with a mixture of disgust and jealousy. She always thought of Lacey as having been created and then shellacked, all five feet ten inches of her. There was never a hair out of place, never a nail broken or a chip in her nail polish. She applied her makeup as if she were following a road map—a dab here, a dash there, blended, blended, blended. She was a farther uptown version of Christie Brinkley with none of the model's winsomeness. Everything about Lacey was perfect, from the top of her fashionable hairstyle to the tip of her manicured toes. Hard, glittering eyes, high, sharp cheekbones, small, elegant nose that was usually in the air, and a thin mouth that rarely, if ever, smiled. There was nothing real about Lacey. The feathery eyelashes, the porcelain caps on her teeth, the artificial nail tips and silicone breast implants. Where, she wondered, was the real Lacey Bucka-lew?

Lacey's hackles rose. Why couldn't she and Ivy be nice to each other? Why did they have to end each meeting, each conversation, on an angry note? Or was it a jealous note? As they made their way back to Tess's bedroom, Lacey decided it was all her mother's fault.

Tess's narrowed eyes took in the dull brown dress and the string of pearls. The dress did nothing for Ivy's figure. She blinked, her eyebrows arching at the clear, rosy, almost ethereal complexion of her younger daughter. Even so, she looked dowdy next to her glamorous sister, who had poured herself into a black sheath skirt with a sparkling sequined top. So very fashionable; a mannequin, hard and glittering.

Tess sighed. She just knew that the way Ivy was dressed was some kind of omen. Things were not going to work out. She didn't like the calculating look in Lacey's eyes, either. She'd seen that look before. It meant Lacey was determined to do something, something her mother wouldn't approve of. It had to be Cole Tanner. Lacey hadn't been the same since they'd broken up. Thrown into the same company with Cole, she might do something tonight that she'd regret later. She'd talk to her in the car, Tess decided. Better yet, she'd warn her. Cole would have to be history.

How many times she'd dreamed about this place called Sunbridge, Julie Kingsley thought, and now she was finally here. She'd soon be seeing it, for the first time, in all its splendor.

They were passing under the high wooden arch proclaiming that this was Sunbridge. Miles of white rail fencing stretched into the distance. Tall, leafless oaks lined the drive, and on either side were wide expanses of lawn, dull brown now, with the tiny heads of the sprinkler system showing. Julie let her breath explode in a long sigh. She'd known it would look like this from Billie and Thad's description. Thad said when the oaks were in leaf it was like driving through a dappled tunnel of green with golden shards of sun shooting through the leaves.

Far up the drive, daylight shone, and when the car rounded the final turn, the house came into view.

Sitting on a gently sloping rise, the great house basked beneath the overcast Texas sky. Julie thought, as they came out from the tunnel of trees, that here, in this place called Sunbridge, the sun would be its warmest and most golden.

The house was a three-story brick of the palest pink, flanked by two wings, which were also three-storied but set back from the main structure. The expanse of prairie rose was accented by white columns that supported the roof of the veranda that swept the entire frontage. As the driver pulled the limousine up to the portico, Julie noticed the multipaned fanlight that crested the huge double front door. The design was repeated again over each window on the top floor. Ornamental topiary trees and crape myrtle hugged the foundation, and surrounding the house was the magnificent rose garden Billie had spoken of, dry and brown now, but complete with trellises and statuary. Julie drew in her breath again. Fairy-tale land. "Is this what you call a spread?" Julie asked in awe.

The driver smiled. "Here in Texas people do call it a spread. Sunbridge does spread over two hundred and fifty thousand acres. It's needed to raise the cattle and thoroughbreds. Mostly they're kept in the back acreage. You're not seeing Sunbridge at its best, though, miss. When the sun is shining, it's one of the most beautiful spots on this earth. I've been here a long time and I've never seen its equal anywhere."

"I can see why they call it Sunbridge. With the sun shining down on it, it must be breathtaking," Julie said in awe.

"They say when the first Mr. Coleman saw this land, that would be Seth Coleman now, he felt as though he could almost reach up to the sun. They say he came from very dark beginnings, and building this place was like making his dream come true. They say he wanted the great house to bridge his past with what he wanted for the future. The whole thing, all of this, the house, the landscaping, everything, was what he wanted. No one knows for sure if the first Mrs. Coleman had a say in the way things were done."

"I'm sure she did," Julie said generously.

"We're here, miss. You go along inside now. I'll carry your bags into the front hall."

At the front portico Julie looked around. She took a moment to imagine the ethereal beauty of the rose garden and the feminine sweep of the clematis vine surrounding the heavy oak doors, knowing for certain that they were the first Mrs. Coleman's contribution to Sunbridge. The outside did nothing to prepare her for the inside of the house. Shining oaken floors, massive beams studding the ceiling, thick, dark Oriental carpets, and man-size leather furniture, shabby and worn. Standing there, alone for a moment, Julie imagined masculine voices and thudding high-heeled cowboy boots. Panoramic paintings filled the walls, all of them depicting burly, tanned men at some manly endeavor—branding steers, breaking horses, riding the range. The driver had been right: Sunbridge was a man's house. It was Seth Coleman's domain, and every detail of the worn shabbiness attested to that fact. Then she heard, not cowboy boots, but the light tapping of her Aunt Billie's high heels.

"I'm so glad you're here," Billie Kingsley said warmly as she embraced her husband's niece. "It affects everyone this way the first time they see it," she said softly. "I'll never forget how petrified I was when I arrived here as a new bride. I was so high on being married to Moss Coleman, I didn't come down to earth till I walked into this . . . mausoleum. Don't look for feminine touches, because there are none. This house looks the same as it did when I first arrived, and that was forty-five years ago. I hope you aren't too disappointed."

"I don't know if I am or not," Julie said honestly. "I'm not quite sure what I expected. Hearing about a place for so many years makes it easy for a person to add his or her own little touches. I'm guilty of imagining a Bavarian crystal chandelier in the central hallway, and I added a marble floor, too."

"Someday," Billie said, "I'll tell you what I imagined this place would look like, but not today. Everyone is anxious to meet you, so let's get the introductions under way. The whole clan is in the library, gathered for this momentous occasion— and your arrival just adds to the excitement."

Billie led Julie down a long corridor lined with framed photographs and into a cozy room where a fire was burning in a huge fieldstone fireplace. Her heart pounding with excitement, Julie squared her shoulders and followed Billie into the room.

It was Amelia who put her arms around Julie in welcome when Billie introduced her. When she blushed with pleasure, Amelia winked at Billie. It seemed nobody blushed these days, and when a prospective thirty-niner did it, it was refreshing. She would do.

Amelia looked hard at Julie and saw an attractive, buxom woman with laughing eyes and a crinkly smile. Light-colored freckles, the same shade as her hair, marched across the bridge of her nose, giving her a winsome look. She wasn't young, nor was she old. Amelia knew that Julie's thirty-ninth birthday was only months away and that she'd never married.

Amelia took Julie's elbow, and began to introduce her around. "This is Maggie and Rand. They live in perpetual Hawaiian sunshine all year long, while we shiver and shake. Rand is my son, but then, I'm sure you already know that. I just love to say it," Amelia gurgled.

"Welcome to Sunbridge, Julie," Maggie said, a smile in her voice. "Any time you're in Hawaii, feel free to spend time with us. Amelia's right, this is too cold for us. That's one of the reasons we moved."

"And in this corner," Amelia went on, "we have my niece, Sawyer, and my two nephews, Cole and Riley. They officially run Coleman enterprises. Sawyer and Cole operate Coleman Aviation, Sawyer from Japan and Cole here in Texas. Riley's in charge of the cattle and oil end of things."

"I've heard a lot about you," Sawyer said warmly, "and now that I'm meeting you, I see everything Thad and Grand said about you is true. Welcome to Sunbridge, Julie." Her handshake was every bit as bone-crushing as Cole's and Riley's. They nodded their approval.

"Don't let Cole talk you into going for a plane ride with him," said Sawyer. "And Riley is equally as dangerous on a horse, so watch it."

Julie grinned across at Cole. "I always wanted to wear one of those flight suits and a billed cap. Any time you're looking for a passenger, I'd be glad to go for a ride."

"It would be a lot simpler if you'd buy a flight suit from Banana Republic. Trust me, this guy is a devil in the air." Sawyer grinned.

"I really should do something before I turn forty." Julie looked at Riley. "How fast do horses go?"

"We have a mare named Doolie that goes about a mile every three hours." Riley laughed.

"Don't trust these guys, Julie," Sawyer warned again good-naturedly.

"Don't look at me, young woman," Amelia said as she led Julie in the direction of the bar. "They all talk a different language than I do. Sawyer is probably right, though."

"My niece Susan and her husband, Ferris. They live in Minnesota and head up the Spina Bifida Foundation. The whole family is very proud of them."

"I would think so," Julie said warmly. "Billie and Thad talk about the marvelous work you both do. Someday, Susan, I hope I get a chance to hear you play the piano. Your mother told me she could listen to you play all day long."

"Was that with or without earplugs?"

"Moving right along here," Amelia said with a laugh as she guided Julie to a man seated in a chair by the fire. "This is the second most wonderful man on earth. Mr. Hasegawa. We call him the Coleman savior."

"Please, don't get up." Julie dropped to the hearth. How ill he looked. She extended her hand and was surprised at the firm handshake. "Someday I hope to visit your country."

"It is my pleasure to meet Thaddeus's niece. He has spoken of you often. I wish I could say I have a desire to visit Vermont, but I don't. Thaddeus has schooled me on your small state. I will, how do you say, pass on it." His voice was gentle and cultured. "I think you would like my country. Whenever you would like a job on one of my magazines, you have only to ask."

"That's very kind of you, Mr. Hasegawa. I'll remember your kind offer. Tell me, what did you think of Miranda?"

"I subscribe to the theory that every man should have a dream. I am very happy to be a part of Mr. Assante's dream. Do you have a dream, Julie Kingsley?" the old Japanese asked gently.

Taken off guard, Julie hesitated, but only for a second. "Yes, I suppose I do. Nothing grand. Rather simple, really. I want to get married someday. I want to know what it's like to love and be loved. I want to be as happy as my Uncle Thad and Billie are." Julie flushed a bright pink when the old man stared deeply into her eyes.

"Ah, but your dream is important. It is what we all wish and dream of. No one should be alone. We all need someone. You Americans say something about a knight on a horse, do you not?"

"A white knight, and he doesn't *have* to be on a horse. If he knocked on my door, I'd be just as happy if he had on running shoes."

"This is a joke?"

"No. What that means is, I'll take him any which way I can as long as I love him and he loves me."

"Ah, so, I understand."

{ 24 }

"I'm glad I finally got to meet you, Mr. Hasegawa. We'll talk again before I leave."

"Can I get you anything, Mr. Hasegawa?" asked Amelia.

"Nothing. But you could send my grandson over, if he's not busy."

Amelia's eyes raked the room. She didn't see Riley anywhere. Or Cole. "I'll find him." She turned to Julie. "I guess that's the family, except for Cary, and I have no idea where he is. Oops, I see him. Stay right here and I'll send him over. I have to find Riley."

Julie looked at the man who had just entered the room, and she was aware of two things instantly. First, Cary Assante was one of the handsomest men she'd ever seen. Second, in all the years her uncle and Billie had spoken of Amelia and Cary, they'd never once mentioned the couple's huge age difference.

"I've heard a lot about you, Julie. I'm Cary, Amelia's husband."

None of the men she'd ever known or heard about would have tacked that little phrase onto an introduction, Julie thought. She smiled at him.

"I love this family," he went on. "The day I married Amelia, they adopted me. It was the happiest day of my life. I truly believe I'd lay down my life for any one of them."

Julie wondered if marrying Amelia or the family's adopting him was the happiest day of his life. Probably both, she decided. Cary Assante was obviously a happy man. But he must be twenty years younger than Amelia! "I'm so glad I finally got to meet all of you. I've heard about this family for years. It was like getting the next episode on your favorite soap opera. I've been following your progress with Miranda. It's magnificent. You must be very proud."

Cary's voice was suddenly shy. "I didn't do it alone. The Colemans and Mr. Hasegawa backed me. Amelia was with me every step of the way. I created it, but they made it happen."

"The way I heard it, you were a hands-on builder all the way."

"I did do some of the work. Most of it, though, was on the drawing board."

"Whatever will you do for an encore, Mr. Assante?"

"I don't think I could ever top Miranda, and I don't think I want to. All I want now is to spend some time with my wife. Perhaps take a vacation. Or maybe I'll help Amelia with what she's working on, housing for the elderly. Did she tell you about it?"

"No, she didn't, but Billie did. I think it's wonderful of her to give so unselfishly of her time. Sooner or later we're all going to be old, and I, for one, would like to know that I'll have a clean bed and a roof over my head. Not to mention my dignity. What she's doing is so very important."

Cary blinked. He'd never heard such a passionate defense. "I am proud of Amelia. She has one hundred percent of my support." What a strange young woman this was. He looked at her closely in the filtered afternoon light. Very attractive, but then, Amelia had said she was, and Amelia would know. Soft. Warm. Gentle. Nothing hard and brittle about this lady. Good eyes and one of the nicest smiles he'd ever seen. He wondered why Thad and Billie had never brought her here before. She seemed to fit into the family like a hand into a glove. He was glad. Amelia would probably invite her from now on.

"A lot of people don't like to talk about the aged," Julie was saying. "I guess we all tend to think we'll never get old —or else we think, let someone else do it. But we should all do our share. I'm going to tell Amelia if she needs any help, I'd be glad to offer my services."

"Did I hear my name mentioned?"

"This young woman offered her services to you."

"Julie, did you really? I can use all the help I can get. I've recruited Billie and Maggie and Sawyer. I'm working on a mail campaign to the state legislators. Can you type and stuff envelopes?"

"I work nine to five. My time after that is yours."

"What about your social life?" Amelia asked.

"I'm afraid there isn't one," Julie said ruefully. "Even if there were, I'd still find a way to help."

"Bless you, child. When you get back to Vermont you'll have a package of materials waiting for you. This is pretty much a one-shot deal, so don't feel you're locked into this for a long period of time. I want these letters to reach the legislators before the New Year. Maybe they'll think twice over the holidays about us old people."

Cary's noticeable flush made Julie uncomfortably aware that she was intruding on a personal issue, but Amelia's arm was still around her shoulder and Cary's eyes were locked with her own. She couldn't extricate herself without embarrassing all of them.

"Old! Surely you can't be referring to yourself, Amelia," Julie exclaimed. "Billie has always said you have more vim and vigor than anyone she's ever met."

"I used to, but time does take its toll. Now I'm on a downswing, but I don't seem to mind. My work with the aged is very fulfilling."

"I think it's time for me to go upstairs and get ready for this evening," said Julie lightly, relieved to note Cary's blush had subsided. "I've been promising myself a long, leisurely soak. I went straight to Miranda from the airport."

"Did anyone give you a room? Come along, I'll show you where you'll be staying for the next couple of days. If there's one thing Sunbridge has, it's plenty of room. On second thought—Cary, you take Julie up and I'll save myself the stair climbing. The room next to the nursery has its own bath. I think you'll be comfortable there." Her voice was gay, her eyes merry as she kissed Julie on the cheek.

Julie trailed behind Cary as he led her up the wide center-hall staircase. She should be saying something to keep the conversation going, but she felt at a loss. Cary's shoulders appeared stiff and his jaw was tight. Undercurrents of some kind were bothering him. Whatever it was, it wasn't her business. She opted for silence until they reached her room.

"Thanks. And congratulations again. You've made quite a statement with Miranda."

Cary leaned against the door frame. "Right now it's like Christmas night after all the food is eaten and the presents opened. Kind of a letdown, if you know what I mean. I feel like I should be planning something or at least have some idea of what I'm going to do next, but I don't have the slightest idea."

"I always felt that way about Christmas myself. The anticipation is better than the actual event. But then you go on to the next day and hope something will come along to get that anticipation working again. I'm sure a plan will surface before you know it, and you'll be in it with both feet."

Cary laughed, a charming, manly sound that delighted Julie. "You, dear lady, are a boost to my ego. I know something will come along, especially if I give a little push. I'm not one to sit around and rest on my laurels. I have a lot of years ahead—" He stopped, a stricken look on his face. "Ah, if you need anything, just ask. I guess I'll see you later this evening. Amelia and I are going on ahead, but the rest of the family is going together." As if she didn't already know all of this. He gave Julie an airy wave and closed the door softly behind him.

Julie looked around at the spacious but rather Spartan bedroom. She couldn't make up her mind if she was elated or disappointed. For years she'd heard her Uncle Thad and Billie speak of Sunbridge. Her uncle's voice had always sounded so enthusiastic, and Billie's had always sounded . . . sad. Of course, that could all be explained away, she decided. Moss Coleman, Billie's first husband and heir to Sunbridge, had been her Uncle Thad's best friend all during the war and up until the day he died. She didn't think she'd have liked the former heir to Sunbridge. The bits and pieces she'd heard over the years convinced her that Moss Coleman hadn't been the gentle, loving, caring man her Uncle Thad was. As far as she was concerned, the man hadn't been born yet who could come close to her uncle.

If it hadn't been for Uncle Thad, she wouldn't have gone to college, she wouldn't have her job, and she wouldn't be standing here in Sunbridge. She'd been seventeen and in her last year of high school when her family's house burned to the ground. It was a wonderful old house with mullioned windows and a glorious staircase with a perfect shining banister to slide down in the mornings. It had an attic full of secret hidey-holes for little girls to play in, and trunks and boxes, each full of surprises for a rainy day. There were little nooks and crannies all over the house, perfect places for hiding treasures from one's parents. The kitchen with its braided rugs and floor-to-ceiling windows, allowing for all the light in the world, had been her favorite place to drink lemonade and munch on fat sugar cookies sprinkled with cinnamon. She had a dog named Jasper who followed her wherever she went and slept in the crook of her arm. When she was twelve, a nasty old woodchuck bit off Jasper's tail; he died from an infection three weeks later. Dog after dog was paraded in front of Julie, but all she would do was shake her head. There were certain things in life that could never be replaced, and Jasper was one of them.

A magnificent elm tree stood outside her bedroom window, hundreds of years old with perfect branches for sneaking out to meet boys. Going down was always easy; shinnying back up yielded more scraped knees than she cared to remember. The tree had burned along with the house, and to this day she didn't know which she grieved for more, the tree or the house.

She'd had her best years, her fondest memories, in that old house. Once in a while she suffered frightful attacks of guilt because she'd shinnied down the elm the night of the fire; she was a mile away while her parents were trapped in their bedroom by the thick, black smoke.

After the funeral she drew into herself and managed to escape reality and herself for a whole year. It was her Uncle Thad who brought her back to the land of the living with his patience and kindness. He helped her select a college, settled her in, explained to the dean about his career as a naval officer and stressed that he could always be reached for the important events like Parent's Day, Homecoming, and graduation. He hadn't failed her once.

Thad had helped her land her first job as a graphic designer for a mail-order catalog. She'd worked there for seven years, and when there were no more challenges and no more pay raises, she left and found a job that paid more money and was chock-full of challenges, one of which was a man who made her heart skip a beat. But when the relationship didn't progress, and she pressed for a commitment, he'd told her he was already committed—to a wife and two babies. She became wary after that, not trusting men. There had been other relationships, but for some reason they never lasted more than a few months. Normally cheerful by nature, she refused to allow the lack of a man in her life to depress her. She loved Vermont and the invigorating outdoor life. She worked long, hard hours, and filled the void in her life with activities and work. She was reasonably happy and felt she was well adjusted, but she was coming to that time in her life when she wanted a change more than a challenge.

Of all the Colemans, Julie decided she liked Billie the best. Next to Billie she liked Amelia. The boys, Riley and Cole, and Maggie and Sawyer were great, too, so normal, just like the people in Vermont. She'd expected glamour, pretentiousness, perhaps even a certain amount of phoniness. People with money, the rich and powerful, according to magazines and the media, were shallow and artificial. The Colemans weren't like that, though; they were warm and kind, welcoming her with affection. Sunbridge itself was old, worn, and inviting, shabby yet genteel. She decided she loved it. She felt a prick of envy that she hadn't been here to grow up next door or down the road. There was no comparison between Vermont maple syrup and Texas oil, she thought with a grin. Simple little Julie Kingsley, daughter of Thad's oldest brother, Simon, here at last in what she'd always thought of as fairy-tale land.

For a minute she wished she were younger, prettier, shapelier. But then, if she were all those things, she wouldn't be Julie Kingsley.

There was enough change going on in her life now. The first of the year would find her in New York City with a new job and, with any luck at all, a new social life. Anything had to be better than Vermont. She considered the move a challenge and she was looking forward to it.

She felt alive and vibrant as she twirled about the room. For a little while she could be part of this wonderful place called Sunbridge. For now she was one of *them*.

How good it felt. How *right* it felt.

Enough daydreaming. She unpacked her overnight bag, hanging her evening dress carefully on a scented hanger in a cedar-lined closet.

The exquisite-smelling bath salts in the crystal decanter made Julie gasp. The little decorative container, along with the bath salts, probably cost more than she earned in a week as a graphic artist. She slid down into the fragrant wetness. A bath, she sighed, had to be the most relaxing thing on earth.

The thick, thirsty towels were bordered and monogrammed in satin. She knew she could get used to this kind of living with very little effort. Now that she was so relaxed, a catnap might be in order.

Julie's last conscious thought before she shifted her mind to nothingness was that Amelia Coleman Assante was one lucky woman.

Cole stood with his hands on his hips, staring through the kitchen window at his cousin. "Christ, he's going to freeze out there!" he muttered. He was in tune with Riley these days. Their feelings for each other had changed and deepened when they went their separate ways to different colleges. Their hostility and competitiveness had given way to good-natured camaraderie, and while they didn't live in each other's shadow, they were there for one another when the going got tough. Right now, for Riley, it couldn't get any tougher, Cole thought. Should he go outside and offer his ear? Hell, Riley knew all he had to do was look at him in a certain way and he'd drop whatever he was doing and give him the benefit of his own twenty-eight-year-old wisdom.

Riley turned, feeling Cole's gaze. Cole offered a crooked grin through the glass.

"You got an icicle hanging off your nose," he joked when Riley finally got inside.

"Wouldn't surprise me. It's as cold as a witch's tit out there. Where is everyone?"

"In the living room trying to decide if they should have another drink or a nap to rest up for tonight. Aunt Amelia sent me to find you—your grandfather wants to talk to you."

"I know. I'm trying to get myself together first."

Cole slapped his cousin playfully on the back. "Why? Since when do you have to?" The strained look on Riley's face finally registered. "Jesus, you didn't know he was sick?"

"I didn't think it was this serious. Sawyer said he wasn't feeling well. That's all she said."

"Haven't you talked to him, written?"

"No," Riley said curtly.

"I know this is none of my business, but don't you think—"

"Do you want the truth? I think I've known for months. I'm sure you know what it all means."

"For now, what it means is your grandfather is ill and wants to talk to you. You can't avoid it, Riley. His illness isn't going to go away. He will, though. How will you handle that? I don't think you have to make any earthshaking decisions in the next few hours. They're all waiting in there to see what you do. No matter what your decision, this family is one hundred percent behind you."

"I've been thinking about something lately." Riley waved his hands about to show that what he was going to say was vague at best. "The thought came to me one night, from out of nowhere. You should have been me and I should have been you. You'd love operating Rising Sun. I'd hate it. I love what I do here and . . . you hate it. You never actually said you hate . . . What I mean is . . . ah, forget it. This is what happens when you box yourself into a corner and can't get out."

Cole digested Riley's words. The thought of operating the Rising Sun publishing empire was so awesome, so mind-blowing, so . . . He shuddered.

"Can I help . . . ?"

"No one can help me," Riley said miserably.

"I think you're wrong. I think your grandfather will understand if you talk it out with him. He might not like your decision, but he'll understand and respect it."

"My mother must be anguishing in her grave. I was taught from the time I was . . . It's expected. . . . I'm the only male grandchild; it was all my grandfather used to talk about. My mother would have expected it of me. I knew this day was going to come and I didn't prepare for it."

"What you thought, Riley, was that your grandfather would die peacefully in his sleep. You thought he wouldn't be around when it was time to make the decision. Saying no to the old man could be the toughest thing in the world to do. If you can admit that, we have something to work with. Well, am I right?"

"About as right as can be. Cole, I haven't been around, haven't seen death or sickness. My father died before I was born. My mother died quickly; there was no illness. She was at my side and then she was gone. I'm going to have to live with this every waking minute of my life until . . ."

Cole glanced at his watch. "We've been out here too long. Come on, let's go talk to him together. I'll stick with you and babble up a storm. That way you can postpone the moment till later, when you're alone."

Only Maggie noticed the strain on their faces as Cole and Riley burst through the swinging door. The Coleman men. The only Coleman men. Her eyes shifted to Shadaharu Hasegawa and then to her mother. Conversation picked up and she could hear Sawyer's tinkling laugh as she tried to describe her miniature house in Japan. She turned to her husband. "Cole's there for him. That's all I needed to see. What do you say, Mr. Nelson, let's you and I take a long, I mean really long, warm —as in very warm—shower together?"

"You're leering at me, Maggie."

"Ah, a man with a keen eye. What's your feeling on silk sheets?"

"The same as yours. You mean there's silk sheets upstairs?"

"Only because I brought them with me, and that delicious soap you like . . . and the scented coconut oil."

"Show me the way home, honey."

"We don't want to be obvious, now, do we?"

"God forbid. Should I take the back stairs and you take the front?"

"Sounds good to me." Maggie giggled.

"Darling, we don't see enough of you anymore," Billie complained to Sawyer.

"It's tough running Coleman Aviation from a foreign country, Grand. I wish I could get back more often. I'm seriously thinking about hiring a couple of assistants. So far, the thing that's held me back is the language barrier. I can speak pidgin Japanese, but that's about it. They're such good workers, Grand, they put me to shame, and you know I'm no slouch. And look, let's not get into the oil thing this afternoon, okay?" Sawyer added a bit of nonchalance to her next question. "Has anyone heard from Adam Jarvis?"

Thad smiled. "I saw him in Washington a couple of months ago. He asked about you."

"He did, huh? He never writes. We've lost touch. I heard about his wife and I wanted to . . . I didn't think I should."

"You should have—Adam is a good friend," her grandmother admonished. "I'm surprised, Sawyer; that's not like you."

"I know it isn't. To tell you the truth, I wanted to take the next plane home. I had to fight with myself. It's one of those things, Grand, where he has to make the first move. I know I let it hang there, but after my surgery and recovery I couldn't bind him to me in any way. We both knew that. Adam chose to go a different route, and I was happy for him. Sad at my loss, but as long as he was happy, that's all that mattered. You see, Grand, I learned how to put other people first, just the way you taught me."

"I shouldn't be carrying tales," Thad said, "but then, Adam didn't swear me to secrecy. He told me his marriage was one of convenience more than anything else. He has a stepson, you know. A troubled boy, from what he told me."

"I believe, and I have always believed, that Adam loves you," Billie said gently. "I think the two of you have to sit down and have a long talk before one of you does something that can't be corrected."

"I'm going to work on it, Grand," Sawyer said, just as gently.

Billie noticed that Sawyer's eyes kept sweeping the room,

{ 33 }

always coming to rest on Riley and Shadaharu Hasegawa.

"I wish there was something I could do," Sawyer said, knowing her grandmother would understand what she was referring to.

"I can feel Riley's torment, and I know just how Mr. Hasegawa feels. If they can meet at some point, things might be all right." Billie's eyes brimmed with tears. Thad reached out to clasp her hand in his. He, too, understood.

"Don't count on it, Grand," said Sawyer. "Riley wants it all. Mr. Hasegawa wants all of Riley. Culture, honor, duty— an awesome threesome, if you follow me. Riley is in an awful position, or as Cole would say, between a rock and a hard place. I honestly don't know what he'll do. I lie awake nights worrying about him, and when I try to talk to him, he says he's working on it. I feel we should be doing something, at least talking to him."

"No, that's the worst thing we can do," Thad interjected. "When and if he needs our help, he knows we're here for him. Riley has to work this out himself."

"Thad, darling, perhaps you could talk to Mr. Hasegawa. Tell him of Riley's torment. He'll listen to you. You've been friends for so many years."

"Darling Billie, I would cut off my arm for you, but in this instance I cannot, I will not, interfere. And for the very reason you just mentioned. We have been friends for many years, and Shadaharu himself was the one who drew up the boundaries that were not to be crossed. I've always respected them, as he has."

"I know, I know. I'm grasping at straws. I still can't believe he traveled all this way in his condition. He's not mentioned his illness once. I couldn't say anything, unless he did. I feel so helpless."

"Welcome to the club," Sawyer said wryly. "I don't know about you two, but I think I'm going to take a nice warm shower and a nap. I understand we're all going to dance the night away, and I want to be prepared."

"I think you're right, darling," Billie said, getting to her feet. "The part about the shower and the nap. I'm not sure I can dance the night away. What's your feeling on that, Senator Kingsley?" she asked playfully.

Thad laughed. "It's my feeling—and mind you, it's just my feeling—that those of us who can dance the night away will, and those of us who can't, won't."

"And he's off the hook again," Billie said. "Spoken like a true politician."

As the room emptied, Cole shifted from one foot to the other. Riley's slight nod told him he, too, could go upstairs. He touched the old Japanese on the shoulder and poked Riley playfully. "Five-thirty in the central hallway, Coleman."

"We'll be there," Riley said lightly.

In the quiet of the room, with only the logs crackling in the fireplace, young eyes stared deeply into old eyes. No words were spoken. Riley lowered his head first, in deference to his grandfather. He let go of the thin, veined hands he'd been holding. He got up from the ottoman and jammed his own hands into his pockets to stop their trembling.

The old man leaned back and stared up at his grandson. He was so American. Even his height. By Japanese standards, six feet three inches was of monster proportions. He would have to listen to his grandson's tortured words. He thought he knew what Riley was going to say, and he dreaded hearing it. He waited patiently for him to collect his thoughts. Nothing in his long life had prepared him for this moment. How was it possible, he asked himself, to love one person so much, to the exclusion of all else? He could feel his own hands start to tremble. He knotted them together and was rewarded with pain.

"I love this place," Riley said, waving his arms about. "Leaving all of it would be like tearing my insides out. I sleep in my father's bed in the room that belonged to him. My baseball cap that was my father's hangs on his peg on the hat rack in the hall. Aunt Maggie turned over half of Sunbridge to me because it was meant for my father. Grandma Billie turned over the oil and cattle end of the business to me to run. You sent me here. You saved this family in its darkest hour!" Riley cried passionately.

To visit, the old Japanese wanted to shout, not to stay. Yes, I helped save this family because of a man's dream, and you were part of that dream. He could say none of those things, even in a whisper. The boy hadn't said he *wouldn't* return, only that leaving would be like tearing out his insides.

The old man's eyes were heavy and his stomach pained him. At the moment hope and anticipation were exhausting emotions.

"I have not forgotten my old life, Grandfather. I think of it every day. I compare my life here and my life as I remember it in Japan. I know you feel I am dishonoring our family, and I feel shame with my inability to...Cole should be your grandson, not me. Cole would be everything you want and what I can't be. Why...why did this have to happen? My mother would have understood; why can't you?" Riley cried in a torn voice.

The anguish in his grandson's voice ripped at the old man's heart. "Coleman Tanner is not of my blood. You are," Shadaharu Hasegawa said softly.

"Then you should understand why I want to remain here. My blood is here, too. I'm one of the Colemans. I belong. I'm one of *them*. I don't want you to ask me to give this up. Please, Grandfather, don't ask that of me." Desperately he threw Cole's name into the exchange a second time. Later he realized it was to get himself off the hook. "It isn't fair. Cole doesn't want all of this. I do. Cole won't leave because he... He doesn't want to belong....Forget it, Grandfather. I see that you're tired and..."

"It has been a long day, my grandson. Please, help this old man up the stairs so that I can sleep before this evening's events. By help, Riley, I mean that you will walk behind me." The old man swallowed hard. If he pretended not to hear the words, they wouldn't eat away at him like the disease in his body.

"Yes, Grandfather," Riley said respectfully. This way you will not see my tears, nor I yours.

The second level of Sunbridge was quiet. Riley paced the floor with frenzied steps, smacking one balled fist into the other. It wasn't fair. For years Sawyer had drummed into his head that life wasn't fair and no one had a right to expect it to be. Sawyer herself was a perfect example of an unfair life. She'd loved Rand Nelson and had to give him up when he fell in love with her mother, Maggie. She'd survived. She'd survived the brain tumor, too, and Adam Jarvis's marriage. Grandmam Billie had survived the death of her husband and married Thad. His own mother had died at the hands of a drunken driver. That hadn't been fair, but he and his grandfather had survived. Aunt Amelia had survived bypass surgery and a host of other terrible events. Cole. Cole was different. Cole had his troubles, but he always managed to come out on top. Aunt Maggie was perhaps the most beleaguered and traumatized of all the Colemans, and yet today she was getting ready to fill her mother's shoes as head of the family. They were all survivors. Why should he be any different? The same blood ran in his veins. He dropped his head into his hands. It wasn't going to be enough to win the battle. He had to win the war as well and not come out a casualty. He had to believe he would be a survivor, like the rest of the family.

The bed that he thought of not as his own, but as his father's, welcomed him. He rolled over on his side and was asleep almost instantly, his sleep tortured by a parade of tiny Japanese girls following him up the hill to the cherry blossom grove. He was playing a haunting melody, a favorite of his mother's, on a flute that was a gift from his grandfather. Cries and pleas for help from the edge of the clearing were drowned out by his music and the voices of the little girls. The children pointed, their voices raised in excitement, to the edge of the grove, where the family, one by one, slipped off the embankment. "You're the only one left," the little girls shouted. "The only one!" Then they laughed, high, shrieking sounds. He stopped playing the flute long enough to hear the first little girl say he was their savior. Japanese people didn't say such things. A savior. A word from his own Catholic faith. He woke drenched in sweat and with a pounding headache.

Standing under a pelting shower, he decided that if he did nothing, then nothing would happen. Don't commit, don't make a decision. Look to the future, not the past. For now, it was the best advice he could give himself.

{{{{{{{{ CHAPTER TWO *}}}}}}}}*

It was one of Texas's finest hours.

Miranda was getting a salute that only Texans could give. The city might have been built by Cary Assante, but it was the Coleman family whom the crowds came to see and pay tribute to.

Amelia's dedication of the Jessica Coleman Library was private. The family had voted unanimously to keep it small and personal, and the crowds and press respected their wishes.

It was snowing lightly when the family made its way from

the library to the grand ballroom in Assante Towers.

"This is the part I always hate," Billie muttered. "Being on display."

"Smile, darling, this is for Cary and Amelia," Thad said, looking around at the crowd. "Lord, all of Texas must be here."

"And all the other forty-nine states," Billie giggled. "Half the Senate is here—who do you think is minding the store? I've seen at least twenty Congressmen. I expected the governor and the lieutenant governor, but this . . . this turnout is like a Capitol Hill funeral without the body. If you tell me the president is here, I'll die."

"Not the president, but the second in command," Thad said. "And I had nothing to do with it," he added.

"Mam, I'm stunned!" Maggie gasped. "Who did all this? I just saw Henry Kissinger, and if I'm not mistaken, he was talking to Ted Koppel."

Billie's eyes widened. "Ted Koppel! Thad, is that true? Where is he?"

"Down, girl." Thad laughed. "Maggie, to answer your question, Cary hired publicity people, and Amelia sent out invitations to the governor asking him to invite anyone he wanted. They're old friends, as you know. That accounts for the governors on parade. I guess the Senate and House can be laid on my doorstep. I invited them all, but I didn't think they'd show up. I'm happy they did, but I didn't expect—"

"Thad, this is the first time I've ever seen you at a loss for words," Maggie said. Thad grinned sheepishly.

"Sawyer told me the Beach Boys are playing, and Cole said Elton John and John Denver are singing. They must have been putting me on. They love to see me get excited and then prick my balloon," Maggie cried happily.

"We'll know soon enough, once everyone gets inside."

"I don't know about the rest of you, but I'm going to stand here and gawk," Sawyer stage-whispered behind her hand.

"Me, too," Maggie whispered back. "You-all go inside, and Sawyer and I will report back later. In detail."

Billie's eyes warmed. How happy she was that Maggie and Sawyer were at last not only mother and daughter but friends as well.

"There are more Rolls-Royces, Ferraris, and Jags in the parking lot than in Saudi Arabia," Cole whispered in his mother's ear. "And I saw two sheiks talking to Mr. Hasegawa. Old friends, I believe."

"You look handsome, Cole. Run along now and join the penguin brigade. I appreciate the effort you put into that dinner jacket."

"For you, Mother, anything."

Maggie smiled. She knew he meant every word. It hadn't always been like that. There'd been some rough times, but they were mother and son now, just as she and Sawyer were mother and daughter. How blessed she was.

"This is better than an Academy Awards celebration," Sawyer giggled. "There're movie stars all over the place. I feel like I'm sixteen."

"I feel like I'm nineteen—I have to be older." Maggie laughed.

Mother and daughter stood off to the side, admiring the latest fashions as a parade of glamorous women swept through the wide central doors.

"This ballroom is at least three city blocks wide and long —what do you think, Mam?" Sawyer asked.

"It sounds right to me." Maggie's face turned suddenly serious. "How bad is the oil business, Sawyer? Are you in love with Adam Jarvis?" Nothing like blurting it all out at once, she thought.

"Now, where in the hell did that come from? It's bad, but we have a couple of options. And yes, I'm still in love with Adam. Look at that Fisher mink! Jeez, it's Tess Buckalew!"

"My lord! Lacey's wearing one, too. I thought you said the oil business was bad."

"Ivy looks like a poor relation," Sawyer announced. "I always liked that kid. She's got more on the ball than all the Buckalews put together. Coots looks rather dashing, don't you agree? My goodness, Mitzi Fanny is wearing a Russian sable. Bill looks elegant."

Maggie agreed. "I've seen enough," she said. "Let's go inside and gawk at the gowns and jewels."

Sawyer and Maggie made their way to the family table.

"Mam," Maggie whispered to Billie, "you won't believe —just look around. Galanos, Adolfo, and every major designer in the fashion industry. And Van Cleef, Tiffany, and Cartier! And *we're* all wearing Billie originals. I haven't seen one other Billie outfit. Too expensive, I guess."

"I don't know if that makes me happy or not," Billie said.

"Be delirious, Mam," Maggie said. "We're unique."

"You wouldn't believe how long and hard I worked on your dress, Maggie. I couldn't get the right shade of tangerine to save my life. I wanted it just right for your hair and coloring. You are satisfied, aren't you, honey?"

"Mam, it's perfect. The Popsicle colors in Sawyer's dress amaze me. You have your Blink Pink in there, I see."

"It's my trademark now. You both look lovely. Professional models couldn't show off the dresses better than you two."

The crowds swelled till there was barely inching-around room in any direction. Sawyer craned her neck to see the banquet tables; she was hungry.

The grand ballroom was the size of a football field, and thanks to Cary Assante's efforts, it had been turned into a magical fairyland for the night's festivities.

Five-star chefs dressed in crisp white smocks and crisper starched hats stood behind their culinary masterpieces. The tables were forty feet long and draped in shimmering silver with garlands of red satin ribbon stretching from one end to the other. A three-foot-high ice sculpture—models of Assante Towers—rose up from the center of each table. The crystal chandeliers overhead shone down on the sculptures, bathing them in a red and silver glow, and winked down on the sterling silver serving dishes that held lobster, shrimp, filet mignon, duckling, pheasant under glass, and fresh mushrooms from Japan. Baccarat crystal dishes held colorful vegetables decorated with sprigs of holly and feathery greenery. Cheeses flown in specially from Wisconsin sat on wheels of silver next to platters of beluga caviar. Dom Perignon trickled from hidden spouts in the ice sculptures. "Vintage fifty-nine," one of the chefs whispered to the governor as he waited for his glass to fill.

Waitresses wearing short scarlet swirling skirts trimmed in white fur, like the Dallas Cowboys Cheerleaders, walked through the crowds carrying silver trays with crystal glasses of champagne. In their wake, waiters who could have doubled for the famous Chippendales, wearing skintight scarlet trousers and silver waistcoats, moved through the huge room on light feet, their upraised hands carrying trays of caviar and shrimp.

Before Sawyer asked her brother Cole to sweep her out onto the dance floor, she let her eyes travel once more around the room so she would never forget the most splendiferous sight she'd ever seen. She blinked and shook her head in awe as her eyes went to the four corners of the room, banked with tier after tier of poinsettias. She smiled at the revolving bandstand. Every inch of space that wasn't occupied by the orchestras was covered, with the brilliant red Christmas flowers. "Someday," she muttered to Cole, "I hope someone tells me how much this cost and how much the IRS absorbed. Come on, twinkle-toes, let's cut it!"

Cole smiled woodenly at Sawyer and dragged deeply on his cigarette. He rarely smoked, and when he did, it was out of nervousness or anger. He must be nervous, because he didn't feel angry. This was a hell of a place to soul-search.

He looked around the table at his family. He'd go to the wall for any one of them. He belonged; he was one of *them*; for now. He wondered, as he had many times before, what would happen if he simply picked up and left. The thought made his heart pound. When and if he decided to leave, the only person who would truly understand would be Riley. And possibly his grandmother Billie. She always said, don't marry the Coleman business, make a life for yourself outside the family. How in the living hell was he ever going to *do* that?

"Well?" said Sawyer, holding out her hand to him.

One of these days he was going to sit down and confide in Sawyer. Sawyer was modern, a woman of the eighties, as she was fond of telling everyone. Often over the years when things were bad for her or himself, they'd talked things out.

Sawyer had this thing about family, though. As far as she was concerned, the sun rose and set on the Colemans. Sawyer could be tough as rawhide and soft as marshmallow. Cole's stomach lurched when he remembered the family vigil at the hospital and how Sawyer almost died of a brain tumor.

You needed guts to be a Coleman, and he didn't have the requisite amount. Thank God his name was Tanner. In the end, that and that alone might make it easier for him to make the break.

Cole drained the last of his drink, which was more water than alcohol. He wished he had another.

"Come on, little brother, what say we boogie?" Sawyer said, finally getting up and throwing her arms about him.

"So you can torture me by stepping all over my feet! Everyone knows you have two left feet. How the hell you ever got to be the head of Coleman Aviation is beyond me," Cole grumbled good-naturedly.

"I am the head of Coleman Aviation because I am the best goddamn aeronautical engineer ever to come down the pike. An M.B.A. and a Ph.D. in aerodynamics ain't nothing to sneeze at, little brother. You could say my instincts for business rival only our great-grandfather and grandfather's. And," she said loftily, "I and I alone, with only legal advice, managed to license Grandpa Moss's plane and keep the copyrights intact for you, you little shit. Does that answer your question?"

"Yeah, it does. Can I ask you something, Sawyer? And if I do, will you tell me the truth?"

Sawyer sat down; the dancing would have to wait. It was coming; she could feel it. She'd sensed Cole's tension as soon as she sat down next to him. "You bet," she said lightly.

"Have you ever thought about getting out? Moving on, doing something . . . unrelated to the family."

So that was it. The old identity thing that plagued them all from time to time. "At times. You know what a coward I am. I know what I have and I don't know what I'd step into out there. The unknown frightens me."

"Come off it," Cole growled.

"Seriously," Sawyer said gently. "Even when I knew I'd die if I didn't have the brain operation, I couldn't make myself agree to have it. I was so afraid. . . . I didn't know. . . . If it wasn't for you and Adam and Riley, and of course all the family, I never would have . . . You know what I'm trying to say."

"You're saying you'll run Coleman Aviation until you drop because you're a Coleman and it's expected. That sucks, Sawyer!"

Sawyer snorted. "When you put it like that, I guess it does. Look, if a white knight named Adam Jarvis showed up on my doorstep and offered me the proverbial vine-covered, picket-fenced cottage, I'd snap him up so fast both our heads would spin. Until that happens I am committed to this family and this company. But I *could* leave, as long as it was for my own happiness and survival. Did I help?" she asked anxiously.

Cole grinned. "Yeah, you always help." She hadn't asked him any pointed questions; Sawyer never did.

"On your feet, woman! Let's show these people the two Coleman illegitimate bastard children know how to dance!" Cole quipped.

"I'm with you, little brother," Sawyer laughed. Her hand

was on Cole's shoulder as he fought his way to the crowded dance floor.

As brother and sister edged their way off the dance floor, Cole grabbed Ivy Buckalew and dragged her back among the dancers just as the band started to play "The Shadow of Your Smile."

"You having a good time?" Cole asked. Hmmmnn, Ivy looked good. She smelled sweet and clean. He drew her closer, but not until she answered him.

"No. I wish I was home."

"You and me both. Unfortunately, this is one of those things that are a must."

"Maybe for you, but not for me. This isn't my . . . I don't fit . . . you know . . ."

"Yeah, I do know," Cole said softly. Gently he edged her away from him. He looked into her eyes and was stunned at how pretty Ivy was. Christ, she'd grown up and he hadn't even noticed. "Ivy, sometimes wanting something isn't enough. Sometimes you have to go out there and slug your way through the crap to get what you want."

"If you're talking about what I think you're talking about, I'm the first one to admit I'm no match for . . ." Ivy jerked her head in her sister's direction.

"Look at me, Ivy. Do you want to be like that?"

"A little," Ivy admitted miserably.

"Trust me, you don't. You're real, kid. You hang in there and before you know it, Sir Galahad over there is going to wake up and start paying attention. Time will do it, Ivy. The white knight over there," Cole said, inclining his head in Riley's direction, "still thinks of you as one of the guys. We've all been friends for so long, it takes us a little while to notice the changes in one another." He chuckled when he said, "Remember how you could always climb the trees fastest, get the worm on the hook quicker, hit the softball a real whack for a girl, not to mention how you outbreaststroked him in the swim meet? If I remember correctly, your backhand was a smidgen better than his, and how many times did you get a hole in one? On top of that, each time you bested him, you clapped him on the back so hard he almost fell over. I'm the first one to admit I know nothing about women, but I do know about guys. You didn't let him win, ever, Ivy. If you want the truth, I think you intimidate him."

"But . . . I just did it to . . . so he would notice me. . . . Jeez, he writes such great letters, you know, real buddy-buddy stuff. He never gave a hint of . . . how he felt," Ivy said miserably.

"Oh, he noticed, all right," Cole drawled. "He'd rather have a stick in the eye than let you know how he feels about your prowess."

Ivy stepped back from Cole a little. "I don't know how to be a limp doll, and I'm not a clinging vine. I am what I am. So what if I'm better at something than he is?" She laughed, a sound of pure mirth. "God, how I hated those slimy little worms. I'll tell you what, I won't clap him on the back anymore. That's the only concession I'll make, not that it matters anyway: He's so tight with Lacey, he doesn't know I'm alive."

"Ivy, trust me when I tell you he knows. He knows," Cole said soothingly as he swept her across the dance floor.

When the dance was over, Ivy slipped away. Cole watched her till she was out of sight. When he turned, he was staring directly at Lacey. He nodded curtly and headed back to the family table.

Lacey Buckalew was history.

"I thought you always said you were graceful," Cole complained to Sawyer as he joined her at the table. "All you did was step on my toes."

"That wasn't me, and I am graceful. Ask Riley. He just got sandwiched into a corner over there with Lacey and can't get out. By the way," she said, "I saw Lacey give you a look that means she'd like to get you onto the dance floor. It isn't any of my business, but I don't think Riley—"

"You didn't see me dance with her, did you?"

"Touchy, aren't we?" Sawyer kidded. At the look on Cole's face, she drew back. "I'm sorry, Cole. It's just that Riley is so . . . so sensitive. You and Lacey had a thing going for several years. I thought . . . we all thought you were going to make it permanent. I am out of line. Forget I said anything."

"She wanted to get married, I didn't," Cole growled. It was almost a relief to talk about it even though he was giving Sawyer, out of habit, a hard time.

Sawyer sipped at her wine. "If I drink any more of this stuff, I'll have a good buzz on." She tried for a light tone. "Who's driving?"

"I am, and I'll get you home in one piece. And it won't be the first time I've had to sober you up."

"That's unkind, little brother. Circumstances . . ." she let her voice trail off.

"I think she's stringing Riley along. I also think she talked him into picking up her father's oil leases."

Sawyer's face set into hard lines. "If he did, that's his problem now, isn't it? Riley's all grown up and has to take responsibility for his actions. He's not as fast track as you, but he's got to learn how not to be taken. If that's what's happening."

"Aren't you being kind of hard on him?"

"Ah, to your cousin's defense. I like that, Cole. I can't get used to the idea that Riley would pick up your leftovers. I'm sure he was flattered when she came on to him, but engaged . . . Come on!"

"It's none of our business," Cole said flatly.

"Was it your business when she came on to you this evening? I wasn't spying, but I couldn't help overhearing."

"Then you know my response. It's over. I'd never do anything to offend Riley. We trust each other."

"Then somebody should tell Lacey before Riley gets downwind of his intended's intentions."

"I already did."

"Let's change the subject. Did you see the look on Thad's face when that Saudi sheik asked Grand to dance?"

Cole hooted. "Yeah, but the look on Grandmam's face was what got me. It was the first time I've ever seen her at a loss. Dancing with a guy in a dress!"

"Robe. He was doing some serious talking to Mr. Hasegawa. Thad said he ordered thirty million microchips. Just like that. We're in the wrong business, little brother."

Cole wanted to tell her she was right, in regard to himself, but he kept quiet. He wished he had more of Sawyer's blasé attitude toward life.

"Well, I'm off to the ladies' room to powder my nose, providing I can find it. Hold down the table," Sawyer said.

"Don't fall in," Cole cracked.

"I'm not drunk, not even close to it. I feel good. Any time you want to talk some more, I'll listen. I've known for a long time that something's bothering you, and it isn't the Lacey thing, either."

Cole's face was serious. "I'll keep it in mind. Go on, before you wet your pants."

Sawyer squawked. "How—"

"Because you're hopping from one foot to the other. If you don't think you can find the ladies' room, I can show you where it is."

Cole laughed when Sawyer wobbled off. When she came back her hair would be combed, she'd have on fresh lipstick, and there would be a serious expression on her face, and she'd look every inch the professional aeronautical engineer that she was. His sister. And he loved her.

Tess Buckalew fought her way across the crowded room, jabbing and poking with her bony elbows. She had to find Lacey. She'd just heard one of the photographers say they wanted pictures of the family. Lacey was soon to be family, and if Lacey was family, so was she. She could already see her picture on the front page of the *Crystal City Times*, standing or sitting next to the Coleman family. When she'd told Coots to head toward the Coleman table, he'd disappeared. Maybe it was just as well. He looked like he'd been rode hard and put up wet. Drink did that to Coots.

"Lacey honey, there you are." Tess made her way to Lacey and Riley a few steps away, champagne goblet in hand. "The photographers sent me to fetch you two. They want to take some pictures of the family," she said. Riley groaned as she grabbed their glasses and set them on the nearest table.

"Come on, Riley. Mama wants to have her picture taken. Don't you want to see yourself on the front page tomorrow?"

"Not really. I must have posed a hundred times today."

"That many?" Tess cried in dismay. That meant they'd sift through the best for the front page. Her spirits drooped, then brightened. Surely, though, the last picture of the evening would be the one they'd choose.

"Stay behind me and I'll plow through," Riley grumbled.

"Mama, where's Ivy? I haven't seen her all night."

"She went home," Tess said curtly.

Riley stopped and turned. "Why? Why did Ivy go home?"

"For heaven's sake, Riley, I don't know," Tess shrilled. "I suppose because no one paid attention to her. You know Ivy; she has two hundred reasons why she does things."

"How did she get home?" Lacey demanded.

Riley stood rooted to the floor. "I promised to dance with her."

"Riley Coleman, you can dance with her at your wedding.

Move along, now. I can see the photographers from here and they look impatient."

"You don't suppose she walked home, do you, Lacey?"

"It would be just like her. Or else she hitched a ride. Ivy is very self-sufficient. Don't worry about her."

"Someone should—it's freezing outside," Riley said curtly.

As soon as he reached the table, Riley stepped over to Thad. "Thad, have you seen Ivy?"

"Not for a long time. Why? Is something wrong?"

"Probably not."

"I saw her talking to your grandfather," Cole volunteered. "I think he arranged for one of the Saudis to take her home. Check with him—but first, smile pretty, we're news tonight."

Riley fixed his face into a grimace. Out of the corner of his eye he could see Tess Buckalew push Lacey next to Sawyer. It annoyed him, but what annoyed him more was the look on Lacey's face as she stared across at Cole.

The moment the photographers departed, Riley sought out his grandfather. "Did you arrange for Ivy to get home, Grandfather?"

The old man nodded. "I offered to go with her, but she declined. She's a remarkable young woman. She says what she thinks. Very down-to-earth. A pity there is no one to show approval."

"She is outspoken," Riley agreed. "What did she say?"

"She said"—the old man pursed his lips into a round O—"that this affair . . . sucked." Riley burst out laughing. "It was obvious to me that you hurt her feelings by promising to dance with her and then . . ."

So he was to be charged with neglect on top of everything else. "I'll make it up to her. Ivy and I have been friends for a long time."

"No, my grandson, this you cannot make up for. The slight was too real to Miss Ivy."

Riley swallowed past the lump in his throat. "I'll still try. Tell me, Grandfather, how do you like Lacey? Doesn't she look beautiful?"

The old Japanese was quiet for so long, Riley thought he'd dozed off. "My preference," he said quietly, "runs to ugly ducklings."

Riley winced. Then anger shot through him. "You barely know Lacey."

"I was going to say the same thing to you, my grandson. What looks beautiful on the outside isn't always beautiful on the inside. One doesn't have to live many years to know this simple truth." The old man rose with difficulty. "Thad is trying to gain my attention," he said. "I must leave with them."

"I'll see you back at the house, Grandfather. I have to take Lacey home."

"Say good night for me," the old man said softly.

Riley watched his grandfather make his way around the table. He didn't approve. Somehow he'd known he wouldn't. None of the family approved. Jesus, what had he gotten himself into?

Cary and Amelia walked around the empty ballroom. "What do you think, babe? Was this a party to end all parties?"

"That about sums it up. All I want to do is go upstairs and take off my shoes."

"Everyone had a good time. I don't know about you, but I think those Saudis made the night. When they came trooping in, all eyes were on them. And when Billie danced with one of them, I couldn't believe it. That's the picture that's going on the front page. You wait and see."

Amelia yawned. "I wouldn't be surprised. I'm just grateful we don't have to clean up this mess." She looked at her watch. "It's two minutes after twelve. It's history now. Don't look so forlorn, darling. There will be other projects for you to work on. You deserve a rest."

Cary swept his wife into his arms. "Tonight, my darling, you get a free ride, and I'm going to carry you over the threshold. Hang on!"

Amelia squealed with delight. A perfect ending to a perfect evening.

The overpowering stretch limo pulled into the long drive of Buckalew Big Wells. Ivy didn't wait for the turbaned driver to step out and open her door. She scrambled out and muttered a breathless "Thanks." The driver frowned. The young lady was supposed to wait. These Americans, they were all so impatient. He bowed low and offered his arm to escort her to the door. Ivy giggled and then sobered when she saw a look of horror spread across the man's face at the sight of the reindeer on top of the roof.

Ivy was mortified. "It's . . . it's an advertisement. This is fine; you don't have to walk me any further. I can manage from here on. Listen, would you mind . . . What I mean is, oh hell, what do you guys wear under all those white sheets?"

The driver grinned, his teeth as white as the turban on his head. "As little as possible."

"Uh huh, that's kind of what I thought. Thank you for driving me home. I really appreciate it. I know you must want to get back to the party and all. . . ."

"Yes, the party. I will sit in the car and wait. You are the wise one to leave so early. It sounded like a . . . rousing party."

"It was rousing all right. Thanks again."

Ivy grinned in the darkness when she saw the driver glance back over his shoulder at the garish Christmas display on the roof. She laughed aloud when she saw him shake his head in disbelief.

Ivy closed her bedroom door and stripped off the ugly brown dress, a defiant purchase made years ago to annoy her mother. It had backfired, though, when Tess said, "It suits you."

Snug in a beautifully tailored mauve robe with satin piping down the front, a Christmas gift last year from Lacey, she settled herself in a chair by her bedroom window. She stared into the black, cold night waiting for the first sight of Riley and Lacey's return.

She'd been so sure Riley would ask her to dance. She'd boned up on the latest steps so she wouldn't appear awkward and nervous in his arms. Not only didn't he dance with her, he didn't come near her all evening. Three times she'd fought her way to the banquet table, and then to the bar when she saw Riley heading that way, but she'd been stonewalled by the crowds. The highlight of the evening was her dance with Cole, and their serious conversation, and her meeting with Riley's grandfather. She loved the old Japanese on sight.

Damn Riley Coleman!

The evening wasn't a total loss. Shadaharu Hasegawa had liked her, she could tell. She'd made him laugh aloud and she'd made him smile and she'd made him talk. When he arranged for her to get home, he'd patted her on the head and then clasped both her hands in his frail ones. "We have something in common, little one: my grandson." She'd blushed furiously and the old man had pretended not to notice.

Ivy hated formal, stiff good-byes, so she threw her arms around the old man and kissed him soundly on the cheek. He'd beamed his pleasure while, out of the corner of her eye, she saw Lacey glaring at her. "Thank you," she'd said, "for making this evening bearable. I really enjoyed our talk. Have a safe trip home. If I ever get to Japan, I'll look you up," she'd said breezily, to cover her awareness of the old man's condition.

And that was the end of her evening.

Ivy dozed but jerked awake at the sound of the Bronco's engine and the headlights arcing onto her bedroom wall. She peered out but couldn't see a thing beyond Riley's high-beam lights. What had she expected? Absolutely nothing. What she wished was for Riley to jump out of the Bronco, minus Lacey, and have him throw a pebble at her window. Real Romeo and Juliet stuff.

Ivy dropped to her knees, something she did every night before sleep. She offered up several prayers and then asked the same thing she asked for every night: "Please God, don't let me hate Mama and Lacey, and if you can, make them stop hating me. I work so hard, God, trying to be nice to them, but I always get whacked in the face. I can't turn the other cheek anymore. I know You must have a reason for making me hurt like this, and it would help if I knew what it is. Bless them all, and if You can fit Riley into my scheme of things, I'd really appreciate it. Sometimes, God, you just know certain things, and I know I'm meant for Riley Coleman. He doesn't know that yet, so if You could intercede a little on my behalf, I can do the rest. And while you're working at that, try to make Lacey happy, but not at Riley's expense. If You decide to help, that is."

Lacey Buckalew was annoyed, though she tried not to show it. Riding in a Ford Bronco while wearing a Fisher mink wasn't her idea of class. That was for starters. Riley wasn't with her mentally, which probably meant he was ticked off because she'd been talking to Cole. Her mother had been on her back all evening to make more of a show of togetherness with Riley. Her father had managed to get a gibe in twice during the course of the evening. Then the business with Ivy. Leave it to Ivy to screw things up! It was amazing the way Riley had come to Ivy's defense, but then, he'd always had a soft spot for her.

She'd been dating Riley now for almost seven months. Her parents expected an engagement announcement over the holidays. She'd pressured Riley, backed him into a corner, aware instinctively that his honor would be in question if he didn't come through. Not that he'd gone to bed with her. It was another kind of honor, something she sensed but didn't fully understand. She doubted if Riley understood it himself. When she asked him if he was going to give her an engagement ring, he'd blinked and said, "Is that what you want?" She'd nodded, even though that wasn't what she wanted at all.

What she wanted was an engagement ring from Cole. Just hours ago Cole had told her to get away from him, not to make a fool out of both of them. He'd hissed the words through clenched teeth. She wondered now if any of the other guests had been aware of her flaming cheeks and her shame. And his final insult as she was trying to gather her dignity: "You'll do anything to get into this family, won't you?" Somehow or other she'd managed to smile because her mother was looking at her and the message was clear: Cole Tanner was not in the best interests of the Buckalews; Riley was.

But she didn't love Riley Coleman. She loved Cole and probably always would. How stupid she'd been, how unrealistic to have assumed she could demand that Cole marry her! They'd had a long-standing relationship, but according to Cole, she'd imposed on that relationship because she knew full well he wasn't ready for marriage. She'd cried at first, knowing Cole was always moved by her tears, but when he appeared unmoved, she'd turned into a shrew, swearing and threatening all kinds of wicked things. The disgust in Cole's eyes was still with her. She'd run to Riley to lick her wounds and he'd consoled her, telling her Cole was a fool, something she needed to hear. He'd told her how pretty she was, how elegant she looked, and he reinforced each compliment by reassuring her that Cole would come around, Cole would realize his mistake. But it hadn't worked that way. And somehow or other she'd started dating Riley—casual, friendly dates for dinner, a concert, a movie, or just hanging out at the ranch.

Riley was a great guy. She wished she could love him, and in a way she did, but not the way she loved Cole. It bothered her that he hadn't put any moves on her. Did he consider her Cole's leftovers? Of did he worry about what his family would think? Apparently he was going to go through with the engagement, and engagements led to weddings. Sooner or later. Riley was a handsome young man, all six feet three inches of him. The slight slant of his eyes and the delicate coloring made him look sensual and mysterious. He was gentle and sensitive, but she knew he could be a hard-driving force in business. Her father had attested to that.

Suddenly she realized that Riley was taking her home, not back to Sunbridge. She wanted to be angry, to say cruel things, but she held her tongue. Going back to Sunbridge would have meant she could see Cole again. Already she'd forgotten her shame and humiliation. Seeing Cole, even if it was just across the room, was all she wanted. And Riley was denying her that pleasure.

"A penny for your thoughts, Riley," she said lightly.

"Do I come so cheap?"

She could tell by his voice she'd offended him. Cole would have taken the comment in stride. "It's just that I want to share things with you, and that includes your thoughts. If something is bothering you, we should talk about it." She hoped the guilt she was feeling didn't show in her voice when she asked, "Did I do something you don't approve of?" She wouldn't mention Cole. Let him be the one to bring up his cousin's name.

Did she? Riley wondered. He'd felt anger when he saw her talking to Cole, but when she turned and gave him her brilliant smile, it was all right. After all, it was a social occasion. Why shouldn't she talk to Cole? That was over and done with, and both of them had to be civil. Take the easy way out, he told himself. Don't answer her question; ask one in return. Make it casual. "What did you think of my grandfather? I saw you talking to him."

Lacey let a moment go by as she searched for the right words. Words and how they were spoken were important to Riley. "I think you're very lucky to have such a dear, wise grandfather," she finally said.

There was no need to tell Riley she'd spent most of the ten minutes of their meeting trying to calculate his vast wealth and how much of that wealth would be allocated to her when they married. Her parents would want to know, right down to the penny. The old man was sick; she could tell by the yellowish tint in his eyes and his skin. Death had never touched her life in any way. She almost hoped he would die before they were married so she wouldn't have to go to Japan for the funeral. Buddhists yet. Oh well, her mother would probably know what to wear at such a funeral, or consult the stars if she didn't. If the old man died after she was married, the Coleman jet would transport the whole family. She'd be part of that family. Cole would of course attend. He loved the old man. She could picture Riley grieving, Cole and herself at his side, consoling him. She would probably be the only one not grieving, but she could learn how to act it out. She was, after all, Tess Buckalew's daughter.

Lacey inched as close to Riley as she could, but she was hampered by the Bronco's console. The heavy fur didn't help either. The car was moving, the heater was purring, and Riley simply wasn't with her. Well, if it was her relationship with Cole that was bothering him, he was going to have to get over it. She couldn't change the fact that she and Cole had been lovers. Lots of women had lovers. Most women were not meant for a nunnery. But a small worm of fear told her it wasn't just Cole; there was another reason for Riley's remoteness. For a brief moment she felt insulted. She should be all he thought about.

"You've never been to Japan, have you? I'm going to drop you off, Lacey, and get back to the house," Riley said, all in one breath. "I want to spend some time with my grandfather."

Lacey blinked, her incredible blue eyes darting swiftly to Riley. Now, what was *that* supposed to mean? Good God, surely he wasn't thinking about going back to Japan to live. She could never live with Orientals on a daily basis, unless, of course, they were servants. Drop her off! Riley never just dropped her off. As a matter of fact, she usually had to tell him to leave. She was warm now and her teeth had stopped chattering. When she spoke, her voice was as soft and warm as her body.

"No, I've never been to Japan because to go to such a wonderful country by yourself would be a disaster. Perhaps we can honeymoon in Japan and you can show me your country. I'd like that. You know, Riley, I barely had a chance to talk to any of your family this evening. Things were so hectic, and time got away from me. Let me go to Sunbridge with you—I can borrow a car from someone and drive myself home."

"Not tonight." His tone was sharper than he intended, but he didn't apologize. "Tonight is family night, and I want to spend time with my grandfather." He hated it when he had to repeat things to Lacey. He'd certainly told her often enough the way Colemans did things. He always felt at a disadvantage when Lacey put him on the defensive.

"And I'm not part of that family; is that what you're saying?"

Riley refused to be baited. "Not yet," he said lightly.

Her mother was going to have a fit. Dropped off like some high school date. She could hear Tess now. "What do you mean you didn't go to Sunbridge with the family? Riley didn't want you in Cole's company because you behaved like a damn alley cat for everyone to see. That's it, isn't it?" Then her father would start by telling her she better not screw up, and he needed this or that from Riley, and the only way he could get it was for her to be tight with him. He wouldn't mince words, either. "What's this family shit that you aren't good enough?"

She'd have to say she was sick and had wanted to come home. Her parents wouldn't buy it one hundred percent, but it would get Riley off the hook. Damn, now she was actually getting a headache. Okay, play the game.

"Okay, darling," she said softly, "I'm tired, too. I just thought you might want some moral support, but I certainly don't want to go where I'm not wanted." Dig in the knife a little, the way Tess would have done it. Guilt always worked with Riley. She waited for a comment, but when Riley didn't respond, she knew he hadn't heard a word she said.

"Riley, slow down; there's the gate."

"I saw it," he said testily as he cut the wheel hard and careened through the arch that proclaimed this tract of land as Buckalew Big Wells. Every time he drove under the arch he had to fight with himself not to laugh at the ridiculous-sounding name, but not tonight.

Buckalew Big Wells was flooded with light, inside and out. All manner of Christmas decorations blazed in the dark night, including a gigantic sleigh and reindeer prancing across the roof. The spotlights trained on the roof could be seen for miles. He wondered what the garish display had cost.

"I'll make it up to you, Lacey. I guess I'm not with it tonight. Don't be upset."

Riley's voice was too cool and flat. Lacey reached over and touched his face. "I can't be upset with you, Riley. When you love someone you can't get upset with him. Look, don't get out of the car. I can see myself to the door. Call me tomorrow. How will you make it up to me?" she asked sweetly.

"How would you like to go to Rio with me next week? We'll be back before Christmas." The minute the offer was out of his mouth, he regretted it.

"South America! Goodness, Riley, I'll have to think about that. I do have a job, you know." She'd have to confer with her parents. Tess could have her packed and out the door in thirty minutes. Her father would carry her piggyback to the airport. "That would be one sweet way of making things right. The only thing is, Riley, you didn't do anything wrong that you have to make right. Y'all know what I'm sayin'," she drawled. Her mother would kill or at least cripple her for what she'd just said. Better get back to playing the game. "Good night, Riley. Give my regards to your family, and sleep well." She blew a kiss in Riley's general direction and was out the door before he could respond.

Riley sat for a few moments before he backed the Bronco out of the long driveway. He knew Lacey had been trying to make him feel guilty, and he was guilty. Was it the shock— the reality—of his grandfather's condition that was consuming his thoughts and allowing no one to intrude? Definitely. The old one was supposed to live forever, or at least till Riley had his life in order.

He wished he could cry, but Japanese men didn't cry. He knew it was fashionable for American men to reveal their feelings, to shed tears, show their sensitivity. What did half-

Japanese, half-American men do? The pull was there . . . and would always be, until he decided who he really was. Not for the first time this evening, he realized he had some serious thinking to do about a lot of things, and Lacey was one of them. He didn't need any more mistakes in his life.

Ivy was about to turn out her bedside light when Lacey poked her head in the door.

"So you are home! You'll be happy to know you had everyone in a tizzy wondering where you were. You did it on purpose, didn't you? It was the only way for you to get some attention. Admit it!"

"If you say so. Kind of early for you, isn't it? Did Riley get tired of you salivating all over Cole?"

"Grow up, Ivy! I came home because I had a headache. I wasn't in the mood to go to Sunbridge. You'd give your eye-teeth to go over there, wouldn't you?"

"And my back molars," Ivy said honestly. "I like the Colemans."

"Yeah. I watched you sidling up to Cole and Riley's grandfather all evening. Brownie points? Cole only danced with you because he felt sorry for you," Lacey said coolly.

Ivy snuggled beneath the covers. "First of all, Mr. Hasegawa isn't a Coleman. He's a very nice old man and I enjoyed talking to him. Cole and I had a wonderful conversation, and I know in my gut you'd kill right now to find out what he said about you, and I'm not going to tell you. Don't let the door hit you on that skinny rear end of yours on the way out."

"You are a nasty, obnoxious child. I don't know why I waste my time talking to you. I told Riley he shouldn't be concer—"

Ivy's face lit up. Lacey was stunned at how pretty her sister was in the bedroom light. She suddenly lost all desire to hassle Ivy. "Good night, Ivy. Riley said to tell you he was sorry he didn't get to dance with you, like he promised. I only danced with him once myself. I'm sorry about tonight, Ivy, I really am. I wish you'd had a better time."

"Yeah, right," Ivy said bitterly.

Lacey stormed over to Ivy's bed. "Why is it every time I try to be nice to you, you lash out at me? I give up. Mama's right, you're nothing but a spoiled, belligerent snot."

Ivy sat up in bed. "Nice! Since when were you ever nice to me? The only time you're ever nice is when you want something. I wonder what you want now. Oh, I know; you want me to tell you what Cole said. Forget it! You're the one who is like Mama, Lacey. Go to bed. I'm sick of looking at you."

"How can you talk that way? You should get soap in your mouth. Shame on you, Ivy."

"It's real easy when you walk in my shoes," Ivy said smoothly.

Lacey closed the door behind her. She knew Ivy would cry when she turned out the light. She almost turned back, but she didn't. She had enough problems of her own. Ivy would have to handle her own the best way she could. She didn't have time to go into the lifesaving business.

"What is this palaver, Thaddeus?" Shadaharu Hasegawa asked quietly. He and Thad sat side by side on a small sofa in front of the fireplace in the Sunbridge library.

Thad spoke gently to the old man. "I suppose it's something like you Japanese call Move the Shade. You know, your warrior Miyamoto Musashi's guide to strategy." The last time he'd seen Shadaharu, he'd had more hair. Now it was thin and wispy, almost frondlike. He'd been heavier, too, by a good thirty pounds. It was clear that this long evening had been too much for him. Thad's heart thumped. Time was taking all his old friends. Already he could feel the grief building in him.

"Ah, so, I understand. Tell me, Thaddeus, when will you retire from your government office?"

"Is that a gentle reminder that I'm getting old?" Thad laughed.

"Absolutely not," Billie answered for him. "But I'd kind of like to know when myself."

"At the end of this term," Thad said flatly. "Then I'm all yours." Billie's smile caressed her husband. Thad grinned. Shadaharu smiled. Riley felt sick.

Across the room Cole watched his cousin. Something was wrong. His heart leaped in his chest and then settled down to a fast thump. He'd dreaded Riley's arrival, certain he'd have Lacey in tow. But he was alone, and Cole didn't know whether to be glad or sorry. What he did know was that something was bothering Riley, and he didn't think it was Lacey. Maybe he'd search him out later and talk. They'd done that at school, one calling the other when things got tough.

A devil perched himself on Cole's shoulder. "This looks like a wake. What's happened to this family? I remember when we all would party till dawn and then sit down to breakfast and still be full of vigor. It's the shank of the evening, two-thirty, to be exact."

"Listen to my son," Maggie booed. "We're tired. You know that feeling that comes over you when you've put in twenty straight hours with no sleep? Go to bed, upstart!"

A chorus of yeahs echoed around the room; one by one everyone got up. First Amelia and Cary, then Thad and Billie. Susan and Ferris clapped Cole on the back and told him to party somewhere else. Mr. Hasegawa struggled to his feet, perspiration dotting his forehead. He bowed low to the room and followed Billie and Thad. Sawyer was the last to fall into line as she poked Cole on the arm.

"You want to party, call me tomorrow for lunch," she said, laughing. She kissed Maggie lightly and smiled at Rand. "Good night, all."

"Allow me to accompany you upstairs, Grandfather," Riley said.

"It is not necessary, Riley. I am asleep on my feet. Tomorrow we will talk. Before I leave. Will you be driving me to the airport?"

"Of course." He laid a gentle hand on the old man's shoulder and was stunned at how bony it was. Sadness swept through him. He nodded miserably, meeting Cole's compassionate gaze.

"Do I know how to clear a room or what?" Cole grinned.

Riley grinned back. "You ass. Are you telling me you did that on purpose?"

"I can smell the trouble you *think* you're in," Cole said. "Remember when I heisted the statue of Knute Rockne from school and you called me at three in the morning and told me you could smell the trouble I was in? Same thing. Come on, what's up?"

"You and I have come a long way, Cole. We are friends, aren't we?"

"Yes. And cousins."

"Blood, eh? Thicker than water?" Cole nodded. "He . . . What he wants . . ."

"He wants you to go back to Japan and take over his business. If I were in his place, I'd probably want the same thing. What are you going to do?"

"That's just it; I don't know what to do. I was going to talk to you tomorrow. I have two families. No matter what my decision is, I'll be betraying one of them."

"It's tough to be between a rock and a hard place. No way out. Someone always gets hurt. And that old man up there is hurting real bad, and I don't just mean physically."

"I know that," Riley said miserably.

"You've done a hell of a job with Coleman Oil. I don't think we could replace you."

Riley beamed. "You mean I'm leaving my mark?"

"If you left, and I said if, yes, you'd leave your mark. Right now you are Coleman Oil. We'd be the ones caught between a rock and a hard place. Same thing for your grandfather if you stay here. I wish I could help, Riley."

"Thanks. I think you're going a bit overboard, though. There are others who could do what I'm doing. Like you and Sawyer with Coleman Aviation."

"Maybe down the road, but not right now. Aren't you going to Rio next week? I heard Sawyer telling Susan you were leaving on Friday. For how long?"

"Ten days, tops."

Laughter wafted down the circular staircase. Cole and Riley both looked toward the second floor.

The family.

"I've never seen this hallway so busy." Maggie laughed. "I do love it when we're all under the same roof."

Amelia put her arm around Julie's shoulder. "We need some nice young blood around here." She liked this gentle young woman; somehow she reminded her of Billie when she arrived at Sunbridge for the first time.

Cary watched Amelia with Julie. He felt pride and love when Amelia bent down to kiss Julie on the cheek. Amelia always made everyone feel welcome, and now she was including Julie in the family. That said it all. He was glad. He liked Julie Kingsley.

"Would anyone mind if I went down to the kitchen and made some hot chocolate?" Julie asked.

"I mind that you have to make it yourself," Amelia said. "Cary, take Julie downstairs and fix it for her. Put marshmallows in it. That's the one thing Cary excels at, hot chocolate." She laughed. "It will do you good, too, darling. Drink two cups. It will help you simmer down."

"Bossy, bossy," Cary said affectionately. "I guess we have

our orders, young lady, so we'd best march to them. Hut two, or however you say it." Julie laughed and proceeded to march down the hallway. The others watched indulgently.

"Now it's time to remove Estée Lauder and crawl between the sheets," Amelia said. "What would any of us do without that lady's miracle products?"

"Look ugly?" Billie queried.

"Close," Amelia laughed. "Good night, all."

When the door closed behind Maggie and Rand, he asked who Estée Lauder was.

"She's a cosmetic legend. See this, and this, and this? And smell this! It's all Estée Lauder. Mam always used her cosmetics, and we just sort of followed her. Mam looks great, doesn't she?"

Rand grinned. "And all this time I thought it was the natural you. And don't confuse the issue here—you just want me to say your mother looks great and then say you look just like her. I'm not falling into that trap!"

"A trap, is it?" Maggie said throatily. "Am I the spider and you're the fly?"

"You got it, beautiful lady. I seem to recall we came home to do something."

Maggie pretended to think. "Sex," she exclaimed. "That was it. We came home to make love. Watch this," she whispered as she twirled away from her husband.

Her movements were sensual and unhurried as she loosened the soft tie that held her gown together at the shoulder. One scandalously high heel sailed to the left, its mate to the right. Legs the envy of any Vegas showgirl were sheathed in provocatively sheer black stockings. Never taking her eyes from Rand's burning gaze, she rolled them down and stepped out of them. Her lacy bra and silky bikini were next. And then she stood naked, allowing her husband to drink his fill of her. She was tall, but he was taller still. Their silence spoke of lifetimes, past, present, and future. She moved closer, her heady perfume wafting around her like a scented aura.

"Let me," she whispered. Her fingers were hot, feverish, as she undid the buttons on Rand's shirt. When the last of his clothes rested next to hers, she stepped closer. Her eyes glowed darkly in the bedroom light. Rand shuddered when her warm mouth met his. He closed his eyes, giving himself to the moment. Her mouth sucked him sweetly, rhythmically, teasing him into groans of pleasure.

Maggie sensed his deepening excitement and allowed herself to be carried with it. One moment his arms cradled her, soothing her, the next they became her prison, hard, strong, and inescapable. She loved him like this, when she could feel the wildness flooding through his veins and know that it was she who had aroused these instincts in him. She yielded to his need for her, welcoming his weight upon her as he gently lowered her to the silken sheets.

His hands were in her hair, on her breasts, on the soft flesh of her inner thighs. He stirred her, demanded of her, rewarded her with the adoring attention of his lips to those territories his hands had already claimed. When he posessed her, it was with a joyful abandon.

She murmured her pleasure and gave him those caresses he loved. Release was there, within their grasp, but like two moths romancing a flame, they played in the heat and postponed that exquisite instant when they would both plunge into the inferno.

"Love me, Rand, love me," she implored, her voice deep, throaty, almost a primal cry of desire. The sound in the silent room made his passions flare anew. He covered her with his body, holding her fast with his muscular thighs, while he skillfully caressed her. She drew his head down to her breasts, offering them. His lips closed over one rosy crest and then the other, nibbling, teasing, drawing tight, loving circles with his tongue. He traveled downward to the flatness of her belly and the soft, darker recesses between her legs.

Maggie arched instinctively against his mouth, her head rolling back and forth on the pillows as though to deny the exquisite demands of her sensuality. Her fingers curled in his thick, blond hair, her body moved of its own volition against the excitation of his caress. Release, when it finally came, was the ebbing of the flood, seeping from her limbs. There was the sudden exhalation of breath and she was floating, drifting on a cloud, the whole of her world consisting of his lips and her flesh and the contact between them.

Still, his movements were slow, deliberate, and unhurried, despite the roaring in his ears that echoed in the pulses of his loins. His hands grasped her hips, lifting her, drawing her against him, filling her with his bigness, demanding his needs be met. His breathing was ragged, and his chest heaved as though he had run a mile. Lips met, lingered, tasted, and met again. He moved within her imprisoning flesh insistently, rhythmically, bringing her with him to another plateau, very different from the first, yet just as exciting. He rocked against her, feeling the resistance she offered, knowing that as she tightened around him as though to expel him from her, she was coming ever nearer to that climaxing sunburst where he would find his own consolation.

Panting, Rand covered her body with his, calming her shudders and comforting her until their spasms passed. And then, reluctantly, he withdrew from her and silently pulled the covers over them, taking her in his arms to cradle her lovingly. Maggie rested against him, sweeping her hand down the length of his body and finding him moist from her own wetness. Curled together in a dream of their own, they murmured love words until at last they slept.

Shadaharu Hasegawa struggled to the side of the bed. It took all his will to stand erect. He wished he were home. The long trip yawned ahead of him. He had hoped that Riley would accompany him on his return trip to Japan. But he shouldn't be thinking of his grandson now. Now he had to get ready for the day. A shower, but first he had to take two of the dreaded painkilling pills. Months ago, when he'd been informed of his condition, he'd made up his mind that he wouldn't take them. He'd carry his sickness with dignity and he'd suffer, the way his ancestors had suffered. No samurai ever took pills. His hand trembled as he shook the little tablets from the bottle. He wondered what would happen if he swallowed the lot of them. Would it kill the pain or would it kill him? If he did that, he would bring dishonor on all his daughters and their husbands, and on Riley. He had to suffer. His faith willed it. Within minutes the raw, knife-sharp pain had dulled, and queasiness in his stomach and chest had lessened. He would be able to brush his teeth now, confident the pills and bile wouldn't spew out. The shower would feel good. His hand shook only a little when he shaved. Perhaps today wouldn't be so bad after all.

How forward would it be of him to go downstairs to the kitchen for tea? The family had told him repeatedly that he was to consider Sunbridge his home. Right this minute he felt like he could eat *sashimi* and *soba*. A trace of a smile played around his mouth when he thought of the Lipton tea bags he would find in the kitchen. Americans didn't know the first thing about making tea.

He dressed in his impeccable custom-made suit, the one he'd had made just for this trip. His tailor, a fussy man with a long, thin white beard, had assured him that his weight loss would not be as noticeable with the expert padding in all the right places. The Colemans had all been kind, not mentioning the way he looked. He'd appreciated the concern they tried to hide, but he wondered what they would think when they found out he wanted Riley to return to Japan with him. Thaddeus and Billie would understand. All of them, he decided, would understand. All but Riley.

Eight daughters he'd been blessed with, and now he had several sons-in-law, but he wanted Riley to run his empire. Riley was a Hasegawa, no matter if Coleman blood ran in his veins. Blood. Riley was of his blood. He hung his head. The shame he was feeling had no words. He never thought the day would come when his only grandson would turn against him.

He was pacing the room slowly now, waiting for the dawn to bleach the long, dark night. He ignored the first wave of dizziness, willing it to go away. The second wave stopped him in his tracks and forced him to grab hold of a chair. He tried to square his shoulders, to make his feet work again. But he was no samurai. He accepted his own silent declaration with sadness, his distress at not being able even to stand erect making him want to weep.

He sensed another presence, but before he could turn around, he felt strong arms around his shoulders. This was what he'd been waiting for, his grandson. He turned in time to see the blinding tears in Riley's eyes. "You mustn't feel sad, my grandson. Buddha wills this. When you come to Japan you must promise me that you will light the joss sticks. Promise me, Riley. Your Jesus will forgive that promise to an old man."

"I promise, Grandfather. It hasn't been decided that I won't return. I need time. Tell me you understand."

The words were an effort, but Shadaharu forced them past his thick tongue. "I understand, Riley, and you must understand that the one thing I don't have is much time. This disease that started out creeping through my old body is now running. There is nothing to stop it. A year at the most, the doctors say."

There was anger in Riley's voice. "Then, Grandfather, you should have preserved your strength and remained in Japan. This trip has cost you too much." The anger turned to anguish at the thought of his inability to do anything for his grandfather's physical comfort.

"Our families are intertwined now," Shadaharu said. "I had to come to give my support. I and other members of our family invested in Mr. Assante's inner city. How could I bring shame on us? Surely you understand."

"What I understand is that you are ill. Everyone would have understood. There are fine doctors here, the best. Sloan Kettering in New York City." The word, cancer, that people were afraid to say didn't have to be spoken aloud. Just the mention of Sloan Kettering made the old Japanese nod in recognition.

"It is too late for me," Shadaharu said sadly. "I will return home today and pray that I will live to see the cherry blossoms one last time." He wanted to tell his grandson not to grieve for him, but his tongue was too thick—or was it that he didn't want to say the words?

"Come, I wish to have some tea, even if it is in little bags. Join me, Riley."

"I'll do better than that. I'll fix the tea myself." Before Shadaharu could protest, Riley scooped the frail body into his strong arms. "There is no shame in what I'm doing, and no one is stirring in the house. Enjoy the ride, Grandfather."

The old Japanese tried to bluster, but in the end he laid his head on Riley's chest and, for the first time in his life, allowed himself to be fussed over.

The Sunbridge kitchen was warm and fragrant. Once he had asked the cook why the room always smelled so good, and she said she heated pine needles and cinnamon sticks in the oven to give off the aroma.

Riley busied himself with the boiling water and teapot. He knew now that he couldn't allow his grandfather to return to Japan alone. He'd just have to put Coleman business on hold and go back with him. He would make it clear, though, that he would return to Texas.

His heart ached as he watched his grandfather grasp the mug of steaming tea with both hands to steady it. He looked away when he saw the amber liquid dribble down the old one's chin. This was the first he knew that his grandfather had difficulty in swallowing. He gulped his own tea and excused himself.

Long legs were pounding down the circular stairway, and he barely missed Cole at the foot of the steps.

Cole swung around and raced after his cousin. "What the hell's going on?"

"I have to go to Japan. I can't let him go alone."

"No, you can't. Is there anything I can do?"

"No. Yes." Riley was throwing underwear and clean shirts into a duffel bag. "Call Lacey and explain. It's too early to call now; they like to sleep late."

"Riley, I . . ."

Riley reached for his sheepskin jacket. His eyes locked with his cousin's. "I trust you, Cole." Cole's arms reached out, and Riley grasped both of them. "I do, you know," Riley said huskily. "Past is past."

"If you need me . . . anything . . . I can be there in hours."

"In that crazy Dream Machine?" Riley's laugh was forced. "You think I don't know they call you Top Gun at Coleman Aviation? You're up there buzzing the heavens and I'm down here busting my ass drilling oil."

Cole relaxed; the bad moments were over. "That oil is what keeps the home fires burning and Coleman Aviation in the air, Coleman."

"You made your point, Tanner." Using last names went back to dorm days and public telephones. Hey, Tanner. Yale's calling. Hey Coleman, Notre Dame is on the horn.

"I'm coming back, you know."

"I know that," Cole said softly. "I'm glad, Riley."

They were at the top of the steps. "It should be fish-or-cut-bait time," Riley said in a muffled voice. "But I can't do it. I want it all."

Cole stepped in front of his cousin. "There's nothing wrong with that if you can handle it. And if you can't handle it, what the hell do you think the rest of us are here for? Family, Riley. Remember the time the family came from all corners of the world for us when Ben Simms accused us of raping his daughter? They'll do it again and again. You taught me that, you asshole. I didn't know you didn't believe your own words. I'll never forget that day, Riley, when your grandfather stared into my eyes and said he believed us. Your grandfather changed my life that day. It was almost as if he looked into my soul. That total, absolute belief is something I never saw before and will probably never see again. I can't tell you how often I think of your grandfather and that day."

Riley shrugged. "Death is so final. I'll work it out, Cole."

* * *

"I'm coming back, you know." Riley remembered his words to Cole. Two short weeks ago, but it seemed like a lifetime. He patted his jacket pocket to make sure the return ticket was safely there. It was his last day in Japan. His last day with his grandfather. He shivered. He pressed the bell hidden in the intricately carved teakwood gate, then took a moment to savor the beauty before saying good-bye, again, to his childhood home. It was palatial compared to Sunbridge, low and sprawling and constructed of concrete trimmed with teakwood. Every branch, every leaf and shrub of the gardens, was manicured to picture prettiness. It had always been this way, he supposed. As a child he'd never paid much attention to his surroundings, caring only that he was warm, well fed, and comfortable. Now he could appreciate the beauty of the place.

It was quiet, peaceful. There were no sounds of the city, no birds chirping, no children making noise. Just silence. The silence; it was one of the things he hadn't liked as a child. Once he'd bounced a ball against the side of the house and his mother had taken him by the hand and told him to bounce the ball on the lawn. It hadn't been any fun. He wondered where the big red ball was now.

This was another world, alien now somehow. The Hasegawa family had always lived behind thick walls, shut off from the rest of the city. For privacy. Too much privacy. Even now, in winter, he couldn't deny the beauty of his old home, but he didn't want to live here. He was sure of it now. He tried to remember if he'd liked it as a child. Probably not, he decided.

Japan was a beautiful country. Someday he'd come back and really see it. He'd been so sheltered, so sequestered here as a child; he'd gone only to school and to the newspaper offices, once in a while. The rest of his time he was behind these walls. He didn't belong here even then, and he certainly didn't belong here now. He didn't want to belong. He knew he could never be a newspaperman.

The old one was sleeping. Riley prowled his great bedroom. The last words he'd spoken to his grandfather, before the strong drug took effect, burned in his brain. He was leaving, going back to America, back to his father's home—*his* home now.

He looked around. How often as a toddler, and then as a child, and then as a young man, he'd come to this room for

{ 66 }

long talks with his grandfather. No problem was ever too big or too small. He never left the room without feeling better. Today was the first time he was going to leave more confused than when he'd entered. And miserable. A word that was almost impossible to associate with this tranquil, peaceful house.

He looked down once more at the sleeping man. He leaned over, his hands clenched. If only he could breathe some of his own healthy life into this frail figure. His lips caressed the crinkly cheek that felt like old rice paper. Tears burned his eyes. His heart ached.

He propped up the letter he'd written earlier, after the doctor told him his grandfather would probably sleep for twelve hours or more. He couldn't wait twelve hours. He had to catch a plane to the States. He had responsibilities there. His family was there.

A tortured sigh escaped Shadaharu when he heard the door close softly for what he was sure was the last time. There was nothing left now, no point in fighting. A tear trickled down his cheek. He felt a moment of shame. It was the first tear ever to leave his eyes. It would be his last.

Then he slept again, the heavy narcotics killing his pain.

Riley walked through the dimly lit house and into the garden.

The precise symmetry of the Zen garden startled him, as though he were seeing it for the first time. The moon created a dramatic pattern of light and shadow. Not a leaf, not a pebble was out of place. It was as though he had stepped back into his childhood. He could picture his mother smiling at him as he ran about.

Calm settled over Riley, a feeling he hadn't had for a long time. Lately he seemed to be on overload, meeting himself coming and going. An accident waiting to happen, Lacey had said. Lacey wouldn't like this garden. It was too sculptured, too perfect. There was no glitz here, no pizzazz. Just tranquillity and beauty. Ivy would like it, though. . . .

Riley checked his watch. It was almost time to leave for the airport. He would sleep on the way back, but he'd still have jet lag when he landed. One of these days he was going to have to learn to eat properly before an overseas trip. Little goose bumps on his arms surprised him. He rolled down his shirt sleeves. His body felt cold and his heart felt cold. There was nothing here to warm him.

When Riley Coleman left the Hasegawa house he didn't look back. His life changed in that instant.

"Airport," he said tersely to the limo driver.

The raw, cold days gave way to late December's tundra weather. Christmas passed with no festivities at Sunbridge, and the New Year was ushered in quietly—just another day.

Amelia delighted in the New Year. She loved new beginnings. Her determination to do something about the nursing home problem had intensified over the holidays. So many lonely old people with none of the small comforts that give meaning to life. She'd spent almost all her time going from one home to the other with piles of magazines and books just to get the lay of the land. Cary didn't understand. She could see it in his eyes. When she'd explained that she was about the same age as most of the residents, and but for the grace of God she could be in the same position, he'd been kind and indulgent, but he really wasn't interested. Why should he be? To a man his age a nursing home must seem like a lifetime away. She'd shrugged. It would happen to all of them at some time, even Cary. He had no children. Who would take care of him when she was gone? Would he . . .

She wished she felt better. Stamina was required for the job she had cut out for herself. Already she had Cary's study filled with manuals and pamphlets, thanks to Billie and Thad, who'd sent her every bit of passed legislation known to man in regard to geriatric nursing care. But it was the interviews she'd done with patients that took up most of the shelf space. After taping and playing them back, she sent them out for typing and binding. Each interview was accompanied by the patient's history. She filed them in alphabetical order by name, being as professional as she knew how. This wasn't a job to skimp on, not when it dealt with human life and dignity.

Amelia tapped the blunt end of her nail on the desktop. If only Cary were more supportive instead of just indulgent. If only . . . those days were gone. She didn't deal with "if onlys" anymore. Everything was either positive or negative.

The pencil moved swiftly. A line, a dark black line on the paper. The bottom line. There was always a bottom line to everything in life. She had one. Cary had one; all the Colemans had a bottom line. She already knew what hers was, but she wasn't one hundred percent sure of Cary's. He seemed to be floundering, searching for a new project but finding nothing to challenge him. Lately he seemed to be moving away from her too. Or was she moving away from him? She had to admit she was consumed with the nursing home project. It was so important. Did only older people like herself, Billie, and Thad understand? How important the last years are, Amelia thought. Every human being has the right to dignity, and by God, she was going to do her best to make sure they got it. If it meant moving further away from Cary, so be it. Someday, when age caught up with him, he'd understand. He'd come to that special place on the hill, high above Sunbridge. He'd kneel down and talk. If he didn't forget, he'd bring flowers. He'd apologize. There would be tears in his eyes. She wondered if he'd be alone. A tear dropped on the dark black line. The paper puckered. A second tear fell on the paper. A sob caught in Amelia's throat. She didn't want to be old, and she didn't want to die. If only she could have yesterday back, just for a little while.

With all the force she could muster, Amelia straightened her shoulders. This was no time to be maudlin. No matter how she felt, she had work to do. Important work. Work that was more important than . . . yes, than anything else in her life.

Cary poked his head in the doorway. "What say we chuck all this and buzz into town for lunch?" He gave her a playful leer. "You get gussied up."

Amelia leered back. Then she laughed. "Ah, the idle unemployed. How nice it is. Sorry, but I have to go over the last three interviews I did this week. I want everything in order before I meet with the state commission."

Amelia felt a flutter of panic as her eyes went from her handsome, virile husband to eighty-six-year-old Jethroe Evans's interview. Old Jethroe was suddenly more important than her husband. She smiled to take the sting out of her refusal.

"Can I help?" Cary asked.

"Nope. This is something I have to do myself. Something I want to do."

Cary felt his throat closing. There seemed to be a chill in the room, which was in fact stifling. Amelia liked it warm these days.

He sensed he was losing her. Like now, she was talking to him, smiling up at him, and yet the rest of her was somewhere else—with those old people. People her age and older, she had told him bluntly when she took on her project. Her age.

Cary refused to think of the numbers. They'd had such a wonderful life, and there was no goddamn reason why they couldn't continue to have a wonderful life. He loved her. He didn't give a damn how old she was. Something was taking his place. He didn't like it, and worse, he didn't know how to fight it.

"Listen, babe, do you think you could take off a few days next week and go to New York with me? Some money boys will be in town, and they asked me to sit in on some meetings. I'd like to. I've been at loose ends since the holidays. We could take in a show, do some shopping, walk through Central Park, have a champagne breakfast. Unwind." He held his breath, waiting for his wife's answer. He knew it would be no, but still he hoped.

Amelia opened her bright red appointment book, which was stuffed with loose papers. He could tell by the scrawled memos that she'd been busy, and from the way she was riffling through the pages, she was going to be a lot busier. "Darling, I can't possibly make it. I've got something going every day. I might, and it's a real iffy might, make it Friday night, and I'll have to come back early Sunday morning. There's an important luncheon Sunday at Grey Oaks. I arranged it myself. The governor and the mayor will be there. How about if I take a rain check? You go and enjoy yourself. Call me and we can talk all evening. Remember how we used to do that when we were first married and you went away on business? We'd both fall asleep with an open phone wire. Lord, those bills were astronomical."

"I miss those days, Amelia," Cary said. "I miss you. We don't have any time together anymore."

"I know, darling. While we don't have quantity time, we do have quality time. Don't you think that's more important?"

He didn't think so at all. He felt like smashing something. Couldn't she see how much he wanted to be with her?

He felt like a fool, standing around begging for quantity time, for God's sake, like some yuppie's toddler. He could feel Amelia's uneasiness and knew she wanted him to leave. He was sorry now that he'd gone with her to one of those old people's homes. He'd let her see how appalled he was, how shocked. He was not ready to deal with mortality. Some of the nursing home residents *were* Amelia's age, as she'd been quick to point out to him, but it was hard to compare her to any of them. He'd never, ever, no matter what happened, commit her to such a place, no matter how good the care was.

She'd laughed when he said so. "Darling, if I lose control of my bodily functions and my mind goes, will you still take care of me? Life is for the living. What I'm trying to do is make sure these old folks get the best possible care. I want people to treat them gently and kindly, not like flotsam and jetsam. I can't explain it any better. I have to help."

"You can't do it alone, Amelia. It's . . . it's too awesome," he'd said.

"I'm going to try, and when I can't do it anymore, someone else will carry on. I refuse to believe I'm the only person out there who cares. I can see you're uncomfortable. I shouldn't have brought you. I'll drive you home and come back." Her voice had been firm and hard.

He'd gone, too, like a chastened schoolboy. He just couldn't bear the thought of Amelia ever being in a nursing home, being feeble. Who was he fooling? Amelia's heart attack had taken its toll on both of them. Was he being selfish? He was glad she was alive and happy, doing something she liked doing. Love, true love, was unselfish, wanting the other person to be happy.

"I guess I'll read the paper," he said quietly. "Can I get you some coffee?"

"I'd love a cup of tea, if you don't mind."

Mind? Jesus, he'd dig a well for the water if he had to. "Coming right up."

Amelia smiled to herself. She was floating in tea, but if it made Cary happy, doing something for her, she'd drink it. She smiled again when he returned, carrying a tray with two cups, two muffins, and a sprig of something green stuck into a mug. She pretended not to see the little granules of dirt that fell on the tray from the greenery. Poor darling, how lost he was.

"Darling, you go to New York. I can't bear to see you at loose ends while I'm so busy. Promise me you'll go even if I can't join you."

Cary nodded. "Was it like this for you when I was working twelve and fourteen hours a day?" Not waiting for an answer, he continued. "It was, I know it. I'm sorry for that, Amelia. We lost so much time. Hours, days, even years. My God, I'm so sorry."

"Cary, look at me and listen. I did miss you terribly and I wanted to be a part of it all. I lived for the time you came home at night, and then you'd be so tired you could hardly stand up. I understood, and I wouldn't do it differently if I had another chance. All I wanted was for you to be happy. If you're happy, I'm happy. I have no complaints, and just look at what you've accomplished. You've left your mark. I'm so proud of you." Her voice softened. "I love you so very much."

Cary could feel the tears gather in his eyes. He blinked. He wasn't the sort of man who was ashamed to show his feelings. "You always know just the right thing to say at the right time. What would I have done without you all these years?"

Amelia wiped at her own tears. "We found each other, so we don't have to speculate. Go along now and make your reservations for New York. Promise to bring me a present."

Cary leaned over to kiss his wife. Her perfume wafted about him. He squeezed her shoulder. "You're my reason for living; always remember that, Amelia. I love you so much I ache with the feeling." Amelia bit down on her lower lip and leaned into the crook of his arm. Their lives. Love.

{{{{{{{{ CHAPTER FOUR }}}}}}}}

Cary didn't know if he loved or hated New York. He'd been walking aimlessly for hours now, gawking at street vendors selling cheap plastic belts and sunglasses, peering into shop windows, hoping the perfect gift for Amelia would beckon him inside. What the hell, he had nothing better to do. As far as he was concerned, he was out of the real estate deal with the high rollers. There was something wrong, and he didn't want to take the time to figure out what it was. It wasn't the big numbers that scared him, it was the nervousness of two of the investors, big-money men who shouldn't even blink at such a deal. He'd known, early in the meetings, that this project wasn't the right one for him, and he'd excused himself, saying he'd give them his decision in a day or so, which meant he had to kick around the city on his own.

Cary walked on, oblivious to the admiring glances he was getting. The wind tousled his hair. He gave up trying to smooth it down and jammed his hands into his pockets. He stopped at a vendor and bought a wind-up toy of two bears, one riding piggyback on the other. Farther on he bought Carrera sunglasses in their minicase along with a god-awful lime-green leather belt big enough to go around a horse's belly. Amelia would laugh. On another street he bought a fold-up umbrella with lace on the scalloped edges and a scarf splattered with chartreuse and purple flowers, to match the belt. He laughed at the look of outrage on the black boy's face when he asked for a bag. It was a deep, delighted sound of humor, and people around him smiled. He nodded slightly to two young girls admiring the brilliant scarf. He looked around to get his bearings and decided to walk to Bloomingdale's for a shopping bag. For fifty cents he could dump all his purchases in one bag. Maybe he should get two shopping bags. The decision to spend a dollar for two shopping bags made him laugh again. Two hours ago he could have made a decision to commit seven million dollars to a fancy hexagonal, copper-colored high rise. Amelia would laugh and say, "Penny-wise and pound foolish," whatever that meant.

The colorful Bloomie's bag felt good in his hand, as if he'd accomplished something. The second bag was folded neatly inside the first for anticipated purchases.

A sweet-smelling clerk motioned him to the Chanel counter and held out a sample of perfume. Cary looked at the little vial, wrinkled his nose to show he approved of the scent. Coco, the girl called it. Her name tag said she was Betsy Gill, and she wore a yellow flower in the buttonhole of her suit jacket. Cary ordered a large bottle, dusting powder, and some fragrant soap. He peeled off two hundred-dollar bills from his money clip and pocketed the few dollars change. Amelia was going to love this. He hoped she wouldn't stint when she sprayed the sheets. He decided to get a second bottle. Betsy smiled and said she wished she were the recipient of such a lavish gift. Cary smiled shyly. "It's for my wife," he said.

A flock of women descended on the perfume counter. He moved out of the way, but not before he heard a vaguely familiar voice ask for a sample of Coco. He tried to peer into the group of women but couldn't see anyone he recognized. Annoyed with himself, he headed for the men's department, not that he needed anything, but at least he could tell Amelia he had checked out New York male fashion. He plunked down $480 for a cashmere sweater, knowing she would be delighted. It was perfect for lounging around in. Casual but elegant, as she would put it.

It was past his lunchtime and his stomach growled. A New York deli pickle would go great right now, he thought, along with a pastrami on rye and gobs of spicy brown mustard. An ice-cold beer to top it off would make him delirious. He marched out onto Third Avenue in search of a deli.

The deli was crowded with shoppers and businessmen. Standing inside the brass rail to wait for a table, he heard a voice ask for a pastrami and corned beef on rye with plenty of mustard. "A diet Coke," the voice added. The same voice he'd heard in Bloomingdale's.

Two ladies got up from their table and Cary sprinted for it. As he slid into his seat he noticed a woman emerge from the crowd at the counter. Now he knew who "the voice" was.

"Julie! Julie Kingsley!" he called, jumping to his feet.

"Mr. Assante! What are you doing here?"

"Same thing you are. Join me. Let me help you. On second thought, I can either hold this table or help you." He'd noticed two men eyeing the situation. They wore three-piece look-alike suits. Madison Avenue. Something else to report at home: all the men still dressed alike!

"Hold the table," Julie called in her sparkly voice. "You have to take the offensive in New York during lunch hour. It pays to carry an umbrella with a long point at the end. Survival, it's called."

Cary held Julie's chair and then seated himself.

"Mr. Assante, what are you doing in New York? Is Amelia with you?"

"I thought we settled that 'Mr. Assante' business back in Austin. Why do you call me 'mister' and my wife by her first name?"

Julie blushed. "I really got to know Amelia, maybe because I felt like I knew her even before I met her. Thad and Billie speak of her on a daily basis. I adore your wife . . . Cary. Billie and Amelia are two of the finest people I've ever met."

"I'll agree with that. But from now on, it's Cary, and you're Julie, okay? Now, what are you doing here?"

"I work here. I just love New York. I decided to move down here, start the New Year off right, and it was a job offer I couldn't refuse. I'm adjusting nicely. I just wish New Yorkers were a little more friendly."

"I know what you mean. Do you work far from here?"

"A couple of blocks. What are you doing here without Amelia?"

"Business. Amelia couldn't make it. I've been shopping for her—I love to buy presents."

Julie laughed. "I do, too. I spend hours and hours looking for just the right gift. I don't care how much it costs as long as I know the person is going to like it. I so enjoy the look of surprise and pleasure when they open it."

"You sound like you don't receive too many presents. A beautiful girl like you should be getting baubles by the basket."

Julie smiled. "Girl? I'm thirty-eight, thirty-nine in two days. I think that takes me out of the 'girl' class."

"All women are girls to me," Cary said. He grinned. "Amelia loves it when I call her a broad. I just do it for fun," he added hastily. He liked the way she bit deep into the thick sandwich. Good appetite. He'd always heard that New York women starved themselves to model slimness or didn't eat so they could afford the sky-high rents. Julie was chewing industriously, savoring the spicy sandwich. A man's sandwich.

"You're staring," Julie said. "Do I have mustard on my chin?"

Her wide grin exposed square, perfectly aligned teeth that had never seen an orthodontist. He didn't remember them being so white. Of course, he'd spent only a half hour with her over a cup of cocoa in the Sunbridge kitchen, and the light had been dim. He'd been on a self-made high that night and into his own success. He'd missed the parade of light freckles on her cheekbones. He liked freckles. Amelia had "freckles" —large brown spots on her arms and hands, some on her neck, too. "Not at all. You're a neat eater, Julie."

Julie's eyes crinkled up at the corners. "At least you didn't say I was a big eater, which I am. I love food."

"That makes two of us. Have you ever had a gyro?"

"I'd kill for one of those. I prefer it to pizza or even a deli sandwich. There aren't too many places that serve them. I'll find one, though; count on it." She leaned over the table. "What I don't understand is how people can give up meat and become vegetarians. I guess I'm basically carnivorous."

"Me, too." How comfortable he was, sitting here with Julie, just talking about food.

"Shame prevents me from marching back through the line for another sandwich," Julie giggled. She leaned back against the cane chair. "Now for my one and only really bad vice, a cigarette. I allow myself seven a day. I don't recall if you smoke or not. Do you?"

"Unfortunately, I do. I don't usually smoke in restaurants, but it seems to be okay here. It's a touchy subject these days."

Julie drew deeply on the cigarette. She blew a perfect smoke ring. Cary applauded as he lighted his own Camel. "Can you imagine having sex and not smoking afterward?"

Cary choked as he attempted to match her smoke ring. A warning bell signaled something in his head that he totally ignored. "I can't imagine that at all." No virgin here, and why should she be one? Not that it was any of his business. Sex made the world go round . . . and round, and round. No small talk about asking him if he was shocked at her words. No young-girl games. Straight from the shoulder. He did *like* her.

"How long will you be in New York, Cary?"

"A few days. Business. I'll be here through your birthday. If you don't have other plans, I can celebrate with you. My gift to you. Amelia would kill me if I left you alone on your birthday. You're kind of like family."

"I'd like that, Cary. I live on East Seventy-ninth Street." She took a slip of paper from her purse and wrote out the address for him. "I get home about six-thirty and I can be ready by seven-thirty. If I appear eager, it's because I am— you'll be my first date. I mean, I haven't met any men that I want to spend an evening with yet."

She liked him enough to want to spend an evening with him. Her birthday. "Listen," he said impulsively, "we don't have to wait till your birthday. How about having dinner with me this evening? I'm going to have to eat alone, and evidently, you are too. What do you say?" Cary held his breath waiting for her answer. He wasn't sure what he expected, but her words startled him.

Julie made a production out of closing her flip-top cigarette box and nestling it into her bag. She liked Cary Assante. She adored Amelia Assante. She'd liked all the Colemans. She'd enjoyed that late-night cup of cocoa and knew even then that he was someone she'd like to get to know better. Damn, why were the good ones always taken? Dinner was harmless, and so was a birthday. There had to be a rule about something like this. She'd have to think in terms of family. Keep it all in its proper perspective. "Tell you what, Mr. Assante—Cary, I mean—you call Amelia and tell her you're having dinner with me at my apartment and that I'm cooking. If she doesn't object, it would be my pleasure to whip you up some spaghetti and Ragu. Garlic bread on the side and some salad. I might even throw in some baklava if I make the deli in time."

"You're on. I'll bring the wine, and I'll call Amelia. Amelia liked you, Julie. So do I. You're family." He wondered what Ragu was. He'd have to ask Amelia.

Family. It was such a wonderful word. Thad and Billie were her family, but aside from a few scattered cousins, there was no one else. It was nice knowing the Colemans liked her and considered her family. But Cary Assante *wasn't* family. Not really. She wished she didn't like him so much. Perhaps she could think of him as an older brother, one she could talk to, share things with. Like her approaching birthday. Thirty-nine was so awesome. Thirty-nine and not married was even more awesome. Thirty-nine with no children was so awesome it made her want to shrivel up within herself. The biological clock ticking away...

"This was nice, Cary. I'm so glad we ran into each other. Give Amelia my love when you speak with her. I'll see you ... sevenish? Is that all right with you?"

"I'll do that, and I'll also walk you back to the office if you want company. Just let me get my bags together."

"Oh, are those Amelia's presents? How nice. What did you get? Show me. I have a few extra minutes."

Cary preened while Julie lifted out his purchases. Nothing would do but to wind up the piggyback bears. She didn't laugh, she guffawed. Not for the world would she tell this kind man sitting across from her that Amelia would—what would Amelia do with piggyback bears? Smile indulgently and acknowledge that Cary bought the wind-up toy for the boy in himself. The brilliant belt and scarf dazzled her. She could almost see herself strutting down Third Avenue wearing them. Where would Amelia wear them? She wished she knew. The price tag on the perfume made her blink. She sniffed appreciatively. It was too heavy for her but pleasing nonetheless. Amelia would love it. How charming and thoughtful this man was. She nodded, her smile brilliant, as she placed the items

{77}

back into the shopping bag. "A wise, diversified selection," she said.

"I'm not finished yet. I want to go back with a whole cartload of presents for Amelia. These are just fun things, things to make her laugh. She's taking herself very seriously these days, ever since she got involved in those nursing homes."

"You sound as though you don't exactly approve."

Cary reached for Julie's check. She handed it over without protest and walked alongside him to the cashier. She thanked him nicely and smiled. A smile that would linger with Cary for the rest of the afternoon.

Outside in the sunshine Julie poked his arm. "You didn't tell me if you approve or not about Amelia's volunteer work."

"I've never been a crusader. I guess I don't understand people who can devote eighteen hours a day to a cause and get nothing back. I don't mean that to sound selfish. I've always had to work, and work hard, for my money. Right now I'm at loose ends and I feel guilty. I need to work, I need to do things. I guess what I'm saying is I have to contribute. It's wonderful what Amelia is doing, but she's obsessed with it. There's no time for anything else. I *wanted* her to come to New York, but she had wall-to-wall meetings."

"You're lonely. And you're right, you have to do something. Why don't you get involved with Amelia and help her? There are never enough volunteers in any job. A few people end up doing all the work. Or is it that you don't want to get involved in something that deals with aging?"

Right to the heart of things. Cary nodded morosely. "Come along, we have the light." He didn't want to talk about Amelia and her pet project with this young woman. Not now, anyway. He felt disloyal saying as much as he had.

Julie was quick to pick up on Cary's change of mood. She walked along, her long-legged stride matching Cary's. "How's Mrs. Buckalew? You know, she hustled me into having my chart done, but I've never received it. I paid her three hundred dollars. I know it was a foolish thing to do, but astrology has always fascinated me. I read my horoscope every day. When it's good I believe it, and when it's bad I call it hocus-pocus. I'm an Aries. What are you?"

"A Leo. Can't you tell? Tess told Amelia she knew I was a

Leo from the moment she spotted me. Does that mean we're compatible?"

"Very compatible," Julie said quietly. The perfect match. Aries and Leo. The lion and the ram. Tomorrow she'd pick up an astrology book and read up on Leos. And she'd write to Tess Buckalew and ask where her chart was. She had certainly cashed her check in a hurry.

"Here we are. I work on the twenty-seventh floor. I enjoyed lunch, Cary. Thank you for adding some sparkle to my day. I'll see you around seven." With a light wave of her hand she was through the revolving door. Cary watched to see if she'd turn around for a second wave. His hand was poised to wave back. But she didn't. Feeling foolish, Cary turned to get his bearings. For the moment he had absolutely no idea where he was. Well, when in doubt, take a taxi and let the driver do the worrying.

A Checker pulled up to the curb, disgorging two giggling girls and one emaciated male with long hair. Cary tossed his shopping bag onto the backseat and climbed in. "Cartier's."

Discreet. Ultraposh. Amelia would be at home here among the precious gems and black velvet. The subdued lighting added luster to everything. Cary reminded himself that he could buy out the store and still have plenty left over, so he shouldn't feel intimidated.

"I don't exactly know what I'm looking for," he told the haughty-looking salesman.

"I need some sort of an idea, sir. Earrings? What sort of stones are you interested in?"

"Diamonds. A bracelet, I think. Perhaps some earrings. It's for my wife."

"Her birthday? An anniversary?"

Cary felt a sudden desire to punch the man in the jaw. Where was this anger coming from? He was being ridiculous. If he'd gone into a hardware store looking for at tool, the clerk would need a little information to help him make his selection. The difference was that in a hardware store the merchandise was on display. Here the "good stuff" was in a vault, brought out one piece at a time. In a hardware store they asked what price range you were interested in. Here, if you had to ask the price, you probably shouldn't be in the store in the first place.

Forty-five minutes later, Cary made his selection—a lacy platinum-weave bracelet studded with diamonds, and a pair of emerald earrings. He wrote out the check and was suddenly $66,437.28 poorer. If he were the wealthiest man in the world, he'd never get used to spending this kind of money on jewelry. He tossed the gift-wrapped boxes into his Blooming-dale's shopping bag and was pleased to see the clerk's elegant wince. He grinned in return.

Outside he took a deep breath. *That* kind of shopping he hated.

His first thought was to head back to the hotel and call Amelia. His second thought was to take a stroll in Central Park. If possible, the day was even brighter than before.

Cary walked slowly up Fifth Avenue, stopping to peek in at the Children's Zoo. He marveled at the tenacity of a five-year-old climbing the monkey bars, to his mother's horror. He couldn't help wondering what kind of father he'd have made. Amelia had been a wonderful mother to Rand. Still was, for that matter. He and Amelia would have had children, of course, if she'd been younger. His brain seemed to freeze for a brief instant. No, they couldn't have had children anyway, because of Amelia's botched-up abortion. He wished now she'd never told him about it. He didn't feel it as a loss, exactly. It was more like curiosity. Parenthood was too de-manding. He'd probably have been a lousy father. Still, a daughter would be nice, someone to call him Daddy. Amelia would have seen to it that she made a debut. Society. It really was all crap. He tried to picture Amelia with children, Amelia in a housedress with a toddler clinging to her skirt and a baby in her arms. Dinner cooking, the television on, toys scattered all over a small frame house with a picket fence and garden. He shuddered. No, his life was perfect the way it was. Maybe when he was older he would regret it more, but not right now. Jesus, he was only forty-eight. Amelia was sixty-seven. The thought stopped him in midstride. A woman in sweatpants and a headband ran into his back. He apologized. She grumpily accepted his apology, remarking that if he wasn't feeling well, he should sit down. He nodded slightly and headed for one of the benches along the wall on the park side of the avenue.

A vibrant, witty, charming, loving sixty-seven. Younger women couldn't hold a candle to Amelia. So what if she had brown spots on her hands and arms. So what if she had fine lines around her mouth and wrinkles around her eyes. He loved every goddamn spot and wrinkle, and he wouldn't give Amelia up for anything in the world. He'd give up his business, everything he owned, his life, if Amelia needed it. He loved her, body and soul. He always had and always would. She was his life, and by God, he'd had enough of this stupid, aimless walk and people crashing into him. He would go back to the hotel, order a couple of drinks, and put a call in to Amelia. His heart started to beat furiously. Amelia was the only woman who had been able to make his heart beat like this.

Cary got the drinks and tried to call Amelia for the rest of the afternoon. By the time he finally reached her, six-fifteen New York time, he had a buzz on and he was a little grumpy. Her voice turned husky as she realized who it was.

"I've been trying to call you all afternoon, Amelia. I wanted to talk to you. I needed to talk to you."

"You are, darling. I'm so glad you called. I miss you. How's New York?"

"I wish you had come with me. Christ, I miss you. Are you sure you can't drop what you're doing and come for at least one day?"

"Darling, I would if I could. We went through all that before you left. How did the meeting go?"

"It didn't. I don't want any part of it. I'll find something else. I don't want you worrying about me. This deal was never important, just something I wanted to check out. Listen, you'll never guess who I met at a deli where I stopped for lunch. After my shopping spree."

"Spree!" Amelia gurgled. "Spree! Tell me, quick, what did you buy?"

"I bought myself a cashmere sweater at Bloomingdale's. I was all over the place and I have two full shopping bags to prove it."

"Full?" Amelia squealed like a girl. Cary laughed. "Tell me; give me a clue, a hint."

"Nope. You're just going to have to wait."

"I hate it, Cary, when you get me all revved up."

"Well, I love it when you rev me up. I have a hard-on right now, so big it's a killer."

"I love it when you talk like that. Keep it that way till you get home."

"Sure. A cop would arrest me the minute I walked through the door." Amelia giggled. The hard-on stayed. Cary massaged himself and groaned. Amelia giggled again. She loved this game and so did he.

"Who did you meet at the deli?"

"Amelia, I need you," Cary said through clenched teeth. "Julie Kingsley."

"What's Julie doing in New York? Vacation?"

"Hell no. She's working here now. We ate lunch together, and yes, I picked up the check. She said she came here after the first of the year. She likes it, but she's lonely. I guess she's pretty choosy about making friends."

"Did she look as lovely as she did at Sunbridge?"

"She looked okay to me. Did you know she has freckles? I didn't remember the freckles. They aren't as dark as yours, though."

"Darling, mine are called liver spots. I lie when I say they're freckles. They come with age. Julie's are natural, and yes, I knew she had them. She's a beautiful woman. I hope you're going to take her out to dinner. I insist, Cary. Do up the town. I like that young woman. She's my kind of gal."

"I can do that." Cary looked down at his zipper and wasn't surprised to see that his trousers were lying flat against his belly. So much for that. He sighed.

"You don't have to sound so put upon. It won't hurt you to go out of your way and show Julie a good time. Take her to my favorite restaurant, the Lion's Rock. Promise."

"All right. She told me she's having a birthday in two days. I'll take her then. Is that okay?"

"Darling, that's perfect. Now you have to buy her an absolutely outrageous gift. Sign both our names. She's a working girl, so it has to be something she can't afford for herself. She's thirty-nine remember. That means she's almost forty, and that's middle age. Get her something that will make her forget. I hated being twenty-nine and I hated thirty-nine and I hated forty-nine, but I enjoyed fifty-nine. I don't know why. Anyway, it really has to be a stupendous gift."

"Amelia, stop with the age thing. You're going to have to help me here. I don't know what to get her."

"A mink stole. How many working girls do you know who can afford a mink stole?"

"Not many, but isn't it a bit much?"

"Possibly, but if both our names are on it, she'll have to accept. Now, if you gave it to her alone, she wouldn't accept it—that's the kind of girl Julie is. I think they still wear stoles. But maybe it should be a jacket. Mink jackets can be worn with anything, even jeans. Get a jacket.'

"Are you sure, Amelia?"

"I'm positive. Some flowers, too. Nice ones, roses, none of those pompon things. Order Dom Perignon. Fifty-five if you can get it. Do it up grand, Cary."

"I miss you, honey. I wish I was back in Texas."

"Darling, I miss you, too, but trust me, you don't want to be back here just now. We're having a ferocious rainstorm. I had the devil's own time getting home. I'm running a nice steamy bath, darling, and I think the tub is full. Call me later. I'm going to be in all evening going over a lot of paperwork. Keep that hard-on and we can talk it down later. Deal?"

He smooched a kiss into the phone.

Amelia walked into the bathroom and looked at the dry tub. She turned on the tap and felt less a liar. She poured lavishly from a crystal decanter of tinted bath salts. Steam spiraled slowly upward, carrying a heady scent into the air. She was tired, and this bath and a light supper in front of the television would feel wonderful. An entire evening to herself to ponder the progress she'd made with the local and state authorities.

She stripped down, avoiding the full-length mirror on the back of the door. She didn't want to look at the vicious bypass scar. Stretched luxuriously full-length in the tub, she thought about Cary and the phone call. Julie was a fine young woman, the kind of woman her father had wanted *her* to be. Cary couldn't do any better, in her opinion. She felt a momentary sense of loss and then she remembered all the happy times, all the good years. For the most part she'd had a wonderful life. Not in the beginning, but for the last forty years. Forty years. Lord, where had they gone? The best years of all had been spent with Cary. Until she drew her last breath she'd love Cary Assante. It was a miracle that she'd come through her surgery, that she could still live, and love, and do something worthwhile before she called it a day. She knew she'd been saved for something. All those silent prayers . . . Let me live. . . . Let me live and I'll do whatever I can. . . . Let me live and I'll prove I can do more than exist. . . . Please, God, let me live so I can see Cary again. . . . Let me live, let me love. And then, in the recovery room, when she knew, when she felt she would live, that silent prayer of thanks, that vow to do something.

At the time she hadn't known what the something was, but

she knew now. God had given her more time to live and love Cary. Now she had to give back, contribute. She regretted that Cary didn't understand, but *she* understood, and that was all that mattered. She was paying her last and final debt. She'd had it all, more than most people had a right to expect. She'd endured. Wasn't it Faulkner who said it wasn't enough to just endure, you had to prevail, too? Well, she had. That old tired cliché about having her moment in the sun was over. Now she was in the shadowy area of her life, and she had to make it count.

Amelia lifted one long, thin leg, toes stiff and pointed outward. She twisted the faucet carefully, watching a stream of hot water separate the bubbles over the drain. She lowered her foot and let some of the warm water drain away. Little beads of water dotted her knees. She laughed as she turned her leg this way and that way to see if the folds of skin hanging over her knees would disappear. Loss of elasticity, every woman's despair. Once she would have cried or tried to figure out a way to hike the skin back up. Now she simply didn't care. She was alive, she loved, and she had a mission to fulfill. She couldn't ask for more. There was no more. The simplicity of it made her laugh again. She held up her arm, watching the loose skin fall, and made an imaginary toast to Cary and Julie. "To friends and lovers," she whispered.

The tiny smile around her lips was forlorn.

Cary walked through the shabby lobby of Julie's building at seven-fifteen. The elevator operator, who introduced himself as Angel, said he had orders to take Mr. Assante straight up to the sixteenth floor. Cary was amused when Angel waited in the elevator doorway until Julie opened the door. "It's okay, Angel," Cary said. "Thank you."

Julie slid the bolts on three locks. "I'm just not used to the city. I've got bars on the window, too. The fire escape is right outside the window, and this is the top floor. There's nothing but the roof overhead. It's a sublet. What do you think of it? A single girl in New York paying eight hundred fifty dollars for a sublet? I was lucky to get it."

"If you're happy and content here, that's all that matters. I approve of the decor—it looks lived in."

She smiled. "Sit down and I'll fix you a drink. What would you like?"

"Scotch and soda would be fine, thanks. What are you having?"

"A wine spritzer. Liquor goes right to my head and makes me say strange things. I play it safe."

"What kind of strange things?" He was going to have to make an effort to remember everything she said so he could tell Amelia. Amelia liked to hear chatter.

"About how fat I was when I was a child. My first zits, my first bra, that kind of thing. I suppose it's a compulsion—the need to confess how unhappy I was at times."

"What do you talk about when you drink wine spritzers?" Cary teased.

"That I don't really make my carrot cake from scratch; I use a Duncan Hines premix. And my spaghetti sauce is not homemade."

So that was what Ragu was. "You already confessed about the Ragu." It was funny. Here they were, two people who had met only once before, and they were both comfortable, talking about food.

"Did you speak to Amelia?"

His answer was important; he could tell by the anxious look in her eyes. "I finally got her an hour ago. She's happy that you're here in the city. I told her about your birthday, and she suggested I take you to one of her favorite restaurants, the Lion's Rock. I gave her your love and she returns hers."

Julie slipped off her shoes and curled her feet under her. "I just love this sofa. You can get lost in it. When and if I ever get my own place, I'm going to get one just like it. Are you hungry?"

"Starved. How about you?"

"That's what you have to be to eat spaghetti and Ragu. I only use it in a pinch or if I'm in a hurry. Billie and Uncle Thad always say it isn't important what you eat but who you're eating with. I tend to go along with that theory."

"I'll second that."

They laughed and talked. They ate and did the dishes together. They sat on the wheat-colored sofa watching a video of *Puff the Magic Dragon*, something Julie said always made her feel wonderful. Cary handed her his handkerchief when she cried, something she said she always did, but a good kind of crying, it showed she had feeling, and she never wanted to lose that. It was a wonderful, quiet evening. Cary couldn't remember when he'd enjoyed himself more. Promptly at eleven Julie turned off the television, rewound the video, and announced that it was time for him to leave because she was a working person, and if she didn't get a full seven hours of sleep, she was a real grump in the morning.

"Thanks for dinner. Sorry I forgot the wine. I'll make it up to you."

"That's okay. Sorry about the Ragu. I'll make it up to *you*."

"How?" Cary blurted.

"Why...I...somehow." She flushed a brilliant scarlet. Cary was instantly contrite.

"Chance meetings deserve whatever happens. I enjoyed the spaghetti. I had two helpings and you didn't hear me complain."

"I didn't complain about the wine either," Julie said lamely.

"That's true, you didn't. It's just that good-byes are awkward. I feel like I should kiss you. I want to kiss you, but I'm not going to. Scotch and soda makes a confessor out of me, too. If you give me your phone number, I'll call you tomorrow and perhaps we can have dinner out. I'm not leaving till Thursday."

Julie rattled off her number. Cary repeated it three times until it was locked in his memory. "I'll see you tomorrow, then. Good night, Julie."

"Good night, Cary."

He waited outside until he heard the three bolts shoot home. The urge to whistle was strong. He ignored it and rang for the elevator. Thirty minutes later he was back at his hotel. He showered, wrapped a towel around his middle, called down for a drink, and flopped onto the bed. It was a quarter to twelve, not yet ten in Texas. Amelia would still be up.

He was into his second drink when he made the call fifteen minutes later. Her voice sounded alert. "Darling, I was just about to give up on you and go to sleep," she said, "but knowing how you keep your word, I was sure you'd call. What did you do all evening?"

Cary could feel the guilt stampede through his entire body. "I had a few drinks and watched some television. Time got away from me, I guess." It wasn't a lie...exactly. He prided himself on never lying to Amelia. He was copping out and he didn't know why.

"You sound tired, darling. Maybe you should hang up and

get some sleep. It's probably the New York air."

"Maybe. What are you doing, besides talking to me? Did you have a nice evening? Do you miss me?"

"Darling, I miss you when you're just out of the room. Of course I miss you. I went over some papers, made a few notes, and read a chapter in one of your new books. I had a snack a while ago, just some crackers and grapes. I've just been sitting here waiting for your call. I did promise to . . ." Amelia waited to see if Cary would remember the promise she'd made earlier. When he let it slide, Amelia closed her eyes. Almost instantly they popped open. She squared her shoulders and asked lightly, "What did you have for dinner?"

"Spaghetti, salad, some garlic bread, and a couple of drinks."

"Where did you go to eat?"

"Seventy-ninth Street, I think. It wasn't bad."

"I think we should say good night, darling."

"You're right. It's been a long day. I love you, honey. You know that, don't you?"

"Of course I know that, and I love you, too," Amelia said lightly. "Sweet dreams, my darling."

There was a click and the connection was broken. Why hadn't he told Amelia he'd had dinner with Julie? She would have understood. The worst part was he probably wasn't going to tell her about dinner the next evening, either. He felt really rotten. He called room service for another drink. Sleep was out of the question. Guilt was something he wasn't used to, and it didn't make for relaxation.

Amelia pulled back the scented sheets. She moved stiffly, making a production out of walking around to Cary's side. She smoothed the coverlet and sheets till there wasn't a wrinkle or crease to be seen. She slipped out of the lacy Dior robe Cary had given her several years ago for her birthday and laid it neatly at the foot of the bed, on her side. She stared at it for a moment, then padded around to Cary's side and placed it where his own would rest if he'd been home. Her eyes moved to Cary's pillow. She imagined she could smell his scent.

Cary was often away on business, but she'd never reacted like this before. She was missing him in a different way, with a different feeling. She drew the covers up to her chin and stared at her husband's pillow. He always squashed it into a round ball. Goose down made that possible. She preferred a firmer pillow.

It was so quiet she could hear the slight hum of the electronic clock on the night table. Quiet and alone. Peaceful. Sort of like death. She shook herself, not liking her rapid breathing. From habit she took her pulse. Too fast. Way too fast. No medication. She could weather this, she could control it. Shift into neutral and think about something else. What else was there? Cary was her life. True, she was doing other things these days and she wasn't . . . Julie Kingsley. Youthful, vibrant, warm, gentle, loving. Almost family. All the same qualities Cary had. The fur jacket was a mistake. She'd have to call Cary back in the morning. What had she been thinking of? Actually, when you thought about it, it was downright ridiculous. A gold bracelet would do nicely.

Amelia glanced at the humming clock. She should be asleep. Instead, she was wide awake. Well then, she should be thinking about the Health Care Financing Administration and the interviews with nursing home residents she'd scheduled for early summer. She'd been partly responsible for going after the state surveyors who insured that the facilities met the standards set by the HCFA. Everyone was delighted with the progress she'd made, but concerned, even as she was, with the implementation of such a program. Nursing home residents needed leverage. She was going to see that they got it.

Her pulse was normal now, her breathing quiet. Tess Buckalew. Maybe she should have Tess Buckalew do another chart for her. What was in her future, in Cary's future? Did she even want to know? She didn't want Tess Buckalew to know, that was for sure. Some other astrologer, then, anonymous. Rubbish was what it was. Who in her right mind believed the stars could predict the future? Cary laughed at it and he made her laugh, but nobody in the Buckalew family ever made a move until Tess checked the stars. It was a terrible way to live. Yet the Buckalews seemed to be doing just fine. Or were they? Cole said it was a front, that they were in as much difficulty as all the other oil companies. She knew for a fact that Billie and the boys, along with Sawyer, had spent many closeted hours discussing the situation. She'd been reading the papers. Oil was down. Cole was edgy, Sawyer was constantly calling from Japan and snapping at everyone. Riley, on the other hand, was closemouthed, but his eyes mirrored the others' mood. Things weren't going well with Coleman Oil, and if the situation didn't improve soon, Coleman Aviation would suffer. It wasn't her problem. If they needed her, they'd call and she'd do what she could. For now, her time was taken up with something more important than oil.

Julie Kingsley. Cary, forty-eight; Julie, thirty-eight. The numbers were right. She was sixty-seven and Cary was forty-eight. The numbers were all wrong. Nineteen years and a semifrail wife weren't going to do it this time around. If it wasn't so damn late, she'd call Billie, but she knew the Kingsleys turned in right after the evening news. She was on her own. Rechannel your thoughts, she told herself. Think about the HCFA study. Don't think about Cary's tortured, guilty voice.

Amelia leaned back into her plump foam pillow and was asleep almost immediately. She slept soundly until four, but after that she could only doze and dream wild, frightening dreams. When she woke at six, the last of her dreams was clear. She'd been committed to a nursing home because she'd lost control of her bodily functions. Tied in the bed, her hair unkempt, spittle drooling from the corner of her mouth, she waited for Cary's twice-monthly five-minute visit. The nurse who brought him into the room was a beautiful young woman dressed in soft white, her nurse's cap like a halo on her head. Her voice was gentle when she whispered that Amelia was waiting patiently, that he was all she lived for. Tenderly she smoothed back Amelia's gray hair and dabbed at the corners of her mouth. "Cary's here, Amelia. Now, I want you to smile for him." And she'd obeyed the pretty nurse, whose name was Julie Kingsley. Cary hadn't smiled in return. Instead, he turned to allow a second nurse to enter the room with a second visitor. Tess Buckalew waving a thick booklet. "Your future, darling, it's all here! Wait till you read it! You're done for, dearie!" Amelia was convinced it was Tess's cackling laughter that woke her. She shuddered. How real it seemed.

Amelia showered while the coffee perked. Decaffeinated, on doctor's orders. Only for herself: for Cary she brewed a master blend that she ordered from a specialty shop. Once in a while she sneaked a cup just so she wouldn't forget what real coffee tasted like. She was on her second cup when she placed the call to Cary in New York. She talked aloud, first, to the empty breakfast nook so her unused morning voice would sound natural when Cary got on the line.

"Amelia! What a wonderful way to wake up and start the

day. There isn't anything wrong, is there, darling?"

"Of course not." She explained about the fur jacket. Cary said he agreed.

"How did you sleep, sweetheart?"

"Like a log," Amelia lied in a light tone. "How about you?"

"Like a log," Cary lied in a matching tone.

"What's on for today?" Amelia asked.

"I'm going to sit in on the meetings again to see if there's something I missed yesterday. I have nothing else to do. I really should come home, Amelia."

"And leave Julie alone on her birthday? Absolutely not. Billie and Thad would never forgive us. Wine and dine her like you used to wine and dine me when we were courting. I love that word 'courting,' don't you?"

"Amelia, when it comes to you, I have total recall. I haven't forgotten a thing about us. Someday I'm going to write my memoirs."

Someday. Far into the future. She wouldn't be here then. People didn't write their memoirs until they were old and wanted to leave something behind. It would be a long time before Cary was old. And Cary could father a child any time. The thought was so devastating she almost fainted. "Darling, that's a wonderful idea! Make sure I'm on page one. I have to run, darling. Busy day today." She smacked her lips as a kiss, and she could hear Cary do the same before she hung up the phone. Her hands were shaking badly; she jammed them into the pockets of her robe. "Think only HCFA," she muttered over and over as she dressed.

Amelia examined her face in the mirror. Her image seemed vague, distorted. Not whole. Was that because part of her life force, Cary, was slipping away from her? Think HCFA. Her image remained the same, vague, distorted, incomplete.

Her steps dragged as she walked around the luxurious condominium turning off lights, making sure the coffee pot was unplugged, the radio off, the balcony doors locked. Cary always chided her about locking a thirty-fifth-floor sliding door. The pedestal with the sundial, another gift from Cary, caught her eye. She slid open the door and walked out into the early morning, touched the sundial. The symbol of eternal life, the spirit of eternal love. Browning's tender words loomed up at her. "Grow old along with me, the best is yet to be." It was a lie. She'd already had the best. There was no more. It was one of Cary's first gifts, and it had made her weep with happiness. It was probably the one she cherished more than any other. She wondered what would happen to it when she died. Grow old along with me. Well, by God, she had certainly done that! The only problem was Cary hadn't grown old along with her. How could he? Did he think he'd been robbed of the best? She wished she had the guts to ask him. The best is yet to be. "Yes, my darling, for you the best is yet to come," Amelia whispered in a choked voice.

Julie Kingsley munched on a bran muffin in between sips of coffee. She hadn't slept well, and that was unusual. Normally she could sleep through a five-alarm fire. Last night she'd lain awake listening to New York traffic, sirens, and what sounded like a mouse scurrying about the apartment. This morning the mirror warned her that sleep was essential. The shadows under her eyes were too visible.

Nervousness was not a trait of hers, but this morning she was jumpy, just short of irritable. Possibly from lack of sleep. Certainly not from the caffeine in her one cup of coffee.

She put a name to her feeling as she rummaged in the closet for her umbrella. Cary Assante. It had been a pleasant evening. He hadn't laughed at her when she showed him her videotape of *Puff the Magic Dragon*. He'd enjoyed watching it as much as she had. He'd chuckled when she repeated the dialogue ahead of the cartoon figures.

Cary was going to call her today and they were to have dinner. "No," she all but shouted. "No, I can't do that. Tomorrow is different; that's my birthday and I accepted his invitation. But not tonight." That would make it three days in a row, but . . . how nice he was. She could feel the pulse in her throat start to hammer. There was no point in looking for trouble.

Without a second thought she walked to the kitchen phone and called her boss at home. "Eleanor, I was wondering if you'd found anyone to go to White Plains to work on the catalog. If you haven't, I'll be glad to do it. I can get the next train out and catch up on my own work over the weekend, since I have nothing planned." She listened to the sleepy voice on the other end of the line. "I don't mind, Eleanor. I have nothing planned for this evening, and really, I'd like the chance to do the layout for this catalog. Do I sound like I care if I don't get back till midnight?" She listened again. "Well, if you insist, I'll take a limo back." She copied down the number of the limo service. "Okay, I have it. I'll see you tomorrow." She sighed so loudly she startled herself.

Her blunt fingers, the nails clipped short, punched out a second set of numbers. Breathlessly, she announced herself to the answering service and left her message. Miss Kingsley will be out of town on business and won't be back till tomorrow. She can't be reached. When Julie hung up the phone, she felt weak in the knees. She gulped the rest of the coffee. Platonic family birthdays were one thing; intimate dinners were something else. She loved the Colemans and wouldn't single out any of them for special attention. The fact that Cary's name was Assante didn't enter her mind.

She thought she would feel better, relieved somehow, when she left the apartment, but she didn't. Loss of sleep was a real killer.

‹‹‹‹‹‹‹‹‹ CHAPTER FIVE ››››››››

Thad Kingsley rocked complacently in one of the rocking chairs Billie had arranged by the fire. A big old yellow cat that had come with the rented house in Georgetown purred contentedly. Thad watched it with disdain. He was a dog person, and so was Billie. They tolerated the feline, feeding it and changing its litter box regularly, but for the most part, the cat with the plumed tail ignored them both.

It was comfortable here in Georgetown, even though Billie detested the constant nights out and the reciprocal invitations. She called it the Washington fishbowl. Thad laughed, but not with amusement, when Billie told him only a quarter of the deals and decision making went on in the Capitol Hill cloakroom. The other three quarters went on over tea and bridge. Billie likened the women to sharks and barracuda. Late at night, when she and Thad were snuggled in bed, she'd entertain him with tales of the women and their devious plans to get into the limelight.

He'd had enough of politics. Secretly he believed he was the only member of the Senate who hadn't compromised himself. Possibly there were others, but he didn't know them. This was his last term. The rest of his life was his own. Thirty years to the navy, two terms in the House, and another two in the Senate was enough to give to one's country.

Billie deserved more of his time. They'd take trips, walk around the farm, take the truck and go into town for a shopping spree, and just hang out with the dogs. They both had some good years left, and by God, if he had anything to say about it, they were going to be spent together. He was going to stick to Billie like a leaf to a branch. Jesus, he loved that woman, but right now that woman was all wrought up about something, and they were going to have to talk it out.

Billie walked into the den carrying two homemade banana splits. The mound of cream and the cherry perched on top made his mouth water. It was their Friday night special treat. "Are we saying the hell with our waistlines again this week?" Thad chuckled as he licked his lips.

"Mine is only a half inch bigger than it was the day you married me," Billie said. "Yours, however, is two inches bigger. Don't try to fool me, Thad; you let your belt out two notches." She grinned.

"That's a testimonial to your culinary expertise," Thad said, digging into the luscious cream and then raising the spoon aloft. "Here's looking at you, kid!"

Billie giggled. "If I were you, Senator, I'd eat that in a hurry. That crazy cat is licking her chops. She looks like she's ready to spring."

They ate their treat, savoring it as they watched Ted Koppel's late-night news program. Another of their treats. Friday night was always a late night. Saturday mornings were for sleeping late and slow, wonderful sex.

"I think you're wrong, Thad. Ted *is* wearing a toupee."

"Wrong." This was their standard weekly argument. "Look at the part. It's his hair. He's one of the lucky ones." Thad ran his hands over his own receding hairline.

"Nobody's hair looks the same day after day, week after week," Billie said. "Once in a while the barber makes a mistake."

"Maybe he trims it himself?"

"It's a toupee," Billie insisted.

"Is not. It's real!"

"Why don't you ask the boys in the cloakroom? They're supposed to know everything," Billie teased. "Wig."

"Wrong! His own hair! And now that we've finished our Friday night ritual, Billie, let's talk about what's really bothering you. You didn't make a mistake when you turned over the oil end of Coleman Enterprises to Riley. We talked about it till we were hoarse. It's not Riley that's the problem, it's OPEC. I'm sure Riley can handle it if anyone can. He's working hard, and we're all behind him."

Billie leaned into the crook of Thad's arm. "Thad, I don't want Riley to make Coleman Oil his life. I don't want him to be . . . to be like Moss. I want him to have a life apart from this family."

"Riley will do what he has to do. The men and the company respect him. He's not a kid anymore, Billie. I heard Sawyer tell you he's brought in every expert in the country." He paused. "I think something else is bothering you, Billie."

Billie's voice was barely audible when she spoke. "Do you think it has anything to do with . . . with the Buckalews?"

There it was, out in the open. It was Thad's hunch that there was more to the Buckalews than anyone let on. And it wasn't Tess and her astrological forecasts. Lacey. Cole's old girlfriend, Riley's new girlfriend. It was his opinion, and he'd cut out his tongue before he'd voice it, that Lacey Buckalew was trash. Designer trash, but trash nonetheless.

Thad chose his words carefully. "Riley said Oakes has been steering him in the right direction. Perhaps he's relying too heavily on his future father-in-law. Oakes has been in the oil business all his life, but that doesn't mean he knows everything. I think Oakes, Coots if you will, has been slugging away at Riley about the Enhanced Oil Recovery Program. Riley wanted to get into it sooner, but Coots talked him out of it. Just the way Riley tried to talk *him* out of closing down his strippers. Cole told me Riley was sorry he'd listened to Coots. Cole didn't want to tell me that, but I badgered him and told him it would go no farther than you. Let's leave it to Cole and Riley to run the business and deal with the Buckalews. If they need our help, they'll ask."

"Before or after we lose Coleman Oil? It could destroy the family, Thad."

"Don't you think Riley knows that? He's under a tremendous amount of pressure. His grandfather is terminally ill. He's torn. If he has made some fatal errors, the Japanese in him will demand he make it right. The American in him is tearing him apart that he can't go back to Japan to be with his grandfather. A rock and a hard place, Billie."

"Let him have his head and hope for the best; is that what you're saying?"

Thad puffed on his pipe. "Pretty much so, honey."

"What if we go under? What happens to all the people that work for us? Their families, what about their families?"

"We do the best we can. The Colemans know how to fight."

"I think it's time we went to Texas to talk to Riley and Cole. I'll drop by and see Tess on some pretext, make a few phone calls, commission a few charts. See what I can dig up."

Thad pretended mock horror. "Is this the same Billie Ames Coleman Kingsley who can't abide the wheeling and dealing that goes on in Washington?"

"You call it whatever you want. In Texas we call it palavering. I was never very good at it, but I'm going to learn now. When can we leave?"

"I thought you said you wouldn't interfere in company policy or tell anyone what to do? How about this Saturday?"

"We aren't interfering, we're helping. There is a difference. Saturday's fine. Thank you, Thad. Now I'll be able to sleep tonight."

"Is this why you've been tossing and turning? Why didn't you say something, Billie?"

"Thad, you have enough on your mind. I promised you when we got married that I wouldn't let the Colemans interfere with our marriage. I've tried to keep that promise."

"Darling, your family is my family. I love all of them. Surely you know I'd do anything I could to help. All you have to do is ask. I thought you didn't want me to stick my nose in."

"Thad, we aren't communicating here. This is the first time in all the years since we've been married that neither of us knows what the other is thinking and planning. Good lord, how did this happen?"

"It's that stupid cat we were saddled with," Thad said with a grin on his face. "I can't think clearly when I have to clean a litter box, and then there's this other problem of Ted Koppel's hair that keeps bugging me. Who can think clearly with momentous problems like that hanging over him?"

Billie doubled over laughing. Thad always made everything right. No matter how bad things were, he always put

{ 95 }

them in perspective. "You're absolutely right, darling." She pressed the remote control button, cutting Ted Koppel off in midsentence. "Obviously it's a wig."

"Nope. Real head of hair." Thad grinned. "Tell you what, I'll put the dishes in the sink and you lock up. Don't forget to leave the night-light on for the cat, and tell it good night, like the owner suggested."

"Uh-huh," Billie mumbled. The day she said good night to a cat named Penelope would be the day Nancy Reagan did a jig on Pennsylvania Avenue. She would, however, leave the night-light on, since that was written into the rental lease.

Lacey was on a leave of absence from between jobs. It seemed to her that her whole life was either between something or absent from something. From long habit she'd awakened at six-thirty, and now she couldn't go back to sleep. Rain peppered the window. She remembered waking up one other morning with Cole next to her. Rain had peppered the window then and they'd made heavy, intense love and gone back to sleep. They'd spent the entire day in bed.

She liked Riley, and she supposed it was possible that one day she might fall in love with him. Her mother said she would. The stars ordained it. Lacey sniffed and reached for a tissue. A lot of things were ordained in life, she supposed, but loving Riley the way she loved Cole was not to be one of them.

She shouldn't have taken the leave of absence, but the pressure from her parents was too much. She'd screwed up half a dozen accounts and was on report with the company. Her boss told her to take some time off to get her head straight and then think about coming back to work. She'd probably been replaced by now. She wondered if she could collect unemployment. Tess would have a fit. A Buckalew collecting unemployment! Coots, on the other hand, would tell her to go ahead, the state could afford it. He'd also tell her he wasn't supporting her. He'd done his duty by sending her to one of those fancy colleges that cost more than the first house he ever bought.

All indications pointed to money being tight at Buckalew Big Wells. Just last night her mother was telling her father that a windfall was due soon, and Coots had laughed and said if it wasn't real soon, her mother would have to go out to work. But then Tess announced that she'd been commissioned to do some extensive charts for a whole group of wealthy Dallas women. At five hundred dollars a throw, she'd earn enough to put on the biggest, ritziest wedding Austin had ever seen. In the Assante Towers Ballroom in Miranda. Her father had turned green. She'd gone white herself. She didn't want to get married. Not to Riley. Cole was all she wanted, all she would ever want. Riley was just to make Cole jealous, but it wasn't working. Her mother had ordered her, actually ordered her, to beg Cole to take her back. Her father had jumped in with both feet, telling her she was a low-down snot and not fit to carry the Buckalew name. Then, when that didn't work, he'd pretty much told her to suck up to Riley and hope he'd have enough brains to take her on. She'd protested vehemently, but Tess had shown her the way the stars lined up, pointing out a marriage that would end in bliss. Not that she believed it for a minute. She could never be happy without Cole.

The Colemans and the Buckalews, that's what it was all about. A business merger, and she was the stock. She'd agreed; that was the sad part. Now she was one step away from being engaged. After the engagement came the marriage. Then children. One-quarter-Japanese children. She didn't like kids, but the Colemans were big on family, so she'd have to perform. Her father would see to it. Tess, too. Somewhere it was probably written in the stars that she was to have 2.5 children along with the requisite dog to complete the family.

Her father needed the Colemans, specifically Riley. He didn't care about her, he never had. She wasn't even sure if Riley cared. Not that it mattered. The engagement and marriage would come off as planned, regardless of what she wanted.

Sunbridge would be stirring now. It was twenty minutes of seven. Cole should be out of the shower and shaved. He was probably half-dressed. He never bothered with anything but the coffee and juice brought to his room at six-thirty. She knew these things because Cole had told her in the days when they had shared everything. He was probably tying his shoes right now. He'd gulp the last of the coffee, shrug into his jacket, grab his wallet and keys from the dresser, and be out of the house by seven-fifteen. Her shaky fingers punched out the numbers of his private phone. The phone was right next to the coffee cup. He'd pick it up on the first ring.

His voice was rough-sounding as he said hello.

"Cole, it's Lacey. I'm glad I caught you before you left. I

was wondering if you'd take pity on me and have lunch. I'm on a leave of absence, and this place is driving me crazy."

Cole's hand gripped the receiver till his knuckles glowed white. "Not today, Lacey. And not any other day, either. I thought we had an understanding."

A lump settled in Lacy's throat. "What's wrong with having lunch?"

"For one thing, Riley's away. The second thing is it isn't right, and the third thing is I don't want to have lunch with you. We made the break and you're about to become engaged to Riley. That's the way it's going to stay. I don't want you calling here anymore unless it's for him." When Cole replaced the phone, his hand felt cramped and sweaty. He closed his eyes wearily. He didn't need any more problems.

He was out of sync now, after Lacey's call. The day loomed ahead of him like a gigantic dark mass. He'd call Sawyer in Japan when he got to the office. There was business to discuss with her, and if he was careful, he could work the conversation around to personal issues. If there was one thing Sawyer loved, it was giving advice.

He was pacing now, hardly aware of what he was doing. He found himself at the window looking down into the brick courtyard. Memories of his youth flooded back to him. His eyes raked the apartment over the garage, where sexy Luana Simms and her drunken father used to live. His Mercury Cougar and Riley's Berlinetta used to be parked directly below the window. The Cougar had been replaced with a sleek red Porsche, the Berlinetta with a four-wheel drive for Riley. Snug in the garage was Riley's Lamborghini, which he rarely drove.

The rain seemed to be coming down in buckets. It wouldn't hurt to wait a while for it to slack off. The Porsche wasn't real good in the rain. Rain. He'd always liked rain. Lacey had told him many times that she loved to lie in bed and listen to the rain on the roof and splashing against the window. He tried to force thoughts of Lacey from his mind. Lacey and the rain. Lacey and the rain. He could write a song about it if he were musically inclined, which he wasn't.

Freedom, no responsibilities. He supposed a life like that was possible, but it would make him a pretty worthless individual. He wished he had just a little of Riley's blind loyalty to the family, his dedication. He put on a good show, so good that even old Sawyer hadn't picked up on his unhappiness, until just recently.

He'd been brought up on goals and dreams. Hope, too. For what? Maybe what he wanted, what he missed, was the challenge of the outside world. Making it on his own, without the family behind him. That fall-on-your-face, pick-yourself-up-and-dust-off kind of thing.

A sheet of gusty rain slapped against the window. Cole jumped at the sound. He promised himself he would do something about his future, as soon as things in the oil business settled down.

Coleman Aviation was awash in fluorescent lighting. Cole was glad to be inside, away from the dreary, rain-soaked day. Away from the unwanted thoughts that attacked him at Sunbridge like a thief in the dead of night.

His office welcomed him. He'd decorated it himself, choosing restful earth tones and soft leather. Everything in the office was comfortable and useful. The Chagall paintings always had a cheering effect. The tasteful green plants reassured him by surviving in canned air and artificial light. He alone had the responsibility for watering, trimming, and spritzing them. The onyx ashtray, a gift, held paper clips and rubber bands to discourage smokers. When he was forced to halt a would-be smoker, he smiled and said the smoke killed the plants.

For a long time he hadn't felt like a responsible contributor in the scheme of things at Coleman Aviation. When it came right down to it, it was Sawyer who breathed fire and life into Coleman Aviation; he merely fanned the flame. He did what was required, and he did it well, but Sawyer deserved the credit.

He'd known for some time that this wasn't where he wanted to spend the rest of his life. In his own way he was as tormented as Riley. Riley at least knew what he wanted. He, on the other hand, was playing the old family game. His mother's gift of half of Sunbridge had locked him in, just as Riley was locked in. Riley's eyes had glowed like Christmas lights when his mother handed him a copy of the deed to Sunbridge. Riley should have been given the whole package. He and Sawyer could easily manage all of Coleman Enterprises.

When the oil business righted itself, he was going to have to make some real hard decisions. Always, when he thought like this, his grandmother Billie's words surfaced: "Don't ever make the mistake your grandfather made. Don't make this family and this business your life." She'd understand when it was time to make decisions. Not now, while Riley was in hot water and needed his support. He'd see him through, and by summer or early autumn he'd be ready to make a move.

He never felt better than when his thoughts took this direction. A defecting Coleman. He'd read something once that was written by a Dutchman. "If you can't whistle on your way to work, then you don't belong in that job." Hell, he'd never whistled, not from day one. Riley had, though.

Time, and patience, would win out.

He shook his head to clear away his thoughts. Sawyer. His half sister. He owed a lot to her and to his mother. Give credit where credit's due. He smiled ruefully. Two great women in his life. A guy couldn't go wrong with those two in his corner. And if he did, he'd have no one to blame but himself. Straight-arrow Tanner.

His intention to call Japan resurfaced. He'd have to place the call himself since his secretary didn't arrive till eight-thirty. This was the time of day he liked best. He felt fresh and alert. He needed those qualities when he spoke to Sawyer, just to hold up his end. He wondered if she knew Adam Jarvis was back at the ranch with his stepson.

A pity Sawyer and Adam never got together. After Sawyer's operation and long recovery, they'd just drifted apart. Adam had needs, and Sawyer couldn't or wouldn't fulfill them. Eventually he'd married a classy, sassy California girl with a young son. As far as he knew, they'd been happy until the day she'd been caught in the cross fire of a crazed gunman in a shopping mall. They'd all rallied round for Adam until he was on his feet, taking the responsibility for his stepson. Cole couldn't help wondering what kind of father Adam was. Damn good, he was sure. Adam was first-rate.

It was early evening in Japan. Sawyer would be finishing her day as he started his. He could see her propped up on her lemon-colored sofa with a wine spritzer. He was disappointed when her phone continued to ring. He wondered why the answering machine didn't switch on. Concern furrowed his brow. Sawyer didn't exactly sit home at night, that much he knew, but she always went home to shower and relax before an evening out. He replaced the phone, a thoughtful look on his face. The sudden urge to speak with his mother made him punch out a series of numbers that would connect him with lunchtime in Hawaii. At least there would be servants to answer the phone, a human voice telling him his mother or Rand was available and to hold on, or to tell him his message would be relayed and the call returned. He waited, his sense of unease increasing.

The phone was picked up on the fifth ring. Mr. and Mrs. Nelson were on their way to Japan. They would call on their arrival. Would he care to leave a message? Cole's stomach tightened into a knot. He left his name.

Cole walked over to the tropical fish tank. He dusted some powdered shrimp across the top of the water. The fish ignored it and continued to swim in and around the colorful rocks and greenery. The knot in his stomach remained tight. He went back to his desk and opened the appointment book. Something was going on.

The polished brass plate said the occupant of flat 2–B was Chesney M. Brighton. The M wasn't real; it had been added, not on a whim, but rather as a necessity to reinforce Chesney Brighton's identity. The fact that the initial wasn't recorded on her birth registry made it that much more real because she had given the initial to herself. The M stood for Madeline, a name she liked.

Inside flat 2–B, Chesney stood at her bedroom window, watching the gray English dawn. In the soft early light she thought she could see the promise of a beautiful day as the faint pink streaks struggled to announce the sun. Chesney knew she was capable of putting sunshine into her life on this day even if Mother Nature decided to cast clouds over the golden orb. Inwardly or outwardly, today was going to be one of the sunniest days of her life.

Today was the day she was going to visit Sawyer Coleman, the head of Coleman Aviation, halfway around the world. The same Sawyer Coleman who, according to her hard-won information, was involved in a relationship with Lord Randolph Nelson—her father. She was going to ask Sawyer Coleman the whereabouts of Rand Nelson so she could tell . . . tell him what?

That I'm his illegitimate daughter. That I've been searching for years for him. It should be the other way around, she thought. He should be searching for me, but since he doesn't know I'm alive, how can he search for me?

She was going to change all that now. She would announce who she was, ask for an introduction to her father, produce the documentation she had concerning her birth, and then she would walk away.

Her announcement was going to be a bloody shock, one she hoped her father was up to, but if he wasn't up to it, it was his problem, not hers.

Chesney rolled her name off her lips. Chesney Brighton, Chesney M. Brighton, Chesney Nelson, Chesney Brighton Nelson. If her parents had kept her, she wondered what middle name they would have given her. Lillian? Mary? Not Mary, that was too plain. Mary Catherine? Dorothy? Amelia? Amelia was the name of Rand Nelson's stepmother, she'd learned, and one of the powerful Colemans of Texas as well as Sawyer Coleman's aunt.

Yes, she thought, if her father had known about her, he would have christened her Chesney Amelia Nelson.

Chesney's gaze shifted from the creeping dawn to her bedside table and a picture of herself and her friend Sara. It was the only photograph in the entire flat worthy of framing and prominence. It was a somber, solemn picture, but to Chesney it represented who she was *then* and who she was *now*. It was a reminder of what she and Sara had endured. Because they had endured, she would not allow that time to be forgotten. She was Chesney M. Brighton—orphan and airline stewardess. Chesney M. Brighton, seeker of her heritage and her future. If things worked out, she might one day be one of *them*.

Sawyer let herself into her small house at noon. It had been careless of her to leave behind the most important papers she needed for the day. She'd looked them over earlier, when she woke. She'd spilled coffee and had tried to dry them off. Always aware of time since her operation, she'd realized she was running late and simply forgot to stuff the papers into her briefcase. Now she was home, cursing her carelessness. She decided to fix herself a cheese sandwich and tea and to forget about not taking a lunch hour. She was halfway through the sandwich when she heard the tinkle of the bell at her garden gate. She walked to the kitchen window. The gardener never rang the bell. He had his own key. She wasn't expecting any deliveries, either. There was no panic or fear in her as she walked through the Zen garden to the gate—only curiosity. She fitted her key into the lock and pushed outward. Standing before her was a tall woman about her own age. She wore fashionable clothes, and her hairstyle was simple but elegant. Just the tiniest bit of makeup around her eyes. Beautiful, Sawyer thought. And something else. She swallowed hard and asked if she could be of help.

The voice was soft, cultured and very British. "Are you Sawyer Coleman?"

"Yes, I am."

"I'm Chesney Brighton. My name should be Chesney Nelson. I'm Rand Nelson's daughter. I'm trying to locate him. I was told you might be able to help me." No expression. Just cold, hard, matter-of-fact words.

Sawyer struggled to recover her composure. She locked the gate and led the way into the house, trying to quiet her jumping nerves. Rand's daughter! He'd never mentioned having a daughter. The likeness was there, especially around the eyes. Problems. Not for her but for Maggie and Rand. Maybe. Or maybe it wouldn't be a problem at all.

Sawyer could feel her heart beating erratically. Any mention of Rand Nelson made her ache because he was lost to her, married now to her own mother. And while she hurt and ached, she wouldn't have it any other way. Rand and Maggie were meant for each other. Who was she to deny them happiness? She tried never to think about the wonderful relationship she had shared with Rand years ago, and for the most part she was successful, but every now and then, like now, her past reared up and socked her, forcing her to administer a pep talk to herself. But she couldn't do that right now. Later, when she was alone, she'd tell herself how lucky she was to be alive. She'd concentrate on her comfortable life here in Japan, doing a job she loved for a family she'd die for. One day Rand Nelson would be nothing more than an interlude in her life that hadn't worked out.

"Tea?" Anything to stall for time. She had to collect her thoughts.

"I'd love some. I stopped by the Coleman office and was told you'd come here. I must have missed you by minutes. I hope I'm not intruding."

"Not at all, but I don't understand why you've come to me."

"I was told that you and my father were . . . are . . . that you were getting married. I've been searching for years."

"That was all a very long time ago. Rand, your . . . Rand is married to my mother. They . . . they live in Hawaii. I don't understand. . . . If you're Rand's daughter, why are you searching for him?" She thought she knew the answer, but wanted to hear the words spoken aloud.

A sick feeling settled in Sawyer's stomach. Rand never wanted to have children. He'd confessed once that he wasn't fond of the little buggers. At the time she'd merely laughed, convinced that every man wants children at some point in his life, to carry on his name. Rand hadn't laughed in return. Instead he'd turned very serious and said he wasn't getting any younger and he was set in his ways and children would only complicate his life. She'd been so in love with him at the time that she'd accepted his decision without an argument.

Rand with a checkered past? Most men weren't saints, but then, most men didn't have illegitimate daughters who showed up from out of nowhere. Never once had Rand so much as hinted at a child. She could feel herself drifting back in her memory to that long-ago day when Rand Nelson upset her world . . .

"There's something wrong, Rand. You . . . you seem to be avoiding me. . . . Have you had a change of heart?" She held her breath as she waited for his denial.

"Sawyer, there's no easy way to say this. . . . It won't work for us. We're worlds apart. You're young and you have your whole life ahead of you. You deserve children. I don't want children. I . . . I don't think I ever want to get married."

"Is there someone else?" she blurted, unable to stop herself.

He seemed startled that she should ask, even offended. "No, of course there isn't. You know I wouldn't hurt you for the world."

"I don't know any such thing. I don't believe you. It's my mother! You've fallen for my mother!" Sawyer clapped her hands over her ears and squeezed her eyes shut.

She could feel herself start to choke.

She wrenched herself back to the moment and faced Chesney's voice.

"I'm Rand Nelson's illegitimate daughter. I was brought up in an orphanage. I was left on the proverbial doorstep with the proverbial note pinned to my nappie. My mother was part of a touring entertainment group. She was young and wanted some adventure in her life. She met my father in Saigon. My father . . . Rand Nelson was a chopper flyer for your government, on loan, I believe, from the British. My mother was sketchy on the details, and there was something about Mr. Nelson having a dual citizenship. He flew fire flights in country. It wasn't a war, you see, but more of an altercation; that's why my mother agreed to go with the tour. My . . . Mr. Nelson used to go to Saigon on his days off, and that's how he met my mother. His favorite hangout was the Tigress Inn, or so my mother said. My mother believes he saw . . . other women, but he always came back to her. She said she loved him very much. He . . . he was stationed in Da Nang."

She'd heard all this before. From Rand. She hoped what she was feeling wasn't showing in her face. How could this young woman know about the Tigress Inn? She nodded her head for Chesney to continue.

"Trouble developed with the tour group, and the leader went off and left the girls. They in turn got separated. Rand Nelson sort of looked out for my mother until he was called back. She tried to tell him about her pregnancy, but he . . . he didn't want to hear and he had to leave. He gave her money. When the tour leader left, he had all the girls' passports and their last week's wages. They were left high and dry. She used the money Mr. Nelson gave her to buy letters of transit on the black market, and the Red Cross got her safely back to England, which is where she had me. End of sad story," Chesney said ruefully. "When it became permissible for orphans to seek out their parents, I searched for and found my mother. At first she refused to tell me anything. She's married now, with a family of her own, and didn't want to disgrace them. I understood. At first she lied to me, saying she didn't know who my father was. I felt she wasn't telling me the truth and I felt she wasn't a promiscuous woman, so I kept going back to her house, day after day, week after week, until I finally wore down her resistance. There is no place in her life for me now. I recognized that and told her she has nothing to fear from me. I don't know if there's a place in my father's life for me either, but I want to see him. I was told that you and he . . . Well, what I mean is, information was skimpy and I was lucky to get as much as I did. Do you understand what I've been telling you, Miss Coleman?"

"Every word," Sawyer choked out. What was this going to do to Rand and Maggie? Bring them closer together or cause problems? "Does Rand know? What I mean is, did your mother agree to have an abortion? Did she tell Rand she would?"

Soft gray eyes stared directly into Sawyer's concerned gaze. "I have to assume he thought she had an abortion. So to answer your question, no, he doesn't know of my existence."

"And you want me to put you in touch with your father?" Sawyer held her breath. Of course that's what she wanted. If she were in her position, she'd want the same thing. She knew what it was to grow up without a father.

"I was hoping...I thought you could...what is the expression?...pave the way for me so it wouldn't come as such a shock to him."

The young woman's control was too tight, Sawyer thought. She wanted to know what else Chesney knew about Rand, but she was afraid to ask. Should she check her out? She could be anybody. The girl had managed to track her down halfway around the world. She didn't look like she was hurting for money. Searches like this cost a lot.

Sawyer took a deep breath. "If what you say is true..." She let the sentence hang in midair.

Chesney waited.

"I can't, I just can't invade my mother's life and make... and upset their lives. For all I know, you could be an impostor. Do you have any sort of documentation?" As if she needed any. The girl was almost an exact replica of Rand. She could be some sort of distant relative, though, not necessarily a daughter. Rand was a wealthy man.

"I understand what you're going through," Chesney said. "You must be wondering about a lot of things. Where am I getting the money to do this, for one. It would be much too costly under ordinary circumstances, but I'm a stewardess. I can pretty much fly all over the world on my time off and pay only the tax. My job pays well and I've been frugal. It's the best I can offer for now."

"What was your mother's name?"

"Marion Brighton. My mother did one thing to help me. She gave me this." Chesney drew out her billfold, snapped it open, and withdrew a faded and wrinkled snapshot. She handed it to Sawyer.

It was blurred, as if the person who took the picture hadn't focused the camera properly, so it was impossible to tell if the handsome pilot standing next to a smiling young woman was Rand or not. The cocky angle of his cap made her think it was. She'd seen him stand in exactly the same position many times. Loose. Cock of the walk. She handed back the picture.

There was a desperate note in Chesney's voice when she spoke next. "My mother told me things. It's true that most of them must be public knowledge, but there were a few... intimate things, the kinds of things lovers say to one another. I don't think I should repeat them unless it's to my father."

Sawyer's head was bobbing. "Yes, you're right. Look, I have to get back to the office. Why don't we meet this evening and have dinner—seven at the Okura. Will that be all right?"

"That will be fine. I appreciate your seeing and talking with me." Chesney smiled warmly and held out her hand. Sawyer grasped it firmly. She'd always prided herself on her manly handshake. She'd met her match.

The afternoon dragged. Chesney kept intruding into Sawyer's thoughts. It was three-thirty when she picked up the phone to call Hawaii. Should she ask for Maggie or Rand? Should she just blurt her news, or choose her words carefully and try to soften the blow? And it was going to be a blow, especially to Maggie. Rand was going to have to deal with a daughter, a grown daughter who was old enough to have children of her own. Maggie. She'd speak to Maggie. Maggie would know how to deal with it. She sighed with relief when she heard her mother's voice.

"Sawyer! How nice of you to call. I was going to write you a letter today. Now you've saved me the trouble—you know how I hate to write letters! There isn't anything wrong, is there?" Maggie asked anxiously. "Mr. Hasegawa isn't..."

"He's doing as well as can be expected. I don't know if what I have to tell you is to be considered something wrong or not. I've been sitting here for the past few hours trying to decide how to... to tell you...."

"For God's sake, Sawyer, what is it? Damn Rand, he went to Hilo today to see about a sugarcane plantation. He wants to buy it. Stop me from babbling, Sawyer. I know you aren't an alarmist, but goddamn it, you are alarming me. You never call in the middle of the day. What is it, Sawyer?"

Maggie listened while Sawyer told her of her noontime visitor. She heard Maggie's gasp but kept on talking. "I'm supposed to meet her this evening at the Okura. She seems to be legitimate, and Maggie, she looks like Rand, so much so that it's spooky. I don't know what else to say."

"I don't either. How am I going to tell this to Rand?"

"The same way I told it to you. Just say it. Maggie, I'm the last one in the world that would ever try to advise you, but . . ."

"Lay back, is that it?"

"I think so. It's going to be a shock to Rand. Be there for him."

"Of course," Maggie said soberly. "How is everything, Sawyer?"

"Fine. Cole's coming over in ten days. We'll party and liven things up. Every time he comes over here, he roots me out of bed at six in the morning to walk down the Ginza. He really gets off on it. Someday I'm going to find out why."

"He probably saw someone do it in the movies and it stuck with him," Maggie said in a quiet voice. Usually she laughed indulgently when she heard something about Cole she didn't know. Mothers were like that.

"Do you want me to call you this evening after dinner?"

"Yes. If I know Rand, he's going to want to take the next plane out. Thanks for calling, Sawyer. We'll be in touch. Don't be surprised if we show up on your doorstep in the next day or so."

"You're welcome," Sawyer said warmly.

"You really mean that, don't you?"

"You bet." Good-byes were so awkward. No one ever seemed to know how to hang up a phone or get out a door. Sometimes good-byes were longer than actual visits. "I'll be in touch tonight, then. Good-bye, Maggie."

"Good-bye, Sawyer."

Maggie stared at the phone for a long time. She'd been happy too long. Things had been too idyllic. She hadn't actually been sitting around waiting for the other shoe to drop, but she'd known that sooner or later her life was going to be intruded upon. Later always came, no matter how you tried to prevent it. She'd handle it.

Tess sipped her coffee and kept on talking at the same time, no mean feat, Coots thought. His wife always did two or three things at a time. Sometimes Tess awed him. Today she looked cranky, and when she was in what he called one of her star moods, he tried to absent himself as quickly as possible.

"You are one foolish girl, Lacey," she scolded. "You should have insisted on going to Japan with Riley. The configuration was just right. When will you learn to trust the stars?"

"The same time I do." Coots guffawed. He loved poking fun at Tess's astrological jabberings and detested the area of the house that she referred to as her offices. He particularly hated the decor: the bright half moon and the yellow glittery stars she'd pasted on one of her black velvet walls. The weird charts and maps that hung in the room made him nervous, not that he believed for one minute that Tess could predict the future, although at times she came damn close. He knew for a fact that *she* never made a move until she'd consulted the stars. As far as he was concerned, it was devil doings and he wanted no part of it.

"Ah know your opinion all too well, Coots, and ah'd appreciate it if you'd keep it to yourself," Tess said in the affected drawl she pulled out when she was upset. "Ah was talking to mah daughter, so let her speak for herself. Well, Lacey?"

"Mama, Riley was gone before I got up. Cole called and gave me the message. There was nothing I could do. Why on earth would you want me to fly all the way to Japan and deadhead back hours later? You know how those airtight jets suck all the moisture out of your face. Your skin just flakes. I think your . . . configurations must be off this time. I'll go to Japan when the time is right or when the stars say I'll enjoy myself."

Tess nodded. She knew when not to beat a dead horse. Now that her dander was up, she honed in on Coots. "Someday, Coots honey, y'all'll beg me to chart your course. You're in a bad trend right now. Mercury is retrograde, and that bodes ill. Y'all mind my words."

"We'll mind them, Tess," Coots snickered. "What do you ladies plan on doing today?" It wasn't that he cared, but he'd been saying the same thing for years now, and he was a creature of habit. He beamed down at his daughter Ivy, his favorite. She was eating what he called a hearty he-man breakfast, the kind he liked to eat. He approved of Ivy, and she was smart as a whip, something else he approved of.

Lacey watched her father's approving gaze. It irked her. She knew she was her mother's favorite, and she also knew her father didn't care much for her. But she was good enough for him to put the squeeze on when he wanted something from the Colemans. She didn't like these little family scenes. They were never loving and warm. There were never kind words, only bickering and accusations. It was a wonder anyone could eat a bite. Ivy never seemed to be bothered, but Ivy was an entity unto herself. When she was little she used to pretend she was born into royalty, and the hospital had gotten the babies mixed up. She probably still believed it.

"Ivy, it's disgusting the way you shove food into your mouth." Ivy ignored her. "Mama, what do the stars predict for Ivy? Surely an ulcer, or some kind of stomach gas."

Tess also detested Ivy's robust appetite. She was tempted to lie about her daughter's chart, but she took her work seriously where the family was concerned. "Ivy's a true Scorpio and suffers no health problems," she said. Her voice sounded tight, as though the words were being forced from her mouth against her will.

Ivy finished the last of her coffee and lathered a third piece of toast with butter and jam. She looked up at her sister. She neither liked nor disliked Lacey, and the feeling was the same for her mother. They were two of a kind, and both of them had tormented her from birth. Over the years she'd built her own protective shield to ward off the hurt and pain they dished out to her. But she loved her rough, crude father, almost as much as she loved Riley Coleman, who thought of her as a child, a squirt, a pest to be dealt with kindly but brusquely.

She'd chosen geology and engineering as her major and minor because of Riley and her father. She was going to be the best goddamn geologist ever to come out of the state of Texas. Two degrees would be something they couldn't ignore. As soon as those diplomas were in her hand, it would be look out Texas, look out world, here I come. She folded her napkin and stood. Nobody said a word as she walked toward the door.

She'd hoped for at least a good-bye, or maybe drive carefully Ivy, that old car is a death trap. Something to show she was part of the family. She didn't care anymore. Right now, this minute, she could walk away from this breakfast table and away from this family and never look back. When she was little, she'd wondered, like all children, if her family would grieve if she died. She'd decided then, and the feeling was still with her, that they'd put on a good show and a week later say, Ivy who?

"It must be nice to cut classes when you feel like it. For God's sake, Ivy, don't you have any decent clothes? Why do you insist on humiliating us by wearing those bib overalls and those stupid wooden clogs?" Lacey called out.

"To annoy you," Ivy said over her shoulder. "I'm carrying a 4.0 so I can do what I please. Is it my fault you came out of school knowing less than when you went in?" She turned and faced her sister, riled up now. "You're a slut, Lacey. You know it and I know it. Someone should tell Riley what you're really like." She jabbed home with, "Obviously, someone clued Cole in. He smartened up and dumped you, and Riley caught you on the rebound. He deserves better than you." Ivy's voice was bitter and angry. She was annoyed with herself for speaking out. She knew better, but Lacey always managed to get her going.

"And that someone is you, right? I've seen you look at Riley with those lovesick eyes. He wouldn't give you the time of day, so forget it. I'm going to marry him, and where does that leave you?"

Ivy snorted, a manly sound that grated on Lacey's nerves. "Praying that Riley comes to his senses before it's too late. You'll ruin his life. Doesn't that bother you at all? Of course not; you have no feelings. Watch my lips, Lacey. You-are-a-snake-a-tramp-a-slut." Ivy enunciated each word slowly and clearly.

Lacey recoiled. It would be just like Ivy to push her off the chair or take a swing at her. "Testy, testy. Guess unrequited love does that to people."

Ivy wanted to strangle her sister. She hated this gutter talk. She never should have come home, but she'd felt the need to see Riley, to talk to him, even for just a few minutes. Each visit somehow sustained her to the next one.

There was no reason for Riley to even look at her. Compared to Lacey, she was a shaggy dog. If Lacey was a Rolex, she was a Timex. Durability and good service weren't desirable qualities these days. She wanted to cry, to scream that she deserved more. Instead, she favored her sister with a final scathing look. "All I can say is Cole was one smart dude unloading you. I think I'll drop him a note and congratulate him. Have a nice day, and if anyone should ask, I'm driving back to school."

"Good riddance," Lacey sniped. The minute Ivy was gone, she regretted the words. She actually liked Ivy. She felt sorry for her, but for some reason, jealousy probably, they fought like cat and dog. Ivy was going to make it, and when she did, she'd know she'd done it on her own.

Lacey sat at the table for a long time, picking at the loose threads on the cuff of her dressing gown. When she'd unraveled the entire cuff, she tossed it carelessly across the table. It didn't matter. Cole had seen this particular dressing gown before.

Riley pushed the baseball cap farther back on his head. He watched the rusty Mustang eat up the snowy road, the white flakes spiraling backward like a low-slung tornado. He grinned in spite of himself; a storm outside the car and another tornado inside it. The analogy between Ivy Buckalew and a tornado was fitting. Lacey's little sister, Lacey's *intelligent* little sister, black sheep of the Buckalew family. Riley liked her. He saw through her defensive facade of abrasiveness and hostility. Get them first, get your licks in, and you don't get hurt was Ivy's motto. The car drew up beside him.

"Yo, Riley, how's it going?" Ivy shouted over the sound of the engine.

"Yo, yourself," Riley said, grinning. "I can't believe this old car is still running. Don't you ever have it serviced?"

"Every five years," Ivy quipped. She got out and flung her arms around Riley. "I miss talking to you. I do talk about you, though. To my professors."

There was something different about this hug. In the last year Ivy had changed. She protruded and indented in all the right places. The bib overalls and sheepskin jacket were bulky, deceiving, but his arms told the truth. And she must have a new haircut or something. He commented on the change in her.

"I thought you'd never notice. I lost eighteen pounds. Young men vie for my attention, if you can believe that. I'm still a virgin, though."

This was Riley's cue to say, "Keep it that way; you're supposed to save yourself for me." The words were on the tip of his tongue and he could see Ivy waiting, but the old camaraderie between them was gone. Ivy'd grown up when he wasn't looking. He felt a keen sense of loss. He smiled, but it was forced. "You make sure if one of those guys does catch you that I get to put my seal of approval on him. Pretty soon you're going to be my sister, and someone has to watch out for you."

"I don't want to be your sister, Riley."

"Be my friend then. Okay?"

Ivy wanted to cry. She didn't want to be his sister and she didn't see how they could just remain friends. Sooner or later she would give her feelings away, or someone would pick up on it. Her family would mock her and beat her into the ground. Riley would be embarrassed and wouldn't be able to look at her. He'd start to avoid her. Seeing him on her visits home, his chatty letters, and the occasional phone call kept her going. But it was all starting to go awry. Riley, always astute where she was concerned, was picking up on something. When he married Lacey, things would never be the same. Maybe she was naive, but she didn't know how a guy could pick up his cousin's leftovers and still be friends with that cousin as though nothing had happened. Wouldn't he always wonder and be reminded of what Cole and Lacey had had together? Didn't he wonder if Lacey compared him with Cole? Couldn't he see that Lacey was still in love with Cole? Poor, dumb, wonderful Riley.

Ivy smiled, a smile that was no more genuine than Riley's. "I'll always be your friend, Riley. No matter what I have to get going. I have a long drive ahead of me."

"Don't your parents worry about you in that car? It's a death trap. Why can't you fly, like everyone else?"

"I do some of my best thinking when I'm driving. I'm careful, and this little gem only looks terrible. Sound as a dollar. I'll tell you what, you worry about me, okay? Then I'll feel special. My parents have forgotten me already. They know I can take care of myself."

"Now, that's a defensive statement if I ever heard one," Riley muttered.

"The next thing you'll be telling me is I don't have a right to be defensive. Pretty little delicate Lacey, the firstborn and the apple of Mommy's and Daddy's eye. Sweet, wonderful Lacey, who only has to pout to get what she wants. I'm the only one in the whole damn family that has a brain, and you know it. I should have said a brain that's used on a daily basis," she snapped.

Ah, this was the old Ivy. Sharp-tongued and cynical. He said what he always said when she went through her routine. "Use that brain every day and make me proud of you. Call me when you get back to school so I know you got there okay."

"I don't need a wet nurse, Riley, so stop acting like one. If I crash and die on the way, you'll have to read about it in the papers, like everyone else. Another thing. Don't believe everything my father tells you. My old man has been known to lie his way through a few deals. Take that for whatever it's worth. I'm telling you this because you're my friend. That doesn't mean I don't love him," she added hastily.

Riley reached out to her and looked at her closely. She and Lacey were like night and day. He pulled her to him and hugged her, aware now of the warm, clean smell of her. She felt soft and comfortable. Lacey was always hard and stiff in his arms, and she smelled of powder and perfume. He held Ivy a moment longer than usual, savoring the feel of her. He patted her head, and before he realized it, he was running his fingers through her soft curls. Lacy's hair was stiff and sticky, and it was always, "Don't touch my hair, Riley." He found himself nuzzling his chin in Ivy's hair. She made a mewing sound that reminded him of a hungry kitten. Her hair smelled wonderful and it was faintly damp. His grandfather liked Ivy. Come to think of it, everyone liked Ivy except her own family.

It was Ivy who stirred first. Gently, she pushed herself away and her eyes locked with Riley's. "You made a mistake, Riley. Lacey's not for you. Do something about it before it's too late. She loves Cole; she calls his name in her sleep. It's better you know now than later. I'm sorry if I hurt you, and you know I wouldn't do that for the world. I have to go now. I'll call you."

Riley watched the old Mustang wobble down the road, a

cloud of black smoke shooting out from behind it. A small tornado.

Ivy Buckalew. Up front. Tell-it-like-it-is Ivy. Black sheep of the family. There were times when Riley felt himself almost as one with Ivy when he would see the deep hurt in her eyes. A kid, she'd always been a kid, a pesky kid. Until today.

Riley squinted in the cold winter sunshine. He realized suddenly that he hated winter. There were a lot of things he hated lately, it seemed, but Ivy Buckalew wasn't one of them. The ominous warning she'd given him about her father and sister made him hunker into his sheepskin jacket. All she'd done was reinforce his own thoughts. Hearing them voiced by Ivy only made them more serious. He had to pay attention.

He wished now for the thousandth time that he'd never gotten mixed up with the Buckalews. Coots had offered his expertise, and he'd been grateful. Unfortunately, he'd listened to him and made some serious mistakes. Coots was an old saw, a wildcatter from way back. He did things by gut feeling, guffawing at Riley's modern technology. The same thing applied to Coots's peers. All cut from the same bolt of cloth. He'd been pleased when Coots offered to take him under his wing and show him the real way Texas oilmen did things. Riley'd been dazzled by old Coots and his cronies, no doubt about it. Instead of going with his knowledge and his own instincts, he'd been swayed. Now, with the price of oil down to rock bottom and the wells not pumping, he found himself between a rock and a hard place. Along with all the other oilmen in Texas.

Enter Lacey Buckalew, fresh from a soured relationship with Cole. He'd been flattered by her persistent attentions. Dating her had gotten Coots off his back. Temporarily. Cole had moved on. Riley'd never asked for details, preferring to think Lacey had given Cole his walking papers, not the other way around.

Now, after all these months, he still didn't know how he'd arrived at the place he was in. Soon Lacey was going to announce their engagement. He'd gone along with it, which didn't say much for him. Lately he couldn't make a decision to save his life. Why? He knew why; he just didn't want to think about it. Belonging. The family. Pride. Do a good job and you really are part of it all. Instead, he'd screwed up.

"The hotshot kid with the slanted eyes" was falling short of the mark. "Well, what the hell did you expect—he's a Jap. They can make microchips and stereos, but oil?" He'd heard the whispers all over Austin. They'd called him a loner, too, the type who preferred to take all the glory, and the defeat, too, if it came to that.

He'd wanted to talk about it with his grandfather, but he hadn't. Why should the old one have to share his shame? And it was shame. He wasn't measuring up—pure and simple.

Maybe he should cut and run. Back to Japan. Give it all up, this dream of belonging to his father's family, being one of the Colemans. Which was he anyway? The Jap who was going to turn Coleman Oil around and return it to its past glory? Or the Jap who went home to Japan with his tail between his legs to take over his grandfather's publishing empire?

How could one person be so torn? He wasn't going to find the answer standing here in the cold, that was for sure. The Japanese in him told him to take things one day at a time. Patience and a clear head would win out in the end. A pity the American frenzy in him had the edge.

The last of the black exhaust from Ivy's Mustang was long gone now. So was the last of the sunshine. Thick gray clouds moved slowly across the sky. Snow. More snow.

Riley swung his long frame into the Bronco. His thoughts shifted to Ivy again. He remembered the times he'd called her a dreamer. We all need to dream, he thought. To have no dream is to have no hope, and to have no hope is to have no reason to live. Ivy would be okay. But he was assuming that, and he had no right to assume anything. His mother had told him in childhood that it was a cardinal sin to make assumptions. Riley piled Ivy Buckalew on his shoulder on top of his other worries.

Cary walked up Third Avenue, his step light, his mind lighter. He was making a social call on his New York attorneys, Friedman, Leeds and Schornstein. He'd take Marty Friedman and Alan Kaufman to lunch, one of those long, expensive lunches with at least three drinks and a couple of bottles of wine. He'd bring them up-to-date on what was going on and tell them about the big deal he was passing up. Marty would smile that special smile Amelia called endearing, and Alan would grin, twiddle the ever-present pencil in his fingers, tip back on his chair, and nod approvingly.

Good guys. He'd learned a lot from them. At first he was concerned that they wouldn't take him seriously, because he'd married Amelia and was younger. He'd worried needlessly. It was like anything else—prove yourself and the respect is there because you deserve it. He was his own man.

The receptionist smiled regretfully. Alan was in court and Marty was out of town on business. He left a jar of macadamia nuts for Alan, a box of Godiva chocolates for Marty's wife, and his hotel number. He had the better part of the day to kill until it was time to pick up Julie for dinner. He was shopped out and it was too raw and windy to trudge around. He opted for the movies and popcorn after a deli lunch. He woke ten minutes before the film was over. A trip to the men's room and a cigarette in the lobby kept him long enough so he got back to his seat just as the credits were rolling by for the second showing. For the first time he realized what the name of the movie was, *Nine Deaths of the Ninja*. He watched transfixed while a man with a face mask twirled himself at such an alarming speed that he actually dug himself into the ground. He munched on popcorn as the other eight deaths took place.

It was four o'clock when Cary walked out of the theater. He hailed a cab and directed the driver to Saks Fifth Avenue. He strode through the perfumed aisles like a man with a purpose. He slowed down at the better jewelry department, scanning showcases of winking gold. A pin? Bracelet? He'd better not press his luck. Amelia said bracelet, and a bracelet it would be. It took him fifteen minutes to make his selection— a dainty, thin, braided gold circlet. He waited another ten minutes while it was gift-wrapped and the Saks silver seal affixed. He heaved a sigh of relief as he sailed through the revolving doors. He'd paid $150 for the bracelet, and it was probably $75 more than Julie would feel she could accept. She'd be gracious in her uncertainty, though, that much he was sure of. But a Tiffany or Cartier bracelet, as Amelia had suggested, would be handed back to him in a second. He'd bet his new cashmere sweater on it.

For one split second, as he marched through his hotel lobby, Cary was tempted to give the bracelet to the smiling desk clerk. But it was still in his pocket when he hung his coat on a hanger. He checked for phone messages and returned Alan Kaufman's call to say he couldn't make dinner, he already had plans. Amelia had called, too, at three-thirty. It was after five now, three o'clock in Texas.

He almost fell off the swivel chair as he tried to reach the portable bar and a can of Budweiser. He had the can in his hand, ready to pop it, when Amelia's voice came on the wire. He heard her greeting, but what he was really hearing was Amelia telling him, long ago, that women didn't like beer breath. She especially detested it. The beer went back into the small bar. He plucked out a can of root beer and grimaced.

"You are prompt, darling," Amelia said. "I just called to see if you'd picked out a dazzling bauble for Julie. Tell me what you got."

"Honey, I got a bracelet, just like you said. It's gold."

"What does it look like? Would I like it? Any gems in it, or did you get a plain one? How much did you pay for it?" There was excitement in Amelia's voice, and something else he'd never heard before.

"It looks like a bracelet, honey. It's kind of twisted. It's plain but elegant, and it would look good on your arm."

"How much was it? You aren't going to shame me, now, are you?"

"How much?" Cary hedged. "Sweetheart, aren't you the one who keeps telling me if you have to ask the price, you can't afford it? I don't remember asking. I just charged it." Caught. He'd paid cash. Amelia would be waiting for the slip when the bill came. Saks always sent copies of the bill. Wait a minute, she'd think he charged it on his American Express or Visa.

"That must mean it was simply outrageous. I just love the way you do things, Cary," Amelia cooed. That something he couldn't define was back in her voice. "Did you make the reservation for dinner?"

"Christ, I forgot. Thanks for reminding me, honey."

"Darling, look, it isn't going to be all that bad. You're taking a lovely young woman to dinner on her birthday. Get into the spirit of things and really make an effort to show Julie a wonderful evening. Why don't you top it off with a hansom cab ride through the park? Promise me, Cary, that you will make a pleasant evening of it."

"I promise, honey." Why did he feel like a liar? He hadn't said a word that wasn't true.

"That's better. I'm going to let you go now so you can call for the reservation. Call me when you get back and let me know how the evening went. I'll wait up for you."

"What are you going to do this evening? I wish you were here, Amelia."

"I do, too, darling, but I have four solid hours of paperwork in front of me. I'm making headway, though. I might give Billie and Thad a call later. Well, have a wonderful time this evening." The broken connection sounded extra loud. Cary stared at the phone. His knuckles were white on the receiver and he literally had to pry off his fingers.

He ripped off his jacket and tie, then called down to the desk to make a reservation at the Lion's Rock.

Exhausted, Cary turned on "Live at Five," lay down on the couch, kicked off his shoes, and was instantly asleep.

When Julie Kingsley circled the apartment for the third time, she forced herself to sit down for what she called one of her heart-to-hearts with herself. She'd never been so jittery. She'd never been thirty-nine before either, she told herself. That's what it was, all right, the big old thirty-nine. Next year it would be the big Four-O. Thirty-nine and not married was awful. Forty and not married would make her a first-class old maid. Women were still having babies at forty, but unless she opted for artificial insemination, her chances of motherhood were dim indeed. She'd probably make an awful mother, anyway. She wanted love and total intimacy with the man of her choice. A baby would interfere with that. If she didn't watch it, she'd get maudlin.

A shower was quick, the steaming, pulsating spray soothing to a tired, aching body, but a long, leisurely bath full of bubbles would be the epitome of relaxation. She could slide the shower doors open and watch her reflection on the mirrored walls. She'd pin her hair on top of her head, double the bath crystals, and sit in bubbles up to her neck. A glass of zinfandel and two cigarettes to celebrate her birthday would do nicely. Then a warm shower to wash away all the soap, followed by scented body lotion and powder, the only luxury she allowed herself in the way of perfume, and she would be ready to wine and dine her thirty-ninth birthday away.

Tonight after dinner she would place a call to Amelia to thank her for allowing Cary to take her to dinner. Tacky, her mind muttered. A note, a week or so later, sent to both Cary and Amelia would be better.

When the foamy bubbles threatened to spill over the side of

the tub, she turned off the water and slid down into the satiny wetness. Damn, she'd forgotten her cigarettes and wine. No matter. She would have them later—over dinner.

Dinner. A birthday celebration. With Cary Assante. Amelia Assante's husband. It didn't mean anything. What was wrong with her? She'd been out with men before, lots of men. She was no virgin and didn't pretend to be one. She liked Cary Assante. Perhaps she liked him more than she should, considering that he was another woman's husband. She had a rule, and it was that she didn't date married men. He's not a date-date, she scolded herself. As usual, she was putting the cart before the horse. This dinner was simply a warm, kind gesture on Cary's part. Nothing more. So there was no call for her to sit here luxuriating, as if she were preparing for the man of her dreams. It was true, though, Cary Assante was the kind of man dreams were made of. Too bad those dreams belonged to another woman.

Julie stretched her leg from the bubbles and let her toe search out the drain stopper. Water gurgled. She gazed at herself in the mirrored wall. Size nine feet. Freckles, not just on her face but all over. Even on her breasts. Oversize hips that made finding clothes difficult. Too tall. Small breasts, big feet, big hips. Millions of freckles. Blunt nose. Mustn't forget that. Good teeth, though. Wide, toothy smile and clear eyes —that was another plus. Bushy brows that she refused to tweeze. Brooke Shieldsish. God, what was she doing? She hadn't picked herself apart like this since she was dating Ian Matthews, an architect who had let her down easy by telling her he didn't much care for tall women. He might as well have said tall women with big feet, big hips, small breasts, freckles and wide noses.

She stepped out of the shower and wrapped herself in a fluffy blue towel that matched the bathroom tiles. Her toes dug into the soft pile of the matching carpet. She dried briskly, then used the towel to wrap up her head and padded naked into the bedroom in search of her robe. She had plenty of time to do her nails and her toenails. She'd sip on some wine and perhaps have that cigarette while her hair dried. She could be dressed and made up in fifteen minutes. She already knew what she was wearing: an electric-blue jersey dress with its own belt. A matching scarf shot through with silver threads, a Billie Coleman original. Black alligator shoes and pearl earrings would complete her outfit.

While she wiggled her toes and waved her fingers so the polish could dry, Julie let her thoughts go back to Cary Assante—thoughts she'd been pushing away for the past hour. She'd suggest they walk to the restaurant and back home. Even if they dawdled over dinner, she should be back no later than ten-thirty. She'd thank him for a wonderful evening and see him on his way. Tomorrow was a working day and she had to get her sleep. When she was back snug in her apartment, she would laugh at herself for being so uptight over a simple birthday dinner. It would be history, a memory for her scrapbook.

Cary had such warm, gentle eyes and one of the nicest smiles she'd ever seen. But most important, he had the knack for making a person feel special. Humor, don't forget humor, an inner voice chided. He could laugh with you or at himself. A genuine sense of humor, a rarity in these days of maliciousness and the me-first people.

She was afraid of Cary Assante.

Riley finished his steak and potatoes. Even if he felt like it, he would never suck on a bone in a restaurant, as Coots was doing. He hadn't wanted this meeting, but Coots had backed him into a corner by showing up at the office.

Coots waved off the waitress. The signal to start talking business.

"I warned you not to close off the strippers, Coots. You should have listened."

"Hell, boy, they were only giving out four or five barrels a day, and it was costing me fifteen dollars apiece every day to operate them. Show me the sense in that."

"You piss away that much every day on one thing or another," Riley said tersely. "You've been in this business much longer than I have; you should have known better."

"You're going to be in the family soon, son. You should be sharing all that fancy information, that technology stuff you went to school for."

Riley seethed. He wanted to tell the old man what he could do to his anatomy. He and his cronies were the ones who'd said they wanted no part of EOR. Now here he was, old Coots, practically begging for help. Sure, my expertise. Coleman money, that was what he wanted.

"That technology stuff, as you put it, is the only answer from here on in. Every oilman in Texas is sorry he didn't go for it. Technology is our only way out. Coleman Oil is hurting, too, just like everyone else."

"Not so's you'd notice," Coots snapped. "Everyone in Texas knows about the Coleman oil leases in Venezuela."

"Then everyone should know they aren't going to do us any good. They'll let us go in, drill, use our expertise, and then refuse to let us ship the oil. I cut my teeth on that story, and it hasn't changed."

"Talk is you have an in down there with those Spics. Ain't that so, Riley?"

"We have leases. I talk to the officials, like everyone else. They promise everything and give nothing. Coleman Oil doesn't have the money to pay out for nothing in return."

"Those Spics don't know how to get the oil out. You do, Riley. Talk is, you're heading that way next week. Why not take me along with you?"

"That's impossible, Coots. Look, I have to get back." He tossed some bills on the table. He'd bet five dollars there would be a message for him sometime during the afternoon from Lacey saying she'd go to South America with him after all. If Coots couldn't go, Lacey would. He wondered if Ivy would tell him not to trust her sister, either.

Outside in the crisp air, Riley took a deep breath. He felt sorry for Coots. There was nothing worse than the look of a defeated old man. Probably the worst thing in the world, because he was too old and too beaten to try again. No oil. The end of the world.

Riley gunned the Ford Bronco and roared out to the highway. His grandmother was coming this weekend. He knew what that meant. An accounting, an up-front confrontation. Tell it like it is, Coleman. If Coleman Oil goes under, so goes Coleman Aviation.

{{{{{{{{{ CHAPTER SEVEN }}}}}}}}}

Sawyer sat across from Chesney Brighton, trying to find words that would say something but mean nothing. It was like searching for just the right birthday card for an old lover you wanted to stay in touch with. "Rand and my mother will be here tomorrow. I'll arrange a meeting, and the rest is up to you and them," she said.

"It must hurt unbearably," Chesney said softly.

There was no use pretending she didn't understand what Chesney meant. "For a while it was very painful. But I've accepted it, and my life is pleasant, even enjoyable. Rand and Maggie are very happy. I would hate to see that happiness disturbed."

"It won't be disturbed. All I want is to meet my father. I'll leave after I've done that. I'd never force myself on him or your mother. You probably don't understand why I need to do this. . . . I never had a family. I don't know what it's like. I don't know how it feels to pick up the phone and call a sister or a brother, any relative. I have none. I've accepted that. All I want is to see him. That's all. He should know I exist. He has that right, and so do I. Someday he might want to get to know me. Then again, his life may be so full, there is no room, now or ever. I can accept that, too. Do you understand?" Soft gray eyes implored Sawyer.

"Of course I understand. More than you'll ever know."

"I've carved out a life for myself. I have a job and nice friends. I have my own flat and a small nest egg. I'm doing all right. It's just that there was a piece missing in my life, and now I've found it. I'm so grateful to you."

"I'm glad I could help."

"What are they like—your mother and my father?"

"They both have the courage of their convictions. They knew what they wanted and weren't afraid to reach out for it. They found each other. They belong together."

"They sound wonderful."

"They are, and I love them very much."

"I should be getting back. If I want to look decent tomorrow, I have to sleep. My flight leaves at sundown."

"You're leaving tomorrow?" Sawyer gasped.

Chesney smiled. "I'm a working girl; I have commitments. And friends I want to get back to. Surely you didn't think I was going to stay on and force myself on my father?"

"Well, no, but . . . What I mean is . . . they're coming all the way here to meet you."

"And meet me they shall. Then I'll leave, and the next move, if there is one, will be my father's. Please, let me pay my share. I insist, Miss Coleman."

In the end Sawyer agreed. "I'll walk you to your hotel and

then catch a cab to my house," she suggested. "I think this cold air will do us both good. You understand, you are to come to my house at noon tomorrow. Rand and my mother will be there. I'll be at work. If you get a chance, call me before you leave, and if you ever get back here, call me. I'll give you my number in Texas, too, in case your travels take you to the States."

"I'd like that. And if you ever find yourself in England, you call me."

Sawyer smiled. "Don't be surprised if I turn up on your doorstep one of these days." They stood awkwardly facing each other in front of Chesney's hotel.

"I feel as if I've known you for a long time, like you're really a good friend," Chesney said shyly.

"I . . ." Sawyer paused, unsure of what she felt, what to say. "Good luck tomorrow. Whatever happens, go with it. Understand that it's a shock and they're both going to have to—"

"I understand. Good-bye, Miss Coleman."

"I think you can call me Sawyer, don't you?"

"I'll call you, Sawyer, and thanks again for everything."

"I'm glad I could help. Remember now, call me."

On the walk back to the house Sawyer realized she'd meant every word she'd said to Chesney. She *was* glad she could help, and she looked forward to seeing Chesney again. As she'd found out, you can never have enough friends.

The little Japanese house seemed to crackle with electricity. It was almost noon.

Rand paced the narrow kitchen area, his thoughts far away. For the first time in their married life Maggie realized she was not in sync with her husband. Feeling shut out and alone, she paced behind Rand, bumping into him from time to time. He didn't seem to notice.

"It's a scam of some sort," Rand said. "Something inside me would know if I had a daughter. How could I have a daughter by a woman whose face I don't remember? I'm telling you, it's some kind of scam to extort money out of me. I'm not buying it."

Maggie tried for a gentle tone, but wasn't sure she'd achieved it when she spoke. "Then why are we here? Rand, Sawyer is not an alarmist. She said she believes the girl. Please, for your own sake, keep an open mind. See her and at least talk to her. We're here now. I'll help you in any way I can."

It was as if she hadn't spoken. Rand continued his frenzied pacing. Maggie sat down on one of the Western-style chairs Sawyer had brought to the tiny house. All she could do was wait . . . and listen.

"Most of the girls in the troop were pregnant. I know that doesn't say much for myself or the other pilots, but it was an awful time for the lot of us. We were constantly being pulled back to country, to the DMZ. We never advanced. The strain of flying those choppers, dropping supplies, picking up wounded, looking for POWs, flying low under radar . . . We'd go to Saigon because it was neutral and . . . They were English, some American, and even a few French girls. Then the guy who was the head of the entertainment troop took off, with the girls' wages and their passports. They came on to us even stronger then. I'm not excusing myself. I did what I wanted . . . took what I wanted. We all did, and then we pulled back even further. I knew I'd never see her again. I gave her what money I had. I remember thinking it was a shame she was going to have to go it alone. I did tell her to go to the Red Cross. Later on I could have checked on her, but I didn't. She said she *thought* she might be pregnant. Honest to God, Maggie, I never thought about her again until Sawyer called us. I blacked it out completely.

"We were back and forth in country. There were no enemy lines, so to speak; the enemy was all over. Guys were dying from five-step Charlie by the dozens. Snakes called green mambas dropped out of trees onto a man, bit him, the man took five steps and died. . . . It wasn't a real war, Maggie, it was worse. We couldn't drop bombs, we couldn't really fight back. We were there to protect the people. There were those among us who were worse than Charlie. I blacked that out till now, too. The girls . . . they were so young. . . . They thought they were on a camping trip. The men used them. Most of them got pregnant . . ." He let his words hang in midair. Maggie said nothing.

"And as for me giving money to Marion for an abortion, well . . . I did give her money, but the word 'abortion' never came up. She wasn't sure. . . . I used . . . Goddamn it, I'd remember! She's an impostor!" Rand shouted.

"It was so long ago, Rand. . . ."

"It wasn't pretty, Maggie. But I'm making excuses . . .

{ 125 }

trying to justify . . . I'm not sure . . . or is it that I am sure and don't want to take the responsibility?"

"I don't know, darling. That was another life, and the rules weren't the same as they are now. I'm here for you, no matter what. The last thing I would ever do is judge you, Rand."

"Bless you, Maggie. You've been a rock these past hours. What time is it?"

Maggie looked at her watch and remembered she was still on Hawaii time. She calculated quickly. "Two minutes to twelve."

"Christ!"

"Pray that he helps you," Maggie said softly.

The bell at the garden gate tinkled. Rand's eye twitched; that only happened, Maggie knew, when he was under pressure. "I'll go," she said quietly. "Take deep breaths, darling."

All the way down the path Maggie cautioned herself to show no emotion when she swung open the gate. Polite. Don't bring shame on Sawyer or Rand. Or Billie or Thad, or anyone else in the family. She drew a deep, searing breath. She pushed at the gate and waited.

The young woman standing before her smiled. Rand's smile. Rand's eyes. Rand's mouth. Rand's hair color. "Come in; I'm Maggie Nelson, Rand's wife. Of course you're Chesney. Come along, it's cold out here." How normal her voice sounded. She knew now. Just as Sawyer had known.

"Darling, this is Chesney," Maggie blurted. The look on Rand's face was shock.

"Mr. Nelson, it was good of you to come all this way to see me. I really appreciate it. May I sit down? I would imagine you have all sorts of questions you want to ask me. I'll do my best to answer them."

Rand's mannerisms. The most direct gaze Maggie had ever seen, with the exception of Rand's.

Rand motioned to a chair. "Why don't you just tell us your story." Looking at the young woman was like looking at his own reflection all those years ago. The same cheekbones. If he dressed her up in his old flight suit, she'd be an exact replica.

Chesney spoke calmly and simply. When she finished, she stood up and began buttoning her coat. "I would hope, Mr. Nelson, that at some time in the future you might want to see me again, so I took the liberty of writing down my address and telephone number for you. Please, I don't want you to say

{ 126 }

anything now that both of us might regret later. I'm going back to England on the afternoon flight. I give you my word that I won't ever try to intrude on your life. I don't even know where you live. As I said, I wanted to see you. I felt I deserved that right and you deserved to know you have a child.

"It was wonderful meeting both of you. I especially want to thank you for not asking me what I want from you. But if you had asked that, my answer would have been, nothing. I just wanted you to know I'm alive. I can see myself out."

"I'll . . . I'll show you the way," Maggie stuttered. Clearly, Rand was in no condition to do anything but what he was doing—which was staring.

"It was a pleasure meeting you, Mrs. Nelson," Chesney said as they walked to the gate.

"Yes, Chesney, it was . . . my pleasure as well."

"Mr. Nelson is a fine man. Your daughter has such high regard for you both. Perhaps that was the wrong way to express what I wanted to say—she loves you both very much."

"Yes, she does, and we love her."

"Perhaps one day that love will include me."

"Perhaps," was the best Maggie could manage.

Maggie locked the gate and stood for a moment listening to Chesney's heels click as she walked away. She was really leaving. Maggie's shoulders slumped, but only for a moment. She had a husband to take care of.

"Looks don't prove anything," Rand said hoarsely. "For Christ's sake, Maggie, don't you think I would've felt something all these years? A child . . . ?"

"Darling, only mothers feel that way. It's that inborn thing women have. I don't think men feel it. Are you denying that Chesney is your daughter?"

"You're damn right I'm denying it. She's a slick one, though, I'll give her that much."

"Then why are you so upset?"

"I'm upset because . . . because this person dares to come here and upset our lives with . . . with false claims."

Maggie swallowed hard. "I don't think that's why you're upset at all. I think you believe her. You said those things happened every day. Now, today, it sounds terrible and you're feeling guilty. I'm glad Chesney's mother didn't have the abortion. I'm glad that beautiful young woman is alive. Every day when I wake up I thank God Mam didn't let me have an abortion. Furthermore," Maggie continued bravely, "I think that young woman is exactly who and what she says she is. I don't believe for one minute that she wants anything from you. She didn't even ask for acknowledgment from you."

"She'd damn well never get it!"

Maggie sighed. "Rand, we have to face this together, or it will hang between us, and our lives will be ruined. Denial, my darling, is not truth. Look, she told us who her mother is. We could make discreet inquiries, perhaps even speak to her ourselves and reassure her that we won't disturb her life. We could go to the orphanage. We could check out her employment record. Colleagues are always good references. Her church, her friends. Please, Rand, don't be hasty. Don't do something you'll regret later."

"Mother Maggie."

"Yes, Mother Maggie," she said. "Is there something wrong with that?"

"I'm going for a walk," Rand said, patting her on the head as he passed her. "I need to clear my head. You look tired, Maggie. Take a nice hot bath and a nap. We'll take Sawyer out to dinner this evening."

"That sounds good to me. I'd like it better if you joined me in that tiny tub, though. Just think about how close we could be. No, huh? Okay, take your walk and wake me when you get back if I'm asleep. Oh, Rand, while we're here, let's stop and see Mr. Hasegawa." Anything for normalcy.

"Fine. I won't be that long."

Any other time Rand would have had eyes only for the seaside town of Kamakura. It had been his idea for Sawyer to move here during her stint in Japan. She claimed the ride to work took her twenty-five minutes on a good day and two hours on a bad one.

It was cold now, even though the sun was out. The light jacket and sweater vest wouldn't keep him warm. He should have had the sense to put on his overcoat. Maggie usually reminded him, but she was just as upset as he was.

He should have said something to her, something firm and hard about her acceptance of the girl. Women were so quick to side with other women. Sawyer, too. Two against one. He knew if he never uttered another word about Chesney, they wouldn't either. What had he said? He'd told her to take a hot bath. And she'd played the game and tried to tease him into joining her.

His wonderful life with Maggie was disturbed now. Even if he did nothing, it wouldn't be the same. Maggie's family would chastise him, since they were so family oriented. Amelia would call him a horse's rear end and remind him that if it hadn't been for her taking him over when he was a child, God alone knew what might have happened to him.

And if he accepted the girl, what would happen then? His life would be even more disturbed. The Coleman clan would be larger by one member. He'd had no experience at being a father; he could never feel like one. He'd missed the growing years, the years when a parent bonded with his flesh and blood. He couldn't simply put his arm around a grown woman he'd never seen before and say welcome home, daughter. She . . . Chesney would be a contemporary, not a kid. She'd have opinions, likes and dislikes. Goddamn it, she'd intrude in his life. His and Maggie's life.

Who could he talk to about this? Cary? Warm, generous Cary would tell him to grab the girl and bring her home. Amelia would second him. No, this was something he'd have to come to terms with himself.

The rickety bench along the seawall beckoned him, but he sat down gingerly. He needn't have worried. Years of wear and tons of sand had anchored it firmly. He let his mind shift to the water lapping against the wall. It was dirty and murky. His eyes hungered for the sparkling blue Pacific that was his and Maggie's daily treat. He wondered if Chesney had ever been to Hawaii.

An old Japanese with a yoke on his shoulders approached and pointed to the baskets of fish that balanced it on each side. The old man's eyes were deep-set and sad, his face lined with grooves so deep they could hold a pencil. He was toothless, and his straggly mustache and beard were yellow and dirty. The straw hat that was part of every Japanese villager's attire was set at a jaunty angle, and Rand knew it covered a shiny bald head. Probably a hundred years old. He wondered what he would look like if he lived to be a hundred. Little worry of that. Smoking, liquor, and life in the fast lane had already taken their toll.

"I'll take them all." No old man should have to hustle for a living and carry such a heavy load. The old man didn't appear to understand. Rand waved his hands to make a circle. The old Japanese nodded politely. In a flash he had newspaper out and the fish from both baskets wrapped. Rand didn't even bother to count the money he handed over. He knew it was far too much, but he didn't care. Now the old one could go home and sit by the fire. A place he deserved.

An hour later Rand was still on the bench, his thoughts still tortured. His jaw dropped when the old man passed him a second time. His shoulders were as bowed as before, the baskets still as heavy and full of fish. Rand supposed there was a lesson to be learned here. One had to make the effort, had to get up and do each day what he did best. How lonely the old man looked. Rand understood the feeling. He'd never felt so alone in his life.

Guilt. That's what it was all about. He had to be honest with himself. He'd been cock of the walk in those days. A hotshot pilot, a handsome one to boot. Girls danced about him, and he had his pick. He'd always gone for the prettiest, the wittiest, and had his pleasure. And yes, there was one he'd seen more than the others. One who said she *thought* she might be pregnant. He'd emptied his pockets before he left. Had turned over chocolates, cigarettes, and nylons. Hell, at the time it had seemed he'd got the better of the deal. No conditions, no commitments. And there were no rules.

But what goes around comes around, eh, Nelson? Now this girl, his daughter, walked into his life and threw those same things back at him: no conditions, no commitments, no rules. She'd stated her case and walked away. How could she have done that?

"The same way you did, you son of a bitch!" he shouted into the wind.

I didn't know. I wasn't sure. Wrong, Nelson. You didn't give a good goddamn. You had more missions to fly, more girls to seduce, more liquor to drink. You didn't care! Own up to it, old man, and take what's coming to you.

Guilt. It was going to ride his shoulders like the old man's yoke. It would bend him, but would it break him? "Jesus, I don't know," he muttered.

In the taxi on the way back to her London flat, Chesney heaved a deep sigh. She had a real flesh-and-blood father now, as well as a mother. A mother who wasn't interested in her and a father who wasn't one hundred percent convinced that she belonged to him.

Big Ben struck the hour. It was a comforting sound, one she'd come to take for granted. She wondered how many years, months, and days Old Ben had been striking the hour. Someone probably knew, if she was interested enough to pursue the question. Someday she just might do that. Her hands trembled as she searched in her bag for a cigarette. Maybe she should be devoting her time to the present and the future, her own life, instead of anguishing over Rand Nelson, and her mother, and her own sad childhood.

She'd laid down strict rules for herself when she started on her search for her parents: She'd find them, introduce herself, let them know where to find her—and then leave. At first she wasn't going to search for them at all, but the more she thought about it, the more she convinced herself that she had every right to know if she had any living relatives. Suppose one of them might be sickly or crippled, in need of her? That thought, more than anything else, had spurred her on. The rules she set out for herself were necessary because she didn't want what happened to Sara to happen to her.

Sara had been her closest friend at the orphanage. Almost nightly, from the time they were eight years old, they talked late at night about how they were going to try to find their parents someday. Sara was obsessed, confident that her parents were just waiting somewhere for her to make an appearance so they could take her in their arms and weep with joy. Sara worked two jobs to get the money for her search. It had taken her almost three years of following down leads and clues. By the time she found them, she'd worn herself to a frazzle. She'd become stick-thin and her face was set in hard, desperate lines. Her parents, Sara found, wanted no part of her, refusing at first even to acknowledge that they knew each other. Her mother, a tavern waitress, supported six children in a mean, dark flat that smelled of cabbage and urine. Her father, a factory worker with his own brood of children, said he didn't care if she could prove he was her father or not. He had enough mouths to feed and didn't need a bastard kid to boot. And what the hell did she want from him, anyway? He'd told her to go away and find a man to support her.

Chesney had cradled her in her arms and tried to soothe her the way a mother might do, but it wasn't the same. Sara had dreamed of a pretty mother with warm, loving eyes, a woman who would hold her close and say wonderful, endearing words and promise to make up for all the years she'd been lost to her. Instead, a work-weary, slovenly barmaid had sent her packing with harsh words and cold, glittering eyes. She'd convinced herself that her father was a businessman, a gentleman who went to a fancy office every day wearing a three-piece suit and carrying an alligator briefcase. He drove a fine car with a lap robe on the backseat. She'd described in detail to Chesney the picnics and shopping trips he'd take her on. He'd dress her like a fashion model and give her tiny pearls, real ones, for her ears. He'd write down the date of her birthday in his appointment book and always remember it. He'd take her to his big house and introduce her to his other children, who would be jealous at first but who would come to love her. He would not be married. He'd had a wife, of course, but she'd met her death tragically. Sara and her father would console each other over brandy after dinner.

Faced with the reality of her parentage, Sara had simply given up. She withdrew into her cubbyhole of an apartment and read family novels.

One day, returning from a three-day flight, Chesney had gone round to her friend's apartment. The door was locked. She'd rapped and shouted for Sara to open up. An unfamiliar but awful odor seeped from under the door. Panic-stricken, she'd run to find the super, who opened the door and then ran back outside. The police and ambulance came while Chesney waited, tears streaming down her cheeks.

She'd paid for the modest funeral, and she alone had stood at the grave and mourned her friend. The medical examiner had said Sara died from natural causes, but he hadn't said what the natural causes were. Chesney knew Sara had died of a broken heart.

She'd packed Sara's meager belongings in a cheap plastic suitcase and taken them back to her apartment. All the papers, all the documents of Sara's long, long search filled two paper bags. She stored them on the top shelf in her closet. Weeks later, on one of her days off, she'd gone through the papers to find the addresses of Sara's parents. She'd written them each a stiff, formal note, informing them of Sara's death. She'd included her address, but she was not surprised when neither of them wrote back.

To be born unwanted and to die unwanted, Chesney decided, was the most awful thing on earth.

It was after Sara's death that she'd made her rules. She would abide by them no matter what.

Her past was behind her and she'd carved out her future, one of her own making. She didn't *need* Rand Nelson or Marion Brighton. She might *want* them, but she didn't need them.

Chesney paid the driver and ran into her apartment. Frederick, her Persian cat, greeted her by rubbing against her legs. She bent down and scooped him into her arms. How warm and soft he was, almost like a baby. Fred licked her chin and then nuzzled her neck. "Aha, you're hungry. Well, come along and let's see what I can find. But first, I'll put the water on for tea."

Fred, an adoring look on his whiskered face, sat on his haunches and waited patiently for his fish and milk.

The kitchen Chesney bustled around in was tidy and compact. A new stove and refrigerator were recent purchases. She'd found the cane chairs and oak table in a thrift shop. She'd sanded them down and recovered the chair cushions. She'd shellacked the cupboards and laid down the shiny tiles she'd bought. She was proud of her little kitchen, with the African violets on the windowsill and the fern hanging in the corner. The rest of the small flat was just as tasteful. She'd bought one piece of furniture at a time, saving so she could pay cash and not be in debt. For almost a year she'd slept in a sleeping bag until she could afford her brass queen-size bed. She had her own wide-screen telly and a VCR, and she'd recently bought a telephone answering machine. She had almost enough money in the bank for her first car. A daffodil-yellow Lotus. With a car, she could take some of the orphanage children to the country on her days off.

She'd done what she set out to do. She'd found both her parents. She'd made it known that she was alive and well. She'd been up front when she told them she wanted nothing from them. There was no way she was going to end up like Sara.

Early evening was a bitch of a time to get a taxi, Cary decided. Twenty minutes of stomping his feet in the cold angered him. He should have rented a car. He was about to give up and walk when a cab slid to the curb.

The apartment on Seventy-ninth was almost as neat as its attractive occupant. In a vase in the foyer was a large bouquet of fresh tulips. Julie laughed. "My birthday present to myself. I love flowers. Do you?" Cary had to think a minute. Did he like flowers?

"When they're growing in their natural environment, I do," he finally said. "I've always been a giver or sender of flowers, but I never thought much about it. They do brighten up a room. But I don't like to pick them. I could never kill an animal either," he blurted. "I brake if I see a bird flying too low."

Julie's eyes were serious and there was no trace of a smile on her face. Her voice was so soft, he had to strain to hear the words. "Thank you for sharing that feeling with me."

"Would you like a drink?" He shook his head. "Well, then, why don't we consider walking to the restaurant. It's not far, and it will be my quota of fresh air for the day. I'll get my coat."

Cary held the coat for her. She smelled wonderful, sort of warm and spicy, like a kitchen on a snowy winter day. He held the collar while she adjusted a long, multicolored scarf. She turned and smiled. They were so close. "Happy birthday," Cary whispered. He bent to kiss her on the cheek to seal the birthday greeting, the way Amelia had taught him, but Julie moved. Their lips touched lightly. Then Julie took a step back. Cary read confusion and sadness in her warm eyes. "It doesn't mean anything, Julie. It doesn't *have* to mean anything. People always—"

"It's all right. I'm just antsy today. Birthdays do that to me." There was no need to tell this man that her entire body was charged with electricity.

"Me, too." The intense moment was over. But he had another problem. Should he give her the present now, at the restaurant, or when they got back to the apartment? Restaurants were so public, and he had no wish to embarrass Julie. Chances are she'd say good night in the lobby, so that left now. He reached into his pocket and withdrew the gaily colored box. "This is from Amelia and me. I picked it out, so if you don't—"

"Sometimes you talk too much," Julie said huskily. "You shouldn't have. I always say that when someone gives me a present. I guess I don't know how to be a recipient. It's so much easier, and safer, to be a giver."

Cary felt warm all over. He'd always felt exactly the same way. Amelia was a wonderful recipient. She oohed and aahed and squealed her delight.

"Thank *you* for sharing that feeling with me," Cary said.

I'd probably share my life with you if it were possible, Julie thought. "It's lovely, Cary. You shouldn't have gotten me something so . . . special. A box of candy would have been fine."

"Amelia's orders," Cary said cheerfully. He was quick to see the smile leave her face, but it was back in a second. "Here, let me close the clasp. It has one of those safety things so you won't lose it." Amelia would immediately calculate the cost of the gift, catalog the store it came from, before she oohed and aahed. How unkind he was being in his thoughts. Amelia had a right to expect expensive, wonderful things from him. He'd learned early on that candy and trinkets didn't do the trick. Trinkets and a pricey label, now, that was different.

Julie pretended not to see the slight tremor in Cary's hand when he fastened the bracelet on her arm. Possibly the tremor was in her own hand. She was certainly jittery. She thought for certain Cary would hear the sigh that escaped her lips when the tiny safety catch clicked home. Cary immediately jammed his hands into his pockets.

He was so close. He was wearing a different after-shave or cologne this evening. It made her want to take deep breaths. Kind of intoxicating. She hadn't felt this way in years.

Out in the chilly night air Julie impulsively linked her arm with Cary's. He drew her closer to him as they walked against the wind. It was a nice feeling, Cary decided. "You're sure you want to walk?" Julie giggled and said she came from hearty peasant stock.

"I'm not sure what kind of stock I come from. Sometimes I wish I knew. Other times I don't care. I am what I am."

"I feel that way most of the time. Either people like me for what I am or they don't."

"That's the right attitude. Don't ever change."

"I'll try not to. Unfortunately, there aren't too many people beating at my door wanting to get to know me better." She laughed, a forlorn sound.

Julie ordered a Scotch on the rocks. Cary raised his eyebrows in surprise. Scotch was a man's drink. Julie grinned. "Actually, I hate Scotch. I order it and can sip and not have to worry if I'm going to get light-headed. I rarely order a second one."

Cary ordered the same and watched as she settled herself more comfortably. With the dim candlelight softly dramatizing her features, Cary thought her one of the most beautiful women he'd ever seen. "What do you think of the restaurant? It's one of Amelia's favorites."

One of Amelia's favorites. Julie blinked, then smiled. "I think it's wonderful. How do you suppose they ever got that enormous rock out there?" Julie asked, pointing toward the large plate glass window at the end of the room.

"This is New York. Haven't you learned yet that they can do anything in this city? I asked the same question. It's real, that much I can tell you."

"I wonder if any of their tipsy patrons ever try to climb it," Julie said. "In my younger days I'd have wanted to take a shot at it!" She giggled.

"I said exactly the same thing to Amelia the first time we came here." He laughed ruefully. "That was a very long time ago."

"You make it sound as if time is your enemy, Cary."

He took a long, deep swallow from his glass. "I suppose I did. There are times when I feel that way. Right now I'm at loose ends. Everyone else is doing their own thing, and I'm just marking time. I don't like this feeling. I'm used to being involved, right up to my neck."

"But you just completed a magnificent project. Don't you want to sit back for a while and rest on your laurels?"

"And let someone else get the jump on me?" Cary said in mock horror.

"Would that be so bad?" Julie asked curiously.

"I'd like to take a vacation, but Amelia is too busy. I've never gone on a vacation alone, so I don't think I'd enjoy it. How about you?"

"Usually I go alone, and the vacations are more restful than anything else. Occasionally I go with a girlfriend. We've gone to the standard places: Aruba, Puerto Rico, Florida, the Virgin Islands. When you've lived virtually all your life in a place like Vermont, even Florida seems like paradise. I'm taking my vacation early this year. Two whole weeks in Hawaii. Four days in Maui, and I'll take in several of the other islands. My tickets arrived yesterday."

"Hawaii is beautiful. You'll enjoy it. I envy Maggie and Rand their life there. Will you be staying in Oahu?"

"Right in Waikiki, at the Waikiki Beach Tower, I think. The travel agent keeps changing my accommodations."

"You'll have to stop and see Maggie and Rand. They live on the North Shore. If you play your cards right, Rand might even take you to see the Banzai Pipeline; it's a favorite spot of his."

"Surfing scares the day lights out of me. I'm pretty much a pool person. I hate to get sand up my ass."

Cary threw back his head and laughed. "My sentiments exactly. I do, however, like to walk on the beach, especially in the morning and then again at sunset."

"I do, too. It's a great way to start the day. And then a big, as in enormous, breakfast. A whole pot of coffee, two large glasses of orange juice, along with hotcakes and two eggs over easy."

"I always order the same thing. Usually it's Number Three on breakfast menus. Amelia says I'm a glutton."

She didn't like that word; gourmand was nice, gourmet even better. "I guess I'm one, too. But I only eat like that on vacation."

"Me, too." Cary laughed. This compatibility thing was reaching incredible proportions. He didn't mind.

"When are you leaving?" It was suddenly important for him to know.

"March first. I'll send you a card; how's that? I'll say, 'Eat your heart out!'"

"Cruel and inhuman."

"Okay. I'll say, 'Having wonderful time. Wish you were here.'" The moment the words were out, Julie regretted them.

Their eyes locked. "I wouldn't want you to write that unless you meant it," Cary said quietly.

"Well, I . . . I probably won't send cards. They usually get there after I get home. Anyway, the card would be to you and Amelia. I never . . . never say things I don't mean. I mean, people get . . ." She was flustered, and Cary was doing nothing to help her. Damn. "Maybe I'll send you some pineapples." Pineapples could be eaten. That was safe.

"I'd rather have a card." Now, where in the hell was that stubborn sound in his voice coming from? His gaze remained locked with Julie's. "I'd rather have a card," he repeated.

"Then you shall have a card. Oh, look, here's our dinner. I'm starved."

An hour later, Cary leaned back in his chair. "I think we should have dessert."

"Dessert!"

"Ah, here it comes now."

Julie turned to see a waiter bearing a cake with one candle. She blushed as she noticed the other diners smile.

It took her three tries before she could blow out the one

candle. "I don't know what's wrong with me," she muttered nervously.

"I had nothing to do with the cake, Julie. Amelia called and ordered it. Please, don't be embarrassed."

"I feel conspicuous, that's all. People were staring."

"Staring, yes, but with admiration and envy. Birthdays bring out the child in all of us. They were admiring you and envying me for being with such a beautiful woman. Now, eat your cake, and ask the waiter to wrap the rest so you can take it home. Aren't you supposed to put a piece under your pillow and make a wish?"

"Isn't that just for bridesmaids?"

"I'm not up on that sort of thing," Cary said. "But try it. Will you tell me what your wish is?" he asked devilishly.

"And spoil my wish? Not on your life!"

"If it comes true, will you tell me then?"

"If it comes true, I'll take the first plane to Austin and tell you personally."

"It's a deal." Cary stretched his hand across the table to shake on the deal. Julie grasped his hand, intending to shake it, but instead, she felt her hand go limp in Cary's. He reached across the table with his other hand. Impulsively, she brought her other hand to cover his. They stayed that way till the waiter arrived with their coffee. "Friends?" Julie whispered across the table.

Cary nodded. He knew if he uttered even one word it would come out like a hoarse croak. He was drawn to this woman with the beautiful eyes and delicious sense of humor. He felt her attraction to him too, but she was fighting it, just as he was.

The walk home was a silent one, the wind buffeting them along at a fast pace. In the lobby Julie reached up and kissed Cary on the cheek. "Thank you for a wonderful evening. It will go in my memory book." She stared deeply into Cary's eyes in the yellow light from the wall sconces. "If I ask you up, we'll both be sorry. Please understand. It's me I don't trust. I find myself very attracted to you, and if I'm reading you right . . ." The miserable look on Cary's face confirmed what she was thinking.

"Can we stay in touch?" he said.

"I don't know. It's . . . We shouldn't."

"I want to. I'll call you from time to time."

"I don't want you to say that to me, because then I'll stay home all the time so I won't miss your call. Let's just say good-bye, and if you ever find yourself in New York, call me. If I'm ever in Texas, I'll call you. Good night, Cary." She turned quickly and called over her shoulder, "Give my regards to Amelia."

The elevator door closed and she was whisked to the sixteenth floor in seconds. She opened all three locks with machine-gun speed and locked them behind her just as quickly.

Safe.

For how long?

She didn't know.

Amelia stood on the balcony, wrapped in her fleecy robe, waiting for Cary's call. The lights of Miranda seemed to blend with the stars in the darkness. She hugged herself for warmth, just out of habit, though, for the heat from the apartment gushed through the balcony doors and seemed to envelop her. It was a beautiful evening, one to be shared.

Overhead light from the balcony next to hers startled her. The tenants obviously were doing the same thing she was, savoring the crisp, cool evening before retiring. She looked down at the bronze sundial, gleaming in her neighbor's light. "Grow old along with me, the best is yet to be."

Time to go in.

The sliding door swooshed along the grooves and clicked to a close. If she sat on her favorite chair; she'd be able to see the sundial.

It was twenty-five minutes past nine, Texas time, when Cary called. Amelia imagined she could see the phone vibrate at her elbow. She picked it up on the fifth ring. "Darling," she trilled.

"I thought you might have gone to bed. I was about to hang up, Amelia."

"And miss hearing about your evening? I'd have waited up till—" she was about to say sunrise and thought better of it "—till at least eleven."

"I stopped in the bar for a nightcap. The Celtics were going at it, so I watched a while. Did you have a nice day?"

His voice is too flat, Amelia thought. But she didn't let on. "I had a busy, productive, boring day, if you know what I mean. I'm pleased with what I've accomplished. Now, tell me about your evening with Julie. Did she like the bracelet?"

"She said she did."

"Cary, what exactly did she say? I want to hear."

"She said she wasn't good at receiving presents, that she was better at giving them. Something to that effect."

Amelia's eyes snapped shut. "How wonderful of her to admit something like that. You see, you two had something in common after all."

"The dinner was good and she admired the rock. She liked the cake, too. She took it home."

Amelia had never heard such flatness in his voice. "To put under her pillow to make a wish on, a birthday wish," she said brightly. "I hope she gets what she wishes for."

"I do, too. She's a nice person. She adores you, Amelia."

My darling, please don't sound so offended, Amelia wanted to say. "And I adore her. I just knew you'd have a pleasant evening. What did you order?"

"I had ham in raisin sauce, and Julie had calf's liver with bacon and onions."

"How brave of her to eat onions." Amelia almost giggled.

"Yes, I suppose it was." Now that he thought about it, it was probably Julie's declaration to him that it was a dinner and nothing more. "I'm kind of tired, Amelia. Too much wine at dinner and then a nightcap sort of did me in. If you don't mind, darling, I'll say good night. I'll see you about two tomorrow. Will you be home when I get there?"

"I'll do my best, darling. Have a safe flight and dream pleasant dreams."

The connection was broken. He hadn't said he loved her. She didn't have time to tell him she loved him. He'd simply hung up the phone.

Amelia crawled beneath the covers. Falling asleep was going to be difficult unless she relaxed. Part of her almost wished now that Cary hadn't called. The other part wanted to know everything, all the things Cary *hadn't* said.

Her body was statue-still as she forced herself to take long, deep breaths the way the doctor had instructed. But, like everything else, there was a trick to relaxing. You had to make your mind blank, and concentrate, and will your body to respond to the relaxation techniques, all at the same time. Over and over she repeated the words: I now release all my fears and worries; I now relax completely. Minutes later she drifted into an unrestful sleep full of scattered dreams.

She knew she was dreaming when her mother entered her

dream with arms outstretched, beckoning Amelia to come closer. "Not now; it can't be time for me to join you," she'd cried. "I'm not ready, Mam." She wasn't beckoning to her, she was pointing. But where? "What, Mam, what is it you want?" They were in a mist, a cloud of fog. "I don't understand what you want, Mam. I'm dreaming Mam; is that why you won't speak to me?" Again, the arm pointed. She was running now, trying to get closer to her mother. Her feet seemed to be moving, but she was standing still. Jessica remained where she was, a serene, happy smile on her face as she continued to point toward something Amelia couldn't see. Over and over she kept saying, "What, what is it, what are you trying to tell me?" A sound catapulted out of nowhere. A giant balled fist followed on the heels of the sound. Thunder echoed from somewhere. Seth her father! His face was menacing and hateful. "You should have been drowned when you were born!" "Mam, wait!" The fist came closer and closer. "No!" she screamed. "Get away from me. No!"

Amelia woke, her body bathed in wetness. She lay in the big bed, gasping for breath. Her heart fluttered frighteningly. Once again she drew deep breaths and forced herself to calm down. It was only a dream, a bad dream.

Sleep was out of the question now, so she might as well get up. Nobody does anything constructive at three in the morning, she told herself as she turned up the thermostat. Television, then; there must be something on the tube that would lull her to sleep.

Gooseflesh dotted her thin arms as she reached far back into her closet for the ratty, old flannel robe left over from her England winters. It was like an old friend when she slipped into it. She looked down at the frayed sleeves and smiled. She supposed she should have tossed it out years ago, but it was a reminder of those war-torn days when heat was a luxury. She never wore it when Cary was home, only when she was alone, like now. Cary preferred satin and bows and frills.

Amelia padded into the kitchen. Noise, she needed noise. The radio went on, and so did the small portable television on the kitchen counter. She paid little mind to the jumble of sound as she set about making tea.

Back in the living room with her feet curled under her, she sipped at the blackberry tea. Her thoughts were as jumbled as the sounds in the kitchen. For days now she'd been thinking about her mother and father and about her childhood. Last week she'd dreamed of her mother three times, and again tonight. Always when she woke, as she had tonight, she had the feeling Jessie had been trying to tell her something, something she couldn't grasp. And then her father would appear, his face angry and spiteful. He'd mouth hateful names and repeat what he'd said hundreds of times over the years; "You should have been drowned the day you were born." In the dream she'd try to go to her mother, but every time she took a step, Seth beat her back with a hard slap to the face.

God, how she hated the old bastard. Even now, at this stage of her life, her hatred was alive and pulsating. Old Seth had been dead for seventeen years, but she knew she'd carry her hatred to her grave.

Why hadn't she mellowed with age and forgiven her father? "Because," she said through clenched teeth, "he made my life and Mam's a veritable hell, and he doesn't deserve forgiveness." Her mind whirled back over the years as she recalled the hurts, the slurs, and the hatred, climaxing with the memory of the time she'd purchased her mother's childhood home after her death and renovated and refurbished it, only to burn it to the ground the day it was finished, trying to exorcise the ghosts. "Lord, why am I thinking about things like this in the middle of the night?" She sighed wearily as she carried her cup back to the kitchen.

Back in the living room she let her eyes go to the mantel and all the family pictures. Mam in the garden with a bouquet of daisies. Her brother, Moss, and Billie. A shot of Maggie, Susan, and Riley: Moss and Billie's children. A mug shot of her two nephews, Cole and Riley. One of Maggie and her husband, Rand, with the spangled Pacific behind them. The last picture in the long line of photographs was of her and Cary on their wedding day. There was no picture of her father. She wanted no reminders of old Seth.

She slapped at the side of her head. Reminders . . . memories. Of course. There might not be any pictures of Seth in the apartment, but in the last bedroom off the hallway, all his business records were stored in boxes on the shelf. She couldn't even remember now how they had come into her possession. Somehow, she and Cary had ended up with them.

Cary had muttered something once about boxes of records, and the fact that he was storing them in the back bedroom, but she'd been so busy with the decorators that she'd just waved her hand at him. She'd forgotten about the boxes until she was looking for something one day and came across them. She'd wanted to destroy them right then and there, but Cary had said he would take them back to Sunbridge and store them in the basement. But he hadn't. Well, by God, now was as good a time as any to drag the lest vestiges of her father to the front door. Never mind taking them back to Sunbridge. They'd go into the incinerator first thing in the morning.

Amelia stomped down the long hallway to the back bedroom, her face a mask of fury.

Angrily, she yanked and pulled at the heavy boxes until they toppled off the shelf. Ledgers, notebooks large and small, scattered across the pearl-gray carpeting. She tugged again and stepped out of the way as a third box tumbled to the floor. Letters, loose bills, memos, and all manner of notes, some scrawled, some typed, spilled about her feet. "Oh, shit," she wailed.

Clean it up or leave it . . . If she left it, it would stay with her, a reminder of how much she hated the old man. Clean it up, her mind shrieked; drag the boxes to the door and boot them out to the hall. You'll never have to look at them again. Get rid of it all. Now!

Amelia looked down at the boxes. Her father's life rested at her feet. Garbage. She laughed as she kicked at one of the ledgers. Shreds of yellowed paper slid from the leather covers. She laughed again.

Amelia dropped to her knees. Angrily, she gathered the loose papers and bills together, shoving them into one of the boxes any old way. The last of the loose papers was a packet of letters with a rubber band around them. When she picked it up, the band crumbled and fell away. The return address on the envelopes made Amelia blink. United States Government, Washington, D.C. Gingerly, she separated the envelopes and withdrew the two thin sheets of paper in the top envelope. She grimaced. An order for beef. Tons of beef. Stapled to the order was a Coleman bill of lading. Down in the right corner in her father's handwriting were the words "Not Paid," and they were circled in red. Curiously, Amelia opened the other envelopes. They were all the same, orders from the government for beef, planes, electronic equipment, and horses. And stapled to each was a Coleman bill of lading, and the words "Not Paid," circled in red.

Amelia sat back on her heels. What did it mean? Didn't the government pay its bills? Most businessmen would kill to supply the government because it was like money in the bank. Money in the bank . . . Her father had been a barracuda when it came to business. He'd never let something like this slide unless . . . unless he had a reason.

Amelia's hands shook as she emptied the box where she'd been stuffing the loose papers. Bundles of letters bearing the return address of the United States Government stared up at her. These bundles were different. They were orders for the same thing, and bills of lading attached—four, sometimes six copies of bills. The only difference was the words circled in black, "Paid in Full." There were bundles and bundles, at least a hundred or so. Carefully, Amelia went through each bundle. When she returned the last letter to its bundle, there was a smile on her face. "You goddamn foxy old buzzard!"

Night was bleeding into the dawn when Amelia made her way to the kitchen to put on the coffee. She was still smiling when she washed her hands at the kitchen sink. She hummed along with Fleetwood Mac and "Little Lies" on the radio. She waited until the song was over to turn it off. She pressed the off button on the television, and the kitchen was in silence. She continued to smile.

Coffee cup in hand, she retraced her steps to the back bedroom. She sat on the bedroom chair, her coffee next to her, and the first bundle of letters in her lap. It was when she was turning the letters over that she saw the message her father had scrawled on the back of the last envelope. It was written to Agnes, Billie's mother, who had taken over the office work when she and Billie came to live at Sunbridge. The message was simple and self-explanatory:

Aggie, mail one bill, no more. Send it registered and hang on to the receipt. This will cover our asses if we ever fall on hard times. This is just between me and you, Aggie, so keep your lip zipped.

A large S was scrawled for a signature.

Amelia could almost hear her father's raspy explanation to Agnes Ames. "The first rule in business, Aggie, is you cover your own ass. Everyone knows a passel of jackasses runs Washington, so it ain't too hard to stay one jump ahead of them. I been dealing with the government for a long time, Aggie, and they don't never pay their bills first crack off the bat. If we don't send reminder notices, these here bills will get lost in the shuffle. The longer they stay lost, the more interest they build. A man never knows when he might fall on hard times. It's an ace in the hole, Aggie. I'm on top now, and I plan to stay there. These here bills will make that possible. I guess you could call it a stick in the eye. Back there in Phil-a-del-phia, you fancy blue bloods would call it . . . leverage.

"Let me tell you something else, Aggie. Those same jack-asses I'm talking about will think they put one over on this old okeydokey Texan who don't know shit form Shinola, and don't go pursing up those lips of yours, Aggie. A man says what he has to say to get his point across. Jackasses, Aggie, is another name for ring-tailed bastards. I cozy up and jerk their strings, and they think they're the ones doing the jerking. It's how I do business, like it or lump it."

Amelia had heard Seth talk like this many, many times. Now—decades later—his words rang clear and true. And she knew just what they meant.

Amelia threw her head back and roared with laughter, tears streaming down her cheeks. She gasped. "Well, Pap, it's my ass that's going to get covered. As Clint Eastwood would say, you made my day."

It was seven-thirty when Amelia dialed her sister-in-law's number in Washington. Her voice was calm for the thirty min-utes or so that she kept Billie on the line.

Billie herself was laughing. "I say go for it! Seth was your father, and I see no problem."

"What about the others? Coleman Oil is in such diffi-culty. . . ."

"The others will agree, but if you want, I'll call them and get back to you. Coleman Oil is not your problem. Do it, Amelia! Wait, call Valentine Mitchell and get her over there as soon as possible. Old Dudley, too. I think you're going to need a few sharks on this one. Lord, I can't wait to tell Thad. Good luck, Amelia. I'll get back to you later in the day, but I know I'm only going to have good things to report."

"Billie, I've been dreaming about Mam this past week. The dreams were all jumbled up, and Pap kept interfering, but I had the feeling she was trying to tell me something. . . . This must be it. . . . Do you believe in things like this? Like when Maggie said she heard the angels sing when Sawyer had her operation . . . that kind of thing. . . . Billie?"

"Of course I do," Billie said quietly. "You were meant to find those things. You said God gave you a reprieve after your surgery so you could do what you're doing. I'd say His hand is right there next to yours."

Amelia's breath came out in a long sigh. "That's how I feel, too. Thank you, Billie, for agreeing. I needed to hear the words. Call me," she said happily.

Amelia held the packet of bills close to her chest, as though it were her mother's Bible. She raised her eyes. "This doesn't quite even up the score, but for now it will do. You hear me, Pap?"

Valentine Mitchell, the Colemans' lawyer, looked as gorgeous and as professional as she had the day so many years ago when she walked through the doors at Sunbridge to save Cole and Riley from the trumped-up rape charge brought against them by the handyman's daughter.

She grinned at Amelia. "You got 'em, Amelia. I'll take all of this to Dudley and the others and let them look it over. We'll get back to you tomorrow. And may I say, well done!"

"As my Pap would say—we got those suckers by the balls, and now we can squeeze."

Valentine laughed. "How about crush?"

"How about it?" Amelia grinned.

"I'll see myself out. Nice seeing you again, Amelia."

"Give Dudley my regards."

"You bet."

"Thankyouthankyouthankyouthankyou," Amelia whispered.

On her way to the bathroom Amelia reached for her mother's picture on the mantel and carried it with her. "There are some things you don't ever tell anyone because they'd think you were loony. Billie understands, Mam. I knew you were trying to tell me something in those dreams. This was it. Oh, Mam, you must know what I'm going to do. What I don't understand is how you knew. Pap said only he and Aggie knew. I guess up there you know everything. If by some chance Pap is there with you, tell him I said thanks." She blew a kiss in the direction of the picture before she climbed into the shower. She didn't feel foolish at all. Life was full of wonderful, unexplained things.

Cary tossed and turned all night. He wasn't sick, that much he knew. Finally, at four o'clock, he got out of bed and switched on the television. Strange feelings were rushing through him. Feelings he wanted to explore. There were things he wanted to say aloud.

At five o'clock he stood under the shower. The hard-on he'd had since coming back to the hotel finally disappeared. He felt drained. At six o'clock he was the first customer in the coffee shop. He ordered the Number Three breakfast special with an extra glass of orange juice, but when the plate arrived, he realized he wasn't hungry. He drained the coffee cup and smoked four cigarettes. He was back in his room at seven-twenty. He packed his bag, checked his briefcase. He walked around the suite of rooms to be sure nothing was forgotten.

At 7:31 he walked to the telephone and called Julie's number.

"Hi," she said in her unused morning voice. "You sound wide-awake this morning, Cary. I do want to thank you for a wonderful evening."

"It was my pleasure. The reason I'm wide-awake is I didn't sleep all night."

His candor was frightening. "I didn't sleep very well myself. I did put a piece of cake under my pillow, though, and made my wish."

"I wanted to say good-bye."

"We said good-bye last night."

"I know, but I wanted to say it again. I don't like good-byes."

Julie drew a deep breath. "Cary, this is no good. The only thing in this whole world that you can't count on are your emotions, and right now mine are at an all-time high. I don't want to be hurt. I don't want you to be hurt, and I certainly don't want Amelia to be hurt. There's the family, and Cary, I'm not good at sneaking around. I'm an up-front person. Now, I have to get to work or I . . . Go home, Cary, where you belong."

"Julie, please don't hang—" He cursed at the sound of the broken connection. He wanted to call her back, more than anything in the world. Maybe he could explain that . . . explain what? That he was married? That he had the hots for her? She knows that, he told himself. She has more sense than you do, Cary. Go home, back to Amelia and your life in Texas. Amelia is your life.

By five minutes past ten Cary had picked out an answering

machine in Macy's. He gave Julie's address, paid extra to have a messenger service deliver it after six. He paid cash. He didn't know if he felt better or worse. He didn't care.

At 11:27 he boarded the 747 for Austin. He was going home, where he belonged.

{{{{{{{{{ CHAPTER EIGHT }}}}}}}}}

The extra-long dining room table at Buckalew Big Wells was a joke to everyone in the family but Tess. She'd seen one like it in a movie and determined to have one. A monstrous centerpiece of dried flowers resting on a lacy doily stood in the middle. At each end was a candelabrum with pale lavender candles. Tess loved the color purple in all its variations.

Tonight she sat at one end, Coots at the other, just the way it was done in the movie. What did she care if Coots had to shout to be heard?

"This is stupid," Coots yelled. "No one is here but us. No point in wasting heat and electricity in this dining room. We could eat just as well in the breakfast nook. No need for all this, Tess. I keep telling you this ain't Tara and you ain't Scarlett."

"And for sure you ain't Rhett," she shouted. "If I want to think of Buckalew Big Wells as my personal Tara, I will, Coots Buckalew, and there is no call for you to be so feisty. We're dining the way decent, normal folks dine. You never did have any manners." She stabbed at her chicken breast.

Defiantly, Coots picked up the half chicken on his plate with his fingers. He sank his teeth into the soft white meat, ripped off a piece and then another, paying no attention to the sticky, sweet sauce that stuck to his chin and fingers.

"Bastard," Tess hissed.

"Bitch," Coots bellowed with his mouth full.

"You know what you remind me of, Coots? A tick getting fat off a big ol' hog. You're the hog."

"Bitch," Coots repeated. He wiped his fingers on the fancy

lace tablecloth. Then he burped. Tess watched as Coots lifted one heavy thigh off the chair.

Tess screamed. "Don't even think about doing that in mah dining room, because if you do, you'll get these mashed potatoes right in your face. You are an ignorant man, Oakes Buckalew."

"And you're a fine lady married to this ignorant old warthog," Coots bellowed.

"You don't have to scream. I can hear you just fine. Now that we have the endearments out of the way, would you mind telling me what's wrong besides the fact you have a tick in your Jockey shorts? Or is it the clap?"

"You ain't got no class, Tess. Leastways none that I've ever seen. I admit I ain't got none, and I don't want any."

"You do have a burr biting into you, don't you? Come on, Coots honey," she cooed, "tell me what it is that's making you so nasty."

"You want to know what's bothering me, I'll tell you what's bothering me. We're broke. I been telling you that for the past year and you don't pay me no mind. Spend, spend, spend. Instead of helping me, you and your children are putting me deeper into a hole."

"Now, don't go picking on the kids, Coots. What's between us is between us. They haven't done anything."

"Lacey's shiftless and you know it. She don't do what she's told. She's hankering after Cole Tanner, and he don't want no part of her, so what does she do, she sidles up to Riley. A Jap. If she cared anything for this family, she'd have convinced Riley to take over some of these oil leases. Did she do that? Hell, no. She calls Cole on the sneak and tries to get him to take her back. No account," he said bitterly. Coots cleverly ignored mentioning that he was the one who sicked Lacey onto Riley. "There's still hope for Ivy, but I ain't counting on it. So what do you have to say in defense of the kids, Tess?"

"I'll tell you what I have to say. Lacey doesn't have to pull your chestnuts out of the fire. If you ain't man enough to do it, don't send a woman to do it for you. Ivy is a hooligan, just like her father. The case is closed, Coots honey."

"It's closed when your charge accounts get cut off and I cancel the lease on that fancy suite in the Assante Towers. That's when it's closed. You better cut back on these house bills or you'll be on the street with the rest of the hookers in Austin."

The threat of eviction always scared Tess, no matter how much money she had in the bank. Being homeless was a terrible thing to imagine. People would talk. She loved Buckalew Big Wells. She'd had a dream once that Coots had tossed her out with only the clothes on her back and the latest astrology book. In her dream she'd become a bag lady doing horoscopes in a moldy train station for ten cents each. The dream was so real she'd sweated for days every time she thought about it. Beads of perspiration dotted her high brow right now. Men were the kings in Texas and she knew it, just like every other woman knew it.

"Coots, look me in the eye," Tess said, coming around to his end of the table. "Look me in the eye and tell me the truth—could we lose Buckalew Big Wells?"

"I think it's already lost," Coots mumbled. "Everyone is in the same boat we are. Ain't no place to get it, Tess. I thought for sure I'd have the Jarvis place by now, but that kid ain't selling. That was my ace in the hole."

"You waited till now to tell me this?" Tess screeched. "If I didn't bring it to a head, when were you going to tell me, the day they put the notice in the newspapers?" Coots shrugged.

"You might be an oilman, but you ain't no businessman."

"Did the stars tell you that?" Coots guffawed. If he didn't laugh, he'd cry.

"No, the stars didn't tell me that," Tess said nastily, "but the stars might get us *out* of this mess. If I bring the mortgage payments up-to-date, will you put Buckalew Big Wells in my name?"

"Sure, why not? But you got about as much chance of pulling that off as I have."

"How much cash do we have?"

Coots hung his head. "Ten or twelve thousand. I been telling you, but you wouldn't listen."

Tess screeched a second time. "That's all? Did you pay the lease on Assante Towers?"

"First quarter. They're coming due again."

"I'm going to take over that suite, and I don't want to hear another word about it. I'll rent it out or sublet it. Tomorrow morning, Coots, you have all the bank papers here on this table. You hear me? Then you meet me at the bank at one o'clock to put this house in my name. You got any objections, you say so right now."

"Anything you say, Tess. I can just see you as a bag lady. You look the part. Now all you have to do is get Neiman-Marcus to make you up a bag lady outfit, and you'll be all set." He laughed again, but it was a bitter, defeated sound.

Cole was just ready to leave the office when his phone buzzed. His sister was calling from Tokyo. "About time," he muttered.

"How's it going?"

"You tell me, Sawyer; what the hell happened? I thought you were going to call me after the big meeting."

"I had business to attend to. Nothing happened as far as I know. Chesney met Rand and Maggie for about twenty minutes, then left to go back to England. Maggie says Rand doesn't believe her, but Maggie does. So do I. If you want to call, they should be back in Hawaii by now, trying to come to terms with their jet lag. Even as we speak they're probably both lazing on the delicious white sand, while we freeze our butts off. Take some advice and don't call. This is their problem. Let them work it out. If they need us, they know where we are."

"I was thinking about taking the Dream Machine and going over. I could use some white sand and blue water. But if you don't think it's a good idea, I won't go."

"It's just my opinion. The decision is yours. How's everything going? How's Riley holding up?"

"He's not doing much talking these days. I think he's trying to shoulder the blame for the whole goddamn oil industry. Have you seen his grandfather lately?"

"I'm going out tomorrow. I try to stop by once a week or so. He's not good, Cole. I wish Riley . . . Never mind."

Cole sighed. He really liked the old Japanese. "Thad and Grandmam are due this weekend. Riley told me this morning, and now he's more skittish than I've ever seen him. He says they're coming to him for an accounting."

"Stay out of it, Cole."

"I will. Jesus, you're still as bossy as ever."

"I'll ignore that," Sawyer laughed. "What else is new?"

"Bet you'll never guess where Riley and I have been invited this evening. For dinner—barbecue, actually."

"I don't have an inkling. Tell me."

"Adam invited us to the ranch. I met him in Miranda the other day. He had his stepson with him. He asked about you."

"Oh."

"Oh? Is that all you can say? I told him you were real ugly these days and that you have to pluck your mustache."

"You egotistical shitbox. Tell me you didn't say that, and yes, I can call you a shitbox. You're my little brother."

"We're contemporaries. I caught up. Haven't you noticed? I'm not a little brother. I am your brother. Period. That's what I told him."

"I don't pluck, I tweeze. And I don't have a mustache, I have fine hair above my upper lip. I hear *you* have a brand-new feather duster above *your* lip. Riley, too. Jeez."

"Makes us look older. Dealing with fifty-year-old oilmen requires suavity. Riley talked me into it."

"I thought you said you were grown-up," Sawyer teased. "Must drive the girls crazy."

"I'm beating them off with a stick morning, noon, and night."

"You wish. This is costing money, so I think I'll hang up. Say hello to Adam, and tell him to write me a letter. Or tell him I'll be home in the spring and perhaps he'll invite me for a barbecue."

"You've stayed in touch with Adam, haven't you?"

Her hesitation was noticeable. "Not really. Christmas cards, that kind of thing. I knew he was married. I . . . I had a bad time over that. I guess I thought he was going to wait forever for me to make up my mind."

"If you're angling for sympathy, you won't get it from me," Cole said flatly. "I'm one of those guys who thought— still do for that matter—you two were meant for each other."

"It's my loss, Cole."

"He's free now."

"I can't start something, Cole. If it's meant to be, it will be. Give Adam a chance. Look, let's drop it, okay?"

"Okay by me."

"Give Adam my regards and let it go at that. I miss all of you, I really do. Sometimes I feel so cut off over here."

"Someone's got to do the dirty work." Cole laughed. "Love you."

"Love you, too."

* * *

{ 152 }

Cole pulled alongside of Riley. "If you wait, we can go together. I want to get out of this suit. Ten minutes tops."

"You got it."

Riley sat in the Bronco staring up at the apartment over the garage. How long ago that all was. For a while he'd thought his life was going to be ruined. He wondered where Luana was now. And her father. Maybe Cole knew. Now his problems were even bigger and, from where he sat, insurmountable. He and Cole had shed the skins of boyhood that day when Luana accused them of raping her. They'd become young men in a matter of minutes and had remained young men. Now he had to shed that skin and become a man. A man who could take charge of Coleman Oil and his own life. Why had he put Coleman Oil first and his life second? Maybe because he could make sense out of the business, but his life was too torn and jumbled to even try to understand what he should do.

"Ready when you are," Cole said, buckling his seat belt. "I brought you an apple. Adam's a lousy cook. I hope he's going to feed us inside and not out on the patio."

"Adam's not that stupid."

"Sure he is," Cole said, biting into his apple. "Remember that time in New York when he packed sandwiches and told us we had to sit in the park to enjoy the beauty of it? If we didn't sit, we didn't get a sandwich. Egg salad, if I remember. With some kind of little seeds in it."

"Too much mayonnaise. I hate mayonnaise."

"So eat your apple. By the way, Sawyer called just as I was leaving the office. She sends her love. She really thinks I'm going to kiss you on the cheek." Cole brought Riley up-to-date on his mother and Rand. "What do you think, Riley? Is she for real?"

"What would be the point otherwise? She walked away from it. Like Sawyer said, she came, she said what she had to say, and she left. It's up to Rand to make the next move. He won't. Not now. He'll torture himself and your mother. He'll worry it like a dog with a bone."

"Biodegradable," Cole muttered as he tossed the apple core out the window. "My mother will do what she can. They were so happy."

"Yeah, she's going to shoulder Rand's burden. Look at us; if it wasn't for her, we'd be sweating it out in some federal pen or something."

"Or something. Do you know whatever happened to Luana? Every time I look at that damn garage apartment, I wonder."

"I have no idea, and I don't want to find out, either," Riley grated.

"You hear that?"

"Chain saw." Riley raised his eyebrows. "Adam?"

"Maybe he saw it in a movie or something." Cole grinned. "Maybe he thinks if you own a ranch, you have to saw wood. He's a cartoonist," he said, as if that explained everything.

"I can't believe he's thinking about giving up his career and managing this ranch. He doesn't know the first thing about it."

"Who's going to tell him, me or you?"

"I think we should let him find out the hard way. We can send him our own brand of cartoons if things look really bad."

First came the manly handshakes, and then the bear hugs. "Jesus, you guys are all grown-up," Adam said. "Sunbridge's saviors. Kind of a ring to it. I remember when you were both little shits and Sawyer and I wet-nursed you. I'm doing it again, but no Sawyer," he said ruefully.

"Sounds like it isn't going too good."

"No. It isn't. Jeff hates it here. I was sort of hoping you two might have some kind of . . . I don't know what the hell I was hoping. How about a beer?"

"Best offer I've had today," Riley said, grinning and re-membering his stomach—he'd have to nurse it. "Who's using the chain saw?"

"Jeff. You notice it stopped. Damn kid probably sawed off his leg. Hey, Jeff! Come here."

The boy's eyes were old, but his body was that of a gan-gling teenager. "Come over here. Jeff, I'd like you to meet the two guys I was telling you about."

"The two Ivy League dudes from down the road?" the boy asked.

Cole looked at Riley. "You an Ivy League dude, Riley?"

Riley frowned at Jeff. "If you don't behave yourself," he said, "Cole will hang you up on that hook over there. See it?" There was an oversize nail protruding from the patio wall.

"Gee, the Ivy League dudes are big and tough."

"Here, hang him up," Cole said.

Riley was stunned at how thin the boy was under the heavy

flannel shirt and stiff jeans. His legs were beanstalk-thin. The worn sneakers were the only thing that seemed to go with a boy his age—a kid without worn sneakers was like a baby without a diaper. "Now you're going to get a hole in this nice new shirt."

"You bastards!" the boy screeched. "Adam, get me down!"

"Behave yourself, and maybe we'll let you down for dinner," Cole assured him. "By the way, when is dinner?"

In the kitchen, Adam leaned against the sink. "Maybe I should have sent him to his aunt on Long Island, but he can't stand her, and she's not too fond of him. I'm literally all he has, and from where he sits, or rather hangs, it looks like I'm not much of a bargain. Now go get him, you guys, and let's enjoy this here-now barbecue I've been slaving over."

"That was an experience I won't soon forget," Riley said on the ride home.

"That kid makes liking him a challenge, but he's not all bad. He's just a kid, and this kind of living has to be strange to him. I think he'll adjust. That tough-guy act he pulls is just a front to mask his feelings. You and I used to do that. God forbid one of us should have known how the other one *really* felt. He seemed real interested in food and how it's prepared. Maybe he has the makings of a chef," Cole laughed.

Riley snorted. "The kid is real big on four-letter words. I have to hand it to Adam, he didn't blink twice. I guess it's how a parent handles things. If you make a fuss, the kid does it more. If you ignore it, maybe it won't happen again . . . that kind of thing. I told Adam he could have our old mopeds and ten-speed bikes that are in the garage. Maybe the reward system will work."

"Was I that bad back in the beginning? The truth."

"On a scale of one to ten, I'd give you a five in those days. This kid is about a three. Adam is going to have his hands full."

"Don't you mean the three of us are going to have our hands full? Didn't you see how neatly old Adam included us in? Who the hell can walk away from a kid like that and not be affected?"

"Just what we need, another problem. That dinner was awful. Let's get home and get some decent food. You cook the eggs, Cole."

"I'll flip you." Cole laughed.

"Adam needs Sawyer's cool head for that kid. The only thing is he doesn't know it."

"Like hell he doesn't. Why do you think we were invited? We're the second string, because the first string is otherwise occupied. When the top gun arrives, we can sit back."

"I'll be damned," Riley muttered.

"Sometimes you Japs are so damn slow, and other times you're faster than the speed of sound." It was one of Cole's standard put-downs. Riley grinned.

At twelve-thirty Amelia closed her briefcase with a decisive click and left the Austin courthouse, her spirits high. If traffic permitted, she'd make it home a little before Cary was due. She'd have enough time to freshen up and perk some coffee. She'd stopped on her way to the courthouse earlier to pick up a box of the coconut macaroons that Cary liked.

Her spirits remained high as she rehearsed what she would say to Cary about her planned trip to Washington to testify before the House Select Committee on Aging. She'd made a lot of contacts, and her hard work was paying off. She told herself she had a right to be impressed with her accomplishments. What would Cary say?

Amelia felt a rush of pleasure at the thought of Cary's homecoming. He'd be in a lusty mood. She was herself, so the afternoon she planned would be wonderful. First they'd have coffee and Cary's cookies. He would tell her in great detail all about his trip, then tease her a little about the presents he bought her and make a Cecil B. De Mille production of the presentation. She'd do her bit, and Cary would be pleased with his selection, and maybe nibble at her ear. That would be a good time to tell him about her trip. He'd do his best to look interested and offer comments and suggestions and end up by saying how proud he was of her. And of course, the best part was always saved till last. She'd give him a massage with some sweet-smelling balsam oil and casually mention that the Jacuzzi was waiting for them, along with the chilled champagne. She must remember to put a bottle on ice the minute she got home. They'd make long, leisurely, wonderful love. They'd nap, make love again, and then she'd whip up some scrambled eggs and bacon and they'd eat in front of a fire. Amelia smiled.

She all but ran to the door the moment she heard Cary's key in the lock.

"Amelia! You're home!"

"Waiting for you, darling. I'm your welcoming committee of one, and I missed you."

"I missed you, too," Cary said absently. "God, it's cold out there."

Amelia watched as he hung up his coat. Usually he threw it over the back of a chair. He geometrically aligned his brief-case on the shelf. He turned, pecked Amelia on the cheek, and walked to the bedroom. "I brought you some presents. They're in the bag. I'm going to take a shower. Do you think you could make me a sandwich or something?"

Or something. Amelia jammed her trembling hands into the pockets of her new raspberry-colored wool dress. She'd bought it just to please Cary. He loved the color and he said he liked the way the new fluted skirts swished around her legs. "I picked up some macaroons and I'll make some of that master-blend coffee you love," Amelia called to his retreating back.

"Don't bother. I'm about coffeed out. Drank too much on the plane, and my belt says no more sweets for a while. A cheese sandwich and a glass of milk will be fine. If it's not too much trouble."

Trouble? She'd milk the damn cow if necessary. So her plans were sidetracked. She'd rustle up the sandwich and have it waiting in the bedroom when Cary got out of the shower. She'd open her presents while he was still wrapped in his bath sheet. All she'd have to do was whisk it off and *voilà*—love-making Assante-style.

Amelia marched to the kitchen. She peeled three slices of American cheese and slapped them between two pieces of white bread. She looked at the dry sandwich. Butter and may-onnaise and a leaf of lettuce would make it more palatable. She arranged the plate on a silver tray with three sprigs of parsley and some Chilean grapes. She plucked a ripe peach, also from Chile, and set it on the tray. Cary loved fresh fruit. The milk carton refused to open. In the end she had to search the drawers for scissors to cut the stiff cardboard. She poured generously into a large crystal glass. A fresh linen napkin on the tray and she was ready. She carried it gingerly across the long living room.

Tears pricked her eyes when she saw Cary sprawled across the foot of the bed. Droplets of water beaded his shoulders. He hadn't even bothered to dry off. For one brief instant Amelia wanted to dump the contents of the tray all over his slick body. Instead, she set it down on the dresser, covered him with an afghan, and left the room.

Amelia's hands were steady as she held them toward the fire. There were no tears in her eyes. The rest of the afternoon and the long evening yawned ahead of her. Cary would sleep for hours. Well, everyone's dreams were dashed once in a while. And there was always the never-ending pile of paperwork to be tackled. She had a new book from the book club. She could read and gorge on Godiva chocolates. She could start dinner, something that took a long time to prepare and an even longer time to cook. She could also unpack Cary's bag, or she could watch a couple of soap operas. She could call friends and catch up on the gossip or arrange a dinner party. She did have obligations to reciprocate. And if none of that appealed to her, she could go for a walk. She could even drive out to Sunbridge. Maybe it was time for a trip up to the knoll.

Amelia tiptoed into the bedroom. The raspberry dress slid to the floor and was replaced with fleece-lined sweatpants and a cashmere sweater the color of a shiny topaz. Her walking boots with the warm lining and her shearling coat made her ready for the trek to the one spot that gave her comfort.

In rapid succession she made two phone calls: one to the garage to have her car brought to the front and the second to the florist in the lobby.

Amelia's mittened hands nestled the florist's box of violets into her huge carry-all bag. It would protect the violets for the climb up the hill.

Sunbridge looked desolate in the afternoon light. She'd never found the place warm and inviting, no matter what the season. If it weren't for the small cemetery up on the knoll and family gatherings, she'd never choose to set foot on Coleman land.

Amelia picked her way carefully as she searched for the path that led to the knoll. Medallions of ice and patches of crusty snow crunched under her boots.

It was bitter cold now, the wind whipping angrily through the naked, arthritic trees. She gasped, thankful that she was almost at the clearing.

Breathing hard, she leaned against her father's headstone. Defiantly, she sat down on the base of the stone. Her mother's smaller marker was next to it, a florist's vase in shards at its foot. Someone in the family hadn't forgotten Jessica. Cole probably.

It was as desolate here as down on the path. The ground was frozen, with bits and pieces of twigs and old leaves sticking out every which way. She was having trouble breathing. Maybe it wasn't just the climb but the anxiety over Cary's return. Coming here today, she decided, wasn't one of her better ideas. She'd be here soon enough anyway, she thought grimly.

Amelia pulled the scarf from around her neck to cover her mouth. When her breathing returned to normal, she reached into her bag for the violets. The delicate petals would crystallize in seconds in the frigid air.

Now it was time to talk, time to unburden herself.

"It's happening, Mam. I'm not ready. Thinking about something and actually doing it are two different things. It hit me between the eyes, Mam. Handpicking my successor for Cary was just a whim I had, at first. I don't have a right to do that, and I never would have except that Julie Kingsley was so perfect. I was going to arrange everything, but if I'm going to be truthful, I can't go through with it. Not now. It would have been better if it had happened after . . . when I'm here with you.

"On the drive out here I kept thinking about things like fate and destiny. If something is meant to be, it will be. Some things are ordained, you know. In my mind I had it all planned out. Cary would retreat into himself, mourning for me, and Julie would draw him out of his grief with kindness and patience. Mam, I saw the scenes played out in front of my eyes. I'd be up above somewhere, looking down. I wanted to play God, and now He's punishing me. What do you think the chances are of Cary running into Julie in New York City? There's something like nine million people in New York. I couldn't begin to check the odds on a meeting like that taking place.

"It's out of my hands, Mam. I don't know what to do. I'm sure that nothing's happened yet, but Cary is feeling the impact. He doesn't know how to handle it. How supportive and loving can I *be*? What I had planned was for when I . . . when I was gone. And, Mam, I know I don't have all that much time left. Cary's been my whole life—I don't think I can share him.

"Billie says one either loves unconditionally or not at all. If Billie's right, then I have to stand back and give Cary what is best for him. I can give that, Mam, without Cary even knowing I'm the one doing it. It will be new for me, since I've always been on the receiving end of things. Giving is such hard work. There can't be any of that me-first stuff this last time round. I've got Pap's guts." Tears trickled down Amelia's cheeks. She brushed at them impatiently with her mittened hands. "I think I can bear it, Mam, but what if I'm wrong? What if I can't? What if I say something mean and spiteful? What if I drive Cary away from me? I'd die. I wouldn't want to live, Mam, when jealousy takes over, and it will. I know it will. What if I destroy Cary? My heart is so full of love for that man, sometimes I think it will burst right out of my chest. I've had it all. More than I or anyone else deserves. I don't want to let go, Mam." Amelia sobbed. "Should I throw myself into my work? Fill up my hours and let Cary fill up his hours in his own way? I ache with the hurt, Mam. Having guts and strength are two very different things.

"Mam, those dreams . . . For a little while they frightened me, and then I had a talk with myself. I knew . . . just knew you were trying to tell me something. . . . I even called Billie and told her. . . . What I'm trying to say is, thank you. I found the papers. I had Billie call the family for their okay. We're winning this one; I can feel it in my bones."

Amelia was surprised to find herself smiling—and warm. She blew a kiss at her mother's grave. "I'll be back, Mam. Maybe just to talk, but maybe it'll be to . . . rest. Either way, you can count on it."

The old shearling coat she'd had since she was nineteen snagged on a piece of protruding masonry from her father's stone. She tugged at the coat, and in her impatience she pulled too hard. The sound of it ripping was like a thunderbolt. She turned, her eyes full of hate, her lips pulled back into a snarl. "You always ruined everything. Even here, you can still do it. But I finally got you, you old buzzard. Mam helped me; what do you think of that? All your life you hated me, and now when I . . . Never mind, you aren't worth the explanation. Bastard!" she hissed through the scarf covering her mouth.

Amelia imagined she could hear her father's taunting reply as she made her way down the hill. "Bitch!" She laughed.

Amelia let herself into the apartment quietly. She removed her boots and placed them carefully on a rubber boot tray in the hall closet. She jiggled both arms as she shrugged out of the coat and hung it on a special wooden hanger that could take the weight. She'd take it to town tomorrow to have it repaired.

It was almost dark. The apartment looked gloomy. Cary must still be sleeping. She snapped on light switches as she made her way to the kitchen. Food was the furthest thing from her mind, but cooking would give her something to do. Perhaps she should make something creative, something she'd never made before, so she could concentrate on the recipe instead of her thoughts.

The freezer was a disaster. Pillsbury frozen pancakes and waffles. Weight Watchers lasagna. Six Swanson Hungry Man dinners and turkey pot pies. Pushed in the back was a twenty-pound leg of lamb. An assortment of vegetables lined the shelves on the door. Amelia slammed it shut in disgust.

The refrigerator was no better. A container of orange juice, four eggs, half a loaf of bread. Four strips of bacon in a Ziploc bag had little blue spots all over them. Butter and blueberry jam nestled in the corner next to two jars of dill pickles. The bottom shelf was full of Coors Light beer and California Wine Coolers. She'd have to make a grocery list and have her thrice-weekly cleaning lady shop for her.

"Amelia! Babe, is that you?" Cary shouted from the living room.

Amelia sucked in her breath. "In the flesh, darling."

"You scared the hell out of me. One minute you're here and the next you're gone. Where the hell have you been? You usually leave a note," he said accusingly. "I only slept for twenty minutes. I needed a few Zs. You know how my eyes dry up in airplanes."

Zs? It must be New York talk. Twenty minutes? Then why was he still wearing the bath sheet? She'd just bet the tray was the same way she'd left it and that his bag wasn't unpacked either. She hadn't lived with this man all these years not to recognize the fact that he'd awakened just minutes ago. Why did he have to put her on the defensive?

"I'm sorry, Cary; I thought you'd sleep the afternoon away. I went out to Sunbridge."

"At this time of the day? Without me?"

Was she hearing outrage in her husband's voice?

"I didn't think you'd want to make a trip to the cemetery so soon after getting home. Why don't you get dressed and I'll fix you a drink. We can sit in front of the fire. I can attest to the nip in the air—actually, it's more than a nip. It's twenty-three degrees."

Cary marched out of the kitchen. This was Amelia's cue to follow him. Instead, she went into the den to add another log to the fire.

In the bedroom, Cary whipped off the bath sheet. It sailed through the air, landing in the corner next to a ficus tree that was made of silk. Amelia knows, he thought. Knows what, for God's sake? You didn't do anything. So what if you bought an answering machine; you didn't leave any messages on it. There was no harm in kissing Julie. Nothing happened. You wanted it to happen, admit it. No, I love Amelia. I belong here. He looked around wildly. His eyes settled on the tray. Amelia had probably tried to make it look appealing, but now the bread was curled up, the parsley wilted. The milk had scum on the top. The grapes looked lifeless and the peach was starting to pucker. No goddamn wonder. It had to be ninety in here. He stomped to the thermostat. He wasn't far off: eighty-two degrees. He turned the dial down to seventy. Amelia would just have to wear a sweater.

His bag wasn't unpacked. That was the first thing Amelia always did—she'd throw the dirty clothes in the hamper, put suits and jackets in the hall closet to be taken to the cleaners. His shoes would be treed and neatly aligned in his own closet. She hadn't seen her presents either. Christ, she knows. Amelia was like a kid when it came to gifts. It was one of the things he loved about her. The sparkle in her eyes, her infectious laughter. The crazy desire to call Julie to ask her what he should do now made him gag.

He'd brought home a list of lies, and he was already adding to it. He'd lied when he said he only slept twenty minutes; her key in the lock had jerked him awake. He'd waited minutes to see if she'd peek into the room, lying back against the pillows, his hard-on at full mast. She hadn't opened the door. Jesus, she knows.

He dressed quickly, comfortable jeans and a worn yellow sweater that Amelia said made her want to attack him. He skipped the shoes and socks, opting for his scruffy slippers.

A night at home with his wife.

Remember now, Cary, one lie leads to another, and before you know it, it's too late to get out. Your life has been wonderful up till now. You're at loose ends. The Julie thing is history now, so forget it. Your marriage is too precious to tamper with. Watch it, bub.

Amelia was curled up on the oversize love seat in front of the fire. On the table next to her was a tray with a pot of hot chocolate and a plate of macaroons. Hadn't he said something about not eating sweets? If he had, this wasn't the time to mention it.

"Let's sit on this sofa, honey," Cary pleaded. "I don't feel like having my eyebrows singed. Your face is flushed." Little mottled red splotches. Where had he heard that word?

"It's so toasty here. You sit on that one and sort of lean back, darling, and we can hold hands while you tell me about your trip."

He would never be an actor. Even though he tried to inject gaiety into his voice, he knew it was coming out forced and flat. He did manage to go on for thirty minutes about the high rollers and the lawyers. He skimmed over Julie and ended with "God, I forgot to give you your presents."

"We have all evening. What do you feel like for dinner? And before you make your announcement, I think you should look in the refrigerator. Trust me when I tell you it will be a wild and wicked selection you'll be forced to make. We could order in if you have a yen for Japanese or Chinese. No pun intended."

"Crackers and cheese?"

"Crackers but no cheese. I used the last of it to make your sandwich." The one you didn't eat, she felt like saying.

"An omelet?"

"Scrambled. We have four eggs."

"Toast and coffee?"

"I can even throw in some butter and jelly," Amelia said lightly.

"A feast fit for a king," Cary said just as lightly.

"Now?"

"Later. I want to give you your presents. Promise to be appreciative."

"Aren't I always?"

Amelia's smile disappeared as soon as Cary was out of the room. She wondered if Julie had helped him pick them out. She'd know instantly if he'd had help. The smile was back on her face when Cary walked into the room with the two scrunched-up Bloomingdale's bags he'd shoved into his suitcase.

"Bloomingdale's, hmmnn."

Cary watched as Amelia oohed and aahed and complimented him on each item. When she came to the wind-up toy, she giggled like a girl. She slid from the sofa and sat on the floor, laughing and playing with the second toy.

"Do you like your presents, babe?" Cary asked.

"Cary, I love everything because you cared enough to think of me while you were away on business. If you gave me two pencils, I'd love them, too." She hoped he didn't hear her sigh of relief when she realized he'd indeed made his own purchases.

"Come here, babe," Cary said. He kissed her. It was a long, hard kiss that demanded she return his passion. He was kissing *her*. When his lips became gentle and searching Amelia knew she'd been replaced by Julie Kingsley.

Cary listened to his wife's even breathing for a long time. He usually slept like a hibernating bear after sex, but not tonight. Hell, he might as well get up. And do what? A radio or television would wake Amelia immediately, and she needed her rest. Damnation. If he didn't fall asleep, he'd lie here and start comparing Amelia to Julie and Julie to Amelia. Half his problem, he decided, was that he'd been idle too long.

It wasn't natural for him not to be working. He'd worked all his life. A man could get into serious trouble just hanging out, watching his wife work. Shit! He'd really believed Amelia when she told him they would take a long vacation after the opening of Miranda. He'd never told her, but he'd actually bought tickets for a cruise around the world. A surprise, he thought. Some surprise. He rolled over carefully so as not to disturb Amelia. He punched the soft pillow till he had it in a ball, just the way he liked it. Twenty minutes later he was still wide-awake. He supposed he could go out to the living room and read. Reading was quiet. Too damn quiet. He could even get dressed and go for a walk. Fresh air and all that. He knew he wouldn't do either.

The blueprints for Miranda flashed through his mind. He knew every inch of the print, remembered every notation scribbled with the thick yellow pencil. The cost of everything, right down to the penny, ricocheted across the moonlit ceiling. A mini Miranda, half the size, maybe even smaller, but for what? He wouldn't have to get any kind of backing for a mini, he could swing it himself, but to what end? Amelia gurgled in her sleep. He had to get out of bed...now! He slid to the edge, then waited a moment to see if he'd disturbed Amelia. Her breathing was deep and regular.

In the kitchen he set about making hot cocoa. While the milk warmed he scribbled notes in his own brand of shorthand, notes Amelia would never be able to fathom if she came across them.

His cocoa finished, Cary washed and rinsed the cup and saucepan. There was no need for Amelia to know he couldn't sleep. He stuffed the notes into his robe pocket. Tomorrow would be soon enough to start a file.

A tear trickled down Amelia's cheek when Cary crept back into bed. She lay quietly, listening to his breathing. She was still awake when the last of the dark night disappeared. Her eyes were loving yet sad when they gazed down at her sleeping husband. She couldn't afford to dwell on last evening's loss. Today was new, and it would be whatever she made it. The kiss she dropped on her husband's cheek was warm and sweet. "I love you so," she whispered tenderly.

{{{{{{{{{ CHAPTER NINE }}}}}}}}}

Riley wolfed down his lunch and popped two Rolaids to ward off the indigestion he knew was coming. The burning in his stomach made him draw up short. The doctor had warned him that ulcers were nothing to fool around with. Ulcers at his age! First chance he got, he was going for a second opinion. Cut the stress out of your life. Easy to say.

Right this instant he was so full of stress, he felt as if he were going to explode. Time to call Sawyer. If it was noon here, it was midnight in Japan.

He didn't mince any words when Sawyer's faraway voice came on the line. "How's my grandfather?"

"I saw him yesterday. He's the same as he was last week when you called. Riley, please call him. Just say hello. He's waiting so patiently."

"All Japanese wait patiently," Riley said flatly.

"If you won't call him, write him a letter—it would mean

{ 165 }

so much. And don't go giving me that crap that you can't. I'm not here to do your dirty work, Riley. What you're doing is unforgivable, and you know it. I don't want to hear that old line that we all have to do what we have to do. It's bullshit, and you damn well know it. Be a grandson, not a bastard."

"You don't understand, Sawyer."

"The hell I don't. You want it all. Well, it doesn't work that way, Riley."

"My grandfather understands. Do you tell him I call you?"

"No," Sawyer lied. She was no shrink, but she'd had enough experience with them to recognize the trouble in Riley's agonized voice. "That old man doesn't know how to play this kind of hardball, Riley. He doesn't deserve your attitude."

"Do you think I don't know that? This isn't easy for me either. You don't understand the Japanese way."

"If you'll forgive me, Riley san, I think it is you who don't understand the Japanese way. Enough said. How's everything in Texas?"

"Rough. Cole and I went over to see Adam the other day. I think your old friend bit off more than is palatable. His step-son is a problem. It looks like Adam's saddled himself with a kid who doesn't even like him."

"Adam will work it out. That kind of thing takes time. Thank God Adam was blessed with patience. Give him my regards when you talk to him."

"I'm leaving for Rio next week in case you need to reach me. I think it pays to stay on top of our oil leases. The office arranged the accommodations, so if you do need to call me, they can give you a number where I can be reached."

"Okay. Don't slay any dragons. Talk to you soon."

Riley hung up the phone. His stomach was killing him. He searched his pockets for the medicine the gastroenterologist had prescribed. Instead of taking one, he took two. Cole would have a laughing fit if he ever found out about the ulcers. The rest of the family would probably ship him back to Japan ASAP.

It wasn't his time yet.

The phone in the Georgetown house rang four times before it switched over to the answering machine that informed callers the Kingsleys were in Austin, Texas.

Maggie blinked as she listened. It was daring of her mother

and Thad to leave such a message. It announced that the house was empty, unless you counted the crazy cat, and he was probably at the kennel. It was like Mam, though. She always wanted her family to know where she was.

Maggie dialed a second time. Her mother picked up the phone on the third ring. "Maggie, how nice to hear from you. Did you try us in Washington?"

"Yes. Mam, you shouldn't leave messages like that. What if someone breaks into the house?"

"Darling, all they can do is steal something, and if they need it that bad, they'd find a way to do it even if we were there. Thad must leave his number at all times, and I don't ever want any of you to call and not know where I am."

Maggie's voice warmed. "I need some mothering, Mam, and some advice."

Billie's voice was immediately full of concern. "What is it, Maggie? It isn't Rand, is it?"

"It's Rand, but he's fine. I mean, he's not sick or anything."

"Darling, what is it? You sound terrible."

Maggie repeated the past week's happenings in Japan.

"Poor Rand. How he must be agonizing. All you can do, darling, is be there for him. Just try to imagine yourself in his place, Maggie. At one time your own life was similar."

"Mam, I never denied Sawyer. What I did was worse. I tried to tell that to Rand, but I can't reach him. All he does is sit under the monkeypod tree pretending to sleep. He had a wonderful opportunity to invest in a sugarcane plantation in Hilo, but I think he's going to lose out because he won't return phone calls. He goes through the motions of eating, but he isn't tasting the food. I could give him poi and he wouldn't know the difference, and you know poi's like eating glue."

"Waiting is so hard," Billie said, "and it always seems to fall to women. It must be because God blessed women with patience, some of us with more than others," she added gently.

"I could do it all for him, Mam. I could hire the private detective. I could call the orphanage. I would, too, if—"

"No, Maggie, you can't. This is something Rand must do."

"How long can he go on like this?"

"Till he can't stand not knowing for another minute."

"Rand has always been so adamant about not wanting children."

"Do you suppose this girl is the reason? If, and I say if,

Rand did give her mother money for an abortion, there is every possibility it left a scar. Taking a life, an embryo, a fetus, whatever, is traumatic. Giving money toward that end places that person in as much moral danger as the woman having the abortion. We're speculating, Maggie, and we have no right to do that. We're invading Rand's innermost secret thoughts and his privacy. He's in a bad place right now. When he's ready to reach out, grab hold and don't let go."

"I knew you'd have the answer, Mam."

Billie laughed. "I only said aloud what you were already thinking, but if you want to give me credit, that's fine."

"I miss all of you."

"I miss you, too, darling. I wish I was there with you now. I left ten inches of snow in Washington and came here to six inches. There's nothing I would like more than six inches of warm sand between my toes."

"You have a standing invitation, Mam. Everyone does."

"How was Sawyer when you saw her? She's had no setbacks, has she?"

"She's fine. She's operating on a clean bill of health. She says she gets tired if she parties too much, and once in a while she forgets things, but the doctors told her that's all part of her recovery. She goes to see Mr. Hasegawa regularly. I went with her. Mam, I cried when we got outside. And I found out something I didn't know before—why is it when a parent hears something wonderful about his child, it's hard to believe?"

Billie laughed. "We all fear disappointment, so we tend to wrap ourselves in cotton wool. Then when we hear something really good, we can throw off that protective wrapping. What did you hear about Cole?"

"How did you know it was about Cole?" Maggie demanded.

"Because you use two tones of voice. Both are loving, but one is for Sawyer and one is for Cole. I picked up on that a long time ago. What did you hear?"

"Cole has been corresponding on a regular basis with Mr. Hasegawa. Cole writes his letters in longhand, and Mr. Hasegawa dictates his. He didn't let me read them, he just told me of them. I think it's in the nature of a secret, since he told me and not Sawyer, so don't mention it. He said Cole shares many things in his life with him. I'm very pleased."

"Isn't it wonderful when our children do kind things?"

"Yes. Mam, what are you doing in Texas?"

"I'm concerned about Coleman Oil. And if you can believe this, I'm here to have Tess Buckalew do my horoscope. I got a bunch of Senate wives to commission theirs, too, so I'll have a good excuse to spend some time with her. I think the Buckalews are a little too involved with our family. And I want to talk to Riley and Cole. There are too many families who depend on us for their livelihood. I don't want anything to change that."

"So you're going to look to the stars for answers," Maggie shrieked with nervous laughter.

"In a manner of speaking. I'd like to hear what Tess has to say. Perhaps I am, as Thad would say, barking up the wrong tree, but I have this feeling..." Billie didn't finish her thought.

Normally Maggie would have pursued the conversation, but today her thoughts were with her husband. "I'll call you in a day or so, Mam. Thanks for listening."

"Maggie darling, if there's anything I can do, or Thad, call us. We're here for you." Billie sat for a long time with the phone receiver in her hand. At one time she'd expected, like most parents, that the older a child gets, the less worry there is. It doesn't work that way, she thought ruefully. Little children, little problems. Big children, bigger problems.

"This is our first dinner invitation, and I don't want you blowing it so we're not invited back," Adam said. "You got that, Jeff?"

"Yeah," the boy said sullenly.

"You're gonna love dinner at Sunbridge. Jonquil puts on a fine spread, and both of us can use a good meal. Let me take a look at you."

"I look like a fruity faggot," the boy complained.

"You look fine. You look the way a goddamn kid is supposed to look."

"Tell me the last time you saw a kid wearing a string tie."

"I always used to wear one. If it was good enough for me, it's good enough for you. What else?"

"Yeah, well, you lived in the dark ages. This is the eighties. Why can't I dress like everyone else? You keep saying you want me to belong. I look like a freak."

"Loafers, dress pants, and a button-down shirt make you a freak, huh?"

"I been telling you that for weeks, but you won't listen. Only old men who wear panama hats and live in the tropics wear this stuff, whatever it is these pants are made of."

"Seersucker. I used to wear them. In the summer," he said lamely.

"Right."

"What do you want to wear?" Adam asked. As if he didn't know.

"What I always wear. What the other kids wear. Jeans and a T-shirt and my sneakers."

Adam capitulated. "Okay. Sorry. I wanted you to look nice. I want people to know I take care of you. Did you wash your ears?"

Jeff called over his shoulder. "Do you want to see the rash behind my ears from the soap? I'm no slob. I brushed my teeth, too, and changed my underwear."

Adam had to admit the boy looked normal when he came back down the steps. "One last thing. One dirty word out of you and I'll fan your ass in front of everyone. You will be polite. You will be civil. You will say yes, sir, no, sir, and you will thank Jonquil for dinner. You can ask for leftovers—but don't say I said that. I taught you what fork to use and how to lay out your napkin. I don't think I forgot anything."

"Jeez, we're only going to your friend's house. They don't care what I do or how I look. What's the big deal?"

"I care, damn it! That's enough of a reason. Get your butt out to the car and let's go before we're late."

They entered Sunbridge through the kitchen door. The huge room was filled with a spicy cinnamon smell. Adam rolled his eyes at Jonquil and moved on to the library. Jeff stayed behind, and Adam overheard him asking what smelled so good.

"Where's your shadow?" Cole said grinning.

"In the kitchen, probably getting a cooking lesson."

An hour later Jeff was still in the kitchen. "Maybe you better check on him," Riley suggested.

Adam was back in a minute, motioning for Cole and Riley to follow him. He cracked the door to the kitchen an inch or so. Three heads peered in and heard; "If you mix the sugar with the cinnamon and sprinkle it lightly, it makes a nice, even brown coating on the top. You can do that for French toast, too. As long as you're copying down the recipe, make a

{ 170 }

note that it goes into a nine-inch pan, not an eight. Now, how many recipes do you have altogether?"

"Four. Five if you count the French toast. I'd like that one for the leg of lamb. Apricots and mint jelly mixed together."

"Here," Jonquil said, handing him a recipe from her file box. "I know this one by heart, so you can have it."

"Gee, thanks, Jonquil. I have over a hundred and fifty at home. I'll share them with you if you want. Some of them look real good. Don't tell Adam, okay? He'd think I was nuts."

"Why?"

Jeff shrugged. "I don't know, I just think he'd make fun of me or something."

"Well, you don't have to worry about me; my lip's zipped," Jonquil said, smiling. "I think you're gonna like this dinner tonight."

The three conspirators backed away from the door, trying to stifle their laughter, but back in the study Riley and Cole hooted.

"It's been food all along," Adam said in awe.

"I can understand that, can't you, Riley? Adam's burnt hot dogs and sticky baked beans would turn any kid into a monster. He told me you made Pillsbury cinnamon rolls the other day that bounced two feet high?"

"It was the microwave. I didn't know you couldn't do them in it," Adam said sheepishly.

"You think the kid is any happier?" Riley asked.

Adam waved his hand back and forth. "I'm hopeful. Yeah, a little, but I've got a lot to learn, too. I had him dressed all wrong to come over here. I asked him what was wrong and he told me."

Dinner was actually enjoyable. Jeff ate appreciatively, answered all questions with "sir," and called Jonquil "ma'am." When they left, at nine, Jeff held out his hand. Riley grabbed it and tousled the boy's hair. Cole squeezed, and Jeff squeezed back. Cole let up first. "You'll be a Texan yet." He could see the boy struggling not to come back with something smart.

"Yes, sir." Adam beamed with pride.

"I was proud of you tonight, Jeff," Adam said on the ride home.

Jeff flushed in the darkness. He felt like he should say something smart, but he realized that he didn't really *want* to.

When Adam reached across and squeezed his shoulder, it felt good.

The following morning when Adam came downstairs, his breakfast was waiting for him. French toast with cinnamon and sugar and four delicately browned links of sausage were on his plate. His napkin was linen and it was folded just right. A long-stemmed wineglass held freshly squeezed orange juice.

"Wow!" he said appreciatively.

"Beats those green eggs you usually make, right?"

"Well, yeah, Jeff, it does. What time did you get up to do all this?"

"Twenty minutes earlier, that's all."

"Jeff, I didn't know you could cook."

"There's a lot about me you don't know," Jeff said, grinning. "I cooked, so you clean up. Gotta go or I'll miss the bus."

Adam sat for a long time at the breakfast table. Food. Simple goddamn food. He knew it wouldn't be as simple an answer as it sounded, but it would do for now.

Adam poured himself a third cup of coffee. He had some heavy decisions to make. Should he wash clothes first or do the dishes? Maybe he should make the beds and clean the bathrooms. He had a pile of ironing to get to, and they needed groceries. Christ, he hated housework and he hated grocery shopping. For some reason he didn't mind sawing wood, though. He was proud of the four cords stacked behind the garage. If only he had a fireplace.

He finished his coffee. He knew what he wanted to do, and it wasn't pissy-assed housework. He practically ran to his workroom. The pencil flew over the paper. It didn't matter if he submitted what he was doing or not. This was for him. This was what he did best.

Tess stood in an agony of indecision, staring into her walk-in closet. What to wear for her lunch with Billie Kinglsey? Vivid stripes? A caftan? Too pretentious, she decided. Certainly not a suit, or skirt and blouse. Too formal for the middle of the day. Skinny fingers plucked at the scented, padded hangers. A dress. Simple but elegant. It would be better to look understated. Tess finally chose a hunter-green wool dress with braided leather belt. This was, after all, a business lunch; she'd be dealing with Billie on a professional level. For which she would receive remuneration. Ten charts at five hundred dollars each would net her a tidy little sum. If nothing else, it would pay some of the utility bills that Coots was bellyaching about.

She couldn't help wondering why Billie Kingsley would pick this particular time to want charts done. Billie must have something else on her agenda. Tess wasn't stupid, even though Coots told her otherwise on a daily basis. Billie had always been polite, like all the Colemans, but this was the first time she'd sounded...chummy. Compared with the Buckalews, the Colemans were old money, and that set them apart. She and Coots were just money, or as Coots said this morning, no money.

How quickly the snooty Colemans had forgotten that old Seth had padded his poke by wildcatting, just like Coots stuck with the only thing he knew, oil drilling. No brains. Tunnel vision. Limited, in every way; that was her husband.

Coots had laughed when she told him Billie was coming to have charts done for her Washington friends. "She's mocking you and that hocus-pocus, and you're too stupid to see it. She'll go back to Washington, and her and all her friends will have a laugh at your expense. Chew on that for a spell." And she'd done just that. Well, Billie Coleman could only make a fool of her if she allowed it.

The visit from the Coleman queen could mean several things, and she'd lain awake all night trying to figure exactly what. Lacey, of course, was at the top of the list. Breaking off with Cole and then rebounding to Riley—the Colemans would do some serious thinking about that. Riley was operating the oil and cattle end of Coleman Enterprises; Riley was where the money was, or so they would think. She'd bet her favorite strand of pearls on it. Somewhere, somehow, Coots had put pressure on Lacey. She could feel it in her bones. Coots would go with the sure thing, and the Jap was it. Coots understood oil money. He didn't know diddly-squat about aviation or electronics. He'd never gotten it through his head that it all came out of the same pot.

Tess picked at her thin hair. It was dry and brittle from too much bleach and teasing. Coots said it looked like a beehive without the bees. She snorted and bared her teeth for the mirror. Glistening porcelain caps glowed in the bathroom light. She grimaced. The price of the caps could have paid the utility bills for Buckalew Big Wells for years. Not that she cared a whit about the bills. They had appearances to keep up. And she still had her nest egg that she'd come to the marriage with, minus the last mortgage payments. It was the first time she'd touched it in all her married years. The last statement assured her she was close to the quarter-million mark. And it was hers. No one else's. Left to her by her daddy.

Lately she'd been having frequent dreams about being homeless. She'd dreamed again that she was a bag lady, with Coots pulling on her leg, trying to get the contents from her shopping bags. Neiman-Marcus bags.

Tess took a final look at her reflection. Billie Kingsley would be hard-pressed to find fault with her dress today. Thank God she'd had the acrylic nails touched up this week. The subdued polish took away some of the shock of the inch-long nails. Coots had hooted with laughter the first time he'd seen them, demanding to know how she wiped her ass. He was just so goddamn crude. Everyone wore them; why shouldn't she? He'd almost choked when she told him it cost ten dollars a nail, and twenty-five to maintain them every week. She just loved to watch old Coots turn blue in the face when she got to him. She wondered idly if she hated her husband.

She still had ten minutes or so till Billie arrived. Time for a quick spritz of perfume and a search for just the right ring.

The bathroom was a complete disaster. Wet towels and the damp floor mat were scrunched in the corner. Mascara streaked the gilt mirror. Trails of striped toothpaste dribbled down the vanity in little squiggles. Discarded panty hose, some gray, some beige, some neutral, all with runs, hung out over the sides of the fake gold wastebasket. Splashes of makeup and blusher dotted the vanity. Hairpins lay in the sink, and two were in the bottom of the toilet. The mirror was coated with hair spray and lacquer, which had sealed the black streaks of mascara.

It took a lot to get Tess Buckalew together.

She walked away from the mess, knowing when she returned, it would be neat and tidy.

Coots hated this bathroom. He'd ranted and raved for days when she'd had the bidet installed. He called it a bid-get and said the day he needed his ass washed by a gold-plated bid-get would be the day the saints marched up the driveway of Buckalew Big Wells. "All you do is piss away my money," he'd roared. Tess had laughed because Coots, who had no sense of humor, had almost made a joke.

The four-carat diamond she slid onto a bony finger made her smile. It was a gift from Coots, one she'd picked out herself after his last indiscretion. Matching earrings were in the safe-deposit box, also a gift, after his two-month fling with a floozy waitress in Crystal City.

She jerked her head upright, her scrawny neck bobbing like a turkey's. She'd been faithful. Men were animals. If they wanted to play, then they had to pay.

The lizard shoes that matched the braided leather belt were perfect for her outfit. She thought she looked like a lady. Billie Kingsley couldn't help but be impressed.

Lunch would be in the breakfast room. She'd spent hours going over the dinnerware and menu, finally settling on her Lenox china for the shrimp salad and chocolate Poor Man's Cake, a recipe handed down from her mother, and one she wouldn't part with for all the diamonds in the world. A centerpiece of fresh tulips with assorted fern and baby's breath rounded everything out perfectly. Not overdone, not underdone. If she'd been entertaining a friend, she'd have gone all out with the gold-rimmed dishes, gold-plated silver, and the fancy cloth she'd ordered from Belgium. Such exquisite lace. She'd have ordered an ice carving for a centerpiece. This understated little lunch was, to her eyes, just short of tacky. But it wasn't her eyes that mattered—it was Billie Kingsley's.

Only to herself would Tess admit that Billie Kingsley was a beautiful woman. She was every inch the senator's wife. Her soft gray hair was casual but expertly arranged. She wore little makeup, but then, she didn't need much. There was barely a trace of wrinkles, but she did have fine lines about her eyes. Laugh lines, character lines. The only jewelry she wore was small pearls in her ears. Tess knew they were real by the pinkish cast. Today she wore a simple navy wool dress with matching scarf; it made Tess suck in her breath. It was so perfect, she knew it had cost a fortune. Billie wore it well, as if it had been designed for her, which it had.

Their cheeks touched briefly. Tess gushed about the cold weather and Billie's coyote coat. Billie repaid the compliment and followed her hostess into the sunny breakfast room.

"Tess, this is so pleasant. I just love sunshine. If I had a window area like this, I'd be sitting in it all the time. We're at that time in our lives, Tess, when sunshine and warmth are important."

Tess agreed, although secretly she resented Billie including her in "that time of our lives." She was at least ten years younger than Billie Coleman.

Billie seated herself. She didn't know what she'd expected, but this pleasurable spot and simple fare weren't it. And Tess herself was almost normal-looking. They'd never been friends, of course, but at times they'd served on the same committees. Tess had always been flamboyant and loud to the point of embarrassment to all around her. She realized now that Tess was suspicious. She could see by the attentiveness in her eyes that she was waiting for the other shoe to drop. She must know that the Billie Kingsleys of the world didn't drop in on the Tess Buckalews just to have horoscopes done.

Billie tasted the chocolate cake. "This is delicious, Tess." It was a warm, sincere compliment, but the look in Tess's eyes didn't change. "I'd like the recipe if you wouldn't mind sharing."

"Not at all. I'll send it on to you." In a pig's eye she would. This was her own special family secret. Billie wasn't the first one to ask for it, and like the others, she would get the old Amelia Earhart recipe. She'd never know the difference, or if she did, she'd simply think it was something she'd done wrong.

"Tess, is there anything I can do to help with the engagement party?"

"Heavens no, Billie. I've got everything in hand. It's a good two months away yet, so that gives me plenty of time. Thanks for offering, though," she added as an afterthought. Of course, Billie hadn't offered to pay half. *That* kind of help she would have accepted.

"If you change your mind, I'm a phone call away. How is Lacey?"

"Just fine. In love. You know how young girls are when they're in love, but Riley's so busy."

"I think every oilman in the state is busy these days," Billie said as she finished the last of the cake. "It's a shame what's happened. How are you and Oakes doing?" She'd be damned if she'd call Tess's husband Coots. "Riley told me he closed off his stripper. Was that wise, Tess?"

So it was business, not love. Not just Lacey. "Wise or not, that's what the man did. Riley didn't tell him about the EOR until after he'd closed them off. I don't know if anything can be done now cr not." There was no harm to either her or Coots talking about this, she decided. All of Austin knew he'd closed them off. All of Austin knew the Jap kid had warned him not to. Everyone knew Coots's back was to the wall. He'd begged Riley to pick up his oil leases, but Riley had refused. If Riley had come through, the Coleman connection alone would make people think Coots had something to offer. But Riley had stood firm, and Lacey wasn't working the magic her father thought her capable of. The Jap kid was no fool. She'd take it one step further and admit, but only to herself, that the engagement and wedding would probably never come off. Everything was going against Coots. First his failure to buy the Jarvis ranch, and then Riley. Even his own daughter hadn't come through.

Tess tried for a light tone. "Mercy, Billie, I don't know the first thing about oil except we all need it. That's man business. We shouldn't even be talking about something we don't understand. You don't understand it, do you?" she asked sharply.

She was like a stringy old bobcat, Billie thought. "I know enough to know we're all in big trouble. If Oakes isn't, I'm happy. I'd heard he had a geological survey done on the Jarvis property. That must be the only ranch in all of Texas that doesn't have oil. Poor Adam."

"Oh, it showed oil," Tess blurted. She was instantly sorry the moment she saw the interest in Billie's eyes.

"Adam told me there wasn't any. I guess I misunderstood him."

Since she'd put her foot in it, she might as well go all the way. "The way I heard it was Adam wouldn't give up the oil leases. He wanted to sell the property but retain the leases. No one, Coots included, would go for a deal like that," Tess said defensively.

Billie nodded to show she was in agreement, and sought to change the subject. "Where are you having the engagement party?" she asked brightly.

Tess let out her breath with a sigh. "In Miranda, of course. Has Riley mentioned where they plan to live? Lacey is so vague, sometimes I could shake her."

"I assume Sunbridge. I believe Maggie said something about Cole moving into the condo, but don't quote me."

"Mercy!" Tess said, smiling widely, all her porcelain

showing. "Mistress of Sunbridge, just like you once were. The wheel does turn, doesn't it?"

Billie did her best to hide her smile. Old Seth must be squirming in his grave over that tidbit. "I'm sure she'll make a fine one," Billie said warmly. "Sunbridge can use a woman's touch and some new blood."

"Whoever would have thought Sunbridge and Buckalew Big Wells would be united." Tess's voice was full of awe.

Certainly not me, Billie wanted to say. Instead she started rummaging in her purse for the slip of paper containing the names of the Senate wives and their birthdays. She handed it to Tess.

"How are Oakes and Riley getting on these days?"

Tess answered absently as her eyes scanned the sheet in front of her. "Not as well as they used to. Coots gets a burr in his hide and takes it out on everyone. Riley is of no mind to put up with that. I 'spect once Lacey and he are married, though, he'll give Coots the respect he deserves."

"Do you know what went wrong? Riley is usually so respectful of everyone."

"Hmmm. Three Virgos. I don't like to work with Virgo. I think it's the worst sign of the zodiac. Riley's young; he'll get over it."

Billie pounced. "Get over what, Tess?"

"Why . . . whatever it was. Land sakes, Billie, you sound like you're grilling me. All I know is Riley used to ask his advice about almost everything, but then something went wrong. Let's face it, Coots knows more about oil than that boy will ever know. If Riley made mistakes, he can only blame himself. I'm sure he can make it right. The world isn't going to come to an end, is it, Billie?"

"I'd say it depends on what those mistakes were, Tess. A lot of families depend on Coleman Oil for their livelihood."

"Seems to me, Billie, that you turned Coleman Oil over to Riley because he was fit to handle it. Are you saying you made a mistake?"

"I'm not saying that at all. I do plan to talk to Riley this evening, though. I, as well as the other members of the family, have a right to know where we stand and just how bad things are."

"I wouldn't worry if I were you, Billie. You have a powerhouse in those two boys. Cole is a whip, and Riley does know his business. They are young and inexperienced, but that won't always be true."

Billie's hackles rose. "They aren't boys anymore, Tess. As a matter of fact, they are very experienced, so I have to argue that point. I trust both of them."

Tess folded the paper in her hand. She leaned across the table. "Then why are you here, Billie?"

She'd been expecting the question. Tess Buckalew was nobody's fool. "Why, the charts, of course. Call me when they're ready. If you like, I can pay for them now."

"When I'm finished will be time enough. I'll start tomorrow." Her eyes bored into Billie.

"I appreciate it, Tess. I know you must have other clients, and you are so involved in your other activities. But this could mean more business for you—my friends have other friends. Things like this do tend to mushroom. Well, I really must be going. Lunch was delightful."

"It was my pleasure, Billie. The next time you come to Sunbridge we'll have to make it a point to do it again."

Tess sat in the breakfast nook for a long time after Billie left. She'd give up all four back molars to have half the class that woman had. Envy was a terrible thing.

In her gut she knew she could never come up to Coleman standards. Buckalew Big Wells would never rival Sunbridge. Coots and she were trash, and it showed, unfortunately. But with Lacey marrying into the Coleman family, she might have a chance of turning some things around. If Lacey didn't screw up. And if Coots would act accordingly. Fat chance of that, she thought grimly.

Jonquil Doolittle, Riley and Cole's part-time housekeeper, served an excellent dinner. Thad's eyes widened appreciatively when the huge leg of lamb was served—his favorite food in all the world next to Yankee bean soup. Billie wondered where Jonquil had found the fresh emerald-green peas and pearly white potatoes at this time of year. A side bowl of bright orange carrots with slivered almonds and fresh parsley, one of Cole's favorites, added just enough color to the table to make one's mouth water. Light, fluffy biscuits with golden butter that looked as if it had just been churned made Riley groan in delight. Two pies stood on the sideboard, one banana cream, one strawberry rhubarb.

This wasn't just another dinner at Sunbridge, and clearly,

everyone at the table knew it. There would be discussion and questions afterward. Billie would have given anything to wipe away the tense, defensive look on her grandson Riley's face. Thad, as always, came to the rescue and regaled them with tales of goings-on in Washington.

When Jonquil carried the last of the dinner dishes to the kitchen, Billie nodded to Thad. It was his cue to go for a walk.

Riley crunched his neck into his shoulders, eyes wary. Cole lit a cigarette, something he rarely did, and never at the dinner table.

Riley's stomach churned as he followed Cole and his grandmother into the parlor. His moment of reckoning. He was glad for Cole's show of support, glad they would sit together while *he* defended his role as the head of Coleman Oil. He wasn't afraid of his grandmother. What was making his stomach churn was the prospect of seeing disappointment in her eyes. He swallowed hard.

Billie put her arms across Riley's shoulders. How miserable he looked. She glanced at Cole; he didn't look any better. She felt like an ogre. What must they be thinking, these handsome, intelligent grandsons of hers? Probably that she was here to fire them, to chastise them, to place blame . . . She had to wipe the stricken looks from their faces. She had to show her support. They were family, and family didn't place blame.

"For heavens sake, will you two wipe the doom and gloom off your faces? All I want is to understand what happened. Now, who's going to tell me?" she asked lightly.

Riley squared his shoulders and took a deep breath. "I'm the one who's responsible, so I'll do the explaining," he said in a choked voice.

"Grandmother, don't listen to him. To hear him tell it, he's the one who's responsible for OPEC dropping the price of oil to eight dollars a barrel. All he does is torture himself," Cole said vehemently.

"I projected our profits when oil was thirty dollars a barrel. I hedged our profits on the commodities exchange, but I didn't hedge enough. I thought oil would stay at that price. It didn't."

"Grandmother, listen to me," Cole begged. "The other oil companies, some of them bigger than ours, didn't hedge at all. Most of the smaller ones, like Coots's, didn't do it either. At least Riley tried to cover our asses. It is not his fault."

Riley ignored him. "I leased other wells that I thought would continue to produce at thirty dollars. I laid out ten million dollars for the mineral rights. I paid out another ten million for labor and materials, and I estimated a thirty-million dollar profit. When oil dropped, I got caught with my pants down. I also leased equipment at fifty thousand a day. I signed contracts with riggers for a year. They earn thirty bucks an hour. I hired five geologists at a thousand dollars an hour. Everyone was under contract. I had to pay off, I'm still paying off. I have to honor those contracts. I spent and spent; I never dreamed the price of oil would drop. We bought real estate, office buildings, other things with my estimated profit.

"My EOR is still in the experimental stage, but it's working for us. That's a high-tech method meaning enhanced oil recovery." Riley's voice was tormented and shaky.

"We're doing all we can do, Grandmother," Cole said forcefully. "You might as well know that Coleman Aviation isn't faring any better. Most of the orders for planes, at least a good portion of them, were from the oilmen. They've canceled, and we're left sucking our thumbs. We could go under, too."

"I was too cocky, too inexperienced. I should have seen this coming, should have hedged more," Riley said miserably.

"If you say that one more time, I'm going to slug you," Cole thundered. "There was nothing you could do. You'd have had to be a mind reader or an insider at OPEC. Tell him I'm right, Grandmother," Cole pleaded.

"He's right, Riley. Where in the world did you get the idea that I or anyone else in this family would blame you? Answer me, Riley," Billie said gently.

"I failed. I also loaned Coots Buckalew a million and a half dollars. So he wouldn't go under. A man works all his life, and then because the banks won't help, he goes belly-up. I had to help."

"Of course you did. I would have done the same thing. All of us would. We're people, not just a business. I think you're losing sight of that, Riley. People, family. We're in this together."

Cole grinned. "I'm glad one of us here has some brains. I've been saying the same thing to him for months now, but he wouldn't believe me. Thanks, Grandmother."

"I think we should all have some brandy and coffee, and in that order," Billie said. "Then I want to hear about the oil leases in South America. Riley, you didn't know your great-grandfather Seth, but I did. I want you to believe me when I tell you he would not be disappointed in you." Billie begged forgiveness for the lie. If Seth were alive, he'd rip his great-grandson's heart right out of his chest and stomp on it.

Riley grimaced. "I find that hard to believe, but because you're the one doing the telling, I do believe. I'll get the brandy."

Cole grinned wryly when he stared at his grandmother. "So it was a little white lie; we all have to tell them once in a while," she whispered. Cole bent over to tie his shoelace to hide his grin.

An hour later Billie walked up the wide, curving staircase with a grandson on each side of her. She kissed them soundly at her door. "We're together on this, and don't forget it for one minute. Now, good night, and sleep well."

Back downstairs in the parlor, a beer in hand, Cole stared at his cousin. "You feel any better?"

"As a matter of fact, I do. I'd hate like hell to have you working against me. Thanks for the support."

"All I did was tell the truth. Grandma Billie wasn't here to do a hatchet job. She's behind us all the way; so is the rest of the family. Now, what say we tie one on and forget about business for one night."

"Hear, hear," Riley said, holding his Heineken aloft. The smile on his lips didn't reach his eyes, Cole noted. But it was a start.

"I'm going to miss you, Riley," Lacey said softly.

Riley stared across at the girl he was supposed to marry. She was beautiful—in a hard, shiny kind of way. Ivy called her a plastic mannequin. His stomach was churning. His ulcer was worse than ever. Nothing seemed to help. He'd made up his mind to talk to Lacey this evening before he left for Rio. It was going to be tricky telling her he wanted to postpone their engagement. He hoped she wouldn't cry.

"I asked you to go with me, and you said you had a job and couldn't go," he began. "Why didn't you tell me you took a leave of absence? I had to hear it from Ivy in her last letter."

"Ivy sticks her nose where it doesn't belong. I was planning on telling you, but you always seem so preoccupied. And it wasn't something I wanted to discuss over the phone. Does it matter?"

"Not to me, but it should matter to you. I don't think Ivy was sticking her nose into things that don't concern her. The way she mentioned it sounded as if she thought I knew. As a matter of fact, she said only the nicest, kindest things about you. Anyway, I thought you loved your job." He knew his voice sounded accusing, but he couldn't help it.

"I do . . . I did. It's just that there's so much to do with the engagement party and all. . . ." She let her voice trail off as the waiter arrived with two delectable-looking shrimp cocktails.

Riley leaned across the table. The candlelight did strange things to his features, making his eyes glow hot and his lips narrow into a thin, tight line. He looked so menacing Lacey could feel her heart start to pound. She should have known something was coming. This invitation to dinner, even if it was his last night in town, was alarming in itself. Riley never socialized in the middle of the week. It was one of the many things about him that irritated her.

"I think we should postpone the engagement party. The way things look, I might have to spend quite a long time in South America. If things don't go well, I'll come back sooner, but then there'll be other problems. Either way, it isn't fair to you."

Lacey reached for his hand. Tears gathered in her eyes. Practiced tears. "Why don't you let me be the judge of what's fair to me? How's this going to look to both our families? Everyone thought, myself included, that you'd give me an engagement ring for Christmas. Are you trying to tell me you think you are making a mistake? Have you changed your mind?"

He felt terrible at the sight of her tears. He *liked* Lacey. Damn, why did he get himself into this mess? *Had* he changed his mind? Of course he had, but then, he'd never made the conscious decision to become engaged in the first place. Lacey had done that, and he'd gone along with it. He was to blame. Now he was going to hurt her, and his stomach would take on additional stress. "No matter how I say this, I'm going to come across as a real heel. I'm very fond of you, Lacey, but I don't think I'm in love with you and I don't think you're in love with me."

"You think I still care for Cole, don't you? Is Cole behind all of this?" Lacey demanded.

"Cole has nothing to do with it," Riley said miserably.

"My father, then. What's he said to you? It's got something to do with my father—I knew it," she hissed.

Riley didn't deny it. "We both need some breathing room. If we're meant for one another, time will help us. I don't want you to feel tied down while I'm gone."

Dumped, cast aside like an old shoe. Again. Little fingers of panic curled in her stomach. Her mother had told everyone who would listen about the impending engagement. Cole . . . Cole would have a laughing fit. She wondered how much the Coleman family had to do with Riley's decision. From the age of sixteen she'd never been without a beau. Always there was a man to be counted on. What was wrong with her now?

"I think, Riley Coleman, that you've decided I'm not good enough for you. The Colemans have such high standards, and the Buckalews don't quite cut it. That's it, isn't it?"

It was on the tip of Riley's tongue to tell her Ivy could cut it, but he didn't. "No, that's not it at all. I have a lot on my mind, Lacey. You know what the oil business is like these days. You also know my grandfather is ill. There's every possibility that I'll return to Japan sometime in the near future. I have to think of all these things and what's best for everyone concerned. Right now I'm not ready to make any kind of commitment. I'd like you to tell me you understand."

She couldn't let this happen. She'd grovel if she had to. "I do understand. Look, I'll go job-hunting tomorrow. I'll tell my mother to put the engagement party on hold. I love you, Riley," she lied with a straight face, "and I absolutely refuse to accept what you're saying. When you come back from South America, we'll pick up where we left off. Please, Riley," she pleaded prettily. He could be swayed so easily, especially where women were concerned.

Riley's heart thudded. This wasn't working out the way he'd planned. His stomach on fire, he gulped at Lacey's Brandy Alexander and felt a momentary relief. Cream of any kind always helped.

He had no wish to hurt her now or in the future. Lacey had gone through hell once before; he couldn't be party to causing her more misery. He knew he was being a first-class fool when he nodded his head in agreement. He missed the triumphant, selfish look on Lacey's face, hidden by the waiter who'd come to carry away the half-eaten appetizers.

The rest of the dinner passed in a blur for Riley. The ride home with Lacey cuddled next to him only annoyed him. He walked her to the door. When she stood on her toes to kiss him, he sidestepped and the kiss fell on his cheek.

On the drive back to Sunbridge he cursed himself over and over. He was still as committed as before. Perhaps more so. Son of a bitch!

Lacey's hopes of making it up the steps without seeing her mother were dashed when Tess practically ran from the living room to follow her up the stairs.

"This is an early evening, Lacey, I thought you'd be gone all night," she said slyly. "What with Riley leaving tomorrow and all."

"You thought wrong, Mama," Lacey said coldly.

"Something's wrong. I can tell by the look on your face. Don't tell me that Jap dumped you. He did, didn't' he?"

"No, Mother, he did not dump me. We have a mutual agreement. We're postponing the engagement till Riley gets all his problems settled. His grandfather is sick. Coleman Oil isn't doing well. There are a lot of things. Riley wants me to be happy, and we agreed that he shouldn't have me to worry about on top of everything else. Relax, Mother; I may become a Coleman yet, but it will take a little longer."

"No need to sound so defensive, honey. I'm just concerned about you."

"Of course you are, Mother. If I don't marry into the Colemans, you'll never get to put on that social-ladder-climbing suit you're dying to wear."

"You are a nasty child, Lacey," Tess sniffed. "No other mother would put up with the way you talk to me. You have no respect." Lacey didn't bother to reply. She slammed the door in her mother's face and locked it.

Lacey stayed in her room for four days, coming out only to make herself tea and toast. She spent the rest of the time reading old letters from Cole, looking at pictures of the two of them, and reading old articles about the Colemans. She tried to call him twenty-six times and all twenty-six was told he was either busy or in a meeting. He didn't bother to pick up the phone in his room early in the morning or late at night. She didn't bathe or brush her teeth. Her hair, stiff with hair spray and mousse, stuck up in bleached spikes all over her head. She looked awful and felt worse. The caricature that stared back at her from the bathroom mirror made her wince. She leaned closer. Her mascara was in clumps on her artificial lashes. She wasn't sure if the dark circles under her eyes were real or from the mascara running when she cried. She looked like a ghoul. She ripped at the sticky eyelashes and dropped them into the wastebasket. Her lips were dry and cracked. Maybe she was dehydrating. Even her skin, usually moist and supple, was dry and flaky. She stepped on the scale and looked at the numbers clinically. Ninety-two pounds. She'd lost nine pounds in four days.

At two in the morning of the fifth day, Lacey staggered from her bed to the bathroom. She showered and washed her hair, brushed her teeth four times, and gargled lustily with mouthwash. Not liking the taste, she brushed her teeth all over again. She pulled on panties and jeans, barely noticing how loose they were over her slight frame. She didn't bother with a bra but slipped an oversize sweatshirt over her damp, curly hair. Her feet rummaged over the closet floor for her Top-Siders. She was ready.

She crept down the stairs quietly, helped by the thick, sculptured carpeting. She made her way through the dark house and let herself out the side door into the garage. Tess's gleaming candy-apple-red 560 SL stood waiting for her. She knew the key would be in the ignition. She pressed the button on the electronic door opener. She shifted into reverse and let the car glide out of the garage and down the driveway. Only when she was a safe distance from the house did she turn on the lights. She drove purposefully, intent only on the road. She refused to think about her destination or what would happen when she arrived.

Lacey cut the lights when she reached the long driveway that led to Sunbridge. She slowed the powerful engine and parked at the far end of the house. She closed the door silently and walked on her rubber-soled shoes to the kitchen door. Doors were never locked at Sunbridge. Quietly, she tiptoed her way to the front hallway and crept up the stairs. The ninth step creaked, so she skipped it. Her heart was pounding now.

At Cole's door she shook her head to ward off the light dizziness she was feeling. Her hand trembled so badly she could hardly grasp the doorknob. She waited a moment and then turned it silently. She closed the door just as silently. She stood a moment to get her bearings. Nothing had been moved; that was good. Her breath caught in her throat when she saw Cole sprawled across the bed, the covers at his feet. The first dawn light ribboning through the slatted blinds lay like silver streaks across Cole's muscular legs. She stepped out of her shoes and shed her clothing. She padded naked to the window to close the blinds. She padded back to the bed and stood for several moments staring down at Cole while she waited for her breathing to ease.

Gently she climbed into the bed and drew up the top sheet. She waited, hardly daring to breathe. When Cole continued to sleep, she moved closer till she lay spoon-fashion next to him. Her hand reached out and at the same time she slid down till her head was between his legs. Her tongue flicked out, snake-like, over the tip of his shaft, once, twice, and then a third time. Cole's immediate erection and his groan of pleasure made her smile in the dark. She knew the moment Cole's surge began to build, and stopped, pulling herself to the length of him. She kissed him hotly, hungrily, her small, round breasts pressing into him. She played with him, delighting in his groans of desire, and always she would stop when the pressure in him started to build. She leaned over him, rubbing her breasts across his lips, tormenting him and loving every minute of it. She was astride him now, that secret place be-tween her legs slick and wet against his stomach. With her hands she cupped her breasts, offering them to him. She al-most stopped when she realized Cole was still asleep, proba-bly thinking he was dreaming. Gently, she parted his lips and thrust one taut nipple into his mouth. She could feel the tense-ness in his belly and knew he was growing hard. She rubbed her breasts and her face into the satiny wetness as she slid lower till she was poised over his stiff shaft. Gently, she low-ered herself until he filled her. "Take me, Cole, now," she cried huskily. "Take me. Love me." She rolled over, her arms about him like a vise locking her to him.

Cole closed his eyes and pushed her back into the pillows as he thrust up into her, his movements desperate and fren-zied. Lacey arched her back, crying out as the thrusts became deep, then shallow, then deep again. A low animal sound escaped Cole's tight lips as he spilled himself into her, bring-ing both of them to a climax.

When his breathing returned to normal, Cole leaned over and switched on the lamp. His face was hateful as he looked down at her. "I can never forgive you for this," he said through clenched teeth.

"Cole, listen to me, please," Lacey begged. "I needed to know if you and I—"

"Well, now you know. We didn't make love. You crept in

here like a thief in the night and I fucked you. That's the beginning and the end of it. Get dressed and go home."

"You liked it; admit it," Lacey sobbed. "You haven't forgotten me."

"And what about Riley? Jesus, I can't believe you came here. I can't believe you'd put me in this position. What kind of bitch are you?"

"I love you. Doesn't that make a difference?" Lacey continued to sob.

"Come off it, Lacey; the only person you love is yourself. What if Riley finds out? How can you face him?"

"The only way Riley will find out is if you tell him. I haven't slept with Riley, so what difference does it make?"

"Lady, you are one cool number. I can't believe you just said what you did. Go on, get dressed and get out of here. Don't make me do something both of us will regret."

Cole leaped out of bed and stood staring down at Lacey, a maniacal look in his eyes. "Are you going to go on your own or do I have to carry you down the stairs and throw your butt out of here, your naked butt?" His voice was hoarse and gruff, his stance as menacing as his eyes.

"I never knew you were so mean and cruel," Lacey whined as she slid her legs over the side of the bed.

"Well, now you know," Cole said. "I don't ever want you to come back here again. Do you understand me, Lacey?"

Lacey didn't bother to answer. She pulled the sweatshirt over her head. She wondered if she told him about Riley's decision whether it would make any difference. But no, it wouldn't matter to Cole one way or the other. He was a cold bastard. Where had she ever gotten the idea that he was a warm, caring person?

At the door she turned to face him. "I guess I needed you to say all those things to me to make me come to my senses. I've loved you for a long time, Cole. When we ... when we broke up I couldn't let go. Riley did his best to help me, and I started to cling too hard. Don't worry about Riley, I'll never say a word."

"That's fine, that's just great," Cole growled. "What about me? How in the name of God can I face him? Every time I'm in his company I'll think about this."

A wry grin stretched across Lacey's face. "I always wanted to be unforgettable. Good-bye, Cole."

Hot, scorching anger surged through him. He lashed out,

kicking the foot of the bed, the chair, the night table, and the door. Pain shot up his leg into his groin. He lashed out with the other foot. He dropped to his knees and beat his head into the mattress. His shoulders shook with the impact of his betrayal.

Cole knew his life would never be the same again.

When Tess came downstairs, she passed what she called their solarium but which was, in reality, a closed-in porch. She backed up a step when she saw Lacey settled in a white wicker chair, writing something.

"Early this morning, aren't you? We don't see you for days and then you're up with the roosters. Are you sick?"

Lacey decided the question held no real concern. She kept on writing.

"Writing to Riley already? He'll be back before the letter gets there. You didn't answer me, Lacey. Are you sick? Why are you up so early?"

"I'm not sick, Mother. I'm writing to Ivy." There was no need to mention she'd already written to Riley, finishing the letter just as the first rooster crowed.

"Ivy!" Tess said in dismay. "Why in the world are you writing to Ivy?"

"Because I want to. Isn't that enough of a reason? It wouldn't hurt you to write her once in a while yourself. She is your daughter. You know, Mother, I don't ever remember hearing you say a kind word to her? Why is that?"

"Aren't we the nosy one this morning," Tess said, hedging for time. She hated it when she got brought up short. "Ah don't have to write to mah daughter, Lacey, ah call her," she drawled.

"Really! When was the last time you called her?"

"I won't tolerate a smart-mouthed daughter in my house, Lacey. It's no never mind to you when and if I call your sister."

Lacey's laughter was mocking. "You won't have to worry about this smart-mouthed daughter living in this house any longer. I've made up my mind to go to New York. I'll be leaving tomorrow. I'll send for my things when I get settled."

"You're what?" Tess screeched. "I knew it, I knew it! Riley sent you packing, and don't think for one minute I don't know where you went in the middle of the night. You have no shame, Lacey Buckalew."

"You're right, Mother. Last night I had no shame. Today I do, and that's why I'm leaving. If once, just once, Mother, you had come to me or been there for me when I needed you as a mother, I might not be leaving. But you never did, for me or for Ivy. I'm writing to tell her she at least has a sister for whatever it's worth to her. I'm probably too late, but at least I'm trying."

"You could have come to me any time, Lacey honey; I'd have listened to you," Tess whined. Lacey ignored her. Tess continued on to the kitchen. She didn't know if she was upset, relieved, or angry. When she couldn't make up her mind, she settled down to breakfast. As she munched on toast she decided Lacey had been a tramp from the time she was ten years old. The realization made her reach for a second piece of toast, which she spread liberally with crab apple preserves.

Only a fool would have asked about the engagement. It was over if Lacey was going to New York. The realization that she wasn't going to be a part of the Coleman family left a bitter taste in her mouth. She swallowed a whole spoonful of preserves, but it didn't help. Tears of frustration filled her eyes. She had no one to blame but herself. The stars had warned her, given off enough clues, but still she hoped the merger would take place. Doomed, she thought morosely. She didn't give another thought to Lacey's leaving or the letter she was writing to her sister.

Tess's brain shifted into overdrive as she tried to calculate a way to approach Riley on his return. She'd be a real bleeding heart. If she did a good enough job, he might take off to New York and bring Lacey back. She felt better immediately. Now the only decision facing her was whether or not to have a blueberry muffin. Maybe the blueberries would stain the porcelain caps, but since she was never one to give up something she wanted, she reached for the biggest muffin in the basket and started to stuff her mouth. That's why they made toothpaste, wasn't it?

Lacey read over her letters to be sure she hadn't left anything out. The first was to Riley.

Dear Riley,
    I've done nothing but think since you left, and I want you to know I agree with everything you said that night

in the restaurant. I do love you, but I'm not in love with you, just as you aren't in love with me.

I've taken a good long, hard look at myself and my life these past years, and I don't like what I see. I'm hoping that my move to New York will make things right for all of us. I'm going to try to get my life in order. By the time you get home I'll be gone, but I know you'll wish me well.

You're off the hook, Riley. It would never have worked. I'm too selfish a person for you. I hope we can be friends, and I do thank you for being there for me when I desperately needed someone.

I hope things go well for you.

Affectionately,
Lacey

The second letter was to Ivy.

Dear Ivy,

I know this letter is going to come as a shock to you. Please, don't throw it away. I want you to read it. I need you to read it.

I'm sorry I haven't been a better sister to you. When I think back, I see now how tough it was for you. I wish I could have been the kind of person you needed, and I hope it isn't too late for us. I need to know I have a sister to love, and who loves me.

I've been such a fool, Ivy. I was so in love with Cole I couldn't think straight. When he dumped me—and yes, he did, I lied when I said we mutually called it off—I did some awful things that I'm ashamed of. For a while I didn't think I could make them right, but I'm going to give it a try. I'm leaving for New York tomorrow. When I'm settled I'll let you know my address.

I was never in love with Riley, nor was he in love with me. I pretty much pressured him into the engagement because of Pop. Gentleman that Riley is, he went along with it. He's in Rio now, but before he left he told me he wanted to call off the engagement.

It's important for you to know that Riley and I never slept together. I know you've always had a real soft spot for him. He for you, too, but he doesn't know it yet. He comes to your defense at the drop of a hat. In the romance department he's a little slow. If anyone can get him revved up, I think it's you.

I'll keep in touch.

Much love,
Lacey

Lacey licked the envelopes and felt as if a load of bricks had been removed from her shoulders. She felt like a real person for a change. An unhappy real person. She knew her about-face had been lightning-quick. Anything else wouldn't have worked. There was nothing like shame and guilt to make a person beat a hasty retreat, only this person wasn't retreating. She was moving forward, her past behind her. She hoped she had the strength and the courage not to weaken and look back. If Ivy could do it, so could she.

Lacey spent the rest of the day packing two suitcases to take to New York. The rest of her belongings went into her three college trunks, to be shipped when she had a permanent address.

The last thing she did before climbing into her bed for the last time was shred all Cole's letters and pictures. The Coleman newspaper clippings were tossed whole into the wastebasket. She wouldn't look back and she wouldn't leave anything behind. New beginnings were exactly what they implied.

Lacey slept deeply and dreamlessly.

The five remaining days till Riley's return were pure hell for Cole. A dozen times each day he made up his mind to confess to Riley. Two dozen times each day he decided to keep quiet and torture himself for the rest of his life. He couldn't ever remember being so miserable. Food stuck in his throat and he wasn't sleeping.

The day before Riley's return, a letter arrived at Sunbridge addressed to him and marked "personal." There was no return address. Jonquil put it on his desk. It was late, almost midnight, when Cole opened his mail. He knew he was half-drunk, but he could still see clearly to read the short note from Lacey.

Dear Cole,

I'm in New York, as you can see by the postmark. I decided this was best for all of us.

The other night was a mistake, one I will regret for

the rest of my life, just as you will. I hope and pray that you won't get any noble feelings and confess to Riley. He's too nice a guy to lay that on him. I've moved on, you'll go on with your life, and Riley will do whatever he has to do.

Please, Cole, if you ever felt anything for me, do me this one last favor and don't say anything to Riley.

Lacey

Cole tossed the letter on his desk with the rest of his mail. He needed someone to talk to. Adam. Adam loved to talk and give advice. He pressed the numbers and waited. Adam's groggy voice came over the wire.

"What the hell time is it, Cole?"

"How should I know," Cole said belligerently. "I called you because I need to talk, not for the time."

Adam's voice was instantly alert. "What's wrong? Are you drunk?"

"Everything. Yes, I'm probably drunk. I only have a little Scotch left in the bottle."

"Was it full when you started drinking?"

"Yesterday or today?"

"You at home? Good; stay put and I'll be there as soon as I can."

When Adam arrived, he stood in the doorway and whistled. "I thought you guys had a housekeeper. What's with this mess?" he asked, indicating piled-up clothing, assorted shoes, books, papers, and magazines scattered all over the room. Wet towels hung from chairs and bedposts. He tried not to look at the parade of liquor bottles on the dresser. Cole was no drinker, nor was he a smoker, but ashtrays had spilled over onto the night tables.

"You want something to drink? If you do, I have to look for it. . . . Maybe I should just go downstairs and get another bottle," Cole muttered as he peered around the room.

"No, thanks. I think I'm going to need a clear head for whatever it is you're going to tell me."

"Not going to tell you anything, going to show you." Cole made a pass at the desk to pick up Lacey's letter. "Read this."

"So you unzipped your pants when you shouldn't have," Adam said cheerfully. "Happens to the best of us. If you keep your mouth shut, like Lacey asks, there shouldn't be a problem."

"Riley's a good guy. We're buddies. Even if I don't say anything, he'll know somehow: he's Japanese."

"Guilt's an awful thing, Cole. You can either carry it around your neck like a lead weight or you can say the hell with it and forget it. I'd opt for the latter if I were you. Please don't tell me you're thinking of confessing all. Nah, you wouldn't be that stupid." But Cole's miserable face told him he'd guessed correctly. "Look, you called me here to talk, presumably to ask my advice. Well, here it is. Don't say anything. Trust me when I tell you you won't feel any better afterwards. Riley will never, ever forgive you. Probably because he's Japanese, as you said. Once words are said, they can't be taken back. Remember that."

"I thought I was dreaming and then . . . What the hell would you have done, Adam?"

"Probably the same thing you did. That doesn't make either of us right," he added hastily. "Put it behind you. You aren't a kid anymore. You want to play in the big leagues, you gotta pay your dues."

"How'm I going to look at him?" Cole dropped his head into his hands. Adam stood by helplessly, patting Cole's heaving shoulders. "He gets home tomorrow. Hell, he doesn't even know she's gone."

"Cole, do you want to come back to the ranch with me?"

"No. Go home, Adam. I'm sorry I dragged you out in the middle of the night. You have your own problems."

"That's what friends are for. Jesus, I hate leaving you like this. Are you sure you'll be all right?"

Cole snorted. "I'm not going to do myself in, if that's what you're thinking. I won't say anything. I'm going to bed. Sorry I dragged you out of bed," he said, eyeing Adam's pajama bottom sticking out from his trousers.

"Hell, I was only sleeping. Strip down; I'll wait till you're in bed." Adam was as good as his word. He tossed a pile of clothing and assorted junk onto the floor and settled himself in a corner chair. He shook his head wearily, his eyes never leaving Cole. Twenty minutes later he was satisfied Cole was in a deep sleep. He got up, massaging his stiff knees. He was tempted, but only for a moment, to tidy the room. Cole was going to wake up with one hell of a hangover. He shrugged as he went about turning off lamps until only one soft pink bulb glowed.

It was a few minutes before two when he headed back to the Jarvis ranch. He wished there were something he could do for Cole, something physical that would make the young man feel better. Life was hard enough without carrying around a load of torturing guilt.

As always when he found himself involved with the Colemans, Adam's thoughts turned to Sawyer. He wished she were here so he could unburden himself to her. She'd know just the right thing to say to Cole, and she'd be free with her advice about how to handle Jeff. God had blessed her with common sense and a blistering tongue. He smiled in the darkness of the car. One day, he hoped, she'd realize she couldn't live without him. Or he'd storm into wherever she was and say something she'd understand, like "Let's cut all this bullshit. I love you and I know you love me, so I'm going to sweep you off your feet and . . ." That's as far as he ever got in his thinking, because he couldn't bear the thought that she might kick up a fuss and scream out that she didn't love him.

Time. Time would take care of everything.

The long working day was over when Riley swung the Bronco into his parking space. Today was Jonquil's day off, which meant the house would be dark and forlorn, unless Cole was home. He looked around for Cole's Porsche, but it was nowhere in sight. He was probably out having dinner or meeting friends for drinks. The thought of food nauseated Riley. An apple or some crackers would do fine for now. What he really wanted was a long, hot shower, some clean clothes, and a stiff drink.

He snapped on the light in the kitchen and looked around. He loved this part of the house. The first time he saw it, his mouth dropped open. He was just a kid visiting Sunbridge for the first time. He'd no idea of what Western living was like, but he knew he liked this warm, comfortable, busy place. He fell in love with the wicker rocking chair next to the fieldstone fireplace. That first time there had been a big old yellow cat snoozing in it. His mother had been with him then. He rubbed at his eyes, not sure if he was rubbing away tears or grit from lack of sleep.

Dark wood beams, gleaming copper, and shiny green plants welcomed him home to the big old kitchen, chock-full of memories. His mother had told him his father used to snitch cookies from the heavy crock in the corner of the cabinet. From force of habit he reached in, knowing it would still be full. It was his only request of Jonquil when he and Cole hired her. He withdrew a soft sugar-coated cookie that resembled a slice of cake, his father's favorite. The delicate flavor delighted Riley. Like father, like son.

Lights sprang to life as Riley walked through the house, the house he loved with all his heart. He stood back, crouched like a basketball player, and aimed his baseball cap at his hook on the hat tree. He grinned when the Yankee cap settled itself. He was home. He should get a dog so there would be someone to greet him on days like this. He bounded up the stairs to his room.

The stinging spray of the shower peppered him as he lathered his body with soap. He felt anxious for some reason as he dried himself and hung the towel neatly on the rack. He and Cole often referred to themselves as the two neatest Colemans, citing Sawyer as the least neat and swearing they could never live in the chaos she did.

Riley's damp toes dug into the coffee-colored carpeting as he made a selection for the stereo. Billy Ocean, one of his favorites, soon filled the room with sound. He wasn't alone anymore.

He knew there was mail on his desk, and out of the corner of his eye he'd noticed the airmail stripes on the top envelope. A letter from his grandfather. He couldn't postpone the moment any longer. He turned on the reading light next to his desk and went through the mail. American Express bill, Visa, a bill from a local garage for the new tires he'd bought for the Bronco. Flyers of every sort found their way into the wastebasket. A card from the dentist showing a set of teeth that looked like piano keys reminded him he was due for a checkup. A letter from Lacey made him frown. Right now he wasn't in the mood for Lacey or a letter bearing her name. He tossed it on his desk and forgot about it.

The stiff drink he'd promised himself was in his hand when he sat down to read his grandfather's letter. Billy Ocean crooned softly, but his melodious voice did nothing to ease the tension in Riley's shoulders.

The letter was short, and written in Japanese in his grandfather's own hand.

My dear grandson,

I beg of you to forgive this old one's shaking hands as I put my pen to paper. Much time has gone since you last wrote me. I know you are in South America as I write this letter, but Sumi assures me you will be back at Sunbridge when this letter arrives.

It is with sadness that I tell you there may be no cherry blossoms this year on our hill. There are so many things this old one finds himself grieving for these days.

Sawyer tells me you are well, and my heart beats in happiness that you find satisfaction and contentment in America. Perhaps you will honor this old one with a visit one day soon. I will keep that wish close to my heart.

I remain forever your respectful grandfather.

Riley folded the letter and replaced it in the flimsy envelope. To write or not to write. What could he say? Wasn't it better to say nothing? He supposed, if he set his mind to it, that he could write a letter full of chatty events and not commit himself to anything. But that would only torment the old one, and he would see through the words in the letter. Or he could write the sort of letter his grandfather expected, full of all the reasons why he didn't want to return to Japan and why he wanted to stay here, in his father's home. He could say he'd made no decision and couldn't make one until he got his life in order. He could tell him his heart ached with love and that he was devastated by his grandfather's illness. He could speak of his obsession with Sunbridge and his American family. He could even write about the cherry blossoms and tell him how often he thought of that peaceful hill. If he wanted to, he could tell him that he called Sawyer once a week to find out how he was. He could write all those things, but he wouldn't. Instead he would write a duty letter so the old one's eyes would fill with warmth when it was handed to him.

Riley rummaged for paper and pen. He would write in English, not Japanese.

Dear Grandfather,

Sumi was correct when she told you I would be in Sunbridge when your letter arrived. I grieve with you for the possible loss of our cherry blossoms. It has been cold here, too. Perhaps next year there will be double blossoms. My mother spoke to me of that once, but I myself cannot remember that beautiful sight.

My trip to South America was just short of fruitless. There is so much corruption and greed there, I find myself at a loss as to how to deal with it. Since it is my responsibility to activate the oil leases, I know I must come up with a solution. I will, but it will take time.

You did not speak of your health, Grandfather. I pray that you are comfortable.

I cannot write the things you want to hear from me, not now. I beg you to understand, my wise grandfather. I have never, in the whole of my life, asked you for anything. I ask now that you allow me the time I need and that you understand my inability to make commitments I might not be able to keep. Because I love you with all my heart, I feel I can ask this one thing of you.

Please, take care of yourself. I remain your loving grandson.

Riley

Riley read the letter over once and then once again. It was the best he could do. He rummaged in his desk for an envelope and stamp. He found only the stamp. He could have sworn he had a whole package of envelopes. Cole must have borrowed them.

Even though they often borrowed from each other, Riley didn't like the thought of going through Cole's desk. Still, he wouldn't feel he'd done his duty where his grandfather was concerned until the letter was on its way. The desire to get the letter downstairs on the hall table for the mailman outweighed his reluctance.

When he opened the door to Cole's room, his jaw dropped. His first thought was that Jonquil had quit. His second thought brought a grin to his face. Cole must have had an orgy. The room reeked of stale liquor, staler sweat, and cigarette smoke. He grinned at the brigade of Southern Comfort and Wild Turkey bottles on the dresser. He thought he could smell stale pot. As a rule, Cole didn't go for marijuana, and neither did he, so that left his guest, whoever she was. He picked his way carefully over discarded sneakers, dirty dishes, and soiled underwear.

Cole's rolltop desk was a mess of papers—some business,

{198}

some personal. There was an assortment of unopened mail. Cole's checkbook, a solar calculator, and his wallet lay among the papers. Riley's shoulders knotted. Cole wouldn't leave without his wallet and checkbook. His eyes swept the room again. No, not an orgy. Trouble.

He reached for the phone then quickly replaced the receiver. Whatever trouble Cole was in, it had nothing to do with him. So that made it personal. And none of his business. He'd come here for an envelope. He'd find it and leave, closing the door behind him. If Cole wanted to talk to him, he'd be just down the hall.

With the envelope in his hand, he closed the desk drawer. In his haste to leave Cole's room he brushed against the pile of papers stacked haphazardly on the desk. They scattered in every direction. He debated a moment as to whether he should pick them up. Cole would never notice with the other mess in the room. But he'd done it, so he'd pick it up. That's when he noticed the red-and-blue-striped envelope and the return address. A letter to Cole from his grandfather. Never in a million years would he invade Cole's privacy. Not till now. The familiar envelope and what it might say taunted him until he opened it. He read it, his eyes narrowing. He replaced it calmly. Then he saw the other letter, crumpled and smoothed out and tossed on the desk. As long as he was spying, he might as well see what it was. The writing was Lacey's.

The envelope that he'd come for lay forgotten on the desk when he slammed his way out of the room. He'd used such force on the door that the lamp on the night table jiggled precariously and then toppled to the floor.

The bastard! Low-down, sneaking son of a bitch!

He paced, he stomped, he cursed. His friend. His cousin. His compadre. Bullshit!

It was ten minutes after three when the headlights of the Porsche shot through Riley's darkened bedroom. He took a deep breath and waited. He listened to Cole's footsteps in the kitchen, directly under his room. The refrigerator door opened. He'd swig half a beer or soda and leave the can in the sink. He was walking through the house now, turning off the lights as he went. That meant he wasn't drunk. No sound on the stairs, then a sound—the ninth step. They'd been aware of it since they were seventeen and creeping in past their curfew.

He was walking down the hall. One, two, three, four. Riley snapped on a light just as Cole reached his door.

"Hey, I thought you'd be asleep by now. Sorry there was no welcoming committee for you. How'd things go?"

"Just the way I expected. The leases mean zip."

A prickle of apprehension made Cole ask, "What the hell are you doing sitting here like this? Did something happen?"

Riley got up from the chair. "I was going to ask you that same question."

"Why—oh, you mean because I'm coming in so late in the middle of the week? I was at Adam's, and time got away from us. We were talking about Jeff and what he was doing wrong and right. Riley, I—" He saw the blow coming at the same moment he realized Riley knew about Lacey. He took it full face, staggering backward.

"You son of a bitch!" Riley hissed. "You waited till I was away and then you moved right in." His fist shot out a second time, landing high on Cole's left cheekbone. Blood spurted from the gash. "Go ahead, tell me some lies, tell me you didn't bring Lacey here, you slimy bastard."

Cole tasted blood, and his front teeth felt loose. "You don't understand, it wasn't what you—" He saw the kick coming, tried to move, but it caught him in the groin. He doubled over as Riley's foot shot out a second time, getting him in the side of the head. Cole fell over, the breath knocked out of him, as he waited for the kick to the ribs he knew was coming. The pain shot through his entire body. He barely felt the kick to his shoulder and the side of his neck. Riley reached down and clutched Cole's suit jacket in both of his hands as he heaved him to his feet. Cole watched through half-closed eyes as Riley drew his fist backward.

"You don't look so bad, you bastard. A broken nose and another black eye won't hurt you. I could smash those front teeth of yours without trying."

"Then do it—why don't you kill me while you're at it!" Cole shouted.

"Because I'd go to jail, and you aren't worth it." He steadied Cole on his wobbling feet and let his fist smash into Cole's face. He laughed when he heard the crunch of Cole's nose breaking. The open gash and rapidly swelling eye made him laugh harder. "You and I are finished, Cole. You ever come near me or speak to me again, and I'll kill you. You got that?"

Cole could barely see, and he knew he was going to black out any second. He tried to stand and couldn't. He reached for Riley's desk chair to pull himself erect. Wave after wave of dizziness washed over him. He knew he had broken ribs. He fought to get the words past his swollen tongue and the blood in his mouth. "Yeah," he gasped, "I got it. But the next time, if there is one, I'll kill you. *You* got *that*?"

"You and what army?" Riley sneered. He reached for Cole's arm and dragged him into the hallway. "Get the fucking hell out of my room and don't ever come back." He shoved him with his hands and then raised his leg to kick him in the small of the back. Cole literally flew down the hallway. He couldn't capture any balance and he tumbled down the stairs.

Riley stood at the top of the railing, a bitter, hateful look on his face. "If you think I'm going to call an ambulance, think again. You can lie there and die for all I care."

Cole wondered if he would die. He'd never been in so much pain. He could barely see, and his face felt three times its normal size. He couldn't walk, that much he knew. He'd have to crawl. He left a trail of blood and curses as he made his way to the kitchen and out to the courtyard. His trousers were in shreds, his hands raw and bleeding, his jacket hanging on strips along his arms. It took him four tries before he could open the door of the Porsche, and another five tries before he got himself into the bucket seat.

He drove like a blind man across the fields, going by instinct more than sight until he reached Jarvis land, his high beams lighting the way. When he saw the ranch, he leaned on the horn all the way in. When he saw the lights spread all over the house, he let go and took his foot off the gas pedal and the clutch at the same time. He fell across the horn.

It seemed like hours before he heard Adam's shout. "Jeff, help me!" He felt two pairs of arms carrying him.

"What the hell happened?" Adam shouted in the bright light of the kitchen. "What's the other guy look like? Who did this, Cole? You're in pretty bad shape. I'm taking you to the hospital!"

"No! You can fix me up. Tape my ribs. Don't worry about my nose, it's been broken before."

"Your face needs stitches. Can you see?"

"I can see your ugly face; what more do you want?" Cole shot back.

"Jeff, go upstairs and get the medicine kit." The boy's eyes were wide with awe. The look on Adam's face and his tone of voice made him run up the stairs. Any guy who could take a beating like that and then make it here in one piece had to be okay. He'd give anything to see the other guy. He was breathing hard with excitement when he returned to the kitchen in time to hear Adam say, "Riley did this? I can't wait to hear what you did to him."

"Nothing. I didn't lay a finger on him. I just took it. I deserved it. Will you tape my goddamn ribs and stop asking questions?"

"It was over some chick, right?" Jeff chirped.

"Yeah," Cole muttered.

"You let your very own cousin whip your ass like this over a fluffball? I don't believe it! Old Adam here has been telling me what superjocks you guys are, and now this?" There was disgust in the boy's face.

"How'd you feel if I'd died and someone brought you the news? Would that make me more of a man in your eyes?" Cole gasped.

The boy shuffled his feet, refusing to meet Cole's eyes.

It was sheer agony for Cole to talk, but he had the feeling that something good could come of this beating if he said just one thing that got through to the kid. "I took this beating because I did something wrong. I committed the cardinal sin of betrayal. I deserve every broken bone, every bruise, and every scar I'm left with. Go to bed and think about it."

The look of uncertainty on the boy's face made Adam squeeze his shoulder. He'd understood. Jeff muttered a good night and left the room. Cole saw him turn to look over his shoulder. He gave a halfhearted wave that Cole tried to return.

"Thanks," Adam said quietly.

"Your reward for patching me up."

"He could have killed you, you know."

Cole tried to laugh, but it hurt too much. "He said he didn't want to go to jail, or he would have. He kicked me down the stairs and said he wasn't calling the ambulance."

"Jesus!"

"Adam, swear to me this won't affect your friendship with Riley."

"Sure. Look, this is the best I can do. I'll put some ice on your face, and I think you better sleep on the couch. I'll snooze on the chair—you know, sort of baby-sit you." He thought Cole would protest, but he didn't.

While Adam was ministering to Cole, Riley was standing under a freezing cold shower. He'd almost killed his cousin. He should be feeling something—satisfaction or remorse—at the brutal beating, but he just felt numb. He knew he had the capability to kill if he had to. Cole was no lightweight himself. In a match, with the odds even, it would be tough to see who came out numero uno. Not that he gave a damn either way now.

In bed, knowing there would be no sleep, Riley wondered what it was Cole had tried to tell him. He knew, no matter what the reason, if someone had attacked him the way he'd attacked Cole, he would have fought back. He winced. His Japanese thinking told him Cole was the better man for suffering the beating, justified or not. He ran the fight through his mind again and again. Physically he'd been beating Cole, but mentally it was himself he was whipping.

It was over and done with. Behind him now, like so many other things in his life. He had to move forward and not dwell in the past. If only he could find a magical way to do that, he'd have it made. No shortcuts, no miracle cures. You paid your dues and took your chances.

He slept fitfully, dreaming he was being buried alive, by Cole, with cherry blossoms. Everyone was laughing happily at his burial. Cole was the only one who wasn't laughing.

}}}}}}}} CHAPTER TEN }}}}}}}}

Julie played a game with herself. The same game she'd been playing every day since the answering machine from Cary was delivered. When she got home from work, she wouldn't allow herself to look in the direction of the living room table where the machine was hooked up to see whether or not the red light was winking. She prolonged the moment of discovery by hanging up her coat, going through the mail, then shedding her work clothes in favor of sweats and slippers. Next she'd walk to the kitchen with her eyes closed, more or less feeling her way. The Mr. Coffee was plugged in, coffee measured. Two cups. The half-and-half and the mug that said she was "Born to Shop" were at the ready. In the beginning she'd been able to measure the actual drips and count the seconds until the water gurgled into a steady stream.

Today she miscalculated by one drip. The last one sizzled on the hot metal. Her coffee ready, she walked slowly to the living room. She set it carefully on a Budweiser coaster on the coffee table.

Now she could look. The tiny red light blinked invitingly. Somehow she'd known there would be a call today. Cary had been calling every Tuesday and Thursday, never when she was home, but in the middle of the day. He always gave the time before he hung up. Either he didn't trust himself to talk to her or he couldn't call in the evening because Amelia was home. She wondered, not for the first time, how he accounted for the calls when the telephone bill arrived. Maybe he called from a phone booth.

The first time she'd come home after the machine was hooked up, she'd almost fainted when she saw the red light. That time it had been a carpet-cleaning service saying they would call back at a more convenient time. So far they hadn't.

She liked the messages. She looked forward to them. She was starting to live for them, for God's sake. By three o'clock she'd have herself in a tizzy of excitement that today there would be a call. She was thirty-nine years old and mentally sick, she told herself.

Her heart thumped wildly while she rewound the message tape. Cary's voice came off crisp and clear, just like the others she'd transferred to a small recorder she kept by her bed. Late at night she played the messages back. By now she had quite a collection. She always had a smile on her face when she fell asleep.

"This is Cary Assante from Austin, Texas, calling." The warm chuckle in the voice always made Julie smile. "I was going to recite a poem for you today, but when I rehearsed it, I felt rather silly. It wasn't my poem to begin with, but something I read in the *Miranda Evening News*. They have this page devoted to what they call the Poet's Corner. Just so you won't be disappointed, here's this little old ditty. Roses are red. Violets are blue. Guess who is missing you? I do miss you, Julie. I think of you more often than I should. That has to mean something. I've been dreaming of you these past few days. That has to mean something, too. There are times when I wish I could walk around a corner and bump into you. I'd scoop you up and whirl you around, all the while saying Julie, Julie, Julie in my best Cary Grant voice. We'd link arms and head to some dimly lit lounge, where we'd sip wine and talk for hours.

"Amelia senses something is wrong. I can feel it in her attitude toward me. I've been toying with the idea of talking to her about the feelings I seem to have for you. I think she'd understand—or she'd *try* to understand. I probably never will say anything though. I never thought of myself as a coward, but I guess I am. I cannot hurt Amelia, but by not hurting Amelia, I am hurting myself, and you, too. It's five forty-five. You'll be home from work soon. I'll think about you listening to this message. I wish I could see you, Julie. I wish that more than anything in the world."

The machine whirred and then stopped. Julie turned it off. The abrupt silence in the room made her blink.

Right now, this very second, he was probably thinking of her. He wanted to see her more than anything in the world. The only thing stopping him was Amelia. Amelia stood between them. For one split second Julie wished Amelia were dead. "No. I didn't mean that. Please, God, I didn't mean that. There's something wrong with me. I would never wish death on anyone. Forgive me. I didn't mean it." What was happening to her?

She'd never written that intended thank you note to Amelia and Cary. Tonight she would do it if it killed her. After she listened to the tape ten more times.

It occurred to her suddenly that she could leave a message for Cary on the machine. Something simple. But if she did that, she would be perpetuating whatever this was between Cary and herself. She could also turn off the machine. Unplug it. Pack it in the box it came in and put it on a shelf in the closet. She could throw it away so she wouldn't be tempted to hook it up again.

She wished she had a close friend, a real confidante. Someone who would listen objectively and not judge or condemn.

Julie beat her fists into the soft pillows on the sofa. Amelia was a kind, warm, wonderful person. "I adore you, Amelia, but I think I'm falling in love with your husband." She beat at the tangerine pillows till she was exhausted. She didn't feel any better. She felt worse.

Julie sat up in bed watching the tail end of the eleven o'clock news. She pressed the remote control, and the newscaster was cut off in midsentence. She grimaced. She didn't like men who blow-dried their hair. She also wondered what shade of tint he used.

The notepad was propped up on a thick magazine resting on her knees. Whatever came off the top of her head was going to be it. She'd procrastinated long enough. When she was finished, she read it back to herself. Then she read it back aloud. She sniffed. It would have to do.

Dear Amelia and Cary,
Please excuse my tardiness in not sending this note sooner.

I want you to know I will treasure the bracelet. I wear it every day and have received many compliments. I truly appreciate your thoughtfulness.

It was more than kind of you, Amelia, to arrange for the birthday cake at the Lion's Rock. It has been many years since I had a real birthday cake, complete with candles.

I hope you and Cary are both well and not suffering from the flu, like most of us New Yorkers. My office was virtually empty last week. I'm keeping my fingers crossed it doesn't strike me down.

I'm looking forward to seeing both of you should you come to New York, as Cary indicated you might.

Affectionately,
Julie

What she should do now was drop a note to Thad and Billie. Or she could take the Eastern shuttle after work tomorrow and pop in for one of her surprise visits. She knew she'd be welcome. She could spend the night and catch the first shuttle back in the morning and still be in time for work.

She needed to talk to someone, another woman. Who better than Billie. Billie would understand. Billie was never judgmental. Is that what you want, understanding, or are you hoping for approval? a niggling voice asked.

"Both," Julie whispered.

"Surprise! Surprise!" Julie cried when Billie opened the door the following evening.

"Julie! How wonderful to see you! Come in, it's cold out there. Is anything wrong?" she asked anxiously.

"Nothing's wrong. I came down because . . . I miss you. I guess I've been a little lonely. I need a little mothering, or comforting . . . or something. I hope you don't mind."

"Mind? Of course not. Will you be staying over?"

Julie nodded. "I thought I'd take the early shuttle in the morning. Is Uncle Thad home?"

Billie made a face. "No. He usually comes in around nine. If he wants an early evening, he has to plan weeks in advance. I can't wait till he leaves office. I really miss the farm. I miss Vermont, and the dogs."

"I know what you mean. I never thought I'd miss home, but I do. More and more I'm thinking about going back."

Billie sensed distress in Julie's voice. "Dinner, Julie? I baked a chicken earlier. I have a great salad and some angel food cake. I don't normally wait for Thad, so if you'll join me . . ."

"I'd love it."

As Billie puttered around the kitchen setting the table and adding dressing to the salad, she kept up a running conversation to try and ease Julie's tenseness. "Are you settled in? How's New York?"

"I'm settled in, but as I told you, I've been thinking about going back home. I like the city and I like my job, but . . ."

"It's all still new to you. Give the city a chance. You'll make friends, and New York is such a wonderful city; there's so much to do every hour of the day."

"It's not lack of friends. I guess it's me. I'm strictly a small-town girl. Did you hear what I just said? Girl! I'm a middle-aged woman now. Men don't . . . they want young . . . you know . . ." she said lamely.

"Julie, don't sell yourself short. There's somebody out there, he just hasn't found you yet."

Julie shrugged. "You might be right, but I doubt it. What

do you think?" she said, pulling her hair aside to reveal the earrings Billie had sent for her birthday.

"They're lovely. Maggie told me onyx is very fashionable these days. Do you really like them?"

"Aunt Billie, I love them. I can't tell you how many compliments I received. It was very thoughtful of you. You shouldn't have, but I'm glad you did."

The bracelet was new, Billie thought. At least, she'd never seen Julie wear it before. Julie kept pushing it up and down her arm as though she wanted to take it off or it was bothering her. Billie forced a laugh. "I always say that, too. How was your birthday? Did you celebrate, or are you at the stage where you'd rather forget it, like me?"

Julie took a deep breath. "I met Cary Assante in a deli one day and he invited me out to dinner to celebrate. It was very nice. We had a wonderful dinner at his and Amelia's favorite restaurant. They . . . they gave me a lovely gold . . . this gold bracelet, and Amelia ordered a cake with a candle. I felt a little embarrassed, but Cary said it was okay, everyone should have a birthday cake. He's a very nice man, and I enjoyed myself." Lord, was that exultant voice hers? She sighed deeply.

Billie hadn't heard Julie sound so elated in years. Usually she was serene and low-key. This new Julie positively bubbled. She couldn't help wondering why.

"Billie, you aren't saying anything. Did I say something wrong?"

"No, Julie, nothing's wrong." Billie had the feeling Julie was about to confide in her. She swallowed hard, knowing what was coming, dreading it.

"Aunt Billie, I . . . I need to talk to someone. I'm finding myself very attracted to Cary, and he to me. I adore Amelia and . . . I need . . . I want . . ." She went on to tell Billie about the answering machine and the game she played with it. "One part of me realizes the danger, the other part of me . . . I don't seem to have any control over my emotions. I could fall in love with Cary so . . . so easily. I don't . . . I never believed in that romantic nonsense that you . . . you can fall in love . . . like . . ." She snapped her fingers. "I never felt this way before. I've had affairs, relationships, whatever you want to call them. I'm not a kid. He sort of swooped into my life, and I reached out. . . . I don't know how else to explain it," Julie said lamely.

Billie sat down across from Julie. "Yes, honey, Cary is a kind, wonderful person and he's married to a kind, wonderful woman. The good ones are always taken," she said ruefully. "I have to ask you something." She paused and looked straight into Julie's eyes. "Do you just want to talk or do you want advice?"

"I don't know. I think I just want to talk. I can give myself the same advice you would give me. You're disappointed in me, aren't you?"

"Please don't think that, Julie. I know how these things can happen. It happened to me once, so I can speak from experience. So many things can go wrong, people who don't deserve to be hurt can be devastated. You have to be prepared to live with . . . whatever you choose to do."

Julie's voice took on a defensive tone. "I know all that. I've done nothing but think about . . . about Cary and Amelia, and myself, since I bumped into him. By accident, Aunt Billie. I had no control over that meeting, nor did Cary. It was like it was . . . meant to be." Her voice was taking on a stubborn note now, and Billie winced. "What about me, Aunt Billie? What about me. I'm thirty-nine years old. I finally met someone . . . someone I'm comfortable with, someone I want to see and talk to again. Why should I have to give that up? My eyes are open. I seriously doubt if I'll ever find myself in Amelia Assante's company again. How Cary handles it will be up to Cary. I have wants, I have needs. . . . Damn it, Aunt Billie, it isn't fair."

Billie chose her words carefully. "I'm a little older than you, honey, not necessarily wiser, but I've found over the years that there is very little in life that's fair. The fair part is inside each of us. Each of us has to deal with it in our own way. This isn't advice, Julie, more a statement of fact, again from my own experience. I don't think you can find happiness at someone else's expense, knowingly or unknowingly."

Julie nodded. "I appreciate your talking to me. I don't feel that I can make any promises to you or to myself, but I will give it a lot of thought."

Billie's heart settled down to its natural rhythm. Julie's promise was more than she hoped for, but it was far from reassuring. She got up to prepare the dessert plates, turning her back to hide her face from Julie. She was very worried . . . for Amelia, but it wouldn't do to show it.

Both women were still at the table when Thad walked in at

nine-thirty. He hugged and kissed Julie, catching Billie's slight nod. He grabbed a chicken leg and excused himself, saying he had a stack of paperwork that needed his immediate attention.

When the kitchen was restored to tidiness, Julie begged tiredness and a need for a warm, soothing bath.

Instead of joining Thad, Billie turned the television on and turned down the volume. She watched the silent screen, but her thoughts were elsewhere. Julie . . . Amelia . . . Cary. Lord, why did these things have to happen to the people she cared about most? In the end, Julie and Cary would do whatever they felt they had to do. Amelia would do whatever was best for Cary.

Amelia walked in the door a little after five. She tossed her warm wool hat in the direction of the coat rack. Her coat found a home on the high-backed chair in the living room. Her left shoe sailed toward the fireplace, the right toward the dining room. Her gloves, bag, and scarf ended up on the coffee table.

There was something different about the apartment, and it wasn't the fresh flowers on the coffee table. The air didn't seem so oppressive.

"Darling, I'm home!" Amelia called.

"I hear you," Cary sang out from the kitchen. "Sit down, put your feet up, and your tea will be served by the man of the house."

Amelia's tired eyes opened wide. She hoped she didn't look suspicious when Cary set the tea tray down and poured. "Two lumps," he said, dropping the little cubes into the cup with a flourish.

"I thought we'd go out to dinner this evening. In fact, I made reservations at Andre's for seven o'clock. We'll only be gone two hours. I think both of us could use a night out. I'm starting to get cabin fever."

"You've got yourself a date." She didn't know what had happened to lighten her husband's mood, but whatever it was, she hoped it could be packaged and bought. She'd order a carload.

"How was your day?" Cary asked. He sounded as if he really wanted to know. She told him. He listened raptly. When she was finished, he smiled. "I'm so proud of you, Amelia. There aren't many people who would take on the challenge you've accepted. I wish there was something I could do to help you. I know, you want to do it yourself, and I applaud that. But I don't want you tiring yourself out and have your health suffer. There must be something I can do. Lick envelopes, stuff them, take them to the post office box, whatever?"

"I'm not running for office, Cary. Believe me, if there was something you could do, I'd shackle you to my left wrist. I'm not tiring myself. This is the best thing for me right now. Are you going to come with me when I go to Washington to say my bit?"

"Babe, I'll be with you every step of the way. I bet you'll even make the news. What's the date?"

"March first." If she hadn't been staring directly at her husband with such a loving gaze, she would have missed the almost imperceptible change in his expression.

"That's not tough at all. We can take a flight the night before so we're both fresh, and take the first plane back when you finish."

"That's not what I had planned at all, Cary. Now is when I can get away. I thought we could do Washington while we're there. As in "do." Billie and Thad will want us to stay for a few days. I was thinking more like a week. Togetherness." She leered.

"A week, huh? Fine with me."

"Are you sure? You don't have anything planned, do you?"

"If I did, I'd cancel it—this is more important," Cary said with forced heartiness.

"Then it's settled. Who gets the shower? You go first, because you hate it when I steam it up. I'll look through the mail. Don't take all day, either. I'm hungry. In fact, I'm starved."

"Me, too. Five minutes."

Amelia's heart raced. A whole week in Washington with Cary and her two favorite people in the world, Billie and Thad. She sighed happily. Sometimes things just worked out right. All you needed was a basket full of patience.

She picked through the mail. Bills, advertisements, a postcard from South America. Amelia smiled. Riley had been back for weeks now.

The small, pale green envelope was caught between an invitation to a black-tie dinner and a letter from the utility company. Amelia held the small square of paper between her fingers as if it were laced with germs. She read it three times.

She sat down with a thump on the padded desk chair. Now she understood. Good lord, could one small scrap of paper make such a difference? Of course it could. It had. Amelia's shoulders slumped. With every ounce of strength she could muster, she forced them back. "All this is is a thank you note from a very nice person. Leave it at that," she muttered to herself when she heard Cary close the shower door.

These days she didn't undress in the bedroom and pad naked into the bathroom the way she used to. Now she carried her clothes into the bathroom, disrobed, and dressed with the door not only closed but locked. The loose folds of skin and the bypass scar were for her eyes only.

In the restaurant Amelia pushed her food around on the plate. Cary ate like a truck driver. "I thought you said you were starved," he said.

"I was then. I had a rather big lunch. But I have eaten two pieces of Andre's magnificent bread and the salad. I always do that and then can't do justice to the dinner."

"This is wonderful," Cary said, motioning to the mess on his plate. For the life of her, she couldn't remember what her husband had ordered. Some kind of fish in a sticky white sauce. She couldn't even remember what *she* ordered. Some kind of chicken. It was buried in a plum sauce that puckered her mouth.

This was the first time she could remember thinking that she and Cary resembled the other diners in the restaurant. You could always tell the married couples. They ate, they drank, and there was little or no conversation between them—until the check arrived and the little woman wanted to know how much her husband spent on her. Lovers, on the other hand, could be drinking Ripple wine and chewing on pickled crab-grass and not know the difference. Quiet whispers and eye contact were the order of the day.

Cary leaned back in his chair. "That was one good dinner. I get points for finishing it all," he said boyishly.

"You certainly do. Are we having dessert?"

"I don't know about you, but I am. That flaming apricot thing Andre is famous for. And let's have some more wine, babe."

Babe. His favorite name for her. Amelia smiled. She remembered the days when he used to refer to her as his broad. She loved it.

Cary gave their order to the waiter. His spirits were high.

"Did you see the note Julie sent us? That was nice of her, don't you think?"

Nobody's voice should sound this happy. Amelia wanted to stretch across the table and slap him. She nodded. "Julie is a very nice person," she said sincerely.

"I know. I couldn't get over how easy she is to talk with. She's fun, too. Wonderful sense of humor. She can even laugh at herself. Most women today are too uptight with trying to get to the top. I think Julie has found her niche and she's happy. She said she likes New York, but at times it intimidates her. I told her you loved it. She thinks the world of you, babe."

"And I of her. She is Thad's niece, so what do we expect?" *Shut up, Cary. Leave it alone. Don't say any more. I can't bear it. You should hear your voice. You sound like you're seventeen and in love.*

"She talked about you a lot. She said you had the most exquisite clothes and knew how to wear them. She admires your dedication. It's hard to believe she's thirty-nine. You could take her for thirty or so, don't you think?" Cary asked, oblivious to the look of pain on his wife's face.

"Yes, thirty or so. I quite agree. Oh, look, here's dessert, flame and all."

"Julie would like this. She's like a kid when she sees something unexpected or something she hasn't had before. Do you know she has this videotape of a cartoon called *Puff the Magic Dragon*? She plays it when she needs a lift. Isn't that amazing?"

Amelia ground her teeth. A lift indeed. But there was no way she was going to fight this. No way at all. *I wish you could hear yourself, Cary.* "I don't think it's amazing at all. I think it's very astute of Julie to know what will relax her, even if it is a silly cartoon."

Cary stopped with the spoon halfway to his mouth. "Why do you say it's silly?"

"Aren't cartoons supposed to be silly? Aren't they supposed to make you laugh? That's why they're silly."

"I thought you were mocking Julie," Cary said quietly.

"Now that you know I wasn't, don't you feel better? It pays to talk about these little things so they don't get blown out of proportion," Amelia said sweetly.

{ 213 }

"You're right, babe. Someday I'm going to learn not to question you. You're always right."

Amelia forced a laugh. "Not always. But most of the time."

"You aren't eating this dessert. You could use a little extra meat on your bones, babe. Come on, this is delicious."

Amelia dug her spoon into the thick apricot sauce. Extra meat on her bones. Like well-padded Julie. Ample Julie. Chubby Julie. Hippy Julie. Julie with the genuine freckles. Julie with the wonderful sense of humor. Julie with the laughing eyes. Wasn't there a song about laughing eyes? Frank Sinatra sang it—when Cary was still in diapers. Amelia hated herself for her thoughts.

She finished her dessert.

It took a full two weeks before Cole could pass for his normal self. The day after the beating, Adam insisted on driving him to the hospital to have his face stitched and his nose set. The intern complimented Adam on his taping job, but Cole's ribs healed slowly. The only visible signs of the beating were a few black and blue marks on his cheeks. He covered them with a bronzing gel.

He hadn't been back to Sunbridge till this evening. And now he'd only come back to get his clothes. The past week had been absolute torture for him as he tried to figure ways to avoid Riley without being obvious about it.

He was on his third drink, trying to gather courage for one last try at explaining to Riley. Two weeks to calm down should be enough, even for Riley, he thought. He'd calmed down a lot himself. At first he had argued with Adam, saying Riley wouldn't listen, and why should he subject himself to another attack? Adam, of course, had the perfect reply. "You have to take a shot at it so you'll know you tried. If Riley doesn't want to listen, then it's his problem, not yours. Do it for yourself, Cole."

Cole burst into Riley's room near midnight. The three shots of bourbon straight up had given him the courage to do what Adam suggested.

"Whatever it is you're doing, stop it! I want to talk to you, Riley. Man to man. We aren't kids anymore. You're going to listen to me if it's the last thing either of us does."

Riley turned from his position at the desk, where he'd been

trying to write a letter to his grandfather. Even this unwelcome intrusion would get him off the hook for a few minutes. "It's all been said. Don't make me change the custom here at Sunbridge by having to lock my door."

"You never used to be so damn pigheaded. Okay, it was wrong. Jesus, she came into my bed in the middle of the night. At first I thought I was dreaming. When I realized it was no dream, it was too late. All this hatred you're directing at me isn't justified. I wanted to tell you myself, and I think I would have if there had been time. It was wrong; I know it was wrong. I wish I could take it back, go back in time and erase it, but I can't. I told Lacey there could never be anything between us. That's why she left. Jesus, don't you understand? She didn't *love* you. She was using you! You can't make someone love you. She, at least, understands that. Why can't you?"

"Get the hell out of here, Cole. I don't want anything from you. Ever."

"I'm not giving you anything. I'm not even offering anything. All I'm trying to do is explain. It's that old rivalry between us, isn't it? I let it go; why can't you? Lacey is off in New York, probably having a goddamn blast, and she's set us against each other. She's a bitch. She set me up, and there's nothing I can do about it."

"Save your breath. I have all the explanations I need or want. Get out of here before I toss you out."

"This is going to affect our working relationship. You're going to avoid me every chance you get. I'm going to be walking on eggs, afraid I'll say the wrong thing. Get off it, Riley. This is kid stuff."

"Is it kid stuff to go behind my back and tell my grandfather lies? Who gave you permission to write to him, to worm your way into his life? Answer me, you son of a bitch! All the old one does in his letters is talk about what a fine young man you are and how lucky I am that we're of the same blood. Ah, you thought I didn't know. Well, you see, I know everything. Not only are you a thief, but you're also a sneak, too. If I never have to talk to you again, it will be fine with me."

"The only lies I ever told your grandfather, I told to cushion his hurt over you. I told him you were away, out of town, all kinds of things so he would think you were working round the clock. I did it for you, you asshole. That old man doesn't deserve the treatment you're giving him. He's not good enough for you anymore, is he? You want to be here with all the rich, big-time Colemans. You like it here. You like it that Grandmam Billie turned things over to you. You like being a big honcho. Admit it, Riley. You don't give two shits about that old man and what he's built. It was all for you, and you spit on it and on him. You have no intention of ever going back to Japan—I see it in your eyes. You talk a good story, but you don't have the guts to do anything about it. I'm sorry I came in here. I hope you do decide to stay here because, by God, you *are* a Coleman. They deserve you."

"Shut up, Cole. Leave my family out of this."

"Which family, Riley? The Colemans or your other family, the one you turned your back on? That family? You're a piss-poor excuse for a grandson. Don't get up. Save the fancy footwork for some other time. If I tangle with you again, one of us will end up dead."

"Fuck you!" Riley shouted.

Cole turned at the door. "I won't come back here. I'm moving into the condo tomorrow morning. Sunbridge is yours, old buddy. Lock, stock, and barrel. When my mother put the deed in both our names, I didn't want it then. I don't want it now. As of tomorrow, it's all yours."

"I don't want anything from you," Riley bellowed.

"Tough." Cole laughed. "It's yours, like it or not."

Riley sat at the desk for a long time. He made no effort to stem the flow of tears running down his cheeks. He crumpled the letter he'd been writing into a ball. He shot it with his thumb and index finger the way he'd shot marbles when he was little. The paper teetered on the edge of the wicker basket, then fell in. He did the same thing with his grandfather's letter.

It was time to make a decision.

The first thing Rand did when he arrived at Heathrow Airport was call to his solicitor to tell him he was on his way.

He whizzed through customs and hailed a cab. It was a typical London day—raw and cold. Rand shivered inside his heavy overcoat, wishing he were back in Hawaii, on the beach with Maggie.

Hiram Laskey was older than Methuselah, Rand thought, but his age in no way affected his brain or his keen eyesight. "You look like you have a problem, Rand," he said in a trembling voice. "How can I be of help?"

"I'll be wanting to make a few changes in my . . . a few changes," Rand hedged. Now that he was here, he was sorry he'd come. He should have made his inquiries first and then come to the solicitor. This man would immediately think, as he had, that it was all a scam. Then again, maybe Hiram wasn't the kind of man who would understand. If only he weren't so ancient-looking. The thin, bald head and straggly beard, with traces of tomato soup, irritated Rand. So did the spots on his tie. He was wearing the same tired old suit Rand remembered from years ago. Clearly, Hiram didn't spend his money on clothing or a barber.

Hiram's voice was gentle, all traces of trembling gone. "Perhaps you might be more comfortable discussing . . . whatever it is you're having second thoughts about with one of the younger men. No offense will be taken, I assure you. As a matter of fact, I insist." He pretended to think while he steepled his fingers. "Arthur Mittington should do nicely. He's at the end of the corridor. Tell him I sent you. You'll get on well."

Rand felt ashamed. Nothing was working out right these days. The old man was right, though; he needed to talk to someone he could relate to.

"It was nice seeing you again, Hiram."

The trembling was back in Hiram's voice. "You won't think it's so nice when you get our bill. And to answer your unasked question, I am ninety-one years old. I will still be practicing when I'm a hundred. I can tell you this now that I've placed you in Arthur's capable hands. You are not, under any circumstances, to tell Arthur how old I am. They keep a running pool going."

The old man's handshake was almost as firm as Rand's.

Arthur Mittington looked like a rugby player. He was forty or so, Rand judged, and carried himself well. He came around from his desk, his hand outstretched. His herringbone suit pleased Rand. Carnaby Street, he suspected.

Arthur listened attentively while Rand talked. When Rand threw up his hands and said, "That's it," he smiled.

"I understand exactly how you feel. I also think you're right in wanting to do all the checking yourself. If we hire on, it might confuse matters. You are the interested party, so to speak. You'll see firsthand and be able to observe everyone. Private investigators tend to be impersonal, and I don't think that's what you want. Might I ask what your intentions are if everything is proved right?"

"I haven't gotten that far. I've never been a father before."

Arthur laughed. "I have, and I can tell you it's no picnic. I will also tell you that out of my four nippers, there isn't one I wouldn't die for. Just knowing you have flesh and blood walking around makes all the difference in the world. You won't necessarily have that feeling, but I am sure if Miss Brighton proves to be your daughter, you will do whatever it is you feel right about. If I can be of any help, call me. I'll jot down my home phone number. Don't be embarrassed to call me at home, even if it's just to talk. Don't you Americans refer to it as unloading?"

"I guess we do."

He'd just used up two hours and hadn't accomplished a thing. But the possibility of a new friend shouldn't be taken lightly, he cautioned himself.

The taxi dropped him off at the Dorchester. He registered, carried his own bag to the lift, and went to his room. He was tired. A shower, some dinner from room service, and a couple of whiskies would be all he needed to sleep. Tomorrow morning would be soon enough to do what he had to do.

The taxi Rand had hired for the day swooshed to a stop in front of the orphanage that had housed Chesney all her young life. It was a dismal place, all gray stone with tiny windows.

He couldn't begin to imagine what a child's feelings would be when brought to this old, forbidding fortress. Chesney had lived here. His heart felt sore and bruised. How would he ever be able to make up for this?

The inside of the building wasn't much better. It was cold and damp. All the women bustling about wore heavy wool jumpers and thick sweaters. No one paid any attention to him. He wandered down the long hallway looking into austere rooms, most of them offices of some kind. He wondered how many homeless, unwanted children lived here. Hundreds probably.

The hallway branched off to the left and right. Rand chose the right. Classrooms. He peered into one through a small pane of glass. Twenty or so children, he surmised. Age five or thereabouts. So small to be so alone. All were dressed alike. He frowned. Did they dress the children this way on purpose so they would lose their identity? Were they numbers on a chart? Did they have real names or made-up ones? He wished he knew. On the other hand, they might be dressed alike so that no child would think he was better than another. He shook his head. He didn't know what he was thinking. Further down the hall he peered into another room. These children were older. To his eye they all looked alike, too. There were no blue jeans and sneakers here. He stood for a long time observing the class. Not one face showed any kind of animation. There was no sparkle. This clearly was not a place of sunshine. How these children would love Hawaii. Perpetual sunshine. Laughter and warmth. He felt sick.

How was it possible that warm-eyed Chesney with the gentle smile was a product of this place? If he'd lived here for eighteen years and then suddenly found out who his parents were, he'd raise hell. Chesney hadn't made one demand, hadn't asked for a thing. She walked into his life and walked out. He felt sicker by the minute.

Rand continued to walk up and down the halls. He wanted to leave these dreary surroundings but couldn't bring himself to walk out. Eventually, he came to a door marked Head. He knocked and opened it at the same time.

"Can I help you?" a pleasant voice inquired.

"I've come to inquire about Chesney Brighton," he said. Rand watched as the thin woman's eyes raked over him; he read dislike in her eyes. And why not?

"Yes, Chesney," she said, her voice no longer so pleasant.

"I remember her very well. She was a wonderful child. Very obedient and never a sassy word out of her."

"What would have happened if she hadn't been obedient and she sassed you?" Rand asked quietly.

"She would have been punished, of course. We pride ourselves on deportment. Each child is made aware, early on, that the outside world is not a playground. We give the children a good education here. Each child has his or her duties, and of course, the older ones look after the younger ones. Chesney was very good with the little ones. She'd tell them stories and make them laugh. Chesney smiled a lot, but she never laughed—now, that's strange; I wonder whatever made me think of that.

"She comes back, you know. At Christmas she brought bags and bags of presents. The child must have used her entire salary for all those gifts. Chesney is one of the rare ones. Most of the others never come back, and I can't say I blame them." The woman stopped speaking and stared at Rand. "Are you the father?"

"I don't know."

"If you are, it's a little late to come calling. You were needed years ago. I don't see what good you can do now," the woman said sourly.

"I don't know either. I just found out. I don't think that will excuse me, but if I had known—"

"That's what they all say. I'm sorry if I sound bitter. You see, so many men and women come here when they get an attack of conscience. All of a sudden they realize their very own flesh and blood has been locked up here or turned loose in the world, and they're full of regret. I've told you everything I know about Chesney."

"She gave me her mother's address," Rand said. "I . . ."

"If you decide to go round to see her, do it in the daytime so you don't disturb her family. Chesney told me she wasn't happy to see her. I felt so sorry for her. They all think there's a parent out there who is just waiting for them to show up on the doorstep. They want to be hugged and told they're loved. We try to hug and love them here, but it isn't the same. They know it, and they keep on hoping."

"Thank you for talking to me. I didn't get your name."

"Ardeth Wilkes. It doesn't matter if you know my name or not. You won't ever be coming back here."

"Good-bye, Mrs. Wilkes."

"It's Miss Wilkes. I'm not married. This place and all these children are my family. Good day."

Rand leaned back and closed his eyes on the trip to Stepney Green. He'd never felt worse in his life. Flogging was too good for him. Right now he'd almost welcome death. He didn't want to talk to Chesney's mother.

"We're here, sport," the driver said cheerfully. "You said I was to stop at the corner, and this is the corner. I'll wait here for you."

It was a neat neighborhood. The houses were pretty much all the same, but different colors. Trees lined the sidewalks. Maggie would call it quaint. A workingman's neighborhood.

Rand swallowed hard before he knocked on the door. He felt light-headed and still a bit sick to his stomach.

Once she had been pretty. Now she looked tired and weary. Raising five children on a carpenter's salary hadn't been easy. She smiled, and Rand remembered. "I'm Rand Nelson," he said.

"I know. Come in."

"How did you know?" Rand asked. It could still be some kind of scam, he told himself, but he didn't believe the thought.

"A woman always remembers her first love. You were so dashing in your uniform. I gave the picture to Chesney. I don't know why I ever saved it. A romantic notion, I guess."

"You must have been surprised when she came to see you."

"I always knew she would someday. When I read that they passed that law, saying orphans had a right to, I knew."

"How did you feel when you saw her?"

"Awful. I wanted to take her in my arms and hold her. I wanted to tell her it would be all right, that she could come here and live with us. I couldn't do that. My husband would never understand. He'd leave me, and how would I ever take care of five children on my own? I was cool, polite. It broke my heart. I still cry when I think of it."

"You should have taken her in your arms—you should have pretended to act like a mother just that once," Rand raged.

The woman stepped back. "Just a minute. Who are you to come here and tell me what I should have or shouldn't have done? Where were you all these years? You fancy chopper pilots had your way with us girls and then left. I don't owe you or anyone else an explanation. You're lucky I'm talking to you now."

"I'm sorry. I had no right to say anything. I went to the orphanage this morning and I came away sick."

"I did the same thing the day after she came here."

"I gave you money. Why did you decide to—not to . . ."

"Have the baby? First of all, it's against God. There wasn't a doctor to be found who would do it, and I didn't want to starve. I used the money to buy a letter of transit on the black market. The Red Cross helped me get back to England. You didn't care. I remember that jaunty wave you gave me when you left. Until Chesney searched you out, you probably never thought of me once."

It was true.

"Besides, I loved you. I couldn't kill a child we created together."

"I did the best I could for her. I left little presents, not much, what I could afford, on her birthday and at Christmas. She told me she kept every single thing. On her birthday I always made a cake and told my family it was for an old aunt I haven't seen in years. It was all I could do."

"I didn't know," Rand said hoarsely.

"And if you had known, what would you have done?"

"I don't know that either," he said honestly.

"Why do I have this feeling you don't believe Chesney is your daughter?" the woman asked.

"At first I didn't believe it. I tried to remember. It seemed to me that I would have known somehow that I had a child. My wife told me only women have those instincts."

"Your wife is right. Is there something I can tell you, something that will prove to you that . . . you were the only one?"

"You don't have to prove anything. You were a virgin. You weren't the kind of young woman to . . . to go with more than one man. I knew you were in love with me, and I knew nothing would come of it. I was going off, maybe get killed. I put it completely out of my mind. I don't even know when her birthday is."

"It's September ninth."

The woman's eyes were kind. "We shared a small, intimate joke and laughed about it together. I've kept all these memories alive. Shall I tell you or will you remember on your own?

We used to talk about our childhood and some of the silly things we did."

"We talked about our pets, our friends. My cat."

"A toy cat. Sally Dearest."

Rand almost blacked out. The woman reached out to him and led him to a chair. Rand realized that they'd been standing all this time.

"You had a real cat with a real name," Rand said softly. "Whiskers."

"Yes. We are Chesney's parents, Rand—you and I. It will be up to you to do whatever has to be done. Will you agree?"

Rand didn't trust his voice. He nodded.

"And will you let me know from time to time how things are? You can address a letter to me in care of general delivery. If you're going to write, do it the first of the month so I don't have to run to the post office every day." Rand nodded again.

"Maybe she doesn't need us," he said. "She didn't ask for anything. She said she just wanted me to know she was real. That I had a daughter."

"She said the same thing to me. I don't honestly know if she does need us. It may be too late. She's an independent girl. I think you better leave now. Please, don't come back. If you need to get in touch, do it through the mail."

"I am so sorry," Rand said.

"I am too. It's up to you to turn it around and make it right, if you can. Good-bye, Rand."

Back in the hotel Rand sat with his head in his hands. His head ached from thinking. So many things to make up for. Could he handle it? With Maggie's help he could. On his own he wasn't sure.

Rand picked up the phone and called Arthur Mittington. They exchanged greetings. "Until I tell you to stop, I want you to send a check for five hundred pounds the first of every month to Chesney's mother. In care of general delivery. I don't know if it's wise or unwise on my part. I just know I want to do it."

"Then consider it done. Shall I enclose a letter?"

"Just the first time. After that just send the check."

"Should I offer you my congratulations?"

"I feel like I've been shell-shocked."

Arthur laughed. "That's exactly the way I felt when we had our first child. It wears off the fourth time around."

"I never much cared for children," Rand confided.

"Not much you can do about it now. I regard them as a blessing of God. Try thinking along those lines. If I can help in any way, give me a call."

"I will."

Sawyer sat in the warm, sunny breakfast nook with her grandmother. She'd flown to New York from Japan for her annual checkup with the brain surgeon, who'd given her a clean bill of health. A quick visit to Billie and Thad was her reward. How wonderful it was to be here, to be with Billie, to have her health back! If only she didn't have a folder full of bad news to deliver. She couldn't put it off any longer.

The cat on the windowsill annoyed her. She'd never been a cat person, not that she was a dog person either. She said so to her grandmother.

"It's a good cat, I suppose," Billie said. "As cats go. But I'm used to Duchess and her pups at the farm. We never had cats. This one came with the lease, so we didn't have much choice. What bothers me is she walks around the countertops."

Sawyer eyed the feline suspiciously. "Why does it stare like that?"

Billie shrugged. "Ignore it, like I do. I'm so glad you stopped to visit. How long can you stay?"

"I have to leave tomorrow. I wanted to deliver this in person. This," she said, pointing to a thick folder, "will tell you where Coleman Enterprises stands."

"Why do I have the feeling wherever it is standing is a place it stood in once before?"

"Because that feeling is right on the money," Sawyer said grumpily.

"But Riley said—"

"Riley never looks at numbers, Grand. That's Cole's and my job."

Billie's throat tickled. She swallowed hard. "But Cole agreed with Riley."

"And I agree with Riley, too. We've just run out of money. There are a few things left to mortgage, but they aren't going to net us the kind of income we need. Sunbridge has not been touched. That will be the last thing to go." Sawyer threw her hands into the air. "We're a hair away from joining the bankruptcy crowd."

"I have some money from Billie, Inc. It's yours."

{ 224 }

Sawyer laughed ruefully. "It may have been presumptuous of me, but I already added in your share. Maggie's, too. Even a loan from Rand. I was going to ask you to call Cary and Amelia. Everything is on paper with them, so I'm not counting on any big loans. We've hit bottom."

"We've been here before, Sawyer."

"Yes, but with a dream and a marketable commodity. We don't have that now. When the loans and mortgages come due, there isn't going to be anything to pay them with."

"We'll have to find a way."

"Grand, do you think I haven't tried? There's not a bank in Texas that would lend us money. Let me make that even stronger—there's not a bank anywhere that will lend us money."

"The boys didn't . . . I thought everything was going to be fine."

"You can't blame Riley, and you can't blame Cole or me. There is no blame. It's that simple. I didn't know myself until yesterday, when I went over the various holdings. We operate on paper, Grand."

"Mr. Hasegawa. He helped us before. He's involved in the EOR. I'm sure he will help," Billie said desperately.

"Grand, we still owe on the Dream Machine. It'll be years before that's paid off. He's already poured money into this project. More than he intended."

"Are you saying he won't help us?"

"I'm saying Mr. Hasegawa is an old man. He is also a dying man. We already owe him millions and millions of dollars. This family will not beg a dying man for money. I won't do it."

"Riley," Billie cried.

"How can you expect Riley to go to his grandfather for money so he can stay here with the Colemans? Riley won't do it. I don't know if he knows it or not, but he's made his decision. He's staying here. Only a fool would advance us money at this stage. Sick as he is, Mr. Hasegawa is no fool. Mr. Hasegawa believes in honor. He's a kind, generous man with what appears to be unlimited wealth. I seriously believe he has become disillusioned with the Colemans, and I think he feels we should have talked Riley into returning to Japan. Grand, he feels that he only loaned us his grandson. Our honor went down the tubes when Riley trenched in. This is only my personal opinion, of course."

"Then we have to make Mr. Hasegawa see his thinking is all wrong," Billie said hotly.

"You're prepared to do that?" Sawyer demanded.

"Yes. No. Thad . . . maybe Thad . . ."

"Grand, you aren't listening to me. Mr. Hasegawa thinks —wrongly, I admit—that we are making life so attractive here that, without meaning to, we turned Riley against his own. He sees that as unforgivable. It goes against thousands of years of Japanese belief."

"He has to be made to understand he's wrong," Billie cried. "I understand everything you're saying, Sawyer. Riley is not a child, he's a very intelligent young man. He makes his own decisions. This isn't Japan."

"Exactly."

"Riley has to talk to his grandfather."

"The Japanese side of Riley will never allow him to tamper with his grandfather's beliefs and his honor."

"You've just given me the biggest headache of my life, Sawyer."

"Welcome to the club, Grand," Sawyer said.

"Do you have suggestions?"

"Nope. It has to be Riley and Cole's decision if we play hardball with those oil leases in South America. If we spend what money we have to persuade them to let us take the oil out, we're gambling all the way. If we do nothing, we lose. Gamble or give up, that's what it comes down to."

"Riley and Cole are in favor of hanging in there, letting things ride with the oil leases, is that right?" Billie asked quietly.

"Yes, but they're making a mistake. I know what those guys are like, Grand. They promise the moon and throw in the stars if you go there to drill for them. I can give you a list this long of Texas oilmen who went down there and fell for that line. Even the big American oil companies gave up and came home. If they couldn't pull it off, I don't see much hope for us."

"A gamble is better than nothing."

"It's also throwing money away. If we can't deal in a position of strength, we can't possibly win. What we are is desperate. The other factor is, Riley is young. They're used to dealing with old, seasoned veterans. They didn't even want to see me, much less deal with me, since I'm a woman and have no place in this business. That's why I didn't make the trip with Riley last month. Riley has the knowledge but not the hands-on experience. I almost think we should cancel the leases and pull out. Lose rather than gamble further."

Billie sighed. Sawyer's good news about her health had been so wonderful to hear. And now this. Every time God opens a window, she thought bitterly, He slams a door. She tried to smile, immediately regretting her bitter thoughts.

The cat meowed loudly and walked across the countertop.

For a second Riley's vision blurred after he read through the reports Sawyer had mailed to him. The projections made him wince. The note at the bottom of the last page in regard to the Hasegawa percentage, and Sawyer's decision not to ask for any more money, threw him into a rage. When he finally calmed down, he felt ashamed. What kind of bastard was he that he would take more money from his grandfather just so he could stay here and continue his life with the Colemans? Even a lowlife wouldn't take advantage of a dying man. Up until seconds ago, he'd been such a lowlife. If it weren't for Sawyer's message at the bottom of the report, he'd have held out his hand again and again.

The moment of reckoning.

His.

Tess decided it was time to find out exactly how deep the hole was that Coots said they were in. She marched through the house to his office. Two hours later she had a vision of herself in a pawnshop with her jewelry box and fur coats, willing to take whatever the sleazy man behind the counter offered, even if he only offered enough to pay the utility bills.

The stack of newspapers on the small table next to Coots's desk attested to how bad things were in the oil industry. Where had she been while all of this was going on? Why hadn't Coots warned her? She admitted that he'd tried to, but she had ignored him and spent, spent, spent. No wonder Coots wasn't sleeping. No wonder he was out chasing anything with legs wearing a skirt. He couldn't deal with it. She sat down with a thump and her eyes fell on the paper she'd set on the desk. It announced an auction to be held at Sidney Laver's ranch, at two o'clock this very afternoon. All monies were to go to the bankruptcy court. Tess knew the Lavers. In fact, she'd done a chart for Lois Laver a year or so ago. Now they were bankrupt. Tess's blood ran cold. Farther down the column, a second bankruptcy notice appeared, a friend of Coots's from the old days, Jack Peters, better known as Boots. She'd never been close to either Carol or Boots, but Coots was. Carol had every charge card issued. Paper—they all existed on paper. No cash. Coots had done the same thing, and she'd gone along with it. Thank God her own nest egg was real and she could get her hands on it. She'd just die if the paper published a bankruptcy notice for her and Coots. Now that Buckalew Big Wells was in her name, that would never happen, but she had to come up with some kind of plan to pay off these bills. She'd start with the ones marked FINAL NOTICE.

How much was she supposed to bear? she wondered. First there was Lacey backing out of her engagement to Riley, which dashed her dreams of becoming united with the Coleman family. Then Coots's confession of how bad things were and her discovery that Coots's drilling equipment was to be repossessed unless he paid off. Lord, *that* might get into the newspapers. She stamped her foot in anger. The stars hadn't indicated any of this trouble. A special reading was clearly called for.

Suddenly she remembered something and her head snapped back as though she'd been stung by a hornet. She didn't really own Buckalew Big Wells! Coots said the deed hadn't been filed. That meant the house could be seized by Coots's creditors. The bottom line was crystal-clear: In order to save Coots's hide and Buckalew Big Wells, she had to dip into her nest egg, even though there would be nothing left for her old age and she would probably end up as a bag lady.

She wondered which one of her two daughters would take care of Coots and herself in their old age if they lost everything. She should write Ivy a letter, she thought in panic. Just a short note. A mother note to a daughter away at school. She'd make it chatty, telling her about Billie Coleman coming for lunch, and all those five-hundred-dollar horoscopes, and Lacey and Riley's decision to break things off. She could even suggest Ivy set her cap for Riley. When the final draft of her short note to Ivy was firmly in her mind, she felt better. Ivy would be the one. She might not take care of her personally, but she'd pay someone to look after her. Yes, Ivy was the one.

Cary's lovemaking was lusty, boisterous, and would have been completely satisfying if he'd been with her mentally as well as physically. There had been no aftertalk this evening.

Cary had fallen asleep immediately, his head resting on Amelia's shoulder.

For weeks now she'd been hurt and angry, and she knew the anger would destroy her if she didn't get it under control. She'd have to learn to live with the hurt because she loved Cary. Love, she thought sadly, is when you want the other person's happiness more than you want your own. All night long she stared at the ceiling. When morning came she felt better. Her resolution to accept things was her first step. The second was to call Billie and tell her about their visit to the nation's capital. She'd do that today, before she left the apartment.

Amelia's mood was light, almost gay, as she dressed. It was as if some unseen being had stepped in and settled things. And she supposed, in a manner of speaking, He had.

Billie brought Amelia up-to-date on Sawyer's visit. "I knew things were bad, everyone is going under, but I thought we were ahead of the pack. Talk to Cary, and if you have any spare cash, get back to me."

"Of course I will. Cary's still sleeping, and I'm about to leave, but I'll put a note on the dresser for him to call you. Have you heard from Rand or Maggie? Rand should be able to help."

"I'm planning to call as soon as the five hours are up. There's no point in calling her in the middle of the night."

"Billie, I don't know what to say, but I do agree with Sawyer about Riley's grandfather. Whatever is that young man thinking of?"

"It's not Riley's fault, Amelia," Billie said generously.

"I didn't mean to imply that it was. I just don't understand his attitude in regard to his grandfather."

"If we pull together, I'm sure we can weather this—we've been at the bottom before," Billie said with false heartiness. "Today must be my day for callers. Julie called before she left for work. She wanted Maggie and Rand's address so she could stop and visit them while she's there."

"Is she going to Hawaii?" Amelia asked in surprise.

"The first of March, I believe. She's very excited. And Maggie gets so little company over there, Julie will be a welcome surprise. She is family, in a manner of speaking."

"More than you know," Amelia whispered.

"I didn't hear what you said, Amelia."

"I said it's wonderful to know that. Get out the welcome mat and be ready for me."

"I'm so excited, Amelia. We can have a real hen party, just you and me, and get caught up on everything. No shopping, though."

Amelia laughed. "You have a deal. I'll call before I leave."

"You did say Cary was coming with you, didn't you?'

"I'm not sure, Billie. That's what we thought originally, but I think he might have other plans. I'll have to let you know."

It was something she'd said, Billie thought, that had changed Amelia's tone. It had to be Julie. Her vacation. First Cary *was* coming to Washington with Amelia, and then he *wasn't*. "I'll look forward to it, Amelia. Take care, now."

Amelia sighed as she hung up the phone. So that was the reason for the look she'd seen in Cary's eyes the night before —that look she'd barely noticed, just as she'd mentioned going to Washington on the first of March. Julie was going on vacation, and he knew about it.

Amelia rushed to her desk. She pulled out pen and paper with a flourish.

Darling Cary,
    Last night was as delicious as that scrumptious dessert at Andre's. I've been thinking, darling. I've decided to let you off the hook for the Washington trip. You will make me too nervous for words. Would you mind terribly if I went alone? I think it would be best. I'll spend a day or so with Billie and come home. We can plan a real vacation for the end of April, if that's agreeable with you. Please say you understand.
                                            Love,
                                            Amelia

She was crazy. No woman in her right mind would pave the way for her husband to . . . Ah, but true love, she reminded herself, was wanting the other person to be happy. She wondered, miserably, if the day would ever come when Cary would think back and see the sacrifices she'd made so he could be with Julie. Only the selfish part of her wanted him to. What did it matter anyway? She wouldn't be around to hear about it, whichever way it happened.

* * *

Cary rolled out of bed at eleven. He did some knee bends and ten sit-ups. He showered, shaved, plucked the note off the dresser, and headed for the kitchen to make coffee.

He read the note several times. Amelia didn't want him to go to Washington with her, which meant he'd have to kick around by himself for a few days. March first, March first, March first, he hummed as he measured coffee into the pot.

Where the hell was that last letter from Rand, the one asking if he'd be interested in a sugarcane plantation in Hilo? He figured he knew as much about sugarcane as he needed to. What would the world be like without sugar? Not very sweet. He grinned at his little joke. Rand had said something about sugarcane being shipped to the mainland for refining and then sold back to the Hawaiians. A refinery. He decided he was interested. He'd wait till one o'clock to call Hawaii to announce that interest.

Maggie picked up the phone on the fourth ring. Her voice sounded breathless.

"Cary! How nice of you to call. There isn't anything wrong, is there?"

"Of course not. I've been thinking about that offer Rand made, the sugarcane plantation."

"Oh. Well, Cary, Rand is in England. I'm not exactly sure when he'll be back. He may have lost out on that little venture. It's this business with his daughter, or I should say, the girl who is claiming to be his daughter. He more or less lost interest in everything else for a while. He's at the Dorchester in London. Give him a call. If it's still possible and you really are interested, I'm sure he will be, too. He thought a refinery was a wonderful idea."

"I do, too. I'll call him now. I was sort of thinking of coming over around the first of the month."

"That's wonderful. You'll stay with us, of course."

"I'm a lousy houseguest. Sometimes I prowl at night; I keep odd hours. I'll stay at a hotel."

"I won't hear of it. We'd welcome the company."

"I'll get back to you; how's that?"

"Fine, but I won't take no for an answer. Rand would be upset if he didn't get to play host in this little corner of paradise. I can't wait to show off my house to Amelia. She's going to love it, and before you know it, she's going to want to move here. Mark my words."

The silence at the other end of the phone startled Maggie. "Cary, are you there?"

"Yes. Yes, I'm here. I'm not sure if Amelia will be coming with me. I don't know if you know this or not, but she's testifying before Congress sometime during the first week in March. First she wanted me to go with her, and then she changed her mind. She said I would make her nervous. I guess I can understand that," Cary said flatly.

"You could wait and come later, or she could come later. Whatever," Maggie babbled.

"Well, enjoy your sunshine, and soak up some for me. I'll call Rand now. Nice talking to you, Maggie." He wanted to get off the phone. He didn't like Maggie's end of the conversation, because he wasn't prepared to give answers and explanations.

Maggie stared at the phone for a long time. She had the feeling something was wrong. Cary coming here, Amelia going to Washington? That by itself didn't necessarily indicate something was wrong, but . . . it was Cary's tone of voice and that slight hesitation, plus the fact that he'd hung up so quickly. It just wasn't like Cary. Amelia and Cary had the strongest marriage in the world, right up there with Billie and Thad, and herself and Rand. It would be so good to see them.

"Jesus, Cary, is that really you? What's wrong?" Rand demanded.

"Nothing's wrong," Cary said, "which just goes to show we don't call one another enough. Maggie said the same thing when I called her. I called because I finally got around to answering my mail and reread your offer about the sugarcane plantation and the refinery. I'm interested, if the offer still holds."

"I didn't have it together there for a few weeks, Cary—I didn't return calls; I didn't go to the lawyers, the way I was supposed to. I may have lost out, and there's not much I can do from here. Call Maggie and ask her to Air Express the blue folder on my desk. You can make some calls from there, get the feel of it. Say you're my partner, and make up some excuse about you being away and me not being able to get in touch with you. You might have to play a little hardball. I can tell you this—there wasn't a waiting line of buyers, and I did my best to tie in the sale of the plantation with the refinery.

Maybe you can come up with better ideas than mine. Right now my head is in a different place."

"How's all of that going, Rand?" Cary asked. "It must be an awesome feeling, now knowing for sure," Cary said sympathetically.

"I do know for sure now. I found out today. I haven't even called Maggie yet. Chesney is my daughter; there's no doubt. The problem right now is she's off on holiday for three weeks. I could go back to Hawaii, but there's some business I can handle here to keep myself busy. I was thinking of asking Maggie to come over."

"I think she's just waiting to be asked. Women like that for some reason. Being asked, I mean. I'll never be able to figure them out. Anyway, I'd like to take you up on your offer. I was planning to fly over to see it March first, if you were still interested. Maggie invited me to stay at the house."

"I'll certainly second that invitation. Even if we're still over here, I want you to stay at the house. Have Amelia join you when she's finished in Washington. That's a magical house for love, you know. Billie and Moss and Thad. Maggie and me. You can't go wrong."

"I'll give it some thought." Cary laughed. "You didn't tell me how all of this feels to you, having a daughter, or is it something you don't want to talk about?"

"It's weird, Cary. I don't know what I feel except guilt. My daughter was raised in the dreariest, most dismal place with no love or affection. The orphanage is like a prison. There are no smiles and no sunshine, Cary. Maggie has made me so aware of sunshine that my heart breaks for those children. If I'd known, I have to believe I would have done something. I'll have to live with it every day of my life."

Cary voiced his sympathy. He knew a thing or two about guilt himself these days.

"Chesney's come out unscathed, and I guess that's what I don't understand. They told me she goes back to the orphanage with presents for the young ones. She must be a very fine person, this daughter of mine. I thought she wanted something from me, but right now I'm angry because she's not here, waiting for me to acknowledge her. It's almost as if she doesn't care. She walked into my life and walked out." There was a long silence. "For Christ's sake, Cary, say something."

Cary shrugged and then remembered that Rand couldn't see the shrug. "I know nothing about children, big or small. I guess God gives you children when you're meant to have them. Being handed a full-grown child, in my opinion, would be a plus. You're contemporaries of sorts. You start out being friends and then you turn into a father when the time is right. I'd go real slow if I were you. I don't know why I say that, it's just a gut feeling. Count your blessings, Rand."

"It's all so sudden. Yesterday I didn't believe she was my daughter; today I'm certain she is. And I don't know what a father is supposed to feel like."

"I can tell you what to do," Cary said briskly. "Hang up and call Maggie. Then *you* can ask her to send me the blue folder."

Cary smiled, pleased with the plans he was making. He wouldn't say anything to Amelia until he had the folder in his hands. He decided he felt so good he'd toast his new venture with a drink. He wasn't going to be sitting around doing nothing; he was getting back into harness. If there was one thing he knew how to do, it was cut a deal. If Rand's negligence had caused him to lose out on the deal, he'd go in as an independent and bring Rand along later. That, he decided, was a minor point. The second important aspect of the arrangement was Hawaii. Land of beautiful smiles, honey-colored bodies, and nine-to-five sunshine. Warm trade winds, gently swaying palm trees, and . . . Julie.

And then the guilt set in. He was planning to cheat on his wife. On his wife, whom he loved with all his heart. An inner voice began a dialogue with him: "A little fun, why not? No one finds out, no one gets hurt, and everyone is happy." Amelia would sense something was wrong. He was no actor. "You can cover it up," the voice argued. "Amelia's had her time in the sun. She wants to curl up by the fire. You've worked like a human dynamo these past years. This is your due. Go for it."

Cary paced the luxurious living room. This is stupid, he told himself. I won't be able to handle it. Let it go. He groaned. The voice continued to argue. "Look, Amelia's needs are not what they used to be. Yours, on the other hand, have accelerated, thanks to Julie. You'll never get her out of your mind. She hit nerves. When you weren't looking, she sneaked into your heart and carved out a little niche for herself. Not intentionally, I grant you. These things happen," the voice niggled. "Besides, if, and it's a big if, Amelia did find out, she'd forgive you because she loves you. You can't lose. Everybody does it. Go for it."

"Shut up!" Cary shouted to the empty room.

He rushed across the room, bumping his shinbone on the sharp edge of the coffee table. He limped to the sliding glass door, slid it open, and stood on the balcony taking huge gulps of the cold, fresh air. He was crazy; there was no other explanation. He'd been sitting around too long doing nothing but watching the boob tube and eating. Fat settled around his brain. Only a fool would do what he was contemplating.

He could cut out the cute phone calls to Julie's answering machine. If he wanted, he could avoid Julie Kingsley for the rest of his life. If he wanted to.

Cary's eye fell on the brass sundial. He knew the words by heart. A poet had written them—Browning, Amelia told him. "Grow old along with me, the best is yet to be." He picked it up angrily. He would have thrown the fifty-pound piece of brass over the rail, but he remembered that pedestrians walked below. He replaced it carefully on the pedestal. It was a lie! He and Amelia had already *had* the best; it was behind them. What was yet to be would never be better than what they'd had. He could have that again with Julie. All the wonderful highs, the few lows that went with life. He could separate the two. Lots of men did it.

His leg ached. He stormed back inside, slamming the door in its tracks. The heavy door frame hit the lock and slid open again. He went back and closed it properly.

Cary continued his frenzied pacing. His eyes fell on a small framed picture of the two of them. Jesus, Amelia was beautiful. Hell, he wasn't so bad himself. He did love her. He'd always love Amelia. He thought bitterly of the litany he'd recited all these past years: Age is just a number; age doesn't matter. We're what matters. He'd meant it then and he still meant it. "Liar," the voice accused. "You see the crepey skin, you feel the sharp bones, the dryness." Amelia was so fragile now, like one of those Japanese porcelain dolls Billie collected.

Jesus, he'd grown old, too, but in a different way. The twenty years had caught up. "I need more," Cary cried to the empty room. Why should I have to settle, be satisfied, when I can have what I want? "Because," the voice inside him cautioned, "you made a deal. You married Amelia. Through sickness and health, till death do you part. That's a deal." The voice, Cary noticed, had switched roles with him. Now *he'd* have to play devil's advocate.

Just this once, just once, Cary pleaded silently. I need this. I need to feel again, to know I'm alive. All I'm doing is marking time. I'm too young to stifle all my feelings and channel my energies into work. What kind of life is that?

"The kind you bargained for. There's a piece of paper that says anything else is wrong." I don't give a damn, Cary argued silently. If you're my conscience, you're supposed to be on my side. "I am on your side. I'm telling you to go for it." Now what? This voice seemed to be contradicting itself again. "You're full of shit," Cary yelled. "You're the devil and you're tempting me." The minute the words were out of his mouth, Cary felt stupid. "I don't have to tempt you; you already did that yourself." "Yeah, with your help," Cary cried. He and the voice had become one.

"Okay, okay, you son of a bitch, the deal is off. I'm going to call Julie right now and leave a message that I've come to my senses. After that I won't call her anymore. Amelia and I will go to Hawaii after Julie leaves."

Angrily Cary dialed Julie's New York number. The color in his face drained, leaving him white and shaken. He listened, hung up, and dialed the number a second time. Julie's clear voice came over the wire. "Roses are red. Violets are blue. I shouldn't be telling you this, but I miss you, too." Cary slammed the receiver onto the desk, missing the cradle completely. When he finally hung up the phone, he noticed he'd scratched Amelia's antique rosewood desk.

Three days passed before Cary decided to say something to Amelia about the blue folder in his top dresser drawer. It took nine phone calls to find out Rand actually hadn't blown the deal. Being a new player to the game, Cary wasn't surprised to hear that the price had gone up $100,000. Plenty of people had tried to jerk him around before. He'd learned more from dealing with Texans than he could ever put into use. A Hawaiian businessman intent on making a killing couldn't be any different than a Texan who wanted a few more notches in his belt. The only thing that bothered him was the fact that two Japanese investors were interested in the same property. Cary's comment was caustic: "They already own half of your island. Hand over the rest and make a clean sweep." The man had chuckled appreciatively. Japanese investors were buying up property and businesses all over Hawaii. Speculation was that they owned more than half the island because the yen was so strong. The real know-it-alls said the Japanese were getting even for what they couldn't take by force during the war, and that left them wide open to buy it all up later. He wondered how much real estate Riley's grandfather owned in Hawaii.

Three more phone calls, and Cary was confident that he had a fighting chance. The next step was to go to Hawaii and clinch the deal.

In Amelia's state-of-the-art kitchen, Cary felt as if he had four left hands. His excitement was at an all-time high as he set about preparing dinner for himself and Amelia. He was no cook, but anyone, he supposed, could broil chicken and pop vegetables into the microwave. A baked potato was child's play. You didn't have to be a chef to scoop out the butter-scotch ripple ice cream, his favorite, from the plastic container. One didn't necessarily have to be a Miss Manners graduate to set the table properly, either.

Cary stood back to view his handiwork. The chicken was ready, seasoned mildly; the potatoes had been washed and were in the microwave; just waiting for him to push the button. The vegetables were thawing, to go into the microwave after the potatoes were done. He looked down at the glass-topped table with the linen place mats decorated with appliquéd butterflies. The Lenox china was plain, but elegant; the crystal winked in the kitchen light. Amelia would be pleased, but something was missing; the table looked naked. A centerpiece, he decided, but where was he to get one? He looked around the apartment at all the beautiful things he and Amelia had collected over the years. Everything was either too big, too small, or the wrong color. He felt annoyed with himself. He should have ordered some fresh flowers from the florist. All the trouble he'd gone to would be spoiled if he didn't have a centerpiece. Amelia was such a stickler for the little things. On his second walk around the apartment he passed the open door of the guest bathroom. On the vanity stood a silk flower arrangement the same color as the butterflies on the place mats. He whisked it to the kitchen and plopped it in the center of the table. It was perfect. His sigh was loud. Finished.

The wine was chilling, the stereo playing softly, some old Nat King Cole melodies that Amelia loved.

Guilt demanded he be a perfectionist.

* * *

Over dinner, he told Amelia about the deal, handing her the blue folder Maggie had forwarded along with all his notes from the phone calls he'd made.

"Darling, how wonderful for you," Amelia said. He was so excited, she couldn't help but smile. Cary hadn't been this animated in a long time. It did her good to watch him and listen to the enthusiasm in his voice. That's all she would think about, nothing else. Not what else that excitement could mean. "I'll clear away dinner and we can sit by the fire," she said. "I have a hundred questions and maybe one or two suggestions."

"Babe, that's what I need, your input. I'm all fired up, as you can see. I'll make the coffee. I like having coffee in front of the fire. God, Amelia, I didn't even ask how your day was."

Amelia laughed. "It had its good and bad points. I'm getting there. This sounds much more exciting. I'm delighted, Cary."

"Me, too, babe," Cary said, hugging her. He was, too. About the deal. Being back in harness was what he needed. All during dinner, up to this second, he hadn't thought of Julie at all. Even now, he pushed her from his thoughts. He wanted to sit by the fire with Amelia and talk about the plantation and the refinery. When it came right down to it, he trusted Amelia's opinions more than his own. She could see around corners, anticipate the unexpected, point out danger areas.

Amelia loaded the dishwasher, then shook out the place mats and folded them neatly. "Does this mean we might eventually reside in paradise?"

"A very good chance. I have a feeling that even though Rand is going to be my partner in this . . . Listen to me . . . it's like the deal's been consummated. . . ."

"It's just a matter of time," Amelia said airily.

"Babe, what would I ever do without you?" Cary beamed.

"Be alone?"

"We're a team. You and me. Me and you. The salt and pepper, the shoe and the shoelace."

"I'm ready. After you, since you're carrying the tray," Amelia cooed. Damn, she felt good. It was like old times. Nothing else mattered. Even if this good feeling between them lasted only an hour, it was worth it. She cleared her mind of everything but Cary.

She felt loved.

They hashed out the proposed deal until eleven o'clock,

when Cary called a halt. "This is going to be a go; I can feel it, babe. I can't wait to call Rand tomorrow."

"Don't be surprised if he isn't as excited as you are. He has other things on his mind right now," Amelia cautioned. She yawned languidly.

"Don't tell me you're ready to go to bed," Cary complained.

"I'm ready to go to bed, but I didn't say anything about sleep." Amelia grinned.

"After you, madame," Cary said with a flourish.

Cary made love to *her* that night. Her heart and her body were those of a sixteen-year-old for a while as she matched Cary's ardent lovemaking. It was well after one in the morning when both Cary and Amelia cuddled, exhausted, in the nest of warm, sweaty bedding. "You know what I'd like right now," Amelia whispered.

"A joint?"

"I still have some Panama Red and a smidgen of sinsemilla."

"We'll get all wired up again." Cary laughed.

"You old men do try a woman's spirit." Amelia giggled.

"Save it for when we clinch this deal." Cary yawned.

Amelia snuggled deeper into Cary's arms. "Uuummm," she said sleepily.

Cary's last thought before joining Amelia in sleep was that he would be a fool to tamper with what he had. He loved his wife.

{{{{{{{{ CHAPTER TWELVE }}}}}}}}

The night air was refreshing. Adam rolled down the windows in the pickup and took long, deep breaths. All the stars were out, and it was going to be a full moon tonight. Sawyer had told him once that when the moon was full, people did strange things—things they wouldn't do under ordinary circumstances. Once he read that there were more births, more deaths, and more violence at the time of the full moon than at any other time. He'd asked his friend Nick Deitrick if it was true; shrinks always know that stuff. Nick had laughed and said he'd heard that old wives' tale himself and he believed it implicitly. And, he'd said, he'd seen some of that strange behavior firsthand, in his patients.

Right now, to Adam, the moon just looked pretty, shining down on him as he drove across the fields to Sunbridge. If his fairy godmother were to appear and grant him one wish, he'd wish for Sawyer to be at his side. They'd walk in the moonlight with all the stars winking at them. He'd have his arm around her shoulder, and because she was as tall as he was, she'd sort of lean into him, her head on his shoulder. They'd whisper to each other, make promises they knew they could keep, and then they'd stop and kiss under the moon.

Christ, he wished Sawyer were here to love him. Sawyer didn't care if he was six feet tall and string-bean-thin. She liked his curly red hair and his homely face. Don't forget your elephant ears, Jarvis, he cautioned himself. That's probably what drove her away—his ears. Maybe he should think about getting them pinned back. Men were getting all kinds of plastic surgery these days—face-lifts, eye jobs, contoured cheekbones, and hair transplants. He'd be happy to have an ear job if it would bring Sawyer back. She was his only love.

Maybe tonight he'd write Sawyer a letter, one of his newsy, flip old-buddy letters. But this time all the good stuff would be in there, if she cared to read between the lines.

Adam rolled the pickup truck to a stop in the Sunbridge courtyard. Riley's car and the Bronco were parked side by side.

"Yo," Adam called loudly. "Anyone home?" He looked at his watch. It was after eight.

Jonquil poked her head out the kitchen door. "Riley's upstairs, Mr. Jarvis. Go on up. How's that boy of yours?"

"Right now he's at the YMCA under the direct supervision of a wrestling coach. I don't have to pick him up till ninethirty. That must have been some cooking lesson you gave him. I can't get him out of the kitchen." Adam laughed. "He keeps making the same thing, though. Do you have any other recipes?"

"I'll write some down and put them in an envelope. I'll leave it here on the counter for you. I hope you encourage the boy, Mr. Jarvis. All the great chefs in the world are men."

"Hey, that's okay with me. I could handle a political cartoonist and a chef in the family. The only thing is, I'm getting fat. I had to let my belt out."

"Encourage him," Jonquil called to Adam's retreating back. He waved to indicate he would.

Adam took the stairs two at a time. He glanced into Cole's room and then backed up a step. This *was* Cole's room, wasn't it? It looked like a spare bedroom.

"Yo, Riley, where the hell are you?" he called.

"Adam. I didn't hear your car."

"This place is a tomb. Where is everyone?"

"Cole moved out," Riley said curtly, "and I took Jonquil on full-time."

Adam's eyebrows shot upward. "Is this one of those things that's none of my business, or do you want to talk about it? I have an hour or so to kill before I have to pick Jeff up. You look like you could use a friend. I'm a real good listener, and I keep my mouth shut," Adam prompted.

Riley hesitated. "Sit down. D'ya care for a drink?" he said, pointing to a bottle of Jack Daniels.

"If you can spare it," Adam said snidely. "It looks to me like you're hell-bent on finishing the bottle yourself. I know you started with a full bottle, because the seal is there on your desk. I knew Cole could heft a few, but I didn't know you hit the sauce."

"There's a lot about me you don't know," Riley snarled.

"Obviously. There's a lot about me you don't know either."

"What the hell makes you think I'm interested in what makes you tick?"

"I won't take offense at that, Riley, because you're drunk and I'm stone-cold sober, and I have a kid to think about."

"I'm sorry, I had no right to come on to you like that. You've been a good friend to me when I needed one. Everything pretty much hit me today."

"Why's that?" Adam questioned.

"Shit! This came in the mail today." Riley grimaced as he handed Adam an envelope.

Adam leaned back in his chair. His eyes narrowed. "This says you are the sole owner of this spread. Cole *gave* you his half? Cole is generous, but not that generous. What aren't you telling me?"

Riley snorted. "We had a fight. A bad one. He said if we tangle again, one of us will be dead. He's a fucking son of a bitch."

Adam drew in his breath. This *was* serious. Riley never cursed.

"He's a goddamn sneaking thief."

"You aren't computing, Riley. The guy just gives you—mind you, the key word here is 'give'—gives you his half of one of the richest spreads in the whole state of Texas, and you're calling him a thief?"

It took Riley thirty minutes to pour out his story. Adam blinked. He was glad he wasn't standing in Riley's shoes. And he thought he had problems.

Saying the wrong thing now could be disastrous. "I never understood the relationship you had with Lacey," he began. "It's not like you to pick up after Cole. What was it, some leftover childish rivalry? Did you know all along nothing was going to come of it? You said you didn't go to bed with her. What the hell were you waiting for? Were you afraid you'd come up short in the sex department? Afraid she'd compare you to Cole? I'm no more stupid than the next guy, but I don't get it."

He paused, but Riley said nothing. He was listening, though, so Adam pushed on.

"You say Cole tried to talk to you, to explain. Evidently his story and Lacey's are identical, but instead of laying the blame where it belongs, you dumped on Cole. Believe it or not, that guy is the best friend you'll ever have. Except for me and Sawyer. C'mon, Riley, let's talk man to man here. It was just a fuck. Once that little jigger goes up and there's a willing body, anything goes. The fact that Lacey took off should prove to you that there is no interest on Cole's part." Another pause; still no response from Riley. "You said you tried to break it off with Lacey," Adam said. "Cole's probably eating himself alive over this. From where I'm sitting, it looks to me like you fucked up. If my feeling this way is going to harm our friendship, say so now."

Riley shook his head miserably. "You're entitled to your opinion."

"You took everything out on Cole. It all came to a head—the business, Coots, your grandmother, Sawyer, and, of course, your grandfather. You made Cole the scapegoat. No one expects more from you than you can give, Riley. You also cannot be all things to all people. You didn't ask for my advice, but I'm going to give you some anyway. Get your priorities straight, and don't do it when your snoot is in a bottle,

{ 242 }

either. If there's anything I can do, I'm here for you."

Riley nodded. "How's Jeff?"

"You aren't going to believe this, but ever since Jonquil showed him how to cook a few things, he's a different kid. He's still surly and snotty, but it's almost like it's an effort to be that way. I dumped him at the Y and told Ed Yeager to work him over. I think I have a handle on it, at least for now. Jonquil said she'd give me some more recipes, so we'll see what happens. Listen, the main reason I came over here was to ask if I could borrow your old mopeds. I figure Jeff and I could ride them together out on those trails you and Cole cut on the old south forty."

"They're in the garage, but there's no gas in either of them. They were drained a long time ago. The maintenance booklets should be in the kitchen. I'll help you."

"That's real kind of you, Riley. I guess you noticed that I have a bad back from cutting all that wood. Thanks for your concern."

"Asshole." Riley grinned.

"Takes one to know one. Have you heard from Sawyer lately?"

"Still carrying the torch five years, one wife and kid later, huh? She flew in and out a few weeks ago, but she stuck to the East Coast."

"If there's no love, the rest doesn't mean anything. So you see, when I hand out advice, I draw from personal experience. What are you going to do with this place now that you're king of all we survey? Sole owner of Sunbridge! That should make the front page the day the deed is filed. I hope you can handle the notoriety." Adam slapped Riley on the shoulder as they headed for the garage.

Riley stood for a long time watching Adam's red taillights. It was a clear night, crisp and cool. Millions of tiny stars winked down on him. It was early morning in Japan now.

On the ride to the airport Amelia had to fight with herself to keep her chatter light and a smile on her face. Cary was really going to Hawaii. Sure, it was a legitimate business deal, but one couldn't conduct business twenty-four hours a day. Cary would have lots of time to explore the islands, to social- ize. If she wanted to, she could call Billie and find out where Julie was staying in Hawaii and the approximate distance to

Maggie's house. For that matter, she could probably look at a map and figure it out herself. If she wanted to.

She'd always felt envy, but not the malicious kind, when Billie and Thad spoke of the house in Hawaii. Rand and Maggie talked about it as though it were the only house in the world for lovers. Maybe, just maybe, she'd get a crack at that wonderful paradise with Cary. She would pray tonight that if Cary sought Julie out, he wouldn't take her there, to that magic house. She wondered how she'd be able to tell if he had or hadn't.

She'd encouraged this trip of Cary's. If her approval could make him smile, if her encouragement could make his eyes light up like hundred-watt bulbs, then she was doing the right thing. She hadn't known she could be so unselfish. But then, she'd never been in this position before. She was learning so many things about herself these days. Her priorities were straight now, thank God.

"I'm glad we decided to come by limo," she said, smiling at Cary. "This way I can come in and stay with you till it's time to board."

"Let's have coffee, okay?" Cary said warmly as he scrunched closer to her in the backseat.

"I could use a cup." God, he was so up, so happy. She'd do anything—absolutely *anything*— to keep this smile on her husband's face.

They sat in the airport coffee shop drinking coffee and holding hands across the table. "I appreciate you coming to see me off, babe. I know you have a busy schedule," Cary said.

"Darling, if you were just taking a bus across Miranda, I'd still see you off. You have your St. Christopher medal on now, don't you?"

Like a kid, Cary fished around his neck and pulled out a dull, worn silver medal on a chain.

"I think they're starting to board, darling," Amelia said, almost in a whisper.

"Amelia, please don't look so sad."

"I wish I was going. Don't have too good a time till I get there, okay?"

Cary kissed Amelia soundly. "Three weeks at the most, babe. I'm going to wrap up this deal so tight, even Rand won't believe it. Should I look for a house for us to buy or rent while I'm there?"

"If it feels right, go for it," Amelia said happily.

"I want you to promise you'll meet me as soon as you can. Swear to me, Amelia. Swear nothing will stand in the way. I want you there with me."

Amelia looked for some sign that Cary was mouthing words with no meaning. Satisfied, she nodded. "Two weeks."

"I'll call you every day, your time."

"You're sure you have everything now, Cary? The key to the house, the map, your tickets and car rental reservation?"

"Right here in my briefcase."

"Do good, darling. Make me proud." Amelia smiled.

"That's what it's all about, babe. You just make sure you're on that plane in two weeks."

"You make sure you're at the airport to meet me."

"I'll be the guy in the flowered shirt carrying a lei. Try and miss me a little, okay?"

"How about a lot. This is the last boarding call, Cary."

I trust you, Cary, I really do, Amelia said silently.

At thirty thousand feet, Cary fished around his pockets for a cigarette. He undid his seat belt and tilted his seat backward. Now he was comfortable. These past weeks he felt like he'd been walking on winged feet. His and Amelia's life was wonderful. The phone calls back and forth to Hawaii and England had been hourly for a few days. Everything was going swimmingly with the refinery deal. Maggie and Rand insisted that he and Amelia use the house. Family was so wonderful. You could always count on family to come through for you.

He hadn't called Julie again after hearing her message. He'd been a fool, temporarily out of his mind. Now he had purpose, direction—and Amelia. All his energies were properly focused. It was coincidence that he would be in Hawaii at the same time as Julie. He was going to be on the North Shore, and Julie would be in Waikiki. He'd checked the map—a good hour to an hour and a half apart by car. He'd be spending a lot of time in meetings and on the different islands. They'd never run into each other.

He was going to the most romantic house in the world, according to Billie and Maggie. For years he'd heard tales about that house. A house for lovers, Billie said. Maggie said it was a house that opened its arms to you and then embraced you. Amelia, she said, would love it. Thad called it Paradise. They told him the story of Ester Kamali and how she and Billie had become friends. When she finally made the decision to sell the house, Billie was the first person she called, and Billie called Maggie. Maggie left Sunbridge behind, with all its ghosts and memories, and embarked on her new life with Rand in the house meant for lovers. Now he and Amelia were going to have a chance to live in the same wonderful house for a little while. If things worked out right, he and Amelia might be the Nelsons' neighbors. He knew Amelia would like that.

Julie was only a memory. Sometimes, though, he wondered what she thought when he stopped calling. Had she guessed that her message had scared the hell out of him? Whatever you sow, you reap, or so Amelia said. He hadn't been fair to Julie, though. Somewhere along the way he was going to be called on to answer for it. What goes around comes around. But Waikiki was a long way from the North Shore.

The view from the penthouse balcony was awesome, Cole decided. The Coleman apartment had a ten-mile view in all directions. Nothing but the best. He shrugged. He could get along with a lot less than the best. Hell, he could probably hack driving a truck overland. He could do anything he set his mind to. He could be a commercial pilot if that was what he wanted to do. It wasn't. He didn't want to drive a truck either.

He rubbed at his arms, tugging at the heavy gunmetal-gray sweater. It was cold out here. But he didn't want to go inside to the heat of the apartment. Out here, up high like he was, he could think better.

Things were bad in the oil industry, prices at rock bottom. Somehow, someway, Riley would save Coleman Oil--for the family. Riley was so obsessed, so dedicated, Cole thought. Compared to his cousin, he was a slouch. No one would ever pin a family business medal on him. Shit, he'd never even get the gold watch on retirement, because he wouldn't be around that long. Riley's watch would be platinum and studded with diamonds. It would be engraved and probably say something corny, like he was a savior or . . . He hated it now when his thoughts returned to Riley.

It was weeks now since he had stormed out of Sunbridge, and he was still smarting. He'd done nothing but dwell on the situation since it happened. He was comfortable here at Assante Towers, in the Coleman condo reserved for visiting businessmen, but it didn't feel like home, and he wasn't conducting any business, and he was sick of feeling like a houseguest in a hotel.

Cole paced the white carpeting, the soft strains of a Billy Joel tune wafting about the apartment. His Nike tennis shoes left deep imprints in the thick pile. He was worried. It now looked as though Coleman Enterprises could go completely down the tube. What would the Colemans do if the good life came to an end? He grimaced. He'd pack up his old kit bag and trundle off into the sunset, he supposed; the decision would be made for him. Maybe that wouldn't be so bad.

He'd done a lot of soul-searching these past weeks. He and Riley were the only ones left, besides Sawyer, who could run the family's affairs. If Sawyer got married and decided to have a family, that would cut her out. Sawyer only did one thing at a time.

He'd winced when he'd gone over the ledgers. Riley had spent millions and millions by listening to Coots Buckalew. They were in over their heads, like everyone else. Sawyer didn't have any magic this time around, and Riley was so trenched in, he couldn't see beyond the end of his nose. Where does that leave you, Cole? Between a rock and a hard place, teetering over a yawning abyss, he answered himself. Now, in retrospect, he realized Coots had very little to do with the way things were. Lacey had nothing to do with Riley's decision making, either. The bottom line was the single-digit price of oil.

The only options the Colemans had at this point were Riley's EOR operation and to wait out OPEC. When there was no other alternative, you opted for the long shot and hoped for the best. That's what he had to put in a letter to Riley's grandfather, and he had to do it now. Ever since he'd started corresponding with the old Japanese, he'd written once a week. He couldn't even remember now how it had all come about. The old man had written first, that much he did remember. He found himself looking forward to the letters and even to writing the replies. He knew it was the old man's way of keeping in touch with Riley without actually doing it. He didn't mind; he liked Riley's grandfather, always had. He'd even confessed to the old man, in his second or third letter, that his and Riley's youthful rivalries stemmed from his own refusal to acknowledge that the Colemans needed help, and the Japanese branch of the family had come through for them.

Cole had set up a home office in one of the bedrooms. His

files, his personal correspondence, along with his portable typewriter and an Apple II, were ready for him when he wanted to work at home, the way he'd done at Sunbridge.

There was no time like the present to do the letter he'd been putting off. The paper rolled into the portable with a snap. The margins were set. All he had to do was let his fingers pick out the words he wanted. First he had to read Hasegawa's letter again so he knew exactly what he was responding to.

Coleman san,

It is this old one's wish that this letter finds you and your family well.

Japan is cold now, just as I imagine Texas is cold. Your mother is a very wise woman to have moved to a warm climate where the sun shines every day. I long for sunshine so I can walk in my garden. If one can free one's mind of troubles, the garden is peaceful. Sometimes I think of it as a sanctuary. Do you understand that, Coleman san?

I particularly enjoyed your last letter. It was three days before anyone could tell me what "overload" meant. You must not tire your spirit, only your body. I did enjoy the phrase "We all march to a different drummer." Once I understood it, I practiced it on my doctor, my attorneys, and some members of my family. They don't understand that I no longer want to be pushed and prodded. They mean well, and I try to be patient with them.

I understood what you meant when you said each of us must be free to sing our song. Understanding and accepting it is difficult for this old Japanese. Old ways die hard. Each day I try. I cannot say I am successful.

You, Coleman san, have brought a breath of fresh air into this old man's life with your witty, cheerful letters. I have no wish to be a burden to you. If you feel you have no time to write to me, do not worry.

My heart aches for my grandson. I sense that his spirit is in a turmoil, much as your own. It saddens me that the path he has chosen to follow is not the one I have chosen for him. I place no blame, Coleman san. I did for a while, but a walk in my small sanctuary showed me that you are right. My grandson must be free to sing his song. If he must sing it, let it be where he is happy—in Texas, where his father lived. Buddha is a gentle god, who forgives me. Finding the strength to forgive myself is something I pray for each day.

Give my regards to all members of your family. If it is not too much trouble, please tell Riley I think of him each day. If you can, explain to him that this old one's anger is abating because my days grow shorter. When he sings his song, Coleman san, ask that he dedicate it to me. Age must count for something.

My warm affection to you, Coleman san, for making this old man's days brighter.

Shadaharu Hasegawa.

"Riley, you are a fucking son of a bitch!" Cole cried. Witty and cheerful, huh? Well, here goes nothing.

Dear Mr. Hasegawa,

The days are cold, the nights colder, here in Texas, and I'm waiting patiently for the first sign of spring, because summer rides its coattails. I've noticed that people in warm climates, where the sun shines most of the time, seem happier and they smile more. Often I wish I was a writer so I could express certain things for other people to read, to see if they share my thoughts. Perhaps when I am old and wise like yourself, I will pursue that dream of mine, one I have shared only with you.

We are all fine. Mother is in England with Rand and his new daughter. Any addition to the family is always welcome. The bigger the better, Texans say.

Cary is in Hawaii and plans to go into business with Rand. Their plan is to buy a sugarcane plantation and build a refinery. Aunt Amelia thinks it's a blast because now we can all get fat. She plans to join Cary in ten days or so. There's even talk that they may buy a house in Hawaii to get away from this cold weather. I can't say I blame them.

Growing up is painful. Just this evening I was wondering what I'd like to be when I grow up. I'm not sure I was meant to be here, doing what I'm doing. I'm doing it because it is expected of me. Riley is here because he wants to be. He's doing what he's doing because he loves it. That can't be wrong. If anyone can turn Coleman Oil right side up, it's Riley. My family, myself included, wish there were some way for us to ease your pain and anguish. Perhaps time, which I understand is your enemy, will make things right.

When you write your next letter to me, use this address at Assante Towers. I'm staying here temporarily.

I will continue to do as I have been doing. Stay well, my friend.

Coleman.

Cole addressed the envelope, fixed the stamp neatly in the corner, filed the Hasegawa letter, and resumed his pacing.

Thoughts of Riley whirled around Cole's head. It was always like this these days. In the shower, out on the street, eating, before going to sleep, thoughts of Riley would attack him. Was he happy now that he was sole owner of Sunbridge? Cole grimaced. Sunbridge, the Coleman shrine. Jesus, how he hated it. Sometimes, he thought, I even hate the Colemans. Adam would tell him life was too short to spend it hating a place or doing something you hate. Move on, Tanner, do what you want, carve out your own niche. Find a nice young woman, get serious, get married. And while you're at it, find a job that will make you happy. Shake the dust off this family and move on.

Cole snorted. Easier said than done. Still, in his gut he knew he would have done just that if the oil crunch hadn't come along. He would have taken off, followed his star. Now it was too late. If he left now, it would be like a rat leaving a sinking ship.

"Damn!" Cole exploded. He rubbed at his throbbing temples. If he didn't put Riley on the back burner and get on with his own day-to-day living, he was going to be in emotional trouble. He forced his mind to other things. He had to fly up to Galveston on Saturday. Maybe Adam would let Jeff go along for company. The kid would have a ball if he let him take the controls for a few minutes.

Sometimes life was a bitch.

Maggie hated London and everything about it. If it were up to her, she'd never come back. She especially hated the elegant, stuffy, old-fashioned hotel. She was surprised at herself; she'd never been one to hate anything. Usually she was the eternal optimist, the one who viewed the glass as half-full rather than half-empty. She knew she wasn't being fair to the lovely city or to the old traditional hotel. It was the circumstances that she hated, she decided. And right now she had a terrible case of cabin fever. Waiting for Chesney to come back from her holiday had been sheer torture.

She still wasn't happy about the letter Rand had written to Chesney and delivered to her flat so she'd find it upon her return. He'd labored over it for days. He hadn't let her read the letter. She'd felt bad, but what made her feel worse was that Rand was counting so heavily on Chesney's response. Somehow, even though she didn't know what the letter said, Maggie wasn't counting on anything. Her Mother Magic, as Cole referred to her intuition, was telling her Chesney was going to say, thanks but no thanks. Chesney would carry it one step further and say, I told you at the beginning I don't want anything from you, I just wanted you to know I'm alive. Period. End.

She was angry, at Rand for his blindness, and at Chesney for her stubbornness. She felt fear for the first time in her married life. Fear that Rand would grow away from her, fear that his daughter would consume him. Fear that she wouldn't be able to handle any of it.

This welcome-home luncheon for Chesney was important, that much she knew. For all of them. She hoped she and Rand would be able to return to the States in a day or so, and then home. Last night she'd made up her mind to return even if Rand elected to stay on. She would stick by her decision no matter what happened at this luncheon.

Maggie watched her husband out of the corner of her eye. He seemed to be taking as many pains getting dressed as she had. She'd changed her clothes three times, finally settling on a cherry-red sweater and matching skirt. It looked more cheerful than she felt. Rand couldn't decide if he should go casual, with a shirt and pullover, or wear a business suit. She was glad when he finally pulled a pale blue sweater over a slightly darker shirt. Gray flannel trousers and gray shoes completed his outfit.

"I think we're turned out rather well, darling. We are not overdressed; we're casual, but not too casual. If you erase the frown lines, you will be the handsomest man in all of London.

Darling, Chesney is going to be delighted to see you. Trust me."

"I'm not ready for this, Maggie." He sat down on the edge of the bed with a thump. "I don't have a good feeling about this meeting. I don't know why."

"I'm sure it's going to be a little strained, but that will be temporary. Think positively," Maggie said.

"How am I supposed to tell this young woman I checked her out, spoke to her mother, and decided yes, she's my daughter and she didn't lie to me? How can I say that, Maggie? For God's sake, the girl has feelings."

"So do you, my darling. Chesney will understand. She told you to check her out. She gave you license to do that. She said she understood that you would resent and reject her at first. Why don't we stop worrying and go along to lunch and see what happens. Unless you've changed your mind."

"No. I'm as ready as I'll ever be. Call down for a cab."

"I did that already, Rand."

"You don't have your coat on."

"Neither do you. I'm waiting for you. It's beastly hot in here. Come along, darling, it's time to welcome Chesney into our family."

Chesney arrived at the restaurant first. She gave her coat to a hatcheck girl, and five minutes later she wished she'd kept it on. The bench-lined hallway where she waited had no heat. She supposed she could ask to be seated. If she did that, she could avoid an awkward meeting in this cold, drafty corridor. She was just about to put her thought into action when the door opened. Maggie and Rand entered briskly, their shoulders and necks hunched into their heavy coats. This must seem like Siberia to someone who made his home in Hawaii, she thought. She smiled warmly and held out her hand, first to Maggie and then to Rand.

Rand ordered drinks. He snapped his lighter to fire up all three cigarettes. Chesney pretended not to see the trembling in his hand.

"Did you have a nice vacation, Chesney?" Maggie asked.

"I had a lovely time. I think, however, the expectation before going away on holiday is greater than the actual holiday. I do love the south of France and go every chance I can. Have you been there?"

Maggie and Rand both nodded. They talked for a while about various restaurants, the weather, the beaches, and the film stars who frequented the glorious beaches.

Their drinks almost finished, their luncheon orders given, Chesney fixed her gaze on Rand. "I was very surprised to see the letter from you in my mailbox when I returned. It was a pleasant surprise."

"I did what you suggested. I went round to the orphanage and to see . . . your mother."

"Has she recovered from my surprise visit?" Chesney asked quietly.

"No. She did, however, tell me something I think you might want to hear. Shall I tell you?"

"If you like."

Rand cleared his throat, not once but twice. "She said she wanted to take you in her arms and hug you. She said she was sorry she didn't do that. Every year on your birthday she bakes a cake and tells her family it's in memory of an old aunt. She said a day never went by that she didn't think of you. The day after your visit she went round to the orphanage."

Maggie watched the girl. Nothing changed in her face. When she spoke, it was as if they were discussing the weather. Don't hurt Rand, please, she begged silently.

"I appreciate you telling me this. She must have her hands full with five children and a husband who isn't too understanding. Our lunch is here. I'm afraid I'm going to have to eat quickly and run."

"Where?" Rand asked bluntly.

Chesney smiled. "I'm a working girl, remember? I have things to do. I must pick up my cat from the vet's, stop by the dry cleaners to get my uniforms, pay a sick call on a friend, and clean three weeks of dust in my flat. In between I have a drinks party to attend that I can't get out of. Plus—" she held up a warning hand "—I must do some grocery shopping since the icebox is empty."

Maggie smiled winningly. "Oh, how I remember those days. It seemed as though there weren't enough hours in the day to do everything. There were times when I got home from work and just went to bed. Can we help you with anything?"

"That's kind of you, but no. This fish is delicious. You aren't eating, Mr. Nelson; don't you like it?"

"Mr. Nelson sounds so formal. I don't expect you to call me father, but how about Rand?"

Rand, Rand, my darling, please don't sound so . . . so desperate, Maggie pleaded silently. She watched Chesney carefully for her reaction.

"If you like. I quite agree that Mr. Nelson sounds out of place. I wasn't sure how you would want me to address you. By the way, how long will you and Mrs. Nelson be in England?"

Rand wanted to say, as long as it takes to get to know you, but he didn't. "We aren't sure at the moment. Our stay depends on several things. When are your days off?"

Chesney laughed ruefully. "Not for a while, I'm afraid. I have to pay back a week of borrowed days from the girls who covered for me so I could have a full three weeks off." She smiled warmly in Rand and Maggie's direction.

What the smile said to Maggie was, "Go home; don't wait for me. I waited all these years; now it's your turn." Maybe she was being unkind to this daughter of Rand's.

"Quit your job. Come to Hawaii with us," Rand said.

Oh, Rand, please don't beg, Maggie wanted to cry. She could tell by the expression on Chesney's face that she'd been expecting Rand to say exactly what he'd said. She sounded, Maggie thought, as if she'd rehearsed her reply.

"I can't do that. I've lived here all my life. My friends are here. I have my flat and my cat. I have a good life, and I made it for myself. I don't want to give it up. For as long as I can remember I had no one to depend on but myself. I've grown accustomed to my independence and I love it. Thank you for the invitation, though," she said soberly.

Chesney's words were warm and gentle, but they knifed through Rand. Maggie could feel the fine hairs on the back of her neck start to prickle. Accept it, Rand. Let it go.

"Perhaps later, then. You can always change your mind." The desperate tone was still in Rand's voice.

Chesney leaned across the table. Her face was earnest, her voice quiet. "I told you when I first met you that I didn't want anything from you. I'm not about to stake out any claims. I'm happy with what I have. I have no desire to change my life. I'm very sorry if I gave you the impression that I would join up, as they say, when and if you came to a decision about my legitimacy. I thought I was very careful to be honest with you from the beginning."

Right, Maggie thought bitterly. You had no intention of changing *your* life, but what about ours? Please, don't be cruel to your father. Father, she realized, was just a title. She certainly could understand that. For so long she, too, had been without a father. But she'd been just the opposite of this girl sitting across the table from her. She'd lashed out and attacked every chance she got. She'd made herself and everyone in her life miserable. This young woman had her life in her own hands, and she wasn't about to transfer one little bit of it to anyone else. Who could blame her? Rand was never going to understand. Never.

"Won't you at least allow me to make up for all those years you spent in the orphanage?" Rand pleaded.

"Nothing could ever make up for those years. That's part of my life, and I think I've become a better person because of those years. I'm not trying to be cruel to you. It shouldn't be important for you to want to make that up. What you're feeling is guilt, and that shouldn't be, either. The only thing that has changed for either of us is we know now that we are father and daughter. I think it's important for each of us to be aware of the other. I'd like it if we could stay in touch. I'm sorry, but I have to run. It was a lovely lunch. Thank you for inviting me. Please, stay and have dessert."

Rand stood. He made a move as if to take her in his arms, but Chesney neatly sidestepped him. With an airy wave of her hand, she was gone. Rand sat down, his face bleak. He turned to Maggie. "What am I going to do?"

"Time, darling, will take care of everything. She is a remarkable young lady, and she means exactly what she says. She has no intention of becoming part of our lives except in a peripheral way. We should go home and pick up our lives, because that's what Chesney wants us to do. Nothing has changed for her."

"I can change her, sway her, make her want to come with us."

"She'll hate you, Rand. Leave her alone. She knows where we are, and if she needs us or wants us, she knows how to get in touch. We have to do what she wants, not what you want. I feel I'm right in this, Rand."

"Maggie, Maggie, I can't just turn my back on her. I have to stay. Please say you'll stay here with me."

"Darling, you'll just torture yourself. The girl's mind is made up. What are you going to do? Hang out where she works, wait till she gets off work, follow her home? Take flights that she's on? Don't do it, Rand."

"I wouldn't do that," Rand said testily.

"Yes you would. I can see it all over your face. And if you didn't do that, would you stay in your hotel room and wait for the phone to ring? What kind of life is that? Trust the girl, Rand, to do whatever she feels is right for her. You cannot make up for twenty-odd years in a few hours."

Rand turned to Maggie, his face full of rage. "Don't you understand? I can't, I won't, abandon my daughter . . . again. If you don't want to stay, then go back to Hawaii. I'm staying here. That's final, Maggie."

In all the years they'd been married, Rand had never spoken to Maggie like this. She felt sick to her stomach when she pushed her pie plate away. "I think I'll walk back to the hotel. You stay here, Rand, and have a few more drinks and commiserate with yourself about how unjust life is." Her tone was sharper than she'd intended.

Rand's eyes were miserable as he watched his wife leave the restaurant. He finished his peach cobbler and ordered a drink. He might just do what Maggie said. One drink, two, maybe even three. When they threw him out to get ready for the dinner rush, he could go to a pub and finish out the night. What the hell did he care?

Chesney forced herself to think only of the chores ahead of her as she made her way back to her flat. It wasn't until she was inside that the tears came. She'd been *that* close to jumping up from the table and throwing her arms around her father. But she'd held back, remembering Sara and the promise she'd made to herself.

She poured a saucer of milk for her cat and put the kettle on for tea. Tea always made her feel and think better. She'd read her father's letter again while she drank the Earl Grey. And she'd cry again, as she had the other fifty times she'd read the letter. Each time the Persian cat hopped on her lap and she nuzzled it close.

Only God knew how she'd prayed all her life for a family. And only God knew how fearful she was of being rejected. She'd insulated herself so thoroughly against that hurt, it was as though she were wrapped in concrete. If you didn't feel, you didn't get hurt.

All those brave words she'd said back in the restaurant were just that—brave words. She'd done a good job of convincing her father . . . yes, he really was her father . . . that she had a perfect life. She'd almost convinced herself. She ached with what she'd forced herself to give up. Would it be so difficult to give him a chance? Yes, yes, yes. If I give even an inch, I'm lost, I'll be just like Sara. I'll expect to be hugged and kissed and catered to. I'll expect an avalanche of loving words. If I give up everything I've fought for, that I've earned, I'll be lost. I can't take that chance. I won't take that chance, no matter how much it hurts now.

A small, mean voice deep inside her made itself heard. "You're up at bat now. Now you can jerk his strings. You can make him pay. You can make him suffer." Chesney dropped her head onto her folded arms. She cried for her past and for the present. She wouldn't cry for the future, because her future would be whatever she made of it. The fluffy white cat jumped on her lap.

With tears streaming down her cheeks, she reached for the letter on the shelf above her kitchen table. She'd read it one last time, then put it away and never look at it again. At least for a very long time. She dabbed at her eyes with a sodden tissue. She read aloud to the cat snuggled in her arms.

My dear Chesney,

I did all the things you suggested. I want you to know I started out convinced one hundred percent that there was no way on this earth you could be my daughter. I am now one hundred percent convinced that you are my daughter.

I have to admit to a certain amount of anger. I told myself, and my solicitors as well, and my wife, that there was no room in my life for a child. I made the decision years ago not to have children because I didn't think I was, as they say, good father material. I'm basically a selfish person. I told myself, over and over, as late as the day I mailed this letter, that I didn't want to be a father. I also told myself I would set up a trust fund for you and then I would leave and go back to my life. I thought it would be easy for me to walk away from you. It isn't.

I found myself going round to a church and having a talk with one of the fathers. He told me God sent you to me for a reason, and I shouldn't question that reason, but just to be happy that we found one another.

I admire what you've done with your life. Had I known about you sooner, I have to believe I would have

{ 257 }

swept you out of that place quicker than you could have blinked. But those are words, and I understand that you might have difficulty believing them.

I would like us to be friends, and perhaps we can go on from there and become father and daughter. That's what I want. It would please me greatly if you would want me as a friend and father. I can't make any wonderful promises to you. I'd like to, but that would be presumptuous of me. What I can do, if you're willing, is introduce you to your grandmother, who is one hell of a lady and who will love you to tears. I can show you our family through pictures in an album that will someday be yours. My wife will love you as I will come to love you, simply because you are my daughter.

I would never ask you to give up your independence, because I think I have some idea of how much it means to you. I ask only one thing of you, and that's for you to give yourself a chance to know the man I am now, not the man I was many years ago. I think that's a fair request.

It would please Maggie and me if you would come to Hawaii with us. If you can't see your way clear to do that now, perhaps you will in time. When you return from your holiday, please call us at the hotel so we can talk again.

Rand Nelson

She was blubbering again and squeezing the cat too tightly. She blew her nose lustily.

"Someday. Perhaps. But not now." She cried again, hard sobs that shook her thin shoulders.

Adam popped a can of beer to fortify himself for the call he was about to make to his best friend, Nick Deitrick, who went back to first-year college days. Nick the shrink. He was probably the kindest, the most gentle, the wisest man Adam knew.

He'd called on him for help at least a dozen times, for friends, even once for a stranger. Nick had been the one to persuade Sawyer to have the risky operation that saved her life. Adam knew if he called Nick from the middle of the Mojave Desert and asked him to come, he'd drop everything and head out. That was the kind of guy Nick was. Adam considered himself fortunate to be Nick's friend. He only hoped Nick felt the same way about him.

Adam swigged from the beer can. This was new—drinking beer at one in the afternoon. Summertime was a different story. He propped his basketball player's long legs on the ironing board and dialed long distance.

Nick picked up the phone on the third ring. "Dr. Deitrick here."

"This is Adam Jarvis," Adam said loftily, "here. That's here in Texas. How are you?"

"Well, if it isn't Farmer Jarvis himself. How's things on the south forty, or whatever it is you guys say?"

"I'm a rancher, not a farmer. Well, sort of . . . if you know what I mean."

"Hell, yes, you're pissing your life away pretending to be something you aren't," Nick said. "How many gopher holes you step in lately? Bet you thought I didn't know about gophers. By the way, you doing any *real* work?"

Adam knew he was referring to his political cartooning. "Haven't had time. This ranching is a hard life. Plus, I have to cook, clean, iron, saw wood, chauffeur, and a whole lot of other shit."

"I understand everything but sawing wood. Why?"

"Why? That's what you're supposed to do. We have a chain saw," Adam added, as if that explained everything.

As if by some prearranged signal the teasing banter between the two old friends gave way to seriousness. "I thought I'd extend an invitation. I'd like it if you'd come for a week, or even just a weekend. Riley would take you horseback riding out on the south forty, and Cole will take you up in the Dream Machine. I . . . I could use some help, Nick. Everybody in Texas is fucked up these days."

Nick's voice was pained when he replied. "I thought this was supposed to be a vacation. With a few little talks on the side—as in therapy, huh? You'd think I went to medical school just to help your friends."

"You know you're coming, so why are you badgering me? You took an oath, remember? To heal the sick in mind?"

"This is the last time I'm coming through for you, Jarvis. I wish to God you'd cultivate some other friends in the medical field."

"They'd never be as good as you. I trust you. When can I expect you?"

"A week from Friday? Best I can do. I have to find someone to cover for me. I hadn't planned on taking a vacation this
soon. By the way, are you working?"

He'd asked the same question the last time they spoke, and
Adam knew he didn't mean was he working on the ranch; he
meant at his profession. "Not yet; well, sort of. I'm getting
some ideas. I can't work when my life is upside down."

"If you'd stand still long enough, it would right itself. You
just look for trouble. I have to cut this short; my next patient is
here. I'll call you Friday before I leave."

"Thanks, Nick. For a shrink, you're okay."

"For a farmer, you're not so hot, but for a political cartoonist, you're the best. Don't be forgetting that, now."

"You son of a bitch!!" He could hear Nick laughing as he
hung up. Adam felt better now with Nick's promise to visit for
a whole week. He didn't like to admit it, but he needed a bit
of professional advice himself. Trouble was, he knew what he
wanted now, and it wasn't ranching after all, but he just didn't
know how to go about going after it. Her.

The phone jittered to life. "Riley! I was just going to call
and leave a message for you. You what? Farewell and adieu?
Jesus, Riley, Japan? For how long?" There was no answer.
Adam changed the subject quickly. "Jeff had a good time the
other day. I was going to ask you to take him out again. He's
hell-bent on becoming a Texas oilman. I tried to tell him there
isn't any oil. And last, but not least, I have to tell you Coots
Buckalew is putting some heavy-duty pressure on me to sell
this property to him. He doesn't have a pot to piss in, so
where is he going to get the money?"

"What did you tell him?"

"What I've been telling him for the past two years. The
Jarvis ranch is not for sale, never was and never will be. My
old man was a rancher, not an oilman, and I don't give a damn
if I'm sitting on billions of gallons of unleashed oil."

Riley would have given all four of his back molars for the
oil leases on the Jarvis property. He'd casually mentioned it
once, and the look on Adam's face made him back off. He'd
never mentioned it again. "How did he take it?"

"Like the bull he is. Said I was being an ornery, unpatriotic
son of a bitch. Now, what would you like from me?"

"Me? Nothing. I just called to say good-bye. Any messages for Sawyer?"

"Naw. Well, yeah, maybe one..."

"What is it? Come on, Adam, I don't have all day. If you can't come up with anything, I can make something up."

"You always were a smart-ass, Riley. Just tell her I love her. Go ahead, say something smart."

"When it comes to love, yours or anyone else's, I butt out," Riley said quietly. "Say good-bye to Jeff for me."

"I'll do that. Good luck, Riley. By the way, Nick Deitrick is coming next Friday. I was kind of hoping you'd want to talk to him."

"I'll work it all out, Adam. See you around."

Adam looked at the pinging receiver. He wondered if everyone in life had problems. He supposed it would be a hell of a world if things went along smoothly. Guys like Nick would be out of business. People like Coots Buckalew would be bored to tears, and people like himself would . . . what, Adam? "Suck my thumb," Adam mumbled. Just sit around and suck my thumb, waiting for the check in the mail. Waiting for Sawyer.

It was midday in England. Maggie sat alone in the hotel suite with her feet propped up on the coffee table. Rand had gone out, to follow Chesney or to see and talk to some of her friends. He hadn't asked her to go, and she wouldn't have gone anyway. She didn't approve of what Rand was doing. She wished now she'd stuck to her original plan and gone back to Hawaii. She'd give anything to walk on warm sand and swim in the spangled blue Pacific. She'd been too long without sunshine. She wanted to make love to her husband in their own bedroom with the warm breezes wafting through the French doors. She wanted to sit under the monkeypod tree and eat pineapples and macadamia nuts with him while they read the newspaper. She wanted to plan her weekly menus and go shopping at Ala Moana. Goddamn it, she wanted her husband back the way he was. And she wanted to go home.

A tear escaped her eye and she swiped at it angrily. She had to do something, make some kind of effort to prove she could still function. What she needed right now was to talk to her mother. She called the hotel operator and placed her call.

"I don't know what to do, Mam," Maggie said tearfully. "I can't blame Chesney. She's held to what she said. It's Rand. Why do I feel like this is the beginning of the end?"

Billie sighed. When her children were hurting, she hurt, too. "Because, darling, you are helpless. There's nothing you can do. This is something Rand has to work out for himself. You can't always be Maggie, the fixer-upper."

"He won't even listen to me. He told me to go home."

"He may have told you to go home, but what he's really saying is, stay with me till I work this out. Why don't you rent a furnished apartment so you will at least have some walking-around room? Whatever happens, you must be strong. Rand's going to take all his bitter disappointments out on you, and you'll have to be able to handle that. Don't create any new problems."

"What if he decides to stay here and . . . and keeps on acting like a bereaved father whose daughter wants no part of him?"

"That's when you deal with the problem, not now. Rand has to experience all his new feelings. It's Rand's problem, Maggie."

"We're married, Mam. That makes his problem mine, too."

"That's usually true, but not this time. This is intensely private. Rand knows you love him and that you'll be there for him when he needs you."

"That's just it, Mam. For the first time, he doesn't need me." Maggie cried.

"Oh, darling, I know. It's such a bitter pill to swallow, but swallow you must. Time, Maggie; give it time."

"This must be what it was like for you with Pap. Was it like this?" Maggie demanded.

"Yes, Maggie, the feelings you're having were the same ones I had with your father. I wanted to be all things, all the time. It simply doesn't work that way. Rand isn't like your father, though."

"Bless you, Mam. Say hello to Thad for me. I'll call you when I decide what I'm going to do."

"Maggie, I want you to promise me something."

"Anything, Mam."

"No matter what happens, don't get angry. Learn patience and practice it. Promise me."

"You're better than Nick Deitrick, and he charges a hundred fifty dollars an hour," Maggie said with a forced laugh.

"Good luck, Maggie. Call me if you need a friendly ear."

"I love you, Mam."

A tear escaped Billie's eye. "And I have always loved you, Maggie dear."

Billie sighed. So many people to worry about. So many problems. Love. Health. Money. Money—that reminded her again of Coleman Oil and the mess they were in. Right in the middle of which, Cary and Rand were investing in a sugar plantation. None of it made sense.

She looked forward to Maggie's visit. It would do them both good to let their hair down and really talk.

{{{{{{{{ CHAPTER THIRTEEN }}}}}}}}

Cary enjoyed the long drive up to the North Shore. The map Maggie sent him was perfect, her directions easy to follow. He recognized the banyan tree that stood sentinel at the Nelson's gate. He saluted it happily. He'd made it! He drove up the long driveway, his eyes trying to take in everything at once. He stopped the car in the middle of the driveway to drink in the beauty of the estate. The thick, spiky grass was a meadow of brilliant green. But it was the back of the house that drew him, made him gasp. There, in all its glory, was the Pacific Ocean. For a moment, he stood in awe. He ran to the white beach, kicking off his shoes as he went. He drew in his breath; Amelia was going to love this. He turned to look at the back of the house. It was postcard perfect. There was the ancient monkeypod tree Billie spoke of so often, the lanai where Maggie and Rand spent most of their time. Everywhere, as far as the eye could see, were brilliant hibiscus, fragrant pink and white plumeria, and, wonder of wonder, orchids by the hundreds.

Cary itched to shed his clothes and sample the warm, blue waters. He walked back to the driveway for his car, garaged it, and carried in his bags. He whistled in awe when he took his first good look at Maggie and Rand's paradise house.

An hour later, with a cold beer in his hand, Cary sat on a lime-colored cushion on the lanai. He had calls to make. People were expecting to hear from him. He groaned. Inside a cabinet to his left was a phone. He pulled it toward him to dial

Thomas Yoneyama's office. He announced himself and waited.

"Welcome to Hawaii, Mr. Assante," a rich, melodic voice greeted.

"Thank you, Mr. Yoneyama. I left subfreezing temperatures in Texas, and I'm real happy to be here."

"Then perhaps you will consider staying for a while to enjoy our hospitality."

"Business first. When can we get together?"

"If you think you will be rested sufficiently by tomorrow afternoon, I can arrange a meeting for, say, three o'clock. Eighteen hundred Kalakaua Avenue in Waikiki."

"I can make it," Cary said.

"It's settled, then. Is there anything I can do for you in the meantime? Where are you staying?"

"The Kamali estate. Or I should say the Nelson estate now."

The man's voice changed slightly and became upbeat. "I know the house well. It was empty for many years. I understand it's a showplace now. I went to school with Ester Kamali. You will have no problem resting there."

"I'm finding that out. I'll see you tomorrow."

The second call was to Ellery Murashige to set up a second meeting in regard to the sugar refinery. After welcoming Cary to Hawaii, he promised to call the other owners and arrange a dinner meeting at the Kahala Hilton. Cary hung up and called Amelia.

"Darling, how is Hawaii?" Amelia asked gaily.

"Amelia, you have to come here. I don't know how to describe this place except to say it's perfect. I can't find a thing wrong with it. I can't wait for you to see it." Cary smiled at the excitement in his own voice.

"Have you been swimming?"

"It's the first thing I did. I'm just sitting here in this warm, beautiful sunshine, missing you and sipping cold beer. What's the temperature at home?"

"Twenty-four degrees." Amelia laughed.

"I set up my meetings, at least the first two. There will probably be two dozen more in the next ten days. I get the impression these people are very formal. No good-old-boy jokes and no backslapping. I haven't called Rand yet. I thought I'd wait till I had something definite to report."

"Darling, hold off calling Rand. I spoke to Billie yesterday." She told him about Maggie's phone call to her mother. "Do what you have to do, and I'm sure if Rand were thinking properly, he'd go along with whatever you decide. Don't be surprised if Maggie pops back; she's really missing the sunshine. I, for one, think she will stay in England with Rand and see this thing through."

"Poor guy. He must be going through hell," Cary said.

"The day always comes when each of us has to pay our dues. Some quicker than others," Amelia said.

"I miss you, babe. I wish you were here."

"Brrr, I wish I was there, too. Soon, my darling. Why don't we say good night so I can go to bed and you can take a nap in the warm sunshine."

"Amelia, there are orchids growing in the backyard. Hundreds of them."

"Save one for me, and I'll pin it behind my ear. I think it's supposed to mean something."

Cary laughed. "That's so some guy can nibble his girl's ear while he's pretending to smell the flower."

"You're probably right. You may nibble my ear on arrival. Good night, darling."

Cary leaned back in the lounge chair after he finished his beer. A nap would be wonderful. He'd probably sleep like a tired marathon runner.

He woke two hours later, bathed in perspiration. He'd been dreaming of Julie. His heart was pounding in his chest, and the stiff erection inside his swim trunks made him dash for the beach.

Dripping wet, he jogged back to the lanai and flopped down on a lemon-colored string hammock to relive the dream. Julie had been standing on the beach, all alone, swaying to some unheard music. He'd been sitting on the lanai, stringing her favorite blossoms into a lei. He'd strung hundreds and hundreds of blooms into an endless string. He'd spotted Julie and ran to the beach, the endless lei trailing behind him. They hadn't spoken. Their eyes met and held. He'd wound the blossoms around her from neck to toe. Still they didn't speak. The scent from the flowers was making him light-headed. Julie, too. He'd woken when they both toppled to the sand, their arms around each other.

He'd successfully pushed Julie from his daytime thoughts, but now she was invading his sleep. There would be more dreams, he was sure of it. On an impulse, he rolled out of the hammock to reach the phone. He sat cross-legged on a reed mat to dial the information operator. He asked for the number of the Waikiki Beach Tower. He memorized the number and quickly dialed. "Julie Kingsley," he said coolly.

Twelve rings later the switchboard operator came back on the line. "Miss Kingsley isn't answering. Would you care to leave a message?"

"No. I'll call back later. Thank you."

He was insane. It had to be the flowers and the sunshine. He was drunk on the island. It happened to people, he was told. He'd sworn he was never going to get in touch with Julie again. "Bastard," he hissed. "Just hours ago you were talking to your wife, telling her you missed her and wished she was here. What kind of bastard are you?" he demanded of himself.

"The kind that's going to shower, dress, and drive into Waikiki. I'm tired of fooling myself. I want to see Julie and I intend to see Julie."

The thought stayed with Cary while he showered and dressed. He splashed some cologne on his cheeks, strapped on his watch, and ran a brush through his hair. He checked his wallet and looked for the car keys. He could make it to Waikiki in an hour and a half, according to the map. Just in time to announce himself to Julie and take her out to dinner.

Cary arrived in Waikiki and its maze of one-way streets. He drove around for an hour trying to find the entrance to the Beach Tower. Frustrated and angry, he stopped a policeman on a three-wheeled bicycle to ask directions.

"Turn around here, go to Ala Wai Boulevard, and follow that till you come to Niu Street. Make a left and stay to your right, and you'll be on Kalakaua. Stay on Kalakaua till you come to Liliuokalani Avenue. There's a McDonald's on the corner; make a left. The driveway is one block down on your left."

Cary turned the car around and narrowly missed two women dressed in brilliant red muumuus. He cursed loudly as his eyes sought out the street signs. Every damn street had at least four Ks in its name.

He drove slowly, caught behind two young boys on bicycles. He'd never seen so many people clustered in one area in his life. They walked aimlessly, carrying their shopping bags, apparently with no destination in mind. He cursed again until he saw the golden arch of a McDonald's. He waited for a crowd of giggling girls to cross the street before he made his left turn. There was the sign—Waikiki Beach Tower. He'd been up and down this street three times and had missed it. A group of women were walking toward his car, so he had to wait again. All of them wore large name tags. The woman closest to him wore a badge that said she was from Poplar Bluff, Missouri.

A valet took his car, and before he knew what was happening, it was gone, tires squealing down the ramp. A second young man approached him and asked who he was visiting. "This is a high-security building, sir. We lock the main gates here, and even the tenants have to use a key to get in. I'll call for you."

"Julie Kingsley. I'm not sure which floor she's on."

The boy grinned. "I think you're too late. She went out about thirty minutes ago, but I'll check."

"Do you know all the tenants' names?" Cary asked.

The boy grinned brashly. "Only the good tippers."

Cary grinned, too. He'd hustled once himself at that age. Hawaiian tourists were noted for overtipping, or so Amelia had warned him. "Fifteen percent, darling, no more," she'd said.

"I was right, sir; she's out. Would you like to leave a message?"

"No. I need my car."

He paid three dollars to get his car back and drove out the way the valet had driven in, tires squealing. He should have known better. Calling would have solved everything. She could be anywhere. Maybe she was with the lady from Poplar Bluff, and he'd missed her in the group. She could be one of the pedestrians he'd seen carrying a shopping bag filled with souvenirs. "Shit."

Now all he had to do was find a street that would take him back to H–1 and Maggie's house.

On the drive home he felt like a forty-eight-year-old fool.

Cary was up the following morning at 4:00 A.M. He was on his way to Waikiki by four thirty-five and chopper-bound for a round-trip to Hilo at six forty-five, courtesy of Mr. Yoneyama. He'd be able to scope out the sugar plantation from the air before their noon meeting.

The pilot looked like a recycled beach bum, Cary thought. He was also quiet. He'd furnished two cardboard containers of coffee which said it came from Apple Annie's.

"Good coffee," Cary complimented. The pilot nodded.

"You don't say much, do you?"

"You're paying me to fly. You didn't say anything about wanting a tour guide. That's Molokai to your left. Maui is a little south, and Hawaii due south of that. Another thirty minutes and we'll be in Hilo. What do you think of our Hawaiian sunrise?"

"Awesome. It beats Key West," Cary said honestly. "You been flying this thing for a long time?"

"About four years. I was a helicopter pilot in the navy. When I got out I came here for some R and R, knocked around the surfing circle, got myself a busted spleen and lost a kidney. Now I'm just an observer on the Banzai."

"You surfed the Banzai?" Cary asked increduously. "Only the best surfers in the world surf the Pipeline."

"Or fools. You must be the dude that's going to buy the old Peralta sugarcane plantation. You don't look British."

"I'm not. My partner is, though. He lives up on the North Shore. The Kamali estate. Do you know it?"

"Used to pass it every day on my way to the Banzai. Where are you from?"

"Texas." Cary sipped at the coffee. It was delicious. "By the way, how did you find out about our interest in buying the plantation?"

The pilot laughed. "They've been trying to unload that plantation for years. You aren't the first man I've flown to Hilo to look it over. You're the first guys interested in building a refinery, though. At least, to my knowledge. I'm no real estate salesman, but I've been here long enough to know a deal when I see one. The plantation is overpriced. Otherwise, the Japanese would have snapped it up by now. They own half this state as it is."

"So I've heard."

"My advice to you would be to play a little hardball. That's just my opinion. We could use a refinery here. Something besides tourism for employment."

"I'll keep it in mind."

"I have a couple of other suggestions if you're interested."

"Let's have it. I can use all the information I can get."

"Check the drainage. Get the weather reports for the past twenty or thirty years and see what the rainfall was. Do a projection. Irrigation is real expensive over here. There's Hilo. Do you want to land or do you want me to circle the plantation?"

"Circle. I want to take some pictures from up here. I assume those shacks are the workers' quarters?"

"Shacks is the right word. Nobody should have to work all day and live in those hovels. There's no running water or electricity. It wouldn't cost that much to put up some military-type housing, maybe Quonset huts. You could take that off the asking price. The main house is in bad shape. There was a write-up about it not too long ago in the *Honolulu Advertiser*. Now, that's going to cost a small fortune to refurbish, if you plan to live in it. I've never been in it, but the pictures were fantastic. Your wife would have a ball getting it into shape. Women see stuff like that as the ultimate challenge. Again, that's only my opinion."

Cary shuddered, remembering the time Amelia refurbished her mother's old house in Texas, spending hundreds of thousands of dollars, and then burned it to the ground the day she finished it. Her words came back to him: "Sooner or later, everyone pays his dues." He shuddered.

"I think I've seen enough. Let's go back to the heliport. I might have time for a visit to the courthouse before my meeting."

"If you plan on doing business here, I'd like to offer my services. I have two choppers. If the price is right, I could keep one on Hilo and ferry you guys back and forth. I'll give you my card when we set down."

"I'll consider it."

"I can't ask for more than that. You should know I have two experienced guys I use when I have more business than I can handle, which isn't often." Cary nodded.

They talked nonstop on the flight back to the heliport. Half the conversation was business, the other half Hawaiian folklore. Cary soaked it all up like a sponge. When Amelia arrived, he'd be able to tell her all about it.

"Where's a good place for breakfast?" Cary asked as the pilot landed the small craft at the heliport.

"When I'm in Waikiki I usually hit the Jolly Roger. They don't skimp, and the food is good. The one I like is on Kuhio. Give it a whirl. Here's my card. Call me if you need me. If I'm out on a run, I turn on my machine. Don't be afraid to talk to it."

Answering machines. Kuhio. Didn't he drive along Kuhio last night when he was looking for Julie? There was a tingling

{ 269 }

in his hands and arms when he climbed into his car. He pulled the map over to the window for light. Yep.

It was only ten-thirty; he had lots of time. He'd have a bite, do a little sight-seeing, stop in an ABC store for toothpaste, call Julie, stop by and see Julie, ask Julie to dinner. See Julie.

This time Cary plotted his course carefully, remembering the one-way streets. If he turned down Liliuokalani Avenue, he could park, and call Julie, then leave his car there while he walked to the corner of Kuhio and the Jolly Roger.

Cary tried to calm his twanging nerves. What tourist in his right mind would be in his room at one in the afternoon? Not Julie Kingsley, according to the attendant.

Cary headed for the Jolly Roger.

While he finished his coffee and Orange Julius, he scanned the map to see how close he was to 1800 Kalakaua Avenue. Satisfied that he could walk, he left a tip and paid the check. He did not give in to the temptation to phone Julie again—but he knew he'd try again after the meeting.

It was ten minutes of six when Cary left the offices of Thomas Yoneyama. The deal was going to go through, he could feel it in his gut. A couple of days of phone calls back and forth would tie things up nicely. He'd kept his poker face intact when Thomas Yoneyama mentioned that several Japanese investors were interested in the plantation. Cary had leaned across the table. "I never make more than one offer. I never dicker and I never renege. What that means in Texas is take it or leave it. All my credentials are in the folder I gave you. You can reach my banker any time—right now if you like. His home phone number is at the bottom of the bank statement. I'll wait to hear from you, Mr. Yoneyama."

Thomas Yoneyama was a peaceful-looking man with honey-molasses skin and a crown of pure white hair. He had great dark eyes which looked like pools of warm chocolate, a sensitive mouth, and square white teeth. They gleamed brightly every time he opened his mouth.

He'd already checked Cary Assante out, as well as Rand Nelson. They fared far better than the Japanese. He had a deal, one he'd been waiting for for years. There was a sucker born every minute. On the other hand, maybe he was the sucker. Both Nelson and Assante were astute businessmen. What did they see that he didn't.

* * *

{ 270 }

There was still no answer in Julie's room. Cary was bushed; he'd put in a long day. He could hang around and continue to make a fool of himself, ringing Julie every ten minutes, or he could go back to the house, call Marty Friedman, his lawyer, and go to bed. He opted for the sensible plan and headed for his car.

It was past midnight when Cary dialed Marty's home phone number. Cary listened politely while Marty squawked about the eleven inches of snow that blitzed the New York area. "Will I come to Hawaii? I'll be on the next plane. I'll call Alan now to save you the call. We should be there by tomorrow evening, your time. I'll have my secretary call you sometime tomorrow with our arrival and flight number. Hold that sunshine!"

A quick dip in the ocean with the moonlight smiling down on him was just what Cary needed. A cheese sandwich and a cold beer would lull him to sleep. A fitting end to a long, hard day.

Just as sleep claimed him, the phone rang. He rolled over, burying his head in the pillow. Was it Amelia, calling him to chastise him for not calling earlier? He was too tired to get up and go into the kitchen to answer the phone. But what if something was wrong at home? He stumbled out of bed and padded to the kitchen. In the dark he reached for the phone, missed, and grabbed a second time. When he brought the receiver to his ear, he heard only a dial tone. "Shit!" he said succinctly. Now he was wide-awake. Should he call Amelia? It was early morning at home. Angrily, he punched out the Texas number. Amelia's cheerful voice annoyed him. "Did you just call me . . . honey?"

"Aha, there's another woman in your life! Sorry, darling, it wasn't me. I am glad you called, though. I expected you to call last evening. I sort of waited up but finally fell asleep. How's it going?"

"Fine. Everything is fine. I was just falling asleep and the phone rang. By the time I got to the kitchen, whoever it was hung up. I thought something might have happened at home."

"My, you are testy. Go back to sleep, darling. We'll talk later. Love you."

"Uh huh," Cary mumbled as he hung up the phone.

Someplace in his dream Cary thought he heard a phone ring a second time. In his nightmare he was running for his very life on Waikiki Beach. Amelia and Julie were both chasing him. His heart beat wildly as he tried to run faster, but the sand and his dress shoes held him back. Long arms, hundreds of them, all wearing gold bracelets, reached for him, dragging him down to the sand. He gasped and woke. It was the phone again. He squinted at the digital clock on the night table— 8:45.

He staggered out of bed to head for the kitchen, only to hear the phone stop ringing. "Goddamn it!" he thundered as he made his way to the shower.

Julie hated bus rides of any kind. She'd taken the tour to Germaine's Luau just so she could say she'd done it. It hadn't been fun for her, although most of the couples seemed to enjoy themselves. There had been only three single people on the whole bus, and it wasn't till they were actually at the luau that she paired herself off with them. She was sorry five minutes later when they announced they were born-again Christians from Sangaree, South Carolina. A devil perched itself on her shoulder at that moment and she said, louder than she intended, "I was born right the first time." She hadn't gotten any laughs, even a titter. The three women, who were also schoolteachers, had moved away from her as though she had underarm odor.

Left to her own devices, and without benefit of an escort, she was afforded the best seat in the house for the show. She enjoyed the Polynesian show, but the song-and-dance team had been awful, in her opinion. The food was something she'd never want again, nor the watered-down blue drink that came with it. She concluded, as she made her way back to the bus, that she'd wasted $38.95. But then, nothing in Hawaii had pleased her so far. Don Ho and his rendition of *Tiny Bubbles* left her as flat as the coconut drink the Hilton Hawaiian Village served during his performance.

She'd done the International Market Place in two hours. Fifty dollars and two straw bags of junk convinced her it wasn't a place to return to even if she was bored to tears. Waikiki Beach, she decided, after the first two days and a vicious sunburn, was worse than Coney Island on a hundred-degree day in August. Diamond Head was beautiful from the highway or from the side window in a plane, but going into the crater was like walking in a field of burnt-out straw. She'd enjoyed the jitney ride around the eighteen-hundred-acre wild-life and botanical gardens of Waimea Falls Park, but again, she'd felt uncomfortable with all the couples holding hands and snapping pictures.

Her itinerary still held places to see: Pearl Harbor, Hilo Hattie's Fashion Factory, the Dole Pineapple Cannery, Nuuanau Pali Lookout, and the Kodak Hula Show. She had made arrangements on her own to see the Kawamoto Orchid Nursery, but she had neither confirmed nor paid for her reservation. She'd signed up for a cruise around the islands but was going to cancel it. She didn't need another whole day and evening of watching happy couples.

The bus was quiet now, the happy tourists thinking about tomorrow's activities. She was tempted to hang out in her room and give her sunburn a chance to cool down.

When the bus ground to a halt at the Waikiki Beach Tower, Julie was the third one off. There was no one to say good-bye to, no one to wave to but the tour guide.

She walked across the road and entered the Tower from the side entrance. After five minutes of foraging for her key, she realized she'd left it in her other pocketbook. She asked to be let in.

The young man at the desk smiled. "That's what we're here for. Guests tell me the islands are so overwhelming, they forget the most ordinary things."

"I guess that's what it is," Julie said tiredly.

"Miss Kingsley, earlier today—twice, in fact—a gentleman called for you. He didn't leave a name, but he has a very distinctive voice."

"For me! Are you sure?"

"I'm sure. I have to log it in the book. The same man was here last night, too, I have his license number, since we parked his car. You were out all three times. Would you like the number of the plate?"

Puzzled, Julie nodded. "Dollar Rent a Car! I don't know anyone in Hawaii. Thank you," she muttered.

It wasn't till she was in her room with the door locked that she started to shake. It was true, she didn't know anyone in Hawaii. Her heart thumped so crazily she had to sit down on the sofa. Cary. It had to be Cary.

Dollar Rent a Car. Well, she'd soon find out. The car rental agencies were open twenty-four hours a day. Information gave her the number. She tapped out the numbers quickly before she could change her mind. The blatant lie that spilled from her lips made her wince. "This is Alice Morgan. I believe a customer of yours sideswiped my car earlier this evening. He drove off before I could call for the police. Yes, I have the license number. Yes. Yes. I'd like to handle this privately if I can. No, there was no damage to *your* car. Just give me the man's phone number and where he's staying. We can avoid calling the police if you cooperate," Julie said briskly.

"This is highly irregular," a young voice declared. She hated it when problems came up on her shift. Personnel had told her the midnight shift was always quiet. She'd taken the job so she could do her homework. This woman was saying she'd settle the matter without calling the police. That was fine with her. It would save her a mound of paperwork and a dozen phone calls. She rattled off the customer's name and phone number and the temporary address he'd given. "If you want his driver's license number, I can give you that, too. He did pay for collision."

Julie walked back to the couch. She stretched out, her arms crossed over her chest. She took long, deep breaths. He was here. He'd remembered the name of the place she was staying. He'd been here looking for her, and he'd called twice. She'd probably gone right by the house he was staying in on her way to Waimea Falls. She'd been *that* close to him.

Her hands trembled when she pulled the phone to the sofa. She pushed the little buttons and waited. She didn't realize she'd been holding her breath till the phone rang for the eighth time. She hung up on the thirteenth ring. Either he was out or sleeping soundly. Tomorrow was another day.

{{{{{{{{ CHAPTER FOURTEEN }}}}}}}}

Nick Deitrick arrived in a lemon-colored Toyota. Adam watched from the window as Nick tried to extricate his soccer-ball body from the little car. The minute he had both feet firmly planted on the ground, Adam opened the kitchen door and shouted a welcome. "What the hell kind of car is that? Looks like one of those things you ride around in in amusement parks." He guffawed.

"The only kind your car rental allowance would allow. I'll

get you for this, you bastard. Do you have any idea of how uncomfortable I was riding all the way out here? Well, do you?" Nick demanded. There was a twinkle in his eye.

"You're getting a whole week's free vacation. Don't quibble or I won't feed you. Let's start all over. Welcome to the Jarvis ranch, Nick."

"Cut the crap. When do we have lunch?"

"It's three in the afternoon. You missed lunch. Dinner is cooking. I can give you an apple."

Nick hefted a canvas bag from the trunk of the car. "You want my brain, you have to feed it."

He devoured the apple; Adam watched him from his perch on the porch railing.

As always, by some unheard prearranged signal, both men turned serious.

"Cole's coming to dinner. I thought you could talk to him while I go to the gym to pick up Jeff. I don't think I've ever seen a more miserable human being than Cole Tanner right now. If I could have helped him, I wouldn't have called you, but I don't know what it is he needs. Cole appears to be open and up front in everything, but I've learned over the years that he lets you know what he wants you to know, and that's it. There's a side of Cole Tanner no one knows. I think of him as a kid, and he's far from a kid. This thing with Riley is tearing him apart. And speaking of Riley, you lost a patient. He's on his way to Japan. He said to say hello, and he'll work out his own problems, thank you."

"Cole knows why I'm here?"

"I told Cole I'd called you to see if something could be done to help Jeff settle in. That was before he and Riley had their knockdown. When I mentioned it again, I said something about him talking to you."

"I can't push myself on him, Adam. Cole's a nice guy. He's also smart enough to know if he needs help."

"I'm not asking for miracles. Just talk to him. Like a friend. He knows you're a shrink. If he wants to open up, he will. We won't know unless we try."

"I'll do what I can. Tell me about Jeff."

Adam dropped his head into his hands. "I don't know, Nick. There are days when I want to throw him back. I want to go back to my old life. I don't honestly know if I want this kid or not. I don't feel much of anything for him, and that bothers me. There are days when I hate the little bastard. He's got a mouth like a sewer. He hasn't made any friends at school because he's so damn nasty. No one wants to be around him. He's smart, though. He's aced every test, written and oral. He's one of those kids that just has to look at something and he remembers it. So far, school isn't a challenge. I've signed him up for everything there is. The kid is so whipped when he gets home, he takes a shower and goes to bed."

"That should make you happy."

"What? That he goes to bed early?"

Nick threw his apple core over his shoulder. "The boy is in school all day. When school is over, he stays for other activities. He comes home, eats, and goes to bed. He's really out of your hair, isn't he?"

"Well, yeah."

"When do you spend time with him? Time when you aren't reaming him out over something. Good time."

"Saturdays are spent at the gym or the Y. Sundays I take him to church. Sometimes we go to a movie or out to dinner. I got some mopeds, but he sneered at them. Riley took him out last week. He had a good time."

"You called him a little bastard before. You and I call each other that, but it's in the fond sense of the word. I didn't get that impression when you spoke of Jeff. Do you hate him, Adam?"

"Do you have to be so goddamn blunt?"

"Yeah, I do."

"Probably."

"Jeff knows it, then. So you aren't doing him any good deeds by keeping him here. Wide open spaces, healthy fresh air, a nice house, good food—they aren't the answer. Do you remember anything at all about when you were thirteen?"

"Yeah. I learned how to masturbate."

"You've forgotten a few things, Adam," Nick said. "What else do you remember?"

"Junior Ranchers. Baseball. Mom and Dad. Nice place to bring friends. Mom always had fresh cookies. Pop always talked to the kids. They all liked him—my friends, I mean. This place was always crawling with kids."

"So you brought him back here, but you haven't given him any of those things. You don't even like him. Why the hell didn't you stay in New York? You didn't have to play the big martyr and throw out your career and make a production of bringing the kid here to make things right. Marrying Jenny was your first mistake. From that point on you kept compounding that mistake. This is where you are now."

"What's the answer, Nick?"

"You tell me. You know us head pounders don't give away answers. I'll tell you one thing, though. It's not Jeff who is standing between you and Sawyer. You're doing that all by yourself. Don't blame Jeff for that."

"Who the hell said anything about Sawyer?"

"I'm trained to see and hear what you aren't saying. That's why I'm a psychiatrist and you draw cartoons. The fact that you make more money than I do by drawing those shitty little pictures doesn't count."

There was a sardonic look on Adam's face. "The truth always hurts. Thanks, Nick. I owe you one."

"No you don't. We're friends. Let's get back to Jeff."

"The closest I've come to seeing this kid happy, or what passes for happy, is when he has anything to do with cooking. He's really into it. He makes breakfast and sets the table for me, always folds the napkins a new way. He's cut a whole stack of recipes out of different magazines. I'll be damned if I know what it means."

"Does it have to mean something? Why can't he simply be interested in good food? He knows you aren't worth shit in the kitchen. Does he serve you breakfast or does he just make it?"

"He goes the whole route. Long-stemmed glasses with crushed ice and orange juice, cloth napkins, a sprig of parsley on the plate to make it look good. He matches the dishes to the place mats. The kid sets a nice table."

"Yet you find that strange."

"Don't you?"

"Not at all. Just because you aren't interested in cooking, or weren't interested in cooking at his age, doesn't mean there's anything wrong with it."

"I know what you're trying to say, Nick. You're right, there's nothing wrong with it. It's just that it doesn't compute. Not with this kid. What thirteen-year-old boy collects recipes? It means something, but I don't know what."

"See, you've made up your mind that there is something wrong. We'll find out what it means. Hey, can I get out of this suit? I feel like an easterner."

"Come on, I'll show you your room. You can take a shower if you want. Cole should be here soon."

"You got running water out here?"

" 'Lectric lights, too. They go on when it gets dark. I'll see you downstairs."

All the way to the Jarvis ranch, Cole tried to rehearse what he'd say in response to the questions he knew Nick would ask. Shrinks always went back to childhood and the parents. Shit. That wasn't his problem and he knew it. Still, if that was what he had to do, he'd do it. He needed to talk to someone. He sure as hell wasn't getting anywhere on his own.

He had all the respect in the world for Nick. He'd seen firsthand the results he'd gotten with Sawyer when she refused to have the operation for her brain tumor. The whole family had tried to reason with her, badgered her, coaxed and pleaded to no avail. She'd have died if it weren't for Nick. He trusted Nick the same way he trusted Adam.

It would be good to see Nick again, and even Jeff. He was beginning to like the kid.

Cole cut the engine and shut off the lights. It was still warm in the car, too warm. All he was doing was postponing the moment when he had to walk into the house and see Nick. He gave himself a mental shake. There was no shame in asking for help when you needed it. "Here goes nothing," he muttered.

The handshakes over, drinks in hand, Cole prowled the room like an anxious terrier. Nick watched him from the corner of his eye. Adam kept up a steady stream of chatter that Cole later couldn't remember.

"Bad day?"

Cole stopped pacing. He looked at Nick carefully, as though he were committing his face to memory. He grinned ruefully. "Not one of my better days, but no worse than some I've had." Nick Deitrick had the shrewdest, kindest eyes Cole had ever seen.

"Ah, we all have those. Take today, for instance. Would you believe I have been given nothing to eat but an apple? A man could starve!" he said, looking at Adam pointedly.

"Just wait till you taste a plate of his favorite beans that he doctors up with soy sauce and raw onions. Now, that's a killer." Cole grinned.

Good old Nick; if there was one thing he knew how to do, it was defuse anxiety. Adam took his cue. "I have never pretended to be a cook, or a chef. I do my best. Beans are good for you. Everything I've ever served you guys is right out of a nutrition book."

"Yeah, but they don't tell you to char it to death, boil it till it evaporates, or fry it till it bounces in the pan," Nick muttered.

"I am a political cartoonist. You expect too much," Adam said loftily. "But you're getting my very best efforts tonight, plus one of Jeff's gourmet desserts."

"If it isn't as good as it smells, you're going out of here in a body bag, and I'm pulling up the zipper," Nick snarled. He winked at Cole.

An hour later the three men pushed their chairs back from the table. Nick loosened his belt. Adam belched loudly. Cole sighed happily.

"I think that's one of the best dinners I've had in a real long time," Cole said.

Adam made a deep bow. "I'll bring fresh coffee and brandy to the parlor if you gentlemen will help clear the table."

"Is there enough left for Jeff?" Nick asked.

"More than enough. His dinner is just waiting for him to sit down. I'm going to pick him up now, while you have your coffee. I should be back in half an hour or so, if the coach lets them out on time."

"Great dinner!" Nick said, following Adam into the kitchen. "No body bags tonight."

Coffee cup in hand, the parlor door closed, Cole looked at Nick, who was sniffing his brandy appreciatively before sipping. "I have this problem," Cole said hesitantly. Nick sipped his brandy and waited. With machine-gun rapidity Cole blurted out the story of his fight with Riley and his relationship with Lacey.

"So?"

"So what? That's the problem I wanted to talk to you about."

"Cole, I've known you a long time. You're a nice guy; you've got a lot on the ball. Someday we're probably going to play racquetball together, when I lose some weight, so don't ruin that promising future relationship by trying to con me. You want my help, I'll give it willingly, but don't try to snow me. Okay? Riley is part of the problem, but he isn't the problem. Get my drift?"

"What do you think my problem is?" Cole asked coolly.

"How in the name of God would I know? What I do know

is that it's an old problem, and the fight with Riley just brought it to a head. If you feel you don't want to talk about it or this isn't the time, I can respect that. It's your decision." Nick watched Cole's expression. He'd seen the same kind of inner turmoil, the same gut stubbornness, in Cole's half sister, Sawyer.

He waited patiently as he sipped his brandy. He let his eyes circle the room for Cole's benefit. Adam's family had good taste. While nothing was new, the old pieces had been shined to a rich patina. Scratches and scuff marks covered. Character. Growing up here had to be wonderful for Adam.

"I never wanted to come here," Cole began, "but when Mother inherited Sunbridge, I had no other choice. I think of Sunbridge as just a house. A place to sleep, eat, and take a shower. I've never spent a lot of time there. I'd go out of my way to work late, stay in town, anything to avoid going back till it was time to go to bed. All it is is a house. Words like shrine and mausoleum come to mind when I have to talk about it. My mother used to practically get orgasmic over it. I know she had some problems there when she was younger, but she got a handle on all of it. She still adores Sunbridge.

"Riley came to Texas at the most vulnerable time of his life. It was as if he was meant for Sunbridge. And vice versa. I think he's counted the bricks it took to build it. He loves that place the way a man loves a woman. Grandma Billie wants no part of it. When she comes to visit, she can't wait to leave. Aunt Amelia hates it. I hate it. I hate it as much as Riley loves it," Cole said vehemently.

"That's okay. A house just gives us creature comforts. Do you know the difference between a house and a home? Don't feel stupid if you don't know the answer. Most men don't."

"A home is a family," Cole said hesitantly.

"And?" Nick prompted.

"A mother, a father, brothers and sisters. Laughter, sadness, and . . . and living together. Yelling and screaming, your own room, fights with your siblings. Punishments, old furniture, pets that crap on the good carpet. Hot dogs and baked beans for dinner on Tuesday nights. Seeing your mother and father kiss each other under the mistletoe."

"You should have been a writer," Nick said lightly. He was shocked to see the color drain from Cole's face. He recovered quickly. "You'll probably find this weird, but I used to write some pretty good poetry. Hell, I even did a short story once.

{ 280 }

Never got either published, but it was a catharsis for me. Tell me more about the fight with Riley."

"I fucked his fiancée, my old girlfriend," Cole said loudly. "That's the bottom line."

"If you think that shocks me, you're wrong."

"When I think about it now, I could have stopped. I didn't. That doesn't say a whole hell of a lot for me, now does it?"

"On the contrary, it says a lot if you care to analyze it."

"You analyze it. You're the problem solver. Every time I think about it, I get tied up in knots."

"You laymen give us too much credit. I'll walk you through it if you want."

Cole nodded.

"Did you think the relationship between Riley and Lacey was a good one? Were they in love?"

"In my opinion, no. Lacey wanted to get married. I didn't. We broke it off. She kept calling me and I tried to avoid her. She went after Riley, and Riley just . . . he just went for it. She told me that they'd never been to bed. She said Riley had too much respect for her to . . . Riley's got a lot of the old Japanese ways in him."

"This is the eighties. Strange that a guy could be almost engaged and have that kind of willpower," Nick said thoughtfully. "Everyone is aware of the AIDS mess, but Riley would have considered Lacey a safe girl, right?"

"I don't know how Riley thinks. Sometimes I think I have him figured out, and then he throws me a curve. To my knowledge, he hasn't had any serious relationships. He did date a lot, though. I don't like talking about Riley like this."

"Why?"

"It's disloyal. He's my . . . he was my friend. Hell, we're cousins. I respect the guy. I'd go to the wall for him."

"That's interesting. Let's sum this up. You'd go to the wall for Riley, you like him, you respect him, he's your friend, or was your friend, and you don't want to say anything bad about him. Yet you allowed his fiancée to crawl into your bed and you made love to her. You could have stopped, you admitted that. You also said you didn't think they were in love the way a man and a woman should be. If you thought they were madly in love and meant for each other, would you have stopped yourself?"

"For Christ's sake, Nick, of course I would have. . . . But if that was true and they were deeply in love, she wouldn't have come to my bed."

"Exactly. Now explain all that to me."

"I can't. I don't understand."

"Would you knowingly hurt Riley?"

"No."

"If you saw him doing something wrong, would you try to stop him?"

"Sure."

"But in a case where love is involved and the woman in question is an ex-girlfriend of yours, would the same rules apply? Or would you have to go about it in a different way?"

"Jesus Christ!" Cole exploded.

"You wanted to shock him. Make him aware that he was going in the wrong direction. Were you going to tell him?"

"Yeah, I was. I wanted to," Cole said lamely.

"Did you anticipate the fight that ensued?"

"No. I thought it would be a verbal battle. I thought I could make him understand."

"But he chose not to understand. I'm not even going to try and get into Riley's thoughts. We're just dealing with you. So you slugged it out."

"He beat me to a pulp. I didn't fight back. I felt I deserved it. He was going for blood. No matter what kind of fight I'd have put up, Riley would have taken me. I have no doubts about that at all."

"So that was the end. For you. You gave him your half of Sunbridge, and may I say, you Colemans are very generous."

"My name is Tanner, Nick," Cole said sharply.

"Cole, I'm sorry. I forgot, okay? When you gave him the deed, how did you feel?"

"Shitty that we let this happen. Relieved that Sunbridge was off my back. I did try to talk to Riley before I moved out, but he wanted no part of me. He accused me of interfering in his life by writing to his grandfather and telling him lies. That's the farthest thing from the truth. I covered for him, made up stories about how busy he was so his grandfather wouldn't be so hurt."

"Did you tell him that?"

"Sure. But he didn't believe me. If he doesn't want to go back to Japan for good, then he should tell his grandfather he plans to stay here. That old man loves him like a son, not a grandson. Goddamn it, it isn't right."

"You hate him for that?"

Cole thought about it for a minute. "Yeah, I do."

"No, you don't. You hate yourself. I don't doubt for one minute that the situation is exactly as you described it, but the same thing is true of you. Isn't it?"

Cole dropped his head into his hands. Nick pretended not to see the tears glistening in Cole's eyes. "Yes."

"You hate Sunbridge, so you got rid of it. You tried to save Riley from making not one mistake, but two. You just now told me your name isn't Coleman, it's Tanner. You don't want to be one of the Colemans. You don't want to be first or second banana for Coleman Aviation. You don't want any part of it. You want to cut and run. Riley knows what he wants; he wants to stay here. You're out in left field and not doing anything about it. Why?"

"They all expect . . . from the time I was . . . I had no other . . . I'm supposed to be a Coleman, and Colemans do what is expected. So I did it."

"You hate it, you want out. You know what you should do, but you aren't doing anything. Riley is doing what he has to do without saying all the words. You want to say the words, but you don't want to do it."

"No guts."

"They're hard to come by. Takes a big man to open up. There comes a time in everyone's life when you have to stand up and say, fuck it all! Now do you see what I mean?"

"Oh yeah."

"Okay. Now I'm going to ask you a question. It's one of those things where when I finish, lickety-split, you answer immediately with what comes to your mind. Truth now. Don't think. I'll know if you're conning me. Ready?"

"Yeah."

"What do you want to be when you grow up?"

"A writer," Cole said promptly. "I'm nuts about words."

"Good for you." Nick laughed delightedly. He held out his hand. Cole grasped it. "Cole, nothing in this world is worth making your life miserable so that you look forward to sleep and dread getting up. You've got a lot of thinking to do. You know where to find me if you need me. I'll be here a week."

"Thanks, Nick."

"Thank Adam. He was really worried about you. You want to know something? I'm worried about Adam. I wish Sawyer loved him."

Cole laughed. "She does."

"What?"

"Sawyer said when the time is right, she'll go for it."

"Are you putting me on?"

"You! You must be kidding. This is just my opinion, but I think she's getting revved up to the first step."

"I always thought they were meant for one another," Nick said.

"You and me and everyone else. It'll happen. Tell Adam to keep his shirt on. Love takes time. I should know. Look, I'm going back to the condo. I have a lot of thinking to do. I don't know how to thank you, Nick."

"Then don't try. Maybe someday you'll write a book about me. Cole, don't try to force anything. Let it all happen naturally. It's easier to deal with that way."

Nick walked over to the portable bar and poured a healthy snifter of brandy. "I love it when it all comes together," he mimicked George Peppard. "Deitrick, you did real good tonight."

{{{{{{{{ CHAPTER FIFTEEN }}}}}}}}

Maggie watched as Rand knotted his tie. A Windsor knot. That meant he was going to try to see Chesney again. For some strange reason, Rand always knotted his tie that way when he was seeking out his daughter.

Maggie and Rand weren't talking at all these past days. She'd made up her mind to leave by the weekend if Rand didn't come to his senses. She'd even toyed with the thought of going to see Chesney on her own, but what would she say when she got there? Love your father, be kind to him? Don't be cruel, can't you see how he's suffering? Can't you see he won't leave until you make him some kind of promise? And what would Chesney say? The same thing she'd said at the first meeting. I don't want anything from you. I just want you to know you have a daughter, and I want to acknowledge that I have a father. No more, no less. That young woman could not be bought, optioned, or leased.

It was almost the dinner hour, and Maggie'd be eating alone again since she refused to hang out at Heathrow Airport with Rand, hoping for a glimpse or a chance to waylay Chesney. Maybe she'd order from room service and watch some television.

The knock on the door wasn't loud, just startling. Probably the bellboy with a copy of the *London Daily Times*.

Maggie picked up a dollar bill to tip the bellboy. When she opened the door she almost fainted. "Chesney!"

"May I come in, Mrs. Nelson . . . Maggie . . ."

"Of course, Chesney. Can I order something for you, a drink or some tea?"

"No, thank you. I won't be here that long. I have the night flight this evening."

"I'll call Rand. He's dressing." His face blanched when she told him Chesney was waiting to see him.

"She's here? In the sitting room? Did she say why she came?"

Maggie thought she knew, but instead of answering, she shook her head. Rand pulled himself together quickly.

"I'm glad you stopped by," he said, formally. "Will you join us for dinner?"

"I'm sorry, no. I came here to . . . to tell you you must stop shadowing me. People are talking about it at the airline. My landlady keeps telling me there is a gentleman skulking about and asking questions all the time. I've seen you in restaurants and even at the movies. I'm asking you to please stop. I want you to go back to your home. Please. Don't upset my life any more. I wish now I had let things alone. I didn't think it would be like this. I'm sorry if this hurts you, but you must think of me, and if you care about me at all, you'll respect my wishes." Maggie thought the girl's voice was too quiet, too controlled.

"Chesney . . . I want to get to know you. If you won't allow me to do that, we'll remain strangers," Rand pleaded.

"Yes, I know. Your reaction is . . . was so unexpected. I can't handle it. I don't want to be rude, and I certainly don't want to have to call the police. I will, you know. I don't want to live like this. I'm sorry if this hurts or offends you. Time, I think, will be the answer for both of us. Perhaps when I next take a holiday, I'll visit you in Hawaii. I'm not promising, but I will try. Will you please give me your word that you'll leave me alone?"

"I've never forced myself on anyone before," Rand said quietly. "My only defense is that I never had a child before. It seems cruel, now that I've discovered you, to walk off and leave you. Please allow me to help you, to be here in case you need or want something. I want to help. Can't you see that?" Rand begged.

"I understand all of that," Chesney said quietly. "But as I said, if you care about me, you'll respect my wishes. For now," she added to take the sting out of her words.

Rand nodded. "Of course, I'll do as you ask," he said coldly. "You won't have to worry about either my wife or myself bothering you again."

Maggie ached for her husband and his daughter. She wondered if Rand heard the tremor in Chesney's voice or knew how close the girl was to tears. Or if Chesney knew how hurt Rand was, and how those cold words were his defense against the bitter hurt. She watched helplessly as Chesney fumbled with her gloves and purse.

"I guess this is good-bye. We'll see one another again, I'm sure." She held out her hand at the last second and then withdrew it quickly when Rand kept his hands in his trouser pockets. She inclined her head in Maggie's direction. Impulsively, Maggie stepped forward and took the girl's stiff body into her arms.

"We wish you well," she whispered. "If you need us, call."

When the door closed, Rand walked to the telephone. "Do you want to make a stopover in Washington to see your mother before going on home?"

"I'd like that, Rand."

"Then that's what we'll do. I think we could both use a little of Billie's mothering."

"I think you're right, darling." Maggie hugged her husband as tightly as she could. She could feel him trembling.

Chesney knew she shouldn't cry. She was going on duty and her eyes would be puffy and swollen.

Regardless of what words she used, she'd closed the door on the Nelsons. There was really no room in her life for either her father or his wife. Well, at least she wouldn't end up like Sara. She wondered why she didn't feel better and why she couldn't seem to keep from crying. Because, damn it, I wanted to go with them. I hated saying the things I said. I lied when I said they were embarrassing me. I only want them to leave so I can *think* clearly. . . .

He'd looked so cold, there at the end when she'd held out her hand. His wife had looked so . . . so kind and gentle . . . the way mothers, real mothers, were supposed to look. She just knew Maggie Nelson had read her children bedtime stories and held their hands when they were sick in bed, had baked gingerbread men and used raisins for the eyes and buttons. She probably used to take them to the park and push them on the swing, and she made homemade birthday cakes and wrapped presents. She kissed her children good night before she tucked them in and turned out the light. She'd just bet Maggie's children had kissed her good-bye every morning when they left to go to school. She was the kind of mother who put little surprises in her children's lunch bags. She knew every lullaby ever printed. She was warm and gentle and loving. She knew how to keep a secret, too, the kind little girls didn't want their fathers to know about. She knew about bras and periods and had rules when it came to boys. Chesney jolted herself back to reality; Maggie Nelson's children were grown-ups now—older than she was.

Her father, now, he probably wouldn't take his little girl to a picture show or let her stay up late and share a bowl of ice cream with a cherry on top—if he'd ever had a little girl, that is. He wouldn't be the type to walk in the Easter parade to show off his daughter's new bonnet, and he wouldn't know the first thing about a skinned knee and that Band-Aids were badges of importance. He'd be afraid to whisper loving words at bedtime. He wouldn't know how to chase away the boogeyman from the closet. He probably didn't even know what a balloon was. He'd never approve of the boys who came to call, and he wouldn't want to pay his hard-earned money for new dresses and shiny black shoes. He wouldn't bring home gaily wrapped presents and stack them under a real Christmas tree. He'd not know the first thing about a flop-eared dog that wet on the carpet. He wouldn't want to share a cup of cocoa long after bedtime. His eyes wouldn't light up when he was called Daddy.

Chesney stopped in the middle of the street, her eyes wild and full of tears. People jostled her, swore at her, and pushed her aside. She stood looking into a shop window, not seeing any of the summer merchandise on display. Her heart was beating so fast, she thought it would leap right out of her chest. *She'd never know what kind of father he would have been.* But she knew he'd be kind and gentle now. He'd regard her as a person. He'd keep his promises. Maggie would be the mother she never had. Sawyer would be her big sister.

She looked around, her eyes tortured. She tried to focus on her watch. She could go back. But she wouldn't. She had too much pride. She held her hand up as she walked to the curb to signal for a taxi.

"My God," she cried aloud. "What have I done?"

The taxi ride to Capitol Hill was short. Too short, Amelia thought. Suddenly she wasn't sure if what she was doing was right or not. Maybe . . . no maybes, she cautioned herself. This is what you set out to do, and you're going to do it. Today!

She wished now she'd eaten a real breakfast instead of nibbling on dry toast. My nerves wouldn't allow it, she said silently. My outfit, is it right or is it too much? She'd changed the high-necked white blouse that covered her thin, wrinkly neck in favor of a round neckline. Let them see that she was as old as the people she would talk about. No cover-ups.

Amelia kept up a silent running conversation with herself for the hour she waited till it was her turn to speak to the one hundredth Congress. She glanced over her notes, not that she was going to use the text she'd submitted ahead of time. She wondered if they could stop her when they heard what she was going to say—throw her out or call the security guards. She wanted to ask Thad but was afraid to. What she was about to do was probably unprecedented, but she didn't care. She'd made up her mind a long time ago that this was the way she was going to do things. If they stopped her, she'd talk to the press. They'd listen. Boy, would they listen.

Her mouth was dry and there was a warning tickle in her throat and chest. No need for alarm . . . yet. She raised her eyes upward—just another half hour, then I don't care. Please, God.

She'd rehearsed her opening statement over and over, timing it, watching her face in the mirror till she had it down pat. If she was as successful as she was in her rehearsal, she could get it all out in seconds. Once she said the opening words, the rest would fall into place.

Her watch told her it was almost time. She said a quick prayer and immediately felt better. He would help her; she was certain of it. He'd let her get this far, and He was holding off now; she could feel it.

A page called Amelia's name and escorted her to the lectern.

She settled herself comfortably. The only thing she removed from her briefcase was a battered old ledger whose pages were yellow and crackly. She leaned toward the microphone. The tickle was still with her; soon it would turn into a flutter. She was all right, though. He was with her.

At a nod from the chairman, Amelia spoke. "My name is Amelia Coleman Assante. I'm here today to talk about the problems of the aged, and I'm also here to collect a debt." She enunciated each word carefully. "I'm also here to shame you. I know I'm deviating from the text that I submitted to you, and I apologize for that." She allowed herself one brief glance at the second hand of her watch. She was on schedule. "The Coleman family has supplied beef to this country and the military for over forty years. We've built planes and electronic equipment for this same government." She was aware of the startled faces of the congressmen, but she continued. "The United States government did not pay us. My father knew this day might come; he saved all those unpaid bills. He left them to me. The United States government owes Coleman Enterprises $11,867,411.18. It's all here, in this book. I'm here today to collect that money, and to use it for the aged, for the aged in my state of Texas. I can't take on the whole country, but I can make a start. Others will come after me." The sound of rustling papers amused Amelia. Let them look. She rushed on. "When I said I was here to shame you, I meant just that." Amelia's eyes searched out her own congressman. She noted a wry smile on his face, and she didn't miss his thumbs-up salute. "People like me and Jethroe Evans and Minnie Mae Johnson put you lawmakers where you're sitting right now. And you don't even know who Jethroe and Minnie Mae are. You know me because I come from a wealthy, influential family. A family, I might add, that pays its bills . . . on time.

"Minnie Mae and Jethroe are wards of the state, residents of a state-operated nursing home that is a disgrace to my state, or any state. For shame!" she cried passionately. The tickle was a flutter now, warning her she had to hurry. She didn't need to look at her watch.

For the next five minutes she spoke heatedly and passionately of the work she'd done for the past two years.

{ 289 }

The wild fluttering in her chest made Amelia stand straighter as she continued. She gripped the microphone tightly. "So you see, I, and people like me, are forced to do your job. The $11,867,411.18 is the principal the government owes us. The interest has not been computed yet, but it will be by the end of the day. I want that money to go into a fund, and a committee set up that is to be monitored by Senator Thaddeus Kingsley. These monies are to be spent for nursing home care in the state of Texas.

"I want to make it very clear that I'm not asking for the payment of this debt on behalf of my family, although, as most of you know, Coleman Oil is in the same position as the other oil companies, due to the sharp drop in oil prices. This money, in Coleman coffers, could solve our immediate problems, but we've decided, as a family, that human life and dignity are more important than a failing business. You will aid our aged. Your payment of this debt will show other states what they can do. That's what our family is going to do for the state of Texas." Amelia paused and drew a jagged breath.

"I've taken the liberty of Xeroxing this entire ledger for your benefit. There is a copy for each of you. I'm sure by day's end you'll see that this wonderful government we live under ... goofed. I thank God it did, because I don't have time for promises and red tape and committees that will only spawn other committees to look into things. Minnie Mae and Jethroe, like myself, are on borrowed time."

"Thank you, ladies and gentlemen, for allowing me to speak here today."

And thank you, God, for giving me the time, she said silently.

She was outside in the hall when she heard the applause. It didn't sound as though they were going to arrest her. She needed air, fresh air. She felt light-headed, and the dancing in her chest was a cramp now, cold and hard. She almost fainted when she saw the horde of reporters coming toward her. From out of nowhere Thad materialized. Even from here she could see the tears in his eyes, or were they her own tears? She allowed herself to be shepherded down a maze of corridors, and finally she was in a dim, paneled room with Thad and several of his aides.

"How'd I do?" Amelia gasped.

"You blew their socks off." Thad grinned. "Mine, too. I didn't know about that money."

"I asked Billie not to tell you. I talked to all of them before I made this decision. Sure, it would bail us out of our present predicament, but this is more important. They agreed. You'll do it, won't you, Thad?" Amelia pleaded.

"Amelia, I'd be honored to monitor the committee; it's something I can do after retirement."

"Wonderful. Now, do you think you could get me out of here? I think I'd like to take a trip to the zoo and just walk around. It's a nice day, and I'm not ready to go back to Georgetown." She had to get out in the air so she could breathe, so she could unwind and pop the pills she was clutching in her hand.

"Absolutely." Thad turned to one of his aides and motioned to the door. "I have to get back for a vote. I'll see you at home this evening. Amelia, well done! I don't know when I've had a prouder moment."

"It was my pleasure."

Outside, in the fresh air, Amelia tried to draw a deep breath, but the vise clamping her chest prevented it. She reached out to . . . nothingness. She felt herself begin to sink to the ground.

In the ambulance, she prayed. You cut it a little close there, didn't You? Thank you, God, thankyouthankyouthankyou-thankyouthankyou.

Billie sat in the breakfast nook watching a precocious squirrel hobble up and down the back steps. She could tell he was old by the way he moved and by his sparse coat, which was straggly and thin. She wondered what he would do when he could no longer forage and dig for the acorns he stashed in the autumn for his winter food. Would he starve or would he lie down and die? She'd been watching this particular squirrel for years now—ever since she and Thad had moved into the Georgetown house.

Billie shook herself. God's creatures had a way of fending for themselves. Weren't people God's creatures, too? Lately, because of Amelia, she'd been thinking more and more about old age and the awful things that happened to people.

A gust of wind slapped against the casement window. Startled, Billie stepped backward and took notice of the day for the first time. Typical March weather, blustery and cold, forty degrees, according to the thermometer on the back porch.

She'd been jittery these past days. Thad had noticed and

had commented on it, last night in bed. She realized now that her jumpiness had started when Amelia arrived. It had gotten steadily worse.

She should be doing something: paying the bills, reading, dusting, something to keep herself busy. For the life of her, she couldn't remember if she'd made the bed or not. She looked down at the breakfast dishes. Amelia had barely touched her scrambled eggs. One corner of a piece of toast had been nibbled. The orange juice hadn't been touched. She'd passed on the coffee, saying she was in a hurry. Billie tried to bring Amelia's face into focus. She couldn't even remember what she was wearing.

She'd never been big on premonitions, but she had the awful feeling something was wrong somewhere. To shake off the feeling, she bustled about the kitchen, clearing away the dishes and tidying up the breakfast area. She threw some laundry into the machine, not bothering to separate it, as she usually did. Thad's underwear, as well as her own, went in with the towels she'd carried down earlier. She opened all the curtains and turned on the stereo. The cat leaped off the mantel at the burst of sound. Now she'd make the bed and take a shower. After that, maybe she'd try sketching some new designs until Amelia returned. Perhaps they could go out for lunch.

Halfway up the stairs, she turned around and walked back to the kitchen. She rummaged in the cabinets till she found the bag of walnuts left over from Christmas. She rummaged some more till she found one of the metal pie tins Sara Lee donated with each pie. She poured out the nuts and set them on the back porch. She stood up, her eyes sweeping the yard. As usual her favorite old squirrel was perched on the lowest branch of the old oak. Even from here she could see that the animal's eyes were dull, as though a film covered them. She felt foolish when she whistled softly and clapped her hands to gain the squirrel's attention. She felt even more foolish when she went inside and hid behind the sheer kitchen curtain. She watched as the squirrel crept up the porch steps, sniffed the nuts, and then scooped one into his two front paws. He stopped a minute and looked back toward the door. Billie stepped back from the window, afraid that if the squirrel saw her, he'd leave the nuts. "I just want to help, little fella," she whispered.

When the phone rang she nearly jumped out of her skin.

Before she picked it up, she had a feeling she was going to hear bad news. She took a deep breath before she answered. She listened to the words but didn't comprehend their meaning at first. "Where is she? I'll be there as soon as possible. Tell her I'm on the way."

Amelia. She'd been doing so well. Now some unknown voice from George Washington Hospital was telling her Amelia was in the intensive care unit. She'd collapsed.

"Amelia?" Billie whispered an hour later. "The nurse will only allow me to stay for ten minutes." Not Amelia; please, God, let her be all right.

"My chest hurts. I think it's nerves. I was so keyed up. I overdid it. They're going to run some tests. They took one cardiogram and they have me hooked up to the monitor. Not a word of this to Cary. Promise me, Billie." Her voice sounded frail and thin, as though it were coming from far away.

"Cary will never forgive me if I don't call," Billie cried. "Amelia, don't you want him here?"

"Promise me, Billie." Reluctantly, Billie nodded. "Call him and tell him I can't make it to Hawaii. You'll have to make up some sort of story. I can't think right now. The medication is fogging things up. I'm not going to die, Billie. I think I'd know if I was. Not yet, anyway."

Billie tried for a cheerful tone. "Of course you aren't going to die. Don't even think like that. I'm sure it's what you said, nerves and stress. Everyone is talking about how powerful you were. You were on the news twice today. I'm so proud of you. Thad said you were eloquent. He led the cheering section. Did you see him?"

"When I was finished he . . . came up to me and . . ." Amelia didn't finish her sentence.

Alarmed, Billie searched frantically for the nurse.

"She's asleep, Mrs. Kingsley," the charge nurse said quietly as she led Billie from the room. "She'll sleep for a few hours. I can have Dr. Katz call you, if you like, since Mrs. Assante listed you as next of kin."

"How serious is it? Is there anything I can do? Should I stay here?" Billie asked fearfully.

"Doctor will talk to you when he comes in. The best thing you can do for Mrs. Assante and yourself is to go home."

"But when she wakes up, I want her to know I'm here, that someone is here."

"I'll tell her I sent you home. She'll understand," the nurse said firmly.

In the end Billie went home. She sat, waiting, by the front window and was out the front door with tears streaming down her face when Thad's car swerved to the curb.

"We'll go back after dinner, Billie. For now, we have to carry on as we always do. Don't let this cripple you. If Amelia said she's going to be okay, let's go with that."

"She just said that to make me feel better," Billie cried.

"Then you'll have to pretend to feel better for her sake. Come inside, it's cold out here. We'll have a drink and decide what to tell Cary. That's the part I don't like, but we have to respect Amelia's wishes."

Together the Kingsleys came up with what they hoped was a suitable story: more meetings with Congress, meetings with different senators, and a possible meeting with the president himself. It was decided that Thad would make the call and deliver the message, making it sound more true.

It took three days to get in touch with Cary. When his voice finally came over the wire, he thanked Thad for calling and didn't leave a message for Amelia. Thad's face was expressionless when he repeated the brief conversation to his wife.

Billie went into his arms, tears streaming down her cheeks. Thad rubbed her hair while he made soft, soothing sounds in her ear. "It will be all right, Billie."

They had their coats on, ready to leave for the hospital, when a yellow cab pulled up in front of the house. "It's Rand and Maggie," Thad called. He raised his eyes upward. "Thank you, God," he whispered.

Maggie and Billie sat in the back of the car, Thad and Rand in the front seat, for the drive to George Washington Hospital. Thad briefed Rand on his mother's condition.

"Did you get in touch with Cary?" Maggie asked.

"Just today. We've been trying for three days." Billie went on to tell Maggie about Amelia's wishes.

"How serious is it, Mam?"

"Serious enough. She's going to need a nurse when she gets home. Lots of bed rest."

"An invalid?" Maggie asked fearfully.

"It's a possibility, darling."

"Does Amelia know?"

"I don't think so. She's been sedated. Most of this is guesswork on my part."

"Amelia always said she didn't want to end up like Grand-mam Jessie. Powerless. Helpless, like a baby."

"Don't cry, Maggie, or you'll have me crying. I put loads of mascara on so I wouldn't be tempted to cry."

"It was something in my eye," Maggie gulped. She whispered to Billie, filling her in quickly on the last difficult days in England and Chesney's visit. "It was awful, Mam. You would have thought someone physically whipped Rand. Now this. I know this sounds crazy, Mam, but there are times when I think this family is doomed. Do you ever feel that?"

"My faith in God is too strong to allow me to think thoughts like that. I will admit there were times, years ago, when I thought so. I don't want you to think like that anymore, Maggie."

"We always seem to be in a state of crisis. Something's bothering Cole. Riley is torn in two directions. Amelia is ill, a possible invalid. Me and you, Mam. We have to hold it together."

"That's the key, darling. Together." She leaned closer to Maggie. "The dear, sweet, wonderful men in the front seat *think* they do it, but we know better, don't we?"

"Right on, Mam." Maggie linked her arm through her mother's. She laid her head on Billie's fur-clad shoulder, something she hadn't done in a long time. Sometimes nothing else would do but the comfort of one's mother.

Back in Georgetown, Billie busied herself making coffee and sandwiches. Maggie popped a cake from the freezer into the microwave. She couldn't bear watching her husband cry. Thad was doing his best to console him, but failing miserably. Only Billie would be able to make Rand come around.

At the table it was Billie who spoke first. "Rand, the fact that Amelia is still with us is a plus. None of us expected her to come through her first heart attack, but she did. She said she had something to do, and with the help of God, she did it. She knew what the stakes were, but she felt God gave her a second chance and she took it. I am so proud of her," Billie said in a choked voice. "I want you to be proud of her, too, Rand. Don't turn this into a wake. Amelia will sense it. She's alive. We have to thank God for that and take it one day at a time. Rand, are you listening to me?"

"Yes, Billie, I am. I thought the first time was bad, but this time, I don't know, it seems worse. Cary should be here. I think we should call him and tell him to come home. The hell with the business deal. There will be other deals."

"Amelia doesn't want him to come home. She'll never forgive us if we go against her wishes. Please, Rand, don't do anything foolish. The doctors are hopeful that she can leave the hospital in another week if she progresses. Thad and I want her to stay here with a nurse until she's strong enough to be flown back to Texas. We certainly have the room. There's no way in hell," Billie said vehemently, "that I will allow Amelia to go into a nursing home; I don't care if it's one of those country club places."

Rand nodded. "We'll stay on, too. We can get a hotel in the city."

"No you won't." Thad spoke up. "This house has four bedrooms. One for Amelia, one for the nurse, one for you and Maggie, and one for Billie and me. Four. You're staying with us."

Maggie's eyes thanked Thad.

"Company, Thad. Isn't it wonderful?" Billie said. "We just rattle around this house by ourselves. We're so glad we can help."

"You're always here for us, aren't you, Mam?"

"I try, Maggie. Come along, we'll have to make up the bedroom for you and Rand."

"Thad," Billie called, "show Rand the videotape of Amelia. Thad made six tapes, one for everyone. Amelia was so wonderful. She really did what she set out to do. I cried when I watched it. Some of those austere congressmen were crying, I could tell."

"And some of the senators, too," Thad said quietly.

Rand had never felt such devastation. It seemed that the world and everyone in it was ganging up on him. First his daughter turned her back on him, and now his stepmother lay critically ill. Except he never thought of Amelia as a stepmother. From the time he was five years old, when his father was killed and Amelia took over his care, he'd never once thought of her as a stepmother. She was his very own mother; his father had said so when he was barely old enough to understand. She said so, too—and still did, every once in a while.

Amelia had never failed him, even once. No matter where she was, no matter what she was involved in, she'd stop what she was doing and come to his aid, saying, "What can I do, son?"

What could *he* do now, for her? Pray for her recovery? Wish for her recovery? He wondered if he'd been a good son, or could he have been better? He flashed back over his life and decided he'd been the best he was capable of being. He had no regrets. He mustn't get maudlin over Chesney or his mother. Amelia would hate it. She'd come down hard on him for what she would call his 'feeling sorry for himself attitude', and she'd tell him to pull up his socks and get on with his life. Everything before the present, she'd say, is history. If you look back, you see only ghosts and shadows, and pretty soon they start to chase you, and then you're forced to run. Live life for the present and the future; the past is gone. Maybe she wouldn't actually say those things to him, but she'd be thinking them.

What would his life be like without his mother in it? Amelia would say you look it square in the face and you deal with it. Death is final, so you *have* to handle it. No choices, no options.

He wondered about that final moment when the casket was lowered into the ground and the first handful of dirt was thrown in. Could he handle that? He shuddered violently. There was something barbaric about funerals, something ritualistic. Maybe it was better to be cremated and cast to the wind. But then there'd be no special place to go to visit, to talk, to hope that a spirit hovered about to hear one's anguished words.

Rand wept for his impending loss, and for the others who would grieve for his mother. He spread his hands out, palms upward, turning his mother's life into Other hands.

{{{{{{{{{{ CHAPTER SIXTEEN *}}}}}}}}}*

Warm trade winds rustled the silky, sheer bedroom curtains, wafting in the heady, hypnotic scent of plumeria. Early-morning sunshine crept into the room along with the scent from the fragrant blossoms. The warmth from the sun created lacy patterns on Cary's bare legs. He inhaled deeply and then smiled. Heaven? Paradise?

Cary scrunched the two oversize pillows into a ball. He propped himself up and leaned back. This, he decided, was something he could get used to. No wonder Rand and Maggie were so happy here.

What a golden day it was! From his nest in the pillows he could catch glimpses of the Pacific each time the curtains billowed apart. It made him want to get up—almost.

A dip in the ocean, a tepid shower, clean clothes, and breakfast out on Kam Highway would be a great way to start the day. A day that was to be all his. The only decision he had to make now was what to do with the rest of his time in Hawaii since Amelia wasn't going to join him. Alan and Marty had left on the evening plane, their briefcases bulging with canned macadamia nuts, chocolate-covered macadamia nuts, and macadamia nuts in the shell. He hated to see them leave, but life in the legal fast track demanded they return to New York's cold, blustery weather. Alan had grinned when they stopped at one of the airport kiosks to buy leis. He'd winced when Cary kissed him on both cheeks as he draped the garland around his neck. Marty bought two extra ones for his wife and daughter, but danced nimbly away when Cary tried to buss him on the cheek. When he waved to them for the last time, Cary knew his business interests were in good hands. His and Rand's, that is.

He didn't know if he was annoyed or angry that Amelia wasn't going to join him. Until this morning, he'd barely given her a thought. If Thad hadn't called and said she was tied up in D.C., he probably would have forgotten to call her. Now that he had free time, he could think about her broken promise. He realized he wasn't just annoyed, he was pissed off—big time. He'd be damned if he'd leave early to go to Washington. This was the first real vacation he'd had in five years, and he was going to enjoy every goddamn minute of it. If Amelia's affairs were more important than he was, let her attend to them.

He could feel his anger start to build. If he didn't watch it, his whole day would be ruined. He wasn't going to call today, either. Every time he thought about calling, it was either too late or too early. The last two times he'd called, Billie said Amelia was out. Since the Nelsons didn't have an answering machine, he didn't know if Amelia had called while he was out. Someone had been calling, seven or eight times in the past few days, but so far he hadn't managed to get to the phone before it stopped ringing.

He punched at the fluffy pillows, settling them more comfortably behind his head. Normally, he never smoked before he brushed his teeth or had breakfast, but now he lit a cigarette—defiantly. He watched a perfect smoke ring circle its way across the room and out the open French doors.

Julie. He'd given up on Julie. If it was meant to be, he'd have been able to make contact by now, probably sooner if he'd left a message.

He had four days and three nights left. He could laze in the sun, or he could take a tour around the islands. Or he could go to the Waikiki Beach Tower and camp out till Julie turned up.

He donned his swim trunks. There was something bothering him, but he couldn't quiet figure out what it was. He trotted down to the beach, his eyes on the brilliant blue of the water. He dropped his towel and hit the surf at a dead run. The shock of the cool, bracing water washed away all lingering signs of sleep. On the way back to the house, he heard the phone ringing. This time he wasn't going to bother to run to answer it. Whoever it was would hang up just as he picked up the receiver. After he dried off, maybe he'd call Amelia. Amelia would laugh about the way they kept missing each other.

He'd seen Amelia on the eleven o'clock news. He thought he was going to burst with pride. From bypass surgery and recovery to the one hundredth Congress. A coup if ever there was one. But the pride was short-lived, replaced now with anger.

Cary felt a twinge of envy at his wife's accomplishment. Not many people could do what she'd done. His inner city seemed dull now in comparison to Amelia reaching Congress, presenting a truly important issue. The sugarcane deal was just another deal. He'd never make the noonday news, much less the eleven o'clock news. And he hadn't been there to share her victory the way she'd shared the grand opening of Miranda with him. The rest of her family was there, though, sharing her big moment. Rand, Maggie—Billie and Thad. Amelia's family. Suddenly he felt like an outsider.

Cary slipped into jeans, a pullover of soft sky-blue knit, and deck shoes.

On the drive to the restaurant, and while he ate, Cary's

mind clicked. Amelia had been so insistent that he come here. He could have sworn she meant to join him, because Amelia never said things she didn't mean. He'd looked forward to showing her around the islands so he could see and appreciate them through her eyes. Could it be that she really didn't *want* him with her in Washington? That she didn't want him there for her big, grand moment? She hadn't even called to tell him how nervous she was. She hadn't called to tell him what it was like to speak before Congress and to see herself on the national news. She hadn't wanted to share that with him, but she was sharing it with Thad and Billie, Maggie and Rand. She'd handpicked her audience.

Cary looked down at the eggs and pancakes he'd been devouring. He pushed the plate away. Even the coffee tasted rancid now.

In the parking lot, Cary sat in the car for a long time before he started the engine. From the day they were married, he'd shared everything with Amelia. All his hopes, his dreams, his failures. He'd left nothing out. Once he'd even cried in her arms and been comforted. He'd shared his vulnerability with her. She was such a rock, always saying the right thing at the right time. He wondered now how many times she'd hidden her own hurt and frustration from him. He'd never wondered about that before. One of the greatest moments of her life, and she hadn't wanted to share it with him! "Don't let this fester, Cary," an inner voice warned. "Stop now at the next place you see with a phone. Call."

The golden arches of McDonald's beckoned him: he figured it was about five miles down the road. When he got there, he changed a five-dollar bill for silver.

The phone in the Georgetown house rang fifteen times before Cary hung up. It was three o'clock in the afternoon in D.C. He searched his billfold for Thad's private number in Washington. He was told that Senator Kingsley was visiting a sick friend and could be reached at his home after six. Cary hung up in disgust.

Cary felt sick as he climbed back into the car. How could Amelia slap him in the face like this? All along he'd felt as though he belonged—been a part of the family. Had they been laughing at him behind his back? Had they poked at one another when Amelia picked out his clothes and gave him crash courses in Texas protocol? Had they only pretended to accept him because that was what Amelia wanted?

The siren behind Cary made him glance in the rearview mirror and then at his speedometer. He slowed and pulled over to the side of the road.

"I clocked you at ninety, sir. We don't drive that way in our state. If you're a visitor, you're expected to obey the speed laws, like everyone else. Take your license out of the billfold, sir."

Cary handed over the license and the car rental papers. He felt like shit. There was no defense, and he wasn't about to offer one. He signed his name carefully so that it was legible, pocketed his license, and drove off at a sedate fifty miles an hour.

The rental car seemed to have a mind of its own as it headed toward Waikiki.

To Julie.

Her reflection in the glaring fluorescent light of her bathroom dismayed Julie. She looked every day of her age and then some, she decided. No amount of makeup would cover the dark circles under her eyes, but it might at least cover the sunburn on her forehead and the tip of her nose. She wished she'd taken her sunglasses off when she was in the sun. Now she looked like a raccoon, with white-rimmed eyes and bright red nose. There was a tight line around her mouth, too, one she'd never had before this trip. She looked tired, unhappy, and disillusioned. Mirrors, like cameras, didn't lie. Before she checked out she was going to fill out the card on the desk that asked for suggestions. Rosy light bulbs in bedroom and bathroom.

Julie gingerly patted some aloe gel on her sunburn, hoping she wouldn't peel. She snapped off the offensive bathroom light in disgust.

She was in an awful mood, one that wasn't going to allow her to sleep. She popped a can of Bud Light and carried it to the balcony. The breeze was warm, drying the tears on her cheeks almost immediately. She gulped at the beer, knowing she'd have another and then another till the six-pack she'd purchased at the ABC store was gone.

Seeing Amelia on the late news had been a terrible shock. Amelia wasn't here, but Cary was. What did it mean? Maybe he'd gone home, and that's why there was no answer. She'd sat, bug-eyed, when Amelia was introduced to the Congress as Amelia Coleman Assante. She'd felt so proud to know her.

Amelia had been absolutely wonderful as she spoke about the problems of the aging, citing herself as one of the more fortunate oldsters. Based on Amelia's passionate voice, she'd have voted for anything Amelia was pleading for. Probably every other woman in America would have, too. Even the men, if they weren't fools. When the camera panned the crowd, she'd caught a glimpse of Thad, but no sign of Cary.

Julie's imagination ran away with her as she sucked on can after can of beer. Amelia and Cary had separated; otherwise Cary would have been at her side for something as important as an appearance before Congress. Cary had come here to find her because she was the most important thing in the world to him. Cary loved her and wanted to be with her, here in the islands, instead of in Washington with his wife. Cary didn't want to be reminded on national television about their age difference. Cary wouldn't want to be standing next to Amelia when she spoke to the reporters. Numbers. Her fantasies were rich and ripe; she pictured Cary knocking down her bedroom door and scooping her up in his arms.

The beer was gone, all six dead soldiers lined up on the glass-topped patio table. She didn't have the buzz she thought she'd have, nor was she sleepy. Instead, she was on overload, ready to erupt at any minute. She'd gone to the bathroom eleven times in the five hours she'd been sitting out here. The sun was up and it was going to be another glorious Hawaiian day.

Enough was enough! She showered, dressed, and gulped down a cup of instant coffee. While she sipped at the hated packaged coffee, she called down to the desk to order a rental car. She copied down the desk clerk's directions to the North Shore.

By nine-fifteen she was on Kam Highway, headed for Haleiwa. Twice she got lost, her nerves pinging in protest at the delay. She pulled over, backed up, and retraced her steps. Eventually she found her way back to Kam Highway. An hour later it was obvious she'd passed Maggie's house. She drove slowly, getting out three times to peer at the house numbers hidden behind glossy banyan leaves. Finally, a half mile down the road, she found the gates to the Nelsons' driveway.

The wheels of her car crunched on the shale in the driveway and should have alerted anyone in the house to her arrival. Two cars, a Mercedes station wagon and an Audi, stood in the open garage. Both cars had Hawaiian license plates.

The Nelsons' cars. Whatever made her think they wouldn't be home? She hadn't seen Amelia's son, Rand, on the news, so they must be here.

Well, she was here now, and she'd have to make the best of it. She rang the doorbell for a full minute, listening to the continuous chime inside. Either they weren't home or they were outside.

Julie could feel the heat of excitement on her face as she walked around to the back of the house. Her heart pounded wildly at the thought of Cary sitting there, reading the morning paper. Or the Nelsons having a late breakfast. She was trembling so badly, she had to stop and take deep breaths. What would the Nelsons think of her, popping up on their doorstep? Surely they'd see right through her and know she was here only to see Cary. She felt as though her intentions were clearly written on her face.

The lanai was empty and there was no sign of anyone on the lawn or the beach at the foot of the yard. A wet towel hung haphazardly over the back of a webbed chair. She tried the kitchen door and found it unlocked. She cracked it open and called a greeting. When she received no response, she opened it wider and stuck her head in, calling louder. When there was still no response, her shoulders slumped. She'd come all this way for nothing.

The house seemed so inviting, almost as if it were beckoning her to enter. She wasn't sure what breaking and entering consisted of. If the door was open, was it the same thing? The Nelsons *had* invited her to stop by if she was ever in Hawaii. Surely they wouldn't mind if she used their bathroom. But what she really wanted was to see if there was any sign of Cary. She decided to go in.

It was a beautiful house—low, sprawling, light and airy. She forgot her need of the bathroom as she walked slowly around the house, savoring the beauty of it all. The French doors leading to the patio were shaded from the sun but allowed the garden, with all its rich, vibrant blooms, to be part of the view. If the doors were open, as they were now, the garden became an extension of the living room. The light bamboo furniture made it a perfect blend of indoors and outdoors. She could taste the tang of the sea far below and feel the ocean breeze wafting through the open doors.

The bedrooms she walked through made her gasp in delight, but it was the open suitcase on the floor that made her eyes light up. He was still here. The light coating of dust she'd seen in the other rooms was testimony that the Nelsons weren't in residence.

She felt more comfortable now that she wouldn't have to concoct a story for Maggie and Rand. Instantly, she made a decision: she'd wait here for Cary, no matter how long it took. She'd wait outside, on the lanai.

She washed her hands in the same bathroom Cary used and dried her hands on a damp towel, probably the same one he'd dried himself with after showering. When she settled herself on the lanai, she altered her plan slightly: she'd wait till five o'clock. If Cary didn't return by then, she'd leave. If she could calm her nerves and still her furiously beating heart, maybe she'd be able to catch a nap. She felt giddy and light-headed.

Cary, I'm here; where are you? she whispered over and over.

The valet attendant at the Waikiki Beach Tower looked at Cary and smirked. Before Cary could get a word out of his mouth, the valet informed him that Miss Kingsley had left about two hours ago. "I'd say she plans to be gone all day, because she ordered a rental car." Cary wanted to kick the desk he was leaning on. The valet added insult to injury when he asked, "Do you want to leave your name . . . this time?"

"Yes, I do," Cary said through clenched teeth. He roared out of the garage onto Liliuokalani Street, narrowly missing a girl in a bikini. He sobered instantly, remembering his speeding ticket. He drove like a ninety-year-old Sunday afternoon driver, up one street and down another.

Since he had nothing else to do, he opted for some sight-seeing. If he paid attention, he should be able to find his way to Pearl Harbor. And he would keep calling the Waikiki Beach Tower each time he saw a phone booth.

Anger, hot and scorching, roared through him every time he thought of Amelia's betrayal. It was still raging in him when he parked the car and slammed down his money for a ticket to view the Arizona Memorial. He followed the rest of the crowd, mostly Japanese, into the theater, where film footage of the bombing of Pearl Harbor was shown. He watched it defensively, aware of all the Japanese around him. He wondered what they were thinking of, or were they like him, thinking only about personal problems? All he could think about was placing another call to Billie's house, and then the Beach Tower. He had to get this searing anger off his chest.

It was four o'clock when Cary dropped money into the pay phone to call Billie. His fist pounded the counter when the receiver wasn't picked up by the ninth ring. He held on a few moments longer. Billie picked it up, gasping for breath, on the eleventh ring.

"It's Cary, Billie."

"Cary! What...How nice of you to call. Is anything wrong?"

"Not at all. Is Amelia there? I've been calling all day and there's been no answer. I called Thad's private number and his secretary told me he was visiting a sick friend."

"Amelia isn't here, Cary. I know it's nine o'clock, but there was this...this...gathering she was invited to. Do you want me to give her a message?"

"Is Rand there?" Cary asked, ignoring the part about leaving a message.

"Ah, no, no, he isn't. He's...he's with Amelia, Cary. Would you like me to have him call you back?"

Cary seethed. "What I would like, Billie, is to have my goddamn wife call me back, if it isn't too goddamn much trouble for her. You can also tell her for me, if she didn't want me with her, all she had to do was say so. She should have told me to my face instead of making up excuses. Forget it, Billie, don't tell her any of the things I just said. I'm sorry I'm taking my anger out on you. Please, forgive me. Just tell Amelia I called, and give my regards to Rand, Maggie, and Thad." Rand was personable and elegant enough to squire Amelia to her "gathering," but he wasn't. Fuck it all!

Defiantly, Cary dropped more money into the phone. "Miss Kingsley doesn't answer," the impersonal voice announced. Cary left his name, and the Nelsons' phone number.

He was back in Waikiki. Cary knew the streets now, turning here, maneuvering to the right or left to avoid a one-way street, beating the major portion of late-afternoon traffic. He was on H–1 a little before five. He paid careful attention to the speedometer; every few seconds he looked into the rearview mirror. He turned off Kam Highway and pulled into a Burger King. For the first time since breakfast, he realized he was starving. He ordered three Whoppers, a double order of french fries, and two cups of coffee.

* * *

It was four-thirty when Julie started her countdown. She'd had such high hopes, and now they were dashed. She couldn't stay here any longer like a lovesick schoolgirl. It was clear now to her that she wasn't going to find Cary. If she was meant to be with him, they would have found each other before this. She'd made a fool of herself by coming here, but thank God, no one knew about it but herself.

She used the bathroom one last time before the long trip back to Waikiki. She brought the still damp towel to her cheek. It smelled like Cary. She wanted to wad it up and carry it with her. Instead, she spread it out neatly on the rack, so it would dry.

He was here—at least, his things were here. So close. She ached with longing as she took one last look around the bedroom. Cary's suit hanging neatly, his dress shoes lined up underneath. Jeans and T-shirts slung over the backs of chairs. Cary's things. His shaving gear, his toothbrush, his aftershave. She closed her eyes, swaying dizzily. She sat down on the edge of the bed, imagining she could feel Cary's body warmth emanating from the tangled bed sheets. She had to get out of here before she burst into tears.

It was two minutes after five when she backed her car out of the gravel driveway.

The Burger King on her left looked appealing to Julie. Her conscience hadn't allowed her to touch the food in the Nelsons' refrigerator. She realized she was starving. She drove to the back of the parking lot and swerved next to a car with a Dollar Rent a Car sign on it. Curious, she bent down to look at the license plate. Her heart skipped at least two beats. With shaking hands, she rummaged in her handbag for the scrap of paper with Cary's license plate number. She leaned against the trunk of the car, a feeling of warmth coursing through her.

She spotted Cary immediately. She slid onto the seat opposite him and reached for one of his Whoppers. "Thanks. I'm starving," she said softly.

Cary stopped chewing for a moment. Things like this only happened in the movies. "I am, too.... That's why ... I bought three. Have some french fries and one of these coffees."

"Thanks. I was waiting at your house all day."

Cary didn't find the admission strange at all. "I went to your place and they said you rented a car, which probably meant you would be gone all day. I just sort of bummed around and kept calling. Those guys know me already."

"They told me someone was asking for me. I never dreamed it was you. This is the best hamburger I've ever eaten."

"I think I've made a fool of myself."

"I don't mind. I've been calling your house at all hours of the day and night. I lied to the rental car place and said you sideswiped me. They gave me your address and phone number."

Cary's eyes were full of awe. "Why?"

"I wanted to see you. You should have gotten more catsup."

"They're all out. I got the last. I thought when I didn't call back . . . you would think . . ."

"I did. Then I decided anything worth having has to have problems attached. All I've been thinking about is making love to you in that beautiful house. I've heard so much about it from Aunt Billie."

"Ever since I got here I've been having dreams about you. In one of them I was going to make love to you down by the water. I had you wrapped up in a lei I made myself. I woke up."

"Were you sorry?"

"Yes. Maybe we should . . . talk about this some more?" Cary said hesitantly.

"If you like. I won't change my mind. There are no strings attached to me. Why didn't you call back after I left that message?"

"No guts. This deal I'm working on. Amelia. I didn't want you to be hurt. I wanted to call. A couple of times I had my hand on the phone . . ."

"We aren't kids. I'm thirty-nine, in case you've forgotten," Julie said gently.

"I haven't forgotten anything. I played our time together over and over in my mind. A thousand times at least. I thought you said you were starving."

Julie fixed her eyes level with Cary's. "I am, but not for a Whopper. You don't seem to be too hungry yourself."

"My appetite seems to have disappeared," Cary said softly. "We should talk."

"Words have a way of coming between people."

"In that case I think we should climb into our respective

cars, with me in the lead, and head back to the house I'm staying in. Jesus, I'm glad you were hungry enough to stop here," Cary said happily.

"Me, too. Cary, there doesn't have to be an afterwards. This is now." He nodded to show that he understood.

Cary drove slowly, constantly looking into the rearview mirror to make sure he wasn't dreaming and that Julie was still behind him. He wiggled a finger and smiled to himself. It was happening. Julie was here. They were going back to the house. Three days and three nights left. Julie's eyes had told him what *she* was expecting. He hoped his answering glance told her his thoughts were identical.

The leaves of the huge banyan tree at the Nelsons' gate parted in the wind, as though they were standing aside for the lovers to enter. Julie took it as an omen. She was meant to be here. Absolutely.

The cars slid to a stop in the middle of the long driveway, both doors opening simultaneously. It was dusk now, that soft, lavender-gray time when the worries of the day were behind and new beginnings were forged. Julie's voice was as light as a summer breeze. "It's so beautiful here. If I lived here, I don't think I'd ever want to leave."

"I feel the same way," Cary said. His arm was around her. Julie leaned into him as they walked to the lanai.

Cary uncapped two wine coolers from the small refrigerator. "I think we should talk. Not that I want to. I can't make you any promises, Julie."

"I'm not asking you for any. I'm here. You're here. This is our time. It will mean whatever each of us wants it to mean. No more and no less. Tell me about the dream again, the one where you wrapped me in a lei and then made love to me," Julie said lazily.

"Why don't I show you instead," Cary said softly as he pulled her toward him. His arms drew around her, holding her close to him. How tall he was, towering over her, lifting her chin with the tips of his fingers to look down into her eyes. His lips, when they touched hers, were soft, giving as well as taking, gently persuading her to respond. His arm, cradling her against him, was firm, strong, but his fingers touching her face were tender, trailing whispery shadows over her cheekbones. A kiss like this was the best possible beginning to a wonderful evening. A kiss. A tender gesture that tempted and demanded.

"Hello, beautiful lady," Cary whispered against her cheek.

"Hello, darling Cary," Julie responded breathlessly. "I've never been kissed like that before," she confided shyly. Cary smiled in the lavender shadows as he squeezed her closer to him.

"We're going to make a lei," he said boyishly. "No one taught me how to do it. I figured it out myself, in my dream."

"I'll help you," Julie whispered.

"Why are we whispering?" Cary whispered.

"I don't know," Julie whispered back. "Maybe because this place is so perfect, so hushed, loud voices will shatter something. Where's the string for the leis?"

"In that little cabinet next to the refrigerator."

They talked of everything and nothing, of Cary's trips to the Beach Tower and Julie's unhappy days in Waikiki. Their voices were as soft and gentle as the warm trade winds billowing about them. They worked on their leis, their eyes on each other.

"I has to be a long one. In my dream I wrapped your entire body in it and there was still some left over," Cary said.

"They should make perfume like this," Julie said.

"No. Then there wouldn't be moments like this." Please, God, don't let this be another dream, he prayed silently.

Cary reached for her. His embrace was so natural, she felt herself melting into his arms as though she'd been doing it for hundreds of years. He felt good. He felt right. His arms tightened, bringing her closer to him. No words were spoken; none were necessary. Gently, she felt his lips in her hair, on her cheek and throat. Tenderly, his fingers lifted her chin, raising her lips to his own. He was pressing her closer to his chest, crushing her breasts against him. His body was hard, muscular. Julie's arms encircled his back. Without reason or logic she felt safe and secure in his embrace, and she faced her tumultuous emotions with directness and truth. She couldn't help it. She wanted this man as much as she wanted to take her next breath.

Their eyes met in the soft dusk. Julie knew that she could drown in that dark gaze and emerge again as the woman she wanted and needed to become.

Seeing her moist lips part and offer themselves to him, Cary lowered his mouth to hers, touching her lips, tasting their sweetness, drawing from them a kiss, gentle, yet passionate. As the kiss deepened, searing flames licked her body, the pulsating beat of her heart thundered in her ears.

It was Cary who broke away first, his hands trembling as he untied the shoulder straps of her loose-fitting dress. Her flesh burned when he undid her bra and slipped her panties down over her hips. The cool, fragrant plumeria blossoms were wound about her body, a balm to her scorched skin. Her own hands were quivering, yet gently, when she undid the buttons on Cary's shirt and loosened the buckle on his belt. She felt his hardness when she slid his shorts down over his muscular thighs. When she laced the last of the plumeria around him, his eyes searched hers for an instant, then time became eternal for Julie. From somewhere deep within her a desire to stay forever in his arms, to feel the touch of his mouth upon hers, began to crescendo, threatening to erupt like fireworks. Thick, dark lashes closed over her blue eyes, and she heard her own breath come in ragged little gasps as she boldly brought her mouth once more to his, offering herself, kissing him deeply, searchingly, searing the moment upon her memory. Slowly, Cary lowered Julie to the emerald-green of the lanai carpeting, the garland of plumeria breaking apart so they could lie among the fragrant blossoms that were an aphrodisiac, heady, bringing all of her senses to a high-pitched frenzy.

She kissed him then as she had never kissed another man, a kiss that made her weak and dizzy. She knew, in that endless moment, that this man belonged to her. She had found him

Cary's fingers were gentle as they danced through her hair. He sensed what she was feeling. There are needs of the soul that go beyond the hungers of the body. His voice was deep, husky, little more than a whisper. "Help me make this a night for all eternity."

He waited for her answer, wanted to hear her say it, commit herself to it. Wordless agreement would not do for him, he realized, not with this woman whose skin was so soft and fragrant beneath his lips and whose eyes were lowered with shyness. "Tell me, Julie," he murmured against the hollow of her throat, sending little tremors vibrating through her.

"Yes, yes," she cried. Was that voice her own? A voice deep and singing with desire, her woman's voice. "Cary," she murmured against his lips, feeling them soft and moist on her own. "I want you to make love to me."

Cary was excited by her voice, each of his senses heightened because she wanted him to love her. He captured her mouth with his own, entering with his tongue, feeling the velvet of hers. Together they knelt and fell back into the soft bed of plumeria blossoms, where she offered herself to him, allowing his hands to move over her body, exciting her, matching his hunger with her own.

She surrendered to his touch. She grew languorous as his hands possessed her breasts, the soft tenderness of her belly, and the smoothness of her inner thighs. His mouth gently opened hers, his silken-tipped tongue exploring, teasing, caressing with a fervor that sent her senses spinning.

When his hands moved between her thighs, rising upward, she moved against his touch, and she heard the response to her passion in the catch of his breath and the deep, deep sound that came from his throat. "You're so beautiful, Julie. So very beautiful. I love the way you want me to touch you." His voice was softer than a will-o'-the-wisp, and she wondered if she only imagined it.

Rolling over on the soft blossoms, he took her with him, trailing his fingers down the length of her spine and returning over and over again to the roundness of her buttocks. He invited her touch, inspired her caresses, always watching her in the dim moonlight, reveling in the heavy-lidded smoldering of her eyes. He wanted her to take pleasure in him, wanted her to find him worthy of her finely tuned passions. Did he please her? he wondered, as she smoothed the flat of her palms over his chest, her fingertips gripping and pulling at the thicket of hair. Her mouth found his nipples, tasting, lowering her explorations to the tautness of his belly and the hardness of his thighs. He reveled in her touch, in the expression of her eyes as he took her face in his hands and held it for his kiss.

Putting her beneath him once again, he kissed the sweetness of her mouth, her eyes, the soft curve of her jaw. Her breasts awakened beneath his kisses; she arched beneath his touch.

She sought him with her lips, possessed him with her hands, her own passions growing as she realized the pleasure she was giving him. The hardness of his sex was somehow tender and vulnerable beneath her hands as she felt it quiver with excitement and desire . . . for her. His hands never left her body, seeking, exploring, touching. . . . She wanted to lie back and render herself to him; yet at the same time she wanted to possess him, touch him, commit him to memory and know him as she had never known another man. She felt her body sing with pleasure.

Julie was ravaged by this hunger he created in her. She wanted him to take her and bring her release, feeling as though she would die if he did not, yet hating to put an end to excruciating pleasure.

He put himself between her opened thighs, his eyes devouring her as she lay waiting for him. Her hair reflected the silver of the moon, her skin was bathed in a sleek sheen that emphasized her womanly curves and enhanced the contact between their flesh. He sat back on his heels, his gaze locking with hers as his hands moved over her body. Julie met his eyes, unashamedly, letting him see the hungers that dwelled there and the flutter of her lashes which mirrored the tremblings in her very center. His hands slipped to her sex, and she cried out softly, arching her back to press herself closer against his gently circling fingers. "You're so beautiful here," he told her, watching her eyes close and her lips part with a little gasp.

He gentled her, fed her desires, brought her to the point of no return, then smiled tenderly when she sobbed with the sweetness of her passion. She climaxed beneath his touch, uttering her pleasure, whispering his name. His hands eased the tautness of her thighs, kneading the firmness of her haunches and smoothing over her belly.

When she thought the sensation too exquisite to be surpassed, he leaned forward, driving himself into her, filling her with his pulsating masculinity. Her body strained beneath his, willing itself to partake of his pleasure, to be his pleasure. The fine hairs of his chest rubbed against her breasts. His mouth took hers, deeply, lovingly. His movements were smooth and expert as he stroked within her, demanding she match his rhythm, driving her once again to the sweetness she knew could be hers.

Her fingers raked his back, feeling the play of his muscles beneath his skin. She found the firmness of his buttocks, holding fast, driving him forward, feeling him buried deep within her. He doubled his delight and she climaxed again, and only then did he quicken his pace, thrusting himself into her with shorter, harder strokes.

Her body was exquisite, her responses delicious, but it was the expression on her lovely face and the delight and pleasure he saw there that pushed him over the edge and destroyed his restraint. The total joy, the hint of disbelief in her clear blue eyes, the purity of a single tear on her smooth cheek, were his undoing. He found his relief in her, her name exploding on his lips.

They lay together, legs entwined among the blossoms, her head on his shoulder as he stroked the softness of her arm and the fullness of her breasts. His lips were in her hair, soft, teasing against her brow. "You're a beautiful lover," he breathed, tightening his embrace, delighting in the intimacy between them. "I could make love to you again and again," he chuckled.

They lay together in the lanai for a long time, saying words only lovers say, but Julie knew that no matter how many times they made love, there would be one small part of Cary that would never be hers. She had sensed it several times during their ardent lovemaking. She'd sensed something else in him, too—a wariness, as though he were listening. Caught up as she was in her passion, she realized she could be wrong, but she doubted it, and in the end it made no difference to her. She was here with Cary Assante. If there were little ghosts between them, she'd handle it.

Cary sighed deeply. He couldn't ever remember being so satisfied, so contented. He hugged Julie to him. Was he falling in love with her? For now, in this wonderful place, it would be all right if he did.

But always, in the back of his mind, he waited for the phone to ring.

"How about a midnight swim?" he asked.

"Is it midnight already?"

"I have no idea. While you're here, we are not going to look at a clock or ask one another the time. For us, now, time has no meaning. Is that okay with you?" Cary nuzzled his face in her hair.

"It sounds too wonderful to be true, and yes, I agree. I also agree to the swim."

For a brief moment she felt self-conscious when she stood up, naked. She knew Cary was staring at her ample breasts, her heavy thighs. She sucked in her breath, waiting to see if the expression on his face changed. When it didn't, she let her breath out in an explosive sigh.

"What was that all about?" Cary laughed.

"I was wondering if my . . . my . . . ampleness shocks you."

For an answer he drew her to him, kissing her deeply. "I think I'm falling in love with you, ampleness and all."

"Shhh," Julie whispered as she laid a finger against his lips. "Come on, last one in the water is a stinkweed."

They swam effortlessly, in sync with each other, out to the coral reef and back. Their energies in high gear, they frolicked like two playful dolphins, laughing and dunking each other. When at last they tired, they made their way up to the white beach, bathed in silvery moonlight. They lay back, exhausted.

They made love again and again when their energies returned, the moonlight bathing their bodies in silver, the stars winking their approval. They slept entwined in each others' arms, Julie deeply, Cary soundly but with an ear to the lanai. Where the phone was.

They breakfasted on fresh fruit and pineapple juice. They swam, they snorkled, they made love. They napped and sat under the monkeypod tree. They even climbed the gnarled old tree and nestled in the deep boughs, swearing their love for all eternity. The twin lemon-yellow hammocks rocked with their pleasure and their giggles. They loved each other until they were exhausted, then napped and loved again and again.

On the afternoon of the last day, they showered and dressed together. Now it was time to talk. There would be no more lovemaking; there wasn't time. Cary had to pack, and then they'd drive to the airport in separate cars. It was Julie who initiated the talk, her heart crying out to know things only Cary could answer.

"Why," she whispered, "didn't you go to Washington with Amelia?" Please say it was because of me, she pleaded silently.

Cary listened to the question, hating to answer but knowing he must. If nothing else, he had to be fair to Julie. His voice was halting at first, then the words tumbled out one after the other. He finished with, "I can't believe she's ashamed of me. I guess she is; nothing else makes sense."

"Cary, you're wrong." Julie leaped from her beach chair to drop to her knees at his side. "I'll never believe that, not of Amelia."

Cary reached for her hand. The desire to make love to her one last time was strong; he thought he would pass out with the feeling. She read his intent and slowly shook her head. "It's over for us. For now anyway."

"I don't care anymore. You notice there were no calls while you've been here. That says it all as far as I'm concerned."

She hated playing devil's advocate, but play she would, for Cary. "Maybe the phone isn't working. Did you try it?" The naked hope in Cary's eyes was more than she could bear. She watched with tears in her eyes as he reached for the white phone on its little table. The pinging dial tone made his face harder than granite. Julie got to her feet and stared down at him. She wanted to ask, to demand, if she was just a fill-in for Amelia, something to while away the time, but she couldn't; the words wouldn't slip past her swollen tongue. Oh, he felt something for her, but it wasn't like the love he felt for Amelia. Her heart was breaking.

"I think we should start back," she said quietly.

"I don't want to leave," Cary said harshly. He grabbed her arm and pulled her toward him. "I love you; I want you to know that. No matter what you think, I do. I can see all kinds of things in your face, and I guess I don't blame you for what you're thinking. I didn't know it was possible to love two women at the same time, but it is. I need to know how you feel about me, Julie."

Should she laugh or should she cry? Truth or lie? Because she didn't know how to lie successfully, she opted for the truth. "I think I love you more than life."

There was a desperation in Cary's voice when he said, "I'll come to New York, I swear I will, every chance I get. I'll write, I'll call every day. I need you, Julie. What will I do without you?"

Tears flowed down Julie's cheeks. How could something that felt so right be wrong? She'd known when she came here, that this was all there was going to be. Once they were back home, he in Texas, she in New York, things would change. You couldn't take paradise home with you.

"Wait here," Cary said. "I want to make one last sweep of the house to make sure all the windows are closed and all the plugs are out." Julie waited. She'd washed all the dishes and the towels. Early this morning she'd laundered the sheets and remade the bed. The owners would find their house the way they left it and probably never know that she'd fallen in love with Cary here, much the same way Billie had fallen in love with Thad, and Maggie with Rand.

She cried all the way to the airport, blowing her nose every few seconds. Thank God she'd brought sunglasses.

Amelia refused to look into the mirror the nurse handed her. Looking into a mirror would only make her feel worse. She pretended, for all their sakes, that she was feeling better and on the mend, but even a fool would know this was the end of the road. It had been a beautiful, wonderful road to travel. She closed her eyes, and the past came alive again. She'd met her first husband, Rand's father, in England during the War. She'd loved him and she'd buried him. His legacy to her was his son—her son now. Further down the road she'd met Billie, her brother Moss's wife then, whom she loved so dearly. Billie, kind and wonderful, the sister she'd never had, who helped her through those awful years with her father, who had hated her from birth. Billie had eased the pain when her mother had died. Billie had shared her own daughter Susan with her; they'd raised Susan together. She could always count on Billie. She was never more than a phone call away with her love and support. She wondered if it was possible to take a mental picture of someone into eternity. If it was, Billie's countenance would be with her.

Her thoughts turned to her own past, her own life and loves. For a while, after she returned from England, she'd hurried down her own long road, stopping often to pick up a stranger to fill the empty spots in her life. The road had been rocky then, but it smoothed out when she met Cary Assante —her reason for living.

Now her road had crested; she was looking at a steep decline. Part of her wanted to backtrack, to return to the smooth sections of the road she'd traveled, that long, lovely stretch where she'd been happiest, but it couldn't be. She had only two options. She could continue to stand at the top of the road, where she was right now, for another six months, a year at most; or she could start her descent to the end of the road.

Amelia leaned back into her nest of sterile white covers. She was needle-thin now, hardly making an indentation in the bedding. Her eyes closed wearily and then she forced them to snap open. She was greedy; she wanted more. The road was still visible. She had to continue down the road until . . .

She thought about her funeral. It would be simple; she'd be on the hill with her mother, a nice place to be for the rest of eternity. All her family would grieve; Billie would grieve the most. Grief was short-lived; life went on. She knew that better than anyone. Life and God had been good to her. She'd never been one of those who asked God for something and then said, if you give me this, I'll do that. No, that wasn't strictly true; she'd done that once, when she was eleven or so. She'd prayed to God that her father would love her. She'd prayed on bended knees, promising to muck the barns for a month if He granted her wish. She hadn't expected an outpouring of love, just a few kind words. When they weren't forthcoming she forgave God with her eleven-year-old wisdom and mucked the barns anyway. God simply didn't have time for lost causes.

She wondered then who would send flowers and who would donate money in her name to different charities. A tear slid down her cheek. She'd never know. What she did know was she'd get a whopping send-off—Texas-style. What the hell, she deserved it. She tried to smile. What she had to remember, what she mustn't ever, ever lose sight of was yes, she was leaving *them*—but she was leaving behind someone who was kind and warm and loving. Someone to take her place.

Amelia marshaled all her Coleman guts, all her love for her family, and sat up in bed. They'd be here soon to take her to Billie's house. A slight detour. It wasn't the end of the road . . . yet.

Ivy stared out of her dormitory window at the scenes being played out below. Damn it, she wouldn't cry! She just wouldn't! Down there, all over the campus everyone was laughing and crying and hugging one another. Graduation! Entire families, from all over the country, were here for their son's or daughter's moment of glory. And what and who did she have? Not one single, goddamn thing. No congratulatory cards, no telegrams, no presents, and not one family member. She hadn't expected . . . but she had hoped. And not even a damn phone call!

Magna cum laude wasn't too shabby. She bit down on her lower lip as her right hand patted her right shoulder. "Well done, Ivy," she whispered. She blinked back the tears that threatened to spill over. "Okay, Buckalew, put that cap and gown on and get over to the auditorium. You're the star today!" Ivy did as she instructed herself. She spent extra moments looking at the honors tassels on her cap. She'd busted her hump for these, but it was worth it. Her head was high as she walked to the door. Her hand was on the knob when the door pushed inward.

"You Ivy Bookalew?" a young kid demanded.

"Yep."

"Then I guess this is for you. I been chasing all over this place looking for you. They told me downstairs everyone was already moved out. Sign here."

Ivy's hand trembled as she ripped at the telegram. Her smile rivaled the bright May sunshine as she read the words on the yellow paper. Congratulations! It was signed, Riley.

Ivy's step was light as she made her way to the auditorium, where the commencement exercises were to be held. All those people, hundreds, maybe a thousand or so, and no one for her. She was the last to take her place in the front row of the platform.

It was a beautiful day, one made especially for graduations. A light breeze ruffled the tassels on her cap. She reached up to straighten them, the small square of yellow still clutched in her hand.

So many people, all dressed in their best, sitting here straining for a glimpse of their son or daughter. Riley's telegram was easing her hurt, but she still couldn't bring herself to look at the front row of seats. Two of them, right in the middle, had been reserved by the dean himself for her mother and father. She should have told the dean her parents wouldn't be coming. She'd meant to, but she hadn't. Why hadn't she told him? Shame, anger, dismay? Those two seats were going to stare up at her like black holes when she was at the podium giving her speech.

Some of the magic left the little square she held in her hand. It couldn't take the place of her family. She bent over to slip it into her shoe and then she saw her . . . right in her line of vision. "Lacey!" she squealed. Lacey waved wildly.

"The plane was late." Lacey mouthed the words, flapping her arms to imitate wings that flew too slowly. She grinned and gave her sister a proud thumbs-up salute. Ivy returned it, tears sliding down her cheeks. It was all right now.

After the commencement exercises, Lacey drew Ivy to the shelter of a tree with a circular bench underneath. "You didn't think anyone was coming, did you?" Not waiting for her sister's reply, she continued. "I saw it in your face. You were in shock when you saw me. God, Ivy, I thought you'd know I'd come. I am so proud of you. There aren't any words. I'm sorry that Mama—"

"It's okay. I guess they were busy. I didn't think you'd be able to come, either. I hoped, though. I never stopped hoping; I want you to know that. We lost so much ground there for a while, and even though you've been writing . . . the trip . . . the cost and all."

"You lost weight," Lacey laughed.

"And you gained some. You look real good, Lacey, real good."

"I have this . . . new boyfriend. He says he likes women with a little meat on their bones. You'll like him, Ivy."

"Why not, if he had the good sense to pick you?" Ivy said warmly.

"Thanks for that, Ivy."

Ivy took a deep breath. Lacey had a new boyfriend. That meant . . . She felt whole suddenly, alive and eager to get on with this new relationship with her sister. "I appreciate . . . God, Lacey, when I looked down and saw you sitting there . . . it was like . . . oh shit, you know what I mean . . ."

Lacey hugged her sister. "I know exactly what you mean. When the plane was late, I wanted to jump out of my skin. I gave the taxi driver twenty dollars to break a few speed laws. I *had* to be here."

The leaves of the sycamore rustled in the warm breeze. Golden sunshine splattered at their feet on the mossy-looking grass. Ivy grinned and pointed at the intricate sunny patches. "That's what we all need, Lacey, sunshine in our lives. I think we finally got it."

"You never answered my letters, Ivy," Lacy said gently. Her eyes went to a cluster of fat pigeons foraging for crumbs from leftover lunches. She couldn't look at Ivy while she waited for her answer. The eyes always said it all. Especially with Ivy.

"I . . . I was afraid I'd say the wrong thing. . . . You know me, I always say—in this case, write—the first thing that pops into my head. I figured if I didn't write at all you'd get ticked off and then I'd know . . . Lacey, you still came to my graduation . . . even when I didn't write." Ivy waved her hands helplessly in the air. "Put yourself in my place, Lacey. It's been . . . years . . . maybe all my life, that I've lived with . . . rejection and hurt . . . I guess I don't know how to act when people are nice to me. Maybe you could . . . sort of help me overcome that."

Lacey laughed, a pure, musical sound of amusement. "The blind leading the blind. My life was no different from yours. You just saw it differently. We've taken the first few steps; the rest will fall into place. Let's go get your stuff and load up your car and catch a bite to eat. A drink, too, to toast your honors. Oh, Ivy, I am so very proud of you."

"I feel like I have the world by the tail," Ivy laughed as she skipped alongside Lacey, their arms entwined. "Riley sent me a telegram!"

Lacey didn't miss a beat. "That's great. Give him a little slack and he'll come around. You'll be the best thing that ever happened to him."

The clump of pigeons scattered suddenly and took wing. Both girls stopped and looked upward. "I feel like I'm flying with them," Ivy said softly.

"You are," said Lacey. "So am I. You can fly with your feet on the ground. Didn't you learn anything in college?"

"Nah. That's what big sisters are for." They both laughed then, a warm, carrying sound that brought the pigeons back in a cluster around their feet. They were still laughing and smiling as they touched each other's arm from time to time, all the way back to the dorm.

"This is a new beginning for both of us, Lacey. Let's not screw up, okay?"

"You got it, little sister."

Little sister, big sister. A unit, part of a family. A twosome.

Sisters.

CHAPTER SEVENTEEN

Billie and Maggie stood side by side. Billie's hand searched out her daughter's. Maggie grasped it tightly. Both were silent, each busy with her own thoughts about how to react when Rand brought Amelia home.

"I feel so awful, Maggie. For days now I've been lying to Cary. What must he think? And Amelia; I can't believe she's given up. She was such a fighter. All she keeps saying is it's her time. I don't believe that. Cary should have been here; tomorrow isn't soon enough. He should be bringing Amelia home, or at least standing here with us."

"Mam, you had to do what Aunt Amelia wanted. Don't start blaming yourself. I refuse to believe she's given up. It's going to take time. I know, I know she's been saying all along she's here on borrowed time, but that was her way of . . . Don't ask me what it is she's covering up. It's just a feeling I have."

"An invalid. Amelia will never accept it. I know her. We've been friends for almost forty years." A sob caught in Billie's throat. "Maggie, I don't know if I can carry this off."

"Mam, all my life you've told me you can do what you have to do. You have to do it for Amelia."

"I am angry with her, Maggie. Cary is going to be angry with all of us, and I can't blame him."

"Mam, I have to confess something. It's so awful I don't even know if I can get the words out. God should strike me dead for such thoughts, but I don't want to keep it bottled up."

Billie was immediately full of concern. "The worst thing you can do is bottle something up. What is it, darling?"

Tears rolled down Maggie's cheeks. "Mam, next to you, you know I love Aunt Amelia best. I never met anyone who could talk turkey to me like she used to do. When we got here Rand was one step away from a nervous breakdown. Amelia's heart attack made him stand back and look at his priorities. Mam, I was glad Amelia got sick, because Rand started acting like a human being again. It took Amelia to bring him back, and when I say back, Mam, I mean back. I thought I was losing him. I saw it all washing away. I feel so awful. I don't want Amelia to be sick. I don't want Rand to have a nervous breakdown either. I want things to be right for all of us. I don't know if you'll believe this or not, but I wasn't *just* thinking of myself, not really."

"Maggie, darling, what you felt was perfectly normal. If Thad were involved, I would feel the same. Don't torture yourself. God works in mysterious ways, as we all know. He has it all in hand."

Maggie dabbed at her eyes. "Thanks, Mam. You're probably the only person in the world who would admit to possibly feeling the same way."

"One time Amelia thanked me—actually she blessed me —for admitting that I wore socks to bed to keep my feet warm. Now, where did that memory come from?" Billie laughed. It was a strangled, crying sound.

"I think I hear the ambulance. Pinch your cheeks, Mam; dry your tears and look cheerful. Smile, Mam; we can do it for Amelia."

"Maggie, she's in a wheelchair. I wasn't expecting a wheelchair. I thought Rand would carry her in or the ambulance attendants would carry her. I wasn't expecting ... Maggie, she's in a wheelchair!"

Maggie's hand in her mother's tightened. "It's temporary. And she'll be able to stay downstairs instead of being confined to bed, like Grandmam Jessica. Smile, Mam, here they come." Maggie herself smiled brilliantly, her arms outstretched in welcome to both her husband and her aunt.

"Just in time for lunch," Billie cried. She leaned over to kiss Amelia's dry cheek. "Welcome home, Amelia."

Maggie followed her mother's lead and kissed Amelia's other cheek. "We've been cooking up a storm all morning, from scratch," Maggie said enthusiastically. Her husband's eyes thanked her as she busied herself with their coats and Amelia's hospital bag.

"The sun is accommodating us today, too. The breakfast nook is warm and bright. All your favorites, the ones you're permitted to have. Your doctor sent a list home with Rand last evening," Billie babbled.

"I don't want you to fuss," Amelia said wanly.

"Amelia, listen to me. I have nothing to do here but sit around and wait for Thad to come home. I like to fuss for the people I love. Maggie does, too, so we made it a joint effort.

Doesn't the house smell wonderful? The cinnamon is real. Rice pudding."

By the time lunch was over, Billie was exhausted. Maggie herself looked weary. Rand was alert, his eyes rarely leaving Amelia's face.

How tired she looks, Billie thought in dismay. How very, very old. This thin stick of a woman was really Amelia. Dear God, what was Cary going to say when he arrived this evening? She pushed that thought as far back in her mind as it would go. All the life seemed to have drained from her friend. Would Cary's return bring back the spark that kept Amelia going? She wished she knew.

"Amelia, how would you like a warm, delicious, delectable bubble bath? I can wash your hair, and Maggie can set it for you. You can get out of those awful hospital things. Rand bought one of those special seats for the tub."

"What I'd really like to do is take a nap."

"That's fine, but let's make sure it's the best nap you can have. A warm bath first and a good cup of tea will do the trick."

An hour later, Billie tucked Amelia between the covers in the guest room. "Amelia, we have to talk, just for a few minutes. Cary is coming home this evening. You . . . what I mean is . . ."

"I will fess up, if that's what you mean. Cary will understand. I'm sorry I put you in such a spot, Billie. Tell me, how sick do I look? And, Billie, please don't lie to me."

"You look like you're recovering. You do look tired. Amelia, hospitals take their toll. You have to remember that you had a heart attack. You don't beat something like that overnight. We'll have you outfitted in your best bib and tucker when Cary gets here. What he'll see is, his wife is getting better."

"I can tell you're a senator's wife; you've picked up the knack of saying a lot of words that mean nothing. I don't have a lot of time left, Billie."

Billie's vision blurred. "Please, Amelia, don't say things like that."

Amelia's words were so matter-of-fact that Billie flinched. "I've known for a long time. If I'm lucky, a year. Possibly less."

Billie swallowed hard. "If what you say is true, old friend, then you have to make the most of the time you do have. Don't give up, Amelia. I want to see that sparkle back in your eyes. Whatever you can do, I want you to do it. Live, Amelia, for me. I'm so selfish. I can't bear to lose you. You're right up there with Thad and the children. Your friendship all these years has meant so much to me."

"Billie, you are the most wonderful person walking the earth. Bless your heart, you are so easy to love."

"Thad keeps telling me that, but what does he know?" Billie said in a choked voice. "I've always been so grateful to you for standing by me, back in the early days. I didn't thank you enough. I should have said the words more often. My life has been so much richer because of you. Some people go through their whole life and never have a true friend. I can't even begin to imagine what it would have been like without your friendship."

"Are you going to cry?"

"I'm trying not to. Are you?"

"For all the good it's doing me. I need a tissue or else my nose is going to run over these pretty sheets." Billie handed her a box of tissues from the nightstand. "I don't want you feeling sorry for me, Billie. You have to give me your promise. No pitying looks you try to cover up. I couldn't bear that." Amelia blew her nose lustily. So did Billie.

Billie swallowed hard. "I'll . . . I'll do my best, but you have to do your part. I want your promise now that you won't . . . that you . . . will do your best. Now what I think we should do is hug each other and cry our eyes out. Is that okay with you?"

"I keep saying I'm not afraid to die, but it's a lie, Billie. I'm so afraid." Amelia sobbed. "No lifesaving techniques. None. Let me go. You have to do it, make the decision. Cary won't be able to do it. Swear to me, Billie?"

"Yes. And if I go first, you do the same." Billie wept softly against Amelia's shoulder.

"All my organs to someone who . . . to the donor bank."

"Mine, too." Billie sobbed.

"Daisies on my grave on my birthday. Will you do that, Billie?"

Billie nodded her head miserably. "Amelia, what will I do without you?"

"Wherever I am, I know God will let me watch over you." Billie was crying harder; her grip on Amelia's thin shoulders was almost fierce. "There will be a letter for you, Billie," Amelia said. "You'll do what I ask in it?" Billie nodded. "You won't forget Cary?" Billie nodded a second time. "He's part of our family, Billie."

They continued to cry for the would-haves, the should-haves, the could-haves, until both were exhausted.

"I feel better, Billie," Amelia lied. "I think I can sleep now."

"I feel better, too." Billie returned the lie. "Rest, Amelia. I'll stay here with you till you're asleep."

"Dear, sweet, wonderful Billie. I knew the moment I laid eyes on you that you would be my friend for all time. I'm so glad I was right. Thank you, Billie, for allowing me to share my life with you." Amelia's words trailed off in sleep, but still Billie sat on the edge of the bed, her hand in Amelia's. If she could have, she would have breathed her own life into her friend.

What seemed like a long time later, Maggie tiptoed into the room. Her eyes went to the tissue box and then to the waste-basket. It looked to her experienced eye like a fifty-tissue cry. She nodded, satisfied. Mam had made it right, whatever it was. Gently, she loosened her mother's firm hold on Amelia's hand and led her out of the room. "After you wash your face, we should start thinking about what we're going to have for dinner. You said you wanted to make bread. I have everything ready on the counter," Maggie whispered.

"What time does Cary's plane get in?"

"Six-thirty. Rand is going to pick him up. I thought we'd eat around eight, if that's all right with you."

"That sounds fine to me. I'll be down in a few minutes."

"It was Rand's decision to brief Cary on the trip home from the airport. Cary shouldn't walk into this cold. Cary isn't some kid who . . . He deserves better."

Billie nodded in agreement.

Cary dragged his carry-on luggage through the concourse, his eyes searching for Rand or Thad. It was Rand who spotted him first. Their handshakes were hearty. Rand grabbed one of the bags. "I think I'm parked at least three miles from here," he said, "so take a deep breath."

"Hold it," Cary said, setting the bag down with a thump. "What happened to 'How was your trip? How did the business go? Man, that's a great tan'?"

"Later."

"No, goddamn it, now! Where the hell is my wife, or is she too damn busy partying to meet me?" Cary all but exploded.

"I said, later," Rand said coldly, aware of the commotion they were causing.

Cary lowered his voice, but it was still angry and belligerent. "Fuck later, Rand. Either you tell me now, while I'm still in this airport, or I'm taking the next flight to Texas."

The hard expression on Rand's face softened. Of course he wanted to know what was going on, and he had every right to ask. Why had he thought the car would be soon enough? The sudden fright in Cary's face made him reach out. "Amelia had a heart attack, Cary. It happened right after her speech. Now can we go to the goddamn car and talk in private? This is killing me, too, you know."

In the front seat of the Audi, Cary turned to face Rand. He couldn't remember how he got to the car, much less where his bags were. If they'd walked three miles, he couldn't remember.

Rand spoke quietly, leaving nothing out. Cary's face was ashen. Rand had to take the cigarette out of his hand to light it for him.

"I thought . . . Christ, you wouldn't believe what I thought. I did . . . You should have told me. Someone should have—"

"I got here after it happened. Billie had already called you. She didn't want to do it, Cary. Amelia insisted. You can't blame Billie."

"No, no, I don't. I should have been there. Instead, I was out . . . Jesus, you don't know what I did."

"Cary, don't tell me. We can talk when we get on the road, away from this airport. Blue zone, yellow zone, red zone. Why can't they say terminal A or B or whatever it is? It's like a war zone with all these cabbies and cars."

"I thought she was ashamed of me. That she didn't want me there for her big moment," Cary said.

"You've been married to Amelia for a good number of years, Cary. You should know her better than I do. How could you think that of her?"

"It seemed like the only answer. I was waiting for her. I had made such wonderful plans, was going to show her all the places I'd seen, tell her all the folklore stuff I'd learned. That house of yours, where everyone was so happy—I could hardly wait for her to see it. When Billie said she couldn't make it, I . . . hell, forget it."

"Seeing her is going to be a bit of a shock. She's in a wheelchair and she's lost a lot of weight she can't afford to lose. Don't let the shock show." Cary nodded.

"What do the doctors say? Did anyone call her doctor at home?"

"The doctors spoke. Cole is going to fly up and take her back as soon as the doctor gives his okay. The prognosis isn't good, Cary." He paused before saying the hardest thing of all. "Maybe a year."

A cold, hard lump settled in Cary's throat. His eyes burned.

"When you say a year, it doesn't sound like much. When you say twelve months, it sounds a little better. Three hundred and sixty-five days sounds like even more," Rand said quietly.

Cary sat back into the softness of the leather seat. His eyes closed wearily, his signal that he didn't want to talk anymore.

Pride. The greatest sin of all. Second on the list was anger. He'd suffered both, and been unfaithful. Nothing was ever going to be the same again. Nothing.

Nothing Rand said prepared Cary for the shock of seeing Amelia. This needle-thin person with the sunken eyes couldn't be his wife. For one brief instant he felt repulsed, but he recovered quickly. The smile he pasted on his face didn't feel right. He guessed that it didn't look right, either. What the others took for dismay and grief on his part was really guilt and shame.

Billie wanted to weep with the effort Amelia was putting forth. What was wrong with Cary? Her eyes pleaded with Thad to intervene.

"I get to push the lady in to dinner," Thad said, a little too heartily. "In case you aren't aware, we've been waiting patiently for the pair of you. Roast leg of lamb, mint jelly, those little new potatoes, homemade bread and homemade ice cream and chocolate cake. Billie and Maggie were in the kitchen all afternoon slaving away for this homecoming dinner. Now, let's reward them for a job well done."

"Hear, hear!" Rand joined in. Maggie and Billie took their bows. Billie linked her arm through Cary's.

"You aren't covering it up well enough. More effort is needed on your part, Cary," Billie whispered urgently.

He tried. God alone knew how hard he tried, but the guilt coursing through him was so intense he could hardly eat. His eyes kept going to Amelia, who did her best to avoid his glances. Her bright patter only made him feel worse. He almost jumped out of his skin when Amelia declined dessert and asked if she and Cary could be excused.

Thad and Rand rose from the table. "I'll carry you up, Mother." Cary mumbled something that sounded like "Excuse me," and went on ahead.

"This is not good. Something's wrong. Do you know what it is, Mam?" Maggie demanded. She felt shaken when her mother's eyes filled with tears. She stared blindly at Thad. Thad wiped at his wife's tears with a napkin.

"Don't cry, darling," he whispered. "Amelia will make it right."

Rand returned to the table and demanded a slice of chocolate cake with three scoops of ice cream. "Move, woman," he said, nudging his wife.

"Hey, I baked the cake. You serve me. Guess who's clearing the dishes, too," Maggie said. Effort made her voice shrill.

"It's my turn anyway," Thad sighed. "For some reason it's always my turn when we have guests."

The bad moment was over.

Amelia seemed lost in the big bed. He'd never seen a frillier room, all ruffles and bows. Even the sheets and comforter that Amelia had pulled up to her chin had little pink bows all over them. It was up to him to say something, but the words stuck in his throat. Any other time, Amelia would have taken pity on him. Either she was too tired or she didn't care anymore.

He turned his back and made a pretense of opening his overnight bag for his toiletries and robe. "You should have told me, Amelia. You shouldn't have gone through this alone."

"Cary, there wasn't anything you could do. I wanted you to go through with the business deal. I didn't want to worry you. That's a woman's lot in life, to shoulder things so as not to worry her husband."

"That's a crock and you know it."

"I can't believe you're angry with me. You have a right to be upset, but not angry. I'm fine. It's going to take a while for me to get on my feet, but I did it before. Come over here and tell me all about your trip and the business deal."

"This isn't something we can gloss over, Amelia. I thought all kinds of things. Billie's phone calls left me feeling you were ashamed of me and you didn't want to share your moment of glory with me. I can't wipe that out in a few minutes. I thank God you're all right, but what you did to both of us was wrong. And yes, I am angry. Because of those feelings, I did . . . Forget it. I should have come home when I finished the business instead of . . . Never mind, it isn't important. What do the doctors say?" he asked grimly.

This was all wrong. Nothing was going the way she'd planned. Cary was supposed to be filled with remorse. Some kind of feeling should be showing on his face. So far, he hadn't said a kind word. Women could cover guilt so much better. She'd given him his chance, at great cost to herself, willingly and selflessly. What was she supposed to do now? Lie about her condition or tell the truth? Make it easy for him? His guilt would probably be less bearable if she told lies.

"Cary, I'm sorry. I was thinking of you. You know I would never be ashamed of you. I always worried that you would be ashamed of me. Like now. I know how I look. I also know how I feel. I understand if you can't . . . can't cope with me or my condition. But to answer your question, the doctors say I have to take it easy, get lots of rest, eat well, fresh air, that sort of thing. I'm mending. If you can forgive me, it will make the recovery process a lot easier on me."

"Amelia, I—"

"Cary, I don't want you feeling guilty. You look guilty, too, so get that look off your face. I won't have it."

Cary sat down on the bed. He took Amelia's thin hand in his own. Sorrow welled up in him. He could feel tears prick at his eyelids. "It's me, babe, who should be saying he's sorry, not you." He started slowly at first and then worked up into a fast chatter. He was pleased when Amelia giggled over some of his tales. At some point during the telling, he'd gotten under the covers. Amelia leaned into his arms, her head resting on his shoulder. She did her best to stay awake. Her last conscious thought before dropping off to sleep was that she'd given and Cary had taken.

Just as she planned.

Adam paced the living room. He felt old, useless, and a tad sorry for himself. Why was it he could get a bead on other people's problems and practically solve them, but he couldn't get past square one with his own?

He knew now he wasn't going to live out his life here in Texas. He belonged in the city, where something was happening every second of every day. If he stayed here, he was either going to saw off his arm with the chain saw or start the biggest bonfire the state of Texas ever saw with all the wood he and Jeff had cut and stacked. Busywork.

He should sell the ranch. Riley might still be interested. Everyone, for the past two years, had been speculating on the oil that might be on his property. Riley would make some kind of fair deal on the oil leases, unlike Coots Buckalew. He was going to have to give the whole thing some very serious thought.

Texas, this ranch, the people—they all reminded him too much of his youth, and Sawyer. Coming here, thinking he'd put down some roots for himself and the boy, wasn't one of his better ideas. He had to put the bullshit aside and get on with his life. But before he did that, he had two immediate problems to handle and resolve. One was Jeff; the other was Sawyer. He could call Sawyer now.

Cole picked up the phone on the third ring, holding it away from his ear when Adam barked out his question. "You want Sawyer's phone number! Why?"

"Because I'm calling her to ask her to marry me. This is her last chance. I've decided to sell this place and go back to New York. If you Colemans want to buy, ante up," Adam barked.

"You're talking to the wrong guy, Adam. I want to shake off the dust of this place as much as you do, and you know it. Riley's the one to talk to. You want to make a deal on the oil leases, right?"

"Damn right. I got a kid to put through eight years of college, and hopefully a wife and kids of my own to support."

"What brought all this on?" Cole asked curiously. Nick, he'd guess.

"I decided it was time to get on with my life instead of sitting on it. If she doesn't want me, okay. I have to know. I haven't asked her to marry me in five years. What do you think my chances are?" Adam asked fretfully.

"As good as they'll be tomorrow or the next day. Go for it; all she can say is no."

"That's my thought. Nothing ventured, nothing gained, I always say."

"I always say that, too." Cole chuckled. "Give me a call and let me know what she says. If it's bad news, don't bother."

"It's a deal. Wish me luck."

"You're nuts, you know. Sawyer's okay. I love her, but she's not exactly marriage material in my opinion. You want to share her with Coleman Enterprises, then I say go for it."

"Thanks, Cole."

"For what?"

"Your blessing. That was your blessing, wasn't it?"

"Hang up, Adam."

Five minutes later, Sawyer picked up the phone.

"Will you marry me?"

"What?"

"Will you marry me?"

"When?" Sawyer's voice squawked.

"Day after tomorrow."

"Why so long?"

"I thought you might want a church wedding with all the family." Of course, he knew she wouldn't.

"How about when I get home?"

"When's that?"

"A couple of months. Soon."

"Was that a yes? Are you shaking your head up and down?"

"Yep. What's taken you so long?"

"No guts. Will you marry me, Sawyer?"

"Yes, Adam, I'll marry you. As soon as I get home."

"Will we have lots of little Sawyers and Adams?"

"At least one Adam. Call Grand and tell her, okay?"

"Are you sure, Sawyer?"

"Jeez, I was going to ask you when I got back. I'm sure, Adam."

"I decided to sell the ranch. I'll tell Riley it's his if we can work out a deal on the oil leases. That okay with you?"

"I love you, Adam."

"You never said that to me before."

"I could never say it before because I wasn't sure. I am now. I knew when I saw you the last time."

"Okay, I'm going to hang up now and get drunk. Write me a letter."

"Okay."

"'Bye."

"Bye, Adam."

In a daze, Adam dialed Cole's number. "She said yes."

"Congratulations; or should I offer condolences?"

"Smart-ass. I'm going to get drunk as soon as Jeff goes to bed. Want to join me?"

"I think I'll pass. Stay happy, Adam. I always said you'd make a great brother-in-law."

"I always said that, too," Adam said happily.

Hell, he didn't need alcohol to feel drunk.

The cold reality of her aloneness depressed Julie. At times these past weeks, Hawaii and Cary seemed more a dream than reality. A wonderful dream.

The harshness of the blustery April wind tore into Julie as she walked up Park Avenue. She felt like crying, but knew that if she did, she wouldn't be able to stop. She hiked the colorful cashmere scarf, a gift from Billie and her Uncle Thad years ago, up over her nose. What did she care how she looked? There wasn't a soul in this city she cared about.

April in New York. It should be warm now, with spring flowers on all the corner stands, and she should be wearing a light coat instead of being bundled up like an Eskimo. Sub-freezing temperatures in April in New York were almost unheard of. "Why not?" Julie muttered under the scarf. "Everything else is fouled up; why not the weather?"

The weather and her aloneness aside, she knew what really bothered her: she hadn't heard from Cary since her return from Hawaii. She'd had an uneasy feeling that something was wrong ever since she'd returned. For one thing, she hadn't heard from Billie or her Uncle Thad. It was unlike Billie not to call and ask how she'd enjoyed her vacation. Any other time she'd have wrapped up the little souvenirs she'd bought for them and mailed them off, but they were still in the ABC bag she'd carried them home in. The last time she'd looked, the bag was on a chair in a corner in the bedroom. She supposed she could have called her uncle and Billie, but she was afraid something would come through in her voice, would give her away.

The wind whipped furiously at Julie's back, driving her forward. She sped around the corner to East Seventy-ninth Street and narrowly avoided colliding with an elderly man walking a shorthaired terrier who was resisting the leash as well as the wind. Maybe that's what she needed—a dog. Animals were loyal and they loved unconditionally. She'd heard stories of animals who killed for their masters or defended them to their own death.

She and Cary hadn't even said good-bye. Both of them knew they'd see each other again; she'd felt it would be soon. Cary had said that he'd be in New York in a few weeks. To her that was soon. She'd gone to the airport with him, just to be with him for an extra hour. She'd waited until his plane took off. She knew he couldn't see her, but she waved until the plane was a dust speck in the blue sky. His plane landed at National Airport in Washington just as hers was leaving for New York. So far apart in distance and miles. But so close in her heart.

The door to the apartment slammed shut behind her. The warmth caressed her cold, numb body. She tossed off her coat and scarf and headed straight for the answering machine. The tiny light blinked repeatedly. She pressed the message button and heard Cary's voice. "I'll call you at nine o'clock this evening." Nothing more. Julie rewound and played the tape four times to see if she could detect anything in Cary's voice. A business voice, cool and impersonal. She had two hours and fifteen minutes to wait.

Tonight would be a good time to make dinner, a real one. She'd had enough sandwiches and soup to last her a lifetime. Frozen dinners in their little metal trays were an indicator that she was alone. She hated them. The freezer yielded two individually wrapped pork chops. She seasoned them, and the broiler would do the rest. A potato was scrubbed; the toaster oven would bake it to perfection. Butter and sour cream were set out to soften. A stalk of fresh green broccoli found its way to a small casserole dish and the microwave oven. Now she could change her clothes and get into her old, comfortable bathrobe and scruffy slippers. While she waited for her dinner she'd call Billie and her uncle. She should have taken the initiative and done it herself long ago. They were family. One didn't ignore one's family . . . ever.

Billie's warm voice was better than a hug, Julie decided.

They discussed Thad and his late hours, the weather, Julie's vacation. "I bought you a present; it's a bit tacky, but remember, it's the thought that counts. It's one of those straw things that hang on a wall to put your bills and letters in. It has a red hibiscus on it."

"If you bought it for us, then we'll love it. I'll even hang it up. I keep my bills in a shopping bag. Thad is always after me about it. How are you, Julie?"

"If this blasted cold weather would let up, I'd be fine. I'm just itching to walk through the park to see all the greenery. I love spring, don't you?"

"Yes, I do, but my favorite time of year is autumn."

"How's all the family?"

"My goodness. I do have news! Adam Jarvis called. He and Sawyer are getting married. A real wedding, with all the trimmings, if we can talk her into it. We haven't had one of those for a long time. I plan to dive in with both feet when the time comes."

"How wonderful," Julie said. "I've caught the bouquet four times. I've given up."

"Never give up. The right man is out there; he just hasn't found you yet."

"I'm thirty-nine, Aunt Billie. He's taking a long time finding me."

Billie chuckled. "Maybe he lost his map. Don't worry, he'll find you."

"Maggie and Rand? I called the house when I was in Hawaii, but there was never any answer." It was the truth; she had called.

"They were in England for a while, then they came back and stayed here for two weeks. They're back in their paradise now. Cole is still in Texas, cleaning up what he calls the mess Riley left for him. Riley's still in Rio." That left Amelia and Cary. Billie didn't want to hear the anguish in Julie's voice, or make her ask about them. Perhaps she didn't know.

"I had a full house for a while," she went on, choosing her words carefully. "Cary and Amelia were here. I don't know if you know this—how could you?" Billie said, answering her own question, "but Amelia had a heart attack just hours after she appeared before Congress. She was in the hospital and came here the day Cary got back from Hawaii. Cole came up and flew them back."

"I thought the bypass surgery corrected her problem." Lord, that strange voice couldn't be hers.

"That's what we all thought. Apparently, Amelia didn't tell us everything. She has to take it easy. I'm sure the nice weather will play an important part in her recovery. I still subscribe to the theory that fresh air, good food, plenty of rest, and a loving husband will do the job."

"I'm sure you're right. I'll have to send her a get-well card. Aunt Billie, I think my pork chops are burning. I'll call you in a week or so. Give my love to Uncle Thad, and keep your eye out for the Hawaiian treasure I'll be sending on."

"Good-bye, Julie."

Death. People who had heart attacks usually died. If Amelia died, Cary would be free. "NO!" she screamed. "No, I didn't mean that. I'm not a ghoul. I won't wait for . . . No! I'm sorry! Please, God, I didn't mean that thought to crop into my head. Make her well. Give her many, many more years."

Anger raged through her. She reached down to unplug the answering machine. It took her a long time to find the box the machine came in. She jammed the machine in, any old way, not caring if she broke the buttons or knobs. She literally threw the box on the top shelf of the hall closet. "That's the end of that," she shouted to the empty apartment. For emphasis she slammed the closet door as hard as she could.

The pork chops were dry and brittle; the thin layer of fat around the edges was black. The baked potato was still hard, the inside mealy, the broccoli overcooked and bland. She ate it all.

When the phone rang at nine o'clock, she was in the shower, washing her hair. When it rang again at nine-twenty, she was creaming her face. When it rang for the last time, at nine-forty, she was doing deep knee bends. By ten-fifteen she was asleep on the couch, the afghan pulled up around her neck.

The following day on her lunch hour she took the time to purchase a witty, cheerful get-well card for Amelia. She stood at the mail desk in Macy's and penned off a short message.

Dear Amelia,
    Please get well soon. I'll look forward to seeing you dance the night away at Sawyer's wedding.
                                    Affectionately,
                                    Julie

Wasn't love putting the other person first?

{{{{{{{{{ CHAPTER EIGHTEEN }}}}}}}}}

Winter, spring, summer—where had they gone? Cole won-dered. He sat in his car, on land between the Jarvis ranch and Sunbridge. He'd taken to checking out Adam's house, more for something to do than for any particular reason.

From here he could see his great-grandmother's rose gar-den at Sunbridge. The house looked mellow somehow, softer in color, bleached by the summer's sun, more pale than a prairie rose. He hadn't been back to Sunbridge, and he didn't miss the old pile of bricks. He was glad that he owned no part of this vast place.

He looked across the grazing lands that were lush from the spring and summer rains. It still held no appeal for him.

Six more months and he'd be ready to leave. He didn't know what he'd do or where he'd go, but he knew he was going. He'd set his own time schedule, late one night when he sat alone, watching the David Letterman show. He was taking charge of his life. His plan included telling the family over the Christmas holidays when they all gathered at Sunbridge. He hoped they'd understand. If they didn't, there wasn't much he could do about it.

He really shouldn't take all the credit for finally coming to his decision. Nick had helped him over the past months. He'd made the time to fly to New York several times, staying four or five days at a time, seeing Nick for a couple of hours each day.

Time was moving too fast in some areas, too slow in others. Time was fleeting for Aunt Amelia and Shadaharu Hasegawa; it was dragging for Riley, and probably for Sawyer, trying to wind things up so she could get married. He had to think about doing something special for Christmas for his Aunt Amelia, making the holidays really festive. With things so slow at the office, he could make all the arrangements. If he read the situation right, his beloved aunt didn't have . . . He swiped at the tears in his eyes. The doctors had said she had a year at the most; and that year would be up next March. This would be her last Christmas. It had to be a good one, as good as he could make it.

Cole got out of his car and looked around. It was something to do, something physical, but his thoughts wouldn't be still. When he was little, in the military school he hated, he used to lie in bed and pretend he had three wishes. First, he'd wish for his parents to come and whisk him home, saying they'd made a mistake in sending him to the school. His second wish was for a motorcycle. The third was for all the blackberry pie he could eat, every day of his life. He played the game now. His wishes were more serious, and for the most part hopeless, except perhaps the last one. He wished for two reprieves—one for his Aunt Amelia, one for Riley's grandfather. His third wish was for Riley to slap him on the back and say, "It's history. I overreacted."

Cole looked at his watch. His lunch hour was over. It was time to go back to the office and tie up some loose ends. Three more cancellations had come in for the DM. Tomorrow there would be more, and the day after that, still more. When prosperous oilmen couldn't make their payroll, they couldn't afford to pay for the jets they'd ordered from Coleman Aviation. Back to a virtually empty office with only a skeleton crew working at a reduced salary. Back to nothing.

It was a sweltering day in late September. Cole sat at his desk way past closing time, going over the reports that came in on a regular basis from Sawyer in Japan. He was tired and he was frightened. Everything was in the red. Two of their best holdings were on the block. Whatever profit they made would only keep them afloat another couple of months.

The rise and fall of the Coleman empire. They'd done about all they could. Soon the vultures would be circling. No more long shots, no magic cures. No one to blame.

It wasn't Riley's fault. He'd done his best. More than his best. Old Seth's bones must be rattling in the ground at what was happening. What would he say? Cole almost thought he could hear the gravelly voice that had been described to him hundreds of times. "Bail out, boy; cut your losses and start over. Use your back, your muscle, and the bank's money. You go belly-up, boy, and there ain't no bank nowhere that will loan you money. Bail out!" Yep, that's what old Seth would say. Riley didn't see it that way. Sawyer was fast coming around to Seth's way of thinking, though; he could tell by the notes she included with her reports.

Cole looked around the office he'd decorated himself. He could either stay here and write to Riley's grandfather or go home to the condo and do it. If he did it here, he could leave it in outgoing mail for the morning pickup. He'd anticipated this very intention by slipping the latest letter from Japan into his briefcase when he left the apartment earlier.

He enjoyed the old one's letters, often reading them three and four times or saving them up and reading them one after the other. For some strange reason, he felt close to Riley's grandfather.

The crackly paper was unlike any other. Cole unfolded it and read slowly:

Coleman san,

My weary eyes appreciated your last letter. It is most kind of you to keep up our correspondence. I look forward to your letters with as much eagerness as my ailing body can muster.

To be sure, your family is anticipating Sawyer's marriage to Adam Jarvis. Your kind offer of wedding pictures will be appreciated. I have come to love Sawyer as my own daughter, as you know. I pray she is blessed with many children.

My heart is full of sorrow for your aunt's frail health. Like all of us, she has become old. She is a remarkable woman with a strong spirit much like my own, I am told. I spoke once with her at great length. We talked of dreams and destiny. Her dream, she said, was fulfilled; her destiny, preordained. I, too, spoke of these same things, something I never thought of myself doing, especially with a woman. I felt a better person for sharing those confidences.

Your grandmother wrote me just last week and told me she is counting the days till January, when Thaddeus retires from his government office. Her plan is to take a trip around the world with her husband. She said she will stop to visit and bore me with all their pictures. My family is blessed to share your own family. East and West, as you are fond of saying. I recall a day many years ago when you and my grandson stood side by side and you asked me, very respectfully, if West could get top billing this one time.

I am proud, Coleman san, that you shared your dream with me. Man must have a dream to make life worth living. All things are within the realm of possibility. I shall pray that you never lose your dream. It is a life force that binds my spirit to this earth. I fear that my dream will go to the grave with me. It is my darkest secret.

Once again I must thank you for sharing your news of my grandson with me. I have received only one letter from Riley since his very brief visit in March. It was a brisk letter inquiring about my health. I searched for some sign of warmth and affection but could find none. I felt like a fighter in the ring who has lost fight. I share this with only you, Coleman san.

My busy daughters are fussing about me and want

{ 338 }

me to take a nap. If they knew about the monsters that invade my dreams, they would not insist, but I must make them happy.

Continue to dream, Coleman san, and one day your dream will be fulfilled. My spirit tells me this is so. You must never give up that which you hold close to your heart. I send to you, Coleman san, my American friend, my best wishes.

Shadaharu Hasegawa

Cole stared at the blank paper in the typewriter for a long time. What did he want to say to this wise old man? Many, many things, he decided, that shouldn't be put on paper. Maybe, instead of writing, he should take a vacation, go to Japan. He could visit and talk as much as the old man wanted. Right now he could use all the wisdom the old Japanese could offer. Anything was better than rattling around the office with no real work to do. He hadn't taken a vacation last year or this year; he was entitled. He could soak up some Eastern culture, dine on sushi, hang out with Sawyer, visit with Riley's grandfather, walk down the Ginza, snap a few pictures to prove to himself he'd really taken a vacation, and rest.

Cole covered the typewriter. The phone was so much quicker. His watch told him it was seven-thirty in the morning in Japan. Mr. Hasegawa was an early riser.

All he had to do was pack, file a flight plan, and he was off. Not wanting to disturb the old one, Cole left a message: Coleman Tanner would arrive by early evening.

Sixteen hours later Cole Tanner rang the bell on the Hasegawa gates. He was ushered in politely and escorted to the Zen garden, where Riley's grandfather sat. The light evening breeze wafted about Cole. He thought the garden the most beautiful spot he'd ever seen. He'd made no sound, yet the old one raised a frail hand and spoke softly.

"Coleman san, welcome to my humble home. Join me here in the garden, where it is so peaceful. My grandson used to play here with his mother when he was a child."

Cole walked over to the wicker chair, uncertain if he should hold out his hand or bow. When he was uncertain about anything, he did what he felt like doing; he dropped down to one knee and grasped the old Japanese's shoulders in both his hands. "It was presumptuous of me to call and announce my arrival as I did. It's good to see you, Mr. Hasegawa."

{ 339 }

"And you, Coleman san, are a welcome sight for these old eyes. I am glad you came to visit me. Sit beside me and talk. If my fussy daughters see me engaged in conversation, perhaps they will allow me to stay up longer. Or you could intervene and tell them to . . . to buzz off."

Cole laughed. "I can't do that, Mr. Hasegawa."

"That is my problem, too. They mean well, but they are . . . pests," the old one said fretfully.

"I can relate to that." Cole laughed again. "Perhaps they will extend your bedtime. A compromise."

"I don't like that word, Coleman san. A compromise means someone wins and someone loses. It is a word I try to avoid. One gives up things and gains things. Winners and losers. I lose and have to go to bed, but I do not sleep."

They talked, intensely at first, and then quietly. West meeting East, and finally understanding. It was after eleven by Cole's watch when a shadow fell across his lap. He almost burst out laughing at the expression on the old Japanese's face

"You see what they have done? My daughter fears my wrath, so she sends in a child, whom she knows I cannot refuse. They call this little spirit Top Gun. She is a buzz saw, meaning she will swoop me up and carry me to my room if I don't follow her docilely."

Cole noticed that the old one rose with difficulty, rejecting the child's offer of her arm. He walked with a cane these days, but at least he was walking. In the dim garden light Cole thought he looked about the same as he had in November, with the exception of the cane.

"I rise at five. If you would like to join me at that time, I have my breakfast, if you can call it that, here in the garden," he said with a grimace.

Cole nodded. "I'll be here."

It was evident to Cole, when he walked to the garden for his early-morning breakfast, that the Hasegawa household revolved around Riley's grandfather. Never in his life had he seen so much quiet bustling. Everyone, it seemed, had her own job. The little girls tittered behind their hands as he nodded formally. He wondered if Riley knew all their names.

They all appeared to be school age. All the little girls were dressed in uniforms—no blue jeans and sneakers here. He doubted if any of the children were aware their counterparts in the United States dressed differently. The United States must seem like another world to them.

"Mush!" the old Japanese said sourly after he greeted Cole. "You will, of course, have the traditional American breakfast of ham and eggs. One of my daughters tells me they prepared something called grits for you. The name alone would prevent me from eating it. You will have coffee and I will have tea. I will pretend not to see you eat, and you must not watch me consume this . . . this mess they say is good for my digestive system. Dig in, Coleman san."

He did. The ham was pink and succulent, the scrambled eggs light and fluffy. The toast was warm, with butter and blackberry jam. The coffee was a blend of aromas that did strange things to his nostrils. The grits, he forced down. He almost laughed when he remembered Riley saying that eating grits was like eating warm snot. His mother had reprimanded him, but she'd never served grits to Riley again.

Cole pushed his plate away. "That was one of the best breakfasts I've had in a long time. Your mush looks . . . awful."

"I know. I complain just to stay in practice. The food I like, I can no longer eat. It tears up my insides. I endure."

"All your family lives here, in this house?" Cole asked.

"Yes, all my married daughters have apartments of their own. I have twelve grandchildren living here. All but two go to school. In Japan space is limited. Children live with their families. It is our way. This house was meant for many people. When Riley was growing up, it was a very happy house. He was the first grandchild. You Americans say, the apple of my eye. Soon I will introduce you to all my family, save my youngest daughter. She is already at the paper, working. She will return late this morning to tell me what she has done right or wrong. Usually it is wrong. She does not want to marry. A career, she says. She wants to be a modern Japanese. When no one is about, she sneaks me a cigar or some sake."

Cole was on his third cup of coffee when the family parade started. First the children were introduced. They bowed formally and left. The daughters approached their father respectfully. He took each one's hand as he introduced them. Each was prettier than the next one. He was surprised; he hadn't expected beauty. He'd seen pictures of Riley's mother, and she'd been pretty, too. The last daughter was the only one to speak. She did so in halting English. "Your breakfast was satisfactory?"

"Yes, thank you."

"If there is anything you wish, ring my father's bell."

{ 341 }

"Nannet, the children will be late for school," the old man said.

"Is Nannet a Japanese name?" Cole asked.

The old man snorted. "This foolish old man you are sitting next to agreed with his wife that she could pick the names for the girls and I would be the one to choose the boys' names. I had no boys. My wife was addicted to the American film stars. Nannet is named after Nanette Fabray. I believe she was a singer. When our last daughter was born, my wife took pity on me and allowed me to name her Sumi. She also permitted me to name Riley's mother, our firstborn. I named my daughter Sumi after my own mother.

"Let us walk about my garden, Coleman san, or my daughters will insist I take a nap. I will tell you what each plant is and when it was planted. A true Zen master planned this garden for my wife and myself. I think it is my favorite spot on earth. If I had more strength, I would take you to a place that is my second favorite spot in the world. I used to take Riley there and hold his hand on the climb. He trusted me then and only wanted to please me."

"Sir, Riley still trusts you."

"Perhaps. I was about to tell you about my second favorite spot. I will ask Sumi to take you there. Beyond my house in the back there is a cherry tree grove. I myself planted the trees when I married. My wife loved the cherry blossoms. At the end of the grove there is a hill. The trees line the walkway on both sides. The top is level, a circle really. My wife planted the trees on the circle, and my Zen master did the rest of the sculpting. I wish to die in that spot. My first choice would be to die here in this garden, but it would leave unhappy memories for my children and grandchildren. None of them love the special place on the hill. My wife is buried there. So is Otami, and next to Otami is a cross that bears Riley's father's name. The only thing buried there is his flight bag. Otami insisted. My wife and I had no objections. In all the trips that Riley made here, he would never go to the cherry blossom hill."

"It would have been too painful for him," Cole said loyally.

"Yes. We must all experience pain and sorrow, for if we don't, how will we know happiness? Come, my daughters are lurking in the windows. You will have more coffee and I will have more tea. Women are only happy when they are fussing about serving food and clearing up. There are days when I feel Sumi has the right idea."

The old Japanese and the young American talked of many things as they sipped their tea and coffee. Every so often a comfortable silence would ensue, or the old one would drift off to sleep. Cole was amazed; he could fall asleep in the middle of a sentence, sleep fifteen minutes, wake, and continue with what he was saying.

"Sumi will be here soon. She always brings me a present, some little thing that catches her eye. Or she will bring a cigar and close the doors so no one can see me puff the evil smoke. Perhaps today there will be a cigar. We could share it, and if my daughters spy on us, you could say it was yours."

"Yes, I could do that," Cole laughed.

Fifteen minutes later the doors behind them slid open. "Ah, here she is. This is my daughter Sumi, Coleman san."

Cole got to his feet. The old Japanese watched Cole and Sumi as they shook hands.

In the blink of an eye, Cole Tanner fell in love. In that first brief moment, he knew all those sensations that a man experiences when he comes face-to-face with his emotional destiny. His entire body was alive with feelings that he had never known before. He knew now, in this briefest of seconds, that he was looking at the one woman who could fill the emptiness in his life, the one woman with whom he would share his whole being.

And, as if nature had planned the meeting, Sumi was aware, for the first time in her life, of what a beautiful sensation it was to look at a man and know he had been predestined to be hers. Yes, in the blink of an eye, Sumi Hasegawa also fell in love.

Because of the intensity of their own experience, neither Cole nor Sumi was aware of the joy on the countenance of the old Japanese as the two of them shook hands.

The day after Cole's introduction to Sumi, the old man took to his bed, but not before he instructed his daughter to look after their guest. The paper could do without her editorial input, he explained to Cole. Hers was just a window-dressing job, to keep her from pestering him to death. Allowing her to work at the paper was his concession to her demand to be a modern Japanese. While Cole was here, she would have another job: to be his guide. And, she'd thought slyly, if her father hadn't found a way for her to be in Cole's company, she would have found one

{ 343 }

herself. She winked at her father, a sign that she was more than a little interested in their American guest.

She spoke, telling Cole what she'd planned; he listened, wishing she'd go on speaking forever. Her musical, lyrical voice intrigued him. Her accent was soft; at times, the way she strung her words together seemed awkward to his ear, but the effect was foreign and exotic. He loved it . . . and her. Why had Riley never mentioned this beautiful young woman?

Cole paced the bedroom Sumi's oldest sister had assigned to him. He was pleased to see it was Western, with no mats or rice paper partitions; for visitors, he assumed. He felt light-headed, and his stomach was queasy—leftover jet lag, no doubt. Or . . . was this how you felt when you were in love? His heart skittered in his chest at the thought.

Cole sat down with a thump on the edge of the bed. He felt his brow the way his mother used to do when she thought he was sick. Cool as mountain water. He'd never been in love before. Oh, he'd had his share of flirtations, affairs, and then his relationship with Lacey. He'd been bewitched and bedazzled by Lacey, the most serious of all his affairs, but he knew from the beginning it wasn't going to be permanent. All that play time was behind him. It was time now for what he really wanted: warmth, laughter, and humor, along with shared insights and gentle touches. Someone to care enough about him to worry if he was warm or cold, sick or well. He wanted someone to argue with, someone to indulge, someone to kiss hello and good night. He wanted someone to encourage him, someone to understand him, someone to listen to him when he had something to say. He wanted love.

Sumi Hasegawa. It has to be the most beautiful-sounding name on earth. Sumi Tanner. Mrs. Coleman Tanner. Mr. and Mrs. Cole Tanner.

The ring of heat around Cole's neck made him touch his brow again; it was still cool. It was possible he was *getting* sick. Sumi could take care of him. She was so fragile, so delicate, so very beautiful. She had such warm, melting eyes, dark and soft like licorice. Those eyes had stared into his soul . . . and what had they seen? He wondered.

She was attracted to him, that much he knew. Tomorrow they were going on a picnic, an outing she said she would arrange. A blanket, a picnic basket, walking hand in hand. Sharing thoughts on the past and the future. Sharing their families. He'd seek her advice about Riley. She'd probably tell him things he didn't know about his cousin, things he needed to know.

Riley was half-Japanese. Sumi was all Japanese. What would his family say? A lump settled in his throat. He had to slow down and think carefully. To his knowledge, no one in his family was prejudiced. He didn't realize he was holding his breath until it exploded from his throat. Thank God. He realized in this second that it didn't matter what his family thought. The ring of heat crawled up to his face. Marry. He'd just met the girl and already he was thinking of marriage. He wondered if it had been like this for Riley's father. Maybe Sumi knew, or maybe Mr. Hasegawa knew. He wondered if it would be all right to ask. He decided he'd voice the question if the right moment appeared. The worst thing they could do was to tell him it was none of his business.

Cole lay back in the deep, comfortable bed and looked around the room. He'd slept here last night, but he hadn't really noticed the room, other than the bed. Now he was aware of everything—the clean, tangy scent of the bedclothes, something that smelled like lemon and eucalyptus, colorful paintings on the wall, the soft carpet which was a peachy cream color, a Sony television, a Sony VCR, a Sony Walkman, a Sony stereo unit, and a host of other gadgets all neatly aligned in a corner. All the comforts of home.

Cole leaped off the bed and raced to the bathroom. If he felt different, he must look different. The face that looked back at him in the mirror was the same one he'd always had. He leaned closer to the mirror. Summer-blue eyes stared back at him. They appeared bright and curious in the smoky mirror. Eyes that were alive, thirsting for... for what? Sumi, of course. He would never be able to drink his fill of her if he lived to be a hundred.

The bathroom was something out of *Arabian Nights*. He had showered and shaved in here, last night or this morning, but for the life of him, he couldn't remember. There were no damp towels to offer a clue. His toiletries were still in their zippered Louis Vuitton bag. There wasn't a speck of water anywhere.

The bathroom itself had to be at least twelve by fifteen feet, he judged. Gold leaf marble walls complemented the sunken black marble Jacuzzi. The faucets and hand grips looked like gold, and probably were. A massive vanity with three black marble sinks took up one entire wall. Cole snapped a switch and wasn't surprised to hear soft music. A second switch produced recessed lighting, a third offered a red heat lamp.

Three fat-bellied china Buddhas sat in a tier, gazing benevolently at him. Cole christened them Mickey, Mike, and Mo. He shook his head in disbelief as he walked back to his bedroom. This was some spread.

Sumi tiptoed around her bedroom; she wasn't sure why she was trying to be so quiet. So she could hear her thoughts, maybe—thoughts of Cole Tanner. She knew she was in love; every beat of her heart told her so. It wasn't just Cole Tanner's handsome presence that was making her heart beat fast, it was all the things her father had told her about him, too. She'd sneaked his letters and read them over and over till she knew them by heart. Somehow, someway, she must have known this was going to happen. All along she'd been preparing herself for this fateful meeting. Now it was a reality. Was she pretty enough, intelligent enough, interesting enough, to make Cole fall in love with her? How did she compare to American girls with their freedom, their panache, their opportunities? She felt something squeezing her heart when she looked into her mirror. She was too tiny, her hair was too black, her skin too honey-colored. Most American women were taller, had golden hair and peaches-and-cream complexions. What could Cole Tanner possibly see in her? Her dark eyes filled with tears.

She was the rebel in the family, and her father indulged her because she was the youngest, the baby. She knew her job at the newspaper was a token concession, but she didn't care. It was a start. That wasn't to say she didn't love and respect the old ways, but time moved on, and she didn't want to be in a gridlock, like her sisters. Life was too wonderful, too precious to remain behind locked walls, seeing to a house and children. She hadn't been willful or adamant; she'd pleaded with her father to understand. If the Coleman family weren't entwined with her family, her father would never, ever have allowed her to work at the paper. In their own way, the American side of her family, as she referred to them, had helped her get where she was now. It was a start.

She loved getting up in the morning to the sound of her alarm clock. She loved dressing in tailored Western clothes. She loved bustling to the kitchen for coffee and juice, the way she'd seen the American film stars do. But the best part was taking the bus to the paper.

Now, in the blink of an eye, her life had changed. She

couldn't help wondering if her older sister Otami had felt the way she was feeling when she met Riley Coleman, Sr. The Colemans had turned their backs on Otami and her young son. No, that wasn't fair; only Moss Coleman had turned his back on her sister and her baby. The other Colemans didn't even know about Otami and little Riley, and when they found out, they came immediately to try to make things right. That was when the Hasegawas and the Colemans became intertwined.

If she could manage to make Cole Tanner fall in love with her, she knew his mother and grandmother would accept her. There was no prejudice in any of the living Colemans—at least, none that she knew of.

Sumi sat down on a hard wooden chair with a thump. She grimaced. And how do I make Cole Tanner fall in love with me? How? She wished she knew how Otami had made Riley's father fall in love with her. She smiled ruefully, knowing full well you couldn't make someone fall in love with you. Either it happened or it didn't. She crossed her fingers, then she crossed her slim legs. She laughed; it was better than nothing.

For the next hour Sumi practiced all manner of makeup tricks in front of the mirror. When she stood back to view her elaborate hairdo, with the sticks poking out at all angles, she giggled. Her painted face made her reach for the washcloth. She looked like a streetwalker on the Ginza.

If Cole Tanner was going to fall in love with her, it would have to be with the fresh-scrubbed Sumi in the mirror.

She wiggled out of her Western clothes, slipped into a kimono, and headed for the kitchen. She would make the food for the picnic basket. Maybe she would make two baskets— Americans loved to eat. So did she, for that matter.

It was almost dawn when Sumi cleaned the last of the flour from the kitchen counter. All the food was stored in the refrigerator, waiting to be added to the two wicker baskets at her feet. The six American cookbooks she'd pored over were back on the shelf. When she walked up the stairs to her room, she felt as if she had created a miracle.

For just the barest instant, her footsteps slowed as she passed Cole's door. She strained to hear any trace of sound. Her smile was tired, but lovely when she heard the light sound of Cole's snoring. She thought it was the most beautiful sound in the world. She hoped the day would come when she would sleep next to Cole so she could listen to his breathing and feel his arms reach out to encircle her in his sleep.

Sumi Hasegawa was in love, a love she would carry with her to eternity.

Cole woke instantly, aware of his surroundings. Today he was going on a picnic! He was out of bed in seconds, showered, shaved, and dressed in eleven minutes flat. It wasn't till he was downstairs in the kitchen, searching for a cup of coffee, that he noticed the time: twenty minutes past six. He groaned. Sumi had said she would meet him in the garden at nine o'clock. Talk about being overanxious.

A walk, he could go for a walk, he thought. If the other family members woke and saw him prowling about, it might not look good. . . . He shifted from one foot to the other trying to decide what to do. Sit in the garden? Walk up to the cherry blossom hill? Go back to his room and wait for nine o'clock? He didn't want to do anything wrong, anything that would make the family think he wasn't good enough for Sumi. Jesus, he was acting like a kid with his first date. He never felt this way before.

In the end, he decided to walk through the first floor of the Hasegawa house to see what it was like. When he saw the shoes neatly lined up at the front door, he hastily slipped out of his Top-Siders. Mistake number one.

Cole spent the next forty-five minutes walking through the spacious rooms, marveling at the costly paintings and rare jade. It was a house full of light and soft furnishings, a house that seemed to be full of promise—of what, he wasn't sure. In what looked to be a music room he saw all the family portraits. He walked from one to the other, memorizing the names of Sumi's ancestors. The portraits dwindled to small oils of the Hasegawa children and on to colored photographs and black and white snapshots, all framed. He stared for a long time at a picture of Riley's mother and father. A picture of Riley at the age of three, in the garden, brought a lump to his throat. He followed the parade of pictures on an eye-level shelf. The pictures ended abruptly with the last picture of Riley, when he was fifteen or so. The bareness at the end of the shelf was so noticeable, so poignant, that Cole had to clench his hands into fists. He swallowed hard past the lump. "Damn you, Riley!" he cursed. He walked around the room a second time till he came to Sumi's pictures. It was like a rogues' gallery. Sumi tumbling in the garden, Sumi in costume at a play in school, Sumi on a pony, Sumi tussling with her sisters, Sumi in a studious pose with glasses perched on her nose. Sumi, Sumi, Sumi. He closed his eyes and willed a picture of himself and Sumi on the shelf. In the picture he and Sumi would be cutting a wedding cake.

Cole stood in the open doorway, looking back at the pictures on the shelves. He thought he'd give up all he owned to have his pictures there with the others. This house, this family, felt so *right*. If he could make a wish, it would be to be one of *them*.

The Zen garden was quiet and peaceful. A flash of red made him turn. Sumi! Sumi was in the garden, and it was only twenty minutes to eight. Sumi!

"I came down early; I didn't think you'd be up yet," Sumi said softly. Her eyes drank in the sight of him. How wonderful he looked, and it was so early in the morning. She hoped she didn't look weary from her own lack of sleep.

"I guess . . . I've been down here since six-thirty. I hope I didn't wake anyone."

"Not at all. When you are here, this is your home. You will do whatever pleases you. I'm sorry there was no family member to greet you on rising. My sisters will feel shame."

"Shame! No, don't let that happen. Sumi, you're laughing. You're putting me on, right?"

"A little. Your face gets very pink when you're upset; did you know that?" Sumi teased. "Come, the picnic baskets are ready. I made them myself last night after everyone went to bed."

She'd done that . . . for him? Cole's voice was full of awe. "You can cook?"

She giggled. "Of course. All Japanese women can cook. It was my first time with an American cookbook, though. I made fried chicken, deviled eggs, potato salad, cole slaw, and something called hush puppies. I have fresh bread, cheese, apples, beer, wine, and pastries. What do you think? Will we starve?"

"Who else is going besides you and me?" Cole asked. Jesus, she wasn't bringing the family, was she?

Sumi's jaw dropped. Good heavens, he wanted her to bring the family. "Just . . . I thought it would be just you and . . . Would you like me to ask my sisters?"

"Hell no!! Let's go, just you and me. I'll eat every bite so it isn't wasted."

They laughed together as they raced through the house with the packed picnic baskets. Shadaharu Hasegawa smiled to himself at the sound of their running feet and happy laughter. He looked like a wise old Buddha as he puffed away on his cigar, alone in his room. Some things were meant to be.

As far as Cole Tanner was concerned, it was a perfect day. He lay back on the blanket they'd brought and contemplated his surroundings. For the first time in hours he was aware of something other than Sumi at his side. Butterflies; Cole blinked as they danced about him. He stretched out a long arm, and one perched on his wrist. "Look, Sumi; shhh, don't make a sound." When the butterfly took wing, Sumi said, "Yellow is my favorite color. What's yours, Cole?"

Did he have a favorite color? He thought about it for a minute. "Blue, I think," he said hesitantly. Was blue really his favorite color?

"That color blue?" Sumi said, pointing to another butterfly. They watched silently, holding their breath, neither knowing exactly why. When the blue and yellow butterflies took wing together, soaring overhead, both of them sighed. Sumi stared boldly at Cole for a second, then lowered her eyes demurely. Cole flushed and rolled over onto his stomach.

"How did you get away from your job today?"

"It really isn't a job, the kind you and Sawyer have. My father allows me to go to the paper and, as he calls it, futz around, and once in a while I write something. I'm not very good," she said shyly.

"I can't believe that. Your people are so meticulous compared to Americans."

Your people. He was comparing. Sumi's heart sank. He was making a point of saying they were two different races. She had to say something, to respond to Cole in a light way. "When I go back to work at the paper, I will write an article about butterflies. My editor will blue-pencil it and say no one wants to read about butterflies, at which point I will stomp my feet and say I'll tell my father, and then they'll run the article. I wouldn't do that, though."

"Good. But if you change your mind, let me know and I'll buy every copy."

"You would do that?" Sumi asked in awe. Cole nodded solemnly. Sumi's heart soared. If she'd been a butterfly, she'd have taken wing herself.

"Who's in charge of all the newspapers your father owns?"

Cole asked lazily. "Listen, if you want to scratch my back, it's okay with me."

Sumi laughed. She rolled over on her side and let her nails trail down Cole's back. She smiled again when he shivered. "Mr. Naomura runs the papers, but he is old and he wants to retire. My father was counting on Riley coming back to take over. Even though my father is ill, no decisions are made until he is consulted."

"What about all your sisters' husbands? Why don't they take over some of the responsibilities?"

"Because they are working for their own fathers. It is our way, Cole. Other men run the different businesses. It is a heavy load of responsibility. Father was counting on Riley. It was his desire to bring everything under one roof, with Riley to oversee all the different companies. There is much confusion right now. Soon my father will have to make important decisions about our different businesses. He procrastinates because in his heart he thinks Riley will return and take over. I do not think that will happen. Do you, Cole?"

Ten different responses ran through Cole's head. He couldn't lie to this beautiful girl. "No. This is just between you and me, Sumi; it goes no further. Agreed?"

"But of course. What is it? What are you trying to tell me?"

"Part of Riley wants to come back here, but the other part, the American side of him, wants to be with his father's people. He is a Coleman, Sumi, through and through. More so than me." He told her then about his fight with Riley, glossing over the reason for the altercation.

Sumi gasped. "How awful for you, Cole. What has gotten into Riley?"

She cared; he could tell by the sound of her voice. She was showing no concern for Riley, only for him. "He wants to be a Coleman," he went on. "He wants to run the business, and he's done well. I gave him my half of Sunbridge, but I gave it in anger. Eventually I would have given it to him peacefully, but he doesn't know that. Sunbridge is where he belongs. Texas is Riley's home now."

"I know that. I tried to make my father understand, but it is—how do you say?—hope springs eternal. He thinks one day the phone will ring and it will be Riley saying he is returning, or he waits for the mail, hoping there is a letter from him saying the same thing. In his heart he knows. That hope is what's keeping him alive. You must never give any indication that—"

"I know. I would never . . . You can trust me."

"And you can trust me."

Cole reached for Sumi's hands and pulled her to her feet. How small and fragile her hands felt. A surge of protectiveness rushed through Cole. He kept one of Sumi's hands in his as they sauntered across the spiky green grass of the park. He wanted to kiss her then, more than anything, but he didn't know if it would be forward, if he would bring dishonor to himself or to her. Clearly some boning up on Japanese culture was called for.

Sumi stopped in midstride. "You could have kissed me back there. Didn't you want to? Are you just being nice to me? I thought you would want to kiss . . . why?" she asked boldly.

"Well . . . I . . . hell, I wasn't sure . . . Sure, I did, more than anything. . . . Jesus, what about your honor and all? . . . Come here," Cole said, pulling her to him. Sumi melted into his arms. How good she felt, how warm and soft, how right. There in the shade of a gnarled old tree, with the blue and yellow butterflies flitting overhead, Cole kissed her, a soft, gentle kiss full of yearning and promise. When he released her, he smiled down into her eyes. "This is the second time that East has met West in my life," he whispered. Sumi burrowed against him.

She was small and slim, tiny actually, the top of her head barely reaching his shoulder, but her figure was womanly— all the curves were in the right places. She wore a simple dress, fashionably long, and on her narrow feet were soft leather pumps. Her long, straight black hair was knotted at the top of her head, and long, feathery tendrils escaped here and there. In the half sunlight the mass of ebony glinted with shimmering blue lights. It looked incredibly soft.

"Your hair is beautiful, and your eyes are like saucers of licorice," Cole blurted. He half expected her to laugh, but Sumi looked up at him, pleasure coloring her cheeks and glowing in her eyes.

"And your eyes are like the skies of summer," she told him simply, truthfully. "It is my favorite time of year."

"Is there . . . is there anyone special in your life?" Cole asked bluntly. He had to know.

"No. Is there someone special in your life?"

"No." Until now, he thought. This girl was special from the

{ 352 }

top of her shiny head to the tip of her toes. There was a certain stillness about her—it was a trait he coveted. He himself always seemed to be churning and stewing about something. She appeared to be shy, yet she wasn't shy; at least, not when it counted. She was sweet and natural. She listened, she smiled, and she interjected her thoughts and opinions in a soft, melodious voice.

Yes, there was no doubt about it; he was in love. When he looked into Sumi's soft, dark eyes, he saw himself as he wanted to be: tender, gentle, manly. He could be all things for this beautiful girl at his side.

Each day Cole spent with Sumi strengthened his commitment to her. He kissed her often now, warm, gentle kisses full of passion and longing. He knew if he pressed her, she would give herself to him willingly, but he couldn't ask that of her— for her sake, not his own. He took more cold showers than he'd ever taken in his life.

They spent each day together, rising early, retiring late. They walked, they went to the movies, to concerts, to the hot baths, and always they returned through the park, stopping to melt into each other's arms under the old tree. Cole carved their initials, and at Sumi's insistence he drew a rough-cut heart around them. As far as he was concerned, that said it all.

When he had only one day left of his vacation, Cole knew he didn't want to leave. As much as Riley didn't want to come to Japan, Cole didn't want to return to Texas. When everyone was asleep he went to the room where the telephone was kept and called Texas. He didn't ask if he could extend his vacation. He simply said that he would be staying on awhile longer. He returned to his room and took a tepid shower. He hated the thought of sleep; it was wasted time. He wished he could knock on Sumi's door and ask her to go for a moonlight walk. Instead, he tossed and turned and daydreamed about the wonderful, intoxicating days he'd spent with her. The days to follow would be equally wonderful; he was sure of it.

Sumi sat by the window in her room, her knees drawn up to her chest. Tears streamed down her cheeks. Cole was leaving tomorrow and he'd done no more than kiss her. He hadn't said all the things lovers say. Tomorrow he would be gone, and she didn't know if she would ever see him again. There were times when she was almost convinced that Cole returned her love; a softening in his eyes, the way he looked at her, the feel of his arm around her shoulder. American men were supposed to be aggressive, chasing women and seducing them left and right, but he didn't want to chase her; he wasn't attracted to her that way . . . maybe because she was Japanese. Her heart shattered in a thousand pieces at the thought.

He was leaving tomorrow. There would be a formal good-bye. Her life would be over the moment he walked out the door. She wished she had someone to talk to, someone to confide in. If only Sawyer were home, but she was off on a long field trip. Sawyer would know what to say and how to say it. Sawyer knew about men. She tried to find reasons why Cole didn't want to make love to her, but she couldn't come up with an answer. Well, there was only one way to find out.

Sumi washed her face and combed her hair. She dabbed perfume behind her ears, a delicious gift from Sawyer, and guaranteed to drive men over the brink, or so Sawyer had said. She'd soon see.

Shadaharu Hasegawa couldn't sleep. He reached for his cane. A walk through his peaceful garden always helped his insomnia. He was standing in the dim shadows of the hallway, leaning heavily on his cane, when he saw his daughter Sumi literally run out of her room and down the length of the hall to where Cole slept. He sucked in his breath. His shoulders drooped wearily. "No," he muttered. "I was so sure . . ." He waited.

Cole struggled through his thick sleep. Something wakened him, a sound, a touch. His heart almost stopped beating when he saw Sumi standing at the foot of his bed. He remembered another time when a young woman had come unbidden to his room. He had to say something, but his tongue was too thick, he couldn't get the words out, the right words.

"I came to say good-bye," Sumi said tearfully. "I promised myself I wouldn't cry. Tomorrow everyone will be around when you leave. . . . I wanted to . . . I need . . . Please, Cole, love me, make love to me before you go."

Cole swung his legs over the side of the bed. "Come here, Sumi." Obediently Sumi walked over to stand before Cole, her eyes downcast. "This isn't what you want. It's not time. . . . I wanted to . . . so many times, but . . . Listen, I'm not leaving tomorrow. I called Texas and said I want to stay longer. I don't want to leave you, not ever; do you understand what I'm saying? I'm not real good at this."

"You don't find me repulsive? You don't mind if I'm Japanese?" Sumi asked tearfully.

"Oh, Jesus, is that what you thought... think?... My God, no. You are the most beautiful, the warmest, the most wonderful girl I've ever met. Don't you know how I feel? Can't you tell that I love you...?" There, the words were out. He waited to see her reaction. Her eyes were like stars when she looked at him, her smile more beautiful than all the moonbeams in the world. "I don't want either one of us to... We have the rest of our life, Sumi, and eternity on top of that. I'll walk you back to your room."

"No. No, you stay here. I want to go to the garden for a little while. Forgive me for coming here. I've brought shame on myself."

"Never!" Cole exploded. "If you hadn't come here, it might have taken me days, weeks, to tell you how I feel. And how do *you* feel, Miss Hasegawa?"

"The same way you feel, Cole. I'm so happy that you will be in all of my tomorrows. I love you more than you'll ever know. I thought... Good night, Cole. I'll see you in the morning."

The cold shower was running as soon as Sumi closed the door behind her.

Shadaharu Hasegawa allowed himself a small smile. So his instincts about Coleman Tanner were right. The young American would bring no shame on the Hasegawa family this night or any other night. His step was light when he followed his daughter to the garden; there were prayers to be said in thanks for his insight. Coleman Tanner could very well be one of *them*.

Sweet, wonderful days followed for Cole and Sumi. At night, in the darkness of his room, there was always a smile on Cole's face as he fell asleep. He loved Sumi, heart and soul. One day he would marry her, but he had to straighten out his life first. If he was lucky, he could fix what was wrong between himself and Riley. Sumi would be at his side; he knew now he could do whatever he had to do. If it was necessary, he could sell Rototillers for Sears, Roebuck.

Should he tell the family? And what about Mr. Hasegawa? The old Japanese deserved to know his intentions in regard to his daughter. And what about Sumi? He hadn't mentioned marriage, nor had she. Did she assume, did she expect... did she want him the way he wanted her?... The night she'd come to his room had never been mentioned again. That was good, he decided. "Anything before the immediate moment was history." The family—telling his family—that was the biggie. But not yet. He wanted to hold on to this time, these feelings. They were his and his alone. Falling *in* love was such a serious business. It meant responsibility for another person, through good and bad, through sickness and health. If he had one wish, it would be that his marriage be as good and strong, as happy and loving, as his grandmother's, his mother's, and his Aunt Amelia's. He decided he would pray to that end. First, he would do it in the Christian way and then in the Japanese way.

While Cole contemplated his love for Sumi, she pored over bridal books, her hope chest, and anything else that related to marriage. There was no way Cole Tanner was going to get away from her. When he popped the question, she intended to be ready, right down to the last pair of stockings. So far, she had not confided in her sisters, knowing they would giggle and chortle and insist on helping. Getting ready for the most important day of her life was something she wanted to do alone, so she could pick out special moments and remember them with ease. She wondered what Texas would be like and how Cole's family would accept her. She knew they would, but her older sister's unhappy experience was something she'd never forget.

When was Cole going to ask her the all-important question? At last count, she had twenty-seven different ways to say yes.

Four days remained of Cole's extended vacation. She had to make them count, to make them the most important in both their lives, so important that Cole would be miserable in Texas without her, just as she would be miserable here in Japan without him.

Sumi fell asleep with a vision of herself in a long, trailing white dress full of lace, the background blurred—Texas or Japan. It didn't matter as long as Cole was next to her.

"Today, Cole, I'm going to take you on the Shinkansen Super Express. Here in Japan we call it the bullet train. Supposedly it is the fastest train in the world. Perhaps it is faster than the plane you fly. By the way, why do you refer to the Coleman plane as the DM or the Dream Machine? But first, do you have the nerve to ride the bullet?" Sumi teased.

"Do I have the nerve? I've traveled faster than the speed of sound. A train is a train," Cole grumbled.

"Very well, Cole Tanner," Sumi smiled. "But when you fall off the seat, I will not pick you up."

"That fast, eh?"

"That fast." Sumi smiled.

"And after the train ride, what then?"

"My father has given us tickets to a Kabuki drama. I think you will love it, as I do. I'm so glad, Cole, that you like all the same things I do. We have much in common."

"Not so fast, young lady. There is one thing here that we do not have in common. You've tested my good nature four times now since I'm here. No more!"

"What? Tell me how I have . . . What have I done?" Sumi could feel a vise around her heart at Cole's strange voice.

"You have the same sickness all my family has, at least the women. I thought you would be different, but you aren't. It's the only thing that I . . . I wish it was different, but . . . you can't change, just like they can't. It's so sad. . . . I was hoping . . ."

Sumi stopped in her tracks. Tears brimmed in her eyes. "Tell me this instant how I have displeased you." She stamped her tiny foot in frustration.

"Sumi, Sumi, I was teasing. Please, don't cry. You could never displease me in any way. I'm sorry if I upset you. I meant shopping. Sometimes I think the women in my family were born to shop. Sawyer is the biggest offender. She can shop for days and then she collapses and says her feet hurt. Then she rushes out to buy new shoes for her aching feet. I was teasing about shopping on the Ginza. Truly, I enjoyed the shops and watching you haggle over the prices. It's an art."

"You are serious about this, aren't you?" Sumi laughed, her eyes sparkling with the tears she held in check.

"Sumi, I love you," Cole said softly.

There on the crowded Ginza with people streaming by, Sumi echoed her love for Cole.

"Later, after the bullet train, if I'm still alive, we'll talk, all right?" Cole asked softly.

"I'll hold you tight so you don't fall off the seat," Sumi smiled. "Yes, I wish to talk . . . about us."

Cole walked around the Hasegawa house for the last time. His heart ached that he was leaving this all behind. In two short weeks he'd come to love everything about Japan, particularly this family. He didn't want to be alone anymore. He didn't want to go back to Texas, but for now he had no choice.

He'd start to put the wheels in motion as soon as he set foot on Texas soil. His thoughts brought him to the music room with all the family pictures. Again, he could feel the mist in his eyes as he stared at Riley and a Sumi he'd never known. His footsteps were leaden, his shoulders drooping as he walked out of the room. Good-byes were so hard.

Where was Sumi? She'd said she would be back in thirty minutes. Something about her father wanting something from the paper. It wasn't like Sumi to be late.

Cole's footsteps took him to the tranquil Zen garden. He would miss this peaceful place. If only...

Startled at the sound of a footfall, Cole turned to see the old Japanese behind him. "There are times when I believe I can hear my soul breathe in this quiet place. Can you hear your soul, Coleman san?"

"Yes," Cole said simply. "I'm happy that you are up and about. You're feeling better, then?"

"Somewhat. Has my daughter pleased you these past days? At times she is willful, with a mind of her own."

Thank God for that, Cole thought. He searched for the right words. He turned till he was facing the old one. He led him to his seat and took one opposite him. "I've fallen in love with Sumi. Your ruse worked. Mind you, I didn't figure this out myself; Sumi told me you would never, under any circumstance, take to your bed, unless there was a reason. I must return to Texas today, but I'll be back. Thank you, Mr. Hasegawa."

"And I thought I was being so clever," the old man said fretfully. "You see, I have no secrets anymore." His tone was still fretful when he said, "I don't suppose Sumi told you she pestered me to come up with a plan so you could spend some time together."

Cole's eyes were full of awe. Then he threw back his head and laughed. "We've been had!"

"Ah, so, now you understand. That is good. Your family..."

"My mother speaks of Sumi often. She loves her. Grandmother Billie says she is like Otami. She, too, loves her. My family will accept her. You need have no fear on that score."

There *was* fear in the old one's voice when he asked, "You will take Sumi away from here?"

"No. I wouldn't do that. I'm surprised at your question. I thought we understood one another."

There was sadness in the old man's voice. "Once, not so long ago, I thought I understood, but I was wrong. One must hear the words, Coleman san, not once, but several times. The more times the words are repeated, the more meaning they hold."

Sumi returned, her eyes soft and compassionate as she leaned over to kiss her father's dry cheek. "What have you been telling him?" she asked.

"All your secrets, you willful child." The old man smiled. "Where are you taking him now?"

"To the Shinto temple, as you instructed, and from there to the airport. You said he must see the fifty different kinds of mosses that grow there. For his Japanese education." Sumi's tone clearly indicated she would much rather do something else.

"One must see these things, be aware of them. In Texas they have no moss, only . . . tumbleweeds. Go along, now. Did you bring me the cigar you promised, and did you leave the sake in my bedroom?"

"But of course, Father. We made a deal, did we not?"

"Yes, but you are a wily one. Sometimes you try to trick me and think I'll forget. Light the cigar for me, Coleman san. Be sure to close the front doors and pull the curtains. Tell your sisters I sleep. I want to smoke it down to the end."

Cole hid his smile as he struck a match to the cigar. A real Havana. He puffed till the tip glowed red. He handed it reverently to the old man, who reached for it greedily. "Go! I want to smoke in peace."

Sumi closed the door softly and drew the curtains. Two of her sisters hovered about. She spoke rapidly in Japanese. Once he heard the word cigar. The sisters nodded and withdrew.

"It's a conspiracy." Cole laughed. "They know!"

"Of course they know. They know about the sake, too. It keeps Father's wits about him. He enjoys tricks and deviousness." Sumi laughed.

"Let's get on with the moss business," Cole grumbled.

"You do not wish to see the Shinto temple?" Sumi giggled.

"I don't care. As long as I'm with you, that's all that matters."

"If you don't mind waiting one more minute, Cole, I want to fetch my raincoat. You will want to say good-bye to my father in private. I'll join you shortly."

Wise, wonderful Sumi. Of course he wanted to say good-bye in private. He had a favor to ask of the old Japanese. His eyes dropped to his flight bag. All the old one could say was no.

Cole squared his shoulders and rapped softly on the garden

{ 359 }

door. When the old man told him to enter, he bent down and hefted his flight bag to his shoulder.

"I came to say good-bye and to thank you for a wonderful visit. I . . . I was wondering . . . I have a favor. . . . It isn't exactly a favor . . . it's more like a request. . . . Would you . . . do you think you could . . ." Cole bent down, to the old man's puzzlement, and then handed something to the old Japanese. "I would like it if . . . if you could put this in . . . in there with the others. If you think it doesn't belong, I'll understand." Cole held his breath, waiting, hoping the reply would be favorable.

Shadaharu Hasegawa's hands trembled. Nothing had prepared him for this moment. He looked down at what he held in his hand and then into Cole's eyes. His voice was soft, barely above a whisper. Cole found himself straining to hear the words. "You honor this old man, Coleman san, but you are too late."

Cole's heart sank. "Too late? I don't understand."

Cole followed the old man to the music room. His eyes searched out Sumi's growing years and then Riley's. He waited.

"My ears followed your footsteps a short while ago. I thought you had seen the family's latest addition. You did not turn on the light; perhaps that is why you missed it. Here, now we have light!" Cole stared about the room. He had missed it, probably because all the frames were the same. Next to the last picture of Riley was a picture of himself in the Zen garden, his favorite place in all of Japan. He was relaxed in the picture, not realizing Sumi was clicking her Nikon.

Cole sucked in his breath. "Did Sumi do this? I'm sorry. . . ."

"No, Coleman san, Sumi did not do this. I myself placed this picture here last night on the eve of your departure. I consider you to be one of my family. I am honored, Coleman san, that you have accepted us as your own."

Cole didn't try to speak; there were no words for this moment. Instead, he wrapped the frail old man in his arms. "It is I, sir, who am honored."

"You will continue to look after my grandson?"

"You bet. He'll be here before you know it."

"Is that a promise, Coleman san?" the old man asked hopefully.

Cole didn't think twice about the lie. "A promise, old friend."

"Have a safe trip, Coleman san. You have much to live for now."

Cole winked at the old man. "Yes, much to live for. Take care of yourself."

"I will see to it, Cole," Sumi said from the doorway. "Come, it is time to say good-bye to my family."

They were lined up in rows, the men in the back, the women in the middle, and the children in front. When they bowed, he bowed. When they smiled, he smiled. He waved good-bye, and they waved good-bye. Sumi giggled all the way to the Shinto temple.

"Will you see about coming to Texas for Christmas?"

"I will do my best. You will not return here?" she asked dejectedly.

"If I can. I'll call every day, and I'll write. You do the same." Sumi nodded, tears gathering in her eyes.

"I will wait for all eternity, Cole."

At the airfield Sumi cried silently. Cole patted her awkwardly. He wished she were going home with him. "I'll call you as soon as I get home. I swear, I'll write every day."

"I will, too. I want to join you for Christmas. I will do my best. Promise you won't forget about me. Absence . . . makes one forget. . . ."

"Never. I'll be back as soon as possible. Be sure to tell your father I . . . enjoyed all the . . . the moss."

Sumi hiccuped. "I will tell him, Cole. Give my regards to all of your wonderful family."

Sumi watched the Dream Machine till it was nothing more than a dot in the sky.

Cole would not forget her. Their lives were linked. The days from now till Christmas would fly by; she was sure of it. Love had wings, or so said the romantic songs.

{{{{{{{{{ CHAPTER NINETEEN }}}}}}}}}

Pale winter sunshine crept lazily into Tess's solarium, a room she'd mistakenly tacked onto the west end of the house. It stuck out at an awkward angle and only allowed for sun around four in the afternoon. The rest of the day it was dark and dreary. She hadn't done much in the way of decorating once she discovered her mistake. For the most part it was filled with odds and ends from the attic, things that had belonged to her mother and that she hadn't wanted to part with. There were several dusty plastic and silk flower arrangements in brass urns—her own contribution. Lacey called it the funeral room waiting for a body.

Tess sat alone this afternoon, the latest astrology book on her lap. Not that she was reading it, but it gave her a reason to sit in the room. She'd felt the need to contemplate her past, her present, and her future today. She knew she couldn't do anything about her past, and the future was up for grabs. The stars weren't giving her the answers she longed for. That left only the present and her own ability to figure out what she had to do to survive. She rarely soul-searched, because she didn't like what she found. For instance: Her nest egg was severely depleted. Coots hated her, and she detested him. Lacey was gone; Tess's dream of becoming a Coleman through marriage had gone with her. Business was lousy: the matrons and the young marrieds of Austin had no money for astrological forecasts, and why should they pay money for the stars to tell them what was staring them in the face? Times were hard, and they weren't going to get any better until the price of oil went up, and even then it might be too late. Buckalew Big Wells could still go on the block if their creditors came after them. She'd probably made the greatest mistake of her life the day she brought the mortgage up-to-date. What she should have done was pay off the creditors who were breathing down Coots's neck. She didn't know which upset her more, the possible loss of Buckalew Big Wells, or not becoming a Coleman. "Six of one and half a dozen of the other," she muttered. Then her greatest fear surfaced, refusing to be shoved into the background: she could become a bag lady. Who was going to look after her? Not Coots. If they went belly-up, he'd head right to the oil fields and hire on like some common hand. Lacey was in New York. She'd written once and asked for her things to be sent on. Tess hadn't heard from her since. She supposed she could have written, but she hadn't. Lacey was her daughter. It was up to her to keep in touch with her mama. "I gave that girl the best of everything; I never stinted. The best years of my life went to that child, and how does she repay me? She slinks off to New York like a thief in the night," Tess wailed. She'd taught Lacey every trick known to woman, and still she couldn't hold on to one of the Colemans. Tears rolled down her leathery cheeks. Lacey didn't care one whit about her. No one else did either. Even Billie Coleman with her fancy friends in Washington didn't care. She'd practically promised Tess that she'd be inundated with requests for charts after she delivered the in-depth forecasts Billie ordered. Tess should have known better. All Billie Coleman wanted was information. Coots was probably right; they must have laughed at her behind her back; sniggering was what he said.

Tess blew her nose lustily into a tissue. When she couldn't find a wastebasket, she threw it in the corner. What difference did it make? She was the only one who ever came into this room.

Ivy stood in the doorway watching her mother cry. If she were any kind of a daughter, she'd be in the room comforting her, wouldn't she? Unbidden, the hurts, the rejections, the nasty barbs, surfaced. Should she walk past the open door and ignore her mother? No, that was wrong.

"Mama, what's the matter?" she asked, entering the solarium.

"Matter? Everything's the matter! Are you blind, girl? You been spying on me again? You're always hovering, spying and reporting—to who?" she demanded.

She should have known better. Stick your neck out and they chop it off. She tried again. "Mama, I heard you crying. I thought . . . I thought maybe we could talk and you'd feel better. It helps sometimes."

"Talk? To *you*! You're like all the rest of them. You don't care two figs about your mother." She searched for a tissue in her pocket. When she couldn't find one, Ivy offered one from her purse.

"Maybe that's because you never cared two figs about us." Ivy's voice was not unkind but sad.

"How dare you talk to me like that? Didn't I put clothes on your back, feed and house you? Who do you think paid for all those years in college? Ah did! Don't you go spouting that ah don't care."

Ivy's words trembled out against her will. "I'm talking about love, Mama. You never showed any. You were never there when I needed you. I know you called me an ugly duckling behind my back. It was always Lacey this and Lacey that. You didn't even love Lacey. She told me you didn't."

"Ah always nursed you when you were sick. I walked the floor at night with you when you were a baby. Ah breast-fed you because you wouldn't take a formula. Ah changed your shitty diapers. Doesn't that count?" Tess wailed.

"No. Not to me. Lacey either. I don't ever remember you saying a kind word to me. You never praised me. You never encouraged me. You don't know how to love," Ivy said sadly.

"Love? You talk about love! Let me tell you a thing or two, young lady. In this life there isn't a whole lot of room for sappy sentiment. Life is cold, and mercy me, it is hard. Ah did the best ah could for you girls, and this is the thanks ah get. Lacey said the same things you're saying. For shame. Ungrateful snots!"

Ivy bit her tongue. She would not say all the mean, hateful things she wanted to say. She would not. She'd bite her tongue off first. "Both of us can't be wrong, Mama," she said quietly. "You didn't even come to my graduation. All these years I studied hard, never socialized, just keeping my nose to the books so you'd be proud of me. You didn't even come. I kept looking all over. Lacey told me you wouldn't be there, but I kept hoping. Everyone had a parent there. Everyone but me!"

"For heaven's sake, Ivy, if it was that important, why didn't you say something?"

"That's what I'm talking about, Mama. I shouldn't have to ask. I thought you'd come because you were proud of me. Daddy said he wanted to go, but you didn't."

"Ah suppose you're going to throw that in my face for the rest of my life."

"No. I'm moving out after the first of the year. I have a good job now, and I've found an apartment I can afford."

"Thanks to my efforts and sacrifices," Tess sniffed. "Your father and I are probably going to lose Buckalew Big Wells. He'll go off to the oil fields and ah'll become a bag lady. Do you care? Does Lacey care? Hell no, you don't, so don't stand there and pretend you do."

Ivy clenched her teeth. She reached for her mother's shoulders. She wanted to shake her till her teeth rattled. She dropped to her knees till they had eye contact. "Mama, I will never let you become a bag lady. I will personally see to it that you are taken care of. Lacey will help, too. Even if we have to sacrifice. There will always be someone to care for you."

"You'll pay someone else to take care of me!" Tess screeched. The meaning of her daughter's words roared through her head. "What if ah have a stroke, what if ah slobber and wet my bloomers? Ah wiped your spit and changed your diapers." She stared up at her daughter as though seeing her for the first time. Ivy was . . . pretty.

"If only you'd put your arms around me, just once. If you'd only said something nice instead of bitching and screaming at me. I'm sorry, I didn't mean to say that. I'm sorry about all of this. I shouldn't have intruded on you."

"*Now* you say that. After you destroy me with all those nasty, cruel things you just said to me. I won't even come to your wedding, *if* you ever get married," Tess said spitefully. "You're a nasty girl."

"It'll be your loss then, Mama. You see, by hook or by crook, I'm going to marry Riley Coleman. He doesn't know it, but he will soon enough."

"You're *what*?" Tess hissed. She took a second look at her daughter. She was more than pretty. She was fashionable-looking. She'd lost weight, at least thirty pounds. Riley Coleman. Memories of Ivy tagging after Riley, calling him at Yale. She'd paid the telephone bills. It wasn't *impossible*.

My God, Tess thought. I backed the wrong horse.

Ivy walked out of the room and didn't look back. She knew she wasn't leaving much behind, and it didn't matter anymore. Lacey had survived and so would she.

Billie and Thad arrived at Sunbridge when the Senate recessed for the holidays. For Amelia's sake, Billie said.

The prairie-pink house had been aired and cleaned, but it seemed empty, with Cole not there anymore and Riley off on another probably futile trip to South America. Thad and Billie, with Maggie and Rand's help, trekked out to the fields to select a twelve-foot spruce, hauling it back in the pickup truck. Rand and Thad argued and snapped at each other as they struggled to get the monstrous tree into the stand. Billie and Maggie clapped enthusiastically when the tree finally stayed erect.

"Artificial trees are easier to handle," Thad said airily.

Billie hooted. "He says that every year until I threaten to go to the attic and get it. Then he says, let's go chop one down. He dragged me, literally dragged me, one year into a raging blizzard to get one of the nicest trees we ever had. It was one of the best times of my life," Billie said, hugging Thad.

"It never seems quite like Christmas in Hawaii," Maggie confided, "but we do our best. One year we had this awful white thing with paper fans and bows for ornaments. I hated it. Then we had an artificial green one with crooked branches. Rand hated that one. Last year we had a real tree. We paid, if you can believe this, two hundred dollars for it. The day after Christmas all the needles fell off and we took it down."

Billie looked anxiously at her watch. "Cary and Amelia should be here by now. Thad, call and see if they left."

"Mam, Cary said they'd be here, and they will," Maggie said. "He brought all of Amelia's things earlier this afternoon. Her wheelchair is in the hall closet; so is her cane, the one with the prongs, and the walker. Cary felt if the things were here, she might use them. Having Cary carry them in in front of everyone seemed to disturb Amelia. I made up her room and it's waiting. I made up separate rooms. Cary said he's a restless sleeper and Amelia needs her rest."

"Since when? Cary always sleeps like he's dead," Rand joked. The look on Billie and Thad's face stopped him. "I'm sorry. I didn't mean that the way it sounded. Obviously, Maggie and I are not in on something that is going on here. If I'm not supposed to put my foot into something, maybe you better tell us what's going on."

"I've had the feeling for a long time that something . . . wasn't right," Maggie said. "You know what it is, Mam; so do you, Thad. I thought we were family. We're supposed to help one another. We never had secrets before."

Thad's nod prompted Billie to confide in Maggie and Rand. There, in the room with the fragrant Christmas tree and the blazing fire, Billie told them what Amelia had told her. Her eyes implored Rand to understand. She offered up a silent prayer of thanks when he nodded and smiled. She wound up her explanation with "I really feel it was a mistake to invite Julie, much as Thad and I love her, but Amelia insisted on it.

She was adamant. Cary, of course, doesn't know Julie's coming. Amelia chose not to tell him."

"How are we going to carry this off, Mam?"

"By being ourselves and showing our love for all of them. It's Christmas and we're together. This . . . this may be Amelia's last Christmas with us, so we must do what she wants. Cary will handle it; he has no other choice. Julie can handle it, too. At first Julie refused our invitation, but when I told her Amelia insisted, she gave in. Cole's picking her up tomorrow at the airport."

Thad changed the subject. As far as he was concerned, things would take care of themselves if left to the parties involved. "I understand Adam and his stepson will be here, and Sawyer has to stay in Japan. Billie, did we get presents for the boy?"

"Darling, we not only got presents for the boy and everyone else, they're all wrapped and in the closet. All you have to do is put them under this tree. Now, if you were awarding efficiency ratings, what would you give me?" Billie teased.

"A ten plus." Thad smiled at his wife. "What's on our menu Christmas Eve?"

"That's been taken care of, too, but it's a secret," Billie said. "Maggie, Jeff and I are cooking it from scratch. We're going to show that boy what a real Texas Christmas is like. It'll cheer Adam up, too. He's patient, but he's chomping at the bit to get married."

"I'm for whatever makes everybody happy. You are looking at one almost happy fella," Thad said exuberantly. "In another ten days I will be Thad Kingsley, private citizen."

"Hear, hear! Hey, I hear a car." Rand peered through the curtains.

While Thad joined Rand at the front door, Maggie whispered in her mother's ear. "Mam, you aren't going to let Cary walk into this cold, are you? It's not fair. I'm sorry, but I don't agree with all of you about that. Julie knows he'll be here, and if she didn't know, I'd want her told, too. It's not right that he should just . . . find her here. It'll be a shock. Drop it in the course of conversation, please, Mam?"

"All right," Billie agreed. She felt better immediately. She hated secrets and tension, especially at Christmas.

Cary settled Amelia on the sofa in front of the fire. "What would you like to drink, honey?"

"Scotch, straight up." Cary raised his eyebrows. "The doctor said I could have it," Amelia lied. "I intend to have a cigarette, too. Don't any of you look at me like that. It's okay. Trust me."

"We do, Mother," Rand said, perching himself on the arm of the sofa. "'Everything in moderation' is what I always say."

"I always say that, too." Cary laughed.

Cole arrived at eight o'clock carrying an enormous Christmas wreath for the front door. "I knew you'd forget. For some reason, I've always gotten the wreath," he said, showing off the fragrant door decoration.

"That's because we can trust you to get the most beautiful, the most perfect, and of course, the reddest bow." His mother laughed. "Now, hang it up!"

They dined by the fire, using little tables, on thick sandwiches and hearty homemade soup. While Maggie cleared away the dishes and the men went to the attic for the decorations, Billie sat on the sofa with Amelia, clasping her hand.

"I'm glad you're going to stay here for the holidays, Amelia. I'll get to see you every day. Tell me the truth, how do you feel?"

"Good some days, bad others. I take it one day at a time."

"How are things with Cary?"

Amelia hesitated for a moment. "I don't really know. He treats me wonderfully. He can't do enough for me. He even reads to me, if you can believe that. I've done everything but push him out the door. He won't leave me, even for a second. Guilt, Billie, is a terrible thing, and I don't want him feeling like this. He has terrible nightmares. I'm the one who made him move to the other bedroom. I hear him thrashing about all night long. Short of telling him I know about Julie and telling him I forgive him, what else can I do? Billie, all I wanted was for him to be happy. Which just goes to show you can't tamper with other people's lives the way I did."

"Cary will come to terms with it all," Billie said softly. "I have to say I disagree with you about having Julie here for Christmas, though."

"Cary needs to see her. He needs to feel her presence. I don't think they've been in touch; I think I'd know if they had. I think Julie . . . broke it off when she heard I was ill. She's a good person, Billie," Amelia said in a choked voice.

"Amelia, *you* are the good person, the best in the world. I've never seen such generosity."

"Because I'm dying and I want my husband to be happy?"

"Yes," Billie said bluntly.

"It gets easier as the days go on," Amelia lied.

"The family is dwindling. We used to be a big gang on the holidays. This year Sawyer and Riley won't be here, but we picked up Adam and Jeff. It's not the same," Billie said bleakly. "Christmas gets to me lately. I want us all together. If only Rand had been able to . . . What I mean is, if things had worked out, his daughter would be here. He wrote and asked Chesney to join us. She declined, but nicely. Said she was flying because she wanted the married stewardesses to be home with their families, and since she had no husband or children, it didn't make a difference to her."

"I don't buy her story one hundred percent," Amelia said sourly. "No matter how hard I try, I can't accept what she's told Rand. Why won't she allow him to be a father to her? She sought him out, she upset his life, and don't for one minute think that happy facade he shows to all of us is real. He's so tormented it breaks my heart. She walks into his life, makes all her announcements, and then walks out. That's dirty pool, Billie."

"She's afraid, Amelia. She doesn't want to get hurt. You and I can't even begin to imagine what life in an orphanage would be like. Being abandoned and rejected—that has to stick with a child for a long time, sometimes all her life."

Amelia stared at Billie for a few seconds. "What goes around comes around, eh? Infancy to old age. How sad."

"Only if you want to be sad. Family, Amelia. I know," Billie said, holding up her hand, "that I've harped on that for years and years, but it's so true. Without family, what is there? Where would any of us be? Why don't you write Chesney a letter, Amelia. Tell her about her father and her grandfather. Tell her about us, how we'd welcome her into our lives. I bet she'd not only answer the letter, but she'd also start doing some serious thinking. It's a start, Amelia."

"This time, old friend, I'm one step ahead of you. I did that two weeks ago. I was hoping for some kind of Christmas response, but as of today, none has arrived."

Billie laughed. "We all want everything yesterday. Time will take care of things, Amelia."

Amelia's face sobered. "It's my enemy, Billie."

"In a way time is everyone's enemy, Amelia. I don't want you thinking or talking like that. This is Christmas. We're going to love and share because that's what this family does best. Put on your happy face—the men are coming with the decorations.

Three strong men to carry two boxes of very light Christmas ornaments." She laughed. "And Maggie supervising."

"I heard that," Thad shouted. "It's not the carrying, it was the seeking that almost did us in. Things like this should be kept in a hall closet."

"Absolutely not," Maggie laughed. "Keeping them in the attic, where you can't see them every day, adds to the mystique. Is mystique the right word? Not seeing them regularly makes the excitement of Christmas all that much more—"

"I think you just botched it all up, darling." Rand grinned.

The evening passed pleasantly. Cole circulated, spending time with his mother and Amelia. He excused himself once to make a phone call. Maggie met Billie's eyes. "I wouldn't swear to it, but I think my son is in love," Maggie said happily. "Wouldn't it be wonderful if there were two weddings in this family?"

"It certainly would," Billie said.

"How can you tell? That Cole's in love, I mean," Cary asked.

Maggie laughed. Billie joined in and Amelia smirked. "His eyes sparkle. He makes phone calls. He looks in the mirror all the time; he's more considerate. That's the biggie—consideration. He can't do enough for all of us. He's better than a trained dog right now. He loves to fetch. I just love the way he's acting. For a while there he was so down, I was getting worried."

"Now that you mention it, Maggie, I've noticed it myself. Cole's always been a gallant young man, but yes, these past days he's been acting differently," Billie agreed.

"Why don't we just ask him?" Thad muttered.

"We can't do that, darling. If Cole wants to share his happiness or his new love, he will. We can't . . . pry. We can't . . . but you or Rand or Cary, that's man stuff. We'll wait right here while you find out." Billie giggled.

Cary started to busy himself by closing the cardboard cartons. Rand gathered stray strands of tinsel from the carpet. Maggie stacked the cups and glasses on a tray. Billie stood behind Amelia's chair, massaging her thin shoulders. Thad was readying the camera for the picture session that was a Sunbridge ritual on Christmas Eve.

Cole's face was stretched wide in a grin when he entered the room. Guilt made everyone stop what they were doing to stare at him. It was obvious he was about to make an announcement. Maggie held her breath.

"Grandma, would you mind an unexpected guest? It's unexpected because I wasn't sure if . . . she wasn't sure if she could get a flight. There was a last minute cancellation or something, so she can make it. Is it all right?"

"Cole, it's more than all right. Who is she? Does she have a name?"

Maggie walked over to her son. He put his arm around her shoulder and drew her closer to him. "Her name is Sumi."

"Cole! Sumi Hasegawa! Sumi! Mam, it's Sumi."

"Little Sumi!" Billie all but squealed.

"The prettiest girl in all Japan," Thad said, not missing a beat as he rolled new film into his camera.

"Congratulations!" Rand said, wrapping his wife and stepson in both his arms.

"I'll second that," Cary said warmly.

"Me, too," Amelia echoed.

"Wait a minute, all of you. She's just coming for Christmas. You act as if I asked her to marry me or something."

"You're going to, aren't you?" Thad queried.

"I might," Cole said uncomfortably.

"Cole, I'm so happy for you," Maggie said, squeezing his arm. "I adore Sumi. She's right for you, you know. Mam, why didn't we ever think of Sumi as a match for Cole before?"

Billie shrugged. "She's just like Otami. The firstborn and the last. I'm very happy for you Cole," Billie said, hugging her grandson.

"You look like you're alive. I'll give you that." Cary grinned. "Treat her like gold and you'll never be sorry. Isn't that right, honey?"

Amelia beamed. "He's on the money, Cole. From the day we were married Cary treated me as if I was gold. We're still hanging together." Only Billie heard the end of the sentence, "but by a very fragile string."

Maggie pushed the dishes out of the way. "Sit down, Cole, and tell me all. I didn't even know you knew Sumi. When did you meet her? Oh, I'm so happy she's coming. Mam," she said, turning to her mother, "this means we hit the stores tomorrow, bright and early."

"I'll make a list. Did you get something for Sumi, Cole?"

Cole flushed. "I picked it out. . . . I wasn't sure . . . All I have to do is pick it up."

"Let me take a picture of this happy group," Thad said, focusing the camera. "Everyone say cheese. Cole, I've never seen you so happy."

"Me either," Maggie said proudly.

"I took a week's vacation and went to Japan. You all know that Mr. Hasegawa has been writing to me. I've been writing . . . . What I mean is, he needs to know . . . I shared Riley with him, those bits and pieces he doesn't have. Riley would probably consider it interfering in his life, but I didn't see it that way. I wanted to see him, to comfort him, so I hopped in the DM. Sumi came in from the office the morning after I got there. I think I fell in love with her the minute I set eyes on her. The Japanese are so quiet and reserved. She says she loves me, but . . ."

Maggie hooted with laughter, and so did Billie. "Sumi quiet and reserved! You met your match, son! Sumi is a modern Japanese."

"Is she still sneaking cigars to her father?" Thad asked. Cole laughed and nodded.

They talked for an hour. Billie told him tales of a little Sumi and a teenage Sumi who gave her father gray hair. Maggie added what she knew. "Sawyer can tell you more. She and Sumi are buddies." Maggie laughed. "This is all so wonderful. Aren't Christmases wonderful?" Everyone agreed.

"I think I'm going to turn in, if you don't mind," Cole said. "Aunt Amelia, how would you like a ride upstairs in these strong, masculine arms?"

"That's my job," Cary said forcefully.

"Then I'll say good night. Grandma, what time do you want me to pick up Julie? I forgot to ask."

Thad immediately demanded that Cary pose with Amelia, just the two of them in front of the tree, for what he called a Christmas Eve *eve* picture. "You can handle it," he whispered in Cary's ear.

Thad squinted into the little window on his ancient camera. Only once before had he seen an expression like the one on Cary's face, which he was about to record. It was his own, the day Billie said she loved him. He snapped the picture.

Amelia sat propped up in bed. She was so tired she could hardly think straight. Each day it seemed she grew more weary, less anxious about life and what was going on around her. The one thing she forced herself not to do was fall asleep before Cary did. It was her special time, when she lay back in her nest of pillows and remembered. She'd stroke Cary's dark head, which was now speckled with gray. Lately, though, even that had been taken away from her, when Cary moved into the guest room. Tonight was a special treat for her. Maggie had apologized profusely, saying she'd made up the room for Cary next to Amelia's, but with Sumi coming, they'd need the room. She'd told Maggie not to worry, and Cary seconded her. They would sleep together, the way they had for years.

"Are you as done in as I am?" Cary asked.

"I'm a little weary," Amelia admitted. "Tomorrow we'll probably be dragging our tails. We're really going to have a houseful."

"I think it's great, honey. It's going to be a little strange without Sawyer and Riley, though."

"They'll both call. We'll all talk to them. We can't have it all. We're blessed as it is."

"You're telling me," Cary said heartily.

"Roll over, darling, and I'll rub your shoulders," Amelia said quietly.

"That's a super offer, but I'll rub yours. Last one to fall asleep has to drink decaffeinated coffee for breakfast."

"Some deal, since I have to drink it all the time anyway," Amelia grumbled.

"Honey, do you need anything done tomorrow, any last-minute shopping?"

"Billie is going to pick up something for Sumi from us. Cole did a lot of my shopping, and I ordered things by phone. Maggie did most of the wrapping. I think we're covered. What did you get me?" she asked sleepily.

"What did you get me?"

Amelia wanted to tell him that her special gift to him couldn't be wrapped. How did you wrap love? "I asked you first."

"Wild horses or stinging bumblebees can't get it out of me." Cary laughed.

"Those same bumblebees and wild horses aren't getting it out of me either."

"So we're back to square one. What did we get Julie? And Jeff?"

We, not you. We, as in together. "We got Jeff a six-week Saturday-morning cooking course in New York. They're moving back to the city as soon as Adam and Sawyer get married.

He can pick the time he wants to attend. I think he'll like it, don't you?"

"He'll love it."

"I didn't actually buy Julie a present. I'm giving her my pearls. The ones that—"

"Were your mother's! Amelia! Why didn't you buy something? Those pearls belong in your family."

I know, and that's where they're going to be, Amelia said silently. "I want her to have them. If you think she'll be offended, I can have Billie and Maggie buy her a new strand tomorrow."

"That's not it, Amelia. How can you give something away to someone who is almost a stranger to you? Something that means as much to you as those pearls have always meant."

"Isn't Christmas meant to be giving? A little to the left— ahhh, that's the spot. Young people today have rediscovered pearls. They're back in fashion. I think Julie will like these. I had them cleaned and polished, and the jeweler gave me a new box. Then I decided she might like the original box, even if it is tattered."

"Amelia, turn around and look at me," Cary said with a catch in his voice. He searched her eyes for a long time. All he could see was love and weariness. "I love you, Amelia. It's damn important that you believe me. I don't ever want you to think that your illness has changed my feelings for you. You have always been and always will be the most important person in my life."

"Darling, Christmas is getting to you," Amelia said lightly. "I was never in favor of bah humbug myself." Her voice turned serious. "I have never, ever, in all the years we've been married, doubted that love. I thank God each and every day, that He has seen fit to keep us together. . . ." Wild horses and raging bumblebees couldn't get her to finish her thought aloud: In sickness and health, till death do us part. That was all taken care of. "Kiss me good night, Romeo."

"Yes, Juliet," Cary said, planting a loud, smacking kiss on her cheek. "Good night, honey."

"Hmmmm," Amelia mumbled.

Cary lay awake for a long time. How in the name of God was he going to carry it off tomorrow, and then again on Christmas Day? Julie. How was he supposed to act? What would Julie expect of him? Amelia and Julie. What did he expect of himself? Before he fell asleep he knew that Julie would make it all seem right. Amelia, he knew, would ease the situation along and make Julie comfortable. The others, if they sensed any kind of strain, would jump in, like Thad did this evening with the camera. Thank God for Thad. If it hadn't been for him, he might have done something stupid or said something that could never be taken back. Words, as he'd found out, were dangerous.

Amelia knew the minute Cary fell asleep. She moved slightly till she was curled up next to him. "Trust me, Cary; everything will be fine." Before she drifted into a deep, restful sleep, she reached for Cary's hand. His grasp tightened in his sleep, something he'd done for years.

{{{{{{{{{ CHAPTER TWENTY }}}}}}}}}

Chesney Brighton shuddered as she listened to the weather report. England was suffering its meanest and roughest snowstorm in years. She wondered if the airport would close down. She should call before she trudged out to Heathrow. As it was, it was going to take her hours to get there. If they closed down, she'd have to make her way back, and then she'd be alone for Christmas. She said a little prayer for the storm to lift. It had started last evening with light flurries, and all the weathermen chortling with glee as they promised a white Christmas. They referred to the snow as a light dusting. The light dusting was now six or seven inches deep and still coming down.

Flying in any kind of bad weather always bothered Chesney, but she dreaded snow most of all. Deicing the wings always made her blood run cold. So much could happen. . . . She wished suddenly that she weren't flying today. She was jittery, and it wasn't just the storm. Christmas was bothering her, too. All her life she'd longed for a family Christmas, and now, when she could have one, she'd turned it down. She'd turned her back on the family that had accepted her as one of *them*. She wished she could backtrack and forget her stubbornness. She'd cut off her nose to spite her face. Because of that stubbornness, she was going to fly on Christmas Eve in horrendous weather.

She continued to listen to the weatherman: more snow coming, temperatures expected to drop even lower. Chesney shuddered. Incoming planes would be stacked overhead and orbiting the field. There would be twenty or more planes on the ground, most with engines running, waiting for clearance to take off. The controllers would be pulling out their hair; the work crews and the snow desk would be a nightmare. Once she'd heard a pilot say that clearing a runway of snow was like clearing several hundred miles of highway. Runways had to be absolutely clear. Her heart fluttered in her chest. Call in sick, an inner voice urged. Instead of listening to the inner voice, Chesney dialed London Air and asked to speak to her supervisor.

"Put on your galoshes and say mush. That's another way of saying Flight 214 is still scheduled. I'll look for you shortly," was the response she got.

Chesney's heart sank as she sat down to pull on her fleece-lined boots. She was buttoning her coat when a feeling of light-headedness swept over her. She knew at that moment that she was experiencing total, absolute fear.

She felt weepy when she turned for a last look at her apartment. The Christmas tree lights were off, the telly unplugged; she'd fixed her two night-lights with their timers to go off at dusk. Four presents from friends, still unwrapped, were under the small, fragrant tree waiting for Christmas morning. Everything was neat and tidy. The Christmas cards were on an end table, colorful and cheerful. She wished she'd sent a card to her father and his wife. She'd gotten one from him, along with a Christmas check so large, she'd gasped. It was still inside the card.

Chesney looked at her apartment through strangers' eyes—strangers who would come in here to go through her things if . . . if she didn't come back. What would they say about her, those strangers who would poke through her things? That she was neat and tidy, that she had a cat. It was an awful summary of her life. She vowed then to mail a card to her father from the airport. Just in case . . .

Chesney arrived at Heathrow three hours later. The terminal was chaos. Thousands of passengers jammed the waiting area. Mountains of luggage were everywhere. Children were crying; parents were screaming and cursing at harried airline employees who were themselves at the screaming stage. She heard the expression "Chinese fire drill" screamed at a reservations clerk, who was Oriental. The young woman threw down her pencil and stalked away from her counter amid cat-calls and loud hisses. Chesney shuddered.

She was exhausted when she finally reached the door marked AIRLINE PERSONNEL ONLY. She looked at her watch. It had taken her twenty-three minutes to fight the crowds through the terminal. She pushed open the door and then leaned weakly against it.

"It's hell out there, isn't it?" her supervisor said cheerfully. She could be cheerful, she wasn't flying in this weather, Chesney thought.

"Dorothy, I can't believe we're going to take off in this. Switzerland is..." She let the rest of the sentence hang in midair.

Dorothy was a string bean of a woman, with bright red hair and two thousand freckles dotting her face. She grinned. "They've been scratching flights for the past hour, but 214 isn't one of them. What you have, Chesney, is a sold-out flight with two wheelchair passengers, one youngster age four traveling alone, and an eight-member Olympic ski team of downhill racers whose final destination is Chamonix. You've flown in bad weather before, and this is no different. Relax."

"This is different, Dorothy. You're wrong about me flying in storms like this. I haven't. Rain, yes; snow, no." Chesney's voice was firm and quiet.

The supervisor's voice took on a hard edge. Chesney was a pro, and the other stews looked up to her. If by look or word Chesney showed doubt or concern, the others would follow her lead. What Dorothy didn't need was a stewardess mutiny on her hands. "If the tower gives permission for takeoff and the pilots are willing to fly, then there's no problem, is there? You look absolutely fearful, Chesney, so I suggest you wipe that look off your face, and while you're at it, forget whatever premonitions you have. You're a professional, so start acting like one."

Dorothy had just given a name to what she was feeling: a premonition. She'd never really had one before. She didn't know if she was foolish or not when she voiced her next question. "What happens if I refuse to fly 214?"

Dorothy had heard this before, from other stews, and it always irritated her. Since making supervisor, she'd had 100 percent attendance from her stews. She cracked the whip and they danced, because they knew she would replace them for even one tiny infraction. She was considered tough and rough. "If that happens, you go on report with an automatic sixty-day suspension. Your case will come up for review in about forty-five days, and two other supervisors and myself will make the final decision as to whether you stay or not. I should remind you that the suspension does not carry your salary. Look"—Dorothy switched to her most motherly tone—"I was a stew for a good many years. I'd never send my girls up to do something I wouldn't do." It was a bald-faced lie, and both women knew it.

Chesney made no comment; the expression on her face said it all as far as she was concerned. She couldn't exist for sixty days without her salary. She couldn't afford to lose her job, either. Because she had no other choice, she would knuckle under and do what she was paid to do: fly and take care of the passengers on Flight 214.

The stewardesses' locker room was bedlam. Girls coming off canceled flights, girls getting ready for various flights, not knowing if they'd take off or not. All wore weary, frightened faces. The room grew quiet suddenly. Chesney looked around, thinking Dorothy had entered the room. Instead, a tall, shapely redhead named Sheila was standing on a bench waving her hands for silence. When she had the stews' attention, she started to speak. "Girls, you all know me; I'm probably senior to all of you, which means I've logged more hours than many of you put together. My flight to Amsterdam was just canceled. We sat on runway four for three solid hours. We deiced seven times. In all my years of working for London Air, I have never seen a storm like this. It's not safe out there. I'm no pilot, and I don't belong to the ground crew, but I'm not stupid. I slogged through seven inches of snow to get back inside. More than three inches on the runway, and snow gets sucked into the jets, and that's dangerous. The ground crews can't keep up with it. I'd like to see all of you band together and talk to Dorothy. There's strength in numbers. It's worth a shot. My crew and myself are staying here, so if you need moral support, we're here to back you up."

Chesney stood up and told the girls about her talk with Dorothy. She could see the dismay on their faces. "How many of you can afford to go without your salary and the possibility of losing your jobs in the end?" Not a single hand showed. Chesney shrugged. "Good try, Sheila," she muttered.

The stewardesses dispersed. Chesney and the nine stews under her supervision walked out to the lounge. She liked all of them and had worked with them before. "I guess we're going to have to make the best of it. I bet a lot of us are wishing we hadn't traded places with the married girls, but it's too late for wishes now. Unless they scratch our flight, we're flying."

A pretty blonde spoke in a shaking voice. "Bobby and I set our wedding date last night. We're getting married February fourteenth."

"That's Valentine's Day." Chesney smiled. "How romantic." The girls congratulated Christine, nicknamed Tiny because of her diminutive size. They immediately started to plan a shower for the first of February. Chesney joined in, knowing they were all forcing laughter and gaiety into their voices for each other's sake. Chesney looked at her watch.

Twenty minutes later, Chesney announced, "We're on countdown. We're leaving from gate six. Don't look so glum, girls. London Air won't send us up if it's dangerous." She hoped her voice carried more conviction than she felt. Her premonition was as strong as before, perhaps more so. She panicked for one split second when she tried to force her thoughts into the future. It was a trick she often played with herself when things weren't going right. She'd focus and try to project, sometimes hours, sometimes days ahead, to "see" where she'd be and what she'd be doing. Now, this second, she could see nothing. There was no Chesney anywhere, just blankness. She shivered.

Patty McIntyre ran up to Chesney. "What . . . what's wrong, Chesney? You look like you just saw a ghost." Patty was the youngest of Chesney's crew and had professed a hatred for flying. She only kept her job because it was a good way to meet eligible, wealthy young men, and sometimes older men, who lavished her with presents. Chesney liked her brash honesty and the fact that she could laugh at herself and her fear of flying.

I saw nothing, so that must be my ghost out there . . . in that void of nothingness. "I think I just realized how cold I am; it's nothing to worry about. Besides, there are no ghosts. Patty, do me a favor; go back there and tell the girls the story you told me about the Greek shipping tycoon who wants to marry you. Make it light . . . it's like a tomb in here. I'm going out to check on things."

"Sure, Chesney; I'll embellish it a little to stretch out the time, so don't give me away, okay?"

"Just ask him if he has a brother the next time you see him. I'll be back in a minute."

Chesney dodged two fistfights, a band of seven-year-olds bent on tearing the airport to pieces, and six elderly ladies saying words that made her blush. Above the babble and anger she could hear the sound of Christmas music. She felt faint as she stepped over two sleeping boys with ski equipment piled next to them. Up above was the airport departure monitor. Flight 214 was still scheduled for a five o'clock departure. It was three o'clock now, and it was Christmas Eve.

Chesney dodged her way through a gaggle of silly girls to lean up against the wall. She needed a breather, a few minutes to get her thoughts in order. Instead of trying to make sense out of the chaos in her mind, she thought about her father. Where was he? Was he preparing for Christmas in Hawaii with his wife, or was he with his wife's family? She could be there, wherever they were—if she hadn't been so stubborn, so . . . hurt. They were probably having a big family Christmas with a huge tree and piles of gifts. There would be wonderful food, laughter and carols, and a church service. She'd tossed all that aside because she was afraid of getting hurt—again. Here she was in Heathrow Airport on Christmas Eve, scared out of her wits, with thousands of angry people who weren't going to get home for Christmas. All she could hope for now was that Flight 214 would be canceled. If it wasn't, she could wish for a safe flight—and survival. She tried once more to focus on the future. She saw only blankness. She was going to die; she could sense it. Her premonition was stronger than ever.

"Merry Christmas . . . Daddy," she whispered. She remembered then her intention to send a card. There didn't seem to be any point now.

Cary and Amelia slept late. Billie and Maggie had already come back from their shopping trip when Cary carried toast and coffee into the living room for Amelia.

"You would not believe the stores! It was fun, though, wasn't it, Mam?"

"Oh yes, fun," Billie said with a grimace. "I bought Sumi one of my own scarves. You just can't believe what these stores charge." Amelia laughed at the indignation on her friend's face.

"What did you get from us?" Cary demanded.

"A pearl bracelet," Maggie said. "Mam picked it out. It's beautiful, and I had it gift wrapped. We got a lot of little things: perfume, some books, a gold comb, a cashmere sweater, and a little teddy bear that looks like Cole. I think

Julie and Sumi will like their gifts. I just can't believe this is happening. My baby, getting married."

"I have to get back to the kitchen," Billie said. "Cary, how do you feel about wrapping?"

"I can take it or leave it alone. Amelia says my corners are sloppy."

"Then you're going to have to straighten them out. Maggie and I have to get dinner started. Julie will be here soon, and we haven't even had lunch. Let's pass on lunch; what do you say?" Billie pleaded.

"Cheese and fruit will be fine. Cary and I will wrap. I'll oversee the corners," Amelia said gaily.

Cole swept in with a blast of cold air along with Adam and Jeff. Blushing furiously, Jeff shook hands with the men and smiled winsomely at the women.

"To the kitchen!" Billie ordered briskly. "Maggie, get the paper and ribbon from the hall closet and then join us in the kitchen."

"Aye, aye, ma'am."

"Mother, could I see you a minute?" Cole asked.

"Sure. Let me get the paper for Cary. Is anything wrong?" she called over her shoulder.

"No. It's just that I need an extra pair of hands or something."

"I feel the same way. Let's go into the study. Oh, Cole, I'm so happy for you. This is all so wonderful. I'm walking on air. We're all together. Well, almost."

"That's what I want to talk to you about. I have to pick Julie up at two-thirty. This was supposed to be a secret, and I wouldn't have given it away for the world, even to you; but with Sumi coming, I'm all fouled up. Aunt Susan and Uncle Ferris are coming, too. They'll take a cab and arrive in time for dinner. Riley gets in around four. And I have to pick up Sumi—and Sawyer!"

"They're all coming. Lord! Does Mam know?"

"No, it was supposed to be a secret. The plan is to stash everyone down in Grandmam Billie's studio till this evening. They all wanted to be here, for Aunt Amelia. We're a full house, Mam. Tell me what to do."

Maggie ran her hands through her hair. "My God, there are no presents!" Maggie exclaimed. "I sent Suse's on to Minnesota. So did Mam."

"They're all here. When Rand took yours to the post office, he had them stick another label on them. Thad did the same thing with Grandmam Billie's. We struck out with Cary's, though, so Rand went out and bought more. Don't open that closet over there or they'll all tumble out." Cole laughed as he pointed to the study closet. "Remember, now, this is a secret."

Maggie smiled. How she loved her two men. "My lips are sealed. You pulled this all together, didn't you?"

"Sort of. Sawyer got through to Riley, and got him a ticket."

"You're a hell of a guy, Cole Tanner."

"You're a hell of a woman, Maggie Nelson," Cole said, hugging his mother.

"I just need to know one thing. Is the game plan the same? I mean, is everyone going to be in Mam's studio till eight o'clock? I turned on the heat before I came in."

"I'm hoping. You just worry about getting Julie, and Sumi and I'll take care of the rest. And be sure Adam doesn't get wind of it. Sawyer insists on surprising him. You'll work it out, Mam. Oh, hey, wait a minute. I want to show you something."

Maggie looked down at the diamond ring in the blue velvet box. "Ooohh, it's gorgeous. Sumi will love it!"

"Do you think it's too small? I wiped out my bank account," Cole said anxiously.

"Size and cost don't mean anything, Cole. To most women, anyway. Sumi is like us. Trust me, this is perfect."

"Thanks, Mam. Hey, you better get cracking or something is going to get fouled up."

"Right. Cracking. Raaannnddd!"

Chesney and her crew heard the p.a. announcement that Flight 214 would take off, three hours behind schedule. She watched two of her girls bless themselves. Patty McIntyre sidled up to Chesney. "Have you looked outside in the past hour, Chesney? I am petrified." She enunciated each word carefully. "I know when we get up above the storm it will be fine, but it's the takeoff and climbing that's bothering me. They can't clear the runway fast enough. What are they thinking of?"

"Performance, a good rating, London Air's reputation. You know the old joke: Fly London Air, we get you there, no matter what," Chesney said tersely.

"Is that dead or alive?" Patty snapped.

"Patty, shh, don't get the others riled up. Each of us has a choice, fly or stay here. We made the choice because we need our jobs. That means we're committed. And yes, I looked outside and couldn't see a thing but snow. Smile, Patty. We're going to do our best to make the passengers comfortable." Patty smiled numbly.

Chesney looked out at the sea of hopeful faces. Didn't they understand? Didn't they know what flying in weather like this was like? Everyone wanted to be somewhere other than an airport for Christmas, but wasn't an airport better than . . . than what? She picked up the small microphone. "Flight 214 for Geneva, Switzerland, is now ready for boarding. Please have your boarding passes in hand. Please, there is to be no shoving and pushing. We are not going to leave till all of you are aboard." Her little speech meant nothing. Men and women who probably never raised their voices at home were shouting obscenities and shoving people out of their way to get to the front of the line. Chesney handed the microphone to Patty and proceeded back to the cabin of the plane. She was trembling from head to toe as the first-class passengers entered the plane. Usually there were smiles and nods and questions. Not today. All she could see was anger at the delay, frustration at the inconvenience, and downright hostility toward all airline employees.

The two wheelchair passengers were brought in and settled, their chairs taken back immediately to the concourse. Next came the four-year-old who was traveling alone with only a raggedy teddy bear for company. Chesney herself buckled the little one into the seat nearest the bulkhead. Three families, with nine children among them, and all under the age of six, were shown in next. Following the three families was the smoking section and then the rest of the passengers. Boarding, Chesney estimated, took exactly thirteen minutes—normally a twenty-minute procedure. She'd never seen so many people at the same time, so eager to fly into . . . nothingness.

Patty reported the head count: the plane was filled to capacity. The aircraft was secured for takeoff. Chesney followed procedure, welcoming the passengers aboard. She doubted any of them heard a thing she said. All 260 passengers had been inconvenienced, and they weren't going to let the stewardesses forget it. It was not going to be a pleasant flight.

Chesney strapped herself into the jump seat, across from the little girl with the teddy bear. She was a pretty little thing, with soft, dark curls and large blue eyes. She clutched her teddy with one hand and had the thumb of her other hand in her mouth. Chesney smiled. She noticed the child's clothing then. She had on a frilly red and white dotted organdy dress with a matching coat of the same shade of red. Short white socks with lace around the cuff, black patent leather shoes, and a small, shiny black purse completed the child's outfit. She looked like a Christmas angel. Chesney smiled again. The child looked at her solemnly. "What's your name, honey?"

The little girl moved her stuffed animal a fraction of an inch to show her name tag. Chesney leaned closer to look at the tiny letters on the self-stick badge. Molly Sanders. "That's a very pretty name. Later I'll get you a pillow and blanket if you want to take a nap. When you wake up we might be in Geneva. Are you hungry?" Molly nodded, but didn't take her thumb out of her mouth. I wish I could suck my thumb, Chesney thought.

They were taxiing now, but the pace was slowing; they must be nearing takeoff. Chesney's heart lurched. She should have sent the Christmas card to her father. She should have done a lot of things. The aircraft was stopped now, with four planes ahead of theirs and probably three or four behind. Until the air controllers cleared them, they had to sit with the engines running, burning fuel.

An hour later the cabin erupted into sound. Passengers started stomping their feet, yelling for food and drinks: free drinks, they shouted, for their goddamn inconvenience. This was the part Chesney hated most—trying to calm irate travelers. The best she could do was make an announcement. She unbuckled her seat belt and went to the cockpit and rapped softly. "The natives are getting restless," she whispered.

The captain snorted. "I heard. Give them the standard announcement, and if they keep yelling, pull out good old number four; you have my permission." Captain Andrews winked at her to show he understood what she and the other stews were going through.

In the galley Chesney reached for the microphone attached to the p.a. system. "May I have your attention, please." She deliberately waited for all sound to cease. When it did, she made her announcement. "Captain Andrews, myself, and the crew apologize for this delay. The captain has asked me to tell you we're next in line for takeoff. Until we get clearance, which could take another hour or so, we all ask that you remain seated. It's against regulations to serve any beverages or food at this time. Thank you." Chesney was on her way back to her seat when the obnoxious catcalls started again. She did her best to squelch her anger as she headed back to the p.a. system. Her hand trembled as she spoke into the microphone a second time. "Captain Andrews has informed me that any of you wishing to get off this plane can do so now. You will, of course, have to find your way back to the terminal on your own. What that means, ladies and gentlemen, is we are apologizing for something that is not our fault. We're all doing the best we can under the circumstances and hope you will help us by doing your part and being understanding. Now, all of you wishing to leave the plane, unbuckle your seat belts and stand up." She knew when she poked her head out of the galley that there would be no passengers wishing to take advantage of the captain's offer. She was wrong. Tiny Molly Sanders was standing on her seat, her teddy bear clutched in her hand. She was crying and calling for someone named Gus.

Chesney walked back to her seat. After the din of the passengers, the silence was almost deafening. She took Molly onto her lap and crooned softly to her. Assuming the child was going to see her mother, she said, "You're going to see your mommy soon. Don't cry, honey."

"My mommy is back there," the girl said, pointing to the window.

"Your mommy brought you to the airport; is that right? Who's going to meet you when we land?"

"My daddy. My mommy is getting me a new daddy. That's why I have to go see my old daddy. I don't want a new daddy. He doesn't like Gus. Gus peed on his shoe; that's why he doesn't like him."

"Who's Gus?" Chesney asked.

"My dog. Mommy said I had to bring Gus so Travis won't hurt him. He's in a cage. My daddy will get him when we get there. He will, won't he? My mommy didn't just *say* that, did she?"

"Of course not." Chesney hoped she wasn't lying to the little girl.

"My daddy is getting me a new mommy, too," Molly blurted. "I'm hungry."

"I know you are, honey. As soon as we get up high, I'll give you some dinner. Are you worried about having two mommies and two daddies?" Chesney asked gently.

Molly sniffed, her eyes brimming. She stuck her thumb back into her mouth. Of course she was worried. Chesney hugged the little girl tighter, then buckled her into her seat and fastened her own seat belt.

The plane was moving now. The engine's tempo was increasing, rolling, faster now, picking up speed, faster, faster. Chesney squeezed her eyes shut, something she'd never done on lift-off. Off the ground. A passenger screamed and then was silent. It was the worst takeoff of Chesney's career. She wondered how many pounds of ice were on the wings.

It was a day of miracles as far as Maggie Nelson was concerned. Things didn't come together till almost eight o'clock. Julie's plane was late by two and a half hours. There was a blizzard raging up the East Coast, but somehow Julie had managed to get the last flight out of Kennedy Airport. Sawyer and Sumi's plane developed engine trouble in Hawaii; they managed to catch a standby flight to San Francisco. From there, Sawyer called on a friend to charter his plane.

Susan and Ferris's plane from Minnesota was delayed by three hours.

Riley arrived an hour early and had to hang out in the airport until Maggie arrived.

Cole was standing at Customs when Sumi and Sawyer walked through. The hell with all this formal stuff! He leaped the railing and scooped Sumi into the air. She squealed with delight.

Cole kissed her soundly. "Do I look as happy as I feel?" he demanded.

"I'm happy you decided to give up on all that Japanese bullshit." Sumi grinned. "I want you to treat me like an American girl. It's time we got this relationship off the ground. I missed you."

"It's off. I told the family. God, I've missed you, too."

"Do they approve?"

"Are you kidding? They love you. It's strange, but when I told them, it was almost as if they'd handpicked you."

Sumi laughed. "I'm anxious to see them all."

"Is this all the baggage you have?"

"Personal baggage, yes. However, my father has sent a mountain of presents. My sisters and myself have been shopping for weeks. Please tell me you have a truck and not your little car."

"As a matter of fact, I do have a truck. A Bronco. It's Riley's." Only then did Cole reach out to hug Sawyer. She stood, a huge grin on her face, tapping her foot in pretended impatience. "Nope," he reassured her. "The cat is *not* out of the bag. Your intended doesn't suspect a thing."

"Riley get here?" Sawyer asked. Cole nodded. "You two still not speaking?" Cole nodded again—grimly this time.

"You let me talk to him. I'll straighten him right out," Sumi said tartly.

"No, no, you can't do that. I have to do it. Promise me," Cole implored.

"Okay. But if your way doesn't work, then I get a chance. Promise?"

"This is Christmas, a time of miracles. Let's pray there is one," Cole said.

"This will be my first real Christmas. I can't wait to see your tree and all the decorations," Sumi cried excitedly.

"You're in for a treat. We sort of get carried away on Christmas."

"That's what my father said. He wanted me to experience what he called a Coleman hoedown, or was it shindig? I can't remember."

"Either will do just fine. Let's get you through Customs and pick up those presents and be on our way. They're waiting for us. I think this is going to be the best Christmas ever."

The Bronco was jammed to the top with boxes of every size and shape. Cole was forced to use the side mirror to see behind him.

"It's snowing!" Sumi cried excitedly.

"It's supposed to snow on Christmas. It's part of the miracle."

"I believe in miracles. My family despaired of me ever finding a man of my own. My father has always said I was too forward. Do you still love me, Cole?"

"More than ever."

Sumi smiled. "I will love you for all of my life," she said softly. In the backseat, Sawyer was still smiling. She leaned back and closed her eyes. Soon she'd see Adam. . . .

"Oh, shit!" Cole said softly. "I wanted this to be perfect. I had this plan. I was going to tell you . . . you know . . . that I loved you. . . . It was going to be romantic. We'd toast each other with wine. . . . I wanted us to be alone with the Christmas tree . . . our first Christmas. . . . You know what I mean. I love you, Sumi."

"I love you, too, Cole. The minute I saw you standing in my father's garden, I knew."

"I've always felt something special for your father. I don't know when it happened or how it happened. I guess it was the time he came to Texas when Riley and I were in trouble. I think it was the look in his eyes. He didn't know me, and yet he believed me. I've never forgotten it. We spoke of it when I visited him."

"My father is a very wise and gentle man. Riley has broken his heart, but he will not admit this. You've mended it for him, Cole."

"No, Sumi, only Riley can mend that break. Listen, can we talk about something else now? We're almost home."

"Your letters were beautiful, Cole. Every day I waited for the postman."

"I wished you had written more often," Cole said.

"A proper Japanese lady does not do anything that could be considered forward."

"I thought you said you wanted to be treated like an American."

"I do. At times. At other times I want to be treated like a Japanese."

"How am I supposed to recognize those times?" Cole grumbled good-naturedly.

"Because I will tell you."

"That's what I thought. Mam said you were a live wire."

"Your Mam is right." Sumi laughed. She turned around in her seat. "I am a live wire, right, Sawyer?"

"Hear, hear," said Sawyer.

"We're here." Cole reached over and took Sumi's hand in both of his. "I'm glad you came."

"I'm glad you had the good sense to ask me. The Japanese in me wouldn't permit me to be forward and invite myself."

Sawyer raced into the house ahead of them, leaving her bags in the Bronco. Cole could hear her yelling, "Surprise!" as she opened the front door. He squeezed Sumi's hand. "Come on, Sumi," he said. "Time to meet the family."

Amelia dabbed at her eyes with her napkin. She knew why they were here. Her family. Her special miracle this Christmas. She wondered which one of the family had arranged all of this. Billie? Maggie? Her eyes circled the room. Cole's roguish wink and his thumbs-up salute made the tears run down her cheeks.

She didn't bother to wipe them away this time.

Family.

Sawyer cuddled with Adam. Cole cuddled with Sumi. Everyone smiled indulgently.

"I guess this means we have to give up our wild, wicked life, eh, Sumi?" Sawyer said devilishly.

"Looks that way," Sumi said.

"No confessions! I can't bear it," Adam said in mock horror.

Cary watched Amelia and Julie talking together. He thought his heart would break. He wondered what they were talking about. Billie was joining them. Billie always made things right. Julie was acting like the invited guest she was, doing and saying all the right things. She'd looked right through him twice when their eyes met. He'd been the one to look away first.

Didn't she care? Didn't she know he cared? They hadn't spoken since their Hawaiian vacation. He'd left one message on her machine, and when he called back, the machine was off. He'd wanted to tell her about Amelia. There were so many things he wanted to tell her. In the end he did what he thought she wanted: he never called again. All the memories flooded back. How could she act so normal? How?

The urge to grab her, to drag her away to some quiet place to talk, was so strong that he had to fight with himself, force himself to walk over to Thad and try to make conversation. Being around Thad was like sitting in a peaceful church, knowing that when you left, things would be all right.

CHAPTER
{{{{{{{{{{ TWENTY-ONE }}}}}}}}}

The passengers were calm now that they were airborne, relieved that they would arrive at their destinations in time for Christmas. The plane was safely off the ground and climbing steadily above the storm. Chesney waited for calm to replace the stress she'd felt since awakening this morning. She did her best to relax, but the fact that the FASTEN SEAT BELT and the NO SMOKING signs were still on meant they weren't out of the woods yet. When they reached their cruising altitude of thirty-five thousand feet, maybe she would be able to relax. The spooky feeling, her premonition, was still as strong as ever. She wished she knew what the others were thinking. She stretched her neck to see Patty. Patty sensed Chesney's gaze, turned, and smiled wanly. She gave an infinitesimal shake of her head. Patty was still scared; Chesney could see it in her eyes.

The L1011 continued to bounce and rock in its upward climb. When it finally leveled off and the captain addressed the passengers, Chesney heard the relief in his voice. "We've reached our cruising altitude, so I suggest you all sit back and enjoy the ride. Miss Brighton and her crew will start serving dinner and drinks. This is Christmas Eve, so the drinks are on London Air. On behalf of the entire crew and myself, we want to wish you all a Merry Christmas."

"What's so merry?" Chesney muttered under her breath.

"I'm hungry and I want Gus," Molly Sanders whimpered. "I want Gus," she repeated.

"The girls are getting dinner ready, Molly. Did your mommy tell you that Gus had to stay in a special place till we land?"

"She gave Gus a pill to make him sleep. Gus can sleep on my lap. He won't pee. I'll tell him not to pee. Can you get Gus?" Molly's thumb went into her mouth as soon as she finished talking.

It was Christmas Eve and a time for special things to happen. Chesney wondered if the captain would okay Gus's release for the little girl. "How big is Gus, Molly?"

"This big," Molly said, holding her hands apart. "He fits on my lap."

In a child's mind, "this big" could mean just about anything. "What kind of dog is he, Molly; do you know?"

Molly bobbed her head. "He's brown." Chesney smiled.

"No, honey, I mean is he a poodle, a mutt, or Yorkie?"

The little girl's head kept bobbing. Her eyes filled with tears. Her thumb was still in her mouth. "He's Gus," she mumbled tearfully.

"Okay, let me see what I can do. Promise me to keep your seat belt on, okay?" Molly nodded, tears streaming down her cheeks.

Chesney made her way back to the cockpit. She rapped softly and was told to enter. "Captain, could I speak to you a minute?"

"Bored already? Nothing to do? The passengers behaving themselves?"

"All but one." Chesney grinned. She explained Molly's request, starting off with "This is Christmas Eve" and ending with "Captain, this is Christmas Eve."

"You made your point. I don't see what harm it could do. Why not? Send one of those boys from the ski team in here. I'll show him the layout of the cargo area and where Gus should be. According to this list, Gus is a seven-pound Yorkshire terrier. I guess we can all hold up if he decides to . . . ah, pee." The copilot burst out laughing. Chesney tried to hide her smile, but when Captain Andrews chucked her under the chin, she laughed, too.

Chesney made her way through first class and into the galley separating the forward section from the tourist class. It was easy to spot the skiers in their green and yellow ski sweaters. She selected a young man sitting on the end of the row and crooked her finger at him. When he mouthed the word "Me?" Chesney nodded. When they reached the galley she explained the situation.

"No problem; I'm a dog lover myself, love. Show me the way."

A short time later, he had the pooch under his sweater. The skier crooned to the frightened puppy.

A sudden wail of distress from the midsection of the plane set the fine hairs on the back of Chesney's neck to dancing. It was Molly. The dog's ears went up, his eyes snapped open, and his tail started to wag, all at once. He was out of the skier's arms in a second, yapping and leaping his way over seats to get to Molly. There was a smile on everyone's face when Chesney announced, "Santa dropped that pup down the hatch for little Molly." No one questioned the word "hatch" or that the plane didn't have one. Everyone was laughing and staring as Gus licked Molly's face and even the teddy bear. It was obvious that Molly, the teddy bear, and Gus were a team. Rules were meant to be broken once in a while.

Chesney forgot her fear for a little while as she set about clearing the dinner trays. From time to time her eyes went to Molly, who was sleeping with Gus in the crook of one arm, her teddy in the other.

Flight 214 maintained its cruising altitude. They were well into their flight when Chesney's nerves started to act up. She looked around to see if the passengers were doing something other than reading or dozing. Everything looked normal; for the moment it was like any other flight. Little Molly was starting to stir. Half the ski team was reading, the other half discussing their racing times and how they hoped to beat their competition when they reached Chamonix, their final destination. Her eyes searched out Patty McIntyre. Chesney motioned for her to come to the back of the cabin.

"Everything under control?" Chesney asked quietly.

"Everything but me. I can't explain it, Chesney, but I've never felt so schitzy. I took Captain Andrews some coffee before, and he said there was a storm in Geneva that would make the one we left in London look like a flurry."

Chesney's heart thumped in her chest. Her mouth felt dry, as if she'd swallowed a tablespoon of peanut butter. "Keep your eye on Molly; I think she's going to wake up any minute. She'll probably have to go to the bathroom, and Gus, too. I have to do a walk-through. I'll join you in a few minutes."

She walked through the plane, stopping to speak to those passengers who were awake. She returned to the bulkhead section just as Molly sat up to rub the sleep out of her eyes.

"Hi, sweetie; did you have a nice sleep?"

"Uh huh. Gus wants a drink."

"I'll take care of it right now." She stooped down to fondle the dog's ears. He whined his pleasure, but snuggled closer to Molly. Molly was briskly rubbing his fat, pink belly, a look of absolute love on her face. Chesney wondered if the little girl ever looked at her parents in the same way.

Chesney was in the midsection of the plane when she experienced a feeling of light-headedness. She gave herself a mental shake to clear her head. She looked around; everyone looked relaxed and unworried. Whatever it was she felt, it was not noticed by the passengers.

"Miss, miss, could I trouble you for a Coca-Cola?" a thin, reedlike voice asked. Chesney looked down at an elderly lady with soft white hair, spectacles perched on her nose, an open paperback novel on her lap.

"Of course; I'll be back in a minute." Her name was . . . Chesney searched her memory for the passenger's name. Edith Neibauer from Akron, Ohio. She'd walked onto the plane with a cane. She'd been angry, stomping both her feet and her cane as she searched out her seat in the midsection—an aisle seat. Because her voice had been so thin and high, it carried backward to Chesney while the boarding was going on. "My son will never wait for hours in a cold airport. He was good enough to send me this ticket, but he isn't a patient man, and his wife is less patient." Later, on one of her walk-throughs, Chesney overheard Mrs. Neibauer talking to her seat companion, and her voice had been tearful. She was being shuffled from one child to the next, like flotsam. "No one wants you when you're old," she said tearfully. "Oh, they're all willing to pay for someone else to see to your wants and needs, but don't infringe on their lives." No one wants you when you're young either, Chesney's mind had shrieked. On her way back to her station a few minutes later, Chesney heard Mrs. Neibauer say, "My daughter, Alice, was sick of me, and she wants to spend the holidays with her in-laws. They don't want to shuffle me in and out of a wheelchair. My chair embarrasses them." Chesney had slowed her steps then and bent down to ask the other passengers if they wanted anything. Her ear was tuned to Edith Neibauer, however. "Getting old alone when you know you have family who don't . . . give a hoot about you . . . you might as well be dead." Chesney had flinched at the woman's awful words.

Chesney returned with Edith's soft drink. She bent low so as not to disturb the woman's seat companion. "Merry Christmas, Mrs. Neibauer."

The woman was touched. "Bless your heart for saying that. You're probably the only one who will wish me a Merry Christmas. There should be love and warmth, but so many times . . . I wish . . . I wish . . ."

"What, Mrs. Neibauer? What do you wish?" Chesney whispered.

"I wish, just once, that one of my two children would call me on the phone or write me a letter and tell me . . . and tell me they love me. I've always told them, all their lives, that I love *them*."

Tears burned Chesney's eyes. She reached out her hand to the old woman. "This visit might be just what you want. Everyone says Christmas is a time of miracles. Can I get you anything else?"

"No, my dear, you've done enough. Thank you for listening. How is the little girl doing?"

"Just fine. Mrs. Neibauer, would you like to go to the back and sit with her for a while? There are some storybooks on her seat. I don't think the child has had many people read to her. It might be good for both of you."

"I'd love to read to her. She won't set up a ruckus if I sit down with her, will she?"

Chesney smiled. "No, I don't think so. The dog probably won't let you touch her, so you might have to wing it."

The old lady had a purpose now. She rose with difficulty and followed Chesney down the aisle.

Molly smiled shyly and squeezed Gus to her chest. The little dog struggled to lick at her face. Molly's giggles made the old lady smile. Chesney was turning, to return to her station, when she felt it again, the light-headedness she'd felt earlier. The look of alarm on Mrs. Neibauer's face frightened Chesney. She forced a smile and muttered, "Turbulence."

Patty McIntyre's face registered shock. She was too young, too inexperienced to cover the fright she felt. One of the skiers excused himself and crawled over his seat companion. "What's wrong?" he hissed.

"Wrong? Nothing. What could be wrong at thirty thousand feet?" Patty whispered over her shoulder.

"Don't give me that crap. I felt something—dizzy. I felt it a little earlier, too. We're losing altitude, right?"

"Turbulence. Only the pilot knows if something's wrong, and he hasn't said anything. You really should go back to your seat and buckle up."

"Why should I go back to my seat and buckle up if nothing is wrong? There's no turbulence at thirty thousand feet. Pilots don't take their passengers into their confidence until it's too late," he said ominously. "And another thing; my brother is a pilot, and I've logged almost as many hours as he has. We've dropped about five thousand feet in the past twenty minutes. Maybe the others aren't aware of it, but I am. Aware, Miss McIntyre. Now what do you have to say?"

"I say you should return to your seat and buckle up," Patty said quietly. "Now!"

"Yes sir, ma'am," he said, saluting smartly. "Whatever you say, ma'am." His voice was sour, almost as sour as Patty's face.

The skier plopped down into his seat and fastened his seat belt, then leaned over and instructed his teammates to do the same. Chesney noticed that he was whispering to the man sitting next to him.

Chesney and Patty watched from the galley in the first-class section as the whisper traveled across the aisle and into the next. They had no way of knowing the message was a terse, harsh alert that the plane had descended five thousand feet, and there was something wrong somewhere in the plane. They watched helplessly as the whispered message was repeated over and over. The whispers had a snowball effect. Twenty minutes later, the entire midsection of the cabin was alerted and aware that something was wrong.

"I'm scared, Chesney," Patty whispered.

Chesney put her arm around the young stewardess's shoulder. "We've all felt tremors and light-headedness before. The captain hasn't alerted us to any kind of malfunction. We're the first to know. I think it's our imagination, and I say we start another round of drinks. Plenty of coffee and tea, too. Smile, Patty."

The soft ping of the FASTEN SEAT BELT sign flashed overhead. The passengers were stirring now, looking at one another . . . silently. Three pings sounded, the signal for Chesney to go to the flight deck. She turned the cart over to Patty and walked nonchalantly through the midsection to first class and then to the flight deck.

"You wanted to see me, Captain?" Chesney asked quietly. Her heart was thumping so loudly, she thought it would leap out of her chest.

"We're experiencing a spot of trouble. We've blown a duct. I've descended six thousand feet, so if any of the passengers —"

"They already know, Captain." She told him about the whispered message.

"There's always one wiseass aboard," the captain said tersely. The second officer nodded sourly. He was only twenty-seven and his heart was pounding in his chest. He wondered if his eyes mirrored the fear he was seeing in Chesney's eyes.

Chesney was halfway through the first-class section when she felt a third wave of dizziness. She turned and headed back to the flight deck and spoke to the captain again. When she returned to her station, her face was chalk-white. She alerted first Patty and then the other attendants to return to the midsection.

The hospitality carts were quickly shoved into their proper places, the cabins cleared of all loose objects. The entire crew rushed up and down the aisles, reaching for glasses and cans, shoving them into their trash bags regardless of the passengers' protests. Chesney was the last to hit the jump seat and buckle up when the captain's voice came over the p.a. system. She tried to force herself to swallow past the lump in her throat as she listened to words she'd heard minutes ago. "This is the captain speaking. As you must have noticed, the Fasten Seat Belt sign is on, and I've just turned the No Smoking sign on. It's just for a while, so please bear with me and the crew. We're experiencing some pressure problems, but nothing to be alarmed about at this time. Staying in your seats now is for your own protection. Our cruising altitude is now twenty-four thousand feet. Forty-five minutes ago it was thirty-one thousand. We're heading into a storm, and there will be some rough turbulence. I'll keep you advised of the storm conditions every fifteen minutes." The captain signed off to total silence.

"How much is forty-five minutes?" Molly Sanders chirped to Mrs. Neibauer.

The old lady's eyes were on Chesney when she replied. "Not long, honey. Maybe as long as it takes for you to have a bubble bath. Did you ever give Gus a bubble bath, Molly?"

"No, the soap gets in his eyes. Gus doesn't get dirty. He has a bib. Do you want to see it?" Molly asked as she rummaged in her shiny black purse. "See?" she said, holding up a small plastic bib with goldfish on it.

"I'll bet he doesn't like that very much," Mrs. Neibauer said in a shaking voice. Chesney was unable to tear her eyes away from the old lady and the little girl. Youth and old age, and where was she? Somewhere in the middle. As alone as each of them. If . . . she wondered who she would help if something happened —providing she was able to help. Every manual she'd read, every lecture she'd attended on crash safety, emphasized the crew first. The crew was to take care of itself first, passengers second. If there was a crash, the passengers would forget the brief demonstration of the oxygen masks. It was never mentioned to passengers that if decompression occurred, only fifteen seconds of life remained. Even in five seconds, without the aid of oxygen, a degree of lessened judgment would occur. Five seconds after that, a state of euphoria would take place. In that state many passengers would opt not to use the masks and lapse into unconsciousness.

Chesney ran the captain's last words over in her mind. "We've blown a duct. It's a slight opening in one of the joints, but it's enough to cause us to lose altitude. We're descending as slowly as we can, but we're picking up some heavy ice. We can't maintain our altitude. The faster we go down, the faster the ice builds up. We're losing our deicing ability. Get back to your station and...pray," the captain had finished grimly. He'd said he was changing course to 240 degrees.

"Oh, God!" Chesney moaned as pandemonium broke out in the cabin. The skier was shouting now, alerting the other passengers. She picked up the microphone and began speaking.

"Ladies and gentlemen, may I have your attention, please. The captain has just informed me that we're experiencing some difficulty with our air pressure. We're also experiencing some icing on the wings, which makes the plane heavier. We're descending slowly so as to take care of that problem, and the captain has changed course. Please buckle your seat belts and remain calm. You must remain calm. The captain will advise us shortly." Chesney no sooner put the mike back into its niche when the skier hopped into the aisle, his face a mask of fear.

"You can't get rid of the ice," he shouted. "There's no way the captain can get this plane down." The boy's voice was shrill and hysterical. Chesney and the other attendants looked on helplessly as he continued his tirade. It was Edith Neibauer who unbuckled her seat belt and limped her way to him.

"Young man, that's just about enough! You are terrorizing these passengers, and I will not tolerate it. I'm too old to die of a heart attack in midair. The law says you're a man, so act like one! The captain will do what he can for all of us. I'm ordering you to *sit down!*" Edith raised her cane threateningly. At the sight of the raised cane, the Yorkie leaped off Molly's lap and tore down the aisle after the skier. The dog bared his teeth, growling as ferociously as only a small dog can do. Passengers were in the aisles, some helping Edith back to her seat.

The first officer growled at the commotion coming through the p.a. system. "Change course two-forty; I'll handle this." The moment the cockpit door opened, the skier barreled through, with the Yorkie in pursuit. The first officer dragged him backward, slamming the door behind him. Gus leaped onto the captain's lap, trembling so badly he couldn't sit. The captain changed course to 240 degrees as he listened to the child's shrieks of "Gus! Gus!" The little dog heard them, too. He was off the captain's lap in a second, growling and whining at the door. Three minutes later the first officer returned, his face as white as the shirt he wore. Gus streaked by him, leaping through the first-class section and on down the aisle of the midsection.

He snuggled in Molly's lap in a flash. A few of the passengers cheered.

"They're applauding Gus, honey," Edith Neibauer said kindly. "He did a very brave thing going after that young man. Gus is a hero!"

"Gus is afraid of sticks. Travis hits him with the broom when I go to nursery school," Molly whimpered.

Dear God, Chesney thought. She'd lost control. Mrs. Neibauer had done her job for her. Tears burned her eyes when she addressed the old lady. "Thank you, Mrs. Neibauer; we all appreciate what you did."

The old lady smiled wanly. "Sometimes old age has its own rewards. I didn't stop to think, and if I did, I guess I thought the young man would think of me as his grandmother and listen to me. It's over now, and Gus saved the day. We're going to"—she spelled the word so Molly wouldn't understand what she was saying—"c-r-a-s-h, aren't we?" Her tone was so calm, so matter-of-fact, Chesney blinked.

It was against everything she'd been told to do, but she spoke anyway. "We're losing altitude very fast. If . . . if we do . . . if anything goes wrong, watch out for Molly . . . and Gus."

The old lady was serene now, so calm that Chesney felt better. "For this little bit of time, these two are mine, Miss Brighton. I'll do my best. You know, when a disaster is about to take place, people usually rally round and pull together. Why don't we sing? It is Christmas Eve, and Santa will be here soon. Why don't we have a rousing chorus of 'Jingle Bells'?"

The captain and first officer heard the song at the same moment that they realized they were on a course of 204 degrees, not 240. They were forty degrees off course and headed west over the French Alps, at an altitude of fifteen thousand feet.

Blame would come later, when the wrecking crew found the black box.

In her jump seat Chesney played her game again as she tried to look into a visual of her future. She could see only blankness. Her fear at the moment was so alive and so real that the words of the song stuck in her throat. She felt Edith Neibauer's eyes on her. She forced herself to finish singing the song. "If you ever feel the need to adopt a granddaughter, I'd like to apply for the position," she said.

"Bless your heart, child. You don't have to apply; the position is yours." Without missing a beat she swung into "Rudolph the Red-Nosed Reindeer." Molly took her thumb out of her mouth long enough to clap her hands in glee. Gus barked happily as he licked at the little girl's face. Chesney was relieved to see the dog was snug in Molly's seat belt. Chesney turned in her seat, trying to catch Patty's eye. When the young stewardess felt Chesney's gaze, she smiled. Chesney smiled back. What would be would be.

The p.a. system came alive. The captain's voice was brisk and cool when he made his announcement. "Due to heavy weather conditions, our blown duct, and the ice accumulating on our wings, we are off course by forty degrees. We're headed toward the French Alps and Chamonix. There are no landing fields that I know of in this particular area. We've lost all contact with Geneva, and at this moment we're descending rapidly. Stay buckled into your seats. If we go down, put your head between your legs. God be with us all."

"Whazat mean?" Molly asked curiously.

"That means we're going to land soon. I'm going to put my knitting bag next to Gus so he's more comfortable." The bulging bag of soft cashmere yarn was secured around the little dog by knobby, arthritic fingers. "Now, listen carefully. . . . 'Twas the night before Christmas when all through the house . . ."

Chesney's eyes were glued to her watch. They were losing altitude faster now, more than a thousand feet a minute. Too much ice on the wings, probably all over the plane. It was colder now, the engines working harder to pump air into the cabin. She estimated their altitude at six or seven thousand feet. The French Alps. She tried to remember what she knew of the Alps. High, dense, snow-capped. Impossible terrain. A belly landing, not head-first. There might not be an explosion. They'd started out with eighty-five thousand pounds of fuel. How much was left? Zip, she thought. She should have sent the card. A phone call would have been better. It was almost Christmas Day. Five thousand, four. The plane was shuddering now, lumbering in midair. From somewhere she heard someone praying, the Our Father. . . . It was Patty McIntyre. She'd never realized what a sweet, clear voice Patty had. If only she'd called . . .

"And I in my kerchief . . ."

Two thousand, one thousand . . .

It happened quickly then. The p.a. system squawked with static, but the captain's voice was lost to the noise. The plane was in total darkness, the lighting extinguished at the moment of impact. The sound was a hundred jets taking off simultaneously. They were down, and almost immediately Chesney felt herself being flung violently to her left, to the side of the plane. Hot, searing pain roared through her arm, shoulder, and neck. She felt not one break, but several. She screamed with pain and almost immediately felt one of the service centers bang into her good arm. If only she could see where she was. She knew her seat wasn't intact. She seemed to be dangling, supported only by her seat belt. "Mrs. Neibauer, Molly, are you all right? Answer me. Molly," she screamed, "answer me! Gus! Bark. Please, Gus, bark." She thought she heard a whimper, either from the dog or Molly, but there was so much screaming and confusion, she couldn't be sure.

She became aware instantly of a searing frigid burst of air circulating about her. "Patty!" she screamed. "Nancy! Martha!" The only thing she could hear that registered in her numb brain were the cries for help. She had to do something, get loose from her restraints. It dawned on her then that her feet weren't touching the floor. Where in the name of God was she?

If only she could free herself, find some flashlights. She drew a deep breath and released the buckle on her seat belt. She dropped, then toppled over a soft mound of flesh. A person, but who? She blacked out for the barest of seconds. The numbing cold woke her, along with flurries of snow that were swirling through the broken windows.

The galley had been to her left and behind her seat. Not sure of her bearings, she struggled backward, tripping and falling as she tried to head in what she thought was the direction of the galley. Over and over she called for Patty, the other attendants, Molly, Mrs. Neibauer.

Airline rule number one. See to yourself first in case of a disaster. That meant she had to find some warm clothes and a flashlight. She forced her mind to ignore the knifing pain in her arm and shoulder. What seemed like an eternity later, she was in the galley searching for a flashlight. When she had it in her hand, she felt better. The sliding closet doors were jammed, which meant she couldn't get at her fleece-lined coat, and her hands and fingers were too cold to try prying them open. She'd have to scavenge the overhead racks for coats or jackets.

The flashlight seemed feeble in the total darkness. Chesney reached up to the overhead storage bin to find emptiness. She waved the beam of light downward; the heavy-duty storage bins lay across the middle row of seats. She felt like a grave robber when she reached inside. Her hand touched wool. Trembling, she pulled out a man's bulky overcoat. She eased it carefully over her injured arm and shoulder. She must make a sling, something to support her arm. She felt sick with the pain. She had to decide what she was going to do next. Who had the warmest clothes? She tried to remember. The ski team, of course. They'd worn heavy fur-lined boots, thick ski sweaters, and down jackets. They probably had warm wool caps, too. There was so much to do, so many people to find. She seemed incapable of moving, but she had to move. Where was the ski team? The light arced and then settled at what Chesney thought was seat-high level. She moved gingerly over still bodies, bodies that were already half-frozen. Over and over she kept saying, "Can I help you? Can I help you?" There was never a response. They couldn't all be dead, could they? Where had the screams come from? Were they her own? Did she hear them before or after the crash? She tried screaming out names. Her voice came out as a soft croaking, little more than a whisper.

"Chesney, is that you?" Patty McIntyre cried.

"God, yes. Patty, oh, Patty, I thought you . . ."

"I'm pinned down under something. I can't budge it. I'm freezing, Chesney. I'm so sleepy."

"You aren't sleepy. Don't even think about closing your eyes, Patty. I need your help. Where in relation to you is the ski team?"

"Up ahead on my left. They're dead, Chesney. Everyone's dead," Patty sobbed.

"Not everyone. We're alive. Keep talking to me while I see if I can find some warm clothes for you. I'm going to need you, Patty."

Chesney scrambled over broken seats, bodies, and luggage to reach the right aisle. She tried to draw a deep breath and almost fainted with the pain shooting through her arm and shoulder. She was alive . . . for now. Regardless of the pain, she had to get to the ski team.

When she found them, they were like rag dolls, their arms and legs twisted crazily, all of them still wearing their seat belts. She felt for a pulse on each young boy. On the last boy she felt a pulse, thin and skittery. He was alive. "Wake up! Oh, please wake up!" Chesney swung the flashlight beam from head to toe. An ugly gash across the boy's temple was deep and dangerous-looking. She worked feverishly to cover him with everything she could find. She called back to Patty, demanding that she answer her. She strained to hear Patty's faint response. She ripped at sweaters and jackets, carried as many as she could back to where Patty sat, tossed the garments to her, and went back for the boys' fur-lined boots. She retched when she pulled heavy wool socks off a dead boy's feet to pull on over her own feet.

Chesney climbed her way back to where Patty sat. She tried to help with the sweater and jacket but had to sit down and take deep breaths. Her exertions were causing her constant pain now, pain so fierce she had to clench her teeth and bite her tongue to keep from screaming.

"Ooohhh, this feels so good," Patty said in a singsong voice. "Now I can go to sleep."

Chesney cursed then, long and loud, saying words she'd only blushed at in the past. She cursed the weather, the plane, London Air, and the manufacturer of the L1011. Something teased at her then, something she'd noticed or heard. . . . It would come to her; she was sure of it. Whatever it was, it was important.

"Damn you, Patty! I told you to stay awake. You can't go to sleep. Come on now, sit up; we have to get these boots on your feet," Chesney said forcefully.

"What feet? I don't know where they are; I can't find my feet." Patty giggled.

Chesney swung the flashlight. Patty was wedged between Marsha Manning and a heavy flight box made of lead. One of the overhead units was upended between the seat in front of the young stewardess and her legs. "Patty, if I pull the woman in front of you out of her seat, I want you to try to push the storage box forward. Even if you move it a little bit, I might be able to tug at it from the front, and maybe you can slide out. I only have the use of one arm, so you're going to have to use all your strength."

Chesney remembered the woman passenger because her reason for going to Geneva had seemed so silly. She was going to buy a Rolex watch for herself because they cost too much in England. It was all Chesney could do to pry the dead woman from her crouched position, but she did it by sheer willpower.

"Now! Push, Patty!" It took them twenty minutes to inch the locker forward; the storage container had no hand grips. Patty finally swung her legs free.

"Quick, massage your feet and legs and then pull these boots on. I need you, Patty."

"Is . . . is everyone dead?"

"Most of them. I couldn't get to the front of the plane. I think there's a tree across the midsection. I couldn't get that close, and my light was too faint. I called and called, but no one answered me. We have to get to the back. I heard voices before. Go ahead of me, Patty. I'm afraid I'll bump into something. My arm is broken in a couple of places. When we get to the back galley, you'll have to fix me a sling. From a dishcloth or something."

This couldn't be happening, but it was. It was more real than any nightmare she'd ever suffered through. In her pain-filled state, her thoughts were chaotic; she was alive, but injured severely. She rubbed warily at her neck and was instantly sorry; the slightest touch to her neck and shoulders set fresh waves of pain roaring down her side.

Molly and Mrs. Neibauer: she had to find them. Surely God had spared them. She tried calling again, and Patty echoed her cries. The muffled yap of the Yorkie brought tears to Chesney's eyes. "Here we are; we're coming! Patty, can you climb over those seats?"

They both shouted then, till they were hoarse, for any survivors to call out their positions. If only they had more light, heat, strength.

"Here, we're pinned down," Mrs. Neibauer called feebly.

"Molly?"

"She's alive, and so is the dog. I think my knitting bag saved him."

When they finally reached the old lady, Chesney cried, sobs breaking from her throat. Edith's knitting bag hadn't saved the little dog and Molly; Edith had saved them—by throwing herself across them. She had unbuckled her seat belt at the last second so as to throw her weight across the little girl and the dog.

"I've been blacking out. I can't move, and I'm afraid I'll smother Molly; you have to pull her out . . ."

They worked feverishly to get the little girl free. "Don't worry about hurting me; I can't feel anything," Edith said wanly. "My body has kept her warm, but she needs to be bundled up, and quickly. The dog, too."

Time lost all meaning as Chesney and Patty did what they were trained to do. From somewhere Patty came up with a prescription bottle of Percodan. She gave Chesney two of them. "There's three left, Chesney. Marsha Manning put them in the storage container. She was taking them for her bursitis. When they're gone, I'll turn you into a drunk. Whiskey will help."

Chesney was functional again, her wits sharp, her confidence at an all-time high. "We can survive, Patty; I know we can. Thanks for the sling; it helps."

What seemed like a long time later, they had a body count. There were nineteen survivors, including themselves, twenty counting Gus, all injured except Patty, Molly, Gus, and Seymour Polkowitz, a sixty-five-year-old disc jockey from New Zealand who suffered from epileptic seizures.

They worked tirelessly, trying to comfort the injured. Molly didn't cry, nor did she ask questions. She clutched Gus and her teddy and kept her thumb in her mouth. Chesney's eyes filled each time she checked on the child.

What seemed like hours later, Chesney took over Mrs. Neibauer's care, and Patty sat watch over the badly injured skier. "I can't wake him up, Chesney," she reported. "He's alive, his pulse is weak, and . . . and . . . both his legs are broken, his left one at the knee and his right leg in three places. He won't ski again. Perhaps for pleasure but never for competition." Her eyes brimmed with tears for the young man.

"He's alive, Patty. All we can do is keep him warm and hope for the best. Keep talking to him. Don't worry about what the future holds for him. We can only deal with the present."

The hours until dawn were the longest of Chesney's life. She prayed with some of the injured, cuddled Molly and the little dog, and stroked Edith's sparse white hair. She listened to the old lady as she spoke of her life and her two children, of her happy times and her sorrows. "I know I'm going to die here. It's not the dying I mind. I'm ready to go to my Maker, but I thought, I hoped . . . my children would be near me so I could at least say good-bye. I hoped they would want . . . they would want to say good-bye. . . ." A spasm of pain passed over Edith's face.

"You're in pain! You said you couldn't feel anything!" Chesney cried.

"One can endure physical pain. This pain," she said, patting her chest, "is . . . a . . . killer."

"Here." Chesney held out one of the Percodan pills. "Swallow this. It will ease the pain."

"No, you keep it. I can see the pain you're in, young lady. You need to function and take care of the others."

Chesney handed the pill to the old lady. "I'm in charge, and I'm ordering you to take this pill. Now!" she said, not unkindly. "You did a very brave thing. You could have been killed, unbuckling your seat belt the way you did. Your chil-

dren will be very proud of you. I'm proud of you, Mrs. Neibauer, and I'm sure that London Air will give you a commen-
dation, not that that's important."

The old lady smiled wanly. "The little one has her whole
life ahead of her. I've lived mine. What I did wasn't heroic, it
was just a mother's instinct to protect her child. At that moment I felt as though Molly was my little Stevie. I'm just a
foolish old woman; don't pay any attention to me. See to the
others, young lady."

"I wish I had more covers for you; I know you must be
freezing, but I'm afraid to move you," Chesney cried.

"My dear, it simply doesn't matter. I've been lying here
staring at this nameplate on the plane. I wonder who Coleman
is. Do you suppose it's the name of the aircraft company or
the name of the people who make the windows? Not that that
matters either."

Chesney gasped at the name. "Where did you see a nameplate?"

"There," Edith said, pointing to a plate near the floor.
Chesney aimed the flashlight to where she pointed. COLE-
MAN AVIATION. She smiled down at the woman under her
mound of jackets and coats. "I think we're all going to be all
right. Rescue teams are probably searching for us right now. I
want you to hang on, Mrs. Neibauer. I don't care what it
takes; I want you to focus on one thing—seeing your children
again. Promise me." Edith nodded her head wearily.

"Now what?" Patty asked when Chesney joined her.

"We wait." She was silent a long time before she added a
comment. "This is a Coleman plane. They'll be looking for
us."

"Sure, sure, and I'm the pope's niece," Patty said bitterly.

"No, no, Patty, you don't understand. My father's family
built this plane. They'll come looking for..." She was going
to say "me," but changed it to "us."

Later, when the first sounds of the rescue team reached the
survivors, Chesney Brighton was holding Edith Neibauer
against her chest. It was her first experience with death, and
she prayed for the ability to comfort the old lady during her
last minutes. "Shhh, don't try to talk, conserve your strength.
The rescue team is here; I can hear the planes overhead. Try to
hang on, Mrs. Neibauer." Pain screeched through Chesney
with the weight of the old lady. She clenched her teeth.

"I want you to do...something for me...later. In my

knitting bag is . . . a rabbit's foot on a chain. Stevie gave it to . . . to me for Mother's Day when he was . . . nine years old. The . . . the colored macaroni necklace . . . is . . . my daughter made it for me. I used to wear it every year on my birthday no matter what kind of outfit I had on."

"What . . . what do you want me to . . . to do with them?" Chesney whispered.

"Give them to . . . to Molly. She needs something to hold on to. It's Christmas morning and she doesn't have a present. Wrap . . . wrap it in some . . . of the colored yarn. Will you do that for me?"

Chesney's thoughts ricocheted. She'd thought . . . wouldn't a mother want her own children to have those things they'd given her? "Do you . . . do you want me to . . . I could call your son or daughter . . . whatever you want, I'll do my best. . . ."

"No, nothing. If . . . there's one small part of me . . . in either of my . . . children, they'll know. I . . ."

She was so still, Chesney knew she was gone.

Chesney's movements were clumsy and awkward when she wrapped the gifts, Edith Neibauer's legacy to Molly, with red and green yarn.

Five minutes later her voice was bright and cheerful. "Molly, Santa left this for you! He left just this one present here and a note saying all your other presents are under the tree at home. Merry Christmas, honey!"

Molly stared intently at the small gifts. She smiled from ear to ear as she looped the macaroni necklace around her neck. She held out the rabbit's foot to Gus, who sniffed at it suspiciously. Sometimes grownups were so silly, Molly thought. She'd seen the little rabbit's foot and necklace in Mrs. Neibauer's knitting bag. She was an expert at not spoiling things for grownups. It was easy to pretend . . . so they would smile.

They waited.

CHAPTER TWENTY-TWO

Dinner was over, except for dessert. Jeff held the door to the kitchen open while Adam and Cole carried the dishes to the sink. The small television set Jeff had been watching between courses was announcing a bulletin. Everyone at the table stopped to listen. Jeff continued to hold the door open. Cole adjusted the volume.

"We interrupt this program to bring you this special bulletin. London Airways has announced the crash of Flight 214. The L1011 bound for Geneva, Switzerland, carried two hundred and sixty passengers plus a crew of twelve. Our latest word is the plane crashed in midflight. No further details are available. Stay tuned to this station."

Rand, Maggie, and Sawyer were off their chairs in an instant and headed toward the hall phone.

"Rand's daughter was the senior hostess on that flight," Amelia said. "He showed me a letter he received some time ago, where Chesney said she was working Christmas Eve. She said she liked Flight 214 because of the particular crew she worked with. Somebody say a prayer." All the heads at the table bowed. It was Julie's quiet, firm voice that said the short prayer. "Merciful father, give all those aboard the plane the strength and courage to handle this disaster. Give each of us here at this table the same strength to handle whatever it is that's in store for those unfortunate passengers."

"Let's all say the Our Father," Billie said. "That prayer makes me feel better."

The heads bowed a second time, each saying his prayer quietly.

No one showed surprise when Rand said he'd just spoken to the prime minister. His eyes were on Maggie when he spoke. "It's not good. There are some survivors. Three of the crew are alive, two stewardesses and one steward. Both pilots are dead. It will be hours, maybe days, before the rescue team can get to them. I have to go."

"Of course you do, darling," Maggie said, getting up from the table.

"The DM. I'll take it."

"Oh, no, you don't," Cole said flatly. "You aren't flying anywhere."

"I second that," Riley said, heading for the hall closet and his jacket.

"I tested that plane," Rand exploded.

"Not when your daughter was in a plane crash," Sawyer said quietly. "Cole?"

Cole looked at Riley. His gaze was cool and level. "I'll flip you because I don't want to fight you."

"I'll be your copilot unless you have any objections," Riley said just as coolly.

"I don't have a one. Aunt Amelia, you'll have to call the governor. There's no way I'll get off the ground without some kind of intervention. This is Christmas Eve. Get me approval and we'll do the rest," Cole said briskly.

"Don't just stand there, get moving. By the time you get to the hangar, your permission will be there," Amelia said. "Cary, hand me the phone!"

"I know everything will be all right, Rand," Maggie whispered. "We'll hold Christmas till you get back. No matter how long it takes. We'll be right here where you left us, and I know you'll have Chesney with you when you return. I just know it. You know it, too, don't you, Mam?"

"Yes, Rand. Good luck. Our prayers go with you."

Julie watched Amelia as she made her call. She listened to the words. Her son, her granddaughter . . . Who could refuse what she asked? She turned to see Cary bend over his wife. She'd never seen such naked devotion in her life. She turned away, blinded with her own tears. Billie's arms went around her. "You have all the time in the world," she whispered.

"I wouldn't dream of . . . Billie, you don't think I would . . ."

"No, darling, I don't think that, but I don't want you torturing yourself. I don't know how else to say this except to say it. This is not the time for anything but family support. That means every member of the family. Your turn will come all too soon."

Julie nodded. "What can I do?"

"The dishes," Jeff said agreeably. "But first we have to have dessert."

"Everyone, listen up," Billie said. "There's nothing any of us can do but pray. We did that and we'll do it again. For now we are going to finish our dinner, do the dishes, and then we're going to sing carols and go to church. We are not going to change our plans. Gift giving will have to wait till the others get back."

Christmas day dawned clear and cold. The ground held just enough snow for the weather forecasters to proclaim it a white Christmas.

Breakfast was prepared with the rising sun, cooked and served by Jeff. Adam played waiter, and Sawyer was the waitress. Morning was spent playing cards and waiting for the phone to ring. At lunchtime, Jeff and Adam made sandwiches. Dinner was soup and salad. Everyone spent the evening glued to the television.

A news bulletin that came on shortly after nine o'clock proclaimed the air crash one of Britain's worst. Film footage was shown. More footage was promised for eleven o'clock.

It was midafternoon on Christmas Day when Cole set the DM down, smooth as silk. Riley congratulated him out of the corner of his mouth. Cole nodded brusquely. They scurried to the far end of the runway, where a helicopter stood waiting for them. They climbed aboard, their eyes gritty with loss of sleep, their shoulders stiff with fatigue. They sat silently while the pilot briefed them.

"You're right on schedule. We just got a fix on the crash site about thirty minutes ago. The first rescue plane took off just as you landed. We'd have had it sooner," the pilot apologized, "but this goddamn snow isn't good for visibility. It'll take us about an hour, maybe more. There's some coffee and sandwiches in a poly bag. Help yourselves, and Merry Christmas."

They swigged the scalding coffee and devoured the thick ham sandwiches. Rand leaned back, his shoulders slumped, his face full of misery. He talked then, the words tumbling out. Later Riley said he babbled. They listened because that was all they could do.

"All I wanted from her was to give me a chance. Christ, what if she . . . if she didn't make it? . . . What if . . ." He dropped his head into his hands.

"You have to think positive, Rand. If you go off the deep end, you aren't going to be any good to us," Riley said briskly. Cole seconded his cousin's words.

"It's Christmas," Rand said.

"A time for miracles. Either you believe or you don't. Which is it?" Cole demanded.

"I've had my second chances, even some thirds. I don't have a right to expect more." A sob caught in Rand's throat.

"That's you. Doesn't seem to me that Chesney got up to bat yet. I'd say she has a shot at a second chance. You're just along for the ride," Cole said quietly.

Hope shot from Rand's eyes. "I never thought about it like that. God, I hope you're right."

Riley sat quietly listening to his cousin and Rand. He wanted to talk to Cole, but this wasn't the time. He had so much to say, so many things to apologize for. When death touched your life, it made you stop and think. He was saved from further thought when the helicopter pilot announced they were ready to set down.

"You have to go on foot for a mile, maybe three quarters of a mile. There should be a makeshift first aid station along the way. Two doctors and three nurses, I was told. Don't ask me where the plane is, because I don't know. I do know there are no landing strips. Two choppers were ahead of the rescue plane."

The pilot held the chopper steady as they leaped, crouching, to the ground. The rotary blades chopped the arctic air about them, kicking up clouds of powdery snow. When the pilot lifted off, they ran to what looked like a path in the snow.

They slogged up the hill, puffing and panting, their lungs burning with the freezing cold air. They were on their hands and knees more than their feet as they fought for toeholds in the hard-packed snow.

"Shock," Rand gasped. "Pneumonia. They could die from exposure."

"Rand, shut the hell up," Cole said raggedly. "Everyone's doing the best they can. Pray, but shut the hell up."

"I agree," Riley said through clenched teeth.

Forty minutes later Cole shouted over his shoulder. "Okay, we're here." Cole staggered into the closest tent. Portable kerosene heaters blazed warmly. Piles and piles of blankets were stacked on stretchers. Cartons of medicine and food left little walking-around room.

"They've been exposed too long," Rand said bitterly. "How many hours has it been—ten, twelve, more? The goddamn rescue team just got here!"

"This isn't the easiest place in the world to get to." Cole's tone was gentle and kind. Christ, what if it were Sumi in the plane, or his mother?

"Be glad you got clearance to get here at all," Riley said. "Calling the prime minister on Christmas Eve is what did it." Jesus, he thought, it could be anyone in that plane. Even Ivy Buckalew. The thought jolted him. He hastened outside and began walking again.

Cole reached out when he saw Riley falter and slip in the snow. The strange look on his cousin's face made Cole forget their differences.

"What is it?"

Riley swiveled to regain his footing. "I was thinking it might be Ivy Buckalew in the plane."

Cole grinned in the darkness. "Ivy Buckalew is back at Buckalew Big Wells eating her heart out over you, just the way she's been doing for years. I'll bet you didn't even buy her a Christmas present."

"You were always a goddamn know-it-all," Riley grated. He felt as if his lungs were going to burst with the climb he was making.

"When you know something, you know something. I happen to know Ivy's been in love with you since she was in pigtails. Stuff it, Riley. I don't give two shits what you do with your love life." Cole grinned again in the darkness. Sometimes you had to take Riley right to where the action was to get him to make a move. "I saw her a couple of weeks ago. She graduated magna cum laude, Phi Beta Kappa. Coots and Tess didn't attend. Lacey was the only one there for her." That ought to shake him up. Riley was real big on education and honors.

This time Riley stopped dead in his tracks. Cole was prepared, and stiff-armed him so he wouldn't lose his momentum. "What?"

"You heard me. Our little Ivy came in a winner, and the only one there to congratulate her was her sister, who, by the way, according to Ivy, is finally getting her shit together. That's a direct quote in case you're interested."

"Jesus," Riley breathed.

"That's what I said." Cole was glad the darkness covered the smirk on his face. He'd hate like hell for Riley to take a swing at him, here on this steep incline.

"I hear voices and I can see lights," Rand shouted.

Riley shouted, too, but the sound was carried away on the sharp-toothed wind blowing through the trees.

When they finally slipped and skidded into the confusion of the crash site, they saw what a nightmare they were confronting. Rand slumped against Cole, his body shuddering with despair.

Cole's eyes raked the scene, as did Riley's. Giant trees were uprooted, lying every which way, across the plane and under the plane, so that it was tilted upward at an awkward angle. "The main body looks like it's intact," Riley said quietly. Fires burned, flashlights beamed as men and women in heavy parkas worked to move the trees.

"It looks hopeless," Riley hissed. "Those trees must be hundreds of years old. A team of horses couldn't drag one of those trees. No chopper could get in here. Jesus, it's starting to snow again."

Rand tore loose and ran, slipping and sliding to where a group of men were huddled by the fire. His face was maniacal as he demanded to know what was being done.

"The best that can be done under the circumstances, which isn't much. Take a look around, mister, and if you have any ideas, I'd like to hear them." He was an older man, his face tough and lined from years of exposure to the outdoors.

"My daughter's in there," Rand shouted.

"I'm sorry about that. We'll get her out as soon as we can. Right now we don't know how we're going to do it, so hang on to your suspenders awhile, okay?"

"What's the situation?" Cole quickly briefed the man on who they were and why they were there.

"More help's on the way. The bad weather isn't helping. What we have is some medical help and not enough muscle and brawn. Christmas, you know," he added, as if that explained everything. "I feel helpless. I've radioed back, but there's another front coming in. I'd say we should pray. I know that sounds callous and . . . inefficient, but it's the best I can do."

"Has there been any contact from within the plane?"

"People are alive in there, but that's all we know. Take a good look, mister. It looks like some unseen hand built a log cabin around that plane. We could use some heavy-duty bulldozers."

"What about moving the plane?"

"The pilot and copilot are dead, that much we know. No one here can fly, and we can't get to the cockpit anyway."

"I fly, so does my cousin, and this guy was a crack fighter

pilot. We're big on electronics, too. What say we scout this out and see if we can lever those trees away from the cockpit."

It took the entire crew of men three hours to hack away branches and debris to get to the cockpit. Acetylene torches flared and flickered. "I'd give my right arm for a chain saw," Riley grunted as he heaved a monstrous tree limb out of the way.

"They're on the next plane. The one that can't get through," said one of the workers. "No time to daydream, boys; we have to keep going."

They worked through the night, breaking only for coffee and five-minute rest periods. Shortly before dawn the snow intensified, slowing down their efforts. A giant tarp was erected over the nose of the plane. The tentlike structure helped, but only a little.

By noon they had the top half of one monstrous tree cleared away, allowing the men with the torches more freedom to work unobstructed. It took four more hours before there was a hole big enough for a man to crawl through.

Cole went first, and then Riley. They crawled on their bellies through the first-class section of the L1011. "We made it!" Cole shouted when he reached the tilted tourist section. In this dim light he could see a small group of passengers crouching in the back of the plane. Numb with cold, they huddled together for the warmth of one another's bodies. "Who's in charge?" he shouted.

"I am, sir," replied a quivering voice. "I'm the senior stewardess on board. We're all hurt. Most . . . most of the passengers are . . . are dead. We . . . what we did . . . was . . . we put them together and took their coats . . . and . . . and their clothes. Several of us can move around. The rest need medical attention right away."

"We're going to try to get you out of here," Cole said with more confidence than he felt. "Now, try to get everyone to a seat and buckle their seat belts. I'm going to try to move this plane. I'm going to be honest and tell you now that I don't know if it will work, but it's our only chance. If this doesn't work, we'll get you out through the hole we climbed through." Cole eyed the enormous tree that cut across the main section of the cabin. You couldn't crawl above it and you couldn't crawl under it. If he could get the plane to move backward, free of the trees, they could torch the back end the way they'd torched the front. He wished he could see better. "I'm going to the front now. Hang on and pray. Which one of you is Chesney Brighton?" He held his breath, willing there to be an answer he could report back to Rand.

"I'm Chesney Brighton," the senior stewardess shouted.

"Jesus." He'd come a long way to hear that. "Buckle up."

Riley was in the copilot's seat, the bodies of his predecessors lying next to each other in the cramped space behind the cockpit seats.

"Chesney's alive. I talked to her," Cole said, sliding into the pilot's seat.

"Great! That's what we came to hear. What say we get this show on the road."

Cole nodded as he studied the panel in front of him. He'd never flown an L1011. He could feel Riley's eyes on him. "This is a Coleman plane, Riley," Cole said in a hushed voice.

Riley's voice was low, almost a whisper. "Yeah, I know. My father went down in a Coleman plane over Vietnam. Let's hope you guys at Coleman Aviation are making them better these days."

"You check this bird out?" Cole asked nervously.

"Yeah. No more talk. Do it!"

"Easy for you to say." Cole's teeth were clenched so hard, he thought his jaw would crack. "If that monster on our left comes crashing down, we're dead meat; you know that, right?"

"You do that, you shithead, and I'll never know if Ivy Buckalew is the one for me."

Cole winced. "Never let it be said I stood in the way of true love. Give me a go." Riley's eyes flew over the indicator lights. Cole's knuckles glowed whitely on the throttle. The behemoth strained, the jet engines thundered. All about them timber cracked, louder than the sound of the jets.

"Again," Riley shouted. "You're sure about Ivy Buckalew?"

"You son of a bitch!" Cole cursed, his face wet with sweat. "What happened to the fucking tree?"

"It's hanging right over our heads. Come on, move this bastard. You built it, you know what it can do. Do it!"

"I hope Ivy Buckalew tells you to take a hike, you asshole."

"Not a chance. I just pissed my pants."

"One more time, baby. Coleman Aircraft, don't fail us now."

Riley's face turned as white as Cole's knuckles on the

throttle. His face was as wet as Cole's, his dark hair plastered to his head.

The sound was like a tidal wave crashing and thundering as the plane groaned and moved backward, slowly at first, then picking up speed. Thunder rolled in their ears as tree after tree crashed downward. They felt the rush of cold air when the bottom and the back end of the plane ripped free. The tree straddling the middle of the plane dropped to the ground.

"You did it! You son of a bitch, you did it!" Riley almost exploded in his excitement. He snapped his fingers under Cole's eyes. "Hey, wake up. You're a fucking hero!"

"Just tell Ivy Buckalew I did it for her!" Cole gasped.

Riley stared at his cousin. This still wasn't the time. "Come on, let's do what we came here to do."

They made their way to the middle of the plane, which was sheared in two. Now all they had to do was crawl over the tree, fight their way to the back, and wait for the men with the torches. Rand would have his daughter in his arms in a matter of hours.

On the second day after Christmas, in the early evening darkness, Riley Coleman carried Chesney Brighton, the last to leave the plane, to her father. "There's a man waiting out there for you. He's come a long way to get you. Welcome to the family, Chesney; we're cousins by marriage. The guy who backed this plane out is your other cousin—he's Maggie Nelson's son. Probably a brother or something to you now. In case you haven't figured all of this out, we take care of our own. We're family."

No matter what the disaster, no matter what the outcome, there were always hordes of volunteers and a reporter. This one was from the *London Times*. Riley blinked in the bright lights. Now they get here. Now, when all the work was done. Christ, he was tired.

He tried not to look at the body bags. His eyes searched for Rand, who was approaching at a dead run over the snow, slipping and sliding. He reached for his daughter, tears streaming down his cheeks.

"Careful, Rand, her shoulder is broken. A couple of ribs, too, I think."

His arms outstretched, Rand gathered his daughter close. He thought he was dreaming when he heard Chesney whisper, "Daddy."

* * *

Three days before the beginning of the New Year, the Coleman family gathered around the television set for the late-night news. The earlier forecast had promised extensive aerial as well as ground footage of the heroic rescue mission of Flight 214.

The aerial footage was shown first. The Colemans sat transfixed.

"I've never seen such monstrous trees," Billie bleated. "However will they get them off the plane? They almost look as if they'd been planted around it."

"Maybe for protection," Maggie said crazily. "Believe it or not, they could be offering warmth of some kind to the passengers." They all nodded. It was easy to accept Maggie's words since they had none of their own.

Dan Rather's professional voice cut through again. "We were told earlier that three Texans, members of the Coleman family, are on the scene. As yet, we don't know why they're there. We'll have more coverage on that development later in the program. As you can see on this particular film clip, the trees are covering the plane; the tree in the middle appears to have sheared the plane in half. The awkward angle of the aircraft, our experts tell us, points to that as the only possibility. Bear with me a moment; this note was just handed to me. The L1011 is a Coleman plane, so perhaps that explains why Colemans are at the scene of the crash site."

"Good God!" Sawyer exclaimed.

They watched the news, the sports, and then the weather. It was about twenty minutes past the hour when Rather's jubilant voice filled the quiet room. "We now have the film clip of the heroic rescue." They watched, hardly daring to breathe, as fur-clad men carried stretchers away from the wreckage. Tears streamed from Billie's eyes at the lost, frightened look on the passengers' faces. It seemed to take forever, but in actuality, it was only minutes.

"There's only nineteen. I only counted nineteen." Sawyer wept with despair. "And I don't see Chesney."

"There's Cole, but I don't see Rand or Riley," Maggie cried.

"There they are! See, that's Riley, and he's . . . he's carrying someone! See, there's Rand!" Amelia shouted in her frail voice.

"He's crying. Rand is crying," Maggie wailed. "I never saw Rand cry."

Billie's arms comforted her daughter as they continued to watch the screen. They watched as Riley transferred his burden into Rand's open arms.

"Is that Chesney? My God, she's dead!" Maggie screamed. "They found her and she's dead!"

"Maggie, look!" Thad cried. The still form in Rand's arms stirred, one arm swinging crazily. They could see the girl struggle to speak. The one word was unmistakable. Daddy.

Maggie fainted.

Adam ran to the kitchen for a wet cloth. Minutes later, Maggie moaned. "Are you all right, darling?" Billie crooned.

"I never fainted in my life." Maggie struggled to get up. "It was real, wasn't it? She's alive and safe with Rand."

"Yes, darling, she's safe. Sit up and we'll get you a cup of tea. According to my wife, that makes everything right side up," Thad said.

"I'll make it," Jeff volunteered.

"Make me one, too, and how about some of those Christmas cookies?" Adam called to the boy's retreating back.

"We have God to thank for this. Always, in our darkest hours, He comes through for us," Billie said quietly. "Always."

Geneva Airport was back to normal. All that remained of the vicious storm was mountains of snow and cold weather. Weary travelers were on their way, thanks to the efficient ground crews, who worked night and day to clear runways so planes could land and takeoff safely. Tired cargo personnel and baggage handlers ticketed tons of baggage and sent it on its way, some late, some on time. The concourse was clear now, and fresh-faced, alert-eyed reservations clerks were going about their business, to the delight of everyone. The nightmare was over.

Steven Neibauer sat in the airport VIP lounge, staring into space. They'd all been kind to him when they told him about his mother and what she'd done on board Flight 214. He hadn't been home, and he wasn't going home now. He was going back to Akron, Ohio, with his mother's body.

He'd called his sister a few hours earlier to tell her about the plane crash. He'd called again to tell her the bad news. He hadn't tried to soften the blow; he'd blurted out the news coldly. He'd never be sure if what he heard in his sister's voice was relief or . . . grief. He thought he told her to go to hell, but he wasn't sure of that either. All he could do now was take his mother's body, and his own guilt, and return to his roots. And try to come to terms with it all. Too much, too little, too late. All that he was, all that he would ever be, he owed to his mother, and he'd never taken the time to tell her. "Mom, I am so sorry," he cried.

Jeff Sanders, unshaven and wild-eyed, stared across at the crying man. He knew who he was; the police had told him. Steven Neibauer. They'd come for him Christmas evening and literally dragged him here, and he'd come, hangover and all, not comprehending what the officers were telling him at first. Then, when realization set in, he'd cried. He'd spoken to his child's mother, who told him in no uncertain terms to "handle it, Jeff; you're Molly's father, and I'm getting married in a few days."

Jesus, he could hardly remember what the kid looked like. The last time he'd seen a picture of her, she was two years old and naked in a bathtub.

He stared at the man sitting across from him; he was still crying. His old mother was the one who saved Molly. He should say something, he supposed, but what?

They talked then, those two men, about everything under the sun.

When the airport manager walked through the double doors with Molly, Jeff Sanders ran to her. She drew back. He reached out a tentative hand to nuzzle the dog's ears. Gus whimpered in delight. Molly smiled and let her father pick her up. He was stunned to see how pretty she was, how warm she felt, how good. "I might not look like much right now, and I might not be worth a whole hell of a lot, but I'm going to give you my best shot. See that guy over there? He said I can call him anytime if I need help."

"Is his name Stevie?" Molly asked. Her father nodded. She wiggled out of his arms and ran to Steven Neibauer. She put her chubby fist into the pocket of her red coat and withdrew the rabbit's foot. She held it out shyly. "Can I keep this?" Molly asked, pointing to the colored macaroni necklace. Steven nodded, unable to speak. Molly put the rabbit's foot into his outstretched hand.

The airport manager spoke. "Mr. Neibauer, if you'll come with me . . ."

Outside in the frigid air, thirty-two young men waited for the courtesy van that would take them to Saint Clare's Hospital. They were going to offer their support to a fellow athlete, the best of them all.

"We have the best sports doctors in the world," an American skier said.

"Bah, in Russia we have the best. You Americans, you are too soft. . . . We know about bones."

"Bullshit," a German youth muttered. "We have the best!"

"You are wrong, gentlemen; France is known for its orthopedic surgeons."

"What the hell," the American groaned. "Between us we'll make sure Mitch has the best. Pile in gang; he's waiting."

They arrived at Sunbridge at ten o'clock on New Year's Eve. Maggie stood rooted to the floor when Sumi ran to Cole, Sawyer to Riley, and Billie to the young woman's side.

"Welcome to Sunbridge, Chesney. I'm Rand's mother-in-law, Billie Kingsley," Billie said warmly.

"She has a broken shoulder and assorted cuts and bruises. We've got her all taped up. Tomorrow she sees our doctor. Right now I think she should be put to bed," Rand said quietly, his eyes glued to his daughter.

"I think you're right," Billie said. She led Chesney up the stairs.

Rand's eyes searched out his wife. He grinned. Maggie grinned back.

"I think I have a daughter, and not just in name only," Rand said happily.

"I think you do, too, Rand. We all prayed," Maggie said, going into her husband's arms.

"Maggie, remember when Sawyer had her operation and you said you could hear the choir? I heard it, too. Not on the ground when we were searching. When we were airborne, right before we landed. I know I heard it. Cole said it was some kind of interference. He won't admit it, but he heard it, too. You should have seen the look on his face. Riley didn't hear anything, or so he says."

"Wasn't it the most beautiful sound you ever heard?"

An hour later the smile was still on Rand's face as he drifted into a sound sleep.

Maggie covered her sleeping husband tenderly. Before she went downstairs, she stopped in her old nursery. How appropriate that Rand's daughter should rest here. She looked down at the sleeping girl, tears filling her eyes. "We have so much to give. All we ask is that you meet us halfway," she whispered. She bent over to brush her lips against the girl's cool forehead and to smooth the tangled hair back from her face.

From the landing on the stairwell she called down to the family. "I think we should all celebrate the New Year by emptying out Sunbridge's water tanks and hitting the sack. Tomorrow is New Year's, and I know it's going to be a wonderful year for all of us. Our numbers are increased by one: We have a lot to be thankful for."

"Hear, hear! I second the lady," Thad said happily. They trouped up the stairs, following Thad as though he were the Pied Piper.

{{{{{{{{{ CHAPTER TWENTY-THREE }}}}}}}}}

Riley walked through the first floor of Sunbridge, touching the back of a chair, straightening a lamp shade, stooping to pick lint off the carpet, anything to keep his hands and mind busy. His home. He then made his rounds to check the windows and lights, wearily heading for the front door to turn off the outside light, the light that welcomed them all back to Sunbridge.

It was all his now. His, because of Cole's generosity. He frowned in the dim light of the hallway. He had to give Cole's deed back to him. There was no way he could claim Cole's heritage as his own. He should have given it back to Cole a long time ago, but the intense feeling he had when he held both deeds in his hands was so strong, so . . . so right, he'd procrastinated, just as he'd procrastinated in making up with Cole.

If there was one thing in life Riley hated, it was admitting he was wrong. It went against everything in him. . . . He wanted to be perfect, to be right about everything. He knew it wasn't possible; it had never been possible. A man was what he was. Two wrongs never made something right. That's what he had to apologize to Cole for.

A sound jarred at Riley, a creak on the stairway. "Cole! I thought you went to bed." Thank God. Cole was making it easy for him. Cole always made it easy for him. Out of stubbornness he'd been deaf and blind to Cole and their years of friendship.

"I did, but I came back down. I thought this might be a

good time for us to talk. Talk, Riley, no slugfest tonight; I'm too tired. I don't know about you, but I *need* to talk to you."

"I'm glad you came down, Cole. You don't have to say anything. It's me who has to talk, to explain, to apologize. I've been meaning to . . . to give you this," Riley said, reaching into his pocket.

"If that's what I think it is, I don't want it. You know that, Riley, and if you don't, then something is wrong somewhere. I thought . . . I would have sworn that you, Riley, knew me better than anyone."

"Cole . . . I wanted to make amends a thousand times, but something always stopped me. I never knew what that something was until just a few minutes ago. I physically beat you within an inch of your life. You let me do that to you. You didn't fight back. All these months I asked myself why, why didn't you hit me back? You could have, you know, but no, you let me pound away at you till you were a bloody pulp. Then you really flipped me the bird when you handed over your half of Sunbridge. You just handed it over like a candy bar. Until a few minutes ago I didn't know why. You gave me Sunbridge in anger, and I accepted it in anger. This is our home, yours and mine. Cole, look at me and tell me if I'm wrong. You *knew* when I was pounding away at you that I was pounding away at myself. Your pain was my pain. You knew that, too. That's why you didn't lift a finger to defend yourself. You took that beating for me. There isn't another person in this universe who would do that for me. I left you there to die when it was me who wanted to die. You *knew* that, too. I let you down, Cole, and I don't know if I can forgive myself for that. What you did for me . . . How . . . how can I ever make it up to you?"

Cole grinned. "That was one hell of an apology! And you don't owe me anything. All I want is for you to have your head on straight. Is it, Riley?"

Riley grinned. "Pretty much so. Cole, I've never spent a more miserable time in my life. I won't admit this to anyone but you: I have ulcers." He paused and extended his hand. In it was Cole's deed to Sunbridge. "Here," Riley said.

Cole shook his head and stepped back. "It doesn't work that way, Riley. Sunbridge can only have one slave. If my words offend you, I'm sorry. I would have said mistress, but the word doesn't fit. You belong here. I don't. The bottom line is, I want *you* to have Sunbridge. Riley, please, don't look at me like I'm giving you my life's blood; I'm not. I'm giving you what you want most in this life: your father's home—yours now."

"What will you do, Cole?" Riley asked softly.

Cole grinned. "I was sort of thinking about going to Chicago and getting a job at Sears, Roebuck. That's down the road. What's important now is to get you on track. Don't worry; if you slip, I'll be here to pick you up and dust you off. Let's forget the past; it's history." Cole wasn't sure if the tears were in his own eyes or in Riley's.

Riley stretched out his hand. "You're right, it's history."

Cole ignored Riley's outstretched arm. "If that's the best you can do, we aren't going to get anywhere," Cole said gruffly. He covered the distance between them and wrapped his arms about his cousin. "I'm not afraid to show you I care. Jesus, Riley, you're the brother I never had. Family, Riley. You and I are family, and I don't want either of us to forget it ever again."

Riley thumped Cole's back. "You're one in a million, Cole."

Cole grasped Riley's shoulders and pushed him backward till their eyes were level. The single tear sliding down Riley's cheek told Cole all he needed to know.

The family, their family; all of *them* would be safe in Riley's hands.

"I know what you're thinking, Cole. I've always been able to read you like a book," Riley said quietly.

"Not all the time, cousin. Only those times that I . . . Yeah, you always could read me."

"I'll take care of *them*; you can count on it."

"I know that; so do they. Listen, you were a rock these past days. I couldn't have done it without you." His tone took on a light, bantering note. "If I were you, I'd call Buckalew Big Wells. This family needs some new blood. Some *more* new blood, I should say."

Riley flushed, something Cole had never seen him do before. "Yeah, I'll do that. By the way, congratulations on . . . Sumi. I should be the one to tell you she's a real buzz saw, and when she isn't buzzing, she doubles as a barracuda. Watch it or she'll have you dancing on a string." Riley grinned.

Cole could feel heat on his neck. "I like to dance. I love her; what can I say?"

"That pretty much covers it. She's perfect for you, Cole, and I'm happy for both of you."

This time Cole's hand shot out. "Friends?"

"You bet," Riley said, reaching out for Cole's offered hand. "You bet."

The New Year yawned ahead of the Colemans like an open abyss. They spoke of the changes in their lives: Thad's retirement, Rand's new daughter, Cole's and Sawyer's late spring weddings. They managed to avoid discussing Amelia's failing health or Riley's business with Coleman Oil.

To Billie it seemed like a time for miracles and sharing confidences, hopes, and dreams for the future. She was happier than she'd ever been. She and Thad could travel, visit, or just hang out with the dogs at the farm. Together, they'd continue Amelia's work with the aged. She'd find a couple of bright young designers to take over Billie, Inc. She and Thad would . . . enjoy life.

Somewhere during these past months, she'd come to terms with the possibility that Coleman Enterprises could go under. They'd all given their best; there was nothing anyone could do. She'd even come to terms with Amelia's failing health. No one, Amelia'd said, was to hang around, or hover. What would be would be. Billie had promised, with tears in her eyes, that she'd go on with her plans.

She looked around now at her brood and the people they'd chosen to share their lives with. All she'd ever wanted, her whole life long, was a family, and to have that family be happy. Thad said she was batting a near thousand.

Cole and Sumi. She'd never seen this open, smiling, unreserved side of her grandson before. And Sumi, beautiful little Sumi. Cole's perfect match. How was it none of them had ever thought of Sumi with regard to Cole? If they had, they would have meddled, and probably ruined this wonderful relationship which was unfurling in front of their very eyes. Cole was happy for the first time in his life, and Maggie positively basked in her son's happiness.

Sawyer, Adam, and Jeff. A ready-made family. How happy they were! God alone had decreed that Sawyer live to unite this little family. Even from here she could see the love in Sawyer's eyes. There were no words to describe what Sawyer called Adam's sappy expression. The boy was beaming, too.

Maggie and Rand. Rand and Maggie. A pair, a matched set, like herself and Thad. Now they were three. Another ready-made family. A daughter for Maggie to fuss over. A daughter for Rand to share with. They were all going back to

Hawaii—together. When she'd asked for how long, Rand had said for as long as it takes for Chesney to mend, to rest, to plan. God's hand again.

Susan and Ferris and Jessie. How happy they were with their lives and the good things their foundation made possible for other children like Jessie, victims of spina bifida. Again His hand had set them on the right path. In doing for others, they found their own happiness. Billie applauded her daughter.

Julie with the warm eyes and crinkly smile. Thad's favorite niece. Her happiness would come. Everything was in perspective for Julie now. She was so much like Thad. She'd shoulder the burden, take the blame before she'd let anyone else do it. It was easy to see why Amelia adored her and why Julie felt so close to Amelia. She'd been blessed with all of Thad's wonderful traits, Billie thought, smiling at her across the room. Julie would be happy. It just wasn't her time yet.

Amelia and Cary. This Christmas had meant so much to Amelia. All her family here to see her. She hadn't been fooled; she knew Cole had arranged it. "You don't usually think of young men caring so much. I never saw that side of Cole. He's deep, Billie. My regret is that I won't be here to see that side of him mature and grow. I don't understand why he felt he had to cover that part of him up. We had a long talk, Cole and I. He said something that astounded me. He didn't beat around the bush or anything—straight out. He said he didn't think death was something to be afraid of but rather something to look forward to. Not with glee or wild expectation. He said whatever good we leave here on earth will follow us. He said the good is like a snowball. When it all catches up, in that place we're all going to, it will be a time of such happiness that we can't even begin to comprehend. Peace and happiness, he said. He spoke with such intensity, Billie. That young man made a believer out of me. I'm not chomping at the bit to go, but I'm not afraid anymore. You keep telling me that God works in mysterious ways, and I know now what that means." Amelia was going to be all right. Cary's life was on hold now. Every waking hour was devoted to Amelia. They'd made their peace.

Riley, her first grandson. Had they placed too heavy a burden on his broad shoulders, or had he done that himself? Sometimes she wasn't sure. She could not help him now. Whatever was to become of Coleman Oil was strictly up to Riley. She was prepared, and so were the others. There would be no blame if things didn't go right. He'd done his best and would continue to do so until he dropped. Old Seth's bones must be rattling in his grave. Thad said Riley was between a rock and a hard place. Her eyes were loving as she looked around. Riley and the others, her family. Whatever would be, would be.

The room seemed lighter, brighter somehow, when her eyes searched out her husband.

Another holiday over. Now his life was about to open for him. He'd done his share, he'd contributed. Now it was his turn. Billie knew that he felt young and almost giddy with relief that Washington would be behind him. No more clocks, no more votes, no more meetings. He wouldn't have to listen to the lies, turn his head so as not to see the wheeling and dealing. Power—let them keep it. He even looked younger, Billie thought.

Her eyes circled the room once more. The mountain of luggage attested to the fact that all these warm, wonderful people were going their separate ways. They'd gather again, many times—for birth or death, celebration or disaster. All it would take would be a phone call, and they would all be on their way. To their home base.

Home to Sunbridge.

Thad looked around the room. It seemed lighter, brighter somehow. He held his arms open, and Billie came to him. She was smiling at him. He should have known. For years now he'd seen Maggie and Billie's smiles light up rooms.

"I'm taking you home with me," Thad whispered.

"And . . ."

"The rest is a surprise."

"A clue," Billie begged.

"I have the secret. If you behave yourself, I might share it with you."

"The boys in the cloakroom finally told you," Billie said, her voice filled with awe.

Thad's face was serious when he nodded. He kissed her on the tip of her nose.

"Finally, the answer. Poor Ted Koppel. But if kissing my nose is the best you can do, I'm staying here." Thad bent down and kissed her, a long, sweet, lingering kiss that promised a lifetime of togetherness. When they drew apart, the family clapped and cheered. They bowed formally, accepting the approval and love.

Their family.

The knock on the front door signaled the arrival of the

airport limo. Ferris, Susan, and Jessie, along with Maggie, Rand, Chesney, and Julie, would be dropped off at their respective airlines. Cole was dropping Sumi off later, but for now he was taking her into town. Sawyer would return to Japan one more time—but not for long. Only Riley would remain behind to operate his EOR program and find a replacement for Sawyer. Only Riley, at Sunbridge.

Cary had his own car warming up. Amelia's bags and wheelchair were already loaded, along with all their Christmas presents.

For two days the family had wrapped parcels to be shipped to their respective addresses so they wouldn't have to carry all their loot on the plane.

The good-byes were tearful and poignant. There were no dry eyes, Billie noticed.

Riley stood alone in the open doorway.

They were gone. All his family was gone. It was hard to believe that just minutes ago, days ago, the house had been filled to the rafters with laughter and love. Now it was as if they'd never been here. Even the Christmas tree had been dismantled, the ornaments carried back to the attic. Riley felt like he was alone in the Astrodome and someone had just turned off the lights.

He closed the front door and walked through the rooms, the silence roaring in his ears. He clapped his hands overhead just to hear the sound. His pace quickened as he switched on every radio and television set in the house. His reward was a jumble of sound that made him clench his fists.

This emptiness was all his now. His father's home. Now it was all his. He'd cut away his past and centered his whole being here. He couldn't go back now even if he wanted to, which he didn't.

Riley uncapped a bottle of Heineken from the portable bar and sat in a big upholstered chair, his feet on the coffee table. He had four hours to kill until Adam and Sawyer picked him up to go to the airport—all the time in the world—time to think, to plan, to dream. He tried to sit still and think, but he was restless, wired up. He heaved himself out of the chair and began to pace the room.

He parted the curtains at the window. It was cold and gray outside. The bare trees looked old, skeletal and arthritic. They had to be over a hundred years old, he decided. There was nothing warm or comforting about the vast expanse of land that stretched before him. He could feel anxiety start to build in him. He could lose all of this—this emptiness, this vastness, this barn of a house. His teeth ground together. His fists clenched at his sides. The desire to put both his balled fists through the pane of glass was strong. He knew in that instant he was capable of killing to preserve what was his father's.

A long time ago Nick had told Sawyer there was nothing wrong with wanting it all. Everyone wanted It All. It was the way you went about getting it that mattered, Nick had said. He'd also said it wasn't important if you won or lost, but how you played the game. If it wasn't important, Riley wondered, then why did they keep score? Or was it himself who was keeping score?

Riley walked back to his chair. He polished off the beer and opened another one. He swigged furiously. He couldn't remember the last time he'd had beer at noon.

On an impulse he picked up the phone. He probably wasn't the Buckalews' favorite person these days, but he didn't care. He wondered why she hadn't stopped by. Ivy always stopped by, if only to pester.

"You didn't stop by," Riley blurted when Ivy picked up the phone.

"You didn't either. My rusty bucket of bolts isn't running."

"You want to use my Bronco, it's yours. It's just sitting here."

"You could have dropped me a card," Ivy said coolly.

"You want to go for a sandwich or something?"

"You gonna pick me up like a date? Get out of the car and ring the doorbell?"

"Hell no. I think your father would like it better if he never saw me again."

"Okay, I'll meet you by the gate. How long?"

"You got another date or something?"

"I might. This is the last minute, you know. A girl could get a bad reputation accepting last-minute invitations."

"Be by the damn gate in twenty minutes."

"I don't know anything about Lacey's love life. So don't plan on asking me any questions about her. You still want to pick me up?" Ivy asked fearfully.

"Just be by the damn gate."

Ivy grinned when the phone clicked.

Twenty minutes. Just enough time to fix her makeup and

put on earrings. Shoot, she should have plucked her eyebrows last night instead of watching television. The gray flannel slacks and electric-blue sweater would do just fine. Riley probably wouldn't notice. He probably wouldn't notice her fashionable haircut, either, or the fact that she now had fingernails all the same size and color. She wondered if she could work in the fact that she'd graduated magna cum laude. The only person so far to be impressed was Lacey.

There was no reason to tell Riley that she and Lacey were good friends these days. They'd even visited each other. Later, maybe she'd tell him. Providing there was a later.

She was waiting at the gate, stomping her feet on the cold driveway to keep them warm. Her heart thumped when the Bronco approached. Her knees felt weak when she climbed into the truck.

Riley looked at her for a long minute. "You look different, squirt."

"That's because I am different," Ivy said sweetly. "I got a haircut and I don't bite my nails anymore. I wear feminine clothes and earrings. And if you plan on mocking me out, say so now and I'll get the hell out of this truck."

"Whoa. I just said you look different."

"You called me a squirt. I don't think I'm a squirt, and I don't look like a squirt. I'm your equal. I managed to graduate magna cum laude. Now what do you have to say?"

"Jesus! You want to climb out and climb back in and we can start over?"

"No. I've said what I had to say. You look awful, Riley. What's wrong? Too much Christmas?"

"I don't really feel in the mood to go public. How about coming back to Sunbridge. There's tons of leftovers."

"That's fine with me. What's with the tons of food?"

"Adam's clearing out of the ranch, and he dumped the contents of his refrigerator into ours. The whole family was home for the holidays. Now it's just me. All by my lonesome, and I'm leaving later this afternoon. One more crack at the South American deal, but I don't have much hope. Then—"

"So this is hello and good-bye?"

"Yeah, I guess it is. Does that bother you?"

"No. Yes. I don't know. Was calling me an afterthought? A way to fill in a few hours?"

"I didn't want to be alone. I walked through that damn house and suddenly I didn't want to be alone. I wanted to talk to someone. You weren't a second or third choice. I wanted to talk to *you*. By the way, you look great."

"I know. I've really been working at it. Have to beat the guys off with a stick. You wouldn't believe the offers I've had," Ivy lied.

"Oh yeah?" Riley said sourly. Ivy tried to hide her smile.

"Yeah. Did you think I was going to wait for you forever?"

"Hell, I didn't know you were waiting. Come off it, Ivy."

"You're a jerk, Riley. Why do you think I was always under your feet? I was happy only when you were chasing me away. When you chased me away you talked to me. You paid attention. I must have been nuts."

Riley ground the Bronco to a halt at the side of the road. "You mean you had a crush on me back then?" he asked stupidly.

"That's a quaint way of putting it. I'd have let you strip me naked in the middle of my father's driveway if that's what you wanted."

"Jesus Christ!" Riley breathed.

"Don't go getting any ideas that I'm easy. You want my body, you're going to fight for it. I should also mention that I'm a virgin. I've been saving myself for you."

"Jesus Christ!"

"You already said that. Be more original. I'm not going to bed with you this afternoon either. I told you I'm saving myself. The only way you get this bod is to marry it. I could probably handle some heavy necking. . . ."

"That's enough of that kind of talk," Riley said.

Ivy smiled as Riley tried three times before he got the Bronco going without stripping the gears.

Riley watched as Ivy carved off thick slices of white meat from the leftover turkey and spread the sandwiches with butter and Russian dressing and a layer of lettuce. She added four cookies to the tray, and some napkins. Riley carried the beer.

They ate with gusto. They talked about everything and anything.

Ivy looked at her watch. "I have to get back, Riley. If that offer of your Bronco still holds, I'd like to take you up on it."

"Sure. Don't run it into the ground, okay? Remember to have the oil checked and put air in the tires once in a while."

"Okay. You can kiss me here," she said, pointing to her cheek. "If you miscalculate, I'll be dragging you upstairs, and

I'm not ready for that. It isn't in my game plan." Riley did as instructed.

Riley watched the Bronco till it was out of sight. He wished he knew what it was Ivy had to do and why she had to leave. He had to shove these feelings he was experiencing as far back as he could. He had other things on his mind.

Inside the house again, he felt as if he were back in the Astrodome. The emptiness shrieked at him. Ivy's presence had filled the room. He'd felt good for a while. Now Sunbridge was just a house again. An empty house.

It was almost dark. Time to turn on every light in the house.

In the kitchen he put away the food and washed off the counter.

There was something he had to do, and if he was going to do it, now was the time. In all the years he'd been at Sunbridge, he'd never climbed the hill behind the house. He'd seen it from the range when he'd been out riding, but he'd never felt the need or the desire to visit the dead. He'd never stood at his mother's grave in Japan, either. That site, too, was a hill. A mountain if you weren't ready to climb it.

Riley clamped his baseball cap on his head. The shearling jacket was old and worn, but warm as toast. He was ready.

Cole and Sumi stood on the balcony of the Coleman apartment at Assante Towers, their arms around each other. There was only an hour left before they'd have to leave for the airport, but Cole knew there was something he had to do in this hour. Even if it meant losing these last few precious minutes with Sumi.

"Sumi, do you mind if I leave you here for a little while?" he asked. He kissed the top of her head. "I have to do something."

"Is it Riley?"

"Yes. I have this feeling that he needs me. Maybe he doesn't. Maybe I want him to need me. I can't explain it. I only know I have to go back."

"I'll be here," she said. "Help him, Cole."

Cole swung his car into the Sunbridge courtyard, noticing at the same time that the Bronco was missing. The whole damn house was lit up like a Christmas tree. He called Riley's name as he walked through the rooms, switching off radios and televisions. He ran up the stairs, taking them two at a time. Riley's bag was packed, his briefcase next to it. Cole ran back down to the kitchen. Something wasn't right. His eyes swept the room. The coat rack was empty. Riley's shearling jacket always hung there. And his baseball cap was gone, too.

Cole yanked open the drawer where the flashlight was kept. It was gone. He ran to the courtyard, straining his eyes in the darkness. Riley had gone up the hill. From here he could see the tiny beam of light, moving farther away.

Grimly, his hands stuffed in his jacket pockets, Cole started the climb after his cousin. Riley had gone straight up over the layered snow, ignoring the path. Cole stopped to take a deep breath before approaching the clearing. The small circle of light showed that Riley was moving about. Cole squeezed his eyes shut, trying to remember the order of the graves. Grandpa Seth, his three horses, all named Nessie; Grandmam Jessie, Grandpa Moss, and then Riley's father's simple cross. That's where he was. The circle of light stopped and then went out. Cole moved closer. He crouched down, ready to spring if Riley had it in his mind to do something stupid. He had no intention of listening to what Riley was saying, but if he were to move now, Riley would hear him and think he was spying. The wind picked up his cousin's words and tossed them into Cole's ears. He listened as Riley bared his soul. Cole bit down so hard on his bottom lip, he drew blood.

He was numb with cold by the time Riley finally moved. The flashlight made a wide, swinging arc, coming to rest on his face. "You were in the area and thought you'd stop by," Riley said quietly.

"How did you know I was here? I didn't make a sound."

"I heard you the minute you stepped on the path."

"I wasn't spying. I thought you might be hurting. I came back because the feeling was so strong."

"I belong here," Riley said, waving his arms wide. "I want to be here."

"I know that, Riley, but you have to tell him."

"I will. I'll write a letter."

"It's easier going down," Cole said quietly, "and I'm not talking about the terrain."

"I'll take your word for it. You've never steered me wrong."

"My ass is frozen; let's go home," Cole grumbled.

"Home?"

"Your home. I'm a visitor. Come on, Riley, we'll all be up

here soon enough; let's not freeze and give them an edge."

Riley went first, his flashlight low to the ground, pointing the way.

A sound behind Cole made him turn. The ground trembled beneath his feet. The disturbance seemed to be coming from the direction of old Seth's grave. Or was it the obscene burial plots of his horses? The ground continued to shake. Cole's lips drew back in a snarl.

"He belongs here, you old bastard. This is all his now; I've seen to that, and don't you ever forget it!" He didn't feel stupid at all when he shook his balled-up fist in the direction of his great-grandfather's grave.

At the bottom of the hill Cole grabbed Riley's arm. "Did you feel that tremor on the hill?"

"What tremor?"

"It felt like the earth was rumbling, you know. Moving, right under my feet."

"Your feet are cold. That's probably what it was. You coming in?"

"I'll take a rain check. I left Sumi back at the condo. I'd like a little time with her before I have to take her to the airport. Good luck, Riley. You need me, call." His hand shot out, but Riley ignored it. Instead, he reached for his cousin. They clapped each other on the back. "See you around."

"Sooner than you think. You didn't tell me who was going to be your best man."

"I'm looking at him."

"Cole?"

"Yeah."

"Thanks."

"Any time."

Riley sat down at the kitchen table with paper and pen. He'd write the letter to his grandfather now. Now, before he lost his nerve. Writing this letter was going to be the hardest thing he'd ever done in his life, worse even than the climb up the hill. He prayed a moment for guidance.

Dear Grandfather,

The only excuse I can offer, Grandfather, for not writing sooner is that your grandson is a coward. For a while I forgot my early teachings and also the teachings of the Coleman family.

Your unworthy grandson wanted everything: you, my family in Japan, and everything here that was my father's. I wanted to give up nothing. For a time I thought it was possible. I know now, after much soul-searching, that it is not possible. I've made my decision.

Please, Grandfather, I beg you to understand that which I am about to write. I do not expect forgiveness. There is no way I can ever make up for the pain and anguish I have caused you. Know in your heart that my own pain and anguish is as heavy as your own.

I plan to stay here in Texas. This is my home. Cole has deeded his half of Sunbridge to me. At first I couldn't believe he would be so generous with me. I've come to learn that my cousin hates this place as much as I love it. I understand Cole now, just as he understands me.

I want to believe, wise one, that in the back of your mind you always knew that I would remain here. It was you, Grandfather, who sent me here to my father's people.

Today, just minutes ago, I visited the Coleman gravesite. There is only a plain wooden cross there with my father's name on it. His spirit was there; I felt it. I talked to that spirit, and when I walked away, I knew I'd made the right decision.

I love you, Grandfather, as I love no other human being on the face of the earth. I must believe that your love for me is as strong. If I believed otherwise, I would not be writing this letter to you. I would cause my own death before I brought shame on you or our family. I say this because I want you to know there is no shame in my decision to stay here.

I pray each day for your health. You are never out of my thoughts. For the first time since my arrival in Texas, as a little boy, I feel free to be who I really am. I must act on that freedom.

Forgive this unworthy grandson of yours. If your heart cannot grant this request, I will forgive you, for I love you as much as life. I sign this your unworthy grandson,

Riley.

Riley read the letter over twice. Satisfied that everything he wanted to say was said, he inserted it in an envelope. He licked a stamp. The letter was ready to go. He'd leave it on the table in the front hall with a note for Jonquil, and she'd mail it tomorrow.

Riley heard the front door open and Sawyer's voice, yelling at him to hurry. He heard the car horn beep twice. A blast of frigid air whipped through the hallway as he grabbed his bags and headed for the open front door. His index finger pressed the light switch a second too soon. The darkness hid the letter, which was lifted in the air and swirled to the floor, where it lay hidden behind the heavy curtains.

Riley drove away from Sunbridge with a light heart. It was time for him to sing his own song.

CHAPTER TWENTY-FOUR

{{{{{{{{{)))))))))

The battery of lawyers worked for seven straight hours to hammer out a working agreement between Coleman Enterprises and Adam Jarvis in regard to the Jarvis oil leases.

For a brief moment Riley felt like a thief when he looked at Adam's face. His voice was gruff but kind when he spoke. "It's only on paper, Adam. The ranch is still yours. If you think for one minute we'd take your family home, then you don't know the Colemans at all."

"But I just sold you—"

"On paper. *This* paper," Riley said, handing a blue folder to Adam, "gives it back. Didn't your lawyers . . . ?"

Adam shrugged, a dumbfounded look on his face. "I suppose they tried to tell me certain things. . . . I had other things on my mind . . . Jeff and Sawyer . . . the wedding. Hell, once you sell something, you sell it. The leases are different. I paid attention to those. Jesus, you guys are something."

"It was Grandmam Billie's idea. She felt, we all felt, the deal we worked out with the leases was more than fair. Now you can come back and saw wood anytime you want. I'd hate to think you wasted your money on that chain saw. What I'm trying to say is, you've given us a chance to regroup. Without these oil leases, we'd go under. Turnabout is fair."

"I wish we'd done this a little sooner. I had no idea you guys were in so much trouble. I've lived a very narrow existence this past year."

"I wish I'd done a lot of things sooner myself, and I wish I'd never set foot in South America. Hey, stick around; we're drilling at six tomorrow morning. You don't want to miss it, do you?"

"Sure do. Just send me the checks. Which field are you starting on?"

"The one bordering Granger's."

Adam raised his eyebrows. "I know from nothing when it comes to rigs and drilling. I draw cartoons, remember. I did drive out there yesterday, though, kind of to say good-bye to it all. Lots of activity going on at Granger's."

"Yeah, I know. I've been watching all that activity myself, and it's starting to make me nervous. They had a small fire the other day. Old man Granger is a tight-lipped man, a private one as well." Adam's look was sharp and questioning. "Not to worry, Adam; from here on in those fields and the adjacent ones are my worry. You can sit back and be a fat cat and collect royalties."

"Guess I'll see you around," Adam said softly.

"It's hard to say good-bye, isn't it?"

"Yeah, it is. Call me when the first well comes in so I can drink a toast to all your hard work."

"We already picked a name for the first well when it comes in." Riley grinned.

"*When*, not *if*?"

Riley laughed, a joyous sound. "Those geological studies were on the money. A perfect teacup formation. Even without it I can smell the oil. Coots smelled it, too. My gut tells me this first one is going to be a pup. Any ideas for names for the *big* one?"

"Surprise me. Kind of like giving birth and not having a name picked out. If the big one arrives before we come up with something, call it Coleman One. What's the name you came up with for the pup?"

"Junior."

Adam hitched up his Levi's. "Sounds okay to me. Do good by me, Riley."

"Count on it. Go on, get out of here. I have to drive out to the site so I can start making you rich."

On his way out of the building, Adam stopped at his lawyer's office. He waved the new contract under the man's nose. "You could have told me. Jesus, I almost bawled and made an ass out of myself."

"I tried, but your head was in Japan with Sawyer and with your son. You told me to take care of things and not bother you. I believe your exact words were, "Wrap it up and send me a check.""

"Well, yeah, but this is different.... They just gave ... Riley told me his grandmother..."

The attorney cleared his throat. "I think you should know that both Riley and Cole would have gone ahead and deeded the ranch back to you with or without Mrs. Kingsley's approval. It was their idea."

Adam shifted his weight from one foot to the other. "I think I knew that all along. I guess I wanted someone to say it out loud."

Adam's step felt light, his shoulders lighter as he exited the legal building. His world was right side up now. He let out a whoop of exultation as he walked to his car. "World, here we come, me and my family!"

Junior arrived almost on schedule, a week before Riley's predicted date. It was a small well by Texas standards, but a well nonetheless. It was christened the moment it was capped. Riley used the field phone to call Adam. "Crack that bottle, Adam; Junior arrived! As you toast me and Junior, make sure you remember I'm out here busting my ass while you're swilling the finest wine."

Adam laughed, a heavy, robust sound that crackled over the wires. "You should be getting back to work, Riley. One victory isn't enough. I want more. M-o-r-e! Well done, buddy."

"You're a son of a bitch!" Riley was grinning from ear to ear when he slammed the phone back into the hitch on the truck.

Two weeks after Junior was capped and drilling was under way for what Riley called the "big one," the Granger foreman showed up at the drill site. He was a tall, greasy man with a body odor so strong it cleared Riley's sinuses. He had a three-day stubble of beard and mean little eyes. Riley watched as the foreman hooked his thumbs in his belt and dug his boots into the ground. "Mr. Granger wants to know if you'd hop in my truck and come over for a talk."

"About what? Why doesn't he come here? Things are pretty wild right now."

"So I see. You struck oil! You got a capable foreman here. Thirty minutes, give or take, ain't going to make you richer or poorer. Mr. Granger is an old man and he wants to see you."

It was always like this—old versus young. It seemed like it was thrown in his face on a weekly basis. Rudy Granger was an old man—a broke old man. "Okay, okay, give me five minutes."

Thirty minutes later Riley was face-to-face with Rudy Granger. The man looked tired and beaten. Riley felt his heart start to flutter. The old man's voice rumbled out of his chest as he stuck out a gnarled, blue-veined hand. His curt nod was his way of thanking Riley for coming to see him.

"What can I do for you, Mr. Granger?" Riley asked. The other oilmen, even Granger's workers, called the old man Rudy. Granger nodded again at Riley's respectful tone.

The voice rumbled to life a second time. "Fifteen miles out I got a . . . poison well. I hear you're about to strike the big one." His arthritic hand waved about aimlessly. "Word travels in this business. If that poison well and the surrounding ones blow, everything for miles around will go with it, and that includes your new one and the 'big one' you're expecting. Biggest goddamn fire this state will ever see." He spat a long stream of tobacco juice that landed a scant inch from Riley's boots. "My foreman here will take you out to see it."

It wasn't a request; it was a demand. Riley had one foot in the Jeep when the old man called to him. "Coleman?"

Riley turned. "Yes, sir?"

"We ain't got no money to fight it."

Riley's shoulders sagged as he settled himself in the Jeep. Talk about being between a rock and a hard place. Just when he was almost ready to jump into the catbird seat.

Forty minutes later the foreman ground the Jeep to a halt. "There it is! We don't go no further."

"I see the flags. Look, I really don't know much about poison wells or fire fighting. What I do know is you need nitroglycerine for something like this. Call Red Adair."

"Adair works for big bucks, and he's out of the country fighting a fire."

"Coots Buckalew, then," Riley said desperately. He was visualizing the disaster the poison well was going to cause.

The foreman cleared his throat and spit out of the corner of his mouth. "Bad blood there. The boss said no."

"The hell with bad blood. I don't want my wells going up because of someone's wounded feelings. Jesus, the fields will be . . ." The idea was so horrible to Riley, he couldn't voice his thoughts.

"The boss was telling you the truth when he said there's no money to fight this. Adair charges a couple of mil for something like this." The foreman's mean eyes turned calculating. "My boss, he's an old man; this is all he has left. It's all me and the others have left, too. We're on half pay as it is. Everyone knows the Colemans have every piece of machinery built by man. You have the manpower and you have the money. The bottom line here is, if we go, so do you."

"Man, you got it wrong. We're hurting just the way you are. The Jarvis leases aren't all ours; we have a deal, a percentage. We'll barely survive until OPEC sends the prices up. In plain English, fella, we don't have the kind of money this fire calls for. No way!"

"Hock something," the foreman said sarcastically. He spit again for emphasis.

"I'm telling you we don't have the funds to fight a big fire. None of us are professionals except Coots Buckalew. We don't have half the machinery you need. The old man canceled Coots out, so where does that leave us?"

"And here I thought all you big-money Colemans were heroes," the foreman sneered.

"Just goes to show you shouldn't listen to gossip," Riley sneered back.

On the ride back to the Granger site, Riley's brain clicked frantically. The guy was right. They'd be wiped out, right down to their shoelaces, if the poison well exploded and fire swept the fields. Adam would say he understood, but he'd never forgive him. All the other oilmen who were hanging on by their teeth would be wiped out.

Riley poked his head into Granger's trailer. "Mr. Granger, I'll get back to you in an hour or so, if that's okay with you. I'd like to borrow the Jeep. My men will bring it back."

"Go ahead, son; do whatever you have to do."

"If—and this is a big *if*,—if I decide there's something I can do, do I have your permission to call Coots Buckalew?"

The grizzled old man stared at Riley for a full minute before he croaked out his answer. "Only if you swear to me that he's the only way to go. That man ain't gonna want to do any favors for me, and I ain't about to toady to him. You hear me, son?"

"I hear you, Mr. Granger. I'll get back to you."

Back at the Jarvis drill site, Riley gathered his crew together. He explained the situation. "I know next to nothing about fighting oil fires. I'm willing to learn because we could lose everything, along with everyone else. If that poison well blows, we might as well move to Rhode Island. I'll give you all a few minutes to think about it. I'll wait here, and I won't hold it against any of you if you vote no." Seven minutes later they were back. To a man they agreed to throw in with Rudy Granger.

Riley made his first phone call. When his grandfather's voice came over the wire, he almost wept. He inquired after the old one's health, the well-being of all his cousins, and the condition of the Zen garden and cherry blossom grove. The amenities over, Riley's voice changed to a hoarse, agonized plea. "Grandfather, I need your help. I need money, a lot of money. I have no right to ask, but ask I must. I'm not asking for myself; but for all the oilmen of Texas and for their families. There is every chance we won't be successful in putting out the fire, but I have confidence in Mr. Buckalew. You met him in Miranda last November. Will you help me, Grandfather?" Riley listened for a long time. He smiled then, the tears glistening in his eyes. "And I you, my grandfather. Yes, out of love. And Cole? You have no objections?" He listened again. The smile turned into a grin. "Make it airtight, Grandfather. Take care of yourself. If I can't call you myself in the next few days, Cole will call you. I am proud to be your grandson. Thank you, Grandfather." Riley wiped at his eyes with the back of his hand. Love, he decided, was a powerhouse.

Riley's second call was to Cole, back in Austin. Once again he explained the situation. "So I don't know anything about fires, I agree. I'm going to learn real fast. Go on, you shithead, tell me you're worried about me. Look, you're going to have to use the helicopter and fly Coots and his crew here, providing he agrees to help out. I think he will. Make arrangements to transport the control rigs, the D-7 Cats, the bulldozers, and all the heavy metal rigging. Coots will tell you how many heavy-duty trucks and Jeeps he needs. He'll have a list as long as his arm. Get him whatever he wants."

Cole's voice was anxious when he spoke. "You're crazy, Riley. Look, you got the money; let Coots and people who know what they're doing handle it. How in the hell am I going to explain this to Grandmam Billie?"

"You tell it to her like it is. You think I'm going to let my grandfather down now? Now, are you going to do what I asked or not?"

"Hell yes, but I'm entitled to protest on general principle. I'll see you in a few hours."

"Thanks, Cole."

Coots's arm swept across the crooked rolltop desk. Papers that were dry, brittle, and coated with stale barn dust sailed in every direction. He didn't need to see the bills and threatening notices to know what the numbers were. The ledgers that held more mildew than entries followed the papers. He had those entries engraved on his brain, too.

This little cubbyhole of an office had originally been the tack room in the barn. When Tess was on her decorator fit, she'd moved him out here, and he'd stayed because it was a place to get away from her nagging tongue. It had proved to be the perfect sanctuary not only for himself, but for Ivy as well.

The other oilmen, his cronies, all had offices in their houses, but then, he wasn't the businessman they were. He'd never had a head for numbers and paperwork. All he needed to know he kept in his head, rounded off to whole numbers. Right now his head told him he had all debits and no credits.

How could he have known, how could any of them have known, that oil would drop to single digits per barrel? He'd been caught with his pants down, like everyone else. Now he wished he had listened to Riley Coleman when he told him to hedge his oil production on the commodities exchange and not to close off his strippers. It had gone against his grain to listen to the young man with his fancy college education. But it hadn't gone against his grain to borrow a million and a half dollars from that same college kid.

He'd worked like a dog and busted his ass all these years, and here he was about to be wiped out. He'd be damn lucky if he could hold on to Buckalew Big Wells. What he needed was a goddamn miracle, and they weren't happening in Texas these days.

Goddamn fucking OPEC. The bastards had flooded the market with cheap oil in their efforts to increase the market share. Did they care that he, like the others, could lose everything? Not likely.

Coots's rough, callused hands raked his hair. He could feel the trembling begin in his shoulders and work through his entire body. Right now he felt lower than a snake's belly. As much as he dreaded it, he was going to have to tell Tess her jewelry and furs would have to go. Anything else they could sell, too. All the silver and crystal. Two of the cars. He'd already cashed in his insurance policies and dropped the premiums on Tess's jewelry and furs. She'd screech for days when she found out. He'd been putting off telling her, but he couldn't postpone the moment any longer.

He wondered, and not for the first time, what his life would have been like if he'd married a different kind of woman, one who worked with him instead of against him. A woman he could talk to, like now, so they could work out their difficulties together. One who would *offer* to sell her jewels and furs. Someone who would pat his shoulder and tell him things would be all right. Or was that the boy in him wanting his mother to make things right? Whatever it was, he needed it and he didn't have it.

A man needed comfort, and he shouldn't have to beg for it. He'd provided, and provided handsomely, all these years. Now, when the bottom was staring up at him, what did he have? Not a goddamn thing. Not even a family.

Coots's eyes went to the cheap little picture frame with a shot of himself and Ivy near one of the derricks. She'd bought the frame and put the picture in herself and had given it to him one year for Christmas. It was one of his few prized possessions.

Ivy used to come out here and hide, and he'd never given her away. He'd sit at the desk and watch her cower in the corner when her mother and sister ganged up on her. Her sanctuary, too. Misfits, the pair of them. Ivy would be all right. He was glad about that. Ivy would make it, and he had to believe it was because of the way he encouraged her—out here in their quiet place. He'd told her she could do whatever she set her mind to do. That had to go for him, too. You do what you have to do. And right now he was going to march into the house and lay it out for Tess. If she balked, if she gave him one second of grief, he'd pack his bags and leave.

Coots pushed the swivel chair back from the desk and got heavily to his feet. He squared his shoulders, something he hadn't done for months now. On the walk back to the house, his thoughts raced. He wondered how much he could cram into his poke. A couple of changes of clothes, his straight razor, some hard soap, an extra pair of boots, and a few dollars cash.

"Tess!" he bellowed.

"You sound like a bull," Tess complained. "Get in the house; you have a telephone call."

"What were you going to do, tell them to call back?" Coots grumbled.

"You told me never to set foot in your . . . office. I yelled, but you didn't answer."

Coots picked up the phone and listened to the crackly voice on the other end of the wire. Tess's jaw dropped when she saw her husband stand a little straighter. It snapped shut when she saw the excitement in his face. She almost fainted when she heard him say he could be ready to leave with his crew in a matter of hours.

Coots stomped his way back to the barn, rummaged for a loose-leaf notebook that held phone numbers, and returned to the house to make his calls. Tess trembled with fear when she heard him talking to his men. If there was one thing Tess was mortally afraid of, it was fire.

Tess stood teetering on her high heels waiting for her husband to make his last call. "Why, why are you going? Who was that on the phone? Coots, y'all answer me right now, this second!"

"I'm going to put out a fire, and when I'm done putting out that fire, I won't be coming back here. If you have a need to reach me, I'll be staying with Joe Wilson. You can get the phone number out of the book. Give the number to the girls if they want to call me. They called me! Not Red Adair. Me! Jesus, they called me! I knew that kid was smart. I was the dumb one," he added generously.

"What kid? Who are you talking about, Coots?"

"Riley Coleman, that's who. Cole Tanner is flying me and my old crew in the Coleman helicopter out to Rudy Granger's fields to put out his poison well. What do you think of that, you miserable excuse for a woman?" Coots bellowed unnecessarily loud to make his point.

Tess had never heard such excitement in her husband's voice. Not even on the day they got married. "Riley Coleman called you!" she cried in shocked surprise.

"I told you your hearing was going. Yeah, Riley Coleman," Coots snapped.

Tess trailed after Coots as he packed his gear and shaving kit. His steps as he moved from place to place were light, like those of a man with a purpose. "Y'all aren't really moving in with Joe Wilson, are you, Coots honey?"

Coots looked straight at his wife. "I said I wouldn't be coming back to Buckalew Big Wells. You wanted it, it's yours. See you around, Tess."

Riley waited impatiently on the makeshift helicopter pad for Cole and the cargo trucks to arrive.

Coots cast a professional eye to the blazing well. "Move those flags back two feet," he barked. He continued to shout orders. When he was satisfied things were temporarily under control, he stomped his way over to Riley. Riley's hand shot out quicker than lighting. Coots reached for it, his eyes level with Riley's.

"I was a little worried you might not want to take this on." Riley had to shout to be heard over the roaring well.

"No time to jaw around now." Coots said gruffly. "You giving me full rein, right?"

"Tell us what you want and we'll do it."

"For starters, everyone wears a red suit and helmet. Only the red suits give instructions. Anyone know what started this hairy beast?" Coots asked. He shrugged into the slick red co-verall.

Riley shouted again. "A wild well they managed to cap, a spark, who the hell knows? Granger is an old man, and he isn't up on the latest safety measures. It's been burning for three days, four wells right in a row. If they go, the whole field goes, and we're all done for."

"You got that right," Coots bellowed. "Will you believe me if I tell you you're in good hands? I forgot more than Red Adair ever knew."

"It's all yours, Coots."

Coots took off on a run to where his men waited for their orders. Cole hung back, his eyes fearful.

"Jesus, Riley, you aren't going in there and . . . You won't . . . You can get killed! You don't know a goddamn thing about fighting a fire. Let the pros handle this."

"I can't ask someone to do something I'm afraid to do myself. What would that make me? I plan to live here, Cole. I'm going to have to deal with men like Granger and Coots for the rest of my life. Where did you get the idea I was a coward?"

"I didn't say you were a coward, I said you don't know anything about putting out fires. You screw up, do one little thing wrong, and bam! That's the end of Riley Coleman." Cole tried for a light tone but didn't succeed. "I'm not planning on sticking around to run Coleman business. I can't put it any blunter."

Riley shrugged, his eyes following Coots as he leapfrogged around the fire site. "You better get out of here unless you're planning on helping."

Cole looked at his cousin. He was so scared he could only nod. "Someone has to watch over you. Where's my red suit?"

Riley laughed. "Over there in that yellow truck. One size fits all." He clapped his cousin on the back. "Glad you're here, Tanner."

The Texas oil fire was carried on the evening news. The late-night news went nationwide. By early morning all three major networks had their camera crews well behind the safety lines for live on-the-hour coverage. By noon reporters from every major newspaper had joined the camera crews. A midafternoon update found one of the newsmen trying to corner Coots as he zigzagged in and out of the safety flag boundaries. Coots's arm swept out, knocking the man's camera off his shoulder. "I got no time for interviews," he bellowed. "Get the hell out of here. Get this guy out of here!" he continued to bellow. Two burly-looking men lifted the newsman and dumped him unceremoniously next to his camera truck.

"You stay put, you hear! You cross that line one more time and your ass is grass, mister!"

"Man down! Man down!" Frantically Riley looked around. A steady stream of red suits was running through the barrier of flags. Riley joined them.

"Who is it?" He shouted to be heard over the roaring flames.

"Cole," Coots shouted back. "He got his leg stuck between two lead pipes. You got any ideas about spitting on this fire, start puckering up; the water line just busted. Get back, Coleman; we don't need another casualty."

Riley elbowed him out of the way. "That's Cole out there." Riley ran then, crouching low to slide under the roped-off flag area. The intense heat drove him backward, but the thought of Cole pinned down so close to the burning well spurred him on. He felt his eyebrows melt away, as well as his lashes.

"Second-degree burns at best," one of the fire fighters muttered out of the corner of his mouth. It was impossible to hear what the man was saying, so Riley watched his lips. His lips pulled back into a snarl of frustration. "Just what the fuck did you think you were doing?"

"Asshole," Cole managed between clenched teeth. "*You* sent me out here to fix the busted water pipe. Just get me out of here, okay?"

"Not so easy. Those pipes are red-hot. We've had to move the flags back; and that means we aren't controlling the fire. Everything that could go wrong is going wrong. Sit tight; a medic is coming along with one of the rigs. Damn good thing you're wearing that asbestos suit."

The look of anguish in Riley's eyes made Cole rally. "You know us Colemans; we lead charmed lives."

The heat was so intense, Cole felt as though he would black out any second.

Riley reached down and patted him with his thick gloves. "The rig is getting ready to pull off the pipes. Coots is having a bird."

Moments later Cole was carried off on a stretcher. A doctor from town cleaned his legs, dressed the burns, and ordered an ambulance to take Cole to the hospital.

"No way!" Cole shouted. "Give me something for the pain —a shot, novocaine, nothing to make me sleep." An argument followed. Coots and Riley drew the doctor aside. Seconds later the doctor jabbed Cole with a needle and handed over three red pills. His face was grim, his eyes worried. He snapped his bag shut. "You belong in the hospital, and I refuse to take responsibility," he said.

Cole was up and hobbling over to Riley and Coots. "What is it?" he demanded. Coots couldn't look him in the eye, and Riley had to swallow twice before he could get the words out. "Somebody has to fly some nitroglycerine in here."

Cole broke into his third sweat in as many minutes. He tried to remember what he knew about nitro, and all he could come up with was, an oily substance used in the manufacture of explosives and sometimes used for heart patients. Deadly if mishandled. His eyes went to the burning well, the orange flames and black smoke shooting upward. Even back this far, the heat was intense. The flags had been moved for the third time. The fire was out of control.

"It's raining," Riley said inanely. He looked upward as a vicious roar of thunder rolled overhead. A jagged streak of lighting raced downward.

"There goes the control head!" Coots bellowed. "Shit! Son

of a bitch! Everybody move it. You two stay here!" It was an order that Cole and Riley both obeyed. They stood on the sidelines watching the men inch forward, only to be driven back by the intense heat.

"This looks like a lost cause," Cole grumbled.

"Without the nitro, it is. It's the only thing left. They only use it as a last resort. Not much time. That well could go in the next six hours."

"Did Coots make the arrangements?" Cole asked in a hollow voice.

"Yeah, he did. We both figured . . . What I mean is . . ."

"What you mean is, if you were in my shoes, you'd do it. Right?" Riley nodded miserably.

"Let's get it together, then, before this stuff wears off." His voice was still hollow-sounding as he limped behind Riley to the trailer.

Reporters swarmed after them, holding out microphones for a quote or even a few cusswords that would be deleted on the evening news. Riley stiff-armed them as he beat out a path for Cole. "Later," he shouted.

"You been saying that for the past thirty hours," one reporter snapped.

Inside the trailer Riley poured coffee into two dirty mugs. The cream he added was as hot as the coffee. Everything was hot—the desks, the chairs, the metal door of the trailer. Even the floor felt hot under his boots.

"You in pain?" Riley asked.

Cole shrugged. "I'm not exactly a happy camper, if that's what you mean. I'll make it. Just tell me where I pick this stuff up and what precautions to take."

"Cole, I don't know. Coots said they'd tell you everything you need to know when you set down. You don't land here when you get back, that's for sure. Coots said the best place for you to land was Granger's third drill site. We'll truck it in from there."

Cole swallowed hard. "Guess I better get going. Thanks for the coffee. . . . Riley. . . ." They slapped clumsily at each other's shoulders. "Why do I feel I've been in this place before?"

Riley shook his head. He'd give anything at this moment to drown out the sound of the fire fighters' frantic voices and the raging inferno. He swiped at his face with his grimy suit sleeve.

"See you in a couple of hours," Cole said softly, so softly Riley had to strain to hear the words.

Cole limped his way to the Coleman helicopter. He'd lied to Riley about the pain. The shot had only taken the edge off it, and now the edge was sharpening, making him gasp for breath. Don't think about anything but what you have to do. You can do it. Pop two more pills and think about the time you won the championship rifle-shooting contest at school. Think about the day Riley crewed for Yale and came in a winner and you were so damn proud of him you shouted till you lost your voice. He forced himself to call up old memories all the way to Galveston, where he was to pick up the nitroglycerine.

Cole listened carefully to the explosives engineer as he strapped the nitro to the seat. "It's all yours, buddy. I'd fly this thing real gentle if I were you. Set this bird down real careful or you won't be here to read about it." His eyes fell to Cole's leg. He hadn't missed the strain and pain in his eyes. "Good luck, fella. You'll get our bill in the mail." It was a feeble joke, and neither man laughed.

Cole adjusted his wraparound sunglasses. He looked down at the wooden box on the seat next to him. Life or death, success or failure. Aloft again, he thought about his family, each member in turn. He refused to think about Sumi; Sumi was his life now. If something went wrong, if he blew this, it would be all over. Cole sweated. His teeth were clenched so hard, he thought his jaw would crack. The pain in his leg was making him gasp for breath. If he didn't think about Sumi, things would be all right. Sumi would be there. . . .

Coots stalked the perimeters of the fire. He'd done everything humanly possible to contain the fire. He knew in his gut that Red Adair couldn't have done any better. They would blow the fire if Cole Tanner was successful in flying the nitro in intact. He didn't envy the young man. He knew experienced flyers who wouldn't touch the stuff for ten grand.

A reporter eased up behind Coots. "What are you going to do now?"

Disgust washed over Coots's face. "Blow it out. What the hell do you think we're going to do, sprinkle water on it?"

"Look, this is all Greek to us. We know you guys are tired; so are we. We're doing a job just the way you are. What do you say, give us a break, okay?"

No sleep and too little food was making Coots hostile. He

looked at the newsman; his face was weary, his voice tired. "When the nitro gets here, we're going to wrap it in asbestos that's soaked in water. We'll attach it to the end of that extension, that one over there that's jutting out." Coots pointed a thick-gloved fist in the direction of a D-7. "Our plan is to blow the two wells on each end at the same time. Timing here is crucial. Then we're going to take a shot at the middle one, the poison one. See those pits over there? The detonator wire leads into those pits. This is the best way since the wire runs are closer together. We'll pack the nitro in a drum. You guys are too close; get back now. That's it; no more talk!" He started to walk away.

"What happens if some of that asbestos comes loose or one of those insulating wires has a hot spot?"

Coots turned. "We won't be around to care. I told you, we're taking every human precaution. We're going to double-wrap the asbestos; we'll check the booster caps ten times, maybe eleven. If the insulated wire is defective, someone is going to have to ask for a refund." The joke was flat-sounding, and the newsman didn't get it at first. "You got any more questions?"

"Good luck, Mr. Buckalew. Okay, guys, let's move back, like the man said."

Coots took a minute to stare at the monster shooting upward. He'd never seen such a fire. For the hundredth time he worried if he really had the expertise to kill the horror that surrounded him. The heat was so intense he could feel the skin on his face peeling. His stubble of beard had been singed off yesterday. The heat was getting worse, an indication that the well was ready to blow. He needed a man to drive the Cat carrying the asbestos. Who? All his men were old, like himself, with children and grandchildren. None of them had the steady nerves required to handle the job. He was going to have to ask for a volunteer. He looked around at the tired men, at Riley and his crew. All were bone-weary.

Two hours later, he heard the sound of the Coleman helicopter. "That's it!" Coots shouted. "He'll set down on Number Three in a few minutes. I need a volunteer to drive the Cat." He waited.

Riley looked around. He'd thought about nothing but this since Cole took off for the nitro. He knew he was that volunteer. He waited a moment longer. Coots hadn't looked his way once. He sucked in his breath. "I got a driving license."

The relief in Coots's face made Riley smile. "You're it,

Coleman! Let's go in the field office and I'll brief you."

Coots poured himself a cup of coffee that was so black and thick, it looked like tar. His eyes bulged when he swallowed it. "Tastes like something Tess makes on the Fourth of July. I ain't gonna kid you, Riley. What you're volunteering for is more dangerous than Cole flying the nitro here. If you ever had thoughts of one-upping your cousin, this will do it."

Riley danced around the makeshift office on tired feet. "Just tell me what to do, Coots. If it doesn't work, none of us will be alive to care."

Coots outlined the job in detail. "The way I see it, boy, is we got maybe another forty-five minutes and then she blows."

"Let's go," Riley said. "I have to see Cole before I do anything."

"Make it quick. We're on a countdown."

Riley stared at his cousin as Coots and his men carried the nitro off the helicopter. "You're an ugly son of a bitch! I was never so glad to see anyone in my life! The doctor is over there waiting for you. Cole . . ."

"Do you think Sumi will still love me if they cut my leg off?" Cole asked groggily.

"Hell, yes."

"Good. Who's driving the Cat?"

"You're looking at him. The least I can do for you is finish what you started. Wish me luck, Cole."

"You're *what* . . . ?"

"I'm driving the nitro. You did your share; now it's my turn. I can handle it! I gotta go; we're on a countdown. If . . . you know . . . you'll know what to . . ."

"I don't plan to dance on your grave with this leg, so you damn well better. . . ." Cole's thumb shot up.

Riley returned Cole's vote of confidence. "What say we tie one on when this is over?" Cole nodded.

Cole watched his cousin as he loped off. For a moment he gave in to the pain, but only for a moment. His eyes went to the stern-looking doctor. "Change the dressing and give me another shot. I'm not leaving here till my cousin is standing next to me. I'll not hold you responsible, Doctor."

"I brought a crutch," the doctor muttered. "Will you at least use it for now?" Cole nodded.

Riley sat in the Cat, his tired mind reviewing what Coots had told him. He crossed his fingers and made the sign of the cross, the way he always did before a test when he was a kid in school.

All about him the fire raged, crackling and splintering in his ears—deafening. His skin felt charred. Even his red suit was black now. Sweat poured down Riley's face and from his armpits. His throat was thick with smoke. He swiped at the sweat dripping into his eyes with a filthy rag. He could use some radar right now. His eyes were on Coots's flag watching for the countdown. He prayed for better visibility. All about him thick gray-black smoke circled like some obscene monster bent on attacking him. The Cat moved backward, the drum holding the nitro in its asbestos cover secure—for the moment. Riley continued to sweat. The rig moved slowly when the flag waved. He wiped the sweat from his forehead a second time. If the nitroglycerine didn't hit just the right spot, it wouldn't kill the fire. He strained his eyes to stay steady with the flag, his mind playing back the picture of the detonator wire that led into the pit and then spliced into the plunger. At the last split second his gaze went to Cole and then to the flag.

Seconds later his part of the job was over. He was still alive! Riley leaped from the Cat and ran, diving for cover the last fifty yards. He crawled the rest of the way to safety. Three seconds later he heard Coots yell "Hit it!" He strained to hear Coots bellow the same order three more times.

When Riley raised his head, the prairie was clearly visible. Just seconds ago the thundering inferno had blocked the view of the prairie. He felt faint.

The shouts that echoed upward and around him made his adrenaline flow. Jesus, they'd done it and they were alive. No casualties but Cole, and he was alive. Being alive was all that mattered.

Riley got to his feet. From here on in, it was Coots's show.

Coots walked away from the aftermath of the fire. He wanted to be alone, to think, but first he needed to strut.

He looked back over his shoulder. Satisfied that his moment of glory with the newspapers and the Colemans was over, he hitched up his Levi's, rocked back on his heels, and then cocked his grimy Stetson at an angle. He squared his shoulders like a gunslinger. He flexed his fingers, filthy with soot, before he hooked them into his belt. He was ready. He was singing the words to "Deep in the Heart of Texas" as he strutted his way to his pickup truck. For those few moments, he felt like a king. It wasn't till he was in his truck and away from the fire site that his shoulders slumped. It was over, behind him now. Past. History. He'd redeemed himself in his own eyes, but what the hell did that mean? A man needed someone to pat him on the back, someone to say, you did a great job, and my God, you could have gotten killed; God was watching out for you, you dumb bastard.

His eyes were watering, probably from all the soot and grime. He rubbed at his eyes with his filthy shirt sleeve. Ivy should have called, or sent a message out to the field . . . something. He'd expected it, wanted her to call. Lacey, too. It was too much to expect Tess to stir herself and come around.

All these years he thought he hated Buckalew Big Wells; now that he was cutting loose, he worried that he'd hate his friend's small apartment with the kitchen he could barely move around in and the stall shower that was made for a midget. He knew the refrigerator would be empty. There wasn't even a decent TV set, just an ancient fifteen-inch black-and-white job. He'd checked it all out.

He had money now. Riley had told him about the fund his grandfather was setting up to bail out the oil industry. He'd be back on his feet in no time, he'd get himself a nice new condo with a spare room for Ivy. He was on a roll now, thanks to Riley.

Coots let himself into Joe Wilson's apartment and headed straight for the midget shower. On his way he noticed the blinking red light on his friend's answering machine. He shivered and he noticed his hand was shaking as he pressed the play button and waited. Lacey's voice spoke to him, halting and unsure at first, but then it changed to a warm, caring concern. "Pop, this is Lacey. I just heard about the fire. I called Mama and she said she didn't know any details. Ivy called me at work and told me what she knew. I've been glued to the television. I saw you after the fire. God, Pop, you could have been hurt. I'm so proud of you, Pop. You're a hero! I realized when you were out there fighting the fire that I. . . . I left home with things unsaid and hard feelings. . . . If something had happened to you, I don't know what . . . I'm glad you're okay, Pop. Here's my number if you want to call. . . ."

Coots's shoulders straightened a little as he waited for the next message. Tess must have told the whole world where he could be reached. The Colemans, one after another, left congratulatory messages. He preened a little when he heard Tess's voice. "You coulda killed yourself, Coots Buckalew, and for what? To get your picture in the paper. You should know that your insurance lapsed." Tess's voice changed slightly when she said abruptly, "I'm glad you came out alive. I mean it, Coots."

Coots felt his eyes start to water again. He knuckled them. Ivy's voice shouted at him. "Pappy! You made it! Man, I was rooting for you all the way. I even brought my TV to the office. I kept telling everyone you were my old man. You know how I feel about Riley, right? Every time I saw one of the news bulletins, I only looked for you. Jeez, Pappy, I'm glad you're okay. Lacey's been burning up the wires asking for details. I told her what I know. She said she was going to call. Give her a break, Pappy, and be as kind to her as you've always been to me. When I spoke to Mama, she was real upset. She said if there was one thing you knew how to do, it was put out a fire. She's real proud of you, Pappy, but she's real upset because you've . . . gone. End of message. I love you, Pappy."

Coots blinked to ease the burning in his eyes. The damn feeling wouldn't go away, even after a steaming hot shower. When he felt whistle-clean, he dressed, shaved, and brushed his hair into place. Now he was ready to make some phone calls. He leaned back in the one comfortable chair and picked up the phone. He'd return the calls in the order they came in. Then he'd get some sleep. All he wanted now was sleep. That's what he wanted, but he *needed* something else; he needed his family.

A tired smile crossed Coots's face. "I can get two extra days early next month," Lacey told him. "Ivy said she could, too, so we'll both be coming home, and it doesn't matter where home is as long as you're there. I love you, Pop, and I'm glad everything ended up okay. Take care of yourself."

Coots knew he should call Tess next, but he wasn't sure he wanted to talk to her. He dialed Ivy's number and grinned at her excited voice. "I knew if anyone could pull it off, it would be you. I'm so proud of you, Pappy, I could just bust! Why don't you get some sack time and let fame and notoriety wait till tomorrow? Take the phone off the hook. Uh, Pappy, how is Riley? He's okay, isn't he? I mean, he looked okay on television and all, but—"

"Lookin' good, honey. That kid has a head on his shoulders. Didja see how he gave me all the credit? Takes a big man to do something like that. Tomorrow I'll give you all the details of what his granddaddy is goin' to do for all us oilmen. Thanks for callin', honey."

Two down and one to go. Coots squirmed in his chair. Should he call Tess or not? It would be the polite thing to do. Jeez, she had called him. The girls said she was concerned. What the hell, he could always hang up if she got a burr in her bloomers and started whining and bitching. It was a good five minutes before he could bring himself to punch out the numbers on the phone. He didn't realize he was holding his breath until the phone went unanswered. He counted the rings —eleven, twelve, thirteen. He slammed the phone back onto the cradle. Thirteen was unlucky. Damn, he should have hung up on the twelfth ring. He felt both aggravated and relieved that Tess hadn't answered the phone. He'd never admit it to anyone, but he missed the stringy old bobcat. They'd been together for a lot of years. An itch that wouldn't go away, a blister that hurt. An old shoe and an old sock.

As Coots reached out to sleep, he could feel the tears slipping down his leathery cheeks. He cried then for the would-haves, the could-haves, the should-haves.

The morning papers carried pictures of Coots's crew, Riley, and assorted Texas oilmen. There was a picture of Cole leaning on his crutch with his fist in the air. The moment he saw it, Riley decided to get a print from the *Austin Gazette* and have it framed for Sumi. A second picture worthy of framing was one of himself and Coots at the poison well site. Coots had his arm around his shoulder, and they were talking earnestly. The caption underneath quoted Coots as saying he was grateful to Riley Coleman and his grandfather, Shadaharu Hasegawa, who had set up a fund to get the Texas oil industry on its feet.

Power . . . the power of love. His grandfather's love.

He was home free. Coleman Oil was intact.

He'd faltered, but he hadn't fallen. His grandfather had seen to that.

CHAPTER
{{{{{{{{{ TWENTY-FIVE }}}}}}}}}

Tess sat alone at her baronial dining room table. For the first time in her life she was alone. Coots had been gone for a month, and she missed him. She picked at her dry toast. Her appetite was gone and she couldn't remember the last time she'd eaten a hearty meal—probably not since the day Coots came by for the rest of his things.

The moment the door closed behind him, it was all downhill. She'd spent hours walking from room to room, and more hours poring over astrology books. Saturn and Pluto were out of alignment. She'd charted and scribbled and finally tossed the whole mess into the trash. She alternated between fear and anger—anger that Coots had walked out on her and fear that she would wither and shrivel up in Buckalew Big Wells with no one to talk to for the rest of her life.

Tears gathered on Tess's false eyelashes. She tried blinking them away, but the glue was sticky and the miserable things were so heavy, she couldn't keep her eyes open. She ripped them off and tossed them into an ashtray. They were trash now, just like everything else in her life. Trash, trash, trash. Even she was trash. "Tess Buckalew, you are nothing but trash, poor white trash," she bleated. She'd pissed her whole life away, and for what? To be alone. Everyone was gone. Her daughters were gone; Coots was gone. Her family. Suddenly all the things she'd wished for weren't important. If she could make wishes now, she'd wish for Lacey and Ivy and Coots to walk in the door. She couldn't hold the tears in check any longer. She sobbed for her loss.

She stopped suddenly. She was a mother. She was a wife. Lacey and Ivy hadn't disowned her. Coots hadn't divorced her . . . yet. Maybe, just maybe.

Before she could change her mind, she punched out a series of numbers on the phone. Her voice was hoarse and choked when she identified herself, saying she wanted to put Buckalew Big Wells on the market. "And," she told the voice on the other end of the phone, "I want to buy a three-bedroom house in town."

The second call was to Eastern Airlines. She booked a seat on the evening flight to New York. Lacey would open the door to her; she wouldn't turn her away, not when she heard what she had to say. It was only too late if you didn't try. She'd stop and see Ivy on the way back. Ivy was in town now, in her new apartment, with a job she loved. Ivy would open the door.

Her heart beat faster when she thought of Coots. They'd come a long way together, and only an old fool would let it all slip through her fingers. If she had to, she'd get down on her knees and beg Coots to take her back.

It took Tess a long time to wash the hair spray and gook out of her hair, and even longer to remove the caked-on makeup. When she emerged from the shower, she put on the dress she'd worn the day Billie Coleman came to lunch. When she looked in the mirror she wanted to cry. She'd never been a beautiful woman, and she hadn't aged well at all. The makeup she'd plastered on her face had accentuated the wrinkles and her scrawny neck. How could she have been so blind? Ivy had always told her she wore too much and had said, "But, Mama, you're pretty; you don't need all that junk." Beauty, then, was truly in the eye of the beholder. Ivy thought she was pretty. Lacey tried to help, and she hadn't listened. Once again she howled her anguish.

Tess sat down on the upholstered toilet seat and reached for a tissue. She blew her nose again and again. "You are a jerk, Tess Buckalew," she said aloud. "Talking to the bathroom walls isn't the answer. You have to go to your family and tell it like it is. You have to hope and pray they are more understanding than you were." She paused, worried. What if they don't want anything to do with me? What will I do then? Then a tiny voice said, 'You will pull up your socks and move forward. You have the rest of your life to make up for the past.'

Tess stared into the mirror again. She should put on a little makeup, at least some moisturizer. Lordy, Lordy, Lordy, she'd scare the passengers on the plane. She looked at her watch. She had three hours before her flight to New York. Time to bake her Poor Man's Cake for Lacey and Ivy. One for Coots, too. They all loved that cake. That's exactly what she'd do. It wasn't much in the way of a peace offering, but maybe if she said the right things . . .

Tess measured out flour and shortening; she knew the recipe by heart. Her mind raced. This feeling, this need of family, was

{ 455 }

what Billie Coleman always talked about, she realized. Tess paused, her whisk in midair. *That's* what made Billie Coleman who she was. That's what she'd always envied about Billie and the other Colemans. Everything Billie did or said was for her family. When you gave, you got. It was that simple.

It was twenty minutes past nine when Tess rang Lacey's doorbell. "I . . . I baked a cake for you and decided to bring it along with . . . with an apology. Will you invite me in?"

The shock on her daughter's face frightened Tess. "I mean it, Lacey. I came here to apologize."

"I heard you, Mama. I'm trying . . . You look so . . . different. You look the way a mother is supposed to look. Did . . . did you really bake that cake for me?"

"Yes, and I almost missed the plane, but I didn't care. It was . . . I baked it for you because . . . you always loved my cake. I baked one for Ivy and one for your father, too. Can I come in, Lacey?"

"Of course. The place is small and kind of messy; nothing like home . . ."

"There's nothing like Buckalew Big Wells. I put it up for sale today. Where do you want this cake? You look thin and run-down, Lacey. Aren't you eating? Are you taking vitamins?"

Lacey was dumbfounded at the genuine concern in her mother's voice.

"I eat when I have time, usually on the run. I'm working two jobs. You have to, to live in this city. I'm managing, though. Oh, Mama, I'm glad you came," Lacey cried.

"Listen, no more crying; I've done enough bawling to last the two of us the rest of our lives. Let's eat this cake and talk. I want to hear all about Ivy's graduation. I want to hear all about everything. I mean everything, Lacey, and when you're finished, I'll talk."

When Tess left for Texas the following morning, she took with her Lacey's love and her promise to return to Texas for a long weekend as soon as she could manage it.

Tess treated herself to lunch at the airport before driving back to Buckalew Big Wells to pick up Ivy's cake. From there she drove her own car back to Austin and got lost three times before she found Ivy's address. It was almost six when she rang the doorbell. The blank look on her daughter's face made Tess's heart flutter. "I baked you a cake, honey."

Honey. A cake. Ivy blinked. Was this her mother standing

{456}

in her doorway? "Mama, what are you doing here?" she asked in a flustered voice.

"I told you, I baked you a cake, and here it is. It's . . . it's all I have to give you. I want to talk to you, Ivy. I *need* to talk to you. Will you invite me in?"

"Well, sure. Is something wrong? Did something happen to Daddy or Lacey?"

"No, they're fine. It's me, Ivy. I need to talk about me."

"Mama, you aren't sick . . . ?" The alarm on Ivy's face made Tess want to cry.

They talked far into the night. They cried and wiped at each other's tears. "I can't change the past, Ivy, but I can change the future, at least my future. All I want is for you to be open with me. I don't deserve it, but I'd like it if you could be kinder to me than I was to you. When you and Riley finally get married and have kids, I want you to ask me to baby-sit for you. You will marry him, you know."

"Did the stars tell you that?" Ivy giggled.

"That astrology stuff is trash. I junked it all. No, this is my motherly intuition. Another thing, Ivy: I don't want you to ever worry about me horning in and wanting to be part of the Colemans. I'll never do that. I finally figured out what the Colemans are all about, and you know something? I have the same thing they have. My family. Now all I have to do is convince your father I'm the girl he married, and we'll be a family again. Do you think I can do it?"

"Heck, yes. All Daddy wants is to be looked up to. He loves it when you ask his advice on things. He's in ecstasy when you say he did something well. He's no different than the rest of us, Mama. He wants to feel important. Not for himself, but for you. He was hurting, Mama, when things went bad. He felt as though he failed all of us. You weren't there for him; none of us were, when it came right down to it. I hope you can make that right."

"I hope so, too, Ivy. Well, you have to get to work, and I have to go back to the house and get his cake. Maybe I'll make another one; that's probably stale by now. I'll take it warm, and if there's one thing your daddy likes, it's warm Poor Man's Cake with a good thick layer of frosting."

Ivy stuck her thumb in the air. "Go for it, Mama."

Tess found her way to Coots's garden apartment by midafternoon, and she wasn't surprised to find the door open. Coots never liked locks of any kind. The apartment was shabby and cluttered, but she could see that her husband had been making an effort to keep the mess to a minimum. It took her three hours to clean and polish the one-bedroom apartment. It was the happiest three hours she'd spent in years. She was sitting at the kitchen table with cake plates and coffee brewing when Coots walked in the door at six-thirty.

"Before you go howling like a banshee, Coots Buckalew, let me say my piece. I'm here with my tail between my legs. I've been a rotten wife and a rotten mother. I admit that, so I don't need you to keep saying it to me. I'm sorry. I didn't know how sorry until you walked out of the house. I didn't know what to do, so I sat there and bawled for two days. I went to New York and poured my heart out to Lacey. I took her a cake. I did the same thing with Ivy. I wanted to give you all something, and for some reason it was the only thing I could think of that might make a difference. I made them myself. I fired the housekeeper and put Buckalew Big Wells up for sale day before yesterday. I ain't much, Coots, but in here—" she thumped her chest "—I never stopped caring for you." Ivy's words rang in her ears. "What you did with the fire, that was the Coots I married. You're a real man, Coots Buckalew. Now, what's it gonna be? You want some of this cake or not?"

"Come'ere, you stringy old bobcat," Coots bellowed. "Whatcha do to yourself? You look the way you did when we got married. I been telling you all these years you don't need that shit you plaster all over your face. I'll make a deal with you. You put some meat on your bones and we'll be Mr. and Mrs. Coots Buckalew again. What d'ya say?"

"See this?" Tess said, pointing to the cake. "This half is yours and this half is mine. You got any ice cream?"

"Four different kinds," Coots said proudly.

"To our family," Tess said, holding her coffee cup aloft. She watched as Coots dripped his all over the table. He slurped at the coffee and then dug into the cake and ice cream. Tess smiled indulgently. You couldn't make a silk purse out of a sow's ear, but who wanted a silk purse anyway?

As the frigid January air gave way to even colder air, messages from the family continued to arrive at the Assante penthouse apartment. Cary carried them into Amelia's room to read aloud, or repeated phone messages verbatim. Amelia would chuckle or smile warmly, happy that her family was staying in touch. She forced herself to concentrate on Cary's words, delivered in his warm, loving voice. She avoided his sad, compassionate eyes whenever possible.

The Colemans and their friends were scattered all over the world. Postcards from Tahiti and the Fiji Islands told Amelia that Billie and Thad were having a wonderful time. Cards mailed from Hawaii said Rand and his family were well, and planning a trip to London soon, so Chesney could wind up her affairs. Cole's cards and telephone messages confirmed that he was a frequent commuter between Japan and Texas. Riley called nearly every day, "just to touch base," he'd say. Adam and Jeff's messages from New York were light and breezy; Adam was counting the days until Sawyer came home to him—for keeps.

In early February a short note arrived in the Assante mailbox, addressed to Amelia and Cary. It was mailed from Burlington, Vermont; Julie had fled New York and gone back home to live. The sap was flowing freely and she was freezing her tush off. She was happy.

Valentines arrived, some with beautiful, meaningful verses, others with witty, even silly messages that made Amelia smile. Julie Kingsley's valentine arrived exactly on Valentine's Day. It bore her signature and a small penned note that read:

Dear Amelia and Cary:
   I decided to make my valentines this year. All the tiny bits of fabric and lace are my own things that I've saved over the years. I wanted to share my heart with all of you at this wonderful time of the year. My design leaves a lot to be desired; the glue was frozen and my fingers are numb. My heart is full of love for both of you.

Affectionately,
Julie

Amelia smiled when Cary read it to her. He propped the funny-looking valentine on the dresser, directly in Amelia's line of vision, and smiled, too, because there was nothing else he could do. His nerves jumping, he excused himself to go to the bathroom. He sat down on the edge of the tub with a thump. His hands were trembling, and they felt hot and dry. He'd touched pieces of Julie's past. Julie with the laughing eyes and warm, crinkly smile. Julie. She'd been his for a brief moment in time. He reached for a washcloth to mop at his perspiring forehead.

Valentine's Day was for lovers. In past years he'd always

bought the biggest, the reddest, the sappiest valentines he could find for Amelia, along with the biggest box of See's candies and dozens of red roses. He'd told her every Valentine's Day for years that she was his heart's desire. And she was. By God, she was. She still was. Amelia always gave him a comical card that made them both laugh. They'd always made wild, raging love on those days.

Memories. Just as Julie was a memory. He wondered if Amelia had kept the cards and letters he'd written her over the years. He'd saved all of hers, romantic that he was. He'd read something once, probably in one of Amelia's magazines, that it wasn't wise to dwell on memories, that life was for the living. He hadn't paid a whole lot of attention to that article. It comforted him to remember Julie and their time together in Hawaii, but guilt and shame allowed those memories to surface only in the lost hours of the night, when Amelia slept. There had been days, these past months, when his guilt and shame rode him like a wild stallion.

He'd been in here too long. Amelia would start to wonder. He folded the washcloth neatly and placed it on the rack. His hand was on the knob to open the door when he remembered to flush the toilet. Guilt.

When the first gusty winds of March ripped across Texas, Amelia Assante suffered her third heart attack. Her voice was frail and thin when she begged Cary and the doctors to allow her to stay home and die in her own bed. They'd agreed reluctantly; Cary hired round-the-clock nurses. He stayed in the room, leaving only to shower and eat.

Amelia slipped into semiconsciousness on the third day of March. The day before, when she'd been feeling a bit better, she'd made her husband promise not to call anyone until she was at rest. He hadn't wanted to give his promise, but in the end he did, because it was what Amelia wanted. He knew Amelia feared her family wouldn't be able to make it in time, anyway, scattered as they were all over the world. She said she wanted to see only his face when she made her grand exit, but he knew she was afraid that only one or two of the family would arrive in time. If she couldn't have all of them, she wanted only him.

He was going to break that promise now. The Colemans would never forgive him. They all needed this last chance to show their love and pay their final tribute.

Once again, Ma Bell worked her special magic for the

Colemans. Or was it a Higher Being? Cary wondered. Borneo, Hawaii, England, Minnesota, Japan, New York, Vermont. He reached everyone. Oddly, the most difficult one to track down was Riley, right around the corner.

Cary prayed—for Amelia's forgiveness and for her family to arrive in time.

The air lanes were filled with chartered planes on the sixth day of March. One after another, they set down at Austin's airport. The intercontinental jet from Japan was the last to arrive. Sumi and Sawyer fell into Cole's arms; he hugged them hard, tears in his eyes, and led them to the waiting Bronco. At Sunbridge, the rest of the family climbed into the car.

The ride to Miranda was made in silence. Cole broke it once when he apologized for the long wait for those who had arrived early. "I thought it would be better if we all got there at the same time." The family nodded wearily. Little Jessie whimpered once, but her mother soothed her by stroking her hair and whispering softly in her ear.

Billie gasped when she saw Cary. He tried valiantly to smile a welcome. How gaunt and hollow-eyed he looked; he'd lost at least twenty pounds.

"How is she?" Billie managed.

"She's been asking for you, Billie. I have this feeling she's been waiting for you. You know she didn't want me to call anyone; she made me promise. You were to be notified . . . after . . . You . . . you understand. Then she started slipping in and out of consciousness and calling for you. I broke my promise. I called all of you."

"Is it all right if I go in now?" Billie asked. Cary nodded.

Billie's eyes flew to the nurse. She rushed to the bed. Surely this tiny person, this thin, skeletal woman, wasn't Amelia. Her heart ripped open with grief. "Amelia," she said softly. "It's Billie."

"I've been waiting," Amelia said in a voice Billie barely recognized.

"I got here as quick as I could. Oh, Amelia, I want to do something. I have to do something for you." Billie sobbed, forgetting the promise she'd made not to cry.

Amelia's hand stretched toward the nurse. "Where is it?"

"Right here, Mrs. Assante. Do you want me to—"

"Give it to me."

Billie could barely make out what the nurse was doing through her tears. Amelia's grasp on the small white envelope was fierce. Billie reached for the envelope, and only then did Amelia's fingers relax. Billie pocketed the envelope, knowing that was what Amelia wanted.

"The family is here, Amelia. They . . . they want to . . . they need . . . Please let them come in."

"Don't cry, Billie, or you'll have me doing it. I can't go with tears streaming down my cheeks. Say good-bye now, Billie."

"Amelia . . . Amelia, I can't . . . please," Billie cried, sinking to her knees at the side of the bed. Thad was at her side in a second.

"Take her out of here, Thad, and don't let her back in this room. Start the parade, will you?"

"Yes, ma'am," Thad said, forcing a grin to his lips. He knew what Amelia's flip words had cost her. He could hear her ragged breathing as he half carried and half dragged Billie from the room.

They walked in, one by one, to pay their final respects. Cary was the last.

The nurse nodded, her fingers on Amelia's pulse. Cary gathered his wife in his arms, a sob catching in his throat. Her breathing was so shallow he could barely hear her. He should be saying something, something Amelia could carry with her to eternity, something meaningful. Words that summed up their wonderful life together. All he could do was hold her close.

"Wait for me, Amelia," he whispered. He thought he could feel her head move.

She was so still, he knew she'd gone from him. He lowered her still body against the mound of pillows. Bending low, he kissed her eyes, her mouth, her hands.

"Wait for me, Amelia," he whispered a second time.

Cary's voice was hushed when he told the family Amelia was at peace. The tears flowed and the sobs echoed around the room. From somewhere Cary's strength returned, his voice became firm and brisk. "You have to stop. This is why Amelia didn't want me to call you. She didn't want you grieving like this. I broke my last promise to her for selfish reasons for all of us. Please, don't compound my guilt. Amelia wouldn't want this."

"The arrangements?" Thad asked hesitantly.

Cary walked to the desk. He handed Thad a slip of paper. "It's all here."

When Thad left the room, Cole and Riley were at his side.

"I had Jonquil make up all the bedrooms at Sunbridge," Riley said quietly.

"Today is my birthday," Sawyer whispered to Cole. "Don't remind anyone, okay?"

"Whatever you say. I think we should leave now. I don't think any of us can handle it when they . . . when they take her out."

Rand stayed near Cary, with the promise to come to Sunbridge when all the arrangements were finalized. Cary watched with unseeing eyes as Julie shepherded the family out of the apartment.

Amelia Coleman Assante's death was announced on the evening news and on the front page of the Miranda and Austin papers the following morning. Those wishing to pay their respects could do so between 7:00 and 10:00 P.M. Services were scheduled at the Little Church of the Flowers for March 8th. Interment services were for the immediate family only.

The church was filled to capacity. The governor, the lieutenant governor, Washington dignitaries, some friends of Thad's, some friends of Amelia's—half the state of Texas came to pay their last and final respects.

The family sat together, directing their grief inward.

Eight pallbearers carried the bronze casket to the waiting hearse.

At the top of the hill behind Sunbridge, Amelia's casket was placed over the open grave. The family gathered in a circle while the minister read the psalm Amelia had requested. Cole stood on the outer edge. Inch by inch, he walked backward, till he was standing on old Seth's grave. He dug his heels deep into the soft earth, his stance rigid. A raging tornado couldn't have toppled him. Billie looked up, their eyes meeting. Only the two of them understood.

The Colemans left the way they'd arrived, full of grief and sorrow. Their numbers depleted by one.

A month to the day after Amelia's death, Cole Tanner woke, drenched with sweat. He lay among the tangled bedclothes trying to recall if he'd had a nightmare, or what else could have awakened him. As near as he could figure, he had been sleeping peacefully. The apartment wasn't too hot, nor was it cold. Somewhere, someplace, something was wrong. He looked at the bedside clock: 3:00 A.M.

Sleep was over for him. He padded into the kitchen to make

{ 463 }

coffee. He sat at the glass-topped table, waiting for the coffee to perk, his thoughts jumbled. He couldn't shake the feeling that something was wrong. He went through the family roll call in his head. Riley? No. Things were all right; they'd spoken yesterday. He was bunking at the oil fields, drilling night and day. Sawyer would have called; she always called. His mother? No. Rand could handle anything. Grandmam Billie? No. He'd spoken with her just the past evening. Not Sumi. He's spoken to her, too. That left only Shadaharu Hasegawa. His shoulders tightened.

Cole didn't bother with a shower. He threw on the same clothes he'd had on the night before. He grabbed his wallet and car keys and was out of the apartment in five minutes flat, the perking coffeepot forgotten.

Twenty minutes later he was sitting in his car outside Sunbridge. He stared at the house for a long time, wishing he knew why he was sitting here at three forty-five in the morning. He didn't even have a key anymore—he'd given it back to Riley at Christmastime—but he did have the electronic garage door opener on the visor in his car. "This is bullshit, Cole Tanner," he muttered. "Go home and go to bed." Instead, he pressed the small device. The doors slid upward. He cut the engine and walked through the garage, his headlights lighting the darkness ahead of him.

First he checked the oil burner and then the water heater. Both were fine as far as he could tell. He walked through the rooms, turning on overhead lights as he went along. Riley had unplugged all the radios and televisions. He made a second pass-through, feeling more foolish than the first time.

Back in the kitchen he felt more convinced than ever he'd done the right thing by giving his half of Sunbridge to Riley.

He shivered.

Cole sat down at the butcher block table that was as old as the house and full of gouges and nicks. He wondered how many meals had been eaten off the table. Nobody in his right mind sits in a cold, empty house he hates at four in the morning, he told himself. Funny, though—he still had the feeling something was wrong, that there was something he should do.

He got up and opened the back door. The air rushed through, warmer than the frigid air in the house. Cole shivered. He switched on the outside light. The courtyard with the double basketball hoops sprang to life. He looked down at two empty milk bottles standing to his left. A wicker hanging basket with a dried-up bird's nest swung crazily in the wind. Nothing here.

Cole walked through the library one more time and into the cavernous front hall. He checked the front door to make sure it was locked, then pulled open the heavy curtains on the side window to look out across the front lawn and down the long driveway. Nothing out there. As he closed the curtains, something fluttered at his feet, something that looked like white paper. He bent over to pick it up. When he looked at what was in his hand, his heart stopped beating for a second. Riley's letter to his grandfather—the one he said he was going to write when they came down from the hill. He must have left it on the hall table for Jonquil to mail, and somehow it had slipped to the floor.

Now he understood Riley's phone calls and the question, over and over, have you heard from my grandfather? This was the letter that was supposed to make things right for Riley and the old one.

Cole raced to the library phone, then stood, the phone in his hand, wondering what to do first. Something told him not to call Japan. He punched out a number in New York. Nick's voice was surprisingly alert, considering the hour.

"Jesus, Cole, do you want me to come down there to mail the letter or what?" he asked after Cole spilled the whole story.

"No. What does it mean, Nick?"

"It means you were meant to find it, I guess. I'm no psychic, Cole. I can't even pretend to understand it."

"Riley must have gone through hell these past weeks not hearing from his grandfather. No wonder he—"

"I think maybe it's the old man who's going through hell," Nick said. "Don't you?"

Cole arrived at the Hasegawa household the following day. He was gritty-eyed, unshaven, and anxious. He found the family gathered in the Zen garden with their heads bowed. His eyes searched out Sumi. Her expression showed no surprise at his sudden appearance.

"Where is he? Am I too late?" Cole barked.

"He's gone to the cherry blossom hill. You must not go there, Cole. We must all respect my father's wishes."

Cole looked around at the Hasegawa family. They sat with their eyes lowered, not concerning themselves with his intrusion. It was clear to him that Sumi was their spokesperson. There was an anxiousness in her voice when she said, "We gave our promise to stay here in the garden."

"Well, I didn't promise. I have something here for him, and he has to see it. Stay out of my way, Sumi."

He took off at a dead run. The path was clear, the soft, loamy earth marked by the cane the old one had used. When he came to the clearing, he stopped short. Was he too late?

"Mr. Hasegawa, it's Cole. I'm not of your family, and I made no promise not to come here. I brought this," he said, holding out the letter. The words tumbled out so fast, he wasn't sure he was saying or thinking them. "I know when Riley wrote it. Did you understand what I just said?"

"Every word, Coleman san. The letter is not needed. I know what is in my grandson's heart. I knew when he called for my help. This humble man thanks you for making your long journey here. Please now, go below with my family. Dry their tears for me and beg them not to grieve."

"No," Cole said emphatically.

"You defy me?"

"No man should die alone."

"It is not my way."

"It is now. If I were Riley, you'd let him stand here. I'm his stand-in. He sent me," Cole lied.

"I knew you were coming, Coleman san. I had a vision before I climbed this hill. I believe it was yesterday. I heard your footfall. My hearing is excellent for a dying man."

The conversation was taking its toll on the old man. His breathing was labored, but still he tried to speak. He appeared to be disoriented, his head wobbling about on his thin neck.

"Can you smell the cherry blossoms, Riley?"

Cole blinked. "Yes, Grandfather." He hadn't noticed them till now. Everywhere he looked there were pink petals.

"You will carry this worthless old body to the bottom of the hill, my grandson."

"I will carry your body to the bottom of the hill, my grandfather," Cole said softly.

"Will this worthless body be covered with cherry blossoms?"

"If this is your wish, Grandfather." Cole blinked away his tears.

"Come closer, Riley. I can't see you."

Cole stepped closer. "I'm here, Grandfather."

"I knew you would come. I prayed for this moment."

Cole felt faint. He had to take something back to Riley, even if it was the delirious words of a dying man.

"I need to know, Grandfather, that you forgive me. That you understand what has happened to me."

The voice was thin, frail, and barely discernible. "My grandson, I would forgive you anything. My happiness is knowing you are happy. It is you who must forgive this foolish old man who turned selfish with the illness that consumes me. Tell me you forgive me so that I may join your mother and grandmother."

"I forgive you, Grandfather. May your spirit and the spirits of my mother and grandmother keep me safe always." Sumi had told him that was the phrase the children used when a relative died. Thank God he remembered it.

When the old one's eyes closed for the last time, Cole walked over to the cherry tree closest to the still body. He reached for a low branch and shook it. The fragile, fragrant petals sailed down gracefully, coming to rest on the old man.

Cole's eyes burned when he picked up Riley's grandfather. He weighed no more than a small child.

He had lied to Riley, Cole thought: it wasn't easier going down. It was the hardest thing he'd ever had to do in his life.

CHAPTER TWENTY-SIX

{{{{{{{{{ }}}}}}}}}

It was a quiet day, but no quieter than any of the other days since Amelia's death. Days spent sitting and staring, or standing and staring, or staying in bed and staring. Long days, endlessly long days with no meaning, no desires. He'd been contemplating his navel, Amelia would have said. It was always like this: as soon as he started to think, Amelia would pop into his head, like now. He had to do something, count for something again. The sugarcane refinery didn't count; once it was off the ground, it would practically take care of itself. He needed a challenge, motivation of some kind, a reason to get off his duff and do some work that would amount to something. He had to come back to the land of the living and start to contribute again. He had to stop acting like an invalid, wallowing in self-pity.

At least once a day he took a stab at pep-talking himself. For a few seconds he'd feel better, then the old guilt would settle in again. His relationship with Julie couldn't have hastened Amelia's death, he'd tell himself. His guilt or lack of guilt couldn't have affected her health, either. The minister told him, in one of his visits, that it was Amelia's time, and nothing could change that. He didn't know if the minister's words were true then, and he still didn't know. Always he ended his guilty thoughts by thanking God that Amelia hadn't known of his unfaithfulness.

Cary leaned back and stretched, trying to loosen his tense neck muscles. He was smoking now, more than ever, almost three packs of unfiltered cigarettes a day. There was always one of the hateful white cylinders between his fingers. The apartment reeked of stale smoke and dirty ashtrays. He didn't care. He watched the ash drop to the carpet, and scuffed at it with the toe of his slipper. That was another thing; half the time he didn't bother to get dressed. He lounged around in his slippers and pajama bottoms, sometimes not bothering to shower because it was too much of an effort. Everything was too much of an effort. The television and radio ran day and night, each vying for his attention. Once in a while he'd use what little energy he had to reach for a picture of himself and Amelia that stood in a gold frame on the end table by his chair. He reached for it now. It was two corny, little pictures in a double frame; he had insisted on displaying it in the living room. He couldn't remember who had snapped the picture, Cole or Riley, but whoever it was caught Amelia's perfection as she dug her shovel into the pile of mud the day they broke ground for Miranda. He'd offered her a pair of work boots, but instead she'd stepped into ankle-deep mud in high-heeled lizard shoes, her fur coat dragging in the mud, too. She'd hefted a damn good shovelful of mud, and then she'd slung it at him for good luck. Slipping and sliding, she'd made her way to him and threw her arms around him, kissing him, mud and all. That was when Cole or Riley snapped the second picture. It was all he had left now: pictures and memories.

Cary stirred, his misery so alive, it frightened him. He mustered all his energies to stumble to the balcony, his arms reaching for the sunshine and fresh air. He struggled to take deep breaths.

All about him the sun shone, glinting off the chrome of the

balcony furniture, shimmering on the artful arrangement of green plants, bathing the pedestal and the. . . . Cary drew in his breath as his eyes searched the balcony for a sign of the gift he'd given Amelia. The sundial was gone. He dropped to his knees, pushing and toppling the plants to see if it had blown off the pedestal or somehow got dislodged. It was gone. The gift Amelia had treasured more than any other, gone. How? When? Why? He searched every inch of the balcony, but there was no sign of the sundial. If Amelia were here, she would say it was one of those little mysteries in life that would never be explained.

He was in the kitchen now, searching aimlessly among the contents of the nearly empty refrigerator. The frosty air of the freezer spiraled outward. As empty as his life. He hadn't been eating right, he hadn't been sleeping right, he hadn't been doing anything right. The apartment was a mess and he was a mess. He closed the refrigerator door, leaned back, and closed his eyes. He felt himself sliding toward the floor and made no move to right himself. He sat there, leaning against the kitchen cabinet and cried, huge, wracking sobs that shook his entire body.

Hours later Cary walked out of the kitchen to look for the phone. He pulled it loose from under a pile of sofa cushions and called a cleaning agency Amelia had used from time to time. Would they please send a crew to do a thorough spring cleaning? He replaced the phone and headed for the shower. Dressed in clean but wrinkled clothing, he left the apartment. He had some thinking to do, serious thinking. He accepted the fact that the sundial was gone. He could live with that. When something was gone, it was gone. That meant it ceased to exist. He might not be whole right now, but he was on his feet, and that was the first step. Amelia was gone, not of this earth. He was alive and life went on. How it went on would be up to him.

Cary estimated he walked fifteen miles that day. A plan took shape in his mind as he walked. Amelia had called ideas embryos. That was all he had, an embryo. Miranda had once been an embryo. When the time was ready, he could do it. He had to do it. Not to prove anything. Do it out of love. Pure, simple love. A memorial to Amelia. There, he'd said the words aloud. An embryo with a name was a fact. An embryo with a name was . . . reality.

There was a certain frenzy in Cary's movements as he rifled through his desk for the thin folder he needed. Remnants and scraps of paper, some notes scribbled on napkins and matchbook covers, ran through his fingers. Some of them, he noticed, were starting to turn yellow. All were ideas and thoughts concerning the building of Miranda. A deep sadness swept over him. It all seemed so long ago.

Why was he having such a hard time finding the right notes and scraps of paper, the memos he'd written to himself? Because part of you doesn't want to remember you made those notes when Amelia was still alive, he told himself. You were already thinking beyond her death to what you would do. Is that what you did with Julie, too, jumped ahead of Amelia's death, envisioning it, preparing for it? His conscience pricked.

A drawing, a sketch of his plan folded in a tight square; goddamn it, where was it? He knew he'd stuffed it here in Amelia's desk. Still, maybe he was wrong. Right after Amelia died, he'd worked on the plan until it became unbearable and he'd shelved it. No, he hadn't shelved it, he'd hidden it. From himself.

Cary upended a third drawer and then he saw it. His mouth felt dry. A warning ricocheted around his brain: Touch this, open it, look at it, make even one mark, one correction, and you're committed. Committed. Are you ready? Can you handle it? Cary's shoulders slumped and then straightened. Yes, he could handle it. He'd built Miranda, hadn't he? What he was contemplating would be small potatoes compared to Miranda. All he needed to get this project off the ground was the desire and motivation.

He picked up the folded square of paper. He was committed now, heart and soul. His memorial to his wife. A retirement city for people like Jethroe and Minnie, for all the people Amelia had worked so hard to help. Amelia had told the one hundredth Congress that others would come after her, would carry on her work. "I'm applying for the job, honey. I don't see anyone else out there forming a line, so I'm it."

Cary perused the rough sketch of the buildings and the surrounding acreage he'd contemplated for his retirement city. Next to his sketch was a map, one of Amelia's, torn and creased. Staring up at him was a large red X. He unfolded the map and smiled. Then he laughed until the tears rolled down his cheeks. Amelia's property. The property her mother's house had rested on, and all the acreage behind it. When she'd burned the house to the ground, years ago, she'd told him that someday something would be built on it. Until that day it would simply wait and grow more valuable each and every year.

A thousand acres of prime land. A thousand acres filled with sunshine. A place with ramps, windows that could be opened, a place where pets would be allowed. If residents arrived without a pet, they'd be given one. No goddamn attendants in white coats, no nurses and doctors except for emergencies. Grass, green and beautiful, trees in leaf with benches underneath. Transportation from one building to the next. Dignity. By God, there would be dignity. No uniforms. A petting zoo, a pool, gardens.

A dream. Built with his blood and sweat. Built out of love.

"I'll make you proud, Amelia. Count on it."

On the first day of summer, a Japanese delegation of seven walked into Cole Tanner's offices at Coleman Aviation. His first thought was that something had happened to Sumi. Then he realized it wouldn't take seven sober-faced men to tell him that.

All the men carried identical briefcases. Even their suits appeared to be made from the same cloth, crafted by the same tailor.

Bewildered, he led the men to the long oval table in the conference room, motioning them to be seated. Damn. Sumi hadn't indicated there would be a problem with their marriage. The only thing she'd said was they'd have to postpone it for a year.

The spokesman for the delegation spoke flawless English. "Mr. Tanner, we represent Hasegawa Enterprises in its entirety." The spokesman's briefcase snapped open at the same moment the others snapped open. Synchronization to the last sync, Cole thought ruefully. Sumi's dowry, or something to do with his own net worth? Shit. When they got a load of his bank account, they'd never let Sumi marry him.

"Mr. Hasegawa asked me to deliver this to you personally. I am to wait while you read it before I continue."

Cole's heart pounded when he reached for the letter. His hands were trembling so badly he could barely hold the paper.

Dear Coleman san,

This letter, my last to you, reaches you from beyond my grave. I am writing this many, many months before my expected demise. I mention this to you so you will know I am lucid and have all my faculties at my disposal. The men who are with you now will attest to this fact.

To you, Coleman Tanner, I bequeath Hasegawa Enterprises in its entirety, with only one condition.

Every man must have a dream, and other men must help bring that dream to fruition. Now you will write. Nothing stands in the way of that dream now. Do it, Coleman san. For yourself, for Sumi, and for all the children she will bear for you with love.

I make no apologies nor explanations. Accept this which I give you with a free, open heart.

Shadaharu Hasegawa

"You have finished, Mr. Tanner?"

"Yes, but . . . Now, wait, this has to be a mistake. Riley is his grandson. I think it's Riley you want. Perhaps he made a mistake. Sometimes Mr. Hasegawa didn't think clearly. . . ."

The second man spoke. "I am Mr. Hasegawa's personal physician. He said you would say exactly what you just said. There are his medical reports. On the date he wrote the letter to you and drafted his will, he was as sane as you and I are at this very moment."

"I can't accept all of this, even if what you say is true. I've heard about the Hasegawa empire from the time I was a kid. It's worth at least a billion dollars. They wrote checks and let other people fill in the amounts," Cole said inanely.

The third man spoke. "Your estimate of the Hasegawa empire is short of the mark. I am the head of the legal firm that handles Hasegawa Enterprises. At the close of business yesterday, we were worth over ninety billion dollars. This is the report."

"That's . . . Only the government has that much," Cole blustered.

"The government deals on paper. You have liquidity. Ninety billion dollars of liquidity."

"I don't believe this. This is all a dream," Cole said desperately.

The fourth man laid a sheaf of papers in front of Cole. "Mr. Hasegawa owned all these companies?"

"He used the names of family members for the companies. Every electronic item you own is manufactured by Hasegawa Enterprises."

"And I thought Sony and Mitsubishi . . ."

The men smiled. Cole felt faint.

The fifth man spoke softly. "There is one condition."

"I knew it. Thank God. Whatever it is, I can't do it. You can all leave now. Tell whoever it is that I thank them, but—"

The fifth man went on talking as though Cole hadn't spoken. "You are to live in Mr. Hasegawa's house and take care of his family."

"That's it? Live in his house and care for his family?" Cole ran his hands through his hair.

"It is a tremendous responsibility. You must look after his family as well as your own. The children must be educated. As I said, a tremendous responsibility. One, I might add, that Mr. Hasegawa said you were up to."

Cole never did figure out who the sixth and seventh men were. The carriers of the contracts, he supposed.

Once his desk was heaped, the men stood back in a precision line. They bowed formally and said in unison, "Goodbye, Mr. Tanner."

The first man turned at the door and spoke. "One month from today you are expected to take Mr. Hasegawa's seat. The meeting is scheduled for ten A.M. Japanese time. You understand, you must come to Japan."

"Well, I . . . Now, listen . . . This is just . . ."

"One month from today, Mr. Tanner."

Cole sat in his office all afternoon reading the letter from Riley's grandfather over and over. Soon he knew it by heart. His secretary came into his office and demanded to know what it was that was piled on his desk and why she hadn't been called to file it.

"Go home, Nancy, and don't fret. I'm not sure what it is. A dream, I think."

"Looks like a nightmare to me. If you're sure, Mr. Tanner, then I'll say good night."

"When you get here in the morning, Nancy, don't touch these papers till I figure out what they are."

"I thought you said they were a dream," Nancy said testily.

"Go home, Nancy."

He wanted to call everyone in the world, but he didn't.

It seemed to Riley that he'd waited all his life for this moment—the moment when Coleman Enterprises would be turned over to him in its entirety. He stood before the mirror adjusting his tie. Was he ready? Could he handle all the responsibility? He felt he was capable, and obviously the rest of the family felt so, too. They'd taken a family vote and agreed to turn it all over to him, no strings attached. This luncheon today was to formally hand over the reins to him. They'd all be there. His family.

Sawyer had flown over, to spend a week with her two favorite men—Adam was joining her at Sunbridge for a long weekend. She had appointed herself in charge of the luncheon and entertainment, something she said she did well. Riley's heart had fluttered a little when he heard the word entertainment, but Sawyer wouldn't . . . or would she? Sawyer could be a real jokester when she wanted to. Her way of paying him back for all the jokes he'd played on her over the years. And right now she was in a real giddy mood—about to give up her work in Japan and settle down to married life.

Nothing was going to dampen his spirits today, not even Sawyer. Whatever she had planned for him, he would smile and behave the way she expected. He wouldn't ruin her fun. His heart swelled with love for his family. Heart and soul, he now believed he was one of *them*.

Riley peered into the mirror. As happy as he was, he knew there was something missing in his countenance. Eyes, they said, were the mirror of one's soul. Instead of mirroring his happiness, his eyes were mirroring his sadness and sorrow. He hadn't grieved yet for his grandfather. Perhaps he would never truly grieve, but one morning he would wake and realize the depth of his loss. The old one had made him promise not to grieve but to go on with life. He had to do his best to honor his promise.

He'd planned it all out the past few days. Tomorrow he was flying to Japan. He wanted to walk up to the cherry blossom hill. He wanted to light the joss sticks. He wanted to walk back down the hill. He *needed* the memory of the cherry blossom hill. There would be other pilgrimages to the fragrant hill, but none as important as this one. He would lay to rest all his ghosts and start clean and fresh as head of Coleman Enterprises.

Riley's hand slicked a stray lock of hair into place. He could have come out of this an emotional cripple, but thanks to his grandfather's love and wisdom, he was now stronger than he'd ever been. He peered again at his reflection. The sadness and sorrow were still there, and would remain until he returned from his grandfather's favorite spot on earth.

Riley winked at his reflection. He was on track.

The Colemans gathered in one of the larger meeting rooms at Assante Towers. Sawyer was in charge, bustling here and there with little cue cards for what she called Riley's entertainment. She cast a critical eye around the room. The tables were perfect, the centerpieces rich with color. Balloons wafted upward in gay bunches tied with gold ribbon. She'd hired a deejay to play what she called triumphant music and to read from the cue cards she'd typed up. The family was sequestered in the small service room off the meeting room, waiting to be called by the deejay. Only Sawyer would be in the meeting room when Riley arrived. She hated the thought that Riley would have a few moments of discomfort when he walked into an empty room with only herself to greet him, but she consoled herself with the thought that the end justified the means.

"Okay, is everybody ready? You all know what to do and say, right?" There was a chorus of yeas. "I think I hear him. Shhhh."

Riley's expression was comical at best. Sawyer felt a pang of regret for what she was doing. Riley didn't deserve even a second of anxiety. "I guess everyone's a little late. They did say they'd be here. Sit down. Relax, cousin. Can I get you a glass of wine? I insist. Sit right there and don't move. I'm going to wait on you hand and foot." She was back in seconds with two glasses of bubbly wine. "Let's not make a toast; that's too corny. This is purely business." She raised her glass to her lips, the signal for the deejay to activate the sound system.

A few bars of music bounced off the walls. The deejay cleared his throat, as though he were testing his equipment. "Riley Coleman, this is your life!" Sawyer burst out laughing at Riley's shocked look. When he recovered, he doubled over with laughter.

"I'll get you for this!"

"You'll never top this; besides, Adam won't let you. I'm getting married, remember. Sit back and enjoy . . . your life. It's just the highlights," Sawyer added hastily. "Nothing long and drawn out."

Behind the makeshift stage, Sumi's voice rang out loud and clear. "I can't personally attest to this, because I was a mere toddler at the time, but my sisters tell me you came into this world feet first, screaming your head off, with your hair standing on end. They said you were rosy-cheeked, bright-eyed, and . . . very, very plump. They also said you turned into a male chauvinist at the age of four. You were the apple of our family's eye . . . and you're still the apple of my eye . . . after Cole. I love you, Riley." Riley stood with his arms outstretched as Sumi ran to him. Riley could feel his eyes smart as he hugged his cousin.

"On with your life, Riley." Sawyer grinned.

Thad's booming baritone came over the sound system. "I take full credit for seeing you first, before any of the Colemans did. You were a rambunctious young fellow . . . outside the walls of your home. You were kind, respectful, and definitely not a male chauvinist. We took long walks, you and I, and I told you stories about your new family by the hour. You always wanted more and more. When I write my memories, you will be included because you are part of my life." Riley was halfway across the room when Thad came out from behind the curtain. They hugged and then slapped each other on the back.

"C'mon, let's not get maudlin; we have a ways to go yet," Sawyer chided.

Billie's sweet voice sounded next. "The minute I laid eyes on you, I loved you, Riley. I thought my heart would burst with happiness. Knowing I had a grandson made my life complete. The day you came to the States to stay with us was one of the happiest days of my life. I will treasure all our times and talks, and I hope you feel the same. I love you, Riley, with all my heart." Once again Riley was off the chair and sprinting across the room. He hugged his grandmother till she squealed for Thad. Tears streamed down Riley's cheeks. He shook his head at Thad's offer of a handkerchief.

"Enough already!" Sawyer shouted. "Next!"

Rand's voice boomed. "I decided I wanted to know you better the night you and I sobered up your cousin Cole. I saw something in your eyes then, compassion, love, integrity, and a spirit that has never let any of us down. I feel privileged to know you, Riley." Maggie's voice came directly after her husband's. "You were the shyest, sweetest young man, after my own son, of course, that I ever met. I remember the time I made grits for you, and rather than tell me you didn't like them, you forced them down. Later Cole told me you said it was like eating warm snot." Maggie laughed, a delighted sound that made Riley smile from ear to ear. "I cannot imagine what our lives would have been without you. You made our family complete, Riley."

They were hugging and kissing him, laughing and crying. Riley didn't care. A guy could do anything when his family was behind him.

"Now it's my turn," Sawyer said in a serious tone. "Adam joins me here because we're almost married. Riley, if it hadn't been for you and Cole pushing and prodding me, I never would have gone for my operation. How do I ever thank you for giving me my life? If you ever need me . . . for anything . . . I'll be here for you." Sawyer's voice ended on a choked sob.

Adam's voice was subdued when he spoke. "You've been a hell of a friend, Riley, the kind of friend a guy wants to keep for the whole of his life. If I had a brother, I'd want him to be just like you. You're okay, Riley."

Sawyer's eyes were flooded with tears as she embraced her cousin. "I love you almost as much as I love Adam." Riley grinned, not trusting his voice.

Cary's voice sounded gruff, but it was filled with love and emotion. "Riley, you're a hell of a guy, and if the chips were down and they were counting time, I'd want you on my side. We have a wonderful family here. If . . . if your Aunt Amelia were here, she'd know exactly what to say and how to say it. She used to tell me not to be afraid to show what I feel. Guys like us think we're macho and tough and all that crap. I know now I'm none of those things; I'm a human being with feelings, and my feeling right now is one of love for you and our family."

"I thought . . . I thought you wouldn't be here," Riley said quietly. "Aunt Amelia . . . I'd give anything if she . . . You know what I mean. . . ."

"Don't kid yourself, Riley," Cary said. "Her spirit is here somewhere. Amelia never missed a family bash." He did something then that made the family draw in their breath in unison. "Hey, babe, this is the kid's moment, right?" The crystals in the light fixture overhead tinkled. "See? I told you." Cary laughed delightedly.

"Thad . . . ?" Billie whispered "Thad . . . ?"

"Shhhh, honey. Let's all believe what we want to believe."

Cole's voice rang in Riley's ears. "If I need an introduction, something's wrong. We've had our moments, some of them good and some not so good. You're one guy I want in my corner for all time. You had my life in your hands on more than one occasion. You're more than a cousin, Riley. You're the brother I never had." They met in the middle of the room, eyes level with one another, hands on each other's shoulders. East and West, joined together not for the first time and certainly not the last.

"Am I supposed to give a speech or something?" Riley asked of no one in particular.

"Not yet, Riley. There's one more testimonial. Sit down next to your grandmother," Thad said gently.

The room grew quiet. Riley waited. Riley reached for his grandmother's hand when his grandfather's voice came gently over the sound system. "My heart is bursting with love as I prepare this message for you. I regret that it was not my own idea, but the idea of Billie and Thaddeus. Your American family's love only exceeds my own. In this world of turmoil that we all live in, a man has the inalienable right to seek happiness. For a short while I forgot . . . how do you say in America? . . . To practice what I have preached for so long. Forgive me, Riley. My love for you has no boundaries and no restrictions. Soon my spirit will soar, and always I will watch over you. You are blessed, my grandson. My last wish to you is to live, love, and above all, be happy."

There was silence in the room. Thad broke it when he said, "We must obey my old friend's order, his direct order! We have the love, we're living, and now we're going to be happy! I propose a toast to Riley, the head of Coleman Enterprises!"

"Hear! Hear!" Adam cried, jumping up. "Now you can make a speech, as long as it only takes one minute. You Colemans are so damn long-winded."

Riley stood up, his hand outstretched to accept the heavy ring of keys Sawyer was holding out to him. "There are no words to tell you how I feel right now, so I won't even try. I love all of you, and I'll do my best to run our company the way you want. If I come up short along the way, I hope you'll come down on me . . . but not too hard. I think my minute's up. Oh, I enjoyed the entertainment. Your day is coming soon, Sawyer!"

It was four o'clock when the party broke up. The Colemans went their separate ways once more.

"Cole, can I talk to you for a minute?" Riley asked.

"A minute, no more. I know what you're going to say, and Riley, it isn't necessary. You belong here. You are one of them now. Just like I'm one of your family. All we did was switch places. I know I have you to thank for all I have, and will have in the future. Listen, if you ever change—"

"Never!" Riley said softly. "That's what I wanted to talk to you about. I'll never regret it and I'll never change my mind. It's as you said, we changed lives. I'm so grateful to you for . . . for just being you. Go along, now, before Sumi sends out a squad to look for you. I'll see you in a day or so. I have . . . I have to go to the cherry blossom hill. See you around, old buddy."

"Any time. Take care, Riley, and be happy!"

Adam executed a wide, flourishing bow and almost tripped over his own feet as he held the door of the low-slung sports car. "Your servant, Mam."

"Mam?" Sawyer chuckled as she swung her legs over the seat the way she'd seen Princess Di do on television. She was still chuckling when Adam maneuvered his lanky body into the seat alongside her.

"Yes. Don't you Colemans call your mothers Mam? Hell, I know you aren't my mother, but you are going to be Jeff's new mother, so I kind of thought . . . what I mean is . . . he has to call you something . . ."

"I love it, Adam. Would you mind terribly if we just sat here for a minute?"

Adam's face registered panic. "Are you . . . are you having second thoughts about giving all . . . all this up?"

Sawyer's touch was gentle on Adam's arm. "Not even a little bit. However, it was all a part of my life for so long, I do feel a little sad. My work at Coleman Aviation helped me through the roughest time of my life. It's Riley's baby now."

"Do you think you can adjust to living in New York?"

"The Big Apple! Lord, yes. I'm looking forward to being Jeff's mam and going to his school and picking out his clothes, like Grand did for me. I'm sorry he couldn't be here today."

"I'm grateful to you, Sawyer. For so long I thought you and I would never get together. I've loved you since I was a kid. You were always in my dreams. What do you see in me? I'm skinny, my ears are too big, my hair stands on end most of the time, I'm sloppy . . ."

Sawyer's face was serious, more serious than he'd ever seen it. "I don't see those things; I never did. What I see is a person who loves other people, and me and Jeff in particular. Looks, my darling," Sawyer said softly, "are in the eyes of the beholder, and I think you are the most beautiful person I've ever met. I'm just sorry we didn't get to this point sooner. I do love you, Adam, with all my heart."

Adam's voice was full of awe when he reached for Sawyer's hand. "And we never even had sex," he blurted.

Sawyer threw back her head and laughed, a deep, throaty sound that sent shivers up Adam's arms. "There are a number of ways to rectify that. We can go back to Sunbridge, or we can drive to a motel, or we could decide to stay over for one extra day and go to the family's apartment upstairs. We could oil each other up and hop in the sunken Jacuzzi and do wild, wonderful things after which I will make you breakfast. It's a king-size bed. . . . I know for a fact there are some silk sheets in the linen closet, and there are thick yellow blankets that are warm and fuzzy and sort of cling to one's oiled body. The towels have satin borders and drink up moisture. I have a stash of the sweetest-smelling perfume . . . guaranteed to drive men over the brink. It's your ball, Jarvis."

"Jesus! I thought Cole lived there. . . . He's so . . . Spartan . . ."

"Bullshit! My brother is probably the most romantic man, next to you, that I know. Who do you think bought all that stuff? He said the oil is scented with honeysuckle."

Adam ground the gears of the car. "Show me the way home, honey!"

"Just follow the yellow brick road, right back to the parking garage." She leered at Adam, who leered back.

Sawyer threw her overnight bag on a wide sofa. She tossed her light coat after it. Her shoes sailed across the room. The overnight bag zipped open, the sound loud in the quiet room. She marched across the room to the stereo unit. It took her all of three seconds to make her selection. Soft, romantic music filled the air. She backed away slowly, beckoning Adam with her finger. Mesmerized, Adam followed her to the bathroom. Never taking her eyes off him, Sawyer bent over to turn on the tap. She pointed to the vanity. "The oil is in there."

"In there, uh huh. Right. I'll . . . get it." But he didn't move. Suddenly Sawyer was like a whirling dervish, her eyes dancing wickedly as she ripped off her clothes. Seconds later she stood before him, warm and satiny, her face alive and beautiful with anticipation. "Need some help?" She grinned.

"Hell no! Yes . . . maybe . . . Get the goddamn oil!" Sawyer danced over to the vanity and withdrew a bottle of oil. She held it aloft, her eyes twinkling. She watched in delight as Adam stripped off his clothes. His mouth dropped open when Sawyer poured lavishly into the palm of her hand. She rubbed both her hands together till the oil was warm. Slowly she started to rub it on Adam's shoulders, back, and arms. Her gaze was sleepy and warm as she moved downward. Adam's gasp made her draw in her breath. Her touch became gentle and sensuous as she worked magic with her fingertips. Adam groaned when she poured the sweet-scented oil into his hands. His hands trembled, then steadied, as he stroked Sawyer's satiny body. His eyes searched hers to see if he was pleasing her with his gentle touches.

"Enough," she whispered. "Playtime!" He lifted her slippery body into the tub and then jumped in beside her. All twelve jets surged to life. For an hour they frolicked, they splashed, they kissed, they touched, and they explored each other's bodies in the warm, swirling wetness.

"Bubbles! We need bubbles!" Adam cried.

"You want bubbles, I'll give you bubbles!" Sawyer laughed as she upended a decanter of bubble bath. Instant bubbles of every size spiraled upward and over the edge of the tub.

"You put too much in," Adam laughed excitedly.

"I know. I always wanted to do that! Where are you, Adam?"

"Here! You better shut this thing off or these damn bubbles are going to go all over the apartment."

"I can't find the knob! Adam, I can't find it! We've been moving around so much, I don't know which side I'm on. I can't see anything," Sawyer gurgled.

"Find the edge of the tub and crawl out!" Adam shouted.

"I'm out, but I can't see anything."

"I can't either. Get down on the floor and crawl to the door. Try and find the door!"

Five minutes later they were both in the master bedroom. Both of them were covered from head to toe with bubbles. "It's like a damn monster; they're coming out here!"

Sawyer couldn't stop laughing. "Shut the door! Shut the door! There's a switch out here to turn it off. Safety reasons or something."

"Or something," Adam groaned. "I'll say one thing for you, Sawyer; you do know how to seduce a guy!"

"Oh yeah? Well, you ain't seen nothing yet! C'mere," she whispered huskily. "See that bed over there? That's where I want to be."

"Me, too. I feel like I've been caught in an oil slick," Adam laughed.

"Oh shit, I forgot the silk sheets," Sawyer grumbled.

"I don't need silk sheets. Do you need silk sheets?" He reached for her, drawing her close.

Sawyer's heart was tripping beneath her breast. Every sense was tuned to Adam, to his every touch and action. Some of her girlhood passion and excitement was stirring, blending with the patience and maturity of a woman. When he moved closer, she melted into his embrace, holding him close, the full length of her body pressed against him, her lips finding the hollow at his neck and nuzzling in the crisp hairs of his chest. She reveled in the scent of him, clean and faintly soapy, but she was sharply aware of the deeper male scent beneath. His hands were in her hair, stroking. His lips were tracing little concentric circles near her temples. It felt so good to be held this way, close against him, almost a part of him. And his tenderness was unhurried. He would woo her, court her, and only when she wished it would he take her. He was kissing her sweetly, gently, the way she wanted to be kissed. He was her master, her teacher and guide, and his only concern was for her pleasure. He was touching her gently, as though she were a delicate flower that would bruise and wither with an indiscriminate touch.

The kisses that he was tracing along her neck sent delicious little quivers down her spine. The hunger in his voice when she touched the tip of her tongue to the base of his throat echoed within her. Expectation plucked at her nerve endings and heated her blood.

As her hands caressed the smooth of his back, those muscles and planes became familiar and intriguing. Her pelvis undulated in a dance, pressing against his stomach and loins with a hungry need of its own. Although the room was dimmed, curtained and shaded against the night, her mind's eye saw him clearly, knowing his body. This was Adam, her soon-to-be husband, the man who would share all of her tomorrows.

His possession of her was tender, sweet and unhurried. A new beginning. Sawyer felt her tenseness melt away, leaving her clean and pink and fresh. She turned her face into the palm of his hand, breathing the scent of herself mingled with his own, feeling the tips of his fingers softly touch her lips.

"My own sweet Sawyer," he whispered, pulling her downward to meet his kiss. It was then, when she felt the moistness on her cheeks, that she realized she was crying. Her tears mingled with his, and the hungry fulfillment of their bodies was secondary to the needs of their hearts. Overwhelming emotions engulfed her, drawing her body closer to his in an effort to touch his soul. Was it to be? Was she at last a part of Adam? Yes, her heart cried joyfully.

She heard her name upon his lips, saw the expression of love in his eyes. Her inner being reached out with long, tender fingers, groping through years of denial and darkness to find him. Her soul seemed to feel him close, so close, closer than a breath away. She lay weeping in his arms, joyful tears of love. As Sawyer drifted off to sleep in Adam's arms, she murmured, "We have all our tomorrows ahead of us."

"Hmmmn," Adam agreed.

{{{{{{{{ CHAPTER TWENTY-SEVEN }}}}}}}}

Cary Assante took a last look around the apartment. Everything was packed, the furniture covered. Maybe someday he'd sublet it, but for now he didn't even want to think that far ahead. He would dive into work. He'd get the refinery operational and move on to his memorial to Amelia, a lifetime of work. His work—to plan and build a perpetual tribute to his wife. A house had been rented, not far from Maggie and Rand's. Maggie promised a housekeeper when he arrived.

The only thing he had to do was lock the door and call Billie from the airport.

Outside in the brisk air Cary noticed for the first time that the trees were dressed for autumn, Amelia's favorite time of the year. He was leaving autumn behind him now but he'd be back for the next one. Warm trade winds, blue skies, and warm water would be the call of the day this year.

His good-bye to Billie and Thad in Vermont was brief but warm. "I'll keep in touch," he promised.

Billie broke the connection and called Julie at her office. "Please, Julie, stop by on your lunch hour or on your way home from work." Thad nodded complacently. He was still nodding when she dialed a second time. "Maggie, darling, I have a favor to ask of you. Do you think you could find a rental house that's close, but not too close, to Cary's?"

"Of course, and I'm not even going to ask why."

"I always said you were the wisest of the lot. I'll talk with you later."

Julie sat at the kitchen table with Thad and Billie, sipping coffee. Billie excused herself and returned a few moments later with a parcel wrapped in brown paper and string. "For me? It isn't my birthday. What is it?"

Billie's eyes filled. Thad looked away. "It isn't from Thad or me. It's for you and it's from Amelia. She said I would know when the time was right to give it to you. This is the right time."

Julie's hands trembled so that she could barely untie the string. Thad clipped it with the paring knife.

"Cary gave that to Amelia years and years ago. I think she loved it more than anything in the world. More even than the pearls she gave you at Christmastime. You do understand about the pearls, don't you?"

"I never understood why she would want me, someone who was almost a stranger, to have something that was her mother's."

"She wanted them to stay in the family."

"But that would mean . . . she knew . . ." Billie nodded.

"Does Cary know that she knew?" Julie asked in a hushed voice.

"I'm not sure, and I don't think it matters now. What matters is what Amelia wanted, and she wanted you to have this." Julie had unwrapped the sundial. "Cary will understand why it was given to you. *Grow old along with me. The best is yet to be.* Please don't cry, Julie. It's Amelia's legacy to you and to Cary. She didn't know how else to say she approved without saying the words outright."

"This is for you, Julie," Thad said, holding out a white envelope.

"What is it?"

"A ticket to Hawaii on the seven A.M. flight tomorrow."

"My job . . ."

"We'll take care of things from this end. When you get to Hawaii, go to Maggie's."

"Maybe it's too soon. Maybe Cary—"

"Cary needs a friend. Be that friend. The rest will fall into place. You better get home now and pack. Thad will take you to the airport tomorrow and close up your apartment."

"Aunt Billie, are you sure this is what Amelia—"

"It's what she wanted," Thad said gently.

Julie walked along the beach, enjoying the early-morning sunrise. Her heart fluttered when she noticed Cary sitting on the sand, staring out at the ocean. "Hi," she said softly.

"Julie!"

"I was sort of in the neighborhood. Would you like to walk back with me? I made coffee. I'm staying about a quarter of a mile down the beach," she said breathlessly, praying he wouldn't refuse her request.

"Sure; why not?" Cary said flatly.

"How's it going?" she asked gently.

"Good some days, bad other days. Why didn't you take my call after we got back?" The tone of anger in his voice surprised him.

"Because Billie told me about Amelia's heart attack. I thought you and I . . . that you just . . . that you were hurt and angry with Amelia and I was someone who was handy. I didn't think I could bear to hear the guilt in your voice. I thought my heart would break," she said honestly, the hint of a sob in her voice.

"I don't feel anything, Julie. I try. I get up, I do what I have to do, but I don't *feel* anything."

"That's normal. I know you don't want to hear this, but time has a way of healing grief. Billie said that to me. It was Thad who bought my ticket to come here. I have a lead on a job I'm to see about tomorrow, and Maggie rented a house for me. I'm all set. I think what I'm trying to say is I'd like to be a friend if you'll let me." She waited for a response. When Cary didn't comment, she turned to walk back up the beach; Cary fell into step beside her.

"Nice little place you have here. Let's have our coffee outside."

"Would you like some toast?" Julie called from the kitchen. When he didn't answer she decided to make it anyway. She stopped in the doorway with the tray in her hands to watch Cary. He was holding the sundial, staring at it intently. The screen door slammed behind Julie, jarring the moment.

"Where did you get this?" Cary asked hoarsely.

"From Amelia. She gave it to Billie to give to me. Billie said when you saw it, you'd understand."

Cary's grief exploded like a bomb. When it was over he lay back in the lounge chair. "I can't believe she knew. She never once—"

"Billie told me Amelia felt you and I were meant for one another, and she would like to see us together after she was gone. I don't know if that was right or wrong of her; I can only tell you what Billie told me. The pearls were to stay in the family, and the sundial was to let you know you have to get on with your life. There's no need for you to feel pressured. You'll make decisions when the time is right. Amelia . . . Amelia tried her best to make it right . . . for all of us," Julie said in a shaking voice.

Cary stared out at the blue jewel of the Pacific. A gentle smile tugged at the corners of his mouth. "Come on, friend, I'll buy you a cup of coffee; yours is lousy." His voice was light, almost breezy, when he reached for Julie's hand.

Their beginning.

By day Cary worked at the building site of the refinery. He wasn't exactly a hands-on carpenter or builder this time around, but more of a supervisor who shouted words impatiently to men he considered slow workers. It took him a full week to realize that no amount of shouting and bellowing would change things. Warm sunshine and bright smiles and affirmative head shakes finally made him smile, too. He learned to relax and let his men work at their own pace. He hired a local foreman who claimed unabashedly to know more than Cary had ever known. He made his statement with laughing eyes and a show of pearl-white teeth. Cary was free to tour the island, take Julie to lunch, meet Maggie and Rand for coffee, visit their house, and swim with Chesney, who was family now.

Evenings were his own, and he made up his own schedule. Every other day he took a long walk after dinner, stopping to see Julie on the way home. It wasn't until the third or fourth visit to Julie's little house that she hesitantly and shyly made a suggestion. Cary's eyes widened in shock that this lovely woman could be so in tune to his thoughts.

"What did I say wrong, Cary? Is it too soon to think about building a memorial to Amelia? Or isn't it a good idea? I could help you. I could quit my job; I have some savings, and I can live off that. I'd like to be part of . . . I want to help," she said simply.

Cary cleared his throat. "For months now I've been thinking

about doing what you just suggested. I came here because I made a commitment to Rand with the refinery, and I have to honor it. I did hire a foreman to give myself more free time. I want my blood and sweat and all my energies to go into building the center. For Amelia. Do you understand what I'm saying?"

"Of course I understand. But you haven't said yet if you will accept my help."

"All I have is notes on scraps of paper." He told her then about the day he thought Amelia's spirit was in the apartment, and about finding the map. She didn't laugh or look at him as if he'd lost his mind. Instead her eyes widened and she smiled.

"Cary, if I tell you something, will you promise you won't laugh or think me insane?" Cary nodded.

"It's nothing like what you just said, but so many times when I would start to think of you and Amelia, I would inevitably feel guilty, but the guilt never lasted for more than a minute. And it wasn't that I shook it off. It was as though Amelia came into my thoughts and drove them away. Are you going to laugh?" Julie asked anxiously.

"No. I think I believe in all that far-out stuff. I believe Amelia's . . . spirit *was* there that day. There is no other explanation. I'll never tell anyone else either."

Julie's heart swelled. "It will be our . . . your . . . experience. Will you show me your notes and tell me more about the memorial?"

Cary shook his head, not trusting himself to speak. Should he share this, his memorial to Amelia, with Julie? He stared at Julie and saw only a warm, caring, wonderful person who would commit herself to him and to his plan for the memorial. She would work beside him. She'd never whimper or complain that he was working twenty hours a day to pay tribute to his wife. Amelia always said true love was unselfish. "I'd like to show you what I have. I can use some input."

Cary's voice grew excited. "I want this to be wonderful, one of a kind, marvelous, extraordinary. I don't want this little city even to hint at illness and old age. I want it to be a modern structure, like Miranda. Glass and steel and perpetual sunshine, and if the sun isn't shining, I'll find a way to manufacture it. I want a zoo with every animal there is, and I want pets, hundreds of pets, and no goddamn goldfish either. I want warm flesh-and-blood animals that shed and eat and crap all over the place. Did you know that pets can make an older person's blood pressure go down if its high?"

Julie's eyes widened. "No, I didn't know that."

"Well, it does. And pets make people laugh, and feel good. Parks and trails, horses and ponies for when the old people's grandchildren come to visit. They can come and stay for weeks. Do you know some of those nursing homes Amelia investigated wouldn't allow grandchildren except for a few hours a week?"

"I didn't know that either," Julie said.

Cary shook his head. "You'd be surprised at the restrictions that are put on the elderly. It's a sin. There won't be any of that in my city."

Julie clapped her hands. "Bravo! Now you see what Amelia was trying to do. She just didn't have enough time." Tears burned her eyes and she looked away.

"Julie?"

"Yes."

"It's going to take me a lot of years to do what I want to do. I have to do it right. I'll be old by the time I finish, if God allows me to finish. Will you . . . would you . . . "

"I don't care how long it takes. Yes, I'll help if you want me to. I owe . . . I want to give back; do you understand?"

"That's just the way I feel. I want to give back for all my good years. I owe so much, and it doesn't matter who I owe it to. It will be my pleasure to have you work with me, but with a salary. It won't be much to start with," he said hesitantly.

"I know how to be frugal. I told you I have some money saved. Just tell me what to do."

"Go back to Texas. I'll draw up a work plan for you. You can start laying the groundwork. Get a lead on the animals."

Go back to Texas. He was sending her away. "If that's where I'll do the most good, then I'm almost gone. But aren't you putting the cart before the horse? Don't you have to build the city before you get the animals?"

"Probably. Amelia always said I did things ass-backwards. It works. Trust me."

"I do, Cary."

He'd expected her to say no, she didn't want to go, she wanted to stay here with him. He knew his suggestion was a test of sorts. Her smile told him all he needed to know. "You can stay in my apartment if you don't mind that Amelia's—"

"I don't mind, Cary, and I won't change a thing."

"When can you leave?"

"Two days; is that soon enough?"

"That's not much time."

"No it isn't, but then, we'll only be a phone call away."

Distance. "Welcome aboard, partner. It's so good to be alive," Cary shouted. Julie smiled from ear to ear.

The last leaves of autumn lay on the ground when Riley brought in Adam's second gusher. He'd worked around the clock for the past three months. A month off, he told himself, as he set about airing out Sunbridge after his long absence. This time when he walked up the hill, he wouldn't have anything in his hands. He'd done what he set out to do. Hail the conquering hero! He grinned. He'd stand tall at his father's marker and tell him what he'd done. Then he was going to ride, walk, and crawl over every inch of Sunbridge land. He had so much to do. Call old friends, call Ivy, mend some fences, call Ivy, lay in a store of food, call Ivy, order a new suit for Sawyer's wedding, call Ivy. Invite Ivy to go to New York with him. Adam had told him to use the loft since he and Jeff were in Japan helping Sawyer close up shop. He and Ivy in New York. Just the two of them. That would be something for the old memory book.

The post office had delivered his mail earlier, two cardboard boxes of God only knew what. The bank had paid all his bills for him while he labored at the drilling site. The cartons probably held little more than junk, but still he had to go through it. It took him thirty minutes before he found three pieces of first-class mail. The first letter was from a Yale classmate. It was one of those keep-in-touch letters, filled with news of old friends. 'Let's all plan on getting together in New Haven the week after Thanksgiving,' the letter said. 'Bring a chick if you have one.' Riley laughed aloud. He wondered what they'd all think of Ivy. He continued to read, catching up on old times and loving every minute of it. Damn, he felt good. He settled back on the kitchen chair to finish the letter. 'Saw you splashed all over the papers. You Colemans must have an in with the publishing industry. You looked ugly as hell! Give Cole my regards. Take your arm out of the sling long enough to write, even if it's just to say hello. Good friends should stay in touch.'

The second letter was nothing more than a piece of paper folded over to look like a card. Inside was a drawing of a soda bottle with a squirt of soda splashing upward. There was no signature. Riley grinned.

The third letter he'd saved for last. It was from Cole and it contained his own letter and two other pieces of paper.

Dear Riley,

I tried to time this letter so it would arrive when your second gusher came in. I know we pretty much said it all when you took over, but you know how I am with the written word these days. It's my opinion that when you see it in black and white, it means more somehow.

Enclosed is the letter that came to me from your grandfather. I have to tell you I am still in shock. I can't believe you knew about all of this and that you gave your seal of approval. It's amazing how our lives have turned around. I hope your faith in me is justified.

Also enclosed is a letter I found in your grandfather's desk. As you can see, it was never finished. There's no date on it. I have no way of knowing whether or not he intended to finish it. I only know I have to send it on.

I have a confession to make. Maybe it isn't exactly a confession, but more a revelation. I knew the moment I laid eyes on you that you were the Colemans' salvation. Go ahead, call me corny if you want. What's even cornier is you knew it, too. Don't deny it.

I'm glad the family took my news so well. Grandmam Billie cried her eyes out. They all kept repeating over and over that they only wanted me to be happy. We've got one hell of a family, and Riley, you are a Coleman from top to bottom.

Here's a rib tickler. I wear those crazy felt slippers you guys are born with. I couldn't get used to taking my shoes off in the house. Sumi cracks the whip, let me tell you. I'm adapting, and I'm hooked on Sapporo beer. Beats Coors. I initiated a lot of noise around here. We now have VCRs, Sonys, and televisions in every room in the house. These little girls think I'm some kind of American magician. There are twelve of them, you know. Just the other day I heard two of the oldest ones saying the Queen Mother of all dirty words. The kind you and I used to hiss at one another. I pretended not to hear. They giggled.

They tell me down at the paper that I control ninety billion bucks. If you ever need some walking-around money, it's yours for the asking.

I'm chomping at the bit to get married. Sumi is keeping me at the proper distance, all the way at the other end of the house. Somehow we manage to meet halfway in the wee hours of the morning. I love her, Riley. Jesus, I never thought I'd feel this way about a woman. And speaking of women, I hope you aren't going to drag your feet where Ivy is concerned. Sumi says we should have a double wedding because there will be more presents. I can't make her understand that half the presents would be yours and Ivy's.

East and West finally merged, thanks to you.

Well done, Riley.

Yours,
Cole

Riley read the letter to Cole from his grandfather. The old one had kept his word. There was no need for Cole ever to know it had been his idea from the very beginning. All they'd done really was to change places in life.

They were one now, the Hasegawas and the Colemans. "Thank you, Grandfather," Riley whispered.

The letter from his grandfather was short—too short.

Dear Grandson,

It is difficult for me to write this letter, for my fingers will not move as I direct them. You will understand if the brush makes mistakes.

My greatest moment came when you called to ask for my help. I knew then, without you saying the words, that whatever it was that lay between us was no more. My heart did sing, as you said yours did, when we spoke of our love for one another.

My heart is proud that you could lay aside your pride to ask for my help, all the while thinking you would cause pain to this old one. It is important to me that you know there was no pain, only joy that you would come to me in your darkest hour and that I, and I alone, could make the light shine for you.

The wheels are, as you say, in motion for your inheritance to be transferred to Coleman. It is, as you say, right to make our families one. I regret

Riley wiped at his eyes. It was finished.

It was time now to call Ivy. Time for his walk up the hill.

Ivy's voice was breathless when she answered the phone. "My father called and told me you would be home any day. I came back to Buckalew Big Wells to head off the realtor. It's off the market; did you know that? My father told me you brought in a second gusher on the Jarvis property. Congratulations! When did you get back to Sunbridge?"

"Strangely enough, only an hour ago. We capped the well this morning, and I'm taking a month of R and R in New York." He waited a second or two to see if Ivy would comment. When she didn't, he spoke again, "Would you like to go with me?"

There was no hesitation on Ivy's part. "I'd love to go!" She'd worry about her boss and the rent payment later. "By the way, do you want the Bronco?"

"Eventually. You didn't call . . . you could have, you know. We have phones at the site. I thought your father would have told you that. . . . " Riley could feel himself flush as he waited for her answer.

"That works two ways, Riley Coleman. If you have a phone at the site, you could have called me. You weren't working twenty-four hours a day, were you? Besides, I was getting settled in my new job and all. I had an apartment to furnish. You know how it is."

"As a matter of fact, I was working twenty hours a day. We were so close to bringing in the well, we only slept in snatches. I have something I have to do. How about if I give you a call later? Will you be in Miranda or at Buckalew Big Wells?"

"Who knows? These days I pretty much move when the spirit strikes me. Do you have a pencil? Okay, here's the number at my apartment. See you around, Riley."

Riley stared at the pinging phone. He felt a loss once the connection was broken. This definitely wasn't the old Ivy. He grinned. He wondered if he'd ever tell her how often he dreamed of her in his hectic snatches of sleep, or tell her he thought of her in his most trying moments. It was so easy of late to bring her face into his line of vision. Sweet, wonderful Ivy.

Something he had to do. It wasn't an excuse, but a fact. For weeks now he'd thought about this moment. Now the moment was here, and he had to act on it. He was being drawn by some inner force to the hill behind Sunbridge. He'd never really shared his thoughts and feelings for the hill, but he knew Cole was aware of them. They'd spoken of it when he came down from the cherry blossom hill in Japan. Cole understood him perfectly. His Aunt Maggie called the hill God's place because all those who rested on the hill had gone to God. He wasn't one hundred percent sure his great-grandfather Seth had gone to God, but if his Aunt Maggie said it was so, then it must be so. He'd only been there twice—once alone, and then for his Aunt Amelia's burial. The others used to go to the hill often, to pour out their hearts as they searched for peace. He supposed some people might think it silly or unmanly to expect . . . what? Consolation, absolution, peace? His mind searched for the word he wanted to describe the hill behind Sunbridge. A sanctuary.

Ivy walked around the empty rooms at Buckalew Big Wells. It was desolate now, with all the furnishings gone. With or without furniture, she'd never been happy here. Should she wait here for Riley to call back? Would he call back? If she waited, she'd feel like a fool if he didn't. On the other hand, he might call her apartment, but if he did that, he'd get her answering machine. It might do Riley good to talk to a machine. It was time for him to appreciate her. She'd wait fifteen minutes and not a second longer. She switched the radio on. Sound blasted through the kitchen, a loud rock and roll tune that made her feet move on the tile floor.

Everything was so . . . hushed. Quiet. Not a peaceful quiet either. An ominous kind of quiet. Ivy leaned over the sink to stare out the window. Her heart started to flutter and she didn't know why. Suddenly the music stopped playing and the announcer came on, his voice somber and mournful. All she heard were the words "tornado" and "Miranda." "Within the hour," the announcer said in clipped tones. He went on to cite statistics of tornadoes in the state of Texas. Obviously the watch had been on for some time. She hadn't heard it, and Riley hadn't said a word. He must not have heard it either.

Riley. She had to warn him. He said he had something to do and then he'd call her back. Her hands trembled as she pressed the little buttons on the wall phone. She knew there wouldn't be an answer. She called her father, and then the Jarvis drill site. No one knew where Riley might be. Her father tried to calm her saying, "Riley would never discuss his personal life with the men. Try some of his friends. Can I help, honey?"

"It's the tornado watch; Riley doesn't know about it. I have to go, Pappy; I have to find him." She broke the connection, cutting her father off in midsentence. In rapid succession, her eye glued to the kitchen window, she called every friend of

Riley's that she knew about. No one had seen him in months or was aware of any special place he might go. Lacey might know. She dialed her sister's work number and waited till she came on the line.

"Ivy, I have no idea. I'm sure he'll play the radio in the car and hear the warning. And speaking of warning, are you safe there at Buckalew Big Wells? Now I'm going to worry, Ivy. Promise you'll call me when it passes." Ivy promised.

Panic rivered through Ivy. She should go down to the cellar, and here she was trying to find Riley. Texas tornadoes were nothing to make light of. There was no one else to call. Cole. If anyone would know, it was Cole. She racked her brain for a full three minutes till she remembered the name of Riley's grandfather's largest newspaper. She made the call person to person. She bit off two of her freshly manicured fingernails while she waited. Cole's voice came over the wire clear and distinct. "Do you have any idea at all, Cole, where he might have gone?" Ivy cried desperately.

"Ivy, don't panic. Let me think. You've called everyone right? This is off the top of my head, but . . . did you say he brought in the second gusher and capped it? Okay . . . he might have gone to the cemetery. In fact, I'd bet ten bucks that's where he went. You know, we all kind of went there when things were either going bad or good—" Cole held the phone away from him. He was talking to an empty line.

Ivy ran then, across the yard and over the fields to Sunbridge property. She was gasping for breath when she leaped the drainage ditch and fell on her face. She wiped at the mud and kept going. She could feel something warm trickling down her knee. Blood probably, she thought inanely. Faster, faster. Her shoelaces were untied, her sneakers slipping up and down. Angrily she kicked them off. Faster, faster, her mind shrieked. Overhead the sky was the color of charcoal. It was so quiet, it was deadly. She tried calling Riley's name, but she couldn't get the one word past her swollen throat. Tears of frustration burned her eyes.

She was on the hill now, on Sunbridge land. She gasped for breath and shrieked Riley's name again, but she was too far away. Faster, faster. She climbed then on all fours, slipping and sliding in her bare feet. Once she looked over her shoulder and almost fainted. She could see it from here, the ugly black funnel coming directly across the hill. She shouted Riley's name again and again until she was hoarse. Faster, faster. Just a few more feet now. Ten feet, seven, five, three, and she was over the edge. Riley was the first thing she saw. He was talking in a low voice, his words muffled in the deadly stillness.

Ivy felt like her lungs were about to burst. She continued to claw her way over to where Riley stood. She was choking now, gasping for air. "Ri-ley," she croaked.

Riley turned, his eyes bulging at Ivy's condition. "What the hell . . ." He turned again to see where she was pointing. "Jesus!"

"I tried to find you. I called everywhere. I heard it after we hung up. Cole told me you might be here. I called him in Japan. . . . No one knew where you might go . . . shelter . . . it's coming our way," Ivy rasped. Riley's face drained of all color.

From the east Riley saw what looked like a giant black Slinky that seemed to be reaching from the earth to the sky. He could see it changing shape, indicating uncontrolled speed.

The long, black funnel became a speeding toy top sucking up everything in its path and spinning it about in a crazy quilt pattern.

Riley now understood the stillness and the quiet he'd been experiencing all afternoon. He moved then with lightning speed. He wrapped his arm around Ivy's waist and pulled her toward a huge oak tree. With his free hand he removed his belt and looped it around a sturdy sapling, an offshoot of the massive oak. His heart thundered in his chest as he struggled to buckle his left arm and Ivy's right arm. With their free arms they clung to each other, their legs entwining for a further measure of security. "Keep you head down and your mouth shut." Riley shouted to be heard above the roaring that was coming closer and closer.

The ugly black funnel thundered across the fields, swallowing everything in its path as it raged toward Sunbridge. Immobile and paralyzed with fear, Riley watched in horror as Sunbridge was lifted from its foundation, a dollhouse in monstrous jaws. Riley stared in numb disbelief as he watched his heritage, his home, disappear from sight.

From their position high on the hill, they could see the center of the tornado roar through the valley below them. Had they not secured themselves in those first seconds, they, too, would have been sucked into the monster's gaping throat.

It was gone, the path of destruction a holocaust. Ivy buried her head in Riley's chest as he struggled to unbuckle his belt.

Freed, they leaned into one another, trembling, holding each other. They were together.

Riley wanted the feeling to last forever. He felt Ivy had reached out to touch his soul. Ivy spoke, breaking the moment. "It's gone, Riley. One minute it was here and then it was gone." Her voice was gentle and tearful, not for herself, but for the anguish Riley was feeling.

"I know. I used to make model houses out of Popsicle sticks and toothpicks. That . . . that thing just took my home like it was a model and crashed it to nothingness. . . . Is there such a word as nothingness?" he asked inanely.

"Oh, Ivy, I busted my ass, I did it by the book, and sometimes I did it by my own book. I worked around the clock, seven days a week, to get where I was before I climbed this hill. I had the world by the tail. I had it all. Ivy, I had it all!"

"No one ever gets it all, Riley," Ivy said softly. "If you were down there, if you hadn't come up here, you'd be dead. It's only a house, Riley. Just bricks and stone and concrete. You can build another one. I'll help you. Didn't you ever, maybe for just a minute, think all this was unreal? I mean what you had, what you worked for?"

"Every waking hour of my life since coming to Texas," Riley said quietly. "I was never sure in my own mind that I could cut it, that I belonged, was one of them. Until the day the family turned the entire ball of wax over to me. At that moment I truly belonged. I finally felt worthy of being one of *them*."

"Riley, this doesn't change anything. You're still who you are. You're just homeless for the moment. If you want, you can sleep on my couch, or you can stay in your grandmother's studio. It's still standing. She lived there for years with Sawyer. If she could do it, so can you."

"Sunbridge was part of it, Ivy. It was so important to me. My great-grandfather built it with his bare hands. My grandfather grew up here, and so did my father. It was their home all their lives, and it's gone now. Wiped away as though it were nothing. Oh God, Ivy, I want it *back*!"

Ivy wanted to tell him how much she loved him. She wanted to do all the things woman has done for man since the beginning of time. Instead she squared her shoulders. "You either pull up your socks and get moving or you stay here and feel sorry for yourself. What's it going to be, Riley?" Her voice was stern, but not unkind.

He still had his arms about her. Ivy was real, Ivy was flesh and blood. Ivy . . . He would never let Ivy go. He knew he could live without Sunbridge, but he couldn't live without Ivy. The realization stunned him.

They looked at one another; an earth tremor shifted them aside. Riley turned to look at his grandfather's grave. Ivy heard him whisper. "Don't be alarmed; I'll build it again, brick by brick, just the way you did. With one exception. I'll use my bare hands to carve out a life for myself and Ivy, for us, not just me. I won't be back up here till it's finished."

Arm in arm they walked down the hill from the cemetery. They walked through the rubble with leaden feet.

"Ivy, did you have Cathy Stamps for a teacher in junior high?"

"Uh huh. Are you thinking about that poem she makes everyone learn?

> "It seems like a long road ahead
>   The road to the right,
> And you're tired at the start
>   Did you say your prayers last night?"

Riley picked up the words and continued.

> "Did you kneel down and pray
>   and keep your hands folded tight?
> Did you look up to heaven for aid—
>   Did you say your prayers last night?"

They finished the last verse together.

> "Our prayers are always answered,
>   We'll be shown the light.
> So let us bow our heads and kneel
>   And say our prayers again tonight."

"Mrs. Stamps always said if you hit rock bottom, say the poem and your spirit will be lifted," Riley said quietly. "That was the hardest poem I ever had to learn, but I learned it. I'm amazed that I even remember it."

"Mrs. Stamps told my class that every year some of her students come back to thank her for the poem," Ivy said softly.

The tears glistened on Riley's cheeks. Suddenly he

dropped Ivy's hand. He started to run, calling over his shoulder for Ivy to follow him.

"What is it, Riley? What's wrong? What are you looking for? Tell me and I'll help you look. I'll help you, Riley, but I have to know what to look for," Ivy cried desperately.

"The hat rack! I have to find it! I don't care about anything else. Please, Ivy, help me find it."

They walked every inch of land surrounding the foundation of Sunbridge. Twice Riley bent down to pick up something. The first time it was his great-grandfather's spittoon, and the second time it was a Humpty-Dumpty doll that had been in the nursery. His Aunt Maggie's doll at the age of four. He cradled it against his chest. Sometime soon he'd send it on to her. They picked through the rubble, the devastation, the bits and pieces that remained of Riley's inheritance. It was Ivy who finally found the hat rack out near the main road, off the long driveway. "I found it!" she shouted. She ran back, the simple pegged rack held out in offering. She knew that in all her lifetime she would never again see such pure, naked joy in the face of the man she loved with all her heart.

"It's just made out of oak and shellacked. My great-grandfather carved it by hand. See, there are four pegs. One for his Stetson, one for my grandfather Moss, one for my father, and one for me. I always hang my baseball cap on it."

"Do you think I could hang my Easter bonnet on it?" Ivy grinned. "Guess our trip to New York is off."

"For now. And yes, you can hang your Easter bonnet on it."

"Riley Coleman, is that a proposal?" Ivy squealed in mock delight.

"I fell right into that one." He turned serious. "Will you marry me, Ivy?"

"You bet! Jeez, I thought you were never going to ask me. That Easter bonnet thing was a nice touch, don't you think?"

"Hell yes. Just remember when we're old and gray and the kids ask how I proposed, that you tell the truth. Do you know how to lay bricks?"

"No. I'm willing to learn. Do you know how?"

"Nope. There's a little more to bricklaying than stacking them on top of each other."

"Are we getting married before or after we build this here house?" Ivy questioned. "I don't think it's going to go real quick, us being novices and all."

"We'll get married just as soon as you're ready. We'll live in the studio. I wonder if this was written in the stars."

"Not on your life! I think God had something to do with it. I used to pray every night that you would fall in love with me."

Riley threw back his head and laughed. "I used to pray to God to send me that special person I was meant to share my life with. You're it, from all indications."

"Just you and me." Ivy smiled warmly as she linked her arm with Riley's.

Riley's voice was gruff and husky. "By the way, do you think you're up to being one of us?"

"Would you marry me if I wasn't? Up to being a Coleman, I mean."

"Hell yes. We're not special; I just learned that about an hour ago."

The sun beamed down on them, golden and bright, embracing them in its warmth.

They walked away from the destruction that was once Sunbridge. Tomorrow would be soon enough to begin building their life and home.

Their own Sunbridge.

TEXAS SUNRISE

I would like to dedicate this book to two very special peo-
ple, Doris and Buzz Parmett. You're always there for me
and besides, you love Fred and Gus as much as I do.

—F.M.

Seth
Coleman
b. Jan. 22, 1892
d. July 30, 1970
m. Sept. 15, 1915

Jessica
Connors Riley
b. May 9, 1896
d. Nov. 1,1943

Cary
Assante
b. Mar. 12, 1947
m. July 20, 1984

Amelia Edna
Coleman
b. May 27, 1920
d. Mar. 6, 1990
m. July 5, 1941

Geoffrey
Nelson
b. Sept. 7, 1917

Moss Seth
Coleman
b. Apr. 9, 1918
d. Jan. 12, 1974
m. June 17, 1942

*Rand Nelson
b. Dec. 31, 1939
d. Mar. 21, 1992
m. Aug. 1, 1986

Margaret Jessica
Coleman
b. Feb. 4, 1943
m. June 1, 1968

Cranston
Tanner
b. April 2, 1936

†Chesney
Brighton
b. June 26, 1964

Adam
Jarvis
b. Aug. 2, 1952
m. July 1, 1990

Sawyer
Coleman
b. Mar. 6, 1956

Coleman
Peter Tanner
b. Apr. 2, 1967

‡Josephine
Jarvis
and
Kathryn
Jarvis
b. Apr. 5, 1991

* natural son of Geoffrey Nelson,
  adopted son of Amelia Coleman
  Nelson
† natural daughter of Rand Nelson,
  illegitimate daughter of Marion
  Brighton
‡ twins

{{{{{{{{{ PROLOGUE }}}}}}}}}

Billie Kingsley blinked. It was the only outward sign that she'd heard what the specialist had said. But inwardly, time stood still for her. What would happen to her family, to her children, her grandchildren? To Thad, her husband? They were her reasons for living. Now this man in his wrinkled white coat was telling her it was all coming to an end. He looked miserable, as if he were going to cry. She had to make the look go away. Her thin hand stretched across the desk. "It's not your fault, Aaron. I've always believed our death is ordained the day we're born."

Aaron Kopelman had known all the Colemans, had been invited to their Texas barbecues, had gone to school with Moss Coleman, Billie's first husband. He remembered being introduced to Billie for the first time and wondering if she would be a match for the robust Colemans. How would this shy, pretty, inexperienced girl from Philadelphia fare among them over the years? It didn't take him long to find out and since then he'd loved her like his own sister. Billie Coleman Kingsley was unique, and God simply didn't make them any better. Or if He did, He kept them for Himself. "How will you tell Thad?" was all he could think to say.

"I don't know, Aaron. I told Thad I was coming to a fabric show, that I was thinking of doing some new designs. I'm not sure if he believed me or not. I've never lied to him, not once in all the years we've been married, but I just couldn't bear to give him even a moment's worry. I think maybe I'll go back to the hotel and do some thinking."

"No you won't," Aaron said spiritedly. "You're coming home with me. We have to talk about . . . treatment." She was so beautiful, Aaron thought, and never more so than at this moment. How was that possible? Was it her essential goodness, her kindness and selflessness showing through? Even now she wasn't thinking about herself, but about her family, her husband, and how her illness was going to affect them. He felt a fierce protectiveness he'd never experienced before, and wondered if it showed on his face.

"No, Aaron," Billie said gently, "I need to be alone. I need to absorb all of what you've told me, and I can only do that if I'm by myself. But I appreciate your invitation. You're a dear, wonderful friend, Aaron. Now," she said briskly, with barely a break in her voice, "let's talk about my . . . limited options."

It was mid-afternoon when Aaron Kopelman walked Billie to the lobby. Promises had been made, commitments would be honored. "I'll be back a week from today, Aaron. Give Phyllis my love. I'll give Thad yours."

Aaron felt hot tears prick his eyelids. He knew they were going to roll down his cheeks, but he didn't give a damn. Why Billie? Why not the killers, the drug dealers, the rapists? "If it were possible," he said, "I'd change places with you. I swear to God I would."

Billie laid a gentle finger against his lips. How dear this homely man was, how sincere, how loving. "Shhh. You're needed here. God knows that. And, if it were possible to change places, I wouldn't do it, you're much too important to leave this earth ahead of schedule. I, on the other hand, am not eager to go, but if it's my time, then I must accept it. I just hope I can meet my Maker with all the dignity Amelia had. I only want to be strong. Do you think, Aaron, that God will allow me that one request? You know, I never bargained with God for anything. I mean I've prayed, but never for myself. Maybe He doesn't know I'm here. Do you pray, Aaron?" she asked fretfully.

"Every single day of my life." His voice sounded just as fretful as hers. "But like you, it's always for someone else."

They said their good-byes, and as he watched her walk away, he said today's prayer there in the open doorway. He asked that God not let her suffer, but instead give her the strength and the dignity she needed.

It was six o'clock when Billie entered her hotel. She was glad she'd rented a suite instead of a room. She liked to walk around, and in its mini-kitchen area she could make a cup of coffee or have a drink without having to call room service. It rather felt like home. She also liked having a telephone in the bathroom, although Thad always said that it was obscene. A small smile tugged at the corners of her mouth.

Billie popped a can of 7UP and kicked off her shoes before she sat down on a dark, chocolate-colored love seat. She stretched out her legs, frowning at their thinness. After pressing the remote to turn on the television, she adjusted the volume to the lowest setting.

She was alone now. Now she could react in private. Howl, yowl, curse, scream, cry, rant and rave. Instead, she thought of all those who'd gone before her and those whom she was about to leave behind. She sipped at her cold drink. She had to call Thad. She had to call everyone. She needed to hear their voices. All those she loved would give her the courage to do what had to be done.

Her husband picked up on the second ring.

"Darling, how are things at home?" Billie asked lightly.

"When are you coming back?" Thad grumbled.

"Tomorrow morning. I want you to meet me with a large bouquet of spring flowers. Artificial will do if you can't find any in bloom." Billie giggled.

"For you, my darling, anything. A slice of the moon, a sunbeam, a sparkling star. Me. What time?"

"Eleven o'clock."

"Wonderful. We can go to O'Malley's for lunch. I haven't had anything decent to eat since you left. I hate eating peanut butter and jelly for breakfast. Actually, it isn't the peanut butter and jelly, it's eating alone. God, I miss you, Billie. Did you find the fabric you were looking for?"

"No. They're going to send me some samples next week. New ones."

"So what's new in the Big Apple?"

"Not much. But I've missed you too, Thad. This city frightens me to death. I can't wait to get back to the farm."

"I volunteered to go with you, but you said no." Thad chuckled. "Serves you right, old girl."

Billie forced a smile into her voice. "A mistake I won't make again. I'll see you tomorrow. I'll be the girl in the red dress."

"Sweetheart, you could be dressed in burlap and I'd pick you out of a crowd of thousands. I love you, Billie."

"Tomorrow you can prove how much. Have a nice evening, darling. I'm going to curl up with a book. Maybe I'll call the children or maybe I'll turn in early. 'Night, Thad."

" 'Night, honey. Dream about me."

"Count on it," Billie said cheerfully.

Exhausted with the effort she'd put into the phone call, Billie leaned back into the depths of the love seat. She realized that Thad was going to fall apart at the news, and the thought made her straighten her shoulders. *She* would have to remain strong for all of them. Lord, how was she to do it? The family she so loved paraded behind her closed eyelids. A lone tear escaped and rolled down her cheek. She wiped it with a trembling finger.

The long, lonely night stretched ahead of her. What to do with it? Eating would take up some time. Tea, lots of tea. Tea always made things better. It didn't make sense; tea had caffeine. Maybe some plum wine. Both she and Thad adored plum wine. No, she needed a clear head so she could think about the situation. She picked up the phone and dialed room service. Her order rolled off her tongue: two glasses of plum wine, two pots of tea, a side of raw vegetables, and a ham and cheese sandwich.

She had thirty minutes until her food arrived. Do something, her mind ordered. Remove your makeup, take off your clothes, put on that snuggly, yellow flannel robe Thad likes so much. Brush your hair, the gray hair Thad asked you not to color. Remove the pearl earrings Thad gave you for your birthday. She found herself staring at her wedding ring, a wide, plain, gold wedding band. Would they leave it on her finger when it was ... when it was time to go? Of course they would. She would need it when it was time to meet Thad in Eternity. *Write it down. Write everything down so there's no problem later.* The words ricocheted around her mind.

She finished writing just as the room-service waiter knocked on her door. With greedy hands, she reached for the wine and drank it in two fiery swallows. Her insides rebelled instantly, and she ran, blinded by watery eyes, to the bathroom.

When she was back in the sitting room, Billie nibbled on the sandwich, which wasn't like any sandwich she'd ever seen. Even Thad, who was a big eater, wouldn't be able to finish it. It was a creation, she thought as she picked at the ham and thinly sliced cheese. It looked pressed, like someone had used a hot iron to flatten it so that more meat and cheese could be added. She had to remember to tell Thad about this sandwich.

Enough already, her mind ordered. A moment later the phone was in her hands.

"Mam, what's wrong?" Maggie whispered fearfully.

"I'm so sorry, darling. I've had this feeling all day that I should call you. Is everything all right with you and Rand?"

"Mam, hold on, I'm going out to the lanai. Don't hang up now." While Billie waited for one phone to be picked up and the other to be hung up, she allowed herself to imagine the lanai, that wonderful, glorious patio, half indoor room and half outdoor room, which was full of colorful, vibrant flowers and greenery. Maggie had said, just a short time ago, that she had reupholstered all the lanai furniture in a wild fuchsia and purple pattern.

"Mam, I'm delighted with this call," Maggie said when she came back on the line. "How are things in Vermont? What's going on? We just talked a while ago.

I know you want to know what I'm going to do about Billie Limited, right?" Billie Ltd. was her mother's design firm. Billie had decided to give up managing it and had asked Maggie to take over.

"Well, I do think you should be doing something besides swimming and sunning yourself. Sun isn't good for you, Maggie. What do you *do* all day, darling?"

"Hang out with Rand, read, walk, swim, cook a little, hang out with Rand, swim some more and hang out more with Rand."

"It almost sounds," Billie said lightly, "as though you can't let him out of your sight." She wondered if Maggie had finally become aware of her husband's wandering eye.

Maggie's voice changed slightly. "It does, doesn't it? I think we're both caught up in this place. We call it our personal paradise. Rand goes to Hilo a few times a week to oversee the sugar refinery. I have to admit that he does more than I do. I've been thinking more and more about your offer. I guess I put it off because ... well, because, you know me, I jump in with both feet and have no time for anything but whatever it is I'm doing. Rand would be ... I think he would be lost. Are you calling for a definite answer or ... ?" Maggie let the rest hang in the air.

Something was wrong. Billie could feel it sing over the wires. Motherly intuition. "Darling, if you could just give me some indication if you feel positive or negative about taking over, I would appreciate it. Otherwise, I've had an offer to sell, although I cannot believe the amount. Can you imagine, the little design business I started when you were born is now worth over a hundred million dollars? I'm sure the Colemans' coffers could use the money if you aren't interested." What she didn't say was that, in her own limited way, she would be ensuring her family's security. Billie Ltd. had always been separate from Coleman Enterprises.

"My God, Mam, you can't sell Billie Limited. Who offered you that much money? The Japanese, right? They're the only ones that have it. What kind of terms?"

"Cash," Billie lied.

"My God!"

"I was stunned, Maggie, considering I haven't really done anything with the company for the past year and a half. It's more or less been running itself, and, I have to admit, going down in revenues. I need to spend time with Thad."

"Let me talk to Rand, and I'll get back to you in a few days. Will that be all right?"

"Of course. Now let's talk about something *really* interesting. Have you spoken to Cole lately, or Sawyer? And how is the weather?"

"My children are fine, Mam. The weather is balmy, I'm here on the lanai, and the breeze is just heavenly. It is paradise, Mam. Did I tell you, I covered the cushions? Bright fuchsia and purple. They keep me awake during the day, the colors are blinding."

Billie chuckled. "And Susan?" she said cautiously.

"Suse is Suse, Mam, you know that. One minute she's the world's biggest bitch, the next she's sweet as sugar. I think she needs to join 'the world' and grow up a little. That whining and helpless act she uses is getting a little dated, if you want my opinion. Listen, Mam, I know you take all this to heart and you blame yourself for Susan's . . . life, but don't do that to yourself. Susan is . . . what, forty-eight? She's certainly old enough to take charge of her life. Aunt Amelia was . . . look, Susan wanted to go to England to study music. She wanted to live with Aunt Amelia. So now she's a renowned concert pianist. Not too shabby."

"No, it isn't, but I never should have sent her. I feel that sending her off like that was the biggest mistake of my life. She was too young, too vulnerable. She needed me, but I gave in to your father and Amelia. What I did, Maggie, was to give my daughter away to Amelia. In my heart I believe she hates me for it."

"Mam, no! You are the dearest person in the world to Suse. That simply isn't true."

"But it is, darling. Susan wanted it all: England, the career, Amelia's twenty-four-hour doting, and all of us. As you say, Susan has to grow up a little. Listen, darling, I've kept you long enough."

"I'm glad you called. Give Thad my love, and I'll call you in a few days with my answer."

"Good night, darling. We'll talk again in a few days. Give my regards to Rand."

"I love you, Mam."

"I love you too. Bye, darling."

Billie wiped at the tears on her cheeks. Her head dropped to her hands. She wished, as she wished every day of her life, that her only son hadn't died during the war. Maggie and Susan both needed a brother, now more than ever. How was she to secure their lives? Should she even try? She needed to know that her family was safe and secure before she ... She would do whatever she had to. All she needed was strength and a little more time. But time was her enemy now. It wouldn't be enough to simply persevere. She would have to prevail.

{{{{{{{{ CHAPTER ONE }}}}}}}}

"So, Coleman-san, you have failed."
Cole Tanner looked around, his eyes widening in stunned surprise, certain what he thought he was hearing was real; his father-in-law, Shadaharu Hasegawa's voice crying on the gentle April breeze. A second later he realized it was his own thought he'd actually voiced aloud. "That about sums it up," he said bitterly, his eyes raised to the umbrella of shell-pink blossoms overhead. He remembered the time he carried the frail old Japanese down the hill, the fragile blossoms covering his wasted body. He'd come many times to this peaceful, tranquil spot in the past three years. He held out his hands, palms upward, and watched as the pale, pink blossoms filled his hands. They were beautiful this year, the petals almost translucent. He wondered if it meant something special or if this was just an exceptional year for the cherry blossoms.

He talked because it was the only thing he could think of to do. "I did nothing different. I studied and followed your methods, and it wasn't enough. I worked hard, stretched myself thin to do all that was required. I never slacked off, not once, and yet I failed to move Rising Sun forward. I don't know what I'm doing wrong. Most of the others, those closest to you, are certain you . . . made the wrong choice. I can see it in their eyes, and right now I feel the same way. I don't know where to turn. I came here to meditate as you used to do. I have to believe your trust in me was misguided, that Riley is the one who should be in control of Rising Sun, not me. I'm not worthy." Cole bowed his head in shame, his eyes burning.

Cole meditated silently, and eventually slept, his weary mind succumbing to the tranquility of the cherry blossom hill. Tortured dreams took him to a faraway place he neither knew nor understood. When he awoke, it was with the name Shigata Mitsu on his lips, though he had never heard it before. Sumi was on her knees next to him.

"I came to tell you that Sawyer called. She will call back in an hour. She says it is important to talk with you." She was panting with her walk up the hill.

Cole felt instantly contrite. "Why didn't you just call me instead of walking all this way?" he admonished gently.

"Because I wanted to come here with you. The exercise was good for me, but I think you can carry me down."

"All ninety-seven pounds of you?" Cole teased.

"Actually, it is ninety-eight and a half as of this morning."

"That's because you ate a bowl of ice cream and a slice of cake for breakfast," Cole continued to tease. "You're worrying too much about me. I don't want you worrying. Things are going to turn around."

Sumi laid her head on Cole's knee. "I know they will. My father chose you, and he never made mistakes in his judgment of people."

He wanted to tell Sumi there was a first time for everything, but instead he asked, "Who is Shigata Mitsu?"

Sumi shrugged her shoulders. "I do not know. Both names are common in Japan, much like the names Michael and Jones in your country. Why do you ask, Cole?"

As Cole stroked his wife's black hair, his voice grew thoughtful, more thoughtful than Sumi had ever heard it. "I was meditating and I guess I dozed off. When I woke, I saw you, and the name was on the tip of my tongue. I don't know if I dreamed it or if it means something. I asked your father's spirit for guidance. Is it possible the name came from him?"

Sumi thought the spirit business silly; she was, after all, a modern Japanese in all ways. She had no time for spirits and legends and the like. She only wanted to deal in the here and now. In her opinion, it was highly unlikely that her father would venture from that nether world where he rested to somehow place a meaningless name on her husband's lips. No. Her father, if he did indeed leave the spirit world, would have asked for a glass of sake and a cigar.

"I do not know, Cole," Sumi said honestly. "The name has a certain ring to it, a cadence, if you will. I personally never heard of it. We can ask my sisters and their husbands. Perhaps someone down at the paper or in one of the offices has heard it. The library!" she said with a sudden burst of insight. "Librarians know everything."

"I knew I married you for a reason," Cole teased. "I'll do that, first thing tomorrow. How are you feeling, Sumi?"

"Wonderful, now that you are paying attention to me." Sumi sighed, loving this warm contact with her husband. These times now were few and far between, much to her chagrin. Her husband was always preoccupied, worried, and lately he was becoming so with-drawn that she was starting to become alarmed. So much so that she was thinking of writing Sawyer a long letter in the hope Cole's half sister would have some in-sight and perhaps offer some advice.

"Have I been that neglectful, Sumi?"

"Yes, Cole, you have. I understand how you feel, but my father did not make a mistake when he chose you to run Rising Sun. You must believe this."

"Then why am I feeling this way?" He caught a lacy pink petal and placed it gently on his wife's lips. "It's almost as beautiful as you are," he said, tracing the line of her lips and the petal at the same time.

"I don't ever remember the blossoms being this beau-tiful. I am sad that my father isn't here to see them. This was always such a special place for him. When I was very little, I would follow him up here and hide be-hind a bush and watch him. He prayed for us and . . . and . . ."

"And what?" Cole asked, curious, as he caught an-other petal. "You know, my grandmother made a dress for Sawyer once that was this color. She took some of the blossoms home with her after a trip over here. Saw-yer looked beautiful in her Billie original. See? I know a thing or two about fashion," he said lightly.

"My father was offering up prayers of thanks. As a child I seem to remember . . . he was talking to some-one, but no one was on the hill. I ran down and told my mother, and she said . . . she said he was probably talk-ing to his . . . friend. Even back then, at the age of seven, I was a skeptic. I demanded to know what friend and if he was invisible like my imaginary playmates. My mother said . . . my mother said . . . what she said was . . . oh, dear, I can't remember. It was so long ago.

Come, we must get back, because Sawyer is going to call you. She said it was important."

Cole was careful to keep his arm around her slim shoulders for support as he helped her to her feet. She was so tiny that she came only to the middle of his chest. If she'd been taller, he would have noticed the wild look in her eyes. As it was, he felt her body tremble and thought it was from exertion. He scooped her into his arms and started down the hill, the gentle breeze sending a wave of fragile, pink petals ahead of them.

"I think, Cole, that it is time for you to go back to Texas for a visit," Sumi said.

"Later, after the baby is born. We'll all go. Don't you want to show off our firstborn?"

"Of course I do, but this time I think you need to go alone. I think you need to talk to your family. You may go as long as you swear in blood you will return."

"In blood? Never!" Cole said in mock horror.

"Ha!" was all Sumi had to say.

When they reached the garden, he set her down and she said, "Sit, Cole, and I will bring you some Sapporo. It is time for me to take my vitamins and drink that awful tea the doctor prescribed. I'll bring the phone to you when Sawyer calls. Now relax."

"You are the bossiest female I ever met," Cole said, whacking her gently on the rump. "Fetch the Sapporo and I'll go for a walk in the garden. Go, go, go!"

Next to the cherry blossom hill, this garden was probably the most tranquil spot in the entire world. It had been planted and sculpted by a Zen master. When Shadaharu was alive, this garden had been his favorite spot. He'd said he wanted to die here, if only it wouldn't leave unhappy memories for his family.

Cole skirted a waterfall and crossed a rustic bridge before he sat down on a nearby bench. When it was time for *him* to die, would he want to die here on foreign soil, or would he want to go back to Texas? He shook his head to clear away these morbid thoughts. Where did they come from? Death was a long way off. He stared off into the distance and barely noticed Sumi when she set down a bottle of beer and the portable phone. She waited a moment, hoping he would ask her to join him. When he continued to stare at a banzai tree, she quietly withdrew, her eyes filled with tears. They were growing so far apart.

Whoever and whatever you are, Shigata Mitsu, you have been here in this garden. I feel it. He thought of words like karma, spirits, and guardian angels, and Shadaharu Hasegawa. There was always something bordering on the ethereal about the old Japanese. He'd mentioned it to Riley's grandfather the first time he set foot in the garden, and the old man had just smiled. He remembered that smile now because it had made him feel so alive and wanted. He also remembered the awe he felt when in the old man's presence. What's more, he had said so, to the old man's delight.

Many times here in this garden, sitting in this very spot, he'd felt Shadaharu's spirit. He felt the old man's hand on his shoulder when he allowed it to slump here in the privacy of this garden. He didn't see ghostly apparitions or trailing bits of fog or even hear singsong words. It was nothing like that at all. He just always knew the old man was there, which somehow made him more aware of the gentle breeze and the sound of his own footsteps. Once, not long ago, when he was feeling very vulnerable, he'd childishly set what he thought was a ghost trap. He'd brought out a small glass of

sake, lighted a cigar and laid it carefully in an ashtray
on a small table. He himself didn't like sake and never
smoked cigars. He sat down to wait, his eyes on the little table. Then one of the children had called him to the
phone. When he returned a long time later, the sake was
gone and the cigar was nothing but a stub. One of the
children, he told himself, or more likely, the cigar had
simply burned out. Until he walked the same path the
old Japanese had so many times, the same walk he'd
taken with him. There, right in front of his eyes, were
little piles of ash. He'd gotten goose bumps that day
and never mentioned it to anyone. It was a secret he
kept to himself. There was no doubt in his mind that
Shadaharu's spirit was trying to help him. If what he
was experiencing wasn't real, then he was losing his
mind. The question was, what was the old Japanese trying to tell him? Was he trying to warn him of something? Cole was tense, impatient, traits the Japanese
frowned upon. He had to relax, meditate. What or who
was Shigata Mitsu?

He realized he was waiting, but he wasn't sure what
he was waiting for. A sign of some kind. He drank his
beer, his eyes on the portable phone. *Shigata Mitsu.* He
whispered the name, his voice soft and full of sadness.
When nothing happened, Cole said, "I understand, old
friend, one clue at a time." He didn't know if he felt
stupid or not, and he didn't have time to think about it
then, for the phone rang. It was Sawyer, his port in a
storm. She was always there for him, whenever he
needed her. He loved his half sister, but not because she
was always lovable; more often than not she was a
royal pain in the ass.

"For Christ's sake, Sawyer, do you always have to
come on the phone like a tornado? I can hear you just

fine. What's up? How are the kiddies, my godchild in particular? How's the weather in New York? Have you ever heard of Shigata Mitsu?" Cole asked, his voice dropping to a low mutter.

"Everything is fine. Kids are fine, Adam's fine. It's raining. My au pair is working out just great. I have time to myself once in a while. That's kind of the reason I'm calling you, Cole. I need some money from that dynasty you control," Sawyer trilled. "What was that name again?"

Cole's stomach flip-flopped. "How much?" he asked gruffly. "Shigata Mitsu," he almost snapped.

"A bunch. Listen, I need to talk with you. I've designed this . . . Cole, it will bend . . . it's a plane that will bend the laws of aerodynamics. I did it in between changing diapers and wrestling with Adam. Coleman Aviation hasn't got the financing I'm going to need. I need big bucks, little brother." Her voice was so airy, so confident-sounding, Cole cringed. "Millions. Maybe a hundred million." His stomach lurched a second time. "Don't you want to know about this splendid plane? Adam is impressed. Riley said, and this is a direct quote, 'It will put us back in the running when Cole comes through.' End of quote. I guess I overwhelmed you. Listen, I see this as tomorrow's *Top Gun*. I'm talking about super-maneuverability, within seconds. A decisive advantage in air-to-air combat. Vectored thrust engine. Canard wings. You interested, Cole?"

"What do I get out of this?" Cole asked coolly.

"The chance to be my financial backer. It'll fly, Cole. Trust me. It's like we're coming full circle. Just like Grandpa Moss did the first time around. It's our chance to get out from under. Megabucks. Are you in, Cole?"

Her voice was fretful-sounding now, Cole thought. She probably hadn't expected any questions, any opposition.

Cole thought about profit margins, his past three years, and his miserable time at the helm of Rising Sun. "Seventy-five percent and twelve percent interest. I could charge fifteen, but since you're family, I'll go with twelve." This must be what he'd subconsciously been waiting for, a sign from the *other side*, from Shadaharu. Jesus, it was his first goddamn clue. What else could it be? His thoughts grew frenzied. Seventy-five percent and twelve percent interest would put him where he wanted to be, in control, showing a profit. For sure he was a believer now. A niggling voice intruded in his thoughts. *At Sawyer's and the family's expense.* His mind continued to race. Was it too high, too much? Guts, he needed a bushelful now. The numbers were high, but given the vagaries of government contracts, it could also alienate the family, plus . . . plus he could be betting the ranch on a *ghost*. Was he losing his mind? Ah shit! He wished now he hadn't rattled off the numbers at the speed of light. He was about to speak when Sawyer's shrill voice pierced his eardrum.

"Did I hear you right, Cole?" she said coldly. "Seventy-five percent and twelve percent interest?"

In his life he'd never heard such a voice from her. He wanted to say no, take the words back. He thought about Rising Sun's profit margin. He thought about his father-in-law, who just happened to be a ghost, a spirit. Well, either he believed or he didn't. He decided he believed.

"I'm open to negotiating this matter," he said. "Nothing is ever carved in stone. Isn't it about time for you to come over here? Let's sit down and hammer out a deal we can all live with."

"In your dreams, Cole," Sawyer snarled. "I guess I did hear you right. You give some people power and money, and it's all over."

Cole didn't think her voice could get any angrier or any colder, but it did.

"Good-bye, Cole."

"Son-of-a-fucking-*bitch*," Cole hissed.

Hovering discreetly at the entrance to the Zen garden, Sumi trundled her way down the winding path to where Cole was sitting. "What is it?" she asked fearfully. "Did Sawyer . . . is it bad news?"

"Depends on your point of view. She wants . . . she expects me to finance a plane she's designed for Coleman Aviation."

"Oh, is that all? I thought it was something terrible, from the way you looked. You told her you would, didn't you? How I admire her ability. To think that both of you, brother and sister, became aeronautical engineers . . . well, it's just wonderful. My father had such respect for Sawyer. It was hard for him to believe a woman could do the things she did. He loved your family very much."

Shame coursed through Cole. "I made her an offer, which she rejected. Obviously, the thought never occurred to her that I might . . . that it is after all a business deal and I'd want to see a profit." When he saw the look in her eyes, however, he grasped her arm, knowing he had to say more. "I know you don't understand, and I really can't explain this, but I did what I did for a reason. I truly believe your father . . ." How was he to say it? "Honey, I believe your father's spirit is trying to help me out of the quandary I'm in. I am doing what is supernaturally expected of me at this point in time." He sounded like a lunatic.

"What *exactly* did you say to Sawyer?" Sumi asked quietly.

"I said twelve percent interest with a seventy-five percent share of the profits."

"I see."

"I've shamed you. That's what that look on your face means, doesn't it?"

"Yes," Sumi said sadly. She pulled her arm free of her husband's grasp. She turned once and almost stumbled on the path. "I wonder what would have happened to your family the first time if my father had acted with your attitude." With one hand on the door, she called out, "My father charged no interest. There was no time limit on the payback and the check was blank. I heard that story so many times I know it by heart."

Cole's eyes were glued to the doors as they closed. He felt like the scum of the earth. Worse. Until this moment, he could do no wrong in his wife's eyes. Now her beautiful, gentle face was full of shame—for him.

Did he have the nerve to say the same thing he'd just said to Sawyer to his whole family? Was there one among them who would understand, even if he could explain the way he felt? He'd boasted when he took over the Japanese empire that he had ninety billion dollars at his disposal. His *personal* disposal. Three years later he still had ninety billion dollars. He knew what all their faces would look like when Sawyer told them, and she *would* tell them, of their conversation. They'd say, among themselves, that ninety billion dollars had turned his head. They would call him a disgusting, greedy bastard. His heart felt bruised and sore.

Cole reached for the Sapporo, but the bottle was empty. He'd taken no more than a few swigs, and hadn't poured any of the beer into the glass on the black lacquer tray. When he picked up the glass, he wasn't at all surprised to discover beer suds in the bottom. The old Japanese had always liked beer with his dinner, no matter what he was eating. Cole looked at his watch. Fifteen minutes past six. He looked around wildly. The late afternoon sun dimmed. Another sign. He was sure of it. Shadaharu's spirit was here, listening. If he truly believed that, then he had to believe he'd done the right thing with Sawyer. Numbers could always be adjusted. Still, his sister was a tight-ass and would view this as a betrayal. Well, he'd just have to convince her she was wrong. Right now he had to concentrate on his loyalty to his father-in-law. The old Japanese came first.

Overhead he could heard the rustle of birds as they readied themselves for flight. He thought it an angry sound. Each rustle, each flap of the wings, seemed to say, Shigata Mitsu, Shigata Mitsu.

Sawyer Coleman Jarvis stared at the pinging receiver in her hand, her eyes full of stunned disbelief. She felt like crying, but she fought back her tears. Behind her, the twins, Katy and Josie, tussled and squealed as they both tugged at a flop-eared rabbit. Both girls were as stubborn as she was. Each of them would end up with one of the rabbit's ears, and then she'd have to sew them back on when they napped. It didn't matter that each had her own rabbit. So far she'd sewn the ears back on both rabbits a dozen times. The terrible twos. She loved and treasured each minute she spent with the twins, who, she said, looked just like Adam, although they had her blond hair and blue eyes.

"Damn," she muttered as she picked her way past an oversize playpen, then tripped over a Raggedy Andy doll, which she kicked out of her way. The twins stopped tugging on the battered rabbit and stared at the colorful doll flying through the air.

"Adammmm!" Sawyer bellowed.

"Are you trying to wake the dead?" Adam bellowed in return. "It's a damn good thing no one else lives here but us, with the crazy hours we keep. What's wrong?"

Sawyer sat down on the high stool at her drafting table, which was alongside Adam's. His and hers drafting tables. Most times she thought it amusing that they could work side by side, Adam drawing the political cartoons that provided their living and she doing her designs. Right now she didn't see anything amusing in it.

She told him about her conversation with Cole. "Do you believe that! He actually said that to me!" Sawyer snorted angrily.

Always the peacemaker, Adam said, "Maybe you caught him at a bad time. Sumi is pregnant, and he's probably worried about her. He's got a hell of a load to carry around. He's responsible for the whole shooting match over there. Cut him a little slack, call him back."

"No way," Sawyer seethed.

Adam's brow furrowed. "Maybe his business practices changed." He was remembering Cole and Riley when they were young, when he acted as mediator, as if he were their big brother. "Do you want *me* to call him? You're a hothead, Sawyer, and Cole's no slouch in that department either. I'm sure this is . . . Jesus, you're asking for a couple of hundred million dollars. I don't know how quick I'd be to say yes. I'm sure he needs time to think about it, to speak with his advisers."

"No, no, no," Sawyer snapped. "He was real quick to say he wanted seventy-five percent and twelve percent interest. Does that sound like he has to confer with his advisers? Cole is the adviser. He's everything. Whatever he says goes. Another thing, Adam. When my family needed money last year to pay off legal suits, you were the first one in line to offer money. Grandmam Billie didn't even have to ask you, so don't go telling me you'd have to think about all this."

Adam scratched his stand-up red hair, the tight curls giving the appearance of corkscrews. He hated arguing with Sawyer, because he never won. She wore him down by sheer persistence. Still, he tried. "I realize this sounds like I'm playing devil's advocate, but has it ever occurred to any of you Colemans that Cole is not your personal banker? Where is it written that he has to come through every time you guys get in a bind?"

Sawyer started to sputter. They'd had this argument once before, and she'd come out on the short end simply because, logically, Adam was right.

"Look," she said hotly, "the point is, I never dreamed he would take the position he just took. He's a little shit, Adam. The money and power have gone to his head."

"But you're willing to tap into that power and money without a second thought." Adam smirked. He was getting to her. Finally.

"If you put it like that," Sawyer snapped, "I guess you're right. But he could have been a little more fair. We'd all make money. You weren't around the first time, when we were scrambling to raise the money for Grandpap Moss's first plane. I remember what *that* was like. It was a nightmare, Adam. It was Mr. Hasegawa who bailed us out."

Adam threw his hands in the air. "I rest my case."

"We didn't ask," Sawyer said tightly, "he offered."

"Has anyone ever questioned how that old Japanese became so successful? What did he do that your family didn't do? I think it was Thad who said at one time Mr. Hasegawa wasn't born with a silver spoon in his mouth and that he came from humble beginnings. At his death he was one of the three richest men in the world."

"What does that have to do with anything? Come here, Josie, Mommy will fix it," Sawyer said, reaching for the Raggedy Andy doll. She looked at the battered face, at the yarn hair, and sighed. "Isn't it your turn to sew this?"

"No, it's not my turn. And it has everything to do with what we're talking about," Adam said. Sawyer reached for the sewing box that was always near her drafting table. Somehow that warmed his heart. His tone softened. "Oh, okay, I'll sew it this time."

"You might be right. Maybe I did come on too strong," Sawyer said, biting off the end of the thread. "So I'll call him back and apologize. In true Sawyer fashion. What do *you* think is a fair percentage?"

"Oh, no, you don't. Don't get me involved. You work this out with Cole and the family." He risked a glance at Sawyer's blueprint. It was Greek to him. Half the time he didn't understand a thing she was talking about. She liked to mutter while she worked. About the only thing he really understood was the term dogfight, and the only reason he knew that was because Sawyer made him sit through *Top Gun* five times. He'd really been out of his depth when his wife, pregnant with twins, had said she wanted to go to England to the Farnsworth air show. She'd been impossible to live with when she got back, with her constant chatter about the MiG-29 that so impressed her by climbing almost straight up, slowing to a stop at about four thousand feet, then sliding back tail first. His wife, the aerodynamicist. Jesus, he even had trouble pronouncing the word.

"There you go, sweetie. Show it to Ellen. In the kitchen, Josie."

"Where's Katy?" Adam said, a frown on his face. "She gave up on the doll too easily."

"In the kitchen getting a cookie," Sawyer smiled. "I have to get back to work. Can you handle things? I mean really handle them?"

"Hey," Adam scoffed, "I know how to hand out all-day suckers and cookies as well as you do. I can also sew and open cans. Ellen's here."

"You're the boss," Sawyer said happily, one hand on the phone, her eyes on a set of blueprints.

Adam snorted. "Get to work."

He could have saved his breath. Sawyer was already lost in the maze of blueprints. He swung back to his own drafting table and the political cartoon he was drawing of President Bush. Political tomfoolery he understood.

It was a beautiful house, perhaps the most beautiful house on the island of Hawaii. Lush hibiscus and fragrant plumeria surrounded the estate. A monstrous banyan tree that resembled a giant umbrella shrouded the timeworn iron gates at the entrance to Maggie and Rand Nelson's estate. The snakelike drive, which eventually widened and became circular, was edged on both sides by regal palms. The house itself was long, low, and sprawling, with the sparkling Pacific as a backdrop.

The house was spacious, yet not overlarge, and it gave off a cozy feeling of coolness and light, so different from Sunbridge, with its heavy leather furniture and somber colors. Every room opened to the outside. The French doors leading to the patio were sheltered from sun and rain by a sloping overhang of the tiled roof. Beautiful gardens were part of the view and seemed to come indoors to blend with the light bamboo furniture and vivid greens and whites of the walls. Graceful paddle fans, centered on every ceiling, created a pleasant breeze, and the tang of the sea far below seemed to fill each room.

Every room in the house had sheer curtains that billowed in the scented sea breeze. The carpets were eggshell-white, bringing into relief the dark tones of the native mahogany furnishings of the bedrooms, while in other rooms it complemented the light bamboo furniture.

Billie, who had been the estate's first owner, had called it her own personal paradise. Maggie and Rand referred to it simply as home.

Maggie Coleman Tanner Nelson, wearing a bikini, settled herself on the lanai. The breeze was gentle today, causing the ferns hanging overhead to dance.

She looked around uneasily. Always when things were perfect, something went awry. She felt a tug at her heart and knew instantly that something was wrong, either with her mother, her son Cole, or her daughter Sawyer. It was a seventh sense the Coleman women had, her mother always said. So far, Maggie thought uneasily, that seventh sense had never been wrong. The feeling had been with her for several days now, and last night's call from her sister Susan accentuated it.

Maggie draped the vibrant beach towel, a Billie original, around her shivering shoulders. It was eighty degrees, so why was she shaking and shivering? Was it Susan's imminent arrival? This visit was unexpected, a total surprise. Susan never, ever, acted spontaneously. That in itself was cause for worry. She'd said her husband, Ferris, was out conquering the medical world, and she'd laughed when she had said it; a bitter sound as Maggie recalled. She'd even mentioned it to Rand, who had pooh-poohed the whole thing away, saying Susan probably just needed to be with her family for a few days.

Maggie walked to the edge of the lanai. How beautiful it was here, she thought, how calm and peaceful. She closed her eyes, forcing her mind to blankness. "Please," she whispered, "don't let anything intrude, don't let anything spoil my happiness."

The towel dropped and she ran straight down the white sandy beach and into the sparkling blue water. Her strokes were strong and sure, testament to the daily workout she gave her muscles. When the tension in her shoulders eased, she flopped over and floated on her back to let the sun caress her body.

Life hadn't always been this idyllic. She'd wasted years both hating and loving her father, Moss. There had been times when she'd hated her mother as well. And she'd caused the family so much grief and sadness when, at the age of fourteen, she'd given birth to Sawyer. A child herself, she knew nothing about babies, but she'd known enough to get herself pregnant. She'd wanted to give the baby away, but her mother and father refused even to consider it. Her mother had taken Sawyer and raised her as her own daughter, while Maggie had been sent to a private school that dealt with incorrigible children. When she came of age, she'd struck out on her own, ignoring her daughter and her family. Eventually she'd married Cole's father and, at the age of twenty-six, became a mother for the second time. Then she'd divorced Cranston Tanner and fought for custody of Cole. The day she had finally settled her son in military school, she attacked the bottle with a vengeance. For a long time her days were spent sleeping off hangovers. The realization that she was an alcoholic came to her the day she received the deed to Sunbridge, her father's legacy. It was then that she had managed to turn herself around. Coleman guts, she told herself every day of her life.

Maggie rolled over in the water and struck out for shore. She hated her thoughts when they carried her back to that part of her life. She always cried when she thought of Sawyer and all she had missed with her.

When Sawyer had been diagnosed with a brain tumor she had turned on Maggie, rebelling as Maggie had with her family. Sawyer had refused an operation. Maggie had tried to talk her out of her decision, to be a mother to her daughter, but Sawyer had told her to go to hell, to get out of her life. Too little too late, she'd said, but Maggie had refused to listen. Instead, Maggie had trenched in and fought Sawyer every step of the way. Her brother Cole and his cousin Riley, sixteen at the time, had joined forces with her, and in the end, tired, weary, and beaten, Sawyer agreed to the operation. Maggie would never forget the day she saw Sawyer's cocky thumbs-up salute as they stood outside the plate-glass window in the intensive care unit. She'd heard the angels sing that day. God, in his infinite wisdom, had given both her and Sawyer a second chance at life.

She was at the shoreline now and could see her husband on the lanai. Leaving the surf behind, she waved as she ran.

Rand's heart hammered with excitement when Maggie reached up to kiss him full on the mouth, but he sensed her inward trembling, saw the concern in her eyes. Something was wrong. Maggie was like Billie, a rock when it came to emotions. It was one of the reasons he loved her. He, on the other hand, only knew one way to deal with emotions.

"C'mere," he said, crooking a finger at his wife.

Maggie laughed. "Oh no, Lord Nelson, I know that leer of yours. Uh-uh, not now. Lela is due to come in here any second to clean, and . . ."

"And . . ."

"And you think I'm easy...." And why now? she wondered.

"Sort of ... we are married, you're supposed to be easy." Rand laughed, his eyes sly.

Maggie's heart fluttered, but her eyes took on a wary look. She supposed she *was* always willing, even when she wasn't in the mood. Yet they hadn't had sex in over three weeks, if you were counting the days. She was counting.

During those weeks she'd done a lot of thinking. Was she becoming unattractive, uninteresting in Rand's eyes? What, after all, did she contribute? All she ever had to talk about was the cleaning lady, her trips to the grocery store, and the latest book she'd read. On a really interesting day when she found a unique shell on the beach or the water changed color, she had to struggle less for conversation.

Lately, all the slick magazines said that the woman in a marriage had to initiate sex at times. What the magazine didn't say was what a forty-nine-year-old woman approaching fifty was supposed to do when she was rebuffed, even if the rebuffing was done nicely.

She was damn tired of pretending it didn't matter, damn tired of being perky all the time, damn tired of struggling after witty, charming conversation. And she was damn, fucking tired of Rand's trips to Hilo and Maui and being left alone for days at a time.

She felt like crying suddenly, but Rand hated what he called her sniveling. To cover the bad moment, she allowed her eyebrows to shoot upward. "How about a swim? In the buff!"

"You're on!" Rand said, stripping off his madras shorts. Maggie squealed the way she always did and ran out across the lanai, her nude husband in hot pursuit.

She hit the deep, blue water of the ocean a moment after her skimpy bikini fell to the sand. She struck out, her powerful arms slicing through the water. Within seconds she slacked off purposely so her husband could catch up with her. When he was almost abreast of her, she jackknifed and her bare bottom upended. Rand whooped and followed her down into the silent, sapphire water. They swam alongside one another as if their movements were choreographed, then together they surfaced, their heads breaking water at the same moment.

"I love you," Maggie whispered.

"How much?" Rand said, locking his body against hers.

"More than yesterday and half as much as tomorrow," she said. "How much do you love me?"

"A lot, you brazen hussy," Rand said hoarsely. He entwined one of his legs with hers to bring her closer. "Want to make love in the water?"

"Yeah," Maggie drawled.

"It might be a little tricky out here."

"Is that your fifty-three years talking, or am I too much woman for you?"

Rand grinned. "More likely the other way around."

"Show me," she whispered. Maybe this time things would be the way they used to be. Maybe this time Rand's lovemaking wouldn't be so . . . mechanical.

He brought his mouth close to her ear and whispered.

"Really!" Maggie laughed.

"Really. And then some." Rand grinned, striking out for the shore line.

A devilish light in her eyes, Maggie jackknifed into the water. She surfaced, her powerful strokes enabling her to overtake him easily. They hit the beach within seconds and rolled on the sand together.

Maggie tensed for what she knew was about to come. Rand's arms tightened despite her pretended struggles. Then he forced her closer, crushing her, his body hard and muscular. She felt herself caught in the intensity of his gaze, aware of the power he had over her. Her pretended outrage was gone, replaced now with passion as he drew her into the depths of his dark eyes.

She lowered her head imperceptibly, digging her body into the soft white sand, bracing herself for his kiss, preparing her mouth for his expected onslaught. Instead, she felt his gentle lips against her brow, slipping into her hairline and descending in a path to the sensitive skin at her ear. She was aware of the faint spicy scent of his cologne, of the close stubble of beard on his chin, of the softness of his lips as they traced patterns across her cheeks.

Maggie felt her body relaxing, yielding, as his hand cupped her face, raising her lips to his own. When she thought she couldn't bear the sweetness another moment, his kiss deepened. The moist tip of his tongue smoothed the satiny underside of her lips and penetrated ever so softly, ever so slowly, into the recesses of her mouth.

Feeling her moist, anxious lips soften and part, offering themselves to him, Rand groaned and moved his mouth hungrily over hers, tasting the sweetness within.

When he released her, his eyes searched hers for an instant, then her long, thick lashes closed, and she heard her breath coming in ragged little gasps of surprise and wonder. How could this man, whom she loved with all her being, still evoke in her these wild animal feelings? She kissed him deeply, and everything was blotted out—the glorious sun, the soft lapping water at their feet, even Susan and the household staff, who had a clear view of the beach. Nothing mattered but this man and the feeling he evoked in her.

It seemed to Maggie that his mouth became part of her own, his white teeth large and square, his lips full, sensuous. It was a clean mouth, tasting of the wine he'd had with lunch. She clung to him, unwilling to allow even the narrowest space between them. His kisses intoxicated her, making her lightheaded, heightening her craving. They strained toward one another, captured by the designs of sensuality, caught in a yearning that penetrated the barriers of the flesh and drove them to join breath and body, spirit and soul.

When at last they could bear to part, he again looked deeply into her eyes. No man could ever take his place in her life. It was fated that his eyes should be looking at her as they were now, filled with desire, brimming with expectation; it was fated that his voice should be so soft, so gentle, yet vibrate through her like the deep, rumbling note of a violin plucking at her senses, casting a spell over her.

Beneath the sun's golden, warming rays he nuzzled her neck and inhaled her fragrance. His tongue blazed a trail from her throat to her bare breasts, and she trembled with exquisite anticipation. All things moved to the distance, nothing and no one existed beyond this moment and place. The only reality was the way her body reacted to her husband. Pleasure radiated upward from some hidden well within her, and she allowed herself to be carried by it, unable to hinder the momentum of her own desire.

Maggie's sensations heightened wherever he touched her; her emotions hurled and spun, wreaking havoc upon her. Her hands were eager, her fingers greedy as she held him to her as closely as a secret.

She watched him now with half-closed eyes, aware of his sun-bronzed chest, of the curling patterns of chest hair that narrowed to a thin, fine fur over the flatness of his belly. His erection pulsated with anticipation. The paleness of his lean haunches delineated the dark patch of hair surrounding his manhood, and his tapered hips flared into thighs thick and strong with muscle.

As her hands moved over him, Rand was filled with a sense of his own power and exulted in her undisguised passion for him. She was so beautiful, this wife of his, with her lips red from his kisses, seductive now, and her languid, heavy-lidded gaze, which hinted at a depth of passion that excited him unbearably. He was so hungry for her, he wanted to spread her beneath him and plunge into her fiery depths, to feel himself become a part of her. Each curve of her body was eloquent: the roundness of her breasts, with their pink crests; the slender arc of her hips, which narrowed into long, lean legs; the golden hue of her skin, gleaming softly with the sheen of her desire. But he would take her slowly, savoring every inch of her, delighting in the pleasure they would share.

When he moved to cover her with his body, it was her turn to protest. As she rolled over on her side next to him, her cloud of dark hair tumbled around her face, grazing his shoulder and tickling his chest. She smoothed his chest with her fingertips, trailing through the patch of dark curls, exploring the regions that were smooth and hairless, then moving to the flat hardness of his belly. He heard himself gasp as her hand wandered close to his groin and then flew upward again. He wanted to applaud her daring, yet he almost laughed at the innocent look in her eyes. "Touch me," he demanded, taking her hand in his, moving it downward again. It was their first time again, something only Maggie was capable of making him feel. "Do you like it when I touch you? Here?" He caressed her breast, feeling its weight in the palm of his hand, relishing the softness of it and the hard little crest that jutted into his palm. "And here?" he asked, sliding downward to the softness of her belly. "Here?" His fingers grazed the satiny flesh of her inner thighs, whispering past the fleecy curls between her legs.

Her hand followed his, combing past the thicket that surrounded his eager shaft. Hesitantly, her fingers explored him, moving upward to touch the velvet-smooth tip, upon which poised a drop of moisture, like a glistening pearl. As she turned her head to watch the progress of her fingers, her hair hung like a curtain, shielding her face from his view. It pleased her to hear his sharp intake of breath as her fingers traveled the length of his manhood downward to the surprising vulnerability between his thighs. She felt desire ripple through him and realized with a curious, proud excitement that she was in command of his passions.

When she lifted her head to look back at him, her eyes were heavy with desire; he was reminded of a sleek cat who has just discovered the cream bowl. The little smile she bestowed upon him was dripping feline self-satisfaction.

She reached out to touch him again, this time watching him, aware of his every reaction, relishing the masculine hardness of him and feeling it pulsate in anticipation of her touch. When she closed her hand over him, a deep throbbing sounded in his chest and rumbled from his lips. Unable to resist her a moment longer, he reached up, pulled her beside him and took the superior position. Only having her, losing himself within her, would satisfy.

A golden warmth flooded through Maggie as he brought his mouth to hers once again. His movements were smoothly executed as he drew a path from one breast to the other, covering each first with his hands and then with his lips. She clung to the strength of his arms, holding fast as though she were fearful of falling in on herself, never to be found again.

His hands, at her waist and buttocks, lifted her slightly. The tortuous, teasing exploration of his tongue made her shudder and heightened her passion. Her fingers clutched and pulled at his dark, ruffled hair as though begging him to stop while her body arched into his, feverishly exposing herself to his maddening mouth. He searched for and found the secret places that pushed her to the brink of release, only to have his kiss follow another path before returning to the first.

A yawning ache spread through Maggie, demanding satisfaction, settling at her core and forcing her to seek relief by writhing and thrashing about restlessly. Rand held her there, forcing her to him, adoring her with his hands and lips until she could deny herself no longer. Her body flamed, her back arched, and her world divided into two parts—her need and his lips. And when the tremors ceased and his mouth covered hers once again, she tasted herself there. She was satisfied, yet discontented. She had feasted, but she was famished. She wanted more, much more. She wanted to share with him the release of his own passion.

She urged him onward. Grasping her hips, he lifted her, and she wound her parted thighs around him. She guided him into her, pulling him forward, driving downward, now with a different desire, cooler than before. As she moved with him, became part of him, Maggie fueled his passion and renewed her own. Together they were flung upward; together they found the sun.

For what seemed an eternity they lay together, whispering and touching. They loved.

"Not bad for an old broad, eh?" Maggie gurgled with laughter.

"Not bad at all," Rand said smoothly.

Stark naked, Maggie and Rand walked up to the lanai arm in arm, their suits draped over their shoulders. They showered together on the concrete pad, and they wrapped themselves in colorful towels.

"Are you still going over to Maui?" Maggie asked as she popped open a can of iced tea.

"Are you kidding? This old man is heading for the bedroom for a nap."

Maggie hooted. "I knew it, I knew it. Let's do it again!"

"You looking for early widowhood?"

Maggie's face became serious. "Don't ever say that again to me. I hate that word. I don't know what I'd do without you, Rand," she said harshly.

He was supposed to say, And I wouldn't want to live without you, Maggie darling. But he didn't. Instead, he said, "I am going to Maui, and yes, I will pick Susan up from the airport on my way back."

"Sounds good to me," Maggie said quietly.

When Maggie heard the sound of Rand's car spewing gravel in the driveway, she walked down to the beach to sit in the sun. Why did she feel so cold, so alone? She ran the past hour over and over in her mind. The lovemaking was wonderful, but it had been *her* idea, not Rand's. She thought of all the excuses he had made over the past three weeks. He had headaches, his back hurt, he had paperwork to do, he fell asleep before she finished in the bathroom. If she had to come up with a word to describe her husband, she would say he was bored. With her. Oh, he still said he loved her, wanted her, needed her, but she wasn't sure if she believed him any longer. Maybe Rand was going through the male mid-life crisis. Maybe, maybe, maybe.

Maggie inhaled deeply, loving the scent of the salty ocean. A spray of frothy blue water rushed about her feet, leaving behind little droplets that looked like tiny jewels on her sunbronzed ankles. It was such a perfect day, the way most were. Not a cloud in the sky, and where it met the horizon, it was impossible to tell where sky ended and ocean began. Breathtaking, utterly breathtaking.

Lord in heaven, she was blessed in so many ways. Why couldn't she just accept that? "Because, damnit, something is wrong," she said aloud. Was it Rand? Her mother, her sister's visit? Or was it her?

A sudden gust of plumeria-scented air swept past. It was so heady, she closed her eyes to savor the fragrant breeze. Next to the tantalizing aroma of fried onions and peppers, plumeria was her favorite smell in the world. Another wave washed against her legs. She looked down and imagined a string of diamonds circling her ankles. A strange sound slid past her lips. Water drops that were like strings of diamonds, flowers that reminded her of frying onions and peppers, mechanical lovemaking. Her do-nothing life. Maybe that was what was bothering her. She wasn't contributing. Instead, she was monitoring her husband, spending as much time with him as possible so he wouldn't spend time with anyone else.

If she took over Billie Ltd., Rand would be left to his own devices. She would have to do a fair amount of traveling, work the same long, arduous hours her mother had put in when the company was at its peak. What it was coming down to, she thought, was Billie Ltd. or Rand. I must not be much of a woman if I can't hold my husband just because I'm nearing fifty, she thought. Fifty. The magic halfway mark in a woman's life. Was it true that women grew older and men grew distinguished? It wasn't fair. She needed a Billie pep talk. Or maybe she just needed to unload on family. A sister could be as good as a mother. Susan might be a good sounding board. Sawyer would be good too, but she had her hands full with the twins. No sense unnerving her.

Maggie dug her toes into the bare sand as deep as they would go. "Nobody ever gets it all," she muttered. "You get close, and then, because you don't deserve it, it's snatched away." Now, where did that thought come from? There were no answers here on this white beach. Her mother said that the answers always lay within one's self, and Billie was never wrong. Never.

A walk on the beach and then a brief snooze under the monkeypod tree might give her some perspective. "All I have are brief moments of happiness," Maggie muttered as she trudged along the water's edge.

As the sun was beginning to set, Maggie woke to voices from the lanai. Her heart fluttered in her chest when she heard her husband say, "Maggie usually takes a nap late in the afternoon. Five will get you ten she's under the monkeypod tree. Maggie doesn't . . . Maggie doesn't do much these days but hover."

Hover. Dear God. She sprang from the hammock,

rubbing the sleep from her eyes. A moment later she was speaking to Rand, forcing a lilt into her voice. "I was reading this awesome book Mam sent a few weeks ago. I'm going to call her later, and I wanted to be able to discuss it with her."

"Are we having dinner this evening?" Rand said. "The kitchen is cool, dim, and there are no fragrant odors," Rand teased lightly.

Maggie refused to look directly at her husband, refused to acknowledge she'd heard his words. *Hover.* God in heaven. Instead, she focused on her sister. "Let me look at you, Suse," she ordered. "Too thin," she said, clucking her tongue. "I don't see a sparkle in your eyes either. Well, we can fix that up in a hurry. The lei becomes you. I made it myself this morning. Doesn't the scent just drive you crazy? I guess Ferris was too busy to come with you. Oh, I get it, this is one of those getaway vacations. Well, this is the right place for a quick getaway. Juice? Some fruit? Come on, I'll show you your room. You can change into a suit and we'll hit the water." She knew she was babbling, but her eyes pleaded with Rand not to question her as she ushered Susan into the house.

"So, this is the magical paradise where everyone has found happiness," Susan said with a bitter edge in her voice. "I'm the only one who's never been here, and yet I'm the one who was conceived here. Can you imagine that?"

"If I remember correctly, you never *wanted* to come here," Maggie said, matching her sister's tone. "I invited you and Ferris dozens of times, but you always had a reason why you couldn't visit."

"Mam *gave* you this place, didn't she?" Susan said tightly.

"Only for a year. Then Rand and I bought it from her. She wanted us to see if we'd like living here on a full-time basis. Where did you ever get the idea it was a gift? Mam is generous, but not that generous. Besides, Rand would never have accepted it. Isn't that right, Rand?" Maggie said, looking directly at her husband for the first time.

"True. But it looks like you two have some squabbling to get out of your system. Why don't you do it while I go to Mickey Dee's and bring home some food?"

He was gone a second later.

"Why are you here now, Susan? What's wrong?"

"Maggie, I'm dead on my feet. I have jet-lag and I haven't been sleeping well lately. Would you mind terribly if I took a nap? Just an hour or so. I ate on the plane so don't worry about me. And don't let me sleep any longer."

"Oh, Suse, I'm sorry," Maggie said, hugging her sister. "Of course you must be tired. We can talk later, stay up all night if necessary. Remember how we used to do that until we got all caught up?"

"I remember," Susan said sadly, her eyes misting.

Maggie pretended not to see her sister's tears. "The bathroom is over there, and in the top drawer are some night things Sawyer keeps here. I'll turn down the bed and all you have to do is hop in. A word of warning, though. Don't sleep on the eyelet ruffle or you'll have creases in your face when you wake. Or," she added thoughtfully, "does that just happen to women my age? I'm forty-nine, you know. What are you, forty-eight? My God! It's awesome, isn't it?" She was babbling again and still didn't know why. "Sleep tight, Suse."

In a flash Maggie was down the hall and into her

husband's small office. As always when she was around her sister, Maggie left her feelings aside; now she spoke boldly to Rand. "Something's wrong. I can feel it. Did she say anything on the ride from the airport?"

Rand stared at his wife. "She said Hawaii is beautiful and she loved the ride up here to the North Shore. We talked about the lei, and I told her you made it just for her. She said they had a hard winter this year. She did say she was homesick, but didn't know where home was. I felt sorry for her. Mother Maggie's magic is what she needs, I think. Maybe she and Ferris had a tiff. She misses Jessie terribly. She hasn't gotten over her death, that's for sure. Don't look so troubled, darling. Susan is a grown woman. She can handle it. Time is all she needs."

"*If* there is a problem, why didn't she go to Mam's? I always want to run to Mam when something goes wrong. It's not just Suse either. I've had this ominous feeling for a few days now that things aren't what they seem with Mam. You know me and my feelings."

"I think you're just overexcited. Let's you and I skip out to Mickey Dee's and grab ourselves some succulent, greasy, deep-fried mahi-mahi, and greasier french fries."

"I'm not hungry. Why don't you go and get whatever you want, or I can make a salad. There's some very good crabmeat in the refrigerator. It's up to you. I want to make some phone calls before it gets too late. You don't mind, do you?" Her tone of voice let him know she didn't much care one way or the other.

"Guess I'll see you in a bit then. I can taste the grease already. Give my regards to everyone."

The soft knock on the door caused both Maggie and Rand to turn around. "Oh, Lela, are you finished?" Maggie said. "Yes, I guess you are. That was a silly question now, wasn't it? I think my checkbook is here somewhere." Feeling uncomfortable about Lela's presence, she rummaged in Rand's desk drawer for the household checkbook.

Lela, the nineteen-year-old daughter of Maggie's housekeeper Addie, filled in when one of Addie's numerous children needed her. Lela was so beautiful, it almost hurt to look at her. Her hair was long and blacker than a raven's wing, her heavily fringed lashes sweeping upward to reveal jet-dark eyes that always seemed to Maggie to be speculating or calculating. She was model-thin, but rounded in all the right places. She was the color of rich honey, perfection dressed in island attire. At the moment, she was engaged in bantering conversation with Rand. Nineteen going on thirty, Maggie thought. Addie should put a leash on her.

Maggie ripped the check from the book and straightened up in time to see Rand tap the girl's derriere. As Lela reached for the check, her eyes playfully challenged Maggie.

"Close the door on your way out, Lela. Tell Addie I won't need you the rest of the week." When the girl had gone, Maggie turned to her husband. "Would you mind telling me what *that* was all about?" she bristled.

"What?" Rand said.

"That little pat on Lela's tush. I don't like it when you do things like that, and I don't like the way that girl looks at me."

"Is that why you told her you didn't need her the rest of the week? That means, darling Maggie, *you* will have to cook and make the beds," Rand said quietly. "Won't that eat into your routine? Anyway, it didn't mean anything."

"If it didn't mean anything, then why did you do it?"

"I don't know. I just did it. Jesus, I'm sorry. It won't happen again."

"See that it doesn't," Maggie said quietly.

"I guess I'll be going," Rand said stiffly. "Say hello to everyone when you make your calls."

"I will," Maggie called over her shoulder as she headed down the hall to their bedroom.

Maggie pulled a mint-green muumuu over her head and slipped into thong sandals, her island attire. She walked down to the beach with the portable phone in her hand. She had decided to call Sawyer. There was a smile on her face when she thought about her daughter's two children, Josie and Katy.

The connection was clear, Sawyer's voice crackling with something that sent chills down Maggie's arms. "I was just going to call you," Sawyer said.

"Is everything okay? Adam? The twins?"

"The girls are eating cookies, Adam is trying to glue a toy together, and I'm . . . I'm pissed to the teeth. Have you heard from Cole?"

"Last week," Maggie said with a catch in her voice. "Why?"

Maggie listened to Sawyer's story until she heard Adam order his wife to lower her voice.

"Well, what do you think, Maggie?" Sawyer asked. She had been calling her mother by her first name since childhood.

"I don't know what to think. That doesn't sound like Cole. Do you want me to call him?" Without waiting for a reply, she rushed on, "For the past few days I've had this awful feeling that something is wrong somewhere. Your aunt Susan arrived today. At first I thought my uneasiness had something to do with her, but nothing she's told me explains the feeling I have. I planned on calling Cole anyway. What should I say?"

"I don't know," Sawyer muttered. "Adam says I should call back and apologize for my attitude. He says it sucks. Maybe he's right. I had no right to assume Cole would be willing to go on the line for us. When you talked to him last, did he act as if anything was wrong? I mean, Sumi is okay. I talked to her a few days ago. It's Cole, Maggie. If you call him, I'd appreciate it if you'd get back to me. I'm going to start beating the bushes for some financing if he doesn't come through. And you can reiterate to him for me that I'm not paying loan-shark rates."

"All right, Sawyer, I'll pass the word along. Now tell me about the girls. Are they talking yet?"

"They're like magpies. All they do is chatter. They seem to understand each other. Adam says they're speaking Greek at an early age. He said to give you his love. Oh, God, Adammmm!"

"What's wrong?" Maggie demanded when she heard a crash and loud wailing.

"They just got into the jelly bean jar and broke it. They climbed up on the table. Ellen, the sitter, is in the bathroom. You can't take your eyes off them for a minute. The terrible twos. And Adam wants to get them a puppy!"

"I guess I better let you go. Give them a kiss for me. Adam too."

"I'll send some pictures. Give Rand and Chesney our love, Aunt Susan too, okay? And call me if you find out anything from Cole."

"I will, Sawyer. Remember now, patience is the name of the game with the girls."

"I always do. Oh God, they threw a pillow into the fish tank. 'Bye, Maggie."

There was a smile on Maggie's face when she dialed Cole's number. She didn't care what time it was in Japan. She loved talking to her son, and especially now that he and Sumi were expecting.

It was hard to believe that Cole was going to be a father, and harder still to believe she, Maggie, was going to be a grandmother for a second time. Grandmother Maggie. She liked the sound of that.

"Cole, how are you?" she asked cheerfully when she heard her son's deep voice.

"Fine, Mother, and no, Sumi isn't ready yet," he said with a chuckle. "She's waddling like a duck and has constant heartburn. She says that means the baby has a lot of hair. Is that true?"

Maggie laughed. "I've heard that. Not to change the subject, but guess who came to visit?" Without waiting for her son to reply, she said, "Susan. She's sleeping right now, so we haven't had a chance to visit, I mean really visit. I'm so excited. I just love it when family comes. By the way, Ivy sent me a picture of little Moss. I can't tell you how much he looks like your grandfather. Even Mam says so. Same name, same face. It's uncanny."

"We got a picture too. Sumi says he has her father's ears."

How flat his voice was, Maggie suddenly noticed, how dead-sounding. She felt her heart thump in her chest. "Have you decided what you're going to call the baby?" Any minute she was going to do what she did best—babble.

"If it was up to Sumi, it would have seven names.

She can't seem to make up her mind. But I get to name it if it's a boy."

"Sounds fair to me. What's your choice?"

"I haven't decided." There was an uncomfortable moment of silence, as if he couldn't think of anything to say. "How's Chesney?" he finally managed.

"She's in Hong Kong. She left this morning on a flight and won't be back till the end of the week. She calls Rand 'Dad' now. He's going through a bit of anxiety, because she's getting engaged to that Navy flier. What's his name? Brian, that's it. He has six more months to go in the Navy and then he's out. He said he's willing to test-fly Sawyer's plane if she gets it off the ground. *That* was what convinced Rand he's an okay guy. Rand flew the test flight for your grandfather's plane, you know. He says history is repeating itself, that we're coming full circle, and I think it's true."

"So you've talked to Sawyer." There was a faint sound of accusation in his voice.

"A little while ago, as a matter of fact. I try to call twice a week. She was . . . upset. Mostly with herself, but she did say she was disappointed in your response. Cole, she loves you so much."

"Sawyer came on real strong. I gave her some numbers off the top of my head. I'm the first to admit they were high. As a matter of fact, I was reworking the numbers when you called. I was going to call her back in the middle of the night and give her a dose of her own medicine."

Maggie strained to hear the chuckle that was usually in her son's voice when he spoke of Sawyer. Not only were they sister and brother, they were friends as well. There was no chuckle. "Cole, is something wrong? I mean really wrong? You've always said that what was yours was ours. I remember thinking that was the most wonderful thing I'd ever heard," she said, then added more firmly, "If you didn't mean it, you shouldn't have said it. You know your sister better than anyone."

"I know that she's damn pigheaded. If you don't do things her way, she takes her marbles and goes home."

Maggie took a deep breath. *God, what was happening to her family?*

Cole snorted. "Look, Mother, don't worry, okay? I'll call Sawyer tomorrow and work it out with her. Give everyone my love, and I'll call in a few days."

"All right, Cole. Give my love to Sumi."

Maggie clicked off the portable phone. She felt like crying and didn't know why. The sun was down now, and the moon was rising. From her position on the beach she could see the ocean's silvery ripples extending to the horizon. Golden by day, silver by night.

"You feel it too, don't you?" Susan said, coming up behind her. She squatted on the sand alongside Maggie and reached for her hand. "I feel," she said, choosing her words carefully, "as if some unseen force is chipping away at the internal workings of this family. You must feel it even more than I do. We all dump on you. That's why I'm here now. I need to do a little dumping. I'm not going to cry, I'm too numb for that. Besides, I've done nothing but cry for months. Just listen, okay?"

"Oh, Suse, I'm sorry. It's Jessie, isn't it?"

"No. A parent isn't supposed to bury a child, and I'll grieve every day of my life for Jessie, but life goes on. Mam made me see that. No, it's that Ferris wants a divorce. He's found a young woman, one who likes to bake cookies and pies and give back rubs. She's a nurse at the hospital. She's drop-dead gorgeous, Maggie. She goes to church and sings in the choir. She has the most beautiful smile, and she's . . . God, she's twenty-two. I went to see her. I didn't want to believe the man I loved would do that to me. But he's been doing it for two years. I never knew. My God, Maggie, I never knew. What does that say about me? He said . . . he said I was boring, that I play boring music. He wants excitement in his life. Martina, that's her name, makes him feel young and alive. I guess that means she's good in the sack. You know, he's always encouraged me to go on tour twice a year. Now I know why." Her voice hardened. "He said I could have the house. Do you believe that? He's keeping the house in the Virgin Islands. I get the Jeep and he gets the SEL. Is that fair or what? He said there's no money to divide. No money, Maggie. He cleaned out the accounts months ago."

"Nothing!" Maggie gasped.

"Zip," Susan said bitterly.

"What happened to the money Aunt Amelia left you, and the money Mam settled on you?" Maggie's voice betrayed her shock.

"Gone. If I'm lucky, I might get seventy thousand for the house. The Jeep is four years old. I have six hundred dollars in my personal checking account and eighty dollars in my purse. I was going to ask you for a loan to tide me over. My God, I don't even have enough to pay the lawyer." She began sobbing. "I guess I'm the world's biggest fool. Jerome did the same thing to me. Can I pick 'em or what?"

"Hey," Maggie said soothingly, "I walked down that road myself. The money is no problem, so don't worry about that. We'll talk to Rand and see what he says. You need a good lawyer, one of those barracudas. We'll work it out, Suse. That's what family is for. Go ahead and cry." Maggie cradled her sister against her breast, patting her shiny blond hair.

"He moved out of the house last week," Susan said vehemently. "He took everything that belonged to him and a lot of the treasures I brought back from my tours. All the jade is gone. The bastard even took the pearls Aunt Amelia gave me for my sixteenth birthday. What did I do wrong, Maggie? Is it because I'm almost fifty years old? Do you think I should get a face-lift, a tummy tuck?"

"I don't think any such thing. You're beautiful just the way you are. Fifty is prime, Suse."

Susan choked and sputtered, then blew her nose. "Get off it, Maggie, fifty is over the hill. Ferris said it. I can see the wrinkles, the beginning of jowls. My ass looks like cottage cheese. My knees are wrinkled, my hair is thinning. Don't tell me I'm beautiful. I've never even been close to pretty. I've always been plain, and you know it."

"You're hurting, Suse, so don't be so hard on yourself. I don't see one thing wrong with getting a face-lift if you do it for the right reasons. And if you want to get your gut sucked out, go to it. But you can't run to a plastic surgeon for every little wrinkle and ounce of fat. I know it sounds corny, but beauty really *is* in the eye of the beholder, and you're a beautiful person inside, Suse."

"Thanks, Maggie." Susan sighed. "I just get to feeling so desperate, and I try to come up with things that will make me feel better. God, Maggie, what *am* I going to do?"

"You're going to stay right here with me. I might even have a temporary solution to your problems. Listen to this. Mam turned over Billie Limited to me as of the first of the year. I don't mean she gave the business to me, but she asked me to run it for her. Rand thinks it's a wonderful idea, so I thought I would take a crack at it and head for the Orient next month on a buying trip. We could go together. We both have an eye for color. I've been working on the colors in my head for the past few weeks. I want to elaborate on Mam's popsicle-colored silks. I came up with a firecracker-red that will blow your socks off. Are you interested?" My God, Maggie thought, I've just made a verbal decision, a commitment. She felt lightheaded.

"Yes, I'll do anything! Oh, Maggie, thank you. Just tell me what to do."

"Tomorrow morning we can draft up letters to all of Mam's clients telling them we're back in business full-time. You can stay here with us. We have so much room, and Chesney is never here for more than a day and a half at any one time. You're going to love her, Suse," Maggie gurgled. "Oh, it's going to be wonderful! See, in some miraculous way, Mam has taken care of you. It's uncanny the way she's always been able to . . . what's the word here . . . you know, step in when the going is tough, when we're at our lowest ebb. She never gives us the answers, but somehow she sends us off in the right direction and we think we did it ourselves. I've never quite figured out how she does it. Let's call her later and give her the good news, okay?"

Susan groaned. "Oh, Maggie, I don't want to upset her."

"Trust me, she won't be upset as long as she knows you're all right. In fact, she'll be thrilled. She's always wanted us to work together."

Susan sniffed and wiped at her eyes. "I don't want to go back there," she muttered.

"Then don't. We'll get a lawyer on the mainland. Hey, let's get in touch with Valentine Mitchell and let her handle the whole thing: the foundation, the sale of your house, the whole ball of wax. You said Ferris took everything of value, so what's the point in going back?"

"My piano," Susan said weakly.

"There's a piano in the music room. Rand has had it tuned every month on the off chance you showed up for a visit." Maggie's eyes filled with tears. "Wasn't that wonderful of him?"

Susan's eyes also misted. "Rand has always been so good to me. He's more brother than anything. You're so lucky, Maggie, so very lucky."

"Am I?" Maggie said quietly. "We do have a good life, I suppose. And now that he's found his daughter after so many years, he's . . . I don't know. It must seem like we have it all, if there is such a thing."

Susan wiped away her tears. "You're worried about something. I see it in your eyes. Let's take a walk on the beach and you can tell me what's going on."

"I guess I'm not very good at hiding it. I wish I were more like Mam. If I could just have her inner serenity, I'd damn well bottle and sell it. She is the most serene, peaceful, loving person I've ever met, and it's just there, she doesn't have to work at it the way we do. We're damn lucky, Suse."

It was after nine when the lights in the lanai beckoned the sisters. They ran back like young girls, the sand spewing up behind their pounding heels.

Over crabmeat and pineapple salad Susan told Rand the reason for her visit. "Maggie said I can stay here until I get myself together. I'd like to take her up on her offer, if it's okay with you."

Rand reached across the table in the lanai to take Susan's hand. "Stay as long as you like. Our home is your home. Forever, if you like. Everyone who comes here says it's a magical place. Maybe its magic will rub off on you. I don't want you to worry about anything. Tomorrow morning I'll call Valentine Mitchell, and the two of us will take a trip to Minnesota. I guarantee you will not be a pauper when we get back. Now promise me you won't worry."

"I promise."

"Good. As for your mother's business, I think it's wonderful that both of you will run it. It's too valuable to let it fall by the wayside. Billie is going to be ecstatic when you tell her." He leered across the table at his wife. "Just don't neglect me."

"Me! Neglect you!" Maggie said in mock horror. "Never happen!"

Maggie turned to Susan. "Billie Limited has very little capital. Mam dug into it to pay off the lawsuits from the plane crash. The lawyers are in the process of settling the last three cases. The Colemans are tapped out, as usual, although Sawyer's plane could swing our fortunes around if she can get it off the ground."

"I never understood why Mam felt she had to pay on top of the insurance company. The final resolution was pilot error, not equipment malfunction," Susan said sourly.

"That's the way Billie is," Rand said quietly. "She felt that if money could make up in any way for the families' losses, then she should give the money. It was a Coleman plane. The family agreed. And it wiped you all out.

"When Billie said the family would start over, Sawyer took her literally and ran with the ball. I can't explain it any better than that. I'm behind her. It's a hell of a plane, and I've committed a good chunk of cash to the project. So has Riley, but she still needs a damn fortune. Cole is her only hope. She might pick up some financing, but she doesn't want investors. She wants this to belong to the Colemans. I think she's right. What did Cole say, Maggie? You did call him, didn't you?"

"He said he was going to rework the numbers. He sounded so . . . so unlike himself. I see this blowing into a major storm of some kind. Sawyer sounded different too. This is the first major rift between them. Knowing Sawyer as I do, I know she's taking this personally. And as yet we haven't heard from Riley. Maybe we should call him."

"I'm sure Sawyer already has," Susan said quietly. "We all know she doesn't let any grass grow under those Nikes she wears."

"Does this mean we kick back and wait, or do we get involved as a family?" Maggie asked, worry creasing her fine features.

"I don't recall anyone asking for family help," Rand said. "I also don't recall you calling a family meeting when your mother handed Billie Limited over to you back in January. What makes this different?"

"Billie Limited was never a part of Coleman Enterprises. Coleman Aviation is. Furthermore, Rand," Maggie said with an edge to her voice, "I'm not asking for a loan of a hundred million dollars. As far as I'm concerned, Sawyer's plane and Cole's financial decisions are a family matter, and a very serious one."

"I agree," Susan said. "This family's financial problems are like a roller coaster. One year we're up and the next we're in a deep ditch. Ferris always said it was poor management, which I guess means Riley isn't doing a good job."

Maggie bristled, as did Rand. The disgust in her voice brought tears to Susan's eyes. "Ferris certainly did a good job managing your money, now didn't he? I don't like what you just said, Susan. Riley has done a great job. Our books are open to all the family. Everything tallies right to the penny. You were sent a year-end report. Did you take the time to read it?"

"Ferris read it, or at least he said he did," Susan said miserably.

"For whatever it's worth, I agree with Maggie," Rand said quietly.

Susan stirred the food on her plate, her eyes downcast. "Okay, I'm sorry. It's just that I relied on Ferris for so long. I don't trust my judgment anymore. Don't be upset with me."

"So do we call Riley or not?" Maggie asked. "I vote we do."

"I agree," Susan said.

The bad moments were over.

"I move we head down the beach and walk off this dinner," Rand said, loosening the button on his shorts. "It's a beautiful evening, so let's take advantage of it. We can re-create old memories under the moon and stars like we used to do when we were kids. Remember that, Susan? God, did you ask questions! How high is the moon, how many stars are there, and why is the sky black at night and blue in the daytime."

"Yeah, and you lied to me. You didn't know the answers any more than I did. I thought because you were five years older than me that you knew everything." Susan snorted.

Rand laughed and Maggie giggled.

"I wish I could go back sometime, be a kid again," Susan said quietly. "We're to the halfway mark, and it's scary. At least to me."

They walked, their arms linked, their bare toes digging into the sand. A long time later they headed back to the house. The moon was mellow, the sky starspangled. Susan thought it an omen as she bid her sister and brother-in-law good night.

"I'm going to sit out here for a while. Should I lock up?"

Rand and Maggie laughed. "We never lock our doors. Don't stay up too late. We're going to have a busy day tomorrow. Rand and I get up at the crack of dawn, and I'm driving him to the airport at seven." Maggie kissed her sister lightly on the cheek. "You can relax now, Suse, everything is in capable hands."

Susan ached with loneliness at the sound of Rand and Maggie's easy banter as they walked through the house. She wondered if they were going to make love. She couldn't remember the last time Ferris had made love to her. She couldn't remember the last time they'd had sex, that bodily release that sometimes made things bearable.

Rand's cigarettes, which he smoked infrequently, lay at Susan's side. She reached for one. A terrible, nasty habit—smoking. She'd started after Jessie's death. Ferris chided her, railed at her, ridiculed her to get her to stop, but she hadn't listened. He posted signs all over the house with the Surgeon General's ominous report. She hadn't cared about that either. It was either cigarettes or sucking her thumb. She lit up a cigarette and blew a whirl of smoke toward the potted plants on the lanai. She wondered if she would die. She decided she really didn't care one way or the other.

Susan leaned back on the chaise. The moon shined through the slats overhead, and in its light the trailing vines glowed like dark emeralds. Tomorrow, when she wasn't feeling so shitty, she would walk through the house and savor its beauty. Tears slipped from between her lashes. She hated herself for wallowing. She was weak, but then she'd always known that. All the Colemans had guts but her. Tomorrow Rand and Valentine Mitchell, the family's lawyer, would go to Minnesota to fight her battles for her. Once before, Valentine and Rand had fought for her. That time they had taken on Jerome, her first husband, and they had made it all work out to her advantage. Could they work their magic a second time? Ferris was a powerful man.

Susan wiped angrily at her tears. She'd promised herself she wasn't going to cry, and here she was, slobbering like a child. Well, by God, she was finished with wallowing. Maggie was helping her to get on with her life, and she was going to take advantage of that.

The moon was working its way into hiding when Susan glanced down at her watch. Her mind raced. Cary Assante, Amelia's widower, was an early riser. Right this very minute he was probably wolfing down one of the huge breakfasts that he said made his day possible. She'd lost track of the times she'd called him over the past year. The first time, he'd choked up when she asked him how she was to get through the days after Jessie's death. The second time, they both cried. Whenever she called, in the darkest hours of the night or during the lightest hours of the day, Cary was there for her. They spoke of everything and nothing: of love, hate, betrayal, birds and cats, mush and grits. She thought she had come to know more about Cary Assante than did anyone else in the world. They'd touched on Julie and Cary's guilt, and on Ferris's and her own. She'd told him how beautiful the young nurse named Martina was, and how young. Cary told her she was beautiful too, both inside *and* outside.

On the first anniversary of Jessie's death, she'd traveled back to Texas and walked up the hill alone, to the smallest of all the graves. When a pair of arms encircled her shoulders, she didn't have to see Cary's face to know it was him. At that moment, she'd thought it most wonderful and remarkable that Cary was so attuned to her that he had showed up at exactly the right minute. Later she found out he'd called the house, and Ferris told him she'd run off like a ninny because she was cracking up. "Losing it," Ferris had said.

The portable phone found its way into her hands, and she punched out the numbers. She sucked in her breath while she waited for Cary's voice to hum across the wires.

"Hi," she said softly.

"Hi, yourself. How's it going, Susan?"

"It's not. Will I ruin your day if I unload a bit?" she asked anxiously.

"Not my day," Cary said cheerfully. "Today we're clearing the last piece of land. We'll be ready by July. Then I'm going to take off on a trip around the world. Want to come?"

"If I can afford it, I'd like that very much." She told him about Maggie's offer. "Rand and Valentine Mitchell are leaving for Minnesota in the morning."

"That's good," Cary said cheerfully. "You're too vulnerable right now. You're thinking with your heart, and we can't have that. Let the experts have a go-round. I'm glad you're with Maggie. Family is important at times like this. You're still planning on coming to Texas in July, aren't you?"

"Cary, nothing could keep me away. And Cary, thanks for talking to me. I think I can sleep now."

"My day is just beginning. I'm going out to play with my dynamite charges while you snooze the hours away."

Susan laughed. "I'll call you next week. Be careful with that dynamite."

"I will. Enjoy the sunshine. Give Maggie and Rand my love."

"I will. Wait a minute, Cary. I want to ask you something. This is none of my business, but did you have an offer to sell Miranda?"

"More than one, but I said no. Amelia would never forgive me. Take care, Susan."

Susan stretched out on the chaise lounge. Sleeping outdoors was rather appealing, if sleep was possible. She was wide awake, *wired*, as the young people said. She sat up and lit another cigarette. There was still one call to make.

Her arm shot up so she could see the time on her watch. Ten o'clock. Three o'clock in Vermont.

"She won't be there. She's never there when I need her," Susan said to herself as she punched out her mother's number. Her face turned ugly when Billie's recorded message came over the wire. She angrily broke the connection. She hated that message machine. So what if it was three o'clock in the morning? Mothers, *real* mothers, were supposed to be on twenty-four-hour call. She called again, but this time she waited for the sound of the beep. "Mother, this is Susan. You know, Susan your daughter. I need to talk to you, but as usual, you aren't there for me. I'm in Hawaii with Maggie, your firstborn, your favorite daughter. Do you think there will ever be a time—" The connection pinged in her ear. Disgust was written all over her face as Susan slammed the phone to the table.

It was always this way when she spoke to her mother's machine, worse when her mother called her back. "Well, fuck you, Mother, I don't need you, wherever the hell you are."

Susan was dozing when the portable pinged to life. It had to be her mother. Who else would be calling at this time of night? Her voice was cautious when she said a wary "Hello?"

"Susan?"

How gentle-sounding her mother's voice was, how concerned. Susan stiffened.

"Who else did you expect to answer the phone— Maggie?" Susan's voice sounded so cold, it was hard for her to believe it was her own.

"I didn't expect you to be in Hawaii, but then you don't write, and the only time you call is . . ."

"When something is wrong. Isn't that what you were going to say, Mother? You're known for telling us you're always there for any one of us, day or night, but for some strange reason you're never there for me. Why do you think I'm here in Hawaii instead of Vermont?"

"Susan, what's wrong?"

Instead of answering the question, Susan asked one of her own. "Where the hell are you this time?"

"England. Thad wanted to visit a few of his friends in Parliament. It's a little after ten. I call three times a day to retrieve our messages. Now will you please tell me what's wrong?"

"Do you remember the last time I saw you in the

flesh, Mother? It was at Jessie's funeral. I think that's pretty sad."

"Why do you suppose that is, Susan?"

"Go ahead, Mother, slam it back to me the way you always do. You go to Texas to see Cary, Riley, and Ivy, you go to New York to see Sawyer and Adam, you come here to see Maggie and Rand, and you were in Japan not too long ago to see Cole and Sumi. You've *never* been to Minnesota."

"You never invited me, Susan. I thought you didn't want me there."

"Are you saying you would have come if I asked you to? If I asked you right now to come here to Hawaii, would you come?"

"Darling, I can't right this minute. Thad is . . . we're in England."

"I knew you'd say that, I just knew it," Susan said spitefully. Then her voice broke and she heard herself scream. "You abandoned me, you gave me up, and it doesn't matter if it was to family or not, you gave me up and let Aunt Amelia raise me! I'm not part of this family, I never was. Just go to hell, Mam, just go to fucking hell." Her shaky finger pressed the button to break the connection. In a fit of anger, she released it and then tossed the phone in the general direction of the beach.

A wave of pure hate, unlike anything she'd ever experienced, rushed through her. She had to pay attention to what she was feeling now, experiencing. All those shrinks she'd spoken to had said her problem was deeply rooted in her childhood, and when she was ready to deal with it, to pull it out and look it in the face, she would be on the right road to understanding why she did the things she did, why she kept making the same mistakes over and over. Tonight, she'd finally used the right word, the word she'd always refused to say aloud: abandoned.

"God, how I hate you, Mother. You should die for what you've done to me. And don't think for one minute I'm going to take your first love up on her offer to work in *your* business. Not in *this* lifetime."

Exhausted with her mental and verbal tirade, Susan curled into the fetal position, the knuckle of her thumb in her mouth. She was asleep within seconds.

{{{{{{{{ CHAPTER THREE }}}}}}}}

Heads turned, male as well as female. The men leered, and the women frowned and sucked in their stomachs. The object of their scrutiny strutted her stuff, her red-gold hair flaming out behind her as she walked impatiently up and down the concourse. At her side she held a Bottega Veneta briefcase. She'd just parked—in a no parking zone—her Lamborghini sports car, which could zip off at 180 miles per hour if one chose to put the pedal to the metal. Valentine Mitchell so chose, and had the traffic tickets to prove it.

She flicked back the cuff of her Armani jacket to check the time on her Presidential Rolex. The jacket, as well as her skirt, had been sculpted for her body by none other than Armani himself.

As the cuff fell back over her wrist, she raised her sleepy green eyes and met those of an aging banker in a three-piece business suit.

"In your dreams, old man," she whispered sotto voce.

The old banker apparently mistook her for a hooker. "I wouldn't give you two dollars," he muttered.

She laughed, and the banker walked out through the door, feeling like a fool.

Valentine was waiting for Rand Nelson. *Lord* Rand Nelson. Now *that* was a hoot. He'd caught up with her in Los Angeles just as she was packing to drive her new

Lamborghini back to Texas. There was no way she could refuse his request, as she was on a retainer from the Coleman family.

Spotting him at the same moment he spied her, Valentine smiled and did a little jig to make sure enough leg showed. Rand whistled approvingly. God, he was handsome, all six feet two inches of him. She approved of his Hawaiian tan, his dark hair shot with silvery strands at the temple. The mustache was new since she'd seen him last, as were the dark glasses he wore to cover his gorgeous dark eyes, which had lashes long enough to kill for. He kissed her lightly on the cheek, inhaling the scent of her perfume.

"Lady," he grinned, "you are a killer."

"And you, Lord Nelson, are as handsome and debonair as usual."

Rand fingered his collar and wondered why his neck felt as warm as it did. He liked her perfume. It suggested faraway places, incense, and veils—veils that came off. For the life of him he couldn't remember what kind of perfume his wife wore. The sudden urge to bolt and run was so strong that he felt he had to dig his feet into the airport carpeting.

"We have time for a drink," he said hoarsely.

"Sounds good. Double scotch on the rocks for me," Valentine said, following him into the airport lounge.

Rand's eyebrows shot upward. "Isn't that a man's drink?" He gave the order to the waitress.

"I work in a man's world, Rand. I've had to join 'em, as the saying goes. Now what are we going to do about Susan and Ferris?"

"I have the key to the house," Rand said, "so we can stay there and map out our strategy. Or we could go to a hotel. Or you could go to a hotel." He held his breath, praying she would say she'd go to a hotel.

Valentine leaned across the table, her perfume wafting about her like a breeze. "The house is fine, Rand. I hate running up a client's bill unnecessarily. By the way, how is the rest of the family? Bring me up to date. It's been four or five years."

"Everyone is fine. You know about my daughter Chesney, of course. Sawyer is designing a new plane, and Cole's wife is due to have her baby any day now. Riley's son is about six months old. Sawyer has twin girls, you know. We haven't seen Billie and Thad for a while but understand they're fine. Cary is about finished with his memorial to Amelia. Maggie and I are doing well, of course, and Susan is the one with the problem. That's about it," Rand said, tossing his hands in the air.

"What's Maggie doing these days?"

The devilish look in Valentine's eyes was upsetting. "Well, yes, there is other news. Maggie and Susan are taking over Billie Limited. I thought you knew. Maggie said she sent you reams of paperwork."

"It's probably on my desk back at the office. I've been in Los Angeles for the past six weeks. These movie people are so hard to deal with."

Rand nodded. He wondered what Maggie was doing.

"Am I bothering you, Rand? You look uneasy, like you want to get away from me."

"Hell, yes, you bother me. I think every man in this bar has a hard-on just looking at you. Can you, you know, tone down or something? Wear a hat or put on a sweater ... or *something*."

"Wait a minute. Are you saying you're attracted to me? Are you worried that I might try to seduce you? For heaven's sake, Rand, I'd never do that. I adore

Maggie. If you're one of those guys in this bar who has a hard-on, then I suggest you squelch it, because you simply aren't my type."

Well, shit, Rand thought. He had to say something, make some kind of comeback to wipe that victorious smile off her face. "You definitely aren't my type either," he said, rather lamely. "Now that that's out of the way, what do you say we get down to business?"

"Yes, let's," Valentine agreed.

It was a pretty house, Rand thought, surrounded by gracious old elms that were in the process of dressing themselves for spring. Once, when Ferris had been in residence, it must have been manicured to perfection. Now the grass was brown and full of wide-leaf crabgrass, and the flower beds were choked with weeds.

"Gardeners cost money," he said tightly.

Valentine nodded.

"This house kind of looks like the one we had in England," he continued. "Very cottagey, if there is such a word. That's an English garden at the side of the house, and I'd bet five dollars Susan tended it herself. She was happy here. So was little Jessie. I thought they had a good working marriage. I mean, the kind of marriage Billie and Thad have."

"Sometimes people grow apart, things go wrong, one changes, the other doesn't," Valentine said quietly.

"That's well and good, but that didn't give Ferris the right to rob Susan blind. I want you to pull out every big gun you have and shove it in that bastard's face. Make it smoke. Guess the file is here already," Rand said, pointing to the bright Federal Express envelope propped up by the front door.

Valentine looked over the low ranch house with its

added dormers. It appeared neat and tidy, much the way she remembered Susan being. The pink and white brick, and the diamond-shaped windows, reminded her of the foster home she had grown up in. She corrected the thought. She hadn't grown up in a home, she'd grown up in a house, a house full of kids who, like herself, were unwanted. The Delroys hadn't been unkind, but neither had they been particularly kind. She'd been fed and clothed decently with the money the state paid for her keep. There were no extras, no spending money, no parties. No love of any kind was showered on her. Yet she hadn't been truly unhappy, and she still stayed in touch with the Delroys. She always remembered to send a Christmas card as well as a present. But she'd never gone back to visit.

At eighteen she'd struck out on her own, working as many as three jobs at a time to put herself through college and law school. She'd done all right for herself too. She'd graduated from college in the top three percent of her class, and was the salutatorian in law school. Then she'd done a lot of pounding the sidewalks, looking for someone to give her a decent job. In the end she'd had to sleep her way through several senior law partners just to be taken on as an associate at a miserly salary. She never looked back, never chastised herself for what she had done. Her big break, as she always thought of it, had come when she took over a case from a law partner when he went into the hospital for an operation. Not only did she get a whopping three million dollar settlement for the firm's client, but she also managed to get her adversary's business. Afterward, she bought a swanky condo full of chrome, glass, and mirrors. End of story. No, not quite. She still didn't have anyone to share her success with.

Valentine sighed as she watched Rand fit the key into the lock.

"Tell you what," he said, "I'll turn up the heat and make some coffee while you read the file and come up with a plan of action."

"Okay." Valentine kicked off her shoes and looked around, trying to imagine Susan living in this place. "It looks like Mr. Clean lived here," she muttered, grimacing. "Is the kitchen cozy and cute?" she called out to Rand.

"Come see for yourself," he called back.

Rand blinked in surprise when Valentine walked in. Without her three-inch spike heels, she was tiny and didn't seem so . . . so seductive.

Valentine nibbled her fingernail. "All this kind of surprises me," she said thoughtfully. "Susan is a world-renowned pianist. I more or less expected a house filled with exotic souvenirs from all over the globe. This . . ." she said, waving her arms about, "just isn't what I expected."

"Me neither. I suppose it has something to do with being sent off to England at such an early age to live with us. This is like our kitchen there. It broke Billie's heart to send her, but Susan's world was music, and England was where it was going to happen for her. She didn't really have a childhood like most children. All she did was practice the piano. I always had the feeling that Susan must have been starved for love. She still hasn't found it, from the look of things. I just fucking hate it when a man steals money from a woman. I thought more of Ferris."

"Not to worry, Lord Nelson, we'll get him," Valentine said airily.

"I wish you'd stop with the lord bit. I never use the

title, and hearing you say it makes it sound obscene. Sugar or cream?"

"Black. See if you can find the deed to this house, and any other papers you think I should have. Income tax records would do nicely. Are they here?"

"Susan said Ferris took them when he left, but she had enough sense to go to the accountant and ask for copies. The accountant didn't want to give them to her, so she went to the head of the firm and got them. They were afraid of adverse publicity, but since her name was on all the returns, they really had no choice. She told me they're in the piano bench in the music room under her sheet music. I'll get them."

Valentine became so engrossed in the file that she barely noticed when Rand laid a stack of tax returns next to her on the couch. Rand tried not to look at the long expanse of thigh exposed through the slit in the Armani skirt.

"I'm going to call home," he said. "If you want me, I'll be in the kitchen or upstairs taking a shower." The minute the words were out of his mouth, he bit down on his tongue. If Valentine heard him, she gave no sign.

He needed to talk to his wife, he thought as he left the room. He didn't like what he was feeling toward Val. Maggie was his wife, his lover, his friend. Maggie would put it all in perspective for him. "Shit!" he said succinctly.

{{{{{{{{ CHAPTER FOUR }}}}}}}}

Riley Coleman stopped his Bronco, the way he did each and every day, before he drove under the high wooden arch emblazoned with the name SUNBRIDGE. His practiced eye took in the miles of white fence stretching into the distance. Tall oak trees lined the winding drive, and on either side were expanses of bright green lawn watered by pulsing sprinklers.

He lightly pressed his foot down on the gas pedal, the Bronco moving slowly down the driveway, Riley savoring the moment when Sunbridge came into view.

The great house, caressed by the sun, basked upon a gently sloping rise beneath the Texas sky. It was three stories of the palest pink brick, and was flanked by twin wings, which were also three stories high, but set back several feet from the main structure. White columns supported the roof of the veranda, which swept along the entire front. There was a fanlight transom over the two huge oak front doors. The same design was repeated above each window on the top floor. Ornamental topiaries and crepe myrtle hugged the foundation, and a magnificent rose garden surrounded the house, complete with trellises and statuary.

It was a hell of a spread, Riley liked to say, and all of it his and Ivy's. One day it would belong to his son, Moss. A grin stretched across his face. Thousands of acres of prime land where thoroughbreds and cattle grazed contently.

Once, the land had been owned by Riley's great-grandfather, Seth Coleman. It was said that when he first saw it, he felt as though he could reach up and touch the sun. He had come from dark beginnings, and this great house was his major achievement. He hoped that building a house upon the rise would bridge his past with his future. He was not a romantic, but the name Sunbridge was entirely his own conception.

Riley brought the Bronco to a stop outside the front doors. He liked going in past the ethereally graceful rose garden and the feminine sweep of the clematis vine that surrounded the oak doors. He remembered how the house had looked before the tornado swept it all away. There had been shiny, dark wooden floors, massive beams supporting the ceilings, thick, dark Oriental carpets, and man-sized leather furniture. Each time he entered the old house, he imagined the smell of his great-grandfather's cigar smoke, the thudding of high-heeled cowboy boots, and the sound of boisterous men drinking hard whiskey. Now Sunbridge was full of sunlight, earth-tone furniture, white walls and light oak floors. The smells were those of his wife and new son. The sounds were popular rock, Ivy's laughter, and Moss's gurgling. The floor-to-ceiling walls were gone now, replaced with half walls, so that the entire first floor was open and inviting.

He almost had it all, he thought as he opened the massive oaken doors. As always, he stood stock-still and pitched his baseball cap toward the peg on the hat rack, the only thing to survive the tornado that had destroyed the house.

"Hey, anyone home?" he called from the center hallway.

"Only us Colemans," Ivy said, and laughed as she stepped toward her husband and gave him little Moss to hold.

"So, what's for dinner?" Riley wrinkled his nose as he tried to discern the tantalizing smells wafting about. Moss squealed, his chubby arms flailing the air. Riley hoisted him high, then nose-dived him downward. "Ooops, sorry, Ivy, I forgot you don't like me doing that. He loves it, don't you, Moss?" he said, setting the baby down on the floor. "Now it's your mommy's turn."

Riley took Ivy in his arms. She smelled so wonderful, just the way Moss smelled, clean and powdered, with a trace of perfume. Ivy was a constant, a given. He knew when he walked in the door, at the end of either a bad or good day, there would be a smile on her face. Dinner would be ready, Moss would be alert and playful, and they'd each have a bottle of 7UP, their drink for the cocktail hour. He looked forward to his homecoming each day with a passion.

They had their soft drink ritual while Moss crawled about, dragging his stuffed animals with him. After dinner, Ivy warmed the bottle of formula and Riley decked out his son in Billie original sleepwear. Together they read him a story, then Ivy crooned a lullaby while Riley cranked up the Mickey Mouse mobile hooked onto the crib. With the night-light on and the door half open, the contented parents embraced in the hallway.

Riley's favorite room, the den, was where they sat side by side to watch the news. During commercial breaks, they talked about the day's events, their hands clasped together, their shoulders touching.

"Cole called today, so did Sawyer," Ivy said, snuggling against her husband. "Cary called right before you got home and said for you to call him early in the morning. I called Maggie this morning, and your aunt Susan is there visiting. Riley," she said, squirming around to face him, "they're going to take over Billie Limited. Isn't that wonderful! Maggie said paradise was getting to her and it was time to get to work. All of which brings me to something I want to talk to you about. How would you feel about me going back to work, at least part-time?"

Riley's eyes softened. God, how he loved this treasure sitting next to him. "You know, you have the most beautiful eyes, and I heard Grandmam Billie say women would kill for those curly chestnut locks of yours." He hugged her to make his point. "Not yet, Ivy, please. We talked about this, and we both agreed Moss needed you full-time for the first year. Of course, if you feel strongly about it, I won't stand in your way, but remember that Jonquil isn't a young woman anymore, and we shouldn't expect her to take over Moss's care. A nurse or nanny isn't in our budget right now. Have you thought about all this?"

"I thought I'd put out some feelers and work here at home. I don't want to leave Moss. I don't have cabin fever and my brain isn't atrophying. But by the same token I want to do more than garden and cook on Jonquil's day off. I'm a good engineer, Riley."

"The best, kiddo. I've never said otherwise."

"If it gets to be too much, I'll give it up. My family comes first. How'd you like the spaghetti I made today?"

"It was great," Riley said, loosening his belt buckle. "Did Cole say what he wanted? It's the damnedest thing, Ivy. All day I've had this feeling that Cole needs me. We've always been so tuned to one another that I can't ignore the feeling. I was going to call him tonight anyway."

Ivy laughed. Riley and Cole were more like brothers than cousins, and one always seemed to know when the other was in trouble. "Cole said he was probably a few hours ahead of your phone call. He sounded . . . sad. Sumi is fine, expecting any day now. I have this . . . this sense that a phone call isn't going to make whatever is plaguing Cole go away. I'll bet you five bucks he does need you, Riley."

"If he does, how would you feel about me going to Japan?"

"Riley! Family first, no matter what. Call Sawyer, she might know what's going on. Go ahead, I'll do the dishes and take out *your* trash." She kissed him lightly on the cheek.

"I'll do it. I forgot it's my night."

"You can fold the laundry later." Ivy ducked the cushion that sailed through the air.

When the door to the kitchen closed, Riley leaned back against the sofa. The soft murmuring from the television set annoyed him. He pressed the remote. The silence around him screamed. He tried to ease the tension between his shoulder blades by squirming and jiggling in the soft cushions. He punched out Sawyer's number with his thumb. Adam answered.

"Yo, Riley, how's the Texas oil king doing?" Not bothering to wait for a reply, Adam, Sawyer's husband, rushed on, "I want to personally thank you for that lovely—as in very lovely—check that arrived last week. Josie and Katy also thank you, as it's their college fund money. I'm just as happy as shit that you're busting your ass for me and my family." It was a standard joke, an inside family assessment of Riley's capabilities. "Seriously, Riley, I'm glad I sold you the old homestead. If you go dry, that's okay too. No sweat from this end. How's Ivy and the cherub?"

"We're all fine. Ivy's talking about doing some consulting work. Moss is getting bigger every day. He's a happy kid."

"If you want to talk to Sawyer, you'll have to wait a minute. She's trying to get the frizz out of her hair. It's been raining here for two days, and she's meaner than a mercenary when her hair frizzes. You'd think she'd save some of that hostility for the important things in life." The banter was suddenly over. "Does this call have to do with Cole?"

"Yeah, I think so. He's been on my mind all day. I was going to call him when I got home, and then Ivy said both he and Sawyer called, so I assume . . . what's going on? Do you know?"

"Listen, Riley, long ago I made a pact with myself not to take sides. I've stuck to it too. You guys iron it all out. Just try and keep a lid on my wife. She's about ready to blow. Here she comes."

Riley grinned to himself as he listened to the conversation taking place on the other end of the phone.

"What's that thing on your head? Are you going to wear it to bed?"

"It's a snood. Shut up, Adam, just because you don't care if your hair looks like a red cloud of corkscrews doesn't mean I don't care about mine. . . . What do you mean, Riley is on the phone!" Sawyer squawked.

"I called you twice, but you had the old dryer going full blast. As for your hair, I'd love you if you were baldheaded. Talk to your cousin and let me get back to my drawing board."

"Adam, would you really love me if I was bald-headed?" Riley heard her coo.

"Bald, fat, and ugly. Hey, watch it, Sawyer. Riley called collect, so all this messing-around time is on our bill."

"You shithead, why didn't you say something?" Sawyer screeched. "Riley!"

"Yeah, I'm here. I envy your compatibility." He grinned. "I'm returning your call, and no, I did not call collect."

"He's such a wise-ass. We've had a bad day, Riley. Listen, the reason I called," she said, shifting to her business tone, "is I spoke to Cole today about financing the plane. He all but turned me down. The financing he did offer was at loan-shark rates. Is something wrong over there? I spoke to Sumi, but she didn't say anything. Have you spoken to Cole?"

"He called today, but I haven't gotten back to him yet."

"Well, he really copped an attitude, and I didn't care for it," Sawyer said bitterly. "What the hell *is* his problem?"

"Hold on to your . . . snood. I'll call him. In fact, I'm prepared to go to Japan if something serious is wrong. I've wanted to go back for a while, but for some reason the time never seemed right. If Cole is in a bad place right now, then this is the time for me to make the trip."

"Riley, I'm not sure . . . You haven't been back since your grandfather's death. If you aren't ready . . . I can handle this. Cole and I have butted heads before, and we've always been able to work things out. Please, don't make the trip on my account."

Riley felt the urge to confide in Sawyer, to tell her about the dreams he'd been having for the past months, dreams he hadn't even described to Ivy. They took place in Japan, and they had no ending, and they made him cry, made his heart ache. His eyes went to the mantel, to the picture of his Japanese grandfather.

"Look, I'll call Cole. *If* I decided to go over, and *if* I get stuck, *then* you can put in an appearance. Is that okay with you?"

"What you're saying is you think I'm a hothead and you aren't. That you can handle Cole better than I can. I'll buy into it all as long as you remember I'm the brains of this outfit."

Riley hooted with laughter. "I'll tell Cole you said that."

"Be my guest," Sawyer snapped. "Give Ivy our love. When are you coming to New York?"

"Never, now that I'm a family man. Ivy said going to New York City is like going unarmed into a war zone. When are you guys coming here?"

"For the opening of Cary's memorial. How is he? We haven't heard from him in a few weeks."

"He called today too. I think everything is right on schedule. You know that he and Julie . . . Julie went back to New York. I guess it didn't work, and Cary said he couldn't let her think . . . she was the one who made the decision. He said they'll always be friends, that kind of thing."

"She must have loved him very much. How awful for the both of them. If she's here in the city, I'll give her a call or invite her over for dinner. Or do you think I should let her well enough alone?"

Riley had the last word before he hung up. "You did say you were the brains of this outfit, didn't you? If you can't make a decision, fall back and regroup or let Adam make it for you. 'Bye, Sawyer."

"How'd it go?" Ivy asked, placing the laundry basket by her husband's feet.

"She's testy, but then she's always testy. Do you have a snood?"

"What's a snood?" Ivy asked, a puzzled look on her face.

"It's not important. Where are you going?"

"To fill the Jacuzzi. The minute you get off the phone, come upstairs and let's ... you know, fool around. I'll take off your clothes, you take off mine. I'll oil you, you oil me. I'll scrub you, you scrub me. The whole nine yards. Coconut oil or avocado?"

"Coconut," Riley groaned.

"The black nightie or the peach?"

"Neither."

Ivy pretended to moan as she reached down into the laundry basket for a bottle of chardonnay and two wine flutes. "I'll be waiting," she said as she sashayed from the room.

Riley calculated the time difference between Japan and Texas. Did he fold the baby's laundry and call Cole, or did he ... ? He bounded from the sofa and took the steps two at a time.

Family first. *Immediate* family, that is.

Riley watched the bright, red numbers on the clock next to his side of the bed. Three-thirty-one and he hadn't closed his eyes. Next to him Ivy slept contentedly, her breathing deep and even. He stretched his long legs, being careful not to disturb his wife. What the hell was wrong? He should get up, go downstairs, make himself some hot chocolate, Ivy's sure-fire cure for sleeplessness, and call Cole. He'd never had the heart to tell Ivy the caffeine in the cocoa gave him a charge of energy instead of putting him to sleep. Ivy took being a wife and mother seriously, and she had cures for everything from sleeplessness to ingrown toenails. Once, she'd forced a cold remedy on him that had curled the hair on his chest. She'd made tea laced with honey, one-hundred-proof whiskey, lemon, and melted Vicks salve. Then she'd stood over him while she watched him down it in two long swallows. She'd pronounced him cured on the spot when his eyes started to water and he nearly choked to death, either from the drink or the Grey Poupon mustard she'd lathered all over his chest. Or maybe it was the string of garlic she hung around his neck. All he knew was that the next morning he was fit to go to work. Not that anyone would come near him. Four days went by before the smell left his system.

Before he could think twice, he swung his legs out of the bed, grabbed his robe, and headed for the hall. He stopped to peek into the baby's room. Moss's chubby fist was clutching the satin binding of his blanket, and his pudgy thumb was secure in his mouth. Riley's heart swelled.

Ivy had spent weeks making the kitchen her domain. The huge fieldstone fireplace that took up one wall was covered with dried herbs, nets of garlic cloves, and shiny copper pots. Tubs of greenery in clay pots graced the hearth along with a basket of logs.

Everything was green and yellow, with touches of red. The floor was red Mexican tile, the cabinets and window moldings honeyed oak. The awning, which Ivy had made herself to shade the huge bow window, was checkered green and white, with a darker green tassel trim. Every appliance was a rich copper color. Bowls of luscious fruit always sat on the counter.

Riley carried the hot cocoa he'd made in a huge mug that said DAD, along with the portable phone, to the old rocker next to the fireplace. The cocoa was cool enough to drink now. Riley sipped, aware that the big old yellow tomcat, Slick, was licking his chops. Slick had wandered up to the back porch one day and had never gone.

Riley leaned back against the cushions. He was diddling, trying to postpone the moment when he had to call his cousin. He ran the time difference over in his head as he punched out the numbers. When he had a clear connection, he spoke in rapid-fire Japanese. He reverted to English when Cole's voice hummed over the wire, though Cole understood Japanese as well as he did.

"How are things back in Texas?" Cole asked quietly.

"Well, it's a quarter to four in the morning, so not much is going on. How's Sumi?"

"Anxious, but then so am I. Look, Riley, the reason I called is . . . What are the chances of you coming over here for a few days? If it wasn't so close to Sumi's delivery date, I'd come to Texas. Can you handle it? I know you said you'd come back when you were ready and not one minute before, but I find myself in need of that cool Japanese head of yours."

"When?"

"As soon as possible. I wish you were here now. Can you clear your decks?"

Riley snorted. "About all any of us are doing is twiddling our thumbs. Yeah, I can get away. Of course, Adam is going to want to know why I'm not tending his wells." The joke fell flat when Cole remained quiet.

"Hang up, Riley, I'll call you back in ten minutes." The connection was broken before Riley had a chance to say anything. He looked at the pinging phone, at the cat who was slinking across the kitchen floor in search of a mouse.

Since he obviously wasn't going back to bed, Riley measured coffee into the percolator and plugged it in just as the phone rang.

"You can get a seven A.M. flight out of Austin, fly to LAX, and from there to Honolulu, where you board a flight for Guam. I'll fly the Dream Machine to Guam, pick you up, and we'll deadhead back. Deal?"

Riley blinked. "Reservations?"

"My girl is taking care of it as we speak. Ivy?"

"No problem," Riley murmured. Guam. His mother had met his father in Guam. They'd been married there and lived in a little farmhouse until his father had been sent to Vietnam to fly night missions over the Mekong Delta, where he was killed.

The coffee was strong, almost as thick as mud. Riley drank it anyway, but not before he poured a generous amount of cream into the cup. It still tasted like mud. Ivy would throw it out when she got up and make her own special blend of Irish cream with a touch of cinnamon. She even ground the beans fresh each morning. Jonquil, their housekeeper, didn't like flavored coffees and kept a can of Folgers for herself in the cupboard, which is what he had used. He decided he didn't like Jonquil's coffee. Neither did Slick when he poured what was left in his cup into the cat's dish.

The first person Riley saw when he stepped off the jumbo jet into Guam's blanket-wet humidity was Cole.

He looks as tired as I feel, Riley thought. He'd never seen shadows under his cousin's eyes before.

When the handshaking, backslapping, and hugs were over, Cole said, "I filed a flight plan. We can either deadhead back or stay over so you can get some sleep. It's your call. I booked a room at one of the hotels we own, just in case."

Riley thought about it for a full minute before he replied. "I slept almost all the way. What I would really like is some ham and eggs and a quick drive around the island. I'd like to see the farmhouse where my parents lived and the church where they got married. What about you, Cole, are you tired? If you are, I can do this some other time. Sumi?"

"Yeah, I am worried. Let's get the ham and eggs. I'll fly you back here when you're ready to return, and you can . . . you can check it all out. You want to be alone when you do that anyway, right?"

"Actually, I'm not even sure I want to do it at all. I feel I should. Let's get the ham and eggs and get back to Sumi. Neither of us will ever hear the end of it if she goes to the hospital and you aren't there. Lead on, cousin. I know you checked this place out already. They're gonna skip the rice, right?"

"Right." Cole grinned.

The two young men who strode down the concourse were almost identical in height and build. The only major difference between them was Cole's blond hair and blue eyes. Riley could have passed for Italian, Greek, Jewish, or Guamanian. Cole's flight suit and the rakish angle of his flight cap immediately identified him as a pilot. Riley's creased blue jeans, low-heeled boots, open-necked shirt, and battered baseball cap proclaimed him a Texan, a fact he constantly wanted to shout to the

world. The slight cast to his eyes that would have re-
vealed his Japanese heritage had been altered surgically
a year before, much to the family's objections, especially Ivy's.

"We must look like giants to these people," Cole said
out of the corner of his mouth. "The tallest man I've
seen so far is around five-eight. I know you're six-four,
and I'm a tad under that. If we lived here, do you suppose it would be an advantage or disadvantage?"

"Well, we'd be able to see far and wide." Riley
laughed as he took his seat in the restaurant. "Like now,
I can see into the kitchen. Looks clean to me." They
spoke of each other's families while eating, then Riley
took a deep breath and plunged in. "Now," he said,
"what the fuck is wrong, Cole? What's with this shit
Sawyer is babbling about? I heard her side. If your side
isn't any better, we're all in trouble."

"I had a bad day. Business is business. You, more
than anyone, should understand that."

"We're talking family here, Cole. Or did you suddenly turn into a loan shark?"

Cole pushed back his flight cap. He didn't like the
edge in Riley's voice. He didn't like the stubborn look
on his face either. "Is that why you're here, to tell me
I fucked up with Sawyer?"

Riley stared across the table at his cousin. "Yeah," he
drawled. He set his coffee cup down carefully. "The
whole purpose of our deal was East and West, remember? United. As one. You agreed. I agreed. Now you're
reneging, like you want to gouge the family. That may
not really be your intention, but that's the way it looks
from where I'm sitting. From where your sister is sitting too. If you have an explanation, I'd sure as hell like
to hear it." This time Riley slammed the empty cup

down on the plastic tabletop. "And, yeah, that's part of the reason I'm here. The other part is I thought you needed me. I'd like to help if you *think* you're in trouble."

"That's big of you, Riley," Cole snapped. "Is this where you remind me that you gave up your Japanese inheritance so I could take over Rising Sun?"

"That's a low blow, Cole, and unworthy of you. I've come halfway around the world to listen to what you have to say."

Cole felt his neck growing warm, a sign that his anger was about to erupt. "That's just another way of saying you're going to interfere."

"Are you afraid of me, Cole?" Riley asked quietly.

Was he? he wondered. "Concerned would be a better word. You control Coleman Enterprises and you still have your hand in Rising Sun. I'm beginning to wonder if I'm not just a goddamn figurehead."

Riley balled up his napkin and then started to shred it. "You control Rising Sun. No strings, remember?"

"*Bullshit!* There's always a string somewhere. I just haven't found it yet, but it will appear like magic if I don't give in and fund Sawyer's plane, right?"

Riley's eyebrows shot upward.

"I'm not aware of any strings, Cole. And you know I've never lied to you. But you and I had a verbal agreement—East and West as one. You're weaseling, and I don't like it."

"I'm not weaseling. I screwed up with Sawyer. I'm sorry about that and the way it looks, so I'm prepared to make a straightforward business deal with her and apologize in the bargain. Does that make you feel better?"

"No. It's not enough."

Cole leaned across the table, his blue eyes burning. "You want me to *give* her the money?"

"My grandfather would have. I would have."

"I'm not your grandfather and I'm not you," Cole snarled.

"Obviously," Riley said quietly.

"Business is business. You don't just give away a hundred million dollars."

"Back in Texas you gave me your share of Sunbridge with no strings. Together we gave Adam back his homestead. That was Coleman money, right? You could be generous with it because you were fed up and didn't give a damn. You thought like I did back then. The bottom line, Cole, is it's the giving that counts. And if you need more proof, just take a look at yourself and what *you* got."

Cole's blue eyes continued to burn. "Let me make sure I understand what you're saying. I give up a hundred million bucks, close the old checkbook and forget about it. Forget interest, forget a share in a plane that will hopefully make history. And at some point in the future maybe five, ten years from now, I'll be paid partial payments on the principal. What kind of fool do you take me for?"

"I never said you were a fool, Cole. You're the last person in the world I'd call a fool. Look, fuck the business end of it. Let's talk about you and me."

"What about you and me?" Cole asked warily.

"We were like brothers, Cole, and now we're not. What is it, we can't afford the phone bills to talk once in a while? I wanted to talk to you so badly while I was waiting in the hospital for Ivy to have the baby. I wanted to tell you how worried I was that something might go wrong, and then when I saw Moss for the first time I wanted to call you and tell you he had all his fingers and toes and that little jigger between his legs was ... I wanted to *share*."

"Then why didn't you?"

"Goddamnit, I did. I called and left messages and even left the number of the phone booth at the hospital, but you didn't call back. Didn't you ever wonder why we sent a cable announcing Moss's birth?"

Cole's shoulders slumped. "I didn't know. I'm sorry, Riley. I was going through ... I've been going through ... I can't sleep, I can't eat right. I drink too much coffee and I'm smoking like a chimney. I'm so wired, I can't think straight these days."

"Is it Sumi?"

"No, of course not. She's upset with me too, and I don't blame her. She'd be entirely justified if she booted my ass right out of the house. I'm not a nice person these days. I have these really awful dreams. I believe—I don't want you laughing at me, Riley—but I believe your grandfather's spirit is in the Zen gardens. Honest to God. I take a bottle of beer out there and set it down. I walk around, and when I come back it's empty. I light cigars, your grandfather's favorite, and then I find ash along the different paths."

"Wait a minute, are you saying that you suddenly believe in ... ghosts?" Riley exploded in laughter, but when he saw that his cousin was serious, he sobered instantly.

"I went up to the cherry blossom hill, and I swear to God he was there. Your grandfather is disappointed in me. I failed. Do you know something, Riley? Rising Sun is in exactly the same shape it was in when I took over. Almost to the penny. I have not made a difference, and I busted my ass. Jesus, I was working eighteen hours a day, and I still am. I have to be doing something wrong, but I'll be damned if I know what it is. I have this feeling your grandfather is watching over me, and he's shaking his head in disappointment."

"Hey, you aren't in the red, so what's the big deal? It takes a while for . . . it's all new to you. The Japanese do things differently than we do back in the States. I think you just need a little more time."

"Riley, I've had three and a half years. If I can't cut it, then I don't belong here. Don't you remember the way you felt when you thought you screwed up and didn't belong in Texas? That's how I feel, but worse. When Sawyer called, I saw it as a way to . . . a deal. I thought it was a message from your grandfather. Call it what you like. I saw this whole line of zeros and I went off the deep end. But I know he's there in the garden, Riley, I swear to God. I figured, what I mean is . . . I thought if you walked in the garden, you'd feel his presence too. He loved you. You'll feel something. Do you think I'm losing my mind?"

Riley blinked, his heart thudding in his chest. Did he think his cousin was losing it? If Cole backed out of Rising Sun, the whole ball of wax reverted to him, which meant he'd have to give up his life in America and return to Japan.

"Hell no!" Riley blurted. He signaled the waitress to refill his coffee cup. "There's a logical explanation for all this. One of my nieces or nephews must have been playing a trick."

"They were in school," Cole said, impatience written all over his face.

"My aunts, then. They're kind of devilish. Maybe even Sumi."

"At four o'clock in the morning? Give me a break.

Grandmam Billie believes in these things. When Aunt Amelia died she and I both felt Seth Coleman's ... well, whatever it was, we felt it. I remember digging my heels into the ground, and I watched Grandmam Billie do the same thing, though no one else seemed to. We talked about it once. Jesus, I don't know what to think anymore."

"Okay, okay. Then where does this leave us with Sawyer and our immediate problem? Are you going to give her the money or not? And by her I mean the family."

"I'm willing to negotiate, but there's no way I can justify *giving* her the money."

"Okay. That's your decision. Now let me tell you what I want. I want one hundred million dollars transferred to my bank in Texas. I want you to put it in trust for my son. I want it transferred by the close of business tomorrow. Remember, it's my money, Cole. You're just the custodian."

"You'd do that to me?" Cole demanded, his shoulders shaking.

"For my family I'll do whatever I have to do. I think you've lost sight of what's important here. Nothing on this goddamn earth is more important than family," Riley said vehemently. "Nothing."

Cole squared his shoulders and drew a deep breath. "An irrevocable trust, Riley. Anything else is not negotiable."

"No," Riley said quietly.

"Yes. Take it or leave it. You know I would never deny you anything."

"Are you going to make me fight you, Cole?"

"You're double dealing and you know it. If it's not an irrevocable trust, you'll give it to Sawyer. Sawyer is business. Little Moss is your son. If you want the whole ninety billion put in an irrevocable trust for the kid, I'll do it tomorrow. I'll close up shop and go to work for Montgomery Ward selling tires." He looked at his watch. "Time to go. Air traffic at this time of day is a bitch. I don't want to be away from Sumi any longer than I have to." He peeled off a twenty dollar bill and laid it on the table.

Riley grabbed his flight bag and loped after his cousin. He'd do it too; the son of a bitch really would close up shop and go to work for Montgomery Ward. When he caught up to Cole, he clapped him on the back and said, "There's no future in tires. The money's in ride-on lawn mowers. We'll work it out, okay?"

"Okay. I'm glad you're here, Riley."

"Yeah, me too, but I'm not giving in. You need to know that."

"I'm not either. You need to know that too."

"At least we're starting out even."

Cole grinned.

{{{{{{{{{ CHAPTER FIVE }}}}}}}}}

Cary Assante settled his hard hat firmly on his head. Just a few more months and his memorial would be finished. In the beginning he'd had doubts that he was doing the right thing, building this center as a memorial to his wife. A wife he'd betrayed in the last months of their marriage. At first he thought he was doing it out of guilt, but later, when it all started to come together, he cast the guilt aside and knew he was doing it out of love for Amelia.

Whenever he came within a few months of completing a job, he grew happy and antsy at the same time. Everyone was going to be so proud at the dedication. He could see it all now, Billie and Thad, the whole family. It was *his* family now, thanks to Amelia. After her death he worried that they wouldn't want anything to do with him. Instead, they'd drawn closer to one another. A week didn't go by without a call or a letter from some family member. For a year now he'd been sending them all pictures depicting the progress he was making on the center.

He looked toward the heavens and spoke to his wife, as he did every day. He no longer cared if people saw him talking to thin air or if people thought he was eccentric. "We're almost there, babe," he said, then trotted off toward the explosion sight.

He was halfway there when he realized he'd forgotten his safety goggles. Should he go back for them or take a chance that nothing would go wrong? Better safe than sorry is what Amelia would have said, but hell, he was a pro. He'd set thousands of dynamite charges over the years and nothing had ever gone wrong. If he went back for the goggles, he'd be behind schedule all day. He loped over to the dynamite charge and raised the red flag. He had it in his mind to stop by Sunbridge and drop off the set of sponge building blocks he'd bought the other day for little Moss. He was, after all, the kid's godfather. Riley and Ivy didn't know it, but after Moss was christened, he'd changed his will. At his death everything would go to Moss, with Ivy and Riley as trustees. Nothing was too good for his family. He would give the shirt off his back to any one of them. Having a family was what life was all about.

"You ready, Cary?" his foreman, Sam Black, shouted. "On the count of three," the foreman said, holding up his index finger. "One, two, three. Hit it!"

Cary was aware of a burst of flame and scorching heat. He reeled backward and heard Black shout, "Jesus Christ! Call EMS, now! Cary, don't move. Son of a bitch, who checked this detonator cap? Move it, move it! Jesus, do I have to do everything myself? It's gonna be okay, Cary, I'm telling you, don't move, not even a muscle."

When Cary heard the panic in his foreman's voice, he figured he was dying. Thank God he'd made the new will. Get ready, Amelia, I think I'm on my way. Hold open the gates. He blacked out a moment later.

When he awoke, he was in a hospital. He could tell by the smell and the sounds. He'd spent a lot of time here when Amelia was ill. He listened to soothing voices telling him to relax, then felt the prick of a needle.

"What did he say, Doctor?" a young voice asked.

"He said, 'Swing those gates, babe, I think I'm halfway there.' He's delirious. Is his family here?"

"Not to my knowledge, just the foreman who came in with EMS. I'm sure they'll be here as soon as they can."

"Well, we can't wait. We'll have to assume we have their permission to operate." The doctor slipped his hands into latex gloves. "What we have here is . . ."

Thad Kingsley stood behind the French doors observing his wife, Billie. The shrill whistle of the tea kettle jarred him from his unhappy thoughts. He hated tearing his eyes and thoughts away from the woman on the chaise lounge. Every minute, every second, was now more precious than ever. God, what was he going to do? "Measure out the sugar, Kingsley, open the tea bag, Kingsley, pour the water, Kingsley," he muttered. His throat felt tight and he could feel his heartbeat accelerate when he shouldered his way through the kitchen door, with the tray balanced precariously in his hands.

"Three sugars, just the way you like it," Thad said cheerfully, sitting down next to her. "I, on the other hand, take mine like a man—lemon and no sugar."

Billie's hands had been jammed into the pockets of her down jacket, under her lap robe. She reached for the cup, her thin fingers greedily absorbing warmth from the heavy mug. "I can't remember such an early spring here in Vermont, can you, Thad?"

"Now that you mention it, no, I can't remember such an early spring. I hope it means a warm summer without too much rain."

"Me too," Billie said softly. She wanted to scream, to say she loved the seasons here at the farm. She couldn't scream, though, couldn't upset Thad any more than he was upset now. She looked down across the lawn to the rolling farm hills that had been in Thad's family for over a century. It was so beautiful, breathtaking really. Her throat constricted.

"Penny for your thoughts," Thad said quietly.

Billie was tempted to lie, but she'd never been anything but honest with her husband. "I was wondering if you can carry your memories into the hereafter or if it's a whole new ball game. I think that's what bothers me the most—not knowing. Thad, we have to talk about this. At least once. Then we can put it behind us and live our days as normally as we can."

Thad was off his seat in a second, his shoulders twitching unbearably. He knew she was right, but he felt cowardly about it. My God, Billie was dying, and he was a coward. He clutched the railing of the deck banister, his knuckles whiter than any sheet. Maybe he could do it if he didn't have to face her. "Okay," he said hoarsely.

"Sit down, darling, so I can see you," Billie whispered.

Goddamnit, he'd fought a war, flown fighter planes, battled for Billie's love, and then waged war in the Senate day after day for years, and nothing was harder, tougher, than this minute. He knew his smile was sickly when he sat down and reached for Billie's hand. How cold and thin it was.

"Now," Billie said briskly, "let's get on with it. I am not afraid to die, Thad. I'm not anxious to go, but it's been ordained. I truly believe that. So you and I have to accept that my time is limited, that I'm going ... to leave you. I need to know you'll be all right, Thad, and that you'll be there for my family. I know they'll be there for you. I need your promise."

Thad nodded, his eyes full of tears.

"Billie, your family ... how am I going to explain ...? What are we going to tell them?"

"I can't burden them with my illness. They would hover, Thad, and maybe that's the way families do things, but I don't want it. Remember the way we all fretted and fussed over Amelia. She didn't want it either. All she wanted was to have the man she loved at her side. She forbade him to call us, but he couldn't keep his promise. Amelia and I had such long talks about death and dying. She wasn't afraid either. Grieving is such a sad, lonely business, and I don't want my family to go through it one minute longer than they have to. We'll deal with July and Amelia's memorial when it's time. Now, Senator Kingsley, what do you say we go into town so you can buy me lunch? And after lunch, let's go to that flower stall at the end of Main Street and buy an armload of spring flowers. Every color of the rainbow. We'll come home late in the afternoon, make a fire and eat leftovers in the den. Double chocolate fudge ice cream with sprinkles for dessert. Are you tempted?"

"You twisted my arm. But I want rocky road ice cream and chocolate sprinkles."

Billie pretended to sigh. "You got it."

"Billie, I would give up my life for you if I could."

"I know that, Thad. But we've had more joy in our short time together than some people have in a lifetime. Always remember that, and don't be greedy. No one gets it all."

Thad threw his hands in the air. "She's a philosopher too."

"And a hell of a cook." Billie laughed as she made her way to the bedroom at the end of the hall. "I'll just be a minute, Thad."

Thad drove his fist into the back of the recliner. "Son of a bitch!" It wasn't fair. People, good people like Billie, were supposed to live forever. "Please, God, just don't let her suffer. I can bear up to anything but that. She's trying so hard. Just this once and I swear I'll never ask You for another thing. Please, God."

It was four o'clock when Thad and Billie walked into the cedar-shingled farmhouse, their arms full of flowers. Billie headed straight for the vases in the kitchen. Just then, the phone shrilled to life.

They both rushed over and, like errant children, waited for the answering machine to click on. Their M.O., as Thad referred to it, was to listen to the message and return the call a few hours later. In the months since Billie's diagnosis, it had proven a successful strategy for convincing people they were on a world tour and only occasionally checked for calls. It was their way of hiding the effects of chemotherapy from the family.

This time a hysterical voice came over the wire. "Billie, Thad, it's Ivy. It's four o'clock in the afternoon on Thursday. There's been a terrible accident. Cary was hurt in a dynamite explosion and is in the hospital. Riley flew to Japan to see Cole. I called and Sumi said Cole flew to Guam to pick up Riley. They aren't back yet. Sawyer and Adam's machine is on. I called twice, but they haven't returned my call. I did manage to reach Maggie. Rand is in Minnesota with Miss Mitchell.

Something to do with Susan. I called there too, and the operator said Susan's phone was disconnected at noon today. Susan's at Maggie's and she's leaving for Texas on the first flight she can get. Riley said you check your phone messages every other day. I thought you'd want to know. I'm waiting for Jonquil to get back from the market and then I'll go to the hospital. Oh, Billie, I don't know what to do. Cary has no family but us. Will I be doing the right thing if I have to sign? I don't know how badly he's hurt. As soon as I talk to his doctor I'll be back in touch."

Billie picked up the phone. "Ivy, we're here. We just walked in the door. As soon as Thad can make the arrangements, we'll leave. We should be on our way within the hour. You hold the fort, darling, and do whatever you have to do. Cary is . . . Cary is tough, he'll be just fine. I feel that in my heart," Billie said. "I'm going to hang up now, darling, so Thad can use the phone. We'll go straight to the hospital. Ivy, are you all right?"

"Oh, Billie, I prayed you would be home. Thank you for being there. If they let me see Cary, I'll tell him you're on the way. It will . . . give him something to hang on to. Please hurry."

"We'll do our best. Take care, Ivy."

"I'll pack our bags while you make arrangements with the airport. Hurry, Thad," Billie called back to him as she ran down the hall.

Thad dialed and talked to his wife at the same time. "I thought you said you didn't want—"

"We switched to Plan B, darling. Family first. Family always comes first."

It was almost midnight when Thad and Billie walked into the waiting room where Ivy Coleman sat, tears streaming down her cheeks. She ran to Billie and Thad, sobbing.

"Shhh," Billie said soothingly. "We're here now, darling. We're sorry you had to go through this alone. Have you spoken to any of the doctors?"

Ivy nodded. "He's got some second degree burns and a few lacerations. He wasn't wearing safety goggles. He's blind."

Billie could feel herself sway as Thad's arms reached for her. All she could manage to say was, "He's alive, that's what matters."

"Can we see him?" Thad asked.

"Not till morning."

"All right, then, we're all going back to Sunbridge and have some coffee."

"Tomorrow is another day," Billie said softly.

There was nothing bright or hopeful about the new day, Billie thought gloomily as she looked out of the new windows in the breakfast nook. Low, swirling fog danced across the spring grass, which meant that it was going to be a warm day.

Billie shivered. As always these days, she felt cold even though she had on slipper socks and a warm flannel nightgown and velour robe. The coffee cup warmed her hands. She wanted a second cup, but she didn't want to get up. She liked this little nest here on the window seat, surrounded by Ivy's pillows. It was all so beautiful now, this new Sunbridge.

She snuggled deep into her robe and curled her legs beneath her. Thad said she was part cat, the way she curled and snuggled. "You even purr like a cat," he would say. She smiled. She always smiled when she thought of Thad.

The kitchen clock chimed softly, pleasantly, in counterpoint with the Wisconsin wind chime on the patio. That too was a lovely sound, so lovely she'd asked Ivy to send her one for the deck in the farmhouse.

The low fog swirled and evaporated from the garden and lawn. The sun would shine soon and the breakfast room would be warm. Ivy would get up and make breakfast, or perhaps Jonquil would do it. Little Moss was already waiting in his high chair.

"Beat me to it again, huh?" Thad said, padding into the kitchen, his sparse gray hair standing on end. "I thought I'd find you down here curled up with your book. How's Einstein doing?" he demanded, referring to Billie's addiction to Dean Koontz, a writer she'd discovered during her "bad time."

"Thad, listen to this," Billie said. " 'During the rest of June, Nora did some painting, spent a lot of time with Travis and tried to teach Einstein to read.' " Billie rolled her eyes. "Nora is going to teach Einstein to read! Page one hundred eighty-five, Chapter Seven. It's a few pages past the halfway mark. Only one hundred sixty-seven to go. It's soooo good, Thad. Do you want me to wait and read to you later?"

"Absolutely. I want to hear firsthand how Nora teaches a dog to read. Don't you dare read another word! Did the hospital call? How long have you been up?" Thad demanded as he poked around the bread box for something sweet.

"I came down around five. The phone didn't ring. I made coffee, but I'd make fresh if I were you. Isn't this a pretty kitchen, Thad?"

Thad nodded. "You're going to cheat, aren't you?" he asked fretfully. "While I make the toast and coffee, you're going to read. I know your M.O., Billie." He smirked with satisfaction when his wife slammed the book shut.

"Okay, Admiral Senator Kingsley. I closed the book. So there! It's half finished, Thad. I hate it when I get to the halfway mark in a good book. We only have one more of his to read and then we'll have read them all. Do you think I should write him a fan letter?"

"Why not?" Thad grinned. "You wrote one to Sidney Sheldon, Clive Cussler, and Robert Ludlum."

"You forgot Tom Clancy," Billie snapped. "I told him I didn't like parts of *Patriot Games.*"

Thad laughed. "I bet he lost a lot of sleep over that letter." It was a game they played. Billie had always loved to read, but since her illness, she read with a vengeance. Most of the time, she read the novels aloud to him. Often she got so caught up in the stories that she forgot about her illness. He made a promise to himself that when he was alone, he would write a letter himself to all the authors Billie adored and tell them how much pleasure they had given her in her last months. He wondered now as he pushed the bread down into the toaster if he would really write the letters or if the thought was just something to make himself feel better.

"Thad, call the hospital," Billie said.

She waited, her heart thumping in her chest while Thad called and identified himself. Her eyebrows rose when she saw her husband's mouth turn grim.

"Of course I'm immediate family. I'm his father. Now, how's my son? Fine, fine, I'll be there by nine."

"Cary's father." Billie smiled. "How is he, Thad?"

"Resting comfortably. The doctor and the ophthalmologist will talk to me at nine o'clock. They won't give out any information over the phone. I suppose that's good."

"Whoa, that's too much butter, Thad," Billie warned. "Remember your cholesterol."

As if he gave a hoot about his cholesterol or his arteries. He scraped off some of the butter because it pleased his wife; he would never give her one moment of anxiety if he could help it. He layered on a thick glob of blueberry jam.

"Remember your triglycerides, Thad," Billie admonished.

He didn't give a damn about his triglycerides either. He scraped off an inch of jam. "Now it's going to taste like shit," he muttered.

"Sit down, Thad, let me do it," Billie said, putting fresh bread into the toaster. "Give me that." She reached for the cold toast and tossed it into the trash.

Thad grinned.

"You did that deliberately so I'd get up and make it for you," Billie grumbled.

"It always tastes better when you make it. Like when you make egg salad and put those little seeds in it. I make it and it doesn't taste the same."

"You're whining, Thad."

"Say good morning, Moss," Ivy said to her son. "My, you're both up early." She looked everywhere but at Riley's grandmother. "The coffee smells wonderful. Jonquil doesn't get here till eight. Usually Riley and I rough it. I'll be glad to make breakfast—eggs, French toast, pancakes. We even have some of your maple syrup left from the last batch you sent."

"Darling, you sit down. I'll make you breakfast. What does Moss eat for breakfast?" Billie asked with a catch in her voice.

"Mashed banana, and then I put some rice cereal in his bottle. I just have juice and toast along with a vitamin. I tend to eat a big lunch. I still haven't lost all my pregnancy weight," Ivy said, fiddling with the suction toy on the baby's high chair.

Billie slipped into her seat across the table from Ivy. "Ivy, please look at me," she said gently, in a voice that would have calmed a terrorist. "It's not the end of the world. Not yet, anyway. Thad and I can handle this. What we can't handle is having this family fall apart. That's the reason we ... we didn't mention my illness. Since my time is uncertain we ... we want ... I don't want hovering, pity, or ... any of that stuff that goes with it. Can I count on you to help Riley through this?"

"Oh, Billie," Ivy said in a choked voice, "of course I'll help him. It's just that he hasn't come to terms with his grandfather's death and it's over three years. I don't know what this will do to him." There was such sorrow in her voice, Billie found herself reaching for Thad's hand under the table.

"This is life's way of coming full circle. I was thinking about this last night before I fell asleep. You, Ivy, are in the same place I was so many years ago. You're a new bride here in a brand new Sunbridge, a house you and Riley built with the help of your neighbors. It's right that the circle should start again. I feel so ... so very positive about this." Billie squeezed her husband's hand. He was feeling the same thing she was feeling, she could tell. He recognized the strength in Ivy's young face, saw the love in that same face for her son and husband. So like herself so many years ago. The sadness that welled in her heart was immediately replaced by the knowledge that the family would survive.

"What's our plan for the day?" Ivy asked. "Are we all going to the hospital? I have to pick Susan up at the airport, so why don't I meet you at the hospital. I'll give Moss his bath and Jonquil can take over from there."

"Sounds like a good plan to me," Thad said, draining his coffee.

"Well, if it's good enough for Thad, it's certainly good enough for me," Billie said breezily. "I do like it when a man takes over, don't you, Ivy?" She chucked the baby under the chin, her eyes misting at the cherub whose face was full of mashed banana.

"I'll bring Susan straight to the hospital," Ivy called over her shoulder.

In the privacy of the bathroom, with Moss splashing and gurgling, Ivy let her tears loose. "Why?" she whispered. "We need her, we really do. I didn't understand about Mr. Hasegawa and I don't understand why You need Billie. Riley's grandfather did only good, just the way Billie does. Yes, I'm selfish and I'm sorry about that, but I have to think about Riley and the rest of the family and what it's going to do to them. Should I tell Susan or let her . . . How can I tell her? Help me, tell me what I should do. Is it my place to tell Susan about her mother? Do I tell Riley and Cole or do I mind my own business?" Oh God, oh God, she railed silently.

As she dried and powdered the baby, she thought back to the first time she'd met Riley's grandfather, Shadaharu Hasegawa. He'd been ill just the way Billie was ill. The family chose not to discuss his condition, and the frail old man tried to disguise his illness just the way Billie was trying to disguise hers by wearing fuller, padded clothing. The old Japanese had fought so valiantly, just the way Billie was fighting. Who was she to take matters into her own hands? Ivy asked herself. Yes, it was going to be hard to put what Riley called a happy face on things, but she could do it. So could the others. If it was what Billie wanted, she would play the part, and the others would have to do the same thing. However, it still didn't answer her question: Did she mention Billie's apparent illness or let the family see it for themselves? She buried her face in Moss's sweet-smelling neck, her eyes filled with tears. She hugged the chubby infant even tighter. Billie was right, the family was coming full circle. She wondered why the thought didn't make her feel any better.

When Cary awoke hours later, he was aware of a presence in the room. The voice was familiar, soft and gentle. Of course, it was Billie. And from a distance he thought he recognized Thad's quiet voice as well.

"We only have ten minutes, Cary," Billie said, reaching for his hand. "Thad and I are here. Ivy went to the airport to pick up Susan. They should be here soon. The nurse told us Sawyer is on her way. Don't try to talk, Cary. We just wanted you to know that we're here for you."

Cary struggled through layers of exhaustion to respond. It sounded as if Amelia's family were all coming to see him.

"I feel like shit," he muttered.

"You look like it too." Thad laughed.

"Open the blinds or pull the damn drapes. It's too dark," Cary said.

"Oh, darling, we can't do that," Billie said quietly. "You're in ICU and there are rules. It's dark because of the bandages on your eyes."

It wasn't a shout, it was a scream: "Why?"

Ms. Baldwin, his private duty nurse, was at Cary's

side instantly. "Why what, Mr. Assante?" she asked soothingly.

"Why are my eyes bandaged?" he demanded thickly.

"Because the doctor wants them bandaged. He was concerned that the light in here might bother your eyes. It's a precaution, Mr. Assante."

Fear coursed through Cary as his adrenaline surged. He was almost wide awake now, aware of everything, of the way Nurse Baldwin smelled of antiseptic, and of Billie's sweet-smelling perfume, so like Amelia's. And then he was aware again of the pain in his arm and chest.

He tried to shout Thad's name, but it come out so weakly, he knew it was little more than a whisper. "Thad, what's wrong with me?"

"You were a little too close to a faulty detonator cap. That's what the EMS filed on your report. At first they thought you had second degree burns, but you don't. You were burned, though. That's the pain you're feeling. Your face took some of the heat, but you're going to be okay. Any plastic surgeon worth his salt can give you new earlobes in a heartbeat. You won't even need them if you let your hair grow."

"Jesus," Cary said, trying valiantly to lift his hand to check his earlobes.

"Cary, it was a joke. There's nothing wrong with your earlobes." Thad chuckled. "I was trying for levity here. I guess it wasn't such a good idea."

"What's wrong with my eyes?"

"I don't know, Cary. I haven't seen your doctor. I understand a call went out to the Wills Eye Hospital in Philadelphia and a well-known ophthalmologist is on his way. All you have to do is hang in there and hold up your end. Let the big guys take over, and things will be fine, I'm sure of it."

Cary sighed. If it was anybody but Thad Kingsley telling him this, he wouldn't believe him. Thad never lied.

"Billie?"

"Yes, Cary."

"I thought I saw Amelia. I swear to God. I've dreamed about her so many times, but this time it was different. I saw her. She was blocking my path and wouldn't let me near her. I begged her; I was crying, and she still wouldn't let me near her. Do you ever see her, Billie?" Cary asked fretfully. "You were closer to her than anyone."

Billie drew in her breath. She wanted to tell him she saw Amelia all the time and that she was always beckoning and saying not to be afraid, but Billie couldn't, not in front of Thad. "Only in my dreams, Cary. You've been through a terrible ordeal, and you reached out to the person who was a constant in your life for so long. Darling, the nurse says we have to leave, but we'll be back later." She reached for Cary's hand and brought it to her lips. "Rest, Cary. You'll need some stamina to hear all about little Moss's antics when Ivy gets here with Susan."

Something was wrong, Cary thought. Her fingers were too thin. Her wrist too. Just the way Amelia's fingers and wrists were at the end. His hand held tight, his limp fingers trying desperately to grasp the twig-thin arm. His hand fell back against the white sheet when Billie ran from the room.

"Thad," he cried in a tortured voice.

"Cary, if there was ever a time when I needed a man to talk to, this is the time. You have to get well, and goddamnit, you have to do it soon," Thad said in a strangled voice. "We need you."

"Ah, Thad, not Billie."

"She doesn't have long. One oncologist said six months, another said less. It's uncertain."

"I'd cry if I could. What can I do?"

"Get better and get out of here."

"Yeah, yeah, I'll be out of here in a day or so. Everything is moving, and if the burns aren't too bad, they might let me go. You can sort of steer me around until they take these things off my eyes. How long are you staying?" He sounded exhausted.

"Mr. Kingsley," Nurse Baldwin said sternly.

"I'll be back later, Cary. Rest and take it easy. If you need anything, have the nurse call Sunbridge. We'll be here for a while yet. At least until you're out of the woods."

Cary was asleep before Thad left the room.

Billie sat quietly in the burnt-orange chair in the waiting room. Her hands were folded tightly to stop the tremor that overtook her every so often of late. She had to prepare herself for her daughter's appearance. Sawyer's too. Perhaps this was a mistake. Perhaps she should have gathered the family and . . . And what? Announced her illness? Instead she was putting herself through anguish each time she saw a family member. Cary, sweet, wonderful Cary, had known. Oh, God, give me strength to handle this, she prayed silently. She dozed, her energy depleted.

They were so alike, mother, daughter, and sister, as they came down the hospital corridor. Beautiful, actually, if one paid attention to the interns' and orderlies' overt glances. Maggie was dressed in a multicolored A-line dress, which brought out the rich highlights in her dark hair and a bloom to her cheeks. Susan, in a sea-foam-green suit with moss-green blouse and a strand of Mikimoto pearls, contrasted sharply with Maggie's earthy look. Sawyer, never a fashion plate, was attired in a Liz Claiborne denim skirt with matching blouse. A three-inch brown leather belt rode low on her hips and matched her well-worn boots. Her long blond hair was tied in a knot on top of her head, in messy disarray. Heavy silver earrings dangled from her ears and matched the clanking bracelets on both arms. Her blue eyes were worried.

"Has it occurred to either of you," she stage whispered to her mother and her aunt, "that Ivy acted strangely at the airport and on the drive here? It wasn't just my sudden appearance either. Or yours, Maggie. Ivy's cool, she can handle just about anything. She even said she more or less expected you, Maggie. She was so quiet, and I had to practically pull tidbits about Moss out of her. If there's one thing a mother likes to do, it's talk about her kids. She didn't have to drop us off by the door and park the car. We could have walked together from the lot. Something's wrong."

"Of course something's wrong. Cary is hurt. That's why we're here," Maggie said as a young nurse went by carrying a tray of medication. "I liked it better when they wore those starched caps," she muttered. "I think Ivy is just tired. Riley's gone, the baby takes a lot of care, and here we all are."

"That's just it. Ivy doesn't ruffle. She's ruffled now, though. What do you think, Susan?"

"Maybe she has PMS. In the scheme of things, does it really matter if Ivy is out of sorts? She picked us up and brought us here, so why don't we just drop it at that? When she joins us in the waiting room, we can all ask her what's bothering her. Come on, I'm anxious to see Cary and Mam," Susan said.

"Let's take bets," Maggie whispered. "I say Mam is wearing something in ... ah, let's see, bright purple. Purple is a spring color. Lace too, maybe on the collar. Five bucks."

"Yellow," Susan said smartly. "Butter-yellow, green accessories."

"Navy-blue-and-white polka dots," Sawyer quipped. Her mother and aunt hooted as the trio moved down the hall.

They were all familiar with the rules of ICU. Maggie led the way to the waiting room, as visiting was limited to ten minutes on the hour. Maggie was almost giddy with the knowledge that she was going to see her mother. Her step slowed as she approached the doorway to the small waiting room.

Three pairs of eyes locked on the sleeping form in the burnt-orange chair. Those same eyes swiveled as one to the hunched-over man with the folded hands. Maggie reached for the wall for support, Susan grappled behind for Sawyer's arm, but Sawyer was slumped against the opposite side of the door. Thad was on his feet in a second, ushering them down the hall.

"Tell me that wasn't Mam," Maggie said in a choked voice.

Susan's world whirled around her. For a moment she thought she was going to faint. Cary ... Mam ... just when they were getting to *really* know one another. Oh, God, it wasn't fair. Why did these things always happen to her? Mam. She squeezed her eyes shut to see which person would flash behind her closed lids. Cary first and then Mam. Mam looked like Aunt Amelia before she died. Cary, I need you. How can I handle this? I'm not strong like the others. I need to lean on someone. I need you to tell me this is all going to be all right. She wanted to cry, to throw a tantrum, but if she did that, Maggie or Sawyer would slap her silly. She bit down on her lower lip.

Sawyer cried quietly into a wadded-up hankie. "I can't handle this," she sobbed.

"Well, you all better handle it," Thad said huskily. "Billie, against my advice, chose to ... to keep her illness from all of you to spare you anguish. When she should have been thinking of herself, she was thinking of you. I didn't want her to come here, but her sense of family is so strong, I knew she'd find a way to get here even if she had to crawl. If you're going to go in there weeping and wailing, I'm taking Billie back to Vermont. I won't have any of you causing her one moment's distress. I mean it," he all but thundered.

"Are you saying you want us to act as if nothing is wrong?" Maggie whispered. "Our world has just crumpled and you want us to act as if nothing is wrong? That's not right."

"I want to hit her," Susan said through clenched teeth. "She can't ... she can't die. I don't want her to die."

"Will you shut up, Susan, and think about someone besides yourself," Maggie said tightly. "Sawyer, get hold of yourself. We have ... we have to agree now how we're going to handle this. We came here for Cary. He needs us."

"I want to go home," Susan wailed. She turned and ran down the hall as fast as her legs could carry her.

Ivy, coming down the hall, stiff-armed her, throwing her off balance.

"I can't even go home, damn you. My home is yours now, yours and Riley's. God, I hate you," Susan screamed.

Ivy swayed, her stomach lurching sickeningly. She was aware of shadowy forms in the hallway as she tried to take control of her emotions. She took a deep breath, then literally dragged Susan around the corner and out to the lobby, and from there out the huge double glass doors.

"Get hold of yourself, Susan," Ivy said sharply. "Let's take this outside."

"Damn you, you should have told us. I thought you were part of this family. You're goddamned living in *our house*, so that must make you family. You should have told us, prepared us. But you didn't have the guts, so you parked the car and let us walk . . . oh, damn you!"

Ivy gulped in more fresh air. "This is exactly why your mother didn't tell you. Now, I think you'd better get yourself together, Susan, because if you don't, I'm going to slug you right here. This is a time when family needs to come together. As for the house, we'll talk about that later—at length if you want."

"I never took the time . . . or had the chance. It's too late for me. I was just talking to Mam. I was so nasty, so unkind. God, I didn't know . . . Cary . . . we came here for Cary. I didn't mean those things I said, I was trying to punish Mam . . . I do love her . . . even if . . . I'm always too late, after the fact. It's like I burn my bridges too soon. Why is that? What's wrong with me? If Cary was here, he'd know what to say to me. . . .

We're not even thinking of Cary now. That isn't right. God must be punishing me," Susan cried.

"It's never too late to make amends," Maggie said, putting her arms around her sister. "It's when you don't try that it becomes a problem." With her eyes, she thanked Ivy.

"Let's all head for the bathroom," Sawyer said in a shaky voice. "I, personally, have three pounds of makeup in my carry bag, and I think we could all use a little repair work."

"*She* said she would slug me," Susan dithered.

"If she hadn't, I would have," Sawyer said callously. "It's time to grow up and face the world, Susan. Mam and Cary need us."

Ivy would have hung back, but Maggie drew her closer. "Don't you ever, ever for a second, think that you don't belong to this family. You do, and if I ever see you with that look on your face again, I'll slug *you*."

Ivy smiled gratefully, her arm linked in Maggie's.

{{{{{{{{ CHAPTER SIX }}}}}}}}

The house was palatial, and Riley thought it beautiful, but not as beautiful as Sunbridge. The huge wrought-iron gates that shielded it from the busy thoroughfare rolled open with barely a squeak as he and Cole drove up.

What if he got locked in and Cole refused to let him leave? The top of the fence was electrified; how the hell would he get out? God, what if he never saw Ivy and little Moss again. He started to sweat.

Cole watched his cousin, correctly interpreting his thoughts. He reached into the gate house and handed over a key. "All you have to do is open it and you're free."

"You always could read me, Cole," Riley said softly.

"And you me. It doesn't matter if you're East and I'm West. Ah, I see you're West now. That's okay, Riley. You're who you are and I'm who I am. Actually I think both of us are more or less straddling the middle ground here. The real truth is we're just people. Cousins. Can we let it go at that?"

Riley fingered the key for a moment. It felt good in his hand, somehow comforting. He handed the key back to his cousin, who merely shrugged.

"It looks the same," Riley said coolly. "It shouldn't look the same. Change . . ." He let his voice trail off as a gaggle of children, twelve of them, his nieces and nephews, rushed out the front door. As he got out of the car he found himself blinking as they bowed and tittered. He knew all their names; he'd studied the family pictures on the flight over. He called them now by name and smiled. He was Uncle Riley, so he played the part, and he liked his role. When the children straggled off, bickering among themselves, Sumi waddled out the door.

She was tiny and very round. He smiled again when he saw his cousin's face light up.

Cole withdrew a small package from his pocket. "Your present," he said with a flourish.

Sumi giggled. "Mexican jumping beans."

"No, no, no. You drop them in hot water and little spongy animals appear. Look, a present is a present," Cole said loftily.

"I shall treasure it always." Sumi continued to giggle, her dark eyes dancing. "Riley, how wonderful to see you again," she said, doing her best to hug him. "Ivy called. She said you and Cole are to get in touch with her as soon as you can. She called from a pay phone."

"Ivy called from a pay phone?" Riley repeated in dismay.

"Person to person." Sumi smiled. "I didn't take the call. One of my sisters did and wrote down the message. I tried to call back, but Jonquil said Ivy was out, and that she was baby-sitting. That's all I know, Riley."

"We'll call, but first we need some food," Riley said. "In the garden, okay, Sumi? And you are to join us. None of these Japanese traditions that the men eat together while the women giggle behind the door."

"I would love to join you, but I must go to town. I have an appointment with my obstetrician. My sister is driving me. We'll visit later. Go, go," she said, making shooing motions with her hands. "My sisters will make tea and sandwiches."

"You're all screwed up, as usual," Cole said, patting her rump. "Make it Sapporo and liverwurst with raw onion on rye bread. We have an American here who doesn't like Japanese food." He made gnashing sounds with his teeth.

Sumi snorted. "This is what *he* eats every day. Do you have any idea how difficult it is to get rye bread? We have to *make* it for him. Fresh. Every single day. We love doing it." She grimaced.

"Ivy walked the same way. Back home we call it the Sawyer waddle. I overheard Sawyer telling Ivy she had to walk like that so people really would believe she was pregnant. She said a protruding stomach didn't count," Riley volunteered. "Sometimes I think your sister is weird, Cole. The twins are just like her and they drive her nuts. Ivy said she's a wonderful mother, so I guess that's all that counts."

Cole nodded. He didn't want to talk about babies, his sister, or duck waddling.

"Let's walk in the garden. It will take Sumi's sisters at least ten minutes to get our food and beer out here. It will be interesting to see if it disappears."

Riley snorted. "My grandfather didn't like liverwurst and raw onion." He fell into step with his cousin. "You know, this must be the most peaceful place on earth. As a child I thought so. When I brought my grandfather back here for the last time when I made my decision to stay in Texas, I came out here hoping somehow I'd gain . . . insight, wisdom, something that would tell me I was making the right decision. I cried. I thought we were all going to live happily ever after. Crazy, huh?"

Five minutes later, in the garden, Cole said, "Shhh. Listen. Okay, the food is out. Come on, I'm going to prove something to you, Riley. I'm going to lock the door from the outside. We both know there's only one entrance to the garden. No other exit. Do we agree on that?"

"Yeah," Riley said, pushing his cap back on his head. He should be calling Ivy instead of playing games with Cole. He watched Cole throw the shiny new brass bolt on the garden side of the door to lock it.

On the glossy black lacquer tray, which had been set on the white iron table, were four sandwiches, two bottles of Sapporo beer, a plate of rice cakes, a small bottle of sake, a yellow rose with delicate petals in a tiny vase, a pair of linen napkins, and two Havana cigars.

Cole clipped both ends of the Havanas, handed one to Riley, and lit them with his gold Dunhill lighter. The cousins puffed until the ash on both cigars glowed. Cole placed his at one end of a huge onyx ashtray. Riley placed his at the opposite end. He felt silly as hell, though his cousin's face was dead serious.

"What now, Sherlock?" Riley said tightly.

"We take a walk," Cole said.

As they moved away from the table, Riley looked over his shoulder. He didn't sense anything unusual. He wondered if his cousin was having a nervous breakdown.

"Keep your eyes on the path," Cole went on, "and observe that there is not a twig, a leaf, or a pebble on this path. It's clean. You wait, you're going to see cigar ash all over the place. There's no wind, no breeze."

"Cole, I know how you felt about my grandfather, but I do not believe he's here. His spirit, his soul, whatever, is at rest. Ask yourself why he would come back here. Such things don't happen." How desperate I sound, Riley thought.

"Then how do you explain the time Sawyer was in the hospital and we heard the angels sing? Even the doctor said he heard it."

Riley shrugged. He'd never come to terms with the angels singing. As the two men walked slowly through the extensive garden, Riley thought about it. He'd heard what sounded like angels. So had his aunt Maggie, Cole, and the surgeon. Cary said Amelia's spirit was always with him, pointing out right and wrong and making chandeliers tinkle. He'd seen that too. He found himself shivering.

"Cole, we should be going back. I have to call Ivy. There may be something wrong. Otherwise, why in the world would she call from a pay phone?"

"Maybe the phones went out. It used to happen all the time, don't you remember? Then one of us would have to go into town and notify the phone company."

Cole was probably right, Riley thought. The phones had gone out twice in the last two months. Ivy had probably gone to town to call him so that he wouldn't worry if he tried to call home. He should have called her from Guam, he thought guiltily. "How long have we been out here?"

"Twenty-five minutes. Maybe you should call out to him."

Riley would have laughed if his cousin's expression hadn't appeared so miserable. But then the fine hairs on his neck started to prickle, and a chill raced up his arms. His eyes dropped to the footpath.

Cole's fist shot in the air. "I told you," he said, pointing to the little pile of ash to the left of their feet. "That ash wasn't there when we walked this way before."

Cole ran down the path back to the little patio, with Riley at his heels. He triumphantly pointed to the onyx ashtray, where only Riley's cigar now smoldered. Half of one bottle of Sapporo was gone, and the tiny sake bottle was completely empty. One rice cake was missing. The napkins remained undisturbed, and the brass bolt was still in place.

"Now do you believe me?" Cole demanded.

Riley shivered. "Where's the cigar?"

"How the hell do I know? I was with you, remember?"

Riley sprinted down the path, poking and prodding every miniature shrub and bush that came within his line of vision. When he reached the small footbridge from which his grandfather loved to view the garden, he took a deep breath. He knew when he lowered his eyes he was going to see the remains of a mangled cigar. He didn't know how he knew, but he knew. He swallowed hard. Then forced himself to look down, and there it was, two inches of mangled pure Havana. He found himself growing light-headed, and would have fallen but for Cole's strong arm.

"What does he want?" Riley whispered.

"I don't know," Cole whispered back. "You ask. You knew to come to this bridge. Maybe he wants us together."

Riley stepped slowly onto the bridge. When he arrived at his grandfather's favorite spot, he whispered, "Tell us what you want. We don't know what to do. Is it the deal with Sawyer? Grandmam Billie? Cole and me? Wait, wait, let's do it one at a time."

But there was no time to wait. Suddenly a furious wind roared outside the walls of the Zen garden. It ripped up and over the wall, feeling almost as strong as the tornado that had leveled Sunbridge.

"Get down," Riley shouted.

All about them the ageless trees and shrubs were uprooted and tossed like twigs. When it was over, the only things remaining untouched were the footbridge and the discarded Havana cigar at their feet.

"All of the above," Riley said softly.

"Jesus. Why would he destroy this? He loved this garden. He told me once he wanted to die here but it would cause unhappy memories for his family and that's why he chose the cherry blossom hill. He loved this garden. Nah, he didn't do this. That was a freak. That was some—What do you mean, all of the above?" Cole asked in a shaky voice.

"I asked him if it was Sawyer, Grandmam Billie, and you and me. That's when the . . . whatever the hell it was hit. Do you have any idea how much those iron pagodas weigh? Hundreds of pounds, at least. Look where they are, all over the damn place. He must be in a hell of a snit to uproot those banzai trees. They're hundreds of years old. It's totally destroyed. I think we should decide *right now*, just the two of us, if we believe my grandfather did this or if this was some . . . fit of nature."

There was such disgust on Cole's face, Riley found himself wincing. "I guess I know what your vote is. As much as I hate to admit it, it *was* my grandfather. I don't think we should . . . you know, tell anyone. Who the hell would believe us?"

The cousins sat together, arms wrapped around their knees, their shoulders touching.

"What does it all mean, Riley?" Cole asked softly.

"I don't know. The Sawyer thing I can figure out. I

guess you're supposed to hand over the money with no strings. As for Grandmam Billie ... she's the head of the Coleman family, just the way my grandfather was head of this family. Maybe she's going to step down and hand the reins over to Aunt Maggie. She already turned Billie Limited over to your mother. As for you and I, I was prepared to go to the wall with you. I would have, Cole."

"I know. I would have let you win, too," Cole said softly.

"You always were a softie, cousin."

"Look who's talking," Cole said, thumping his cousin on the shoulder.

"Come on, we have to protect the roots of the banzai trees. See that one over there by the pagoda? It's eight hundred years old." Riley ripped at his shirt and light jacket. Cole did the same. When they had the roots bundled, they were shivering in their jockey shorts.

Sumi waddled up the footpath, her eyes dancing devilishly at the sight of her husband and his cousin. "Should I call the gardener?"

"I think that's a real good idea. What did the doctor say?" Cole asked wrapping her in his arms.

"He said I'm about ready. One more week, he thinks. He gave me something new for my heartburn."

"Wait a minute, how did you get out here? The door was bolted from the outside."

Sumi held up a steak knife for her husband's inspection. "I just slid it through the crack in the door and wiggled it till the bolt moved. Someone should tell me what happened," she said, eyeing the destruction all about them.

"A crazy wind," Riley said.

"Like a tornado," Cole said.

"Do you really expect me to believe that?" Sumi giggled. "This garden has been through many storms, as well as a war, and it has never been touched. When the Zen master planned this garden, he said it would last till the end of time. My father did this, didn't he? Somehow, some way, he ... so you made a believer out of me," she said, tweaking her husband's cheek. "Besides, no one but the owner of the garden can change it, remodel it, or dismantle it. Ask Riley. Old Japanese proverb."

Cole looked at Riley. Riley looked at Sumi. He shrugged.

"See, I'm always right." Sumi smiled.

As Cole and Riley trekked down the hallway to the bedroom side of the house, they heard titters and laughter. Cole knew Sumi was egging her sisters and nieces on. He heard them making comments about nice buns and Chippendale bodies.

"Jesus," Riley said, after ducking into the first bedroom he came to. "When I left here, the aunts and nieces would never even raise their eyes. What the hell did you do to them?"

"Introduced them to our local version of MTV. They're women of the nineties now." Cole laughed uproariously. Riley thought it a good sound.

Thirty minutes later he was on the phone with Ivy. Cole and Sumi sat directly across from him.

After he hung up, Riley's face was the color of old parchment. He repeated Ivy's news, his vision blurred by the mist in his eyes. He rubbed them and saw tears trickling down Sumi's cheeks.

"You must go now, Cole," she said. "I will pack your bags. There is nothing to worry about where I am concerned. I have my sisters and a very fine doctor. Tell your family I will be with them in spirit."

Cole hugged his wife. "Are you sure, Sumi?"

"I am absolutely sure. You will give my love to all and express my regrets."

"Sumi—"

"It is your family, Cole, you must go. Help me up, please."

Cole pretended to grunt. "Two tons at least."

"At least," Sumi sniffed. Riley jerked back when she whistled shrilly between her teeth. The sisters came on the run, their kimonos flapping in a rainbow of color. With her index finger, Sumi pointed to each sister and issued orders in rapid-fire Japanese. Riley tried to get the gist of it, which was, Snap to it, don't drag your feet, and be here with my husband's bag in ten minutes along with a basket of food.

"Do not move, Riley, I have a present for little Moss. I bought it yesterday on the Ginza and was going to mail it tomorrow. Now you can take it to him and tell him it is from his aunt Sumi and uncle Cole." She waddled away.

"She's one in a million," Cole said quietly.

"Try two in two million," Riley whispered.

"That ... that holocaust out there ... Grandmam Billie ... Cary ... it really is us now."

"Cole," Riley whispered, "I don't have anyone left. My grandfather, Grandmam Billie ... my mother and father."

"I know what you're trying to say here, Riley, but you're wrong. You have Ivy and Moss. Hell, you're the perfect brother. You have all these ditzy aunts coming out of the woodwork, and you have all the Colemans. You said it before—family is what counts. It's all coming full circle. Grandmam Billie says life does that. Your grandfather and Grandmam Billie—they did their best to make it right for us. It's up to us now. We can handle it, Riley, I know we can. While we're in Texas, we are going to unite our families spiritually and financially. From this moment on we are—"

"One family," Riley said in a hushed whisper.

"One family," Cole agreed.

"In alphabetical order," Riley said airily.

"Now why did I know you were going to say that?"

"Coleman-Hasegawa Enterprises. I like that."

"I do too," Cole said.

{{{{{{{{ CHAPTER SEVEN }}}}}}}}

The trees with their budding spring foliage rustled softly in the early morning air. Two plump birds sat atop the barbecue grill, tussling over a fat worm. Inside, peering between the chintz kitchen curtains, Rand watched with interest. He noticed that the bird feeders, placed strategically around the small yard, were empty. He wondered whose job it was to fill them—Ferris's or Susan's? Before he left, he would check the garage to see if there was any seed, and if there wasn't, he'd go to the nearest feed store and buy some. Nobody, human or animal, should have to fight for food, he thought.

Rand turned from the window to survey the tidy kitchen. He loved kitchens. His adopted mother Amelia loved kitchens too. All the Colemans loved kitchens. Kitchens were like nesting places, warm and cozy, where families gathered to eat together, to share their day. He liked Susan's little clay pots on the extra wide windowsill. He leaned over and sniffed. Mint, thyme, parsley, and rosemary. The same herbs Maggie had on their windowsill at home. It must be something sisters did.

The sun would be up in a few minutes, and if it was going to be a nice day, the kitchen would flood with light and warmth. His eye swiveled to the huge Mickey Mouse clock on the wall, and he laughed silently to himself. Susan must have hung the clock for Jessie, to try and teach her how to tell time. Or she hung it for the child in herself. Suddenly he wanted to know why the Mickey Mouse clock was in the kitchen. He stored the question in his mind. When the proper time presented itself, he would ask his sister-in-law.

Time to start breakfast. He realized he was ravenous. As he rinsed the coffeepot and added fresh grounds, he thought about the reasons he was here and what he hoped to accomplish. Two days to pay the outstanding bills and have the phone turned back on. Two days to have Susan's car serviced and filled with gas. Two days to buy a few groceries and pack Susan's belongings in the three large traveling cases in the attic. One case alone was full of sheet music, old contracts, brochures, and playbills.

When he heard the first plop of the percolator, Rand added strips of bacon to the frying pan. He'd just finished whipping the fluffy yellow mixture in the bowl when Valentine padded into the kitchen dressed in a thick, sky-blue terry robe with a matching towel on her head. She looked about sixteen, Rand thought.

"What'll it be, scrambled eggs or pancakes?"

"Both. Lots of bacon and three pieces of toast. I like to dip my toast in coffee. Soft butter, and by any chance do you have strawberry jelly?"

"No, but we have apple butter," Rand said, expertly flipping the bacon.

"Sounds good," Val said, lighting a cigarette. "You do that like a pro."

"I always make breakfast on the weekends for Maggie. In the beginning, she'd make me do it over and over till I got it right. One time I used up four dozen eggs till I got them scrambled just the way she likes them. You should see my pancakes. They're so light they almost float."

Val laughed as she poured herself a cup of coffee, then sat back down. "In the scheme of things, I'd say that's pretty important."

Rand laid the crisp bacon on paper towels to drain, washed the frying pan and added butter just the way Maggie taught him. She didn't like the little specks of bacon that were in the eggs when you fried them in bacon grease. He searched for bowls for the pancake mix. With his head in the cabinet under the sink, he muttered, "You can use the car. I'm going to be stuck here all day waiting for the realtor who didn't show up yesterday."

His glance lingered on her for a moment. She looked cute, he thought, with cold cream all over her face. Cute, for God's sake. How could a legal barracuda be *cute*? Yet he couldn't help but wonder what she had on under that thick robe. The thought tormented him, and he replaced it in his mind with a picture of Maggie.

"If everything goes okay," he said, "I think I can leave tomorrow. I'm going to fly on to Texas. What about you?"

"I think I'm about ready to make my move today too. I have a few phone calls to finish up, and then I have to go over to the bank and wait for some faxed papers I need from a friend of mine."

"How do you think it looks for Susan?" Rand asked.

"Susan will do fine. Why shouldn't she, as long as we fight her battles for her? I mean, this is the second time we've bailed her out and I would be surprised if it's the last. She's forty-eight, Rand, time enough for her to have gotten herself together. I can understand why *I'm* here. I'm the family lawyer. But you? You're putting the house up for sale; you're closing out bank accounts with ten dollar balances, serving a car that's ready to fall apart, shopping for groceries, and packing up Susan's belongings. For God's sake, you even called a used furniture dealer to give you an offer on the contents of this house. Susan should be doing all this herself. And don't tell me how she's a creative talent and creative people aren't like the rest of us. That's bullshit, Rand, and you know it."

Rand stiffened. Val was only saying aloud what he had been thinking since his arrival. Still, he felt obligated to defend Susan. "For God's sake, her only daughter died. That has to be the worst thing in the world for a mother. This thing with Ferris made it a double blow. You don't bounce back from something like that overnight."

"Of course you don't. But you don't run away from it either. Running solves nothing. Susan should be here, fighting for herself." She got up to pour herself a refill.

"I offered to come here."

"To make things easy for her. Everyone makes it easy for her. Somewhere deep inside, Susan knows everyone else will make things right for her, and after a suitable period of time, she'll go right back to her old patterns. She's not stable, Rand."

"What do you think we should do? Everyone isn't as tough as you, Val. There are certain things Susan just wouldn't be willing to do to get what she wants." The moment he said the words, he wished he hadn't. Val looked as if she had been slapped. "God, I'm sorry. You know I didn't meant that."

Val blinked. "Yes, you did." She lit a cigarette. "I offend you, don't I? You've made a judgment about me—or at least my morals. You'd prefer me to be more like Susan—irresponsible, weak, someone who needs you to help her out all the time. Well, I'm a survivor, Rand. I survive no matter what it takes, no matter what I have to do, and whatever that makes me, I'm still the one you come to when you have to pull your sister-in-law's chestnuts out of the fire. So don't you ever, *ever* judge me, *Lord* Rand Nelson. Now, where the hell is my breakfast? On second thought, don't bother, I'll eat out." She ran from the kitchen, the terry robe flapping about her ankles.

Now what was that all about? Rand asked himself as he dumped the eggs in the frying pan; he didn't know what else to do with them. He gagged with the smell of burned butter and looked around helplessly before he threw the mess into the sink. A cloud of smoke rushed up from the toaster. The smoke alarm went off at the same time. He rushed to open the window and then the door. "Son of a bitch!"

He reached down for Val's cigarette, which was still in the ashtray. He brought it to his mouth and puffed furiously. The smoke alarm was still shrieking. In a fit of something he couldn't define, he unplugged the toaster, picked it up and pitched it out the back door. It landed with a loud thwack on the concrete patio. A flock of crows took wing, squawking angrily.

"Goddamnit!" With the cigarette between his lips, he climbed onto one of the kitchen chairs and yanked at the smoke alarm. He ripped it from the ceiling. The sudden silence roared in his ears. He climbed off the chair and slammed the kitchen door shut so hard that the glass in the multiframe cracked. "Oh shit!"

Val's voice was soft, just short of apologetic, when she appeared in the doorway. She looked, Rand thought, gorgeous. She also looked like the professional she was. Her suit was the same Pacific-blue as the ocean back home. She wore a trim white blouse, and at her throat an antique brooch. Her makeup was flawless, her hair perfection. The only thing missing, Rand thought, was the sparkle in her eyes.

"I should be back by four," she said, "no later. I'll drop the car off and call a taxi to take me to the airport."

"Val—"

"I'll be sending you the balance of the old family retainer when I wind things up here. I think it's best if we sever our ties when I wrap this up. You can find a lawyer you approve of."

"Val . . . I'm sorry. What happened here? One minute everything was fine, and then, bam, you're resigning from . . . what the hell *is* it you're doing?"

"I don't want to work for you or your damn family anymore, Rand. You obviously don't respect me, but you're perfectly willing to use me for your own ends."

"Use you? It works two ways, you know. You use the family too. It sure didn't hurt your practice to say you were the family lawyer. With the money we paid you, you started up your own firm." He sounded too defensive. Why is that? he wondered.

Val threw her hands in the air. "Truce." She affected a smile. "Have a good day, and try to get the smell of burnt toast out of the house. The realtor won't like it."

A moment later she was gone, with a flash of leg. Rand felt a strong urge to run after her, but dug his heels into the carpet. At that moment he would have done anything in his power to wipe the vulnerable look from Val's face.

The bank was almost empty when Val walked in. She headed straight for the president's office. Her smile when the balding bank officer looked up was of the five hundred watt variety. Her handshake was firm, and her eyes even twinkled when the president held her hand a moment longer than necessary. She kept right on twinkling as she scanned the papers he was handing her one by one. When the stack of faxed papers grew to forty-five, she raised her head and said, "This is all sooo wonderful. I can't thank you enough, Harry, for being so kind to me. This is just what I need. I really appreciate the use of your fax machine."

"My pleasure, dear lady. Here we believe in service, even if you aren't a customer. I'm sorry though to hear that Mrs. Armstrong is relocating. Very talented woman. Her husband is so well thought of here in the community." He let his voice trail off when he realized what the attorney was holding in her hands. "Of course my lips are sealed."

Val waved a playful finger. "I know where to come if word does leak out." She smiled the five hundred watt smile again.

"Mrs. Armstrong is a very nice lady," the bank officer said limply.

"Thank you again, Harry. Perhaps the next time I find myself in your little town, we can have lunch."

"I'd like that, Miss Mitchell. If I can be of further service, don't hesitate to call."

"Oh, I won't."

Every eye in the bank followed Valentine's exit.

Her next stop was a drugstore on Main Street, where she called Dr. Ferris Armstrong's office and requested a consultation appointment. She said her name was Linda Baker and she was referred by the chief of staff at the hospital. She managed to use the word urgent three times in as many minutes. She smiled when the young voice said Dr. Armstrong could fit her in at eleven-fifteen.

Brody's was an old-fashioned drugstore with a counter, stools, and soda fountain. Danish, English muffins, and corn muffins sat on a lace doily under a plastic dome. Old-fashioned sugar bowls with silver spoons dotted the long counter. It smelled wonderful, Val thought. She perched on a stool and looked at her reflection in the mirror behind the service station. She could see containers of egg salad, tuna salad, and plates of greens and tomatoes behind a glass display case. Probably for the luncheon trade. A huge coffee urn with a real spigot brought a smile to her face. The milk pitcher was pink Depression glass. It was pretty. "Coffee and toast, cream cheese on the side," she said to the waitress in the yellow uniform with brown-and-white-checkered apron. Val assumed she was the pharmacist's wife, and gave voice to the thought.

"Yes, I'm Mrs. Brody. I haven't seen you around here before, have I?"

"No, I'm here on business. I was in a drugstore like this once a long time ago," Val said softly. "It has character; I like that."

"Well, we've lived here all our lives. Our customers are comfortable with things the way they are. Change . . . we're too old to change. There's one of those bright, shiny all-night drugstores out on the highway. Prescriptions are higher out there," Mrs. Brody said, pursing her mouth into a round O of disapproval. "We carry everything that's needed, but not a whole bunch of different brands. We sell only what our people want. We give credit too, and I don't mean credit cards. Not many drugstores do that anymore."

"That's important," Val said, biting into her toast. "Do you have cherry phosphates?"

"We certainly do, and lemon squeezes too."

"No!"

"Yes we do."

"I want one of each," Val said happily. "I want some of that penny candy too. One of each. How can you sell it for a penny?" she asked curiously.

"It's for the children. Most of the time we just give it to them. The little ones come in with their pennies, and it's just a joy to see them take a candy stick and lick it. Mr. Brody and myself never had any children. We didn't put the candy crocks there to make money."

"Do you know Dr. and Mrs. Armstrong?" Val asked quietly.

"Very well. It was a shame about little Jessie. She liked the lemon sticks the best. Mrs. Armstrong was always in here, at least once or twice a week. After Jessie passed away, she would still come in and take a lemon stick. She never bought more than toothpaste or shampoo after . . . She had so many prescriptions to fill for the little girl. It was very sad."

Val nodded. "Does Dr. Armstrong come in?"

"Once in a while. He sends all his prescriptions here. He usually buys pipe tobacco and sometimes candy mints. I haven't seen him for a while now, or Mrs. Armstrong either. Are they friends of yours?"

"I know Mrs. Armstrong quite well. I've met Dr. Armstrong on several occasions. What *is* that smell?" Val asked, sniffing the air about her. "Wait, don't tell me." Her eyes fixed on the frosted flowers on the mirror behind the counter. "It's lemon juice, Max Factor powder, pipe tobacco, and fresh ground coffee." She rolled her eyes as she dusted the crumbs from her fingers.

Mrs. Brody smiled.

Val fished in her purse and laid a five dollar bill on the counter. "Keep the change, Mrs. Brody." She swiveled around on the stool to survey the drugstore. She liked the old oak cabinets with the glass doors and wooden shelves. It was all so tidy and neat, with the toothpaste stacked alongside bottles of mouthwash and dental floss. Everything was aligned according to size and color. Remarkable, she thought.

"Do you make black and white sodas in those old-fashioned glasses, and bananas splits in the boat dishes?"

"We do, and the ice cream is homemade by Wilbur Laskin down at the ice house," Mrs. Brody said proudly.

"I might be back for one of each," Val said, sliding off the stool.

"We'll be here till six."

Val nodded.

The tinkle of the bell over the door when Val closed it brought a tear to her eye, though she didn't know why. She'd been traveling in the fast lane for so long, she had forgotten what small-town America was like. She wiped at the lone tear as she settled herself in the car. She lit a cigarette as she studied the papers the bank president had given her.

Forty minutes later Val rolled the papers into a tight cylinder. She snapped the rubber band into place. "Gotcha, Dr. Armstrong!"

The car in gear, Val drove off through the town of Oxmoor. Two blinks of the eye and she was on the outskirts where the hospital sat nestled behind a backdrop of tall, feathery pines. It was pretty, Val thought, just like the town. Small-town living, no matter how gracious and neighborly it was, simply wasn't for her. She liked city lights, fashionable stores, sleek cars, and good-looking men. "To each his own," she muttered as she parked the car at the far side of the hospital.

Ferris Armstrong's office was on the second floor of the seventy-five-bed hospital, the receptionist told Val.

The waiting room of Ferris's office was cute. Cute because Ferris was a pediatrician. Everything, including the chairs, was geared to children. Bright colors, hand-painted pictures, puzzle carpets, and sturdy toys littered the room. A huge bowl of lollipops sat on a low table with a sign that said ONE EACH. Two little boys, dressed in bib overalls, sat on the carpeted floor playing with checkers as big as dinner plates. Cute.

"Linda Baker. I have an appointment," Val said quietly.

"Come with me," the nurse said, motioning Val to follow her. She was young. Was she the *other* woman?

"I like your suit," the young woman said, eyeing Val from the top of her head to the tips of her shoes. "Did you get it at Mason's?"

Val quirked an eyebrow. "Hardly. It's a Scaasi."

"Oh," was all the nurse said. Val noticed that the heel of her right shoe was run-down and there was a run in her stocking.

Valentine stood by the window and stared down into the parking lot. She had counted thirty-two cars in the lot when Ferris Armstrong walked through the door. The moment Val heard the door close, she turned and smiled.

"Val?" Ferris's eyes dropped to the clipboard in his

hand. "Are you the Linda Baker here for a consultation?" he asked stonily.

"No. I'm not Linda Baker. You look well, Ferris. I'll bet it's been at least five years since we've seen each other."

He was handsome. He had a light, even tan—a sun lamp probably—and he was tall and trim, athletic-looking. The gray at his temples made him seem distinguished, especially in combination with the white surgical coat. His sky-blue stethoscope was wrapped halfway around his neck. It matched his eyes perfectly. She almost laughed aloud.

"What can I do for you, Val?" Ferris asked tightly.

She reached into her purse and withdrew the cylinder of papers. When she held them out to Ferris, he backed up a step. Her laughter tinkled around the brightly decorated room. "It's not a subpoena. Take it, Ferris. It's not even a summons. Come on, a big boy like you, a doctor and all, don't tell me you're afraid of me. Actually, in a manner of speaking, these papers belong to you and your wife. I'm more or less delivering your own property to you." Her tone changed to hard-edged steel. "Look at them. In fact, sit down and read them through. I can wait." She was pleased to see Ferris's hand shake as he reached out to take the papers. She was also pleased to see how jerkily he walked. Rather like a puppet on straw legs.

"My income tax records, so what!" Ferris said coldly.

"Not exactly," Val said in a teasing voice. "What you have there are *amended* tax returns, not the originals your accountant gave to Susan. However, the amended returns *do* carry my client's signature." She clucked her tongue. "Or rather, my client's forged signatures. To the IRS. Shame on you, Ferris. All those assets. My oh my.

I had no idea a pediatrician made that kind of money. It almost makes me think I'm in the wrong profession. Now, let's sit down and talk about how much it's going to cost you to make all this go away."

"How much?" Ferris croaked hoarsely.

"Make me an offer," Val drawled, lighting a cigarette. She blew a cloud of smoke in Ferris's direction.

"Five hundred thousand."

Val laughed.

"Seven hundred fifty thousand."

Val giggled.

"Okay, seven hundred fifty thousand and the house in the islands."

Val shook her head. "Think about the word 'forgery.' Then couple that with the initials IRS. Try again."

"Half the bonds. Half the stocks."

"No way."

"One million."

"Sorry."

"How much is it going to take?"

"You figure out what your ass is worth, Doctor. In jail they don't have any little kids to administer to. What's your life here on the outside worth to you? Personally, I don't think much of a man who can't make it on his own and has to steal from a woman. I'll give you one more shot at an acceptable offer. If it isn't agreeable, I'll walk out of here, notify my friends at the IRS, and by six o'clock you'll be on the Oxmoor news. Oh, I also know what you earn in a year. I factored in what you might have invested during the past five years and have a number at my disposal."

Val watched the pediatrician wilt. She'd seen other men fall apart, but Ferris made it an art form. "Okay."

"Okay, let's do it now. Don't think for one minute

I'm going to give you a chance to split. We'll go together to the bank. There's a notary there. For a small fee, one of Harry's secretaries can type up a general release. You know the one, from the beginning of time to the end of time ... I'll want the title to the Porsche. You can have the other car. Rand can drive the Porsche back to Texas."

"You're only leaving me with a heap of a car, a shitbox of a house, and a hundred thousand dollars in savings," Ferris sputtered.

"That's right," Val singsonged. "And you're out of the foundation."

"You're a goddamn bitch!" Ferris seethed.

"I'll take that as a compliment."

Ferris shrugged out of his white surgical coat and slipped into a cashmere jacket. Val commented on the jacket, and Ferris, ignoring her, stormed out of his office. Val sauntered out behind him.

"Dr. Armstrong, what about your patients?" the nurse asked fretfully.

Val leaned over the desk and whispered. "He's just had some very bad news. Have his associate cover for him. I don't think Dr. Armstrong will be back in the office today."

It was three o'clock when Val walked into Susan's house. Rand was watching "General Hospital" when she dropped a manila folder into his lap. "It's done. I gave him this house, so if you put it on the market, you'll have to take it off. He called it a shitbox, so I thought it was worth giving up. I gave him the car out front and told him you'd drive the Porsche back to Texas. The rest is self-explanatory. Your sister-in-law is now a wealthy woman."

Rand was on his feet. He tossed the envelope on the floor. "Val, wait."

"Sorry, Rand, I want to change, pack, and get to the airport on time. Some other time, okay?" she called over her shoulder.

"Don't you want something to eat, a cup of coffee?"

"I had toast, a cherry phosphate, a lemon squeeze, a black and white soda, a banana split, and three peppermint sticks. I'm not hungry," she called from the top steps. "I might be able to gulp down a cup of coffee, though, if you make it snappy."

Rand raced into the kitchen, stopping long enough to pick up the folder. If Val took half as long as Maggie to change, dress, and pack, he figured he had a good fifteen minutes. He measured out the coffee, filled the percolator, slopping water and loose coffee grounds all over the counter. He wiped at them with the sleeve of his shirt.

While the coffee perked, he spread the contents of the envelope out on the kitchen table. He whistled shrilly, his eyebrows nearly meeting his hairline at what he saw. Whatever Val had charged was worth it. Hell, he'd double her fee. No, by God, he wouldn't pay it. Susan would pay it, and he'd tell her to double it, whatever it turned out to be. Val was right, it was time Susan started to stand on her own two feet.

Rand sucked in his breath when he saw Val standing in the kitchen doorway. She had on jeans, sneakers, and a Greenpeace sweatshirt. Her face was bare of makeup and her hair was tied in a knot on top of her head. He cleared his throat and handed her a mug of coffee.

She smelled like a flower garden.

She looked gorgeous, stunning.

She goddamn *sizzled*.

Val reached into her purse for a cigarette. She made a production of lighting it, then blew a perfect smoke ring. As Rand watched it circle overhead, he felt a ring of heat around his own neck. "You shouldn't smoke so much," he said gruffly.

"I shouldn't do a lot of things. But I *do* get the job done, don't I?"

The slow heat Rand felt around his neck crept up to his face. "I'm impressed. I hope you didn't break any laws."

"If you're worried there will be some heat," she said coolly, "don't worry. Speaking of heat, Rand, your face is flushed. Are you coming down with a bug? Or is something else bothering you?"

"Nothing's bothering me. I said I'd drive you to the airport. There's no reason for you to take a taxi. Why are you being so stubborn?"

"Stubborn? It's silly for you to drive me to the airport and then come all the way back here. I told Dr. Armstrong you'd drive Susan's car over there late this afternoon and pick up the Porsche. That's more important than driving me to the airport. I'm a big girl, Rand. My training wheels came off a long time ago. Besides," she said, "I no longer work for the Colemans, so I'd rather you not do me any favors."

"One thing, Val. How do I explain all this to the family? God only knows what they're going to think. You've been with them for a very long time. At least reconsider your position."

"Don't have to. My mind's made up. I never back down, I never compromise, and I never look back. Give my regards to your family."

Rand's tone grew hard. "Who did you have to sleep

with to get amended copies of Ferris's income tax records?"

Val remained cool. She took a final puff from her cigarette, then tamped it out in the sink. "To reiterate, I don't work for you or your family anymore, and furthermore, it's simply none of your business."

"Maybe I don't like the things you do to get the job done." God, did he really say that aloud? The look on her face clearly said he came through loud and clear.

"Why not? I seem to recall *your* having a torrid affair with Sawyer before you dumped her for her mother. And then we all came to find out you slept your way across England—and that's by your admission—and you have a daughter you never even saw until just recently. You know what I think your problem is? I think you still find yourself attracted to me and don't know what to do about it." She laughed then, a sad, vulnerable sound. "You really thought I was going to come on to you, didn't you? You were going to have such noble fun rejecting me so you could go home with a pure heart and clean hands, right?"

"To a certain degree," Rand said tightly.

"What part is right?" She was suddenly curious. She stuffed her hands into her jeans and rocked back on her heels.

"The part about me being attracted to you."

"That's flattering. Every woman likes to hear a compliment. But I've been around the block. I can't believe we're having this conversation. Look, I really have to go. If I ever find myself in Hawaii, perhaps we could have lunch. And Rand, for what it's worth, I'm attracted to you too."

"Val, don't go," Rand said quietly.

"Rand, I don't knowingly mess around with other women's husbands."

"But you do parade around in front of them before breakfast wearing nothing but a bathrobe and cold cream."

The sudden pain in his shins felt like a mule kick. He saw the swinging purse and ducked. He also saw the tears streaming down Val's cheeks. He heard the taxi horn at the same time.

She was in his arms then, blubbering against his shirt front. She smelled sweet and clean, like Ivory soap and lavender. He knew it was lavender because his mother used to line the dresser drawers back in England with real English lavender. He swayed dizzily as he stroked Val's head, crooning words of comfort. Maggie never cried.

"There's a real person in there, isn't there? One who has feelings and passions but is afraid to show them for fear of being rejected and hurt."

Val sniffed and nodded. "How would you know about being vulnerable and feeling hurt?" she asked.

"Men aren't supposed to show that side of themselves, but I'll tell you a secret, Val. Sometimes I just want to go into a corner and howl. I get so damned tired of being someone's extension, someone's reason for living. Sometimes I want to chuck it all and be a beach bum. I suppose it's what the slick magazines refer to as mid-life crisis."

"You're just feeling your mortality," Val said softly. "You want to do things, experience feelings now because you've realized the future isn't forever. I looked that square in the face a while back. We're the same age, Rand."

"I know," he said, wiping the tears from her cheeks. "I think the taxi left; the horn stopped blowing."

Val took a step back, shivering inside the Greenpeace sweatshirt.

Rand ran a finger around the inside of his shirt collar. "Look, let's go pick up the Porsche and come back here and have dinner. We'll build a fire, open a bottle of wine, and curl up on the floor and talk. How does that sound?"

"Premeditated."

Rand laughed. "I like the sound of that."

He felt like a kid again as he scampered from the house, hot on Val's sneaker-clad heels. He wondered if she took aerobic classes. He asked.

Val gurgled with laughter as she settled herself in the front seat of the car. "No time. I have a fully equipped gym at the office and one at home. I'm lucky if I walk on my treadmill once a week. Aerobics take up a great deal of time. Does Maggie take classes?"

They shouldn't be talking about Maggie, he thought. He shouldn't be thinking about Maggie either. "She takes a two-hour class every day. She swims three times a day. She walks two miles a day in wet sand. That's a workout in itself. She stays in shape. She eats very sensibly and gets eight hours' sleep a night."

"Hey, I didn't ask for a dissertation," Val said coolly.

"I guess it did sound like one, didn't it?"

"Maggie is going to be fifty." Now, where the hell did *that* come from? Rand wondered.

"Whoah, Rand. I think I'm missing something here. Is there a rule somewhere that says we have to talk about Maggie and air all that stuff? I don't think it's a good idea. And just as a point of reference, I'm fifty-four years old. That makes me four years older than your wife. And you, being the astute man that I know you are, should know the grass is not always greener on the other side of the fence. It's a tired old cliché, Rand, but very appropriate in this instance."

They drove for a while in silence. "You're being very blasé about all this," Rand finally said as he swerved into the hospital parking lot. He drove slowly up and down the aisles, looking for a Porsche.

"If I'm blasé, it's because dinner and sharing confidences are okay in my book. As far as I'm concerned, we're just friends spending an evening together."

"Now why did I know the Porsche was going to be red, and why did I know Ferris was going to have a vanity license plate that said 'Doc'?"Rand muttered as he ground to a stop alongside the foreign car.

"Because," Val said seriously, "men are little boys, and little boys are predictable." She climbed out of the car and walked around the apple-red Porsche.

"I don't know if Susan can drive a stick shift," Rand said.

"She'll learn."

"You really don't like Susan, do you? Do you like Maggie?"

"The truth?"

Rand nodded.

"Not really. I absolutely adored Amelia, and I'm very fond of Billie. Sawyer is my kind of girl. She's got chutzpah. I don't like what you did to her, and neither did Amelia or Billie."

"Jesus. Would it have been better for me to marry Sawyer when I didn't love her? In any case, goddamnit, it wasn't the way you seem to think. It was over between Sawyer and myself before I fell in love with

Maggie. If you know a way to be kind in a situation like that, I'd like to hear it."

Val shrugged. "So you say."

"Okay," Rand said quietly, "let's scratch this whole scene."

They settled down into the bucket seats, and after pulling out of the lot, Rand set the car careening down a country road. "Are you still up for some wine?" he asked.

"I'd prefer beer. Coors Light. Wine makes me weak in the elbows."

"You know," he ventured, "now that business is settled, you could ride to Texas with me. If you don't have something to rush back to, that is. Or, of course, there's an early morning flight."

"I'll think about it. I still have a few days to call my own. And I should warn you, I hate car trips. Now, what about dinner? All I really had to eat today was a bunch of sugar. I'm getting hungry."

"There's a lot of food in the freezer and there's beer in the garage. I saw it, so I guess we don't have to stop anywhere. Although technically, we're staying in Ferris's house."

"Oh, Rand, didn't you pay any attention to the papers I gave you? I tacked three days on to the house just in case. I didn't know when you would want to leave. I wasn't sure if you packed all of Susan's personal belongings. What about the attic?"

"I didn't think about the attic," Rand said, slapping at his forehead.

"And the little girl's room?"

"I meant to ask you about that. Everything is still there. The dolls, the toys, the clothes in the drawers and closets. I called last night, but the cook said Maggie left for Texas with Susan. I tried calling the house this morning, and there was no answer. Maybe we should pack all the things in boxes, label them, and send them on to ... where? Texas? Hawaii?"

"What's that *we* stuff, Rand? I'm not packing up Susan's things, which I guess answers your earlier question. I'll be taking the early morning flight since your packing isn't finished. You look relieved," Val added, an edge to her voice.

Relieved wasn't the half of it. For a little while there he'd been temporarily insane with wild imaginings. He felt lightheaded when he climbed from the car, glad that his decision were made for him. As soon as they ate, he'd start packing. Val could watch television and do whatever lawyers did in their free time.

"Who does dinner?" Val asked as she followed Rand into the house.

"I'll flip you. Call it."

"Tails." Val grinned.

Rand flipped a quarter. "You win. Call me when it's ready. I'm going up to the attic."

The phone that had been reconnected at noon took that moment to shrill to life. He reached past Val to pick it up. He knew before he spoke that it would be Maggie. He noticed Val discreetly withdraw from the kitchen. Her absence didn't change his careful tone of voice. He thought about Cary then, and how angry he'd been when Cary had confessed his infidelity.

"What's wrong, Rand?" Maggie asked sharply. He'd never heard her sound this particular way before. "Rand, I need to ... there's been a terrible accident. Cary's in the hospital. It ... it's serious. I had Susan call early this morning to have the phone reconnected so I could talk with you. You should be here ... everyone should be here ... You aren't saying anything. Why is that, Rand? What's wrong?"

"Wrong? Nothing is wrong. What happened to Cary? What kind of accident? How serious is serious?"

"I only know what Thad told us, which isn't much. Cary's eyes have been severely damaged and he has some bad burns. Mam ... I need you here, Rand," Maggie said tightly.

"Maggie, listen to me. I'll come home as soon as I can. Look, I don't want to come back here so let me finish up and I'll leave first thing in the morning. If there was something I could do for Cary I'd leave in a heartbeat, you know that." He thought again about Cary's infidelity and didn't know why.

"You sound strange," Maggie said.

"Well, Jesus, Maggie, you just handed me some bad news. How the hell am I supposed to sound? I'm sure if your mother is there things are under control."

"What have you been doing all day? I tried calling earlier."

It wasn't his imagination, Maggie's voice was ... so down right cold it could chill milk. His eyebrows shot back toward his hairline. "Is there something you aren't telling me?"

"We'll talk when you get here. You still didn't tell me where you were earlier."

"I just picked up the Porsche. Everything is okay on this end with the exception of one thing: What do I do about little Jessie's things? And the stuff in the attic?" He quickly gave her a rundown on Val's day, his voice edgy and cool sounding to his ears.

"I knew Val would come through. I'm glad for Susan's sake. I bet she'll bill us up the kazoo."

"Does that bother you?" Rand asked tightly.

"No. She's worth every penny we pay her. Dudley Abramson says she's the best in the business. I hope you didn't work her to death."

"I don't think so. She's leaving in the morning. She missed her flight this afternoon. She agreed to make dinner, and I'm going to finish the packing. She refused to help."

"At three fifty an hour, I should hope so."

"I thought you liked Val."

"I think she's a fine attorney. I would never hire anyone else. She's just a little too loose and flashy for my taste. Will you be on the same flight as Val?"

"No, I'm going to drive the Porsche back to Texas. Tell me more about Cary."

"He has some burns and he's ... his eyes were severely injured. That's the bad news. The good news is there's no optic nerve damage. But there's something else, Rand. It's Mam ... she's ill. All this time we thought she and Thad were traveling, well, they weren't. She was in Vermont undergoing chemotherapy. She has cancer. She didn't want any of us to know. She looks so ... so different. Susan is behaving like a real witch. Sawyer is here too. Riley and Cole are on their way as we speak. I need you, Rand." Maggie began to sob. "I can't handle this. Rand, say something. Say anything, but talk to me."

"Maggie, I'm sorry about Billie. Truly sorry. I'll be there as soon as I can." He wished he could tell his wife to mix herself a drink, but he couldn't. Maggie hadn't touched alcohol for many years.

Rand looked around the brightly lit kitchen as though seeing it for the first time. Should he leave now and forget about packing Susan's things? Or should he work through the night and leave first thing in the morning?

He could fly back to Texas with Val. He would have to make arrangements for someone else to drive the Porsche, or he could simply park it at the airport lot in long-term parking and hope for the best. Suddenly he hated the Porsche and Susan. He said so to his wife. He listened to the choked silence on the other end of the wire and then hung up.

"Rand, what's wrong? Your face is as white as your knuckles," Val said quietly. He told her.

Val digested the information. She felt a shiver run through her. Billie Coleman Kingsley wasn't *that* old. For some reason, she'd never really thought of Billie as a Coleman, even though she carried the name. Billie was Billie. In her own quiet way, Billie was the backbone of the Colemans. She felt sad, and for once she couldn't control the emotions on her face.

"This must be very hard for you, Rand. Billie is so like your own mother. I wish I had the right words to say to you now, but I don't."

Val stepped away from Rand when she thought he was going to reach out to her. *That* she couldn't handle right now. "Look, I'll make some grilled cheese sandwiches and then I'll help you with the packing. I know I said I wasn't going to do it, but things have changed. We can fly home together. In the scheme of things, that damn car has suddenly lost its importance. So what if someone rips it off? It's insured. All it will take is one phone call in the morning from the airport to the insurance company, and we can fax anything they need when we get home. If we get everything packed up tonight, we can call one of those twenty-four-hour eight hundred numbers in the Yellow Pages and the boxes can be picked up tomorrow sometime."

Rand fretfully combed his hair with his fingers. The

hand that came to rest on his arm was soft and gentle. He looked down through the mist in his eyes.

"I know what you're thinking and what you're feeling," Val said quietly. "It's not the end of the world. I seem to remember that you thought you weren't going to make it when your mother died. We spoke at the funeral. Perhaps you don't remember because of your grief. Life goes on, Rand. Billie . . . she could . . . there's every possibility she could live a long time. They come up with new drugs and procedures every day. The Colemans are a tough bunch. I know you aren't a Coleman, but you *belong*. Someone is going to have to hold them all together, and that someone is you. Cary can't. Thad . . . Thad is going to need you. All of them are going to need you. Riley especially. From what Ivy told me the last time we spoke, he still hasn't come to terms with his grandfather's death. This will be such a blow to him. Cole is very close to Billie. You're the one, Rand. You'll have to hold it all together for them."

"According to Maggie," he said, "Susan is going off the deep end. Sawyer . . . Sawyer will bluster her way through and trample anyone who gets in her way. How do I deal with *that*?"

"Tell Susan to grow up and act like the woman she is. As for Sawyer—you're on your own there. Adam will reel her in and be there for her. He's got a level head. I think you can count on Adam."

Rand placed both hands on Val's shoulders and looked down into her eyes. She had pretty eyes without all the makeup she usually wore. "How'd you get so smart?"

"I don't belong, so I can be objective. It's the lawyer in me."

"You still planning on dumping the family?" His tone was curious.

"Yep."

"Reconsider," Rand said.

"No."

He was too close, she thought, so close she could smell the faint scent of his after-shave. She could also see the late afternoon shadow of his beard. She tensed beneath his fingers. She knew without a doubt that if she took him by the hand and led him to one of the upstairs bedrooms, she could ... She shook her head. "I'm hungry, and you need to go to the attic and ... and do whatever you have to do. I'll call you when dinner is ready." She jerked her shoulders free. A moment later, Rand was gone. She could hear his footsteps overhead.

The urge to cry was so strong, Val opened the freezer door and stuck her head inside. The sharp, cold air restored her self-control. It occurred to her that she might be having a hot flash when she yanked her head back out. Maybe she should have cried. Crying was better than the warm flush she was experiencing. Stress, the doctor had told her months ago, could often bring on the hated hot flashes.

She worked automatically, taking food from the refrigerator and freezer, working the microwave and setting the table. Her thoughts refused to be still. For the first time in years she wasn't able to separate her emotions from the business at hand. Her own desire was suddenly clear to her: she wanted to go to bed with Rand. Wanted to see what it was like to make love with someone she really liked, someone she chose. She thought about all the men she'd slept with and the reasons she'd slept with them. She cringed when she remembered the sagging potbellies, the hairless heads, the kinky things she'd done. So many times she'd asked herself, honestly, if she'd be where she was if she hadn't done the things she felt she had to do to get ahead. The answer was always an honest no. No, she wouldn't have gotten ahead; she wouldn't have her own firm, wouldn't have all the wealth she'd accumulated. She'd never been in love, never borne a child, never had even a halfway serious relationship.

By my choice, she thought bitterly. What good was having all this if she didn't have someone to share it with? And when she died who would she leave *all this* to? Who was going to remember her? Who was going to go to the cemetery and cry for her? Who would *care*? She slapped a piece of Kraft cheese between two slices of frozen bread. The frozen sandwich slid down the counter.

As she rummaged in the oven for a baking pan, she thought about her friends—actually, more acquaintances than friends. All were high-priced, fast-track attorneys like herself. All dressed in fashionable clothes; all of them were eagle-eyed and had razor-sharp minds. Occasionally they lunched, attended the same cocktail parties, cozied up to the same judges. But were they the kind of friends you called up at two in the morning and cried to? Not likely. There were no tears when you worked in a man's world. You just kicked and scratched, clawed and fought, and hoped for the best. She was sick of it. Sick of the families she had on retainer, sick of the whole damn legal profession.

A month ago, possibly longer, she'd received in the mail a bumper sticker from some disgruntled person that read: FIRST OF ALL WE KILL ALL THE LAWYERS. Another time she'd overheard two men in the courthouse say all lawyers were insignificant lumps of snot. At first she told herself they didn't mean her. She was a damn good lawyer and won ninety percent of all her cases. But then, for weeks afterward, she'd taken a good, hard look at herself and her profession. That was when the hot flashes started and her period took a leave of absence. Day after day she shrieked at herself in the bathroom mirror: get out, quit while you're ahead! Move. Make a real life for yourself. Think about adopting a child, get a dog.

Val flipped the sandwich over. Burned. She turned down the flame and prepared another one. She shoved the Tater Tots, whatever the hell they were, into the oven, and turned off the stove.

She found a can of Budweiser in the refrigerator, behind a Tupperware container of ground coffee. There were three more, in case Rand wanted one later. Sipping from the can, she walked out to the garage and brought in the twelve-pack sitting on the floor near the garage door. Was Susan a secret drinker or was this a Ferris leftover? Back in the kitchen, she set the whole package in the freezer and made a mental note to take it out and put it in the refrigerator in twenty minutes.

She thought about Oxmoor then and Brody's drugstore. She *liked* the laid-back, sleepy little town with the Dixon's hardware store on the corner of Main and Elm. She liked the multipaned storefronts, especially the florist shop with its array of spring flowers in the window. There were no franchises here; everything was independently owned, even the tea shop. The library was a small red-brick building trimmed in white, with tubs of spring flowers on the steps. And next to the free public library was the *Oxmoor Sentinel*, a weekly newspaper.

Would she be out of place here in this picture-pretty

little town if she decided to take up residence? Would it be possible to open up a law office and take payment in produce and services? Anything was possible, she told herself. All one had to do was make a decision.

"How's it going?" Val asked when she set the plate in front of Rand.

"I'm about done with the attic. There's nothing up there but junk, and if Susan wants it, she's going to have to come here and do it herself. There was a box of baby clothing I brought down and a box of old playbills from some of Susan's tours. I'm halfway through Jessie's room. I packed the photo albums earlier. There isn't much to pack up so I won't require your help. Does that relieve your mind?"

Val nodded.

Rand bit into the sandwich. "It's good," he said.

Val nodded again.

"You look worlds away, Val."

"Just thinking about where I'll live when I retire."

She began to talk about the town. She told him about the drugstore and how wonderful she thought it was. "The smell was . . . comforting. That's the best way I can describe it to you. Do you know the drugstore I go to has displays of condoms in different colors? Some of them glow in the dark. At Brody's they're probably hidden under the counter."

Rand looked thoughtful. "Do they really glow in the dark?"

Val burst out laughing. The uneasiness between them had disappeared.

"Did you make a fire?" she asked.

"No, but I'm going to do that while you do the dishes. I don't do dishes. I don't do windows either."

"Then what good are you?" Val teased.

"I," Rand said imperiously, "Miss Hotshot Lawyer, am a whiz at a variety of things. If you care to draw me out, I might share some of my secrets with you in front of the fire. I like marshmallows in my hot chocolate."

"I do too, so when you make it, add a few extra to mine. God, I almost forgot the beer." Val was off her chair, pulling the box from the freezer.

"Okay, this is the deal," Val said in her courtroom voice. "I'll clean up and call the moving company. You finish up, make the fire, and I'll pop the beer. There's no hot chocolate. Deal?"

"Deal."

It was fifteen minutes past eight when Val settled herself on a pile of petit point cushions. She flipped on the television. A rerun of "L.A. Law" sprang to view. Val snuggled into her nest of pillows and watched an intense courtroom scene. Her eyes were glued to the set as Grace Van Owen, the prosecuting attorney, grilled a witness. She liked the show, but because of her late hours, she rarely got to watch it. Rand sat down next to her on the floor. A frown crossed her face when the scene changed to the local legal watering hold. Grace was begging her lover, Mickey, to understand why she wouldn't be able to sleep with him for at least five days.

"How real is this show?" Rand asked.

A commercial for an air freshener came on. Val tore her eyes from the screen. "About as real as it goes. When you're prosecuting, or defending a client, you eat, sleep, and drink that case. You leave no stone unturned when it comes to your client's welfare. There are nights when I don't get to bed till two or three in the morning, and then I'm up at five, in the office by six-thirty, and in court by eight."

"You must love it," Rand said.

"I did. I think I'm burned out. I find myself turning most cases over to my associates these days. I oversee everything, though, and that's almost as demanding. I need to get out while I'm still on top. Of course, my saying I'm on top is strictly my own opinion."

"What about financially? Can you afford to pack it in?" Rand asked, curious.

"I've made some wise investments. My bank account is quite healthy. And I can sell my practice. My associates are able, capable attorneys, all handpicked. I might consider doing some consulting work just to keep my hand in."

"So then your decision to sever your relationship with the Colemans doesn't really have anything to do with the family and Susan in particular."

"Yes and no. I *am* sick of the Susans of this world. And I'm tired of the dog-eat-dog world of high-priced attorneys and demanding clients. Maybe it's why I'm thinking of retiring to a small town like this."

"I don't know, Val. It sounds lonely to me."

"I'm used to it. I'm not exactly swimming in companionship now."

"Do you miss not being married?" Rand asked.

"You can't miss something you never had. I suppose you mean the family bit: kids, dogs and cats, the whole nine yards."

"Well, yeah."

"I guess I'd have to say no. You got married late. Did you miss it?"

"Not really. But I think as one gets older one wants the security of marriage."

"Comfort. Familiarity. A nurse for your old age. That surprises me, Rand."

"Oh, why is that?"

"You were always a mover and a shaker. It's hard for me to accept that you live on an island paradise and . . . and just exist."

"I don't just exist," Rand said huffily. "I oversee the refinery."

"And?"

"And what?"

"And you lay in the sun, you play, you laze about. You're at least fifteen pounds heavier than you were the last time I saw you. The good life will do that to you, I guess. What *does* Maggie do?"

What *did* Maggie do? He racked his brain. What the hell did she do? She was always available if he wanted to fly to one of the outer islands; she was always ready to walk on the beach, always available to go out to dinner, always ready to make love. She swam a lot and read a lot. He found himself shrugging. "She's going to take over Billie Limited. I thought I told you that." His ear picked up his defensive tone. He gulped at the last of the beer in his can. "Why, do you have trouble with that?"

"No, I don't. What she does with her life is her business. The same goes for Susan. I can't help wondering, though, how either one of them would have survived out in the world without the Coleman cushion. You too, *Lord Nelson*."

"You're too damn bitter, Val. I could make a gallon of wine from your sour grapes."

Val's eyes sparked, but she held her tongue. She knew she could run rings around Rand, his wife, and his sister-in-law anytime, anywhere. She took a swig of her beer.

Rand added another log to the fire. "I miss the cold sometimes," he said. "I try to come back at least once during the winter months, and when I do, I pray all the way over that there will be snow. I also like fireplaces, like this one."

"I have a fireplace, but I've never used it," Val said. "It's one of those insert things and takes those blue flame logs. The decorator put mirror all around it."

"That sounds god-awful."

"Yeah." Val laughed. "That's why I'm enjoying this one so much. Do you know what I saw in town today? A bookstore. I peeked in. There's this fireplace against one wall, with chairs and a table in front. It's like a nook. They serve coffee and tea, and the book buyers kind of sit around and read half the book before they decide if they're going to buy or not. There was a basket of pinecones on the hearth, and there was a tiger cat snoozing next to the basket. They must have a few local authors around here, because their pictures and their books were on the mantel. Neat, huh?"

"Do you like to read?" Rand asked.

"If I had the time, I'd always have my nose in a book. I cut my teeth reading the Bobbsey Twins and Nancy Drew. God, I would have killed to have a life like Nancy Drew. Remember those old Shirley Temple movies when she was little? I used to eat my heart out over those," Val said, yawning. She thought she was slurring her words. But so what if she was? She wasn't going anywhere. She hadn't had a buzz on for years. She was damn well entitled. She stared into the flames. "Do you ever have regrets about things, you know, the important things in your life?"

Rand thought about it. Did he? Everyone had regrets of one kind or another. He wondered if Val had any.

"Well," she said, "do you?"

Rand sucked at the beer can. "A few. I'm sorry I didn't spend more time with my mother. I'm sorry I came down so hard on Cary when I found out about his affair. He confessed, for God's sake. I'm sorry I hurt Sawyer. I'm sorry I didn't hug Sally Dearest more. . . . She was my stuffed cat when I was little. Does that answer your question?" he asked. "What about you?"

"Nope, not a one. Bet you thought I was going to be riddled with them, huh?"

Damnit, he did think that. She'd bested him. "You're a wise-ass," he said.

"That too. You know what? If someone asked me what I'm proudest of, I'd say . . . Do you have anything you're proud of, Rand?"

"Hell, yes, lots of things."

"Name one," Val challenged.

"I send money to Chesney's mother every month," Rand said defensively.

"*That* doesn't count. You can never make up for all those years with money. You weren't there when she needed you. You have to take responsibility for your actions. Money every month won't cut it, Lord Nelson."

"Stop calling me that. And money *does* count for something. I donate a lot of money to charity."

"And well you should. Those less fortunate deserve help. I'm talking about something big, something that made a difference. You're a man, so I guess you didn't."

"Oh, yeah, what about you, *Lady* Lawyer? What the hell have you done that made a difference?" Rand asked sourly.

"I," Val said, enunciating each word carefully, "marched on Selma. And I attended anti-Vietnam marches on Washington. That's what I'm proudest of."

Rand reached out and put his arm around Val. "You're right, that is something to be proud of." He finished off his beer and reached for the pack he'd brought in with him on the last trip. He yanked at the rings on two cans and handed one to Val. "To Selma and Vietnam."

"I never told anyone before. I don't know why I told you." Val squirmed around so that her face was within an inch of Rand's. "Don't tell anyone, okay? It's like a treasure, just mine, that I pull out and think about from time to time. Please."

"Your secret is safe with me," Rand said solemnly. "You have nice eyes, counselor."

"So do you, my lord," Val said breathlessly. "I think we're drunk. That makes both of us vulnerable. Maybe we should go to bed. You in your bed and me in mine," Val said sleepily.

"It's cold up there. I turned down the thermostat earlier. Why don't we just sleep here by the fire. There's a cover on the couch, one of those knitted things."

"What if the fire goes out?" Val muttered.

"It won't. The grate is one of those fancy things with sides for extra logs. That fire will last four more hours. It's hardwood. Hardwood burns slowly. If we get cold, I'll replenish it."

"I hate to shiver," Val said.

"Me too," Rand said.

"Are you warm now?" Rand asked as he shook out a purple and white afghan.

"Toasty perfect," Val said, snuggling into the crook of Rand's arm. "How about you?"

"Val . . ."

"Yes?"

"Val, I . . ."

"Yes?" Val said, snuggling deeper.

"Maybe this isn't such a good idea."

"Don't worry, I trust you. Be quiet and go to sleep. Do you snore?"

"With gusto. What about you?"

"Women don't snore. Can we go to sleep now? We have to be up early."

"It's just that I've been thinking about us," Rand muttered.

"There is no us, Rand. Get that thought out of your head. You're a married man. That means you have a wife, and husbands aren't supposed to cheat on their wives. Wives say . . . damn, what is it they say?" Val mumbled. She thought she was drunk. She giggled.

"Wives say all kinds of things," Rand said. "All the time. Night and day they say things. They have opinions about everything. Sometimes they don't have opinions and they use their husbands' opinions and turn into clones. What do you think of that observation, Miss Attorney? Brilliant summation, eh?"

"Wives say . . . wives say to their husbands you can look but you can't touch. So look, but don't touch," Val said, her voice suddenly full of inebriated hostility.

Rand frowned. "Now you're mad. What are you so mad about?" Maggie never got mad. Maggie never even pouted.

"Who says I'm mad?" Val said, slurring her words.

"You look mad. You sound mad. I think you're mad at the world. This isn't one of your courtrooms. Unwind, loosen up. How about another beer? We have one left. Or we could open up the wine."

"Wine. We should have candlelight. Wine and candlelight go together."

"That's only if there's going to be a seduction. That would mean," Rand said, struggling for the words he wanted, "you are the seductee and I am the seductor."

"You can get that idea right out of your head, Lord Nelson. You are not going to get in my pants!" Val shrieked.

"Lady Lawyer, that statement dates you. Girls used to say that to me when I was seventeen. What does that mean exactly? How do you get in anyone's pants? It would take me an hour to peel those jeans off you." Rand guffawed and then tittered drunkenly as he slurped at the beer can.

Val wanted to cry and didn't know why. She swung her arm wildly, knocking the beer can out of Rand's hand. Suds shot in the air. "That was a lousy, unkind, nasty thing to say to me. I hate people like you. Get away from me, you're married!" She crawled away, closer to the fire, picking up two of the pillows from the floor and hugging them to her chest. Tears rolled down her cheeks. She sniffled, rubbing her nose on her sweatshirt sleeve.

"You look ugly when you cry," Rand observed. He crawled closer.

Val hiccuped. "I'd rather look ugly than have an ugly heart," Val said. "You have an ugly heart. And I hate that oh so veddy British accent of yours. It's so damn . . . affected. Don't come any closer or I'll . . . I'll . . ."

"What?" Rand blustered. "Tell Maggie? She wouldn't believe you. She loves me. She loves me so much she suffocates me. She's made herself an . . . extension of me. That's true love." He inched closer.

Val inched backward. She was afraid she was losing

control. She didn't like what she was starting to feel. A worm of fear crawled around inside her stomach, which had nothing to do with the alcohol she'd consumed.

"We're crossing over the line, Rand, and I don't like it," Val said. "I'm going upstairs to sleep. I'll strip the bed in the morning. I'll get up early."

Rand's arms snaked out to grab her. She threw the pillow at him as she halfheartedly struggled to get up. She slid backward, then toppled to the floor, holding the remaining cushion against her chest like a shield. She felt herself being pulled forward gently. "I think we should think about this," she whispered hoarsely. "Both of us have had too much to drink, and this fire is—"

"Intoxicating," Rand said, tugging at her Levi's. "We're two people caught up in the moment." His voice was full of excitement. "No one will ever know."

"We'll know," Val said throatily as she felt her jeans slide down over her buttocks. Rand's torso flattened her as his hands worked the jeans lower and lower.

Her weak struggles ceased. It had been so long since she'd been with a man. She forgot about Maggie, about the Colemans, and gave in to what she was feeling. Her arms reached up to circle Rand's head, to bring him closer.

"I've wanted to do this since we met at the airport," Rand said huskily.

"You talk too much," Val said, and mashed her lips against his.

They played then like two lovers, teasing one another with their lips and gentle fingers until Rand thought he would go out of his mind. "I feel like a wild animal," he whispered.

"Then act like one," Val whispered in return.

He did, again and again.

"I think," Val said, a long time later, "that was the best sex I ever allowed myself to have."

Rand preened, drawing her into his arms. "I'll second that."

"We're never going to do this again, are we?" Val said sadly.

"It probably wouldn't be wise."

Val thought his gruff voice sounded desperate. "It wouldn't be the same. Nothing is ever the same after the first time."

"I suppose you're right," Rand said, nuzzling her neck.

"I'm always right," Val said sadly.

"I miss you already," Rand whispered.

"Shhh." Val placed her fingers against her lips. "Go to sleep and dream sweet nothings."

"Don't want to go to sleep. I want to make love to you some more," Rand mumbled. "You're a hell of a woman, Valentine Mitchell."

"Yeah, that's what they say," Val said, her voice raspy. Her eyes filled. A lone tear fell on Rand's cheek when she bent over to kiss him lightly on the mouth.

It took ninety minutes for her to shower, wash her clothes, and pack. She walked out of the house and drove to the airport, leaving the car at the curb. She spent the remainder of the night staring into space until her flight was called at seven A.M. She flew into LAX and retrieved the Lamborghini.

Twenty-four hours later Val unlocked the door of her condo in Assante Towers. Only then did she collapse. She cried until there were no more tears left. Then she slept.

{{{{{{{{ CHAPTER EIGHT }}}}}}}}

*With little Moss on her hip, Ivy walked around the din-*ing room table, checking the dinnerware and wine-glasses. "It looks good," she murmured to the baby. "The tulips look just right. Billie loves tulips. I love tulips. I think everyone in the world loves tulips. Your daddy is going to be here any minute, what do you think of that?" she crooned to the baby. "And Cole is coming with him. Everything is going to be just fine. Cary will be here too, in a wheelchair, but he'll be here. Everything is going to be just fine. Just fine." She knew she was trying to convince herself that what she was saying was really true.

She brought her lips down to Moss's downy head and kissed him. How good he felt in her arms. Her flesh and blood, hers and Riley's.

"Hey, you're snoozing on me, you little rascal." She tweaked the baby under the chin, but the child was too weary to respond with bubbling laughter the way he usually did. Ivy sighed and headed for the stairs. "Guess your daddy is going to have to wake you up when he gets here." Ivy's touch was almost reverent when she laid Moss in the crib. She smiled when his thumb went into his mouth, his other chubby hand groping for his whuppie. "God, Moss, I don't know if I love you more or as much as I love your daddy." Ivy's heart swelled with love, her eyes filling with tears of happiness.

Billie joined her in the baby's room. "He's so beautiful," Billie whispered. "How blessed you are, my dear."

"I know," Ivy said.

"I used to get all teary when I put the children to bed. It's one of my fondest memories. Sometimes when . . . things aren't going well for me, I turn my memory back and . . . what I do is, I . . . I try to remember things in chronological order. I even write them down, and when I have another restless period, I start from the beginning and add a few more memories. At the moment, I'm up to the time when Riley Senior left to join the service. I was still married to little Moss's grandfather then. It wasn't a good time for me," Billie said sadly.

Suddenly Ivy found herself in Billie's arms. Neither woman knew who was comforting the other.

"It's going to be all right, Ivy. Things are a bit unsettled right now, but like Amelia used to say, life's road has to be a little rocky, otherwise one becomes placid and takes it for granted."

Ivy sniffed and wiped her eyes on the sleeve of her shirt.

"Darling, close the door. I need to talk to you about something."

Ivy perched on a huge red building block while Billie settled herself in the wicker rocking chair. "I need you to do something for me, Ivy. I can't ask the others . . . because . . . I don't think they would be able to. Thad will be the worst. Cary was my first choice, but I changed my mind, not because of his accident, but because . . . I'm babbling, Ivy, because I'm afraid you'll say no. Please, darling, hear me out and think about what I'm going to ask you before you give me your answer. And Ivy, I want this kept between us. For now. I don't want you to tell Riley. I know it isn't right of me to ask you to keep something from him . . . dear God, I'm going around the bush, aren't I?"

Ivy smiled wanly, her heart thudding madly in her chest. She watched as Billie withdrew a small square package from the deep folds of her skirt. Without hesitation she reached for it, her eyes full of questions.

"It's my living will, Ivy," Billie said briskly. "I need your assurance that you will do what I want. Thad and my family, they won't be able to. I chose you because you remind me in so many ways of myself at your age, although I do believe you have more guts. Will you do it, Ivy?"

Ivy didn't stop to think, didn't stop to analyze or rationalize. She nodded numbly. Behind her, Moss stirred. Automatically, Ivy reached back to rewind the music box on the colorful mobile hanging over the crib. *Mary had a little lamb.* She cleared her throat. "What . . . I mean, what is in this tape? When do you want me to . . . to look at it?"

"Why not right now? You have a VCR and television set in your bedroom. Perhaps it will be better if we look at it together." She was still whispering, her eyes clouded with worry.

In her bedroom, Ivy slid the tape into the VCR and turned down the volume. She turned to lock the door before she sat down on the bed next to Billie. She couldn't ever remember being this cold, this numb. Billie squeezed her hand. There was strength in Billie's hard, dry grasp. Ivy didn't want to look at the television screen, but knew she had to. As she watched, she cleared her throat again and again. Five minutes later she pushed the eject button and slid the tape back into the case. She carried it across the room to bury it deep in her knitting bag. She felt like a trapped animal.

"You'll give me your answer tomorrow, Ivy?" Billie asked anxiously.

"I don't need to think about it, Billie," Ivy said, returning to the bed. "I don't need a night to sleep on it. If it's what you want, if you're sure, if you have no doubts at all, I'll do it. Yes, I can handle it. I don't want you worrying about me now." Her arms went around the frail woman. She wanted to hug her hard, squeeze her, to breathe her own precious life into Billie's frail body. She felt as protective of Billie as she did of Moss.

"Will you do one other thing for me, Ivy?"

"If I can."

Billie bit down on her lower lip. "Once in a while, when you aren't too busy, will you go up to the hill and kind of . . . tell me what's going on? Bring me up to date on everything. I'll want to know about Moss, Katy, and Josie. Not right at the beginning, but later on. Amelia and I will be busy catching up. Will you do that for me?" Billie's eyes were misty with tears.

Ivy broke down again, and Billie cried against her shoulder.

"This is my last tear," Billie said firmly, reaching for a wad of tissues on Ivy's night table. "In the beginning all I did was cry, wail, and moan. I wanted to be strong like Amelia was. Amelia was so much more to me than a sister-in-law. She was the best friend I ever had. I loved her as much as Cary did. I've been praying to God, asking Him to give me the same strength He gave Amelia. There are times when I feel He's listening to me, like right now, and then there are times when I feel He's too busy to bother with me. I guess that's wrong.

Either one believes or one doesn't. Amelia told me never to bargain with God, so I don't. Just be kind to our family, Ivy. Time to go downstairs now. The others will be gathering. I'll go ahead. I know you want to check on Moss. Thank you, Ivy," Billie said as she hugged the young woman once more.

Ivy didn't trust herself to speak. She nodded. In the adjacent baby's room, she walked over to the wicker rocking chair. There was barely an indentation in the plush velvet padding. She sat down with a thump and thought about Billie's will.

No life-support measures. Pull the plug. Body organs to an organ bank if possible. Those not ravaged by disease. The word euthanasia sent a shudder through her body. What were the ramifications? She racked her brain to remember what she'd read and seen recently on the news. Had she agreed to do something that wasn't legal? The family . . . God, what were they going to say? Would they fight her? She thought of Susan then and imagined her reaction. Her shoulders slumped. Would her husband be on her side?

Ivy was off her chair in a second. The mad desire to fling herself into her son's crib and snuggle with him was overwhelming. What if the family turned on her? What if Riley turned on her? Her hand crept through the bars of the crib. She caressed the downy head. "Then it's just you and me, partner," she whispered to the sleeping baby.

Back in her room, Ivy headed for the bathroom and splashed cold water on her face. She stared at herself in the mirror. How was it possible for her to look the same as when she carried Moss up the steps to put him to bed? She should look . . . awful. Terrible. She picked up the powder puff. Billie wanted to be buried on the hill.

What would it do to Thad to see her buried next to her first husband? Dear God, Ivy fretted, what had she gotten herself into? Billie's words ricocheted in her head. "You, Ivy, are the legal custodian of my living will." Ivy closed her eyes as she visualized the battles that lay ahead of her. Tomorrow, or the next day, she was going to go to Valentine Mitchell's office with the tape. Valentine would help her through this. The decision made her feel better immediately.

Now, she had to go downstairs with a smile on her face and play hostess to the family. She crossed her fingers. *Please, God, don't let Susan get to me.*

Ivy used the back staircase to enter the kitchen. Things looked under control. Beef stew, fresh bread, garden salad, and green peas. Jonquil had trouble cooking any meal that required more than one pot. The whole family loved stew made with prime Coleman beef, which was tender as butter. There would be no complaints, and the pot would be empty when dinner ended. There were never leftovers when Jonquil made stew. The peach cobbler looked wonderful, with its little patches of cinnamon sugar crusting the top. It was one of Billie's favorites. Riley's too.

"You best get in there, Miz Ivy," Jonquil said out of the corner of her mouth. "Miz Sawyer is half snookered. Miz Susan is ... she's been drinking all afternoon."

Ivy took a deep breath and entered the huge family room at the back of the house.

"Well," she said cheerfully, "we're almost all here. Riley and Cole should arrive any minute, and Thad will be here with Cary. Maggie, I'm going to have a ginger ale, want to split it?"

Maggie held her glass aloft. "Beat you to it," she said

quietly. "I told Jonquil to set another place. Rand called from the airport. He's on his way. Guess we'll all be here."

"Well, Miss Hostess of Sunbridge, do you think you can handle *that*?" Susan slurred.

"*Sober,* I can handle anything, Susan."

"Is there a hidden message in what you just said?" Sawyer demanded as she brought the beer bottle in her hand to her mouth.

Ivy forced a laugh that sounded eerie to her ears. "It just means I can handle it. Whatever *it* turns out to be." Her eyes were on Susan when she spoke. "The stew is simmering, and we all know it just gets better the longer it cooks. Why don't we catch up on family matters? I know I would personally love to hear how the twins are. I don't know how you do it, Sawyer. Moss wears me out. Two little girls, it's wonderful. Billie told me about the Easter dresses she designed for them." Her eyes pleaded with Sawyer, who in the past had been her staunchest ally.

"Oh, yes, darling, tell us how the girls are doing," Billie said cheerfully. "And then I'll remind you of the things you did when you were their age."

Maggie's eyes darkened. She hated it when her mother said things like this. She herself had absolutely no memory of what her daughter Sawyer did or didn't do at the age of two.

"You would not believe what they do," Sawyer said proudly. "Adam is better with them than I am. They actually listen to him. Last month they managed to get hold of the phone and called Australia and Greece and a bunch of other places. Adam whacked their bottoms real good. Josie stuck her tongue out at him and Katy kicked him in the shins. Little shits, both of them. However, they're mine and I love them dearly." Her expression became quizzical. "Don't you think it's strange that Katy has straight hair and Josie has curly hair? I mean both Adam and I have curly hair." The question wasn't directed to anyone in particular.

"What's the big deal?" Susan snapped.

Sawyer drained her beer. "I didn't say it was a big deal. I said it was strange. I'm sick of you, Susan. Besides, you're half in the bag, and I don't like talking to a drunk. So why don't you go upstairs and sleep off whatever it is that's crawling in your undies."

"For heaven's sake, girls, what is the problem?" Billie said quietly. "This is a wonderful time. We're all together, and Cary is going to be here any minute. Please, let's not have him come home to a battleground. Now, you're both drunk, and if there is one thing I cannot abide, it is a drunken female. I suggest both of you go to the kitchen and get some coffee."

"Atta girl, Mam," Maggie said tightly. "You tell 'em."

"It was a suggestion, not an order," Billie said, tears forming in her eyes.

"In that case," Susan drawled drunkenly, "I'll pass."

"Well, I won't," Ivy said tightly. "I want both of you to sober up before the rest of the family gets here."

Sawyer set her beer bottle down carefully on the bar. Her eyes were bleak, her hair in wild disarray. "I'm sorry, Ivy. It's just that I felt I needed some bottled courage to face Cole, and before I knew it, I was half lit. I'll get the coffee. Susan, do you want any?"

"Well, I certainly don't want to embarrass *our hostess*, so I guess I will." She tottered after Sawyer, her arms flapping about like a rag doll's.

Billie sighed wearily. Where was Thad? Thad would

have been able to handle this. She looked at Maggie. "What's wrong, Maggie?"

For God's sake, don't you know, can't you see? We're devastated. Right now I want a drink more than I want to take another breath, but if I do that, I won't be any good to anyone. "Susan and Ferris have split up. He pulled a Jerome on her, so Rand and Valentine Mitchell went after him. I'm happy to report, according to Rand, that Suse now has her small fortune intact and will be staying with me in Hawaii. She said she'd help run Billie Limited. It will be good for both of us. Seeing little Moss . . . I guess she thought about her daughter and . . . she's been under a lot of pressure," Maggie said defensively.

"And seeing me like this certainly didn't help matters," Billie said quietly. "Poor Susan, she's been so unlucky in her choice of men." Unbearable sadness engulfed her. She'd never had the opportunity to bond with her daughter, but thanks to Amelia, Susan had the life she'd always wanted, that of a concert pianist. Now, it was too late. She would never be able to help her daughter. Secretly she thought Susan incapable of loving anyone, and for that she blamed herself totally. Susan had never looked at her with love.

The inner trembling that warned of a collapse was starting. She had to get herself in hand or the family would see how weak she was. She brought herself back to the present to hear Maggie speaking.

"That too," Maggie said just as quietly. "You should have told us, Mam. I feel as if we don't count, that we weren't important enough for you to share what you were going through." There was a sob in Maggie's voice that tore at Billie's heart.

"Oh, no, darling, it was nothing like that. I just love

you all too much to make you unhappy for even one second longer than necessary. If it's any consolation to you, Thad badgered me every day. Right or wrong, it was what I wanted. Life goes on, Maggie dear, and when we've resolved the crisis that has drawn us together, Thad and I will return to Vermont."

The steely sound in Billie's voice startled Ivy. She wanted to clap her hands and shout, "Bravo, Billie." Instead, she allowed a small smile to tug at the corners of her mouth as she offered Billie a sly wink.

They all came at once, Thad and Cary, Riley, Cole and Rand. First, there was the sound of three separate car engines, of horns blowing a greeting. Then came the verbal greetings. The men of the family were home.

Ivy ran to Riley, Maggie to Rand, Thad and Cole to Billie.

"Go to your grandmother," Ivy whispered in her husband's ear. She watched as the men crowded around Billie, tears shimmering in her eyes. Billie was so loved, so blessed with her family.

"Hey, what about me?" Cary shouted from the middle of the floor.

"Hey, yourself." Ivy laughed. "What about you? You're here, what more do you want?" she quipped.

"Tell 'em, Thad," Cary ordered.

"We snatched him," Thad grinned. "I couldn't have done it on my own. Rand showed up, and between the two of us, we got him out un-dee-tected."

"Oh, my Lord!" Billie squealed. "Cary, are you well enough?"

"Probably not. It's been four days. I would have signed myself out tomorrow anyway, so a few hours one way or another isn't going to make much difference. Doctors don't know everything. The bottom line is, I wanted to be here. After all, this dinner is for me. I appreciate you all coming like this. I really do. The one thing I have always loved and admired about you all is the way you come together, from all over the world, when one of you has trouble. You stick together like glue, and I'm so grateful to you for your support and love and making me a part of your family. I couldn't have gotten through . . . hell, you know what I mean. End of speech." Cary grinned.

"About time," Susan said. "What would you like to drink, Cary?"

"Suse, is that you?" Cary said, stretching out his hand.

"In the flesh. What would you like?" she repeated.

"Whatever you're having. My nose tells me Sunbridge stew and fresh bread is on the dinner menu. I don't want to spoil my appetite."

Susan's eyes swiveled to Ivy, who smiled. "Soda pop," Susan said. "I had a snootful a while ago and made an ass of myself. As usual. We do have cold beer, though." The tenderness in her voice raised several eyebrows, including Billie's.

"Beer sounds good. Everybody talk so I can get a feel for where you are." Cary laughed when a gaggle of sound erupted around him. "Jesus, not all at once, one at a time. Where's Moss? Ivy, is he here?"

"Afraid not, Cary. He caved in about an hour ago. I tried to keep him up, but he fell asleep in my arms. He might wake up. He does that sometimes when his dad isn't here to put him to bed."

"Here, Cary," Susan said, placing a bottle of Budweiser into his hands. Ivy's eyebrows rose when she noticed how Susan's features softened and the way she touched her hand to Cary's. Her voice was gentle and warm, and she spoke to him in a tone only the two of them could hear. It almost looked as if she was in love with him, Ivy thought.

Cole was the first to break away, his eyes filled with unbearable pain. "So, little mother, how's it going?" he said to Ivy.

"It's going. Some days it's better than other days. The trick is not to get down because it's just too damn hard to get back up. I kind of stick to the middle of the road," Ivy said, hugging him. "How's Sumi? I just know it's going to be a boy. Or a girl." Ivy laughed. Out of the corner of her eye she saw Sawyer approaching from the kitchen. Ivy moved off to stand by her husband. Immediately his arm went around her waist. She laid her head on his shoulder.

Sawyer saw Cole before he noticed her. She stopped. For the first time in her life she was uncertain of what she should do. She told him so.

"When *I* don't know what to do, I just go with my instincts and say fuck it all," Cole said quietly.

"Yeah, yeah, that's pretty much what I do too," Sawyer said hoarsely. "I . . . I guess I got carried away that day on the phone."

"Yeah. I did too. I've been going through a bad time lately. I'm . . ." He wanted to say he was sorry, to take the miserable look from his sister's face, but sorry was just a word. Sawyer wasn't real big on words, not when actions were available. He closed the gap between them and wrapped his arms around her. Her sigh was like music to his ears. Now he could say it. "I'm sorry, Sawyer."

"Me too. Let's pretend it didn't happen and start over. Boy, do I have things to tell you."

"It can't possibly top what I have to tell you," Cole muttered.

"Tonight, when the others go to sleep, we'll talk, okay? Down in Billie's studio. God, I grew up there. I'd kill to have that time in my life back. She's going to die, Cole, and there's nothing I can do for her."

Cole felt like his heart was being wrenched out of his chest. "Smile, Sawyer, or I'll straighten your hair myself. We owe it to Grandmam to be as brave as she is. It's not easy, but you do it because you have to do it. I didn't think I would ever get over Mr. Hasegawa's death. You don't get over it, you just go on. It's part of life. It's that simple, Sawyer. Life goes on."

"But—"

"There are no buts. If we pull together, we'll be able to handle it. God, what *is* that smell?"

"Stew," Maggie said, joining them. "No matter how I try, I can't make it the way it's made here. I guess it's the fresh meat. I plan to make a pig of myself, in case anyone is interested."

"Of course we are," Rand said, slipping his arm about his wife's waist.

Something's wrong, Sawyer thought. Rand was too stiff and his smile didn't show in his eyes. Maggie didn't look right. Sawyer moved away, her eyes full of worry, to where Billie was sitting. She squatted down at her grandmother's feet the way she'd done ever since she was a child. "I've missed you guys. Has anyone heard from Julie?" she asked quietly.

"We've missed you too, but we do love getting the pictures of the girls. We have them lined up on the mantel. They're precious, Sawyer, absolutely precious. And yes, we've heard from Julie."

Thad lowered his voice so it wouldn't travel to Cary

and Susan. "She said she's going to do a bit of traveling and then maybe open her own business in Burlington. She cared deeply for Cary, but like Cary, she was riddled with guilt over their affair. They discussed it all, and both of them agreed parting was the answer. I believe they will always be friends. When we go back, we'll let her know about Cary, but that part of their life is over. Now, what else do you want to know?"

"How do I toilet-train a set of twins?" Sawyer asked ruefully.

"With a great deal of patience, stamina, and fortitude. If that doesn't work, buy stock in one of those diaper companies. You were very difficult to train, darling. You were four years and two months when you finally managed to stay dry," Billie said fondly. "I was about to give up on you."

"But you didn't," Sawyer said softly. "Thank you for that, Grandmam. Did I ever *really* thank you for all the things you did for me?"

"Hundreds of times," Billie said lightly. "You, my darling, were one of the best things that ever happened to me. I wouldn't change one year, one month, one week, one day, one hour of the time we spent together."

"I wouldn't either. My happiest memories were here at Sunbridge. I loved living in the studio. Anyway, thanks again." How husky her voice was. It sounded to her ears like she'd cried too long and too hard. "My God, I'm hungry. When do you suppose we're going to eat?"

"Right now." Ivy laughed.

The family sat down to dinner. Riley said grace.

"Dig in," Thad said happily as he passed one of the three loaves of bread. Riley passed the stew and Ivy passed the salad bowl. Conversation was light, and there were smiles and good-natured bantering back and forth across the table.

When the meal was over, Ivy snapped her fingers. "We ate it all," she chortled. "Every last drop, and we finished the three loaves of bread. Who has room for peach cobbler?" The chorus of groans and opened belt buckles caused a stir when Jonquil carried the plates to the table.

"Real whipped cream!" Sawyer squealed. "Pile it on, Jonquil. Tomorrow I diet!"

"Tuna fish and broccoli tomorrow." Ivy laughed.

The moment dinner was over, the family retired to the huge room at the back of the house, coffee cups in hand.

It was time for family business. An uncomfortable silence settled in the room. Who, Ivy wondered, was going to go first? She nudged her husband.

Riley reacted. "Okay, family, I guess I should mention here at the start of this meeting that Cole and I have more or less come to terms with . . . our families. East and West. We're going to merge these families as one, which was my grandfather's intention all along. I expect things will be bumpy for a while, but I'm confident we can make the transition relatively painless. What all this means is that we will be able to finance Sawyer's plane, and she won't have to seek outside financing. Cole and I agreed to this on the trip back here, so it's not something we thought of on the spur of the moment."

"You're too late," Sawyer said quietly.

Ivy's head jerked upright. Billie squirmed in her chair.

"You're not going to go ahead with it? That's just

like you, Sawyer, get us all riled up, and then you pack it in without telling anyone," Cole said tightly.

Sawyer's tone grew more quiet. "As usual, little brother, you weren't listening. I said you were too late. I didn't say anything about packing it in."

"What are you saying, darling? I'm confused, and I think the others are too," Billie said, matching her granddaughter's tone.

Sawyer was on her feet, her denim skirt swishing about her ankles. One booted foot tapped the oak floor. She moved again to stand behind Cary's wheelchair. "Cary offered me all the financing we'll need. I didn't have to ask. He *offered.* I accepted. What that means, family, is it's a done deed."

"But—" Cole sputtered.

"No buts, Cole. I asked you first and you wanted to gouge the family. This doesn't mean I love you any less, but any profits from this plane won't go into Hasegawa coffers. Coleman Aviation is mine, and don't you ever forget it. Correction," Sawyer said smugly, "I have the controlling interest."

"Why didn't you tell us about Cary's offer?" Riley demanded.

"Listen, I'm not one to let something simmer if I can bring it to a boil. I talked about this to Cary a month ago, and then again the day Cole turned shark. I don't beg anyone in my family to help me. Either you're there for me or you aren't. And let me remind you two," she said, jabbing a finger first at Riley and then at Cole, "it was my husband who pulled your asses out of the fire with his property and his oil. Adam, with my approval—those are the key words, *my approval*—gave this family a chance to rebound. We didn't argue about it, or fight, or make deals. You needed our property, and we sold it to you. I have this absolute, total, blind loyalty where this family is concerned. It was my mistake to think you had it too, Cole."

"That's not fair, Sawyer," Maggie snapped.

"Oh, yeah, what's not fair about it, Maggie? Don't fight your son's battles, he's old enough to do it himself," Sawyer snarled.

"Riley just said . . . you're refusing to take their money, but you'll take money from Cary, an *outsider*?" Maggie railed.

Billie was on her feet and halfway across the room in a second. The slap to Maggie's face was like a gunshot in the quiet, stunned room. "I have never in my life been ashamed of you, but I'm ashamed now," Billie said coldly. "You will apologize this instant," she ordered.

Maggie reeled backward, expecting to find her husband standing behind her, but it was Cole who caught her arm. In all of her life her mother had never laid a hand on her. She was too stunned to do anything but stare at her family. What she saw registered on their faces was shock and disgust. She jerked free of her son's arms and ran from the room. Cole started after her.

"No!" came the iron command.

Cole stopped in his tracks. He'd never heard that tone of voice from his grandmother.

Billie, with Thad's help, walked over to Cary's chair. With great difficulty she dropped to her knees and reached for his hand. "In my heart, Cary, I don't believe Maggie meant what she said. I'm afraid this is all my fault, and I'm perfectly willing to take the blame. This is why I didn't want anyone to know about my illness. It's me Maggie is angry with. She's angry . . .

because ... because she wants me to live forever, like I wanted Amelia to live forever. I think I was the only one who understood what Amelia was trying to do before she passed away. She wanted to spare us, and herself too. But, selfishly, we wouldn't let her. You are not to think for one second that you do not belong to this family. You *are* this family. If you want a chorus of ayes, it can be arranged. Please, I beg you, Cary, don't judge us by Maggie's outburst. I know my daughter, and I know she's already regretting what she said. Words spoken thoughtlessly or carelessly can carry a lifetime of hurt. I can't change that and I have no right to ask you to forgive my daughter. I think it's written somewhere that only a mother will forgive anything her children do because mothers love unconditionally."

Cary took a deep breath. "There's nothing to forgive, Billie. I know how Maggie feels." The warm tears splashing on the back of his hands made his heart thump. He could deny this wonderful woman nothing. Next to Amelia, he loved her more than any other person in the world. He felt Thad lift Billie from her kneeling position.

"Now listen ... family ... if there's a problem with my offer to Sawyer ..."

"There's no problem, Cary," Sawyer said gently.

"Well, if there is, we can work it out. Isn't that what families do?" Cary asked airily.

Riley's eyes sparked in Cole's direction. "No problem, Cary," he said quietly.

"Carry on, folks," Thad said. "I'm giving Billie a ride upstairs. She wants to turn in early. I'll be down later. Cary, do you mind hanging around a bit longer?"

Susan answered for Cary. "No, he doesn't mind. I'm

going to take him for a walk in the garden. It's a beautiful evening and I could use some fresh air."

"That's an offer I certainly won't refuse. Bring some cigarettes, Susan."

"They're in my pocket." Susan giggled. "Hang on now."

"Anyone want a drink?" Rand asked.

"Is it hemlock we're serving tonight?" Sawyer snapped. "Sorry, I didn't mean that."

"I can't believe you accepted Cary's offer," Cole said tightly. "You know that means he has to either mortgage or sell Miranda. You'll be stripping him bare. Is that what you want?"

"Get it through your head, Cole, he offered. He wouldn't have offered if he didn't think he could handle it. It was a drop in the bucket to you, and you . . . look, we're beating a dead horse here, so why don't we just give up, okay?"

"Then what was that business about us meeting down at Grandmam's studio later? I thought things were settled. I screwed up, I apologized, you apologized. Now you tell me . . . ah, forget it."

"Much too little too late. But I *was* going to tell you about Shigata Mitsu. Don't you remember asking me about him? I know who he was . . . is . . . whatever. At first I just recalled the name, and then I asked Thad. He knows all about him. What's wrong with you, Cole? You're white as snow."

Cole forgot about the financing, his mother, and Rand's stony face. "You mean there is such a person?"

"You're a twit, Cole. I just told you so, didn't I? Mr. Hasegawa told me the story once, but it was vague in my mind. Thad repeated it for me. What is it you don't understand?" she asked peevishly, her eyes on Rand.

Before Cole could reply, she said, "Rand, shouldn't you be with Maggie?"

"Why? What she did was unforgivable," he said, pouring himself a second stiff drink.

"I think I'll check on Moss," Ivy said quietly.

"I'll go with you," Riley said, following his wife.

Cole spun around to Rand. "That's a rather unkind remark, coming from you, Rand. I thought you were more understanding. Mother's going through a bad time. Like Grandmam said, she's probably upstairs crying her eyes out and trying to figure out a way to make things right."

"Some things can't be made right. If Maggie thinks of Cary as an outsider, then she must think of me the same way. And what does that make Thad? Ivy? Sumi? Get my point?" Rand said, and drained his glass. "I think I'll go for a walk. Tell Thad I'll go with him when he takes Cary back to the hospital."

"What does *that* mean? That you 'outsiders' are going to band together?" Cole snapped.

"Listen to you, the both of you!" Sawyer said through clenched teeth. "Are you trying to make this family come apart?"

"It's all your fault," Cole snarled. "You started it!"

He never saw the blow, never expected it. He blinked in stunned surprise.

"Goddamnit, Sawyer," he roared, but she was already out of the room.

"Well, that's two down," Rand drawled before he sauntered from the room.

Cole sat for a long time, staring into space. "Sawyer was right," he muttered. "I started this thing, not her. *I'm* making the family fall apart." He was about to get up and search out his sister when Riley and Thad entered the room.

His eyes full of misery, Cole asked, "Is Grandmam all right?"

"She's sleeping. None of this is good for her, Cole. We're going home tomorrow. I'm sure Cary will understand. Ivy and Riley will look after him, and I might be wrong about this, but I think Susan will stay on as well. Billie seems to think they're growing close. It would be wonderful for both of them if they ... you know, kind of got together."

"Thad, how long does Grandmam have?"

"It's uncertain. At least a few months. Every day I see little things. She tries so damn hard. This ... trip, this evening wasn't good for her at all. You must have seen it. She was crying when she fell asleep. She kept saying she failed the family, that she should have done more. Of course that's hogwash. No one could be more loving and devoted to a family than Billie. But all this fuss Maggie caused—and Sawyer too, from the way she just looked—has upset her. By the way, how are *you* doing?"

"Right now I feel lower than a snake's belly," Cole said miserably. "I don't know if I can ever make this right. Where do I start. *How* do I start? Sawyer said this family is being torn apart, and she's right."

"I'm afraid I can't help you, Cole. The only thing I'm concerned with is your grandmother. When we leave here tomorrow, I want to see smiles, and I don't want one anxious word to filter up to Vermont. I want Billie to be worry-free, if there is such a thing. I will not tolerate anything less. If one of you crosses the line, I will simply take her away to someplace where there are no phones and no mailboxes. I want you and Riley to relay this to your family."

"Oh, Jesus, not you too," Cole groaned.

"We'll tell them," Riley said.

Cole nodded. "Thad, Sawyer was going to tell me about Shigata Mitsu before she got all strung out. She said you knew the story. Would you tell it to me and Riley? No, wait. Before you do, let me tell you about what's been going on in my head."

Thad listened intently, then said, "Let me be sure I understand all of this. Are you asking me if I believe in spirits, in the supernatural?"

"Guess so," Cole mumbled. Riley looked everywhere but at Thad.

Thad shrugged. "Damned if I know if I do or not. Cary swears he feels Amelia's presence all the time. I remember getting the heebie-jeebies that day when we played 'This Is Your Life' for Riley. Remember how the chandelier tinkled when Cary raised his head and yelled 'Right, babe,' or something like that? We were all spooked. Then there's that business of the angels singing in the hospital when Sawyer was so near death. If this is a yes or no question, then my answer is yes, I hope so, because I'm going to be looking for Billie when ... when ... you know."

"I believe in them," Cole said flatly. "At least I believe in Shadaharu Hasegawa's spirit. I saw with my own eyes whatever it was rip through the Zen garden. So did Riley. Two of us can't be wrong."

"There are all kinds of explanations for something like that. Earthly reasons."

"You'll never convince me."

"Obviously, Shadaharu doesn't frighten you. I guess that means he's a friendly spirit." Thad groaned. "I can't believe we're having this discussion. At least when I tell Billie, she'll have a laugh. She talks about Mr. Hasegawa a lot. I want to cry every time she says she's going to have so many things to tell her old friends when she gets *there*. She's not at all afraid."

Cole hunched into his shoulders. "Tell us the story of Shigata Mitsu."

Thad sighed. "It's not a long story so don't get comfortable. One day Shadaharu and I were in the Zen garden talking about inane things, and I asked him how he came to be the third wealthiest man in the world. He said it was because of Shigata Mitsu. Shadaharu had been a poor tailor at one time with many mouths to feed. He had very little business and worried himself sick about how he was going to pay the rent and buy food for his family. He was walking home along the beach one night with only six yen in his pocket. He thought about drowning himself because he was so ashamed that he couldn't provide for his family. He sat down on the seawall with the six yen in his hand, and was staring at it when a man sat down next to him. The man was neither young nor old, but somehow seemed timeless or ageless. They looked into one another's eyes. Shadaharu said he saw only himself reflected in the man's gaze, but he knew the man was seeing his soul. He couldn't explain how he knew, he just knew. They struck up a conversation, and Shadaharu showed him the six yen in his hand. The man said that Shadaharu was rich, that some people didn't have six yen or even one yen. He told Shadaharu he had to share with those who had less than he had. Shadaharu said he remembered nodding his head in agreement. They talked a little more and then the man got ready to leave. Shadaharu bowed low and the man placed his hand on his shoulder. Shadaharu said it felt wonderfully warm, and his shoulder remained warm for many days. Anyway, on the way home to his family, he met three beggars and he gave each of them a yen. He said he felt good doing it, knowing the poor souls would at least have a warm meal. The very next day when he went to his shop, a man from the newspaper came in and asked him to make three suits. Shadaharu said he worked all day and night and in two days finished the suits. He delivered them personally. The man from the paper called in some people on his staff and they all ordered suits. Many, many suits. Word spread, and soon Shadaharu was the most sought-after tailor in town. *And what he did, Cole, was give half of everything he earned away to those less fortunate than himself from that day on.* He did that until the day he died. The more he gave away, the more he got in return. God has always said give and you shall receive," Thad said quietly.

Cole was on his feet, his hands jammed into his pockets. "Are you telling me the man Mr. Hasegawa spoke with on the seawall was God?"

"I'm not saying that at all. But do you have a better explanation?"

"Was his name Shigata Mitsu?" Cole demanded.

"No. Shadaharu said he never asked the man's name. He gave the man the name Shigata Mitsu himself. He needed a name to go with the story when he told his wife about the encounter, but he told me he thought he was talking to God. Of course, he wondered why God would speak personally with someone as unworthy as himself, so he convinced himself that the man was an *emissary* from God. The Christian God. I think that was another reason Shadaharu was always so open to Western ways, and why he didn't kick up a fuss when his daughter, Otami, married Riley's father and converted to Catholicism. He believed it was ordained. He was a very wise, wonderful, kind, and generous man. You have no idea, Cole, of the people he helped, of the hospitals he built, the families he supported. He even funded many churches here in the United States. Did you ever wonder why he chose this family to befriend?"

"Of course I wondered. We all did. We still do. We more or less thought it was because of Otami and Riley's father."

"Of course. East and West. He loved this family as much as he loved his own. He expected Riley to carry on, but Riley chose to remain here. You were the logical successor, thanks to Riley. That old man adored you, Cole. He considered you a son."

"And I failed him. Why didn't someone tell me?"

"I think he wanted you to find out yourself. This is just my opinion, Cole," Thad said hastily.

"How did he explain all those . . . giveaways to the accountants and lawyers?"

"I don't think he did. They would never dream of questioning him. He was making so much money, they were hard pressed to keep track of what he did have. Shadaharu said the money just flowed in. So now you sit on ninety billion dollars. Now, as to the tempest in the Zen garden . . . I'd say, if I were a wagering man, that Shadaharu was getting impatient for you to get on the stick. Call it a warning. Call it anything you like. Maybe Sawyer was your test. Hell, I don't know, Cole," Thad said impatiently. References to the hereafter always bothered him.

"Tempest, my ass. Riley and I felt like the wrath of God was coming down around us."

"Ahhh. On that thought, I will leave you to seek out

my charge and return him from whence he was
snatched. Good night, Cole," Thad said, his tone relieved.

The cousins stared at one another. "It would seem,"
Cole said carefully, "that Thad gave us our answer. Sort
of. Now I have to come up with a solution." He babbled
then, nonstop, until he came to the part where he said,
"Sawyer must have been my test, and I flunked. Cary
stepped in, just the way your grandfather did years ago
when the family was about to go down the tubes. Now
I have to make it right. This is my second chance. I
need your help, Riley."

"I'm here. We need a great brainstorming session,
and for that, we need a beer bottle in our hands." He
twisted the caps off two San Miguels and handed one to
Riley.

Settled comfortably with their beers, the cousins
stared unblinking at one another.

"What are you going to do about Sawyer, Cole? And
when are we going to talk about Grandmam Billie?" He
rolled the frosty beer bottle between his hands, enjoying
the cool wetness.

"I'm still trying to accept what happened to Cary. My
mother . . . I can't believe she . . . Jesus, do you have
any idea of what Cary must have felt? I wasn't going
after Mother to console her, but to . . . I guess I was going to blast her. I'm glad Grandmam ordered me to stay.
I thought Rand would go after her, but he looked like
one of those cigar store Indians. He's got a burr scratching him someplace. Cary is what's important now. He
was so matter-of-fact at dinner. I couldn't handle being
blind, even temporarily, and Cary doesn't know if it's
temporary. Did you by any chance notice the little inter-
play between him and Aunt Susan?"

Riley grimaced. "I missed that, but Ivy saw it. She filled me in when we were checking on Moss. I can see them together. Maybe it will be just your mother running Billie Limited. Maybe Aunt Susan needs someone to nurture, someone who depends on her. She didn't have a problem in the world when her daughter was alive. I guess it has something to do with her going to live in England with Aunt Amelia when she was so young. Rand told me once that she never had a normal childhood and that music was her life. It's sad, if you stop to think about it."

Cole set his beer down with a hard thump. "You want sad? I'll give you sad. This whole family is screwed up. It's the 'outsiders,' to quote my mother, who have their shit in one sock. Thad doesn't have problems. Rand is on top of the heap. Adam is . . . Adam is about as perfect as you can get. Ivy and Sumi, they're in a class by themselves. Cary is one of those rare individuals who is totally giving, warm, and caring. He came through for Sawyer with no questions asked, just the way your grandfather did. It's us Colemans that are screwed up. Go ahead, Riley, tell me I'm wrong."

"I wouldn't touch that with a ten foot pole," Riley said, lining up his empty bottle next to Cole's. He opened two more.

"Does it ever get better? How do we get to that place Adam and Cary are in? God, how I envy the inner peace they seem to have. How, Riley?"

"My grandfather had that same inner peace. Grandmam Billie has it. I think Thad does too. I guess you just have to accept things for what they are. Isn't there some kind of prayer or saying about asking God for the strength to accept what can't be changed . . . or something?"

"I know the one you mean," Cole said, pacing up and down the room. "I don't understand how your grandfather could be so peaceful when he knew he was going to die. And look at Grandmam Billie. She seems as if she's completely accepted her fate."

"Listen, Cole," Riley said, by now sounding slightly drunk, "this is a very heavy discussion, and we're on the way to getting fried, but to answer your question, I can only speak about my grandfather. Until Thad told us that story about Shigata Mitsu, I thought my grandfather was born a loving, kind man. If all Thad said was true, then my grandfather achieved that state of peacefulness by doing good. I bet, Cole, if you go through his personal accounts, you'll be in for the surprise of your life. Knowing him as I did, I bet he gave away more than he kept. Hey, I always feel good when I do something for someone. Remember that high we were both on when we gave Adam back his homestead? Does it compute?"

Cole nodded and lined his beer bottle up with Riley's. He reached into the bar refrigerator for two more.

"This last Christmas, Ivy decided we should not give each other gifts. Instead we made Christmas for six families. We went the whole nine yards: tree, decorations, wreath for the front door, food, toys for the children, gifts for the parents, and a promissory note to all six families to help them throughout the year. It was the best Christmas we ever had. I've never done anything like that before, have you?"

Cole shook his head. "The answer can't be that simple. Give and you get. C'mon, Riley," Cole said.

"Forget the *get* part. It's the giving. It doesn't have to be material things. You gotta forget the gimme part. And I never said it was the answer to all of life's problems, but unless you can come up with something better, I'll stick with my theory." Riley knew he was well on his way to becoming drunk as he watched Cole moving in slow motion.

"Thad said he and Grandmam are leaving tomorrow. That breaks my heart, Riley. There must be something we can do."

Riley shook his head furiously. His stomach heaved with the movement. He sat perfectly still until his insides quieted. "We say, Good-bye, we love you, and if you need us, call. We keep our eyes dry and our voices cheerful. That way Grandmam will think . . . think we believe she . . . has a chance. It's what she wants," Riley said mournfully. "It's that . . . giving thing again. It makes sense, doesn't it?"

"Yeah, it does. Thad said he would take Grandmam away if we didn't do what he wanted. He would too. I don't know about that dry-eye part. My eyes water a lot when it comes to this family. Grandmam's been our rock for so long. She's never failed us. Not once. You want to bawl now so she doesn't see us do it tomorrow?" Cole mumbled.

"Men don't cry," Riley croaked.

"Who the hell said that?" Cole snorted.

"Probably Sawyer. Her tongue should get blisters."

"You're talking about my sister," Cole said sourly.

"Your half sister," Riley said just as sourly. He wiped at his eyes. "She's okay. So what if she has a mouth like a truck driver and wears those . . . weird clothes and a . . ." Riley struggled for the word he was searching for. ". . . a snood. She's always there for us too. She has a brilliant mind. She told me that herself."

"She's a pain in the ass." Cole hiccuped. "I didn't come through for her, and she won't give me a second chance, which makes me feel like shit. She won't bend an inch."

"You *should* feel like shit." Riley sniffed. "Furthermore, she lied when she said she would forgive you. Sawyer never forgives. If you don't believe me, ask Adam."

"Naah, he always takes her side. He thinks we're wise-asses."

"He thinks that because Sawyer told him we're wise-asses," Riley said smartly. He peered at the double line of beer bottles. He tried to count them. They were neck and neck. He was searching his foggy brain for something witty to say to his cousin, when he saw Cole's shoulders start to shake. He stumbled his way over to the soft, deep sofa Cole was sprawled on. Clumsily, he put his arm around his cousin.

"Nobody told me it was going to be like this," Cole choked. "I want to be a kid again."

Tears rolled down Riley's cheeks. First my grandfather, then Aunt Amelia, and now Grandmam Billie. He wasn't sure who was trembling, Cole or himself. He clutched at his cousin's arm as sobs ripped from his throat.

They cried then. For the would-haves, the should-haves, the could-haves. Neither of them saw Thad, Rand, and Cary enter and quickly leave the room. Neither of them saw Susan enter and retreat from the room either.

A long time later Cole asked hoarsely, "What time is it?"

Riley squinted at his watch. "Almost ten o'clock. Why?"

"We've been sitting here for a long time. I need to

make some decisions. I feel almost sober. Help me, Riley."

"Sawyer isn't going to bend. That's a given. Were you serious about merging the families?"

"Yes. I wish I knew why I didn't do it sooner. That's going to haunt me forever," Cole said, blowing his nose loudly.

"I don't think it's important anymore. Anything before this moment is ancient history. But if we don't go forward, we're lost. Now that we think we know grandfather's secret to success, we have to follow in his footsteps. Even if for some reason the giving ... wasn't part of his success, I still think we should go ahead. We'll look into foundations. We could do a lot for the homeless. There's churches. I'd personally like to do something for animals. Buy a nature preserve somewhere, fund it so animals don't have to be destroyed. God, we could do so much."

"What about Sawyer?" Cole asked miserably.

"Think about this, Cole. If it wasn't for Sawyer, we wouldn't be uniting East and West. She probably deserves our thanks."

"Get off it, Riley. You're getting carried away. She'll hold it over our heads for the rest of our lives if we admit she was the one who brought us to our senses. You wanna live with that?"

Riley pondered the question. "Yeah, I do," he said quietly.

"Okay," Cole said, "tomorrow we'll kiss her feet and make nice."

He sounds relieved, Riley thought. "What about Cary?" he asked. "With this economy and his present condition, who in the hell is going to lend him money on Miranda? The memorial he's building to Amelia isn't even finished. It was a magnificent gesture on his part to fund the plane, but I don't think he thought it through. They'll kill him with interest payments. He could lose the place. Although we could do it," Riley said slyly.

"Do what?"

"Take the mortgage. We can talk to Valentine Mitchell and see how it's done. Probably a dummy company someplace in New York, or maybe an English one. Cary will never need to know we're behind it. This way he'll never lose Miranda. You control the money, Cole, so once again, it has to be your decision."

"*We* control the money. We shook hands on it on the way over. But what if Cary does find out?" Cole said, a frown building on his face.

"Then we say we're just two wild, crazy kids who got carried away with all that money. The bottom line is we protect Cary. That inner city is his life. You comfortable with this, Cole? The truth."

Was he? "Yes. Jesus, I feel like I've been reborn. And the best part is, we have a secret Sawyer will never know. That gives us the edge." He laughed uproariously. Riley joined in, slapping him on the back.

"Let's make some coffee and work off this drunk," Riley said, teetering his way toward the kitchen.

"You make it, I want to call Sumi," Cole said, lagging behind. "Riley?" Cole whispered.

"Yeah?"

"Thanks."

"You bet."

Sawyer stepped out from behind the wide folding doors of the great room, a gleeful smile on her face. The little shits. She danced a jig and silently clapped her hands. Wait till she told Adam. An hour earlier, when she'd cried her eyes out to her husband, he'd said, "Don't sell those guys short, either one of them. Somehow, some way, they'll come through for you."

When it came down to the wire, when it really counted, you could always depend on family.

Family.

Maggie lay in the darkness. Faint moonlight seeped through the vertical blinds. She had no idea how much time had passed since she'd run up here like a child to throw herself on the bed. She cringed now with shame at what she'd done. How could she have reacted like that? How? She rolled over onto her stomach, burying her face in the pillow. How careful she'd been to stay on her side of the bed. She knew, without having to turn on the light, that there wasn't even one wrinkle on Rand's side.

Rand was the reason she was here cowering like a criminal. Rand was the reason she'd blurted out that hateful word, "outsider." It wasn't just Mam and her illness.

She flopped over onto her back. Ten minutes to twelve. She turned the light off. Earlier she'd heard footsteps in the hall: Sawyer's clumping boots, then Cole and Riley walking past her door. None of them had knocked, none of them had called her name. She was a pariah now. She'd heard Rand talking to Thad and Cary in the courtyard. The three of them had driven off together. She hadn't heard Susan, though. She'd counted on Susan to just open the door and whisper her name, but it hadn't happened.

Her face burned with shame and guilt when she remembered the way she'd pleaded, sobbing at her mother's door, begging her to talk to her, only to have Thad say, "Your mother doesn't want to talk to you right now." Until tonight, no matter what, her mother had never, ever, refused to listen, to offer advice, to help make things right.

That was a separate issue. Tomorrow, today actually, she could attempt to make things right with Cary, to explain why she'd acted the way she had. She could explain to Mam. Mam would understand. Rand. Rand was the problem.

Maggie was off the bed the moment her head started to buzz lightly. She threw open the window, taking great gulping breaths.

Rand was her reason for being. She had no one else. Sawyer was in New York with her family. Cole was in Japan with his. They didn't need her, and that's the way it should be. Mam had Thad. Susan ... would have Cary, even though neither one of them realized it yet. Riley had his family. Rand had his daughter, Chesney.

She'd picked up on the change in Rand during the days he spent in Minnesota with Valentine Mitchell. He'd always admired Valentine, had said so more than once. The two of them had been together in a cozy little house in the Midwest, working side by side, eating together, riding together in the car, having drinks in front of the fire. Rand did love a good fire. She could picture the two of them laughing, talking, sharing secrets of a sort. And then, over drinks, looking into one another's eyes and ...

It had happened. That much she was sure of. As to the date and the exact hour ... well, the poor little wife didn't get to know everything.

How she'd looked forward to Rand returning to Sunbridge. She'd counted on his support. She had needed it to face the fact of her mother's illness. But he hadn't opened his arms to her. She'd run to him, throwing *her* arms around him. He'd had no other choice but to embrace her. He hadn't looked her in the eye, though, hadn't said he missed her, hadn't smiled. She'd known for certain then that he'd slept with Valentine.

Should she confront him? Should she tell him to move out of the house? Cary had done the same thing to Amelia. That's why she'd blurted out that hateful word. Amelia had forgiven Cary, though.

Amelia had confided in her once, late at night. She had admitted she was ill and couldn't give Cary what he needed in the bedroom. She had said she knew about Julie, Thad's niece. She'd gone to extraordinary lengths to cover up her knowledge of the affair and at the same time make it easier for Cary. How noble and unselfish she had been. "Because I love Cary more than life itself, Maggie darling," she'd said. "And I'm so very old, Maggie." Amelia had whimpered then, and Maggie had done her best to comfort her. How could she know then that Cary's betrayal with Julie had happened in her own house in Hawaii?

"Well, I'm not old, and I'm not in poor health. I can't forgive this betrayal," Maggie cried, heartbroken.

Her conscience prodded her. It probably didn't mean anything. These things happened.

Not to me they don't, she told herself. She believed in fidelity, in honoring one's marriage vows. She'd never cheated on him.

Did she have the opportunity? No. She knew she couldn't say what she would or wouldn't do if she were in a similar situation. The right moment, her conscience responded, a drink, your guard is down and . . .

You're wrong, Maggie argued silently. I love Rand. *Loved.* No matter what, she would never be unfaithful.

Rand was going to pretend nothing happened. He thought she didn't know. *I know. Damnit, I know.* He couldn't face her. That's why he wasn't here with her. Under normal circumstances, he would . . . would . . . he would be here with her, consoling her over Mam. She never would have blurted out what she did to Cary if Rand hadn't . . . forget it! Maggie sobbed, running to the bed.

Her conscience pricked a third time. Isn't all this just your jealousy of Valentine? You envy her ability. It's possible she tried to seduce Rand, and he *almost* gave in, and that's why he's feeling guilty. You could be wrong. You must have some doubts.

"None," Maggie said, punching the pillow. "I know, don't you understand?" A woman knows when her husband betrays her. She might not admit it, for whatever her reasons, but she knows. She was relieved when her conscience remained silent.

It was ten minutes past one when the car's headlights arced on the bedroom wall. Maggie slid from the bed and walked over to the open window. Down below she could see Thad and Rand talking in low voices. They must have stopped at a diner for coffee after they dropped Cary off. Would Rand come to the room now? Not likely. Where would he sleep?

Maggie settled herself into a sapphire-blue slipper chair, her eyes glued to the bottom of the door where the hallway light filtered through. Thad had to go past the door. She would hear him or see a break in the light. Through the kitchen, to the back hall, across the family room, out to the center hall and the stairway, and up the steps. She counted, wondering if he knew about the kitchen stairway alongside the refrigerator. Not that it mattered one way or the other. Down the hall now. She waited, holding her breath, for the break in the light at the bottom of the door.

Tears rolled down Maggie's cheeks. She wiped at them with the sleeve of her shirt. As the hours crawled by, she forced herself to think of other things: her mother, her children, Susan and Cary, but she always came back to Rand. Once again her world was upside down.

It was still dark at five-thirty when Maggie washed her face and brushed her hair. An early morning gallop would do her a world of good. A brisk ride in the fresh air might clear the cobwebs out of her head. She was on the landing of the stairs when she sensed a presence nearby. She turned, expecting to see Rand. Sawyer brought her finger to her lips for silence. Maggie nodded and motioned for her daughter to follow her.

"Don't say anything, Sawyer. Please, I'd like you to join me in a ride. I need to talk to someone. What that means is I'd appreciate it if you would listen."

"You didn't sleep at all, did you?" Sawyer said when they were in the stable.

"No, I didn't. Did you?"

"Not really. I'm so used to sleeping with one eye and ear open for the twins, I guess . . . I doubt if anyone in this house slept well last night. But we're talking about you. What's wrong, Maggie?"

Maggie pulled the cinch tighter, then turned to face Sawyer. "Rand cheated on me. He slept with Valentine Mitchell," she said cooly. "Last night, when I said what I did to Cary, it just hit me that he'd done the same thing to Amelia. Nobody knows better than I that it was an unforgivable thing to say. I love Cary. I would never knowingly do or say anything to hurt him. I don't know what to do. I can't . . . forgive Rand. Not now anyway.

The funny thing is, Sawyer, he doesn't even know I know. He didn't come to our room at all last night. That's his guilt. When I was married to Cranston, I became an expert on infidelity. I swore it would never happen to me again. I thought we had such a wonderful marriage. I likened it in my mind to Mam and Thad's marriage."

As they rode off, Maggie took the lead, her heels digging into the horse's flanks. It was still too dark to see well. She's going to kill herself, Sawyer thought. Sawyer's own horse, chomping at the bit to follow the other, reared to show his disapproval. "What the hell?" Sawyer muttered, loosening the reins in her hands. "Follow that horse," she said dramatically.

Forty minutes later Sawyer reined in. They were on Jarvis land. By squinting, she could make out her husband's family home. She wondered if Maggie had lost her bearings in the dark or if this was her destination from the beginning. It was almost full light, that purplish-gray part of the morning that heralds a bright, beautiful day.

"Let's go over to the house and sit on the swing," Maggie called over her shoulder. Sawyer nodded.

This was nice, Sawyer thought. Adam would be pleased that she'd ridden out to check on the house. They really had to think about bringing the girls here for a while in the summer. It would be wonderful to get out of the city in August.

Maggie was already on the swing when Sawyer rode up to the hitching post alongside the house. The mare whickered softly as Sawyer slid from her back. She joined her mother on the swing.

"I always liked this house," Maggie said.

"I always liked it too. Adam had a very happy childhood here."

"I had a miserable childhood," Maggie said.

"I know."

"Thanks to Mam, you had the best."

"I know that too," Sawyer said. "I thank God every day."

"I've always kind of talked to God. I say prayers every night before I go to sleep. I always say . . . said, thanks for giving me such a wonderful marriage. Guess I won't be saying that anymore. In fact, I probably won't be doing much praying from here on in."

"Are you saying you're giving up on God?" Sawyer asked in disbelief.

"I just said I won't be doing much praying. I didn't say I was giving up on God. Only a fool would do that. I'm kind of numb, Sawyer, so don't hit on me right now."

"What are you going to do?"

"Go back to Hawaii this evening. I canceled Rand's flight. I don't want him in the house. I . . . I'll have to tell him, I guess," Maggie mumbled.

"I would think so," Sawyer said.

"Susan is going to stay here. She didn't say so, but I think . . . she will. I'll keep myself busy. There's a lot of work that has to be done to get Mam's old business back in the running. Maybe I'm making a mistake by going back. Maybe I should stay here. I'll be closer to you and Mam. I can get an apartment in town or I can ask Riley and Ivy if I can rent Mam's old studio. What I have to do is make a decision. What do you think?"

"You told me you just wanted me to listen," Sawyer chided gently. She fished around in her jeans pocket and withdrew a key ring. She worked one off and handed it to her mother. "You have to do what is right for you. This is the key to the house. Stay here if you like. Adam will be grateful that someone is here to look after the place."

"What's your opinion of Valentine Mitchell?" Maggie asked carefully.

"I've always thought her a very capable person, and I've always liked her. And yes, she's attractive. That's really what you want to know, isn't it? But then so are you. I've always liked her."

"How could she do this to me?"

"It takes two people, Maggie," Sawyer said gently.

"I'm very well aware of that. It just makes it a little easier if I place some of the blame on Val."

"You said Rand doesn't know you know. How did you find out?"

"No one told me, if that's your question. It's just something I know, something I feel. I'm not wrong, Sawyer."

"You mean you just *think* Rand slept with Val?" Maggie nodded. "What if you're wrong? What if you accuse Rand and you find out it never happened? I just assumed someone told you or you . . . oh, Lord, I don't know what I thought," Sawyer said sourly.

"Come on, time to get back. Don't worry about me, Sawyer, and thanks for the key. If I decide to stay on, I'll let you know. What time is your plane?"

"Eleven o'clock. What time is yours?"

"Five, if I decide to take it. I enjoyed the ride. And the company," Maggie said wanly.

"Me too," Sawyer said softly.

Back at the barn, Sawyer turned the horse over to her mother. "Will you rub him down for me? I have to take another shower and see if I can do something with my hair."

Maggie nodded.

Once the horses were rubbed down and secure in their stalls, Maggie trudged out to the courtyard. She couldn't ever remember being this tired, this discouraged, this betrayed. She wanted to cry, needed to cry, but a release of tears eluded her. How could Rand do this to her? Had he done this before? How was she going to get through this?

She looked at her watch—seven o'clock. She felt like a tired war horse when she struggled up from the milk crate on which she'd been sitting. Time to make the trek up the hill, the only place left for her to go. She brushed at her tears with the back of her hand.

She picked her way carefully, remembering other times she'd gone up to the peaceful cemetery to talk things out. First to her father, then to Riley's father and Amelia. And always she felt better when she walked down the hill.

The path was overgrown, the medallions of stone covered with moss, which was slippery with early morning dew. Obviously Riley and Ivy didn't come to the hill. Why should they? she thought. Thanks to me and Cole, they have everything. She stopped in her tracks and covered her face with her hands. God, what was wrong with her? Why was she thinking like this? She looked at the footpath again, at the overgrown brush and moss. When you were dead, you were forgotten. She sobbed then, in great racking heaves that seemed to echo over the hill.

Maggie hugged herself tighter underneath the shawl as she looked around. The graves were untended. She silently cried out her rage as she dropped to her knees before her father's headstone. This shouldn't be. Riley couldn't be *that* busy. Surely he could afford to have someone clip away the vines and roots choking off the stones. She lashed out at her father's headstone with her clenched fist. Pain shot up her arm, but she didn't care. She stared at her own skin and at the blood trickling over the O in her father, Moss's, name. She reached out with her good hand to wipe it away.

She talked breathlessly then, the words pouring out of her. When she felt purged, she moved on her knees to her brother Riley's grave. She spoke softly there, telling him all about Riley Junior and little Moss. Then she moved to Amelia's stone where she broke down completely.

"He was so changed, Amelia, when he got back. So cool and . . . and almost indifferent. I have this feeling, and it's so hateful, I want to rip out my heart. How did you handle it? I know we talked many times, but you were so . . . accepting, because you genuinely liked Julie. I know you were ill and that made a difference too, but the hurt had to be the same. I'm not wrong, Amelia. I feel it, just the way you did. A woman knows when her husband has been unfaithful. *She knows.* The moment Rand came into the house and looked at me, I knew. My God, I knew. Oh, God, Amelia, you know I didn't mean what I said to Cary. I was lashing out at Rand and . . . and Mam. I hate being helpless. I can't do anything for Mam and Rand, it's a done deal, as the young people say today. It was a double whammy. I almost took a drink, but I didn't. I don't know how to handle any of this. I don't know if I *can* handle it. You know what? There are two words in the English language I hate with a passion. Mortality and infidelity. You know what else I hate, Amelia? That damn saying

that you should be careful of what you wish for because
you just might get it."

Maggie threw her arms around Amelia's headstone
and sobbed.

"I thought I would find you here," Billie gasped,
struggling to get her breath.

"Mam! What . . . why?"

"You needed me. Just put your arm around me and
ease me down gently. I can sit on this little ledge," Billie said brokenly.

"Oh, Mam," Maggie cried, wrapping her frail mother
in her arms.

"Maggie, Maggie," Billie whimpered.

"I don't want you to die, Mam. God, I don't want
you to die."

"I'm not exactly overjoyed at the idea myself," Billie
said tearfully. "This wasn't supposed to happen. I had it
all planned in my mind. It's so hard. I don't have the
words to try and make it right for you. Thad and I will
be leaving right after breakfast. I need you to understand."

"Mam, come to Hawaii or let me go with you to Vermont. Let me take care of you. I'll stay with you night
and day. Please, don't leave us."

"I'm not leaving you, darling. We'll see one another
again. Thad . . . Thad needs to be with me. He needs to
take care of me, and I need him. It's what I want.
Please, Maggie, don't make this any more difficult than
it already is."

"Okay, Mam." Maggie gulped. "About Cary . . ."

"I know you'll make it right, darling. Cary is a very
understanding person. Be kind, darling. Always be kind.
Now, I think we have to figure a way for me to get

down this hill in one piece. Thad is going to be so angry with me for coming up here."

"Then let's not tell him," Maggie said lightly.

"Let's not." Billie smiled.

Billie turned to face Amelia's headstone. "I'm on my way. Don't get impatient," she whispered.

Maggie bit down on her lip so hard, blood trickled into her mouth.

When the two women reached the bottom of the hill, Maggie led her mother over to the milk box. "Sit here and catch your breath. If anyone is awake, they'll think we just came out to see the sun come up." After her mother was seated, Maggie said, "Mam, there's something I want to tell you. I think Rand slept with Valentine Mitchell while he was in Minnesota. I don't know what to do about it."

"Darling, when I don't know what to do about something, I do nothing. You said you *think*. That isn't good enough. Please, don't accuse your husband unless you are certain. Right now, our family is in a bit of a turmoil. There is every possibility you're overreacting to the situation. Think before you speak, is all I ask. Can you at least promise me that?"

"Yes, Mam, I can."

"That's good enough for me," Billie said lightly.

"Billieee!" Thad called.

Billie threw her hands in the air. "See what I mean? He gets hysterical if I'm not in his line of vision. I'm over here, Thad," she called gaily.

My God, how does she do it? Maggie wondered.

"Breakfast is ready. What are you ladies doing out here so early?"

"I was watching the sun come up, and Mam joined me. We were having one of those mother-daughter talks, with the daughter doing most of the talking," Maggie said just as gaily.

"Thad, if you'll just help me. My legs are a little wobbly this morning." For an answer, Thad scooped his wife up into his arms.

"You went up the hill, didn't you? I know you, Billie," Thad whispered against her neck.

Maggie smiled when she heard her mother's response. "Thad, did you *see* me go up the hill?"

"No, but—"

"There are no buts, Thad. Either you saw me go up the hill or you didn't."

"All right, already," Thad grumbled.

Maggie trailed behind, her eyes misty with tears. She reeled suddenly, almost losing her balance. Damn, what was that on her shoulder? She brushed at the loosely woven shawl and then a smile spread across her features. "Thanks for checking in, Amelia. I'll give your regards to Cary," she whispered. Overhead the trees rustled and a huge branch dipped and then heaved upward in the early morning breeze.

The feeling she had now, Maggie thought, was the same feeling she'd had in the hospital when she'd heard the angels sing over Sawyer.

As the family gathered at the front door to see Billie and Thad off, the phone rang loudly. No one made a move to veer off to the living room to answer it. Moss, in his mother's arms, chortled happily, his one bottom front tooth showing clearly.

"He loves the sound of the phone," Riley said huskily. "Hold on, everyone, I'll get it." He marched off stiffly, relieved at the break. This parting was going to be just as horrendous as the one with his grandfather. He barked into the phone, listened, and said, "Hold on,

I'll get him. Don't hang up, for God's sake. Yes, yes, I know. Wait now," Riley babbled.

Riley sprinted back to the wide central hall and tapped his cousin on the back. "The call's for you. I'd snap to it if I were you."

"Did . . . is Sumi ready . . . oh, shit . . ."

"Move!" Thad roared.

The moment Cole was out of sight, Riley whispered, "It's a girl. Eight pounds, eighteen inches long, and she has all her toes and fingers."

"Eight pounds!" Maggie and Sawyer chorused in unison.

"How wonderful," Ivy said, hugging her son. "Now you have three girl cousins to play with," she cooed to Moss.

"Cole will make such a wonderful father," Billie whispered. "I think all firstborns should be little girls. Of course, I'm slightly biased."

"I can't wait to buy a baby outfit," Susan said happily.

"I have a daughter," Cole said, coming back into the room. His face was full of awe. "Eight pounds, can you imagine that? Everyone is fine. I'm a father, for God's sake!"

Riley clapped Cole on the back. "Get your gear together, cousin. I'll drive you out to the plane. You sure you're up to flying back alone? You look like you're about to go into orbit."

"I'm fine. I'm really fine. Sumi picked a name. We agreed that if it was a girl, it would be Sumi's choice."

"Don't just stand there like a ninny, can't you see we're all holding our collective breath?" Sawyer grumbled.

Cole walked over to his grandmother. "Sumi said,

and I agreed, to name the baby Billie Otami Amelia Tanner."

"Oh, honey, I'm . . . I'm overwhelmed. Riley, darling, your mother would be so happy. Thad," she said, turning to her husband, "I think this might be a good time for us to leave."

Cole hugged his grandmother. "Do you ever get the feeling someone is watching over us?" he whispered. "It couldn't have been timed better."

"I know what you mean," Billie whispered in return. "Promise me something, darling."

"Anything, Grandmam."

"Love your daughter unconditionally. Don't ever deviate from that love for even a second."

"You got it. I think you better get out of here while the going is good. Otherwise—"

" 'Bye, everyone. We'll write and call," Billie said, sashaying through the open doorway.

Cole closed the door. The tear-filled faces staring at him tore at his heart. "Listen up, everyone. I don't care if it is ten o'clock in the morning. I want to toast my new daughter. Break out the champagne. Two bottles, one goes to Cary."

"I'll take it over to the hospital," Susan offered.

The toasts and congratulations over, Maggie walked over to her son. "Will you send pictures of little Billie as soon as you get home? Please don't be angry with me, Cole. I . . . ah, I have some things on my mind. I'll be going over to the hospital later to apologize to Cary. I'm going to be leaving late this afternoon. I think Susan will be staying on a bit to look after Cary. I've decided to get started on Billie Limited." She was talking too fast, her eyes pleading with her son for his forgiveness. If she had to grovel, she would. She waited, hardly daring to breathe.

"My Nikon will be clicking every second. I'll FedEx them to you. Hell, I might even develop them myself. Cary is a wonderful guy, Mother, and he's probably the most understanding man I've ever met, next to Adam. Good luck," he said, hugging her tightly. "Listen, now, anytime you want to hop over to see your granddaughter, just do it. We don't stand on ceremony. That goes for everyone!" He laughed happily.

"Wait for me," Sawyer said, her eyes sparkling devilishly. "Adam just called to beg me to come home. It seems the girls woke up at five A.M. and crawled out of their cribs. They squirted whipped cream all over the kitchen, then ate half a jar of sweet pickles and puked all over the kitchen floor. Adam says he thinks they ate a stick of butter too. So I'm going upstairs to pack and head for the airport."

"Oh, we're going to be alone again. I'll miss all of you," Ivy said sincerely. "Susan, you aren't going, are you?"

"No, but I thought I would stay in town. If you need me, I can go back and forth, but I don't have a car."

"Both Riley and I would like you to stay, Susan, but the decision is up to you."

"Town will be better. I'll be open for dinner invitations though."

"You have an open invitation," Riley said. "You can take my car, Susan. The keys are under the mat. I won't be using it for the next couple of days." Susan nodded happily as she made her way up the stairs.

"See? I told you, everything is turning around," Ivy whispered to her husband.

"Wise-ass," Riley said fondly.

"But I'm *your* wise-ass, right?"

"Forever and ever." Riley grinned. "Listen, honey, Cole and I have some business to take care of. Can you make some coffee and bring it into the study?"

"Just as soon as I settle Moss. Where did Maggie and Rand go?"

Riley shrugged.

"Something is wrong," Ivy muttered.

"I know, and whatever it is has nothing to do with Cary. Rand's been acting strange since he got here. He's here, but he isn't here, if you know what I mean."

"Honey," Ivy said, reaching up to kiss her husband, "I think it's a wonderful thing Sumi did by naming their firstborn after Billie and your mother. Billie was so pleased. Did you see how her face lighted? And your own face, darling one, was just as bright. Wait till Cary hears the news. Go, shoo, Cole's waiting for you. Make sure you tell him how wonderful fatherhood is, and don't just tell him the good stuff."

"You want me to tell him about the poopie diapers, and the wakeup calls during the night, and the colic?"

"Yep. If you don't, Sawyer is going to scare the hell out of him. He got a little white when she was expounding away."

"All right. Cole can handle it. Hey, he can call me anytime."

"Don't forget to tell him you always put the diaper on backward." Ivy giggled.

"Enough!" Riley shouted, to Moss's delight.

It was twelve-thirty when Cole leaned back in his chair, his eyes on his cousin. "It's a deal, then. I'll start the legal work the minute I get tired of looking at my new daughter. From this moment on we are ColeShad.

The Cole is from Coleman and Shad is from your grandfather's name. Don't go saying I have a streak of nepotism in me. My last name is Tanner. And we did it in alphabetical order, just the way you wanted." His hand shot out. Riley grasped it in his rock-hard fist.

"You feeling okay about this, Cole?"

"Aside from the headache I'm going to get when restructuring starts, yes, I'm okay with it. I'm sorry it took me so long. You cut me a lot of slack, Riley. I don't know if I would have been as kind if the situation were reversed. I need to know one thing, though. Where's the string?"

Riley thrust his booted feet on top of the desk and hooted with laughter. "There were never any strings. Just the way there were no strings when you deeded Sunbridge to me. We're family, Cole, that's the bottom line."

When the cousins wrapped up business an hour later, it was agreed that Riley would make the appointment with Valentine Mitchell and set the wheels in motion to secure Cary's mortgage on Miranda.

"One last thing, Riley. The moment you . . . as soon as you hear from Thad, get on the horn. I need time to get here."

"I'll do my best, Cole. Grandmam doesn't want any of us hovering and calling all the time. I asked Thad this morning if he would call me every couple of days. He promised. As much as it hurts, we have to do what Grandmam wants."

"Full circle, Riley."

"I think we can handle it now, although it was a little iffy there for a while. Did you ever get the feeling these past years that we—this is going to sound stupid, but—that we were being tested?"

"Every damn day." Cole grinned.

"Me too." Riley guffawed.

"You realize they set us up, your grandfather and Grandmam Billie? Your grandfather with the old switcheroo from you to me, and Grandmam Billie bankrupting the family with the lawsuits. Think about it, Riley, and remember all those trips Grandmam and Thad took to Japan. If it wasn't the lawsuits, it would have been something else."

"It would have been a lot simpler if they had just told us what they wanted," Riley groused.

"Nah, it wouldn't have worked. They wanted us to find out for ourselves. We're it, Riley! From here on in we're on our own. I guarantee there won't be any more ashes in the Zen garden, and no one will snatch my beer and sake. Grandmam Billie will rest easy."

"Jesus," Riley said, his face full of awe.

"Time for me to go, Riley. I'd like to stop and see Cary first, if you don't mind. I want to tell him about my new daughter. He's gonna bust when I tell him her name, and it might take a little of the edge off when my mother goes to see him. I'll meet you by the car. I have to say good-bye to Mother and Rand."

As it turned out, Cole didn't get to say good-bye. Maggie and Rand were nowhere to be found. He scribbled a note saying he would call when he got home. To Jonquil's delight, he kept singing Billie Otami Amelia Tanner over and over as he sailed through the kitchen to meet Riley in the courtyard.

"How did you know where to find me?" Maggie asked from her position on the Jarvis swing, the same swing on which she had sat earlier with Sawyer.

"Process of elimination. That and your favorite horse was also missing."

"Why?" Maggie asked in a disinterested voice. "Since you came back from Minnesota, you have barely said two words to me. You didn't even sleep in our bed last night."

"I was wired up, Maggie. The thing with Cary, it made me realize how fragile our very existence is. Your mother . . . all I could see was my stepmother, Amelia. Your unkind outburst just seemed to bring things to a boil. I felt everything closing in on me. Thad and I stayed with Cary till one in the morning. I didn't want to wake you."

How lame his voice sounds, Maggie thought. She shrugged.

"Don't you think we should be getting back?"

"Why?"

Rand threw his hands in the air. "We have an early evening flight."

"That's not quite true. *I* have an early evening flight. I canceled yours. I don't want you coming back to the house. Ever. I'll pack your things and send them wherever you want. It will be up to you to tell your daughter about your move."

"For God's sake, Maggie, what's gotten into you? I know you're upset about your mother and that . . . whatever that was with Cary, but aren't you carrying this a bit too far? I don't understand. One day things are fine, and the next day you want me to move out of the house! I wish you'd explain things to me. Have you been drinking?"

Maggie shrugged. "No, I haven't been drinking."

"Don't you think I deserve an explanation? Damnit,

Maggie, talk to me." The desperation in her husband's voice brought a smile to Maggie's face.

"I might come back to Texas and work at Billie Limited. Or I can live right here in Adam's house." Maggie held out her hand to reveal a brass key. "Sawyer gave it to me."

"This isn't like you. If it's what you want, fine, but I think I deserve an explanation."

"Why don't we just say I'm crazy and let it go at that? I think this is where you ride off into the sunset. Good-bye, Rand."

Rand reached for his wife and dragged her off the chair. She was like a rag doll in his hands. "Just like that, it's over. With no explanations. Not even a drop dead or go to hell. What the hell did I do?"

"Have you ever been unfaithful to me, Rand?"

The lie rolled off Rand's lips so smoothly, he was stunned. "No!"

"I don't believe you," Maggie said quietly. "I've seen infidelity all my life. My father, my husband, Cary, and now you. I recognize the signs. It's that simple."

"Because you witnessed infidelity in others, you're judging and condemning me!" Rand bellowed, his voice full of guilty rage.

"And found you guilty," Maggie said, anger rising in her. "How dare you! How dare you muck up our marriage like this!" She turned so she wouldn't have to see the awful guilt on her husband's face.

"Maggie—"

"Go away, Rand. Don't make this any harder than it is."

"Maggie, I love you."

"You know what, Rand? I love me too. I don't deserve this. I knew. I knew the minute I heard your voice on the phone. . . . I could hear it in your voice. I felt it. You betrayed me and then you lied to my face. Go, Rand, I can't bear to look at you."

The moment the ground around her was silent, Maggie turned to stare across the prairie. Now she could cry with no one to see or care. *I didn't accuse him, Mam. I asked him and he lied to me. If he'd admitted it . . . no, I can't forgive that. He took something wonderful, something I treasured, and mucked it up. You never forgave Pap for being unfaithful to you. Why should I be any different? I did what you said, though, I asked. I know in my heart what you said to me is . . . is going to be . . . you won't be giving me advice anymore. I followed it, Mam.*

Maggie looked at her watch. She took a deep breath before she got up from the porch swing. She had to make things right with Cary, and she didn't have much time left.

"They all think I'm the strong one, that nothing ruffles me," Maggie muttered as she spurred the horse onward. "Ha. I feel as if my guts have been wrenched out of my stomach."

It was half past twelve when Maggie clicked her way down the sterile hospital corridor in search of Cary's room. Her stomach churned. She swallowed hard as two nurses in starched white crackled by her, medicine trays in their hands. Inside the room she could see Susan sitting on a hard plastic chair, an open book in her hands. Three daily newspapers were piled on the metal table that separated her chair from Cary's. Obviously, Maggie thought, Susan was going to read them all to her charge. How protective she looks. How happy. Maggie's shoulders started to shake the moment Susan noticed her.

"So many flowers," she whispered to Susan. "Would you mind leaving us alone for a minute, Suse?"

"Sure. I'll go get us some coffee." She was gone a second later, the delicate scent of her perfume wafting behind her.

"Cary, it's me, Maggie," Maggie said. She reached for Cary's hand. It felt dry and hot. For some reason, she'd expected it to be sweaty. "I came to apologize. Sorry is just a word, one we all use too often. I want to . . . I need to explain. I'm not sure if . . . what I'm trying to say is I might hurt you even more. . . . Oh, Cary, I . . . Rand . . . Rand slept with Valentine Mitchell. I saw you sitting there and I remembered Amelia and a talk we had and how devastated she was. I reacted badly and I'm sorry. It all sort of slapped me in the face. I had no right to say what I did. I wanted to hurt someone the way I was hurting. Mam . . . Rand . . . your offer to help Sawyer, the look on my son's face. Please, Cary, forgive me."

"There's nothing to forgive, Maggie. I believe I am part of this family. I knew where you were coming from. I felt it. I sensed Rand's . . . guilt. It was so easy to recognize. Don't forget, I've lived with mine for so long, it's part of my skin now."

Maggie nodded and then remembered that Cary couldn't see through his bandages. "I know. I can't be that noble, that selfless. I'm not saying Amelia was wrong, I'm just saying I don't think and feel like Amelia. Betrayal has to be the hardest thing in the world to bear," Maggie whispered.

"I'd say it's right up there with guilt," Cary said quietly. "I live with it every day. Part of me will always love Julie, but I had to send her away. What we had . . . it just . . . I couldn't live with it. What are you going to do, Maggie? What are your options? Wheel me down to the sun room so we can have a cigarette. We can't smoke in the rooms. Don't worry about Susan, she'll find us."

"I am returning to Hawaii tonight. I told Rand to move out. Right now I guess I'll just hang out for a few days and feel sorry for myself. You know, beat my breast and cry a lot. I'm taking over Billie Limited, so that means I have to map out a plan, start up operations, go to Hong Kong and Taiwan."

"It sounds like a good starting place for you. What did . . . Rand say?"

"He denied it. He was never a good liar. I felt it, Cary, just the way Amelia did." Cary squeezed her hand reassuringly. Bolstered, Maggie said, "Cary, I need to ask you a question. Please, for my sake, tell me the truth. If Amelia had asked you, would you have admitted your affair with Julie?"

"Yes. At one point I had, at the very least, one hundred and ten versions of why I did what I did, and not one of them worth the breath it would have taken to utter them. Every single day I waited, expecting Amelia to ask me, but she never did. It's so hard for me to believe, to accept that Amelia knew all along and never said a word. There was nothing about her, no indication. She liked Julie, she approved of her as her successor. Till I die I will never understand *that*. Anyway, I'm glad you came to me."

"Thanks for listening, Cary. Please, I need to hear you tell me you forgive me, that you understand. I think it's a wonderful thing you're doing for Sawyer and the family. Amelia must be smiling from ear to ear. Oh, I forgot to tell you, I walked up the hill this morning, and when I got back I . . . I had this feeling she was touching my shoulder, telling me she was going to look after Mam. Don't laugh at me, Cary. It's important for me to believe this. Anyway, I told her I'd say hello." Maggie leaned over and kissed Cary lightly on the cheek.

Cary smiled. "She's always there when it counts."

Maggie kissed him again. "I know I'm leaving you in good hands. Susan, Ivy, and Riley will watch over you. Susan told you about Cole's new daughter, didn't she? Billie Otami Amelia Tanner. It has a ring to it. Mam was so pleased. I'll be in touch, Cary," Maggie said softly. "Hey, your personal nurse is here, and may I say I love powder-blue," Maggie said, referring to Susan's light wool dress. "Susan, take care, I'll call. You'll be at the condo in Miranda?"

"For a while, Maggie, I—"

"Shhh," Maggie said, hugging her sister. "Take care of Cary." How bright her eyes are, Maggie thought. How wonderful Cary's smile is.

She felt cheated when she made her way out of the hospital to the parking lot.

Four hours later she was airborne. In ten hours she would be home. Minus a husband.

{{{{{{{{{ CHAPTER NINE }}}}}}}}}

Rand stood alongside Riley and Ivy, who held little Moss, under Sunbridge's portico, his face grim, his shoulders rigid.

"I don't know what to do," he said dejectedly.

"Do you want to come inside and talk about it?" Riley asked. "Neither Ivy nor I know what's going on. Aunt Maggie made peace with Cary. When she got back, she said he was more understanding than she deserved. If Cary forgives her, I don't understand what your problem is, Rand," Riley said with an edge to his voice. He loved Maggie like a mother. She'd stepped in and welcomed him to Sunbridge when he first arrived in the States. More than once she'd taken his side over her own son's when squabbles erupted. In his eyes Maggie could do no wrong.

"You two go along. I think this little fella needs a bath and supper," Ivy said cheerfully. "Jonquil made a buffet, so anytime you guys want to eat, just let me know."

"Sure, honey."

"Do you feel like a walk?" Rand asked.

"How about a trip up the hill?"

"No, not the hill," Rand said. "Let's walk around the garden."

They strolled, each busy with his own thoughts. Riley thought he would burst with the silence.

Rand finally spoke. "I think I'll go back to England."

"Now, you mean? Why?"

"Your aunt Maggie told me not to bother going back to Hawaii. She told me to move out and to take my daughter with me. Earlier she mentioned something about coming back here and either renting Billie's studio from you and Ivy or setting up shop in Adam's house."

"I'm in the dark here, Rand. I don't understand any of this. What I do understand is I've never seen my aunt so miserable, so determined. Are you just going to talk or are you going to explain? If you feel it's none of my business, I can deal with that," Riley said briskly.

"Maggie thinks I slept with Valentine Mitchell," Rand said curtly.

Riley's eyebrows shot upward. He thought about his upcoming meeting with the attorney, and then he remembered the three and a half days Rand and Val spent in Minnesota. A vision of the fast-track lawyer flashed before him. He bit down on his lower lip.

"Aren't you going to ask me if I did or didn't?" Rand asked defensively.

"If I did, would you tell me the truth? Aunt Maggie must believe you did if . . . She usually thinks things through pretty carefully before she makes a decision. She used to hammer that into Cole's and my heads. If that was what she was carrying around inside her last night, it would at least explain her outburst about Cary. Maybe she wanted to go back alone to have a cooling off period, to think about things."

"She's already thought about them. Her leaving alone was her decision."

"You didn't put up much of a fight," Riley said coolly.

"So that makes me guilty, I suppose?"

"Don't put words in my mouth, Rand. However, I do remember another time when you and Sawyer were an item, and you didn't have the guts to tell her it was over. That's when she was so sick and almost died. Then you up and married Aunt Maggie a little while later. Hey, I can add, and I can come up with four like everyone else. To this day, you have no idea how you hurt her. Cole and I know, though. Maybe Aunt Maggie is remembering that too," Riley said tightly, his eyes defensive.

"It wasn't like that. The thing with Sawyer was over before Maggie and I got to know one another," Rand snarled. "That was a low blow, Riley, and you damn well know it."

"It's no such thing, Rand. It's a damn fact. You can't change facts. Like Aunt Maggie, I believe in fidelity." He wanted to ask Rand whether Valentine was worth all that he was going through now, but he didn't. How was he supposed to act around Val when he went to her office tomorrow? he wondered. "So what's your game plan?"

Rand shrugged. "As I said, England, I guess."

"You're welcome here. Stay as long as you like. If you want privacy, you can use Grandmam Billie's studio until you decide what you want to do. I'm not judging you, Rand. If it sounded that way, I'm sorry."

"There's always a but," Rand said. "But you aren't comfortable around me. And you still haven't asked me that all-important question."

He's too defensive, too cocky, Riley thought. "No,

and I won't. I don't want to know. This is between you and Aunt Maggie. Did you talk to Thad about this?"

"No. Thad has enough on his mind. And I didn't say anything to Cary either, if that's your next question. But I think Maggie may have said something to Sawyer."

Riley propped one of his feet on the same milk box his aunt had sat on earlier in the day. "I rarely give advice, Rand, but if I were you, I'd go to Maggie and do whatever you have to do to make things right."

"I'll keep it in mind," Rand said in a neutral voice. "I think I'll skip dinner. Do you mind if I use your truck later?"

"Not at all. I'm in for the night. Is there anything I can do, Rand?"

"No, but thanks for the offer. I'll see you later," Rand said, and strode off in the direction of the house.

The room Rand was supposed to have shared with his wife was decorated in soft, earthy garden colors. The only thing out of place was his suitcase, which was still packed and still in the same position it had been in yesterday, when he carried it here himself. Maggie had spent several days in this room, but there was no sign of her at all. The brown and moss-green spread on the bed was free of wrinkles. There were no telltale flecks of face powder, no stray hairpins, no tissues. In the bathroom the towels were folded neatly, the soap looked untouched, and there were no watermarks on the vanity or sink. The lid on the toilet seat was down. Rand puzzled over the fact that there were no tissues in the waste basket. Maggie required at least half a box when she applied makeup. Then he remembered that she wasn't wearing makeup when she left. Her nose had been shiny and her freckles had shown clearly through her tan.

How many times over the years had she repeated the

words, "Be a good houseguest so you're invited back?" What that meant was to remove the bed linens, empty the trash, hang up the towels, and if there are fresh flowers in the room, change the water. Maggie had taken care of everything. He felt like bawling.

Angrily, he pitched his suitcase at the bed. Now the spread was wrinkled. Good. He undid the straps and peered down at the messy array of clothing. Most of the contents were soiled. He upended the suitcase and tossed it on the floor. At the bottom was a pair of wrinkled but clean khaki trousers and a shirt, also wrinkled. He felt victorious when he noted a clean pair of jockey shorts and one pair of rolled-up socks. Then he felt like bawling again.

In the bathroom mirror, he noticed his two-day-old stubble and winced. He looked like a bum. Jesus. He took off his clothes and pitched them in the general direction of the upended suitcase and pile of clothing on the bed.

Thirty minutes later he was shaved, clean, and wrinkled. "Now what do I do?" he muttered. His gaze settled on the chocolate-colored phone on the nightstand. He noticed the flowers then for the first time. Bright red tulips, which looked limp and tired. So Maggie didn't practice what she preached, he thought irritably. It pleased him no end to carry the vase of flowers into the bathroom to pour out the water and add fresh. He was careful to wipe off the bottom of the vase so it wouldn't leave a watermark on the night table. He felt a little better immediately, as though he'd done something worthwhile, something that really mattered in the scheme of things.

He picked up the phone, punched out his number in Hawaii, and listened to Maggie's voice on the answering machine say, "Rand and I aren't here right now, so leave your name and number at the sound of the beep and we'll return your call as soon as we can." He cleared his throat before the beep and spoke loudly and clearly. "Maggie, we *need* to discuss this. You can't just end things without talking to me. I'm calling from Sunbridge, but I'll be leaving shortly. My plan at the moment is to go to a hotel in town. I don't want to burden the family with our problem. They have enough on their minds as it is. I just wanted you to . . . know I care and that I'm thinking of you."

Rand broke the connection and replaced the receiver. It was dark now, and the only light shining into the bedroom was from the bathroom. Rand snapped on the overhead light and for the first time noticed the sapphire-blue chair by the window. It looked out of place, more like a woman's chair, or at least a Billie color. He wondered if his wife had sat on it. Was it okay to smoke here in the bedroom? Ivy had never said if it was or wasn't. Riley smoked occasionally, Ivy not at all. He opened the window before he lit his cigarette, spotting a small ceramic ashtray on the wide windowsill.

Where should he go? What should he do? What exactly were his options? What were his legal options? He groaned. Regardless of the mitigating circumstances, Maggie would bend over backward to be fair if it came down to legal defenses. *What goes around comes around.* That's what Sawyer had said to him. He wished now that there had been bitterness in Sawyer's voice instead of sadness. He'd stepped over the line, and Sawyer knew it. She would never forgive him. They'd all forgiven Cary when he fell off the fidelity wagon because Amelia had forgiven him, had given her seal of approval to Julie. They weren't going to forgive him, though. He wondered how long it would take before they *all* knew he'd crossed over the line. The lie he'd told his wife had made things worse. Amelia had raised him to be truthful, to stand up and take his medicine when he screwed up. His shoulders slumped as he realized what he'd done. He'd been unfaithful and he lied to cover up his wrongdoing.

Goddamnit, just because Maggie said he shouldn't go back to the house in Hawaii didn't mean he had to listen to her. He had as much right to be there as she did. Do what she wants, wait it out, an inner voice cautioned. The right time will come for you to sit down and talk. Maggie won't stay in Hawaii alone. She'll come back. She doesn't do well alone. And then another voice accused: Maggie loved you heart and soul, you bastard. Now you've lost her. You're a low-down, stinking, miserable bastard and you deserve whatever Maggie dishes out, *Lord* Rand Nelson.

Rand squeezed his eyes shut. The burning sensation he was feeling made them water. Too much cigarette smoke.

What goes around comes around.

He felt like a thief when he tiptoed down the steps, through the house and out to the courtyard. Since dinner was a buffet, he more or less assumed Riley and Ivy would be eating in the great room. His thought proved right, and he didn't encounter them. He drove around the house and out the three-mile drive to the main road. He never felt more an outsider in his life.

On the highway, driving at a sedate seventy miles an hour, Rand turned on the radio. He almost ran off the road into a ditch when he heard Rod Stewart singing "Maggie May." Shaken, he eased up on the gas pedal and concentrated on the road in front of him. He ended up in the underground parking lot of Assante Towers.

"Your card, sir," the security guard said quietly. Rand whipped out the plastic card Cary had given to all the family members attached to Riley's visor in the pickup. He waited while the card slid through a coding machine. The guard handed back the card and said, "The elevators to the penthouses are to the right of the B section, sixteen through thirty-two are to the left of the A section. The stairs are next to the C section." Rand grunted as he strode off in the direction of the A section.

He stepped out of the elevator on the thirty-sixth floor and walked slowly up the hall until he came to 36A. He pressed the doorbell. He listened to the soft chiming on the other side of the door. He thought it was a tune, but couldn't be sure. He backed up a step when the door opened.

"You were in the neighborhood and thought you would stop by and say hello," Valentine Mitchell drawled. "So say hello and leave. We said we weren't going to see one another again."

Rand stiff-armed the door, which was about to close in his face.

"How did you get in here anyway? We agreed, Rand."

"All I want is to talk to you," Rand said, stepping into the shiny foyer. He didn't think he'd ever seen such an accumulation of mirrors, glass, and chrome in one place. It seemed as if his and Val's reflections were everywhere. House of mirrors, he thought.

Val stepped aside. "Come into my parlor, said the spider to the fly." She made a low, sweeping bow, her face inscrutable. Rand looked at her bare feet. She was wearing jeans and the same Greenpeace sweatshirt she'd worn in Minnesota.

The plush of the white wall-to-wall carpet seemed to cuddle Rand's shoes as he made his way past Valentine into the low sunken living room he'd seen from the foyer. He settled himself in a white leather chair. "This is different," he said as he looked around the huge room. "I like the pictures." On the wall were oversize hangings that were nothing more than gigantic slashes of brilliant color.

"They're my contribution to the decor," Val said tightly. "Since I live in a black-and-white world twenty hours out of every day, I thought I could use a little color. You didn't come here to discuss the furnishings in my apartment, did you?"

"No, I didn't. Maggie knows."

Val fired a cigarette and blew a perfect smoke ring in Rand's direction. "That surprises me. I didn't think you were the type to kiss and tell." She blew another smoke ring, her face impassive.

"I didn't tell her. She said she figured it out herself. She left earlier this evening and doesn't want me to go back to Hawaii. Maggie is not a forgiving person."

Two perfect smoke rings sailed upward. "The first rule in life is you never admit to anything," Val said. "The second rule is, if you fuck up, you deal with it. Usually I charge three hundred fifty dollars an hour for that kind of advice. For you, Lord Nelson, it's free."

"I didn't admit to anything. Maggie asked me point-blank, and I lied. I want you to back me up. It never happened."

"I never look back, Rand, and I never get involved in messes like this."

"Come off it, Val. I'm asking you to help me save

my marriage. All it takes is one phone call. I don't think it's too much to ask."

"I do." She laughed, but it didn't reach her eyes. "That would be an admission on my part that the alleged incident did in fact take place. No thanks, Rand, I'll pass on this one."

Rand's eyebrows crawled backward. "You're refusing to help me?" he asked incredulously.

Val tapped a fresh cigarette on the glass-topped table, looked at the cigarette in her hand with clinical interest before she hung it in the corner of her mouth and then talked around it. "If the alleged incident were reversed, how quickly would you come to my defense? Let's see." She squinted past the smoke spiraling upward. "I'd say your first inclination would be to cover your ass in a variety of ways. You'd have sixteen of the finest, most upstanding citizens you know swear you were in a card game during the time the alleged incident took place. You'd hang me out to dry without blinking. You see, I gave it a lot of thought on the way home from Minnesota. You play, you pay. Now if you don't mind, I have some briefs I need to look over. I have an early day tomorrow."

"Val, please," Rand said huskily.

"Rand, that night, I told you it wasn't a good idea. But we had too much to drink, and we took advantage of each other. As far as I'm concerned, it never happened."

"It happened," Rand snarled.

Val threw her hands in the air. "You see, there are two sides to everything. I told you, I never look back."

Rand was on his feet, his face full of rage.

Val only laughed. "By the way," she said, "yesterday I returned the balance of my retainer from Coleman Enterprises. Certified mail. I also faxed my resignation so there would be no doubt as to the time."

"The family will view that as an admission of guilt," Rand sputtered.

"I don't care how your family views it. It's the way I view it that's important."

"You just dug my grave, Val," Rand snarled. "I'll see that you never get another legal case in this state."

"Really!"

"Yes, really."

Val crushed her cigarette into the ceramic ashtray. She leaned over the cocktail table and took a fistful of M&M candies from a crystal dish. With cool deliberation she popped them, one by one, into her mouth. "This is just my opinion, Lord Nelson, but I'd say Maggie was well rid of you. You aren't the nice person I thought you were. Now, if you don't leave, I'm going to buzz for security. You weren't announced, so that must mean you came up the service elevator and used someone else's card." Her hand was on the phone when Rand slapped it out of her hand.

"Don't ever threaten me, Val."

Rand's arm swept the contents of the cocktail table onto the floor before he stormed out of the apartment. The moment the door closed, Val ran to it and shot the dead bolt home. As Val sat down on the sofa, she realized her anger had turned into something else—a deep melancholy. She needed a friend, but she didn't have one. Not one *true* friend. God, how had she gotten to this point in her life without making at least one?

Well, it wasn't too late. Friends could still be made. She could change her life around if she wanted to.

She'd lied to Rand about having to work on briefs. The pile of papers on the table represented a proposal of

sale of her firm, which was now worth a cool eleven
million dollars. The six associates were willing to buy
her out if they could get adequate financing. Thirty days
and it would be over. Right now, this minute, she knew
she could walk out of this apartment with her toothbrush and survive the rest of her life in a style that
would be more than comfortable.

She thought about Brody's drugstore in Oxmoor,
Minnesota. She wouldn't take a toothbrush. A toothbrush, one of those bright yellow ones in the cellophane
wrappers next to the mouthwash, would be her first purchase at Brody's.

Fifty-four wasn't too old to start over. Other people
had done it. She could buy a little house like Susan's,
with a garden. She looked down at her acrylic nails and
knew they would be the first thing to go. She could get
a couple of dogs and a cat and one of those birds that
chirped in the morning. She'd go to Dixon's hardware
store and buy a lawn mower, a lawn rake, and a snow-
blower. She'd sell the Lamborghini and get a Range
Rover. She'd stick the Rolex, the pearls, the diamonds
in a safe deposit box and learn to shop at Wal-Mart.

The move, if she went through with it, would be the
biggest challenge of her life.

She thought about Maggie Nelson. She'd once heard
through the Coleman grapevine that Maggie and Rand
had a marriage to equal that of Billie and Thad
Kingsley. How sad that it was coming to an end. How
sad that Rand screwed it up, and with her help. All the
way home on the plane she'd thought about her part in
it all.

"But why can't I get Maggie out of my mind?" she
asked herself. Maybe she should call her. Not for Rand,
but for Maggie. Maggie was sharp; would she believe

her? Not likely. She could tell Maggie the truth. Which would be harder for Maggie to deal with? Or was it better to remain quiet? Rand was right about one thing— the family would view her resignation and departure as an admission of guilt. She had to decide now, this very second, if she cared.

Val reached for another handful of the colored candies, popping all of them into her mouth. She munched contentedly. She didn't care.

Thoughts of Maggie stayed with her as she tidied up the papers on the table. At one time Maggie had been tough as rawhide. Now, though, Val thought, she's just as vulnerable as the rest of us. How devastated she must be. Val stopped what she was doing, a terrible expression on her face. What if Maggie started to drink?

Val bolted from the sofa and started to pace, arguing with herself as she waded up and down the long, narrow living room into the dining room, around the table, skirting the four-foot-high pedestal with the bust of Blackstone on it. Up and down she walked, smacking one clenched fist against the other. She stopped once to yank at the Greenpeace sweatshirt riding up around her waist. If only she had a friend to help her, she thought. If only she had someone to listen.

Then, suddenly, faster than she'd ever moved in her life, she ran through the thick carpet to the door, yanking at the chain and the dead bolt. She pulled the door open, stopping for just a moment before she ran down the hall to 36C. She rang the doorbell and stepped back so the occupant on the other side could see her clearly.

Elliot Morrow, publisher of the *Miranda Sentinel* and a client of Val's firm, opened the door. "Val, is something wrong?" he asked, concerned.

"No, of course not. I was wondering if you would do me a tremendous favor."

"If I can," the rotund little man said. "Come in."

Val stepped into an apartment that was almost identical to hers. "I was wondering if you would loan me Isaac for the night. I . . . I have just decided to get a dog, and I . . . I said I would let the man know first thing in the morning. Since I never had an animal, I would . . . ah, like to . . . what I mean is . . ."

"Sure, Isaac knows you."

Elliot whistled. A four-legged whilrwind skittered to a stop at Val's feet. Val dropped to her knees to scratch the taffy-colored spaniel behind his ears. Wet, adoring eyes begged her to continue.

"Val, is anything wrong?"

"Nothing I can't handle," she said quietly.

"Okay. Wait here." Elliot returned a minute later with a shopping bag filled to the brim. "This is Isaac's bed and his blanket. I've included two of his toys, his leash, his snacks, his brush and comb, his toothbrush, and his breakfast. Walk him at eleven-thirty and again at six. Drop him off anytime between seven and eight. His sitter comes in at eight-fifteen. Don't let him on the furniture, and wash his whiskers after he eats. He hates it when his whiskers get stiff. He goes to sleep right after he's walked for the night. His music box is in there too."

"You know, Elliot, you treat this dog better than some people treat their children."

"Isaac and I have been together for a long time. So I spoil him, so what? It makes me happy, and I don't think you could find a happier dog anywhere in this universe. Take care of him," Elliot said, opening the door. To the spaniel he said, "Go with Val and she'll give you a treat." The dog looked backward once, but followed Val obediently, his eyes on the bulging shopping bag.

Val opened the door to her apartment. The moment it closed behind her, Isaac walked straight into the living room and leaped up onto the white couch. He woofed softly and then began to sniff his surroundings. Val watched as he stretched, trying to reach the candy dish on the cocktail table. He woofed again. "Go ahead, help yourself," Val said, emptying out the shopping bag. "A man could go to war with less gear," she muttered.

The moment the dog's belongings were stashed, Val sat down on the couch next to him. She waited, uncertain of what to do next. She wanted to pick Isaac up, to hug him, to feel his warm body and the beat of his little heart. She fondled his silky ears, her eyes misting with tears. She held her breath when the fat little dog slowly inched his way closer until his front paws were on her jeans. He wiggled again, then again, until he was in her lap. A sob worked its way up to Val's throat. Tears rolled down her cheeks. Isaac squirmed and wiggled until he was on his hind legs, his front paws on Val's shaking shoulders. His silky ears flopped this way and that way as he licked first at one side of her face, then the other.

Isaac allowed himself to be petted and stroked, hugged and squeezed. The spaniel's silky head was so wet with her tears, Val had to dry him with a tissue from her pocket. She clung to the animal, baring her soul.

"I was attracted to Rand. I will never deny that. But I would never have acted on that attraction if he hadn't made the first move. I have never lied to myself, and I know in my heart that I wouldn't have. Drunk or sober.

So, Isaac, where does that leave me?" Val sobbed to the dog. "This is pretty much a moral call here, my friend." She rubbed her wet cheeks against the dog's soft body. Isaac whimpered as he snuggled comfortably in the crook of Val's arm.

They slept. Once during the long night, the spaniel crept quietly from Val's arm to circle the apartment, finally choosing the shiny chrome dining room table leg to relieve himself. He was back in the attorney's arms a minute later.

Thirty-six floors below, Rand sat in Riley's pickup truck. He wished now that he hadn't come here. This was his problem, not Val's.

You play, you pay, Val had said. Rand leaned his head back into the cracked leather seat. It made his back itch. His eyes closed and he took roll call of his life. All things considered, it had been a good life. A few ups and downs. More ups than downs. Scene after scene flashed before his closed eyes. He thought about his favorite stuffed animal, a cat, when he was a child. Sally Dearest he'd called it. He wished he had it now, so he could bury his head in the fuzzy, patched-up animal. Back then it had given him so much comfort. The past. Sally Dearest was history. Everything before this moment was history. Exhausted with his soul searching, Rand dozed. When he woke hours later, he looked at the numerals on his watch. Ten minutes past midnight. Time to go home. Home. That was the laugh of the year.

Rand turned the key in the ignition and backed out of his parking space. He proceeded up the ramp and out into the clear starry night. He drove aimlessly because, he told himself, when you didn't have a home, it didn't matter what you did or where you went. He headed east on 290 with no destination in mind. An hour later he pulled the pickup to the side of the road at a phone booth and used his calling card to call Hawaii. He explained to the operator that the machine would come on and he wanted to leave a message.

Rand shivered when he heard Maggie's voice on the answering machine. All about him cars and trucks whizzed by. Where in the hell was all the traffic going at this hour of the morning? He found himself yelling into the phone. "I'm taking the first plane out in the morning. I need to talk to you, Maggie. After I say what I have to say, you can do what you want. But you're going to hear me out. I love you, Maggie. I've never loved anyone but you. I need you to believe me." He choked, his voice breaking. "I *need you*, Maggie."

It wasn't much, but it was a start. Rand half turned in the narrow booth to lean his forehead against the cool glass. All he had to do now was head back to Sunbridge, drop off the pickup, and head for the airport, where he would catch the first flight to Hawaii.

He pushed at the bifold door in time to hear a loud whoosh as a Ryder truck roared down the road. He gasped at the strong wind and smell of the truck's exhaust. God, where *was* this traffic going? He blinked at the blazing oncoming lights. He brought up his hand to shield his eyes, debating if he had time to get to the truck and close the door before the next vehicle barreled past. He opened the door of the cab, his right hip and leg half on the seat, when he heard the sound of an eighteen-wheeler bearing down so close he could see the license plates in the oversize side door mirror. He knew the finely printed words on the side mirror by heart: Objects in mirror are closer than they appear. He was about to slide the rest of the way onto the seat when the behemoth streaked by at eighty miles an hour, slamming him against the door and ripping it off its hinges with a metallic shriek.

He was dead before he was tossed in the air like a rag doll, then down into the deep culvert alongside the road, thirty feet from the telephone booth, his hand still on the door handle.

The driver looked into his rearview mirror, knowing he'd ripped the door off the pickup. "Damn fool deserves to lose his door," he muttered under his breath.

Isaac stirred restlessly in Val's arms. She too stirred with the strange movement. Her eyes popped open to meet those of the spaniel. How warm he was, how soft and cuddly. But she groaned when she realized the dog needed to be walked. "Poor little thing," she crooned as she struggled from her nest in the pillows.

"Okay, Isaac, I know my duty. I'll get my shoes, and we'll head for the nearest fire plug." When she returned wearing her sneakers, she was in time to see Isaac lift his leg on the dining room table leg. "Guess that takes care of that," she whooped, but made no move to clean it up. She squatted down next to the dog, certain he was going to communicate with her in some way. "Don't you have to do something else? Or do you do that at night?" The dog stared at her unblinkingly. Val stared back. "Okay, how about breakfast? Chicken and noodles. Come on, I'll put it on fine china, howzat?"

Val busied herself in the kitchen, dicing chicken thighs and chopped noodles per Elliot's written instructions. When Isaac's food was ready, she slid it into the microwave oven for forty-five seconds, then transferred the mess from the plastic bowl onto the Lenox plate and tested the food with her index finger to see if it was warm enough. Satisfied, she looked around for the dog. She called him and then whistled. "Hey, Isaac, breakfast time!" When the dog still didn't appear, she walked through the dining room and on into the sunken living room. She didn't know if she should laugh or cry. The papers she'd stacked so neatly the night before were haphazardly arranged on the floor where a rather large pile of poop could be seen. Isaac was trying to hide under the glass-topped table, his head between his paws.

Val squatted down again. "I applaud ingenuity in all forms," she said as she tickled the dog behind his ears. She leaned sideways to peer at the mess of papers. The brown stuff was on her resignation letter. She laughed, a strange sound even to her ears. She scooped up the spaniel and carried him to the kitchen. "Good boy," she said, patting the dog's rump as she set him down next to the Lenox dish.

Reassured by Val's tone of voice and gentle hand, Isaac lapped at his food, his long silky ears swishing among the noodles.

While Isaac ate, Val showered and dressed in a soft peach-colored suit and a peach and white polka dot blouse with a demure bow at the neck. She took one last look in the mirror to check her subtle makeup and the French braid she'd become addicted to of late. She padded out to the kitchen, where she proceeded to re-pack Isaac's gear. "C'mere," she said to the spaniel. Brush in hand, she ran it down the dog's back before she threw it into the bag. She looked at the red, white, and blue toothbrush and muttered, "No way." She did, however, moisten a paper towel and wipe the dog's ears and whiskers. At the door she looked down at the spaniel and said, "I think—mind you, this is just my opinion—but I think you got me through the worst night of my life. You are the only one besides myself who has ever set foot in this apartment. Of course, Rand doesn't count, and neither does the cleaning lady. You are the first *invited* guest, and it doesn't matter if you have four legs or two." Isaac tilted his silky head to the side. He appeared to be listening intently to every word. She was stunned a moment later when the dog leaped into her arms, almost knocking her backward. His little pink tongue lapped at her chin. She cuddled him, her eyes as wet as the spaniel's.

"Time to go home," she said.

She carried the dog, inching the shopping bag ahead of her with her leg. The moment her neighbor opened the door, Isaac leaped to the floor. "Thanks, Elliot." To the dog she said, "See you around, Isaac." She was halfway to her apartment when Elliot called to her.

"Are you going to do it?"

Val stopped. "Do what?"

"Get a dog."

"Oh, yes. Yes, I am," she said, and then muttered under her breath, "at some point."

Back in her apartment, Val wrinkled her nose as she walked past the brown lump on the floor. She made no move to clean it up. She slid her feet into beige Ferragamo heels, always the last thing she did before leaving for work. Briefcase in hand, she headed for the door. She was not in the habit of looking back. This apartment was just a place to sleep. It wasn't a home. It could never be a home. Susan had a home. The Colemans had assorted homes. Maggie and Rand had a home.

Maggie.

Val stopped at the door, set the briefcase down, and

retraced her steps to the kitchen, where she picked up the white phone on the wall. She tapped out the area code for Hawaii information, then scribbled the number on a pad on the counter. With a trembling hand she pushed the eleven buttons it took to reach Hawaii. She held her breath, wondering if Maggie would answer or if she'd let her answering machine take the call. Maggie's recorded voice startled Val.

"Maggie, this is Valentine Mitchell," Val said briskly. "I have something to say to you, and I want you to listen to me. Rand came by last evening and told me what you . . . what happened between the two of you. You're wrong, Maggie. Nothing happened. Rand was and always has been a perfect gentleman." The lie was like a lump of peanut butter in her throat. "I thought you knew me well enough to know I would never in any way compromise your family. I also want you to know I am severing my firm's business relationship with the Colemans. In fact, I'm selling the firm and planning to go into semiretirement. Don't for one minute read anything into this statement but what it is. I want a life outside the legal profession, and I just hope it isn't too late for me. Well, that's all I called to say. If I don't see you again, Maggie, enjoy that paradise you live in. And if you doubt what I've said, ask yourself if I've ever done anything but my very best for your family, or if I've ever lied to any of you. 'Bye, Maggie."

The peanut butter was back in her throat. Her thumb shot upward. "That's one for you, Val," she croaked as she made her way to the door.

It was exactly eight o'clock when Val's secretary poked her head in the door and stage whispered, "Riley Coleman is here. What should I tell him?"

Val's mind raced as she looked around her cluttered office. "Send him in," she said in a resigned voice.

How handsome he is, she thought when Riley entered the messy room.

"Riley, we didn't have an appointment, did we?" Val asked cheerfully.

Riley didn't respond. Instead he held out a white envelope with the firm's name engraved at the top. "Would you mind explaining this?" he said, tossing the envelope on her desk.

"There's not much to explain, Riley. I decided I've had enough of the rat race. I want to wind down and have a life of my own. I'm sorry if it comes as a shock to you," she said quietly. "I did return the balance of the retainer."

"Rather sudden, wasn't it?"

Val's lips tightened. "From your point of view I guess it was, but not from mine. I'm selling the firm. If your family wants to stay here, you can negotiate with the new partners. It will probably be to your benefit, and cheaper." Here it comes, Val thought, the biggie.

Riley pushed his baseball cap back on his dark hair. "I can't argue with the part about wanting a life of your own. It's the suddenness that bothers me. Listen, Val, there's no one in the world I have more respect for than you. Both my butt and Cole's would have been in jail if it weren't for you. So I'm not going to beat around the bush here. Rand more or less implied a problem. Aunt Maggie took off. Rand left the house early last night and never came home. I'd like to know what's going on. Not because I'm being nosy, but because you are terminating your contract with us. I also came here today to conduct some business. Or try to."

Suddenly it was important to her that Riley not view

her with suspicion. She was genuinely fond of him, and she absolutely adored Ivy. She got up from her comfortable chair and walked around to him. "Nothing happened between Rand and myself. This thing, whatever this thing is, seems to be coming out of nowhere. I really don't want to get involved with your family's personal problems, Riley. Now," she said briskly, "you said you came here to do some business. What is it?"

Riley explained.

Val laughed. "A piece of cake. I'll tell you what, Riley. I'll do it. We'll call it my going-away present to you. Once I set it up, one of the new partners can take over if that's agreeable with you. Three days, four at the most."

They were shaking hands when the intercom on Val's desk came to life. "Miss Mitchell, there's a call for Mr. Coleman on line two." Val raised her eyebrows and winked. She busied herself at the file cabinet as Riley stretched across the desk for the phone.

She whirled about when she heard Riley say, "What did you say? Yes, that's my license plate number. I loaned my truck to my uncle last evening. It was early when he left my house. No, no, he didn't come home at all last night, and he still wasn't there when I left this morning. No, he didn't call. I'll be there as soon as I can."

When Riley hung up, Val whispered fearfully, "What was all that about?"

"That was the state police. They said . . . they said Rand's dead." Riley's face was drained of all color.

"Dead!" Val said, lowering herself into her chair. "It must be a mistake. How . . . where do they want you to go?"

"The morgue. They said a passing motorist stopped

around six this morning, just as it was getting light, to use the roadside phone booth. My truck was parked on the shoulder of the road with the door ripped off. The motorist called the state police and . . . they found . . . Rand in the culvert. That's all I know."

"I'll go with you," Val said, reaching for her purse. "I'll drive, too. You're whiter than ceiling paint."

"Aunt Maggie?"

"Not yet, Riley."

Val linked her arm through Riley's as she steered him through the maze of offices. To her secretary she said, "I don't know when I'll be back."

They drove in silence. Over and over in her mind Val thanked God for the wisdom he'd bestowed on her earlier. She was glad now that she'd called Maggie, glad she'd lied to her and to Riley. She longed for Isaac's warm, cuddly body. How cold she felt, how very tired.

Ivy was waiting in the corridor outside the morgue, pacing up and down, wringing her hands, her eyes full of tears. She ran to Riley the moment she saw him, her Reeboks making hard slapping sounds on the marble floor.

The three of them stared at one another. Val squared her shoulders. "I'll do it, Riley. I've done it before. Stay with Ivy."

Val was alongside them four minutes later, her face as sheet-white as Riley's. "I signed the paper identifying the body. There was no mistake. It's Rand. We have to go upstairs now." She bit down on her lower lip. God, she needed air. Lots of air. Her stomach lurched sickeningly. Who was going to call Maggie? Who was going to call Billie?

Later, while they waited for Riley to join them in the

corridor, Ivy said, "Riley told me what you said, about you and Rand. You lied. You never did that before, did you?"

Val shook her head. "I didn't want Riley to remember Rand like that. I think . . . I have to get back to the office. You have a car, right?"

"I borrowed Jonquil's. Susan has mine. Val, I need to talk to you in a few days. Friend to friend, if that's okay. Riley told me you weren't going to represent the family anymore."

"I decided to retire. Well, semiretire. I don't know if lawyers ever really retire. And Ivy . . . I'm very sorry about Rand. If there's anything I can do, let me know, and yes, I'll be happy to discuss whatever it is you want to discuss. Friend to friend."

"I always thought Val was tough as wet rawhide," Ivy said to Riley when he joined her minutes later. "She had tears in her eyes. I don't think I ever thought of Val as anything but an attorney who had her head screwed on right. That's terrible, isn't it, Riley? I've never thought of her as a human being. Just an attorney."

"Yeah, Ivy, that's terrible, but it's the way I thought of her too," Riley said hoarsely. "Come on, honey, let's go home. God, how am I going to tell Aunt Maggie?"

"We'll do it together, Riley," Ivy said quietly.

The services for Rand Nelson were held privately. The family left the mortuary in a tightly knit group. Once again their numbers were depleted. This time, though, there would be no burial on the hill. There was to be no grave, no headstone. On Maggie's instructions, Rand's ashes were to be returned to England and placed in his family's crypt. Chesney, Rand's daughter, volunteered to deliver the urn in person, saying she would return to England to live.

Ivy Coleman presided over the gathering. From time to time she wiped at the corners of her eyes, and she was never far from her husband's side.

They were eating now, an exquisite luncheon prepared by Jonquil. The family's voices were little more than hushed murmurs as they stirred and stared at the food on their plates.

We look like an assembly of penguins, Ivy thought, eyeing everyone's black clothing. Only Maggie, in a vivid scarlet dress with matching hip-length jacket, added color to the room. She looked as out of place as a hare in a hound's lair.

"I have to do something," Sawyer whispered to her husband. "I have to say something to wipe that awful look from her face. She's my mother, Adam."

"She's strung too tight, Sawyer. Leave her alone, and by alone I mean keep that mouth of yours shut. You don't see Cole doing anything, do you?"

"Cole's a guy. At a time like this a woman needs a woman," Sawyer said with a catch in her voice. "My God, Adam, do you have any idea how she must feel?"

"Pretty shitty, I'd imagine." Adam gave his wife a nudge. "Talk to her about anything but Rand."

"All right," Sawyer mumbled as she made her way across the room to where her mother was talking to her grandmother and Thad.

"It looks like one of those Texas storms we've heard about is starting to brew," Thad said, motioning with his arm toward the wide expanse of windows.

"I remember one or two of those, don't you, Grandmam?" Sawyer said to Billie.

"More than one or two," Billie said lightly. "Would

you girls mind sitting down with me? My legs are tired," Billie lied. "Thad, fetch us a drink, please."

"Not right now, Mam. I want to talk to Cole." Maggie looked at her watch and frowned. "If there is going to be a storm, I should leave now. I don't want to miss my plane."

"You're leaving?" Billie said blankly.

"You mean you're going back to Hawaii?" Sawyer said, stunned at her mother's words.

"Is there any reason why I should stay?" Maggie asked coolly.

"I don't think it's a good idea for you to be alone right now, darling," Billie said quietly.

"Why is that, Mam?"

"Under the circumstances, I would think you'd want to be with your family," Billie said gently, her face full of sadness.

"The way *you* want to be with us? It was you, Mam, who said we were to peddle our papers and leave you and Thad alone. I'd like to be alone too. I've been alone before. Excuse me," she said, and walked away.

"Did she say good-bye to Chesney?" Sawyer asked.

"Yes. They shook hands," Billie said. "I found that a little hard to accept, but right now Maggie has to do whatever it takes to get through this. If she is going to leave, I hope she goes before Valentine Mitchell gets here. Ivy told me she called and asked to stop by."

"Oh, God," was all Sawyer could say.

"I didn't think Maggie would wear black. But I never expected her to wear red," Billie said fretfully.

"Whatever it takes, Grandmam," Sawyer said, reaching for the glass of wine Thad held out to her.

Across the room, within earshot of Riley and Ivy, Maggie said, "I'd like to leave now, if you don't mind."

"Are you sure, Mother?" Cole asked.

"Yes, I'm sure. I'll go through the kitchen and slip out the back door. I'll meet you by the car."

"Aren't you going to say good-bye?" Cole asked, stunned at his mother's words.

"You know I don't like good-byes, Cole. They're so final. I've had about all the finality I can handle for one day. If it's a problem for you to take me to the airport, I can call a car service."

"It's no problem, Mother. I'll meet you outside. I have to get the keys from Riley."

Riley's eyes were full of unasked questions when he handed over the keys. Cole shrugged. "I'm not going to try and change her mind," Cole said softly. "Once my mother makes up her mind, there's no changing it. We all know that. I won't be long."

Out of the corner of her eye, Ivy saw movements in the courtyard. "It's Val," she said to Riley. "She must have driven in from the back. Don't look at me like that, Riley. She said she wanted to pay her respects to the family. Think what you want, Riley. I like Val. I like her a lot, and since this is my home too, I don't see why there should be any kind of a problem."

"I was thinking more about Val than the family. She's going to feel awkward, I think," Riley muttered. "It's amazing, you know? When you stop to think about it, no one knows anything. Neither Rand nor Val admitted to anything, and yet . . . oh, skip it. Civility has always been this family's long suit." He gave his wife a gentle squeeze before he walked to where Cary and Susan were sitting.

Ivy made her way to the kitchen as unobtrusively as she could. Damn, Val's timing couldn't have been worse, she thought fretfully. She wondered for the thousandth time if the attorney and Rand had really, as Riley put it, *done it*. She remembered their fight, and how she'd defended Val, her voice shaking with emotion. She'd flounced out of the room yelling over her shoulder, "Valentine Mitchell would never do anything to hurt this family." It had been hers and Riley's first serious disagreement, and one Riley had apologized for two hours later.

Outside, the sky was darkening rapidly. The wind whipped through the tunnel-like courtyard. Maggie had the car door open when Val parked next to her. Maggie turned, the skirt of her red dress fussing about her knees in the whipping wind.

"Val," she said quietly.

"I came to pay my respects to your family, Maggie."

"I have no objection. I'm leaving myself," Maggie said tightly. "Cole's driving me to the airport. I think it's commendable of you to show up like this. If I had even the slightest doubt in my mind that Rand or you told the truth, just the teeniest little doubt, I'd throw my arms around you and weep with sorrow, but, you see, I know. In my heart I know Rand was unfaithful. Under the circumstances, if I were in your place, I might have done the same thing. Then again, maybe I wouldn't have. Emotions are the one thing in the world you can't count on. I've learned that the hard way." Unexpectedly, Maggie's hand shot out. Val reached for it. "Maybe we'll talk about this someday," Maggie said, getting into the car.

"Just call," Val said in a whispery voice.

Only Ivy saw Val knuckle her eyes. Only Ivy saw her slide back into her car, where she leaned her head over the steering wheel, crying. She watched the attorney back the car out of the driveway and head out to the road that ran perpendicular to the house. An immense surge of relief flooded through her. Relief for Val. She ran then up the back stairs of the kitchen, taking the steps two at a time. Gasping with the exertion, she ran down the hall to the baby's room. Only here was it normal. Only here in this bright, colorful room were things the way they should be.

Ivy's eyes fell on the cartoon-figured hamper that held Billie's VCR tape. She'd removed it from her knitting bag and secured it in an airtight Ziploc bag before placing it in the bottom of Moss's hamper, because Riley liked to rummage. She felt like a criminal when she lifted the lid on the wicker chest, and heaved a sigh of relief when she saw the tape untouched in its plastic bag.

"There you are," Susan hissed from the doorway. Ivy dropped the lid, her face full of guilt.

"Susan, you startled me," she chided.

"Sorry." She didn't sound sorry at all, Ivy thought.

"I was just checking on Moss. Maggie left." Ivy whispered until she was out in the hall, the door safely closed behind her.

"I know. Maybe it's best for her." Susan made it sound like no matter what happened or where it happened, it would be for the best. "I just came up to tell you I'm taking Cary back. This whole thing has upset him terribly. This is not a good place to be right now. Things always happen here. Sunbridge was never a happy place."

"That's a terrible thing to say, Susan. A place isn't unhappy. It's the people in the place that are unhappy."

"Maggie was never happy here. Cole wasn't either, since he deeded his half of the place to Riley. Mam wasn't happy here, she said so. Grandfather Seth banished Aunt Amelia, and she hated Sunbridge. Mam said Grandmother Jessica wasn't happy here, so who does that leave? Riley? You? That mean-spirited tyrant who was my grandfather was the only other person who actually lived here, and no one knows to this day what made *him* tick. No, you and Riley are the only ones who *say* they're happy here. Anyway, I only came up here to tell you we're leaving. It was a nice luncheon, Ivy."

As Susan made her way down the steps, Ivy stood at the railing, looking down into the great room.

Riley's family. Hers now. Ivy's shoulders slumped. They straightened almost immediately when Riley looked up and smiled. She smiled back.

It was four o'clock when Sawyer and Adam, the last of the family to leave, said their good-byes. "We seem to be doing this a lot lately, saying good-bye," Sawyer said sadly.

"Good-byes are never easy," Ivy said quietly.

"Aunt Maggie can't bring herself to say those words," Riley remarked. "She'll say so long, see you around, or something to that effect, but she'll never say good-bye. I wonder why that is?"

"I don't think it's important right now, Riley," Sawyer said gently. "Maggie will cope. She's tough. She put up with all of us for a long time, didn't she?"

"Yeah, she did. Cole said he'll take Sumi and the baby to see her as soon as the doctor gives the okay for the baby to fly. Aunt Maggie will like that."

"Yes, she'll like that," Sawyer said happily. "Chesney didn't stay around very long. She didn't say two words to me. I thought that was a little strange."

"What's even stranger," Ivy said coolly, "was how fast she made an appointment with Val to go over

Rand's will. I didn't see any tears in her eyes at the church service, and I looked."

"No kidding. I missed that," Sawyer muttered.

"She was probably in shock, like the rest of us," Riley said.

"Grow up, Riley," Sawyer said nastily. "Months ago, Maggie told me Chesney was never at the house and that the relationship Rand wanted with her never really materialized. Chesney, Maggie said, was ever so polite, but ever so indifferent. For a while Maggie had convinced herself that she had a second daughter, but it turned out to be wishful thinking. Chesney is a very wealthy young woman today. She gets half of everything, and *everything* is considerable."

Riley smiled. He loved it when Sawyer was off and running. "Except the house in Hawaii," he said. "Val told me herself that last year Rand had deeded it over to Maggie because she loved it so. I assume Aunt Maggie knows this, but knowing Rand, he may never have told her."

"That's something, at least." Sawyer turned to Ivy. "Ivy, thanks for putting up with us," she said, hugging her. "Riley, take care of things, and don't let Susan get to either one of you. Production on the plane starts two weeks from Monday. Cary assured me the money would be in the coffers in less than a week. He must know some pretty influential people."

"That's great, Sawyer," Riley said. "Cary is one in a million. I'm glad he's the one who's getting the project off the ground. Cole feels the same way. You really stepped in it, old girl."

"Didn't I, though?" Sawyer said smugly.

Another round of hugs followed. Both Riley and Ivy watched until the rental car was out of sight.

The moment Riley closed the door, Ivy said, "This was such an awful day. All I want to do is curl up in a corner and pretend it never happened. I felt so bad for Maggie. I wanted to slap Susan till she bounced off the walls. That doesn't say much for me, does it, honey?"

"It says you care. Let's put a slicker on Moss and go out for a chili dog with lots of onions ... real greasy french fries and onion rings, and one of those giant-size slushes. Blueberry. Later I'll drink a quart of Mylanta."

"Just the three of us?" Ivy said, her eyes shining.

"Yep."

"You're on. I'll get Moss."

"Ivy?"

"Yeah?"

"I love you."

"Not as much as I love you."

"I'm never gonna win this one, right?"

"Nope."

{{{{{{{{ CHAPTER TEN }}}}}}}}

Maggie's eyes were glued to the sun creeping over the horizon. Sunrises and sunsets should be shared. A soft whimper escaped her lips. She squirmed, the chill of the vinyl lounge cushion sending chills through her body. She struggled with the oversize beach towel she'd used for a cover, yanking and pulling at it to no avail. She had to get up, brave the new day somehow. She had to make coffee and eat something, possibly take a vitamin pill. There were so many things she had to do; the list was growing longer each day. In the ten days she'd been back, she'd done nothing but sleep, drink coffee, and swim. She gave up her struggle with the beach towel and entered the kitchen.

The kitchen was warmer than the lanai. In another hour it would be warm and sunny and filled with the scent of the plumeria outside the open windows. She loved plumeria and all the island flowers.

Maggie carefully measured out coffee, added just the right amount of water to the Mr. Coffee, and pressed the red button. The refrigerator surrendered bread, butter, and mango jelly. There was no milk and no juice or eggs. A jar of pickles with cloudy brine was the only thing left. She was going to have to go to town to the market. "Tomorrow," she muttered. Everything was scheduled for tomorrow.

She listened for the last little gush of bubbles as the water in the machine dribbled down to the pot. Ten cups. She'd drink it all by mid-morning. Her toast popped up. It looked as dark as the coffee. She knew the butter wasn't spreadable, but she tried anyway, finally settling for little pats, which she covered with three spoonfuls of jelly. She chewed slowly and methodically.

When she finished, she donned a clean bathing suit. She poured fresh coffee into a giant-size mug that said MAGGIE on it and carried it down to the beach, where she would sip at it and stare out across the water until her eyes started to burn, at which point she would head back to the house for more coffee, which she would drink on the lanai.

With the exception of her caffeine nerves, she felt better today, more rested and not as restless. She could think clearly now and was probably capable of making a decision.

She shuddered in the warm, fragrant air, her eyes sweeping her private stretch of beach, the beautiful palm trees and the squat palmettos and the gorgeous white sand. It was all so perfect, this place she'd called her personal paradise. If she didn't watch herself, it was a place where she would lose touch with reality.

She brought her mind into the present. She'd given herself ten days to deal with Rand's death. During that time, she'd allowed herself to settle into a dark, emotional place that was full of nightmares and boogeymen. Ten days. Not much, but all she allowed herself to mourn, to hate herself, to wallow in self-pity. Now it was time to rejoin the world.

Maggie ran the list of things "to do" over in her mind. At the top was changing the message on the answering machine, listening to ten days' worth of messages, since she hadn't been answering the phone, going through her mail, then packing up Rand's mail and sending it to Chesney.

Chesney. Rand's daughter. Her stepdaughter.

Nobody was what they seemed, she thought sadly. Not Rand, not Chesney, not even her own mother. She wondered if what you saw was ever what you got.

Chesney was gone, bag and baggage, and Maggie felt only a sense of relief. Chesney had been an intruder. She'd had her own life, had asked for nothing, and had openly said she didn't love her father, though she did admit to liking him. She reminded Rand over and over that she would one day return to England. Brian, her fiancé, she said, was perfectly willing to make his home in England and perhaps fly for the same airline she did.

It occurred to Maggie at that moment that Chesney was as unforgiving as she was. The only difference was that Chesney had said from the beginning—from the moment she found out Rand was her father—that she wanted nothing except to see him, to see the man who'd let her grow up in an orphanage believing she wasn't loved or wanted.

Inheriting half of Rand's sizable estate was poor compensation for spending one's young life in an orphanage. The girl deserved whatever Rand left her. Maggie wondered how long it would take Chesney to stake a claim to this slice of paradise. Not that it mattered one way or the other. Chesney deserved more than whatever Rand had left to her in his will.

"Miss Maggie!" Addie, Maggie's three-day-a-week domestic, called from the lanai.

Maggie stood up and brushed the sand from her bare legs, then drained the last of her coffee before heading toward the lanai. "I'm sorry, Addie, I forgot you were coming today." Addie, Maggie thought, was the neatest, tidiest, nicest person she'd ever met. She was tiny, no more than four feet eight inches tall, but she said her coronet of braids added an entire inch to her height, making her four feet nine inches tall. She took the extra inch very seriously. She had dark licorice eyes with a double fringe of dark eyelashes. Her age was a mystery which she refused to discuss. She also refused to tell Maggie where she bought her muumuus, one-of-a-kind, gorgeous creations, which Maggie adored. Today she was attired in a straight-lined, boat-necked muumuu of a pinkish lavender. On her feet were sturdy L.A. Gear sneakers.

"What would you like me to do today, Miss Maggie?"

Maggie inhaled deeply, letting her breath explode in a loud shoosh. "Today, Addie, I want you to . . . pack up all of Mr. Nelson's things and take them back to town with you. I mean everything. Give them to the Rescue Mission, or if you know someone who needs them . . . I don't care. I would appreciate it if you'd call one of your brothers or cousins to come for the bedroom furniture in my room and . . . and Chesney's. I don't care what you do with it either. I know you might not get to all this today, but if you're free, come back tomorrow and pack up Mr. Nelson's office. There are a lot of boxes in the garage. Ask Mattie when he comes to do the lawn if he'll carry them up to the crawl space over the garage."

Addie's licorice eyes were full of concern. "If we take the furniture, where will you sleep, Miss Maggie?"

Maggie grimaced. "Out here on the lanai, where I've been sleeping for the past ten days. And, Addie, throw away the red dress and jacket. The shoes too," she added as an afterthought.

The black eyes snapped. "There is no food in the refrigerator," Addie said, wagging a finger at Maggie. "I will tell my brothers to stop at the market before they drive up here. Will there be anything else?"

"Would you mind bringing me the leather case in my room? The big one leaning up against the wall. And I'd appreciate it if you'd make some more coffee."

The black eyes snapped again. "You still haven't been out of the kitchen, have you?"

Maggie dug her heels into the sand at the edge of the lanai. "No, I haven't. I've been using the bathroom off the kitchen. I can't . . . I'm not ready . . . Later, when you're finished I'll . . . maybe then I can . . . Right now, it's not important, Addie."

"You've lost weight, Miss Maggie. Tonight before I leave I will cook you some food. You must promise to eat."

Maggie nodded absently, then headed back down to the beach and into the water. She swam till she was exhausted. She rolled onto her back and let the waves rush her to the shore. Exhausted with her effort, she struggled toward the house, where she snuggled into the lounge chair, the beach towel snug around her to prevent an attack of the shakes. The MAGGIE cup was full to the brim, steam spiraling upward. She inched one of her hands free of the towel to the cigarettes next to the cup. Where had Addie found them? Over the past days she'd wanted them desperately, but she wasn't desperate enough to drive to town or to walk through the rooms of the house to search for one. She lit one now, inhaling deeply. Terrible, terrible habit, smoking. Her eyes fell on the Surgeon General's words. As if she cared. She puffed and sipped. Sipped and puffed. Rand loved to smoke, got great enjoyment out of cigarettes. Maggie smoked and sipped until the cup was empty.

"Life goes on," she muttered as she bent to pick up her leather case, which once belonged to her mother. It was full of sketches, color samples, Billie's formulae for dyes, every color of the rainbow and some that weren't in any color formula anywhere in the world. She stuck the cigarettes and lighter into the bra of her swimsuit before she trudged with the heavy case out to the monkeypod tree, where she laid it down and unzipped it.

The sun crawled high in the heavens and then started its downward descent as Maggie studied the contents of the case, scribbling notes, matching colors, writing questions to herself. Once, she looked up and fantasized she was meeting with one of her mother's clients. "Gentlemen, the offices of Billie Limited are under a monkeypod tree." Her adrenaline was flowing, she could feel it coursing up through her body. A good sign. She went back to work, stopping again at four o'clock to stare at the descending sun. "If I can get the color and blend it with . . . what? What I want is a color that's the same shade as the sun over Sunbridge." She would have to do some experimenting with the pots of paint in her bedroom closet. It occurred to her then that she was going to need some work space. "Sorry, gentlemen, I've closed up shop under the monkeypod tree. From now on, Billie Limited will be conducting business out of the garage."

It was a decision. She'd actually made a decision. Out loud. "When you say it out loud, it makes it real, definite. All I'll need is a chair and two folding tables," she mumbled.

"Miss Maggie," Addie called from the lanai, "I have your dinner ready."

Maggie looked around, an expression of shock on her face. The sun was starting to set.

"It's not much this evening, Miss Maggie. Just a chicken pie, but I made the crust myself. There's enough for your lunch tomorrow. The vegetables are from my own garden. My brother's wife sent the dessert. I know you like banana cream."

"Thank you, Addie," Maggie said, sitting down at the table. "It looks delicious. Tell me, where did you find those cigarettes?"

Addie opened one of the kitchen drawers and pointed. She clucked her tongue in disapproval and then pointed to the large glass of milk next to Maggie's plate. Dutifully, Maggie picked it up and drank. Addie gleamed with pleasure.

"Tomorrow I will come back and do the laundry. The office will be finished by noon. What will you do for a bed?"

"I guess I'll have to go to town and get a new one. I have to get some folding tables too. I know you must be tired, Addie. I can clean up here. Go home to your family. And, Addie, thank you."

Maggie stopped eating long enough to thank the cousins and brothers trooping through the kitchen in Addie's wake. She started to eat again, realizing she was ravenous. She dug into the remainder of the chicken pie and finished it off. She finished the milk and poured more. Then she ate two slices of banana pie. Before the night was over, she'd probably finish that too. She could walk off the calories on the treadmill in the garage, if she felt like it.

It would take her ten minutes to wash her dishes and

tidy the kitchen. The night loomed ahead of her. She hated this time of day, that fragile time when day crept into darkness and the blackness was sprinkled with artificial lights.

Was she wrong? she wondered. Would the question haunt her forever? *Don't think about Rand. Rand no longer exists.* The realization brought such an ache to her chest, she doubled over, fighting for her breath. Her eyes started to water. She wiped at them angrily with the back of her hands. She *wasn't* crying. How could she cry when she was dead inside? If I'm dead inside, then why do I feel like this? she asked herself as she slammed her dishes into the sink. Scalding hot water poured from the faucet, steam rushing upward. She added detergent. She watched curiously as the frothy bubbles rose up and poured down the front of the sink. She turned off the water. *You could be wrong. Valentine said you were wrong. You judged and condemned a man you loved based solely on your feelings, on instinct, and now he's dead. You could be wrong. Val said you're wrong. Rand denied . . . Rand said . . . I don't care what he said, he lied. Val lied because . . . Val lied.* "Period," Maggie said coldly. She looked at the pie crust crumbs on the table. She swept them to the floor with her arm. The ants had to eat too.

Now what was she supposed to do? What did she normally do after dinner? Walk on the beach with Rand, hold hands, make love in the sand, play Scrabble, watch television, read. All of the above.

Maggie turned and yanked at the kitchen drawer. She pulled out a pack of cigarettes, ripping at it. She looked around for the MAGGIE cup, but the water in the sink was too hot for her hands. She opened the cabinet door for a clean cup and saw the RAND cup, the mate to hers.

Her eyes burning fiercely, she reached for it, hefted it in her hand, then threw it across the kitchen. The shattering sound was deafening. She ran from the kitchen, through the lanai and down to the beach.

You aren't perfect, Maggie. Admit that just maybe you're wrong. Look it square in the face and admit the possibility. "I saw the guilt in his face," she said aloud, "heard the lie in his voice. I'm not wrong." *What if you are? What if, what if?*

Maggie stomped her way down the beach fighting the tears burning her eyes. "I know! I know!" she shouted, to be heard over the lapping waves.

She walked for a long time, stumbling and righting herself in the wet sand. When she was exhausted, she turned to see how far she'd come. At least two miles, she estimated. She could barely see the lanterns strung on the lanai.

She ran back, tripping and falling, stumbling and cursing, until she reached the lanai, where she collapsed, her breathing ragged and uneven. "I know I wasn't wrong. I know it!" she cried brokenly. "Oh, God, I need you, Mam."

The moment her breathing was back to normal, she reached for the portable phone with shaking hands. She was stunned at how normal her voice sounded when Thad's voice came over the wire. She almost hung up when she realized it was the middle of the night in Vermont. She apologized. "I'm sorry, Thad, I forgot the time difference. I don't suppose Mam is awake."

"No, Maggie, she's sleeping. I'll tell her you called when she wakes in the morning. Are you all right?" The question sounded to Maggie as though he didn't care if she was or not. It was something to say, something polite. Thad was always polite.

"Fine. Look, don't even tell her I called. I know she doesn't want to be bothered ... right now. Take care of her, Thad," Maggie whispered.

"I will, Maggie. Stay well."

Maggie's next call was to her daughter, Sawyer. Adam, his voice groggy answered the phone. "Maggie, is anything wrong?"

"No. I just wanted to talk to Sawyer. I know it's late."

"She's dead to the world. The twins have chicken pox, and we haven't had any sleep for three days. Can she call you first thing in the morning?"

"No, that's okay. I'll call later in the week. Make an oatmeal paste for the girls. It will stop the itching. Good night, Adam."

Susan. Maggie punched out a new set of numbers. She let the phone in the Coleman condo ring eighteen times before she hung up. Where was she? At Cary's? At Sunbridge? She tried Cary's apartment and wasn't surprised when there was no response. Susan once admitted that she never answered the phone after eleven o'clock at night, fearing a disaster of some kind. She had said she could only handle disastrous news in broad daylight. It was all a crock, Maggie thought. Susan couldn't handle anything. It was a wonder she could brush her teeth on her own.

Ivy. Ivy would understand what she was going through. She dialed Sunbridge's private, unlisted number, which only the family knew. She listened to Ivy's message: "Riley and I have gone to Florida for my mother's birthday. We'll be back home on Tuesday. For any of you who are interested, Moss now has his second tooth."

Maggie lit a cigarette from the stub of the old one.

She counted the filters in the ashtray. Six. She snorted in disgust. Did she dare call Cole? He would be at the office now. She closed her eyes, trying to visualize his office number. The moment it came to her, she called. His secretary said that Cole had gone to Kyoto and wouldn't be back in the office until tomorrow.

How unavailable her family was. Each of them had someone running interference for them. As her mother had always been there for her, Maggie had made a point of always being available to the family, no matter what was going on in her personal life. Always. Now who was there for her? Maggie buried her face in her hands. Everyone had someone.

Because she didn't know what else to do, she entered the house, snapping on lights as she went along. She walked into the empty bedroom to where the phone and answering machine rested on the floor in the middle of a nest of tangled wires. She dropped to her knees and pressed the message button, then rocked back on her heels as she listened to the calls for Rand from the re-finery. Those had been made before . . . before anyone outside the family knew . . . One call from Sawyer, one from Ivy telling her about the trip to Florida. There were no calls from Susan or her mother, but there were six, one after the other, from Valentine Mitchell, and one from Cary, who wanted information, if she had it, on the refinery. The last call was from Cole, saying baby Billie was now a pound heavier.

Maggie rewound the tape. They had stayed in touch after all. But she didn't feel any better.

On her way back to the lanai, she passed the foyer, where mail was stacked neatly. Most of it, she knew, would be for Rand, probably refinery business, house-hold bills, charge accounts, insurance bills, tons of magazines, and sale flyers. Nothing really personal or directed to her. Someday she'd look at it.

Someday.

Back on the lanai, Maggie toyed with the idea of calling Valentine Mitchell and waking her from a sound sleep.

She was wired now, there was no doubt about it. Wired and angry. That was good, the anger part, she thought. "Up till now I've been in a stupor," she muttered.

Should I call Valentine Mitchell or shouldn't I? To what end? she asked herself. Call her, ask her again, beg her to tell you the truth. "No!" The word exploded from Maggie's mouth.

Maggie got up and paced. Should she make coffee? Should she light another cigarette? Already her mouth tasted like a pair of old sneakers. Should she brush her teeth? She moaned. God, she couldn't even make a simple decision.

She had to do something physical. Work of some kind. She slid her feet into a pair of zoris and marched around to the garage at the side of the house. The sensor lights came on as soon as she stepped on the walkway, bathing her in six hundred watts of light. She opened the door and put on the inside light. Like all garages, this one was a mess, so messy that she couldn't park a car inside. She looked around. Which one of us was the messy one? she wondered. She remembered her intention to walk on the treadmill. It was in here somewhere, along with a stationary bicycle and a stair machine. Rand said they needed the machines, along with his Nautilus equipment. To her knowledge, he'd never used any of them. Swimming had been their major exercise, that and walking miles up and down the beach.

Maggie worked through the night, clearing away a section of the oversize garage she planned to use as a work space. Once the canvas beach chairs, picnic coolers, bags, boxes of shells, and junk they'd collected over the years was stored on the far side of the room, she realized she might not have to buy folding tables at all. The workbench, once it was scrubbed, would serve nicely as a work surface. The shelves above it, which now held jars and cans of rusty screws, nails, nuts, and bolts, would be perfect for her jars of paint. If she left the garage door open, cleaned the windows, and painted the concrete floor white, she'd have more than enough light to work by. She could bang nails into the walls to hang up her sketches, and stretch a line to hang the wet, painted fabrics that would later be dyed. Who needed five thousand bucks a month overhead? Clients wouldn't be coming here. She'd go to them, the way her mother had.

She did need more paints, though. She ran back to the lanai for her mother's case. Inside was a catalog from which Billie ordered paints. Federal Express could have them to her in twenty-four hours. The swatches too. She looked around to see if there was a phone in the garage. She found the jack but no phone. A simple matter to rectify. A business phone she would answer, the house phone—no.

It was almost full light when Maggie set the scrub bucket on the driveway. *Her* half of the garage literally sparkled. Not only had she scrubbed the workbench, she'd painted it too, along with the shelves. She'd wet-vacuumed the garage floor and slapped a thick coat of paint on it. By evening it would be dry.

"You do good work, Maggie *Coleman*," she muttered.

By eight o'clock she'd showered, washed her hair, braided it, and donned a pair of clean chinos and a polo shirt. She washed the dishes, made coffee and breakfast, washed dishes again, smoked four cigarettes, and was ready for her trip to the Ala Moana shopping center.

Before she left the house, she wrote a note to Addie and left her check on the kitchen table. She blew her horn when she passed Addie in her open Jeep on Kam Highway.

She'd never come to the center this early in the morning. Usually, she had to fight for a parking space. This morning she sailed into one with no cars on either side of her.

Maggie used up an hour buying the first two bed-room sets she set her eyes on. Both were white bamboo, the headboards intricately carved. From there she mean-dered down the outdoor concourse to a linen shop where she ordered sheets and new towels, telling the clerk she'd pick them up at the delivery door later. At a stationery store, she stopped long enough to fill a shopping bag full of pencils, pens, markers, notepads, colored chalks, and construction paper. She was about to pay for her purchases when she saw a decorator phone with numbers so huge, she blinked. "I'll take that too," she said.

Her next stop was a coffee shop, where she ordered a mahi-mahi sandwich, a glass of root beer, and a slice of coconut custard pie. She then walked over to Liberty House, where she bought herself a bottle of Ysatis per-fume and talcum powder. From there she went to Liz Claiborne and bought one of everything in the designer's spring collection. She asked to have it sent to Sawyer.

Out on the concourse again, she stopped at a phone center and made arrangements for the telephone com-pany to install a new number for her in the garage the following day. From there she retrieved her car, picked up her linens, and drove to the market, where she bought everything in sight, completely loading down the trunk of the car.

She was back home at three o'clock. The kitchen smelled wonderful. She was sniffing in appreciation when the phone rang. She stared at it and muttered, "Where were you when I needed you?" She sniffed again when she opened the oven to reveal a plump oven roaster that would provide many lunches, decorated with baby carrots and small red-skinned potatoes. A salad waiting for dressing was covered with Saran Wrap in the refrigerator. The note on the table from Addie said the chicken would be done at five o'clock. The P.S. said all the office boxes were stored in the attic over the garage.

Maggie stocked her cupboard shelves and refrigerator before she carried the shopping bags with the sheets and towels into the empty bedroom.

In the bathroom off the kitchen, she stripped down and donned a tangerine one-piece bathing suit. She carried the shopping bag with her supplies out to the garage. The floor was dry, but she didn't walk on it. Back on the lanai, she opened the catalog to the pages she wanted, dialed the eight hundred number and placed her order. She was promised delivery by ten o'clock the following morning.

She walked the same distance she'd walked the night before, swam for an hour, and returned to the house at exactly five o'clock. She turned off the oven before she curled up on the lounge chair on the lanai. She slept until midnight, when she got up, ate, did the dishes, and slept again until morning.

Her life, Maggie told herself, was under control. For now.

{{{{{{{ CHAPTER ELEVEN }}}}}}}}

Maggie stirred, then stretched, flexing her legs beneath the new blue-and-white-striped sheets. Should she go back to sleep or get up? The realization that she was now a working woman with a real job made her swing her legs over the side of the bed.

Her morning ritual was different these days. She took a five-minute shower instead of one that lasted until the hot water heater ran cold, tied a rubber band around a ponytail instead of wrestling with a braid, and dressed in shorts and T-shirt instead of donning a bathing suit.

Bedmaking, at best, took a minute, unless her pillow was wet, which it usually was from crying in her sleep. In that case, she stripped the pillowcase and put on a new one. Today it was wet. After she had stuffed the pillowcase in the wicker hamper in the bathroom, her watch told her she'd used up eight and one half minutes.

Time for breakfast. Three cups of coffee, a corn muffin with mango jelly, and a glass of orange juice. Two superduper vitamins for women who were fifty or over were next to her orange juice. She swallowed them knowing they made her ravenously hungry during the day. In the last five weeks, since the day she'd cleaned and painted the garage floor, she'd put on seven of the ten pounds she'd lost.

She wasn't swimming as much, and most of her tan was gone. In the scheme of things, she didn't think it mattered. The only thing that made sense to her was her daily schedule. She went around to the garage and sat down to work from seven o'clock to twelve, then ate a huge lunch, and returned to work until three, when she took a break and a fifteen-minute swim. Refreshed, she worked until six, ate a dinner that Addie had prepared in advance, and was back at her workbench by seven-fifteen. With a new Mr. Coffee machine and the MAGGIE cup at her elbow, she worked until she felt her eyes cross with weariness. A mile walk on the beach with an apple in one hand and a banana in the other, followed by a quick shower, allowed her to sleep soundly, if not dreamlessly.

Maggie looked around the garage. It had become a nest. A smile tugged at the corners of her mouth. It seemed as if an artist had gone berserk. Colored swatches, sheets of plain white paper with colored streaks and splashes, were clipped with colorful clothes-pins to a length of dental floss tied to nails on the wall. There were more swatches, more sheets of paper, on a pegboard that was at eye level with her workbench. The workbench she'd painted white was now a rainbow of color, spills, streaks, and dots of mind-boggling hues.

Maggie felt anxious, nervous, when she took her place at the table. Today was a test of sorts. The Baby Ben clock she wound each morning stared at her. Next to the clock was an Amalfi shoe box with three jars of paint, a sheaf of fabric, and a stack of white papers. At exactly ten o'clock she had to run to the beach and stare out across the water to try and match the colors she was working on.

There was nothing on paper, no formulae, no idea of

how, if she succeeded, she was going to present her lines to the people in Hong Kong who would eventually make up the material she needed. In her head she was calling one set of colors Pacific Jewels, the second Egyptian Lights.

Her goal, the same as her mother's, was to set the fashion world on fire with her 1993 line of colors. She'd talked with many of her mother's suppliers, who promised to wait until June for it. Not the end of June, the first of June. She had less than five weeks now till the deadline.

Today she was striving for the electric-blue of the Pacific, the color that appeared where the sky merged with the ocean, a color so vibrant, so alive, she'd so far been unable to capture it on fabric or paper. She'd captured the green of the ocean by staring out at the ocean for endless hours, waiting for that one moment when the water changed color right in front of her eyes. Nile Green was the result.

Egyptian Lights now had two perfect colors: Nile Green and Egyptian White. Cleopatra Gold was giving her as much trouble as Pacific Blue, and she knew she was going to have to go back to Sunbridge, to the hill, to study the sun, then somehow combine that color with the hues of the sun here in Hawaii.

Maggie squeezed her eyes shut. It wasn't the manufacturers' and suppliers' timetables that were really bothering her, it was her mother's timetable, and of course her own timetable for success. Subconsciously, she knew she was putting unbearable pressure on herself, but she was unable to ease the mounting tension that was increasing steadily each day.

Today was momentous in more ways than one, Maggie thought as she stared at the Baby Ben. Late this afternoon she was expecting an overnight delivery from Hong Kong of raw silk, chiffon, and pure silk swatches. And she'd promised herself to go through the three Liberty House shopping bags full of first-class mail. Time permitting, she'd also promised to call the family members and Valentine Mitchell. Half of the mail in the Liberty House bags was from Valentine. What she *really* wanted to do was carry the bags down to the beach and set fire to them.

The Baby Ben ticked on, the hands moving so slowly Maggie wanted to scream. She lit a cigarette and fingered the swatch she called Firecracker Red. She wasn't sure what she should do with it, as it didn't fit either end of her color spectrum. Could it stand alone? She doubted it, but the color was so stunningly beautiful, she knew she had to do something with it.

The Baby Ben continued to tick. She smoked, drank coffee, rinsed the pot with the garden hose, made more. She drank more, smoked the last cigarette in the pack, ripped open a new carton.

Both hands on the Baby Ben settled on the ten.

Maggie grabbed the Amalfi shoe box and sprinted down to the beach, where she settled herself with the open jars of paint. She flexed her fingers before she laid out the swatches and papers and said a silent thank you for a windless morning. Her fingers were feverishly poised over the pots of paint, her eyes glued to the marriage of sky and water taking place in front of her eyes. She worked frantically, smearing, blending, dotting, streaking the colors on both paper and material. She had only five minutes until the colors changed.

Maggie's breath exploded in a loud exhalation. Until this moment she hadn't realized she'd been holding her breath. She blinked as a cotton-ball cloud drifted downward toward the marriage taking place. She dabbed again, smeared, blended, stroked. Blueberry. Dresden Blue. Hyacinth. Cerulean. Cornflower and, God Almighty, Pacific Blue!

She had it! But would it look the same when it was dry? By mid-afternoon, when the swatches had dried, she'd know for certain. Wet paint and dry paint were totally different, but she knew, felt, that she'd captured a true marriage of color. When made into dye it would be perfect. The same way you knew, felt, that your husband was unfaithful? an inner voice niggled.

"Yes, damnit," Maggie said hoarsely. "I wasn't wrong then, and I'm not wrong now."

Maggie withdrew a folding aluminum cylinder from the shoe box and stuck it in the sand. With paint-stained fingers she Scotch-taped each swatch, each sheet of paper, to the pole. The shoe box under one arm, the pole in the other, Maggie made her way back to the garage, where she carefully removed each swatch and paper and hung them on the dental-floss line with bright red plastic clothespins. She crossed her fingers and danced a jig before she poured coffee and lit a cigarette. Tomorrow she'd start to work on the actual dye.

Her mind whirled, her eyes ricocheting from one end of the dental-floss line to the other. More than anything in the world, she wished she could call her mother and give her a progress report. Did she dare? Maybe it would perk up her spirits. The worst thing that could happen was there would be no answer or Thad would say her mother was resting. She could explain to Thad that she wasn't calling to whine and fret or . . . chastize her mother for . . . for dying, for God's sake. She'd been whacked in the face so many times lately, one more time wouldn't matter if Thad got defensive. Or offensive.

Maggie looked at the swatches again. Oh God, oh God, they looked ... they looked just right. She reached for the phone. She was stunned when her mother's voice came over the wire, all quivery and shaky, but still her mother's voice. Maggie started to talk, the words rushing from her mouth. Then she was babbling, trying to get everything out at once before her mother said she had to go or Thad came on the line and said "time's up."

"Maggie darling, that sounds wonderful. I love the names you've given to the lines. Tell me again, what does Cleopatra Gold look like?" Billie asked in a thin, reedy voice.

Maggie told her. "Mam, what do you think of a gossamer scarf with either gold or metallic threads? Oversize, of course, or would it be better to bleed the colors? Both? I think I'm going to go back to Texas this week. I've got the Pacific Jewels collection, I'm so sure of it. I wish you could see them."

"No metallic threads. You have to be careful with metallic thread. You've always had a good eye for color, Maggie. I'll tease myself by imagining them, and when you have them completed, we'll see how close I come. I'm so glad you called, darling. How *are* you?"

"I'm okay, Mam," Maggie lied. "Vermont must be beautiful now. I can hardly believe it's the end of April. I love April. Actually, I love all of the months, December is my favorite, though." She was babbling again. "How's Thad?"

"Thad went to town for a haircut, and he said he was going to stop and pick up some cheese. He wants to make a cheese and mushroom omelet for dinner. He's turned into a rather good cook. Of course, I supervise. I think I hear him now. Call again, Maggie."

Maggie stared at the pinging phone in her hand. She felt worse now than before she called. Tears burned her eyes. She rubbed at them, not caring what the cosmetic manufacturers said about thin eye tissue.

What was she doing? What was she trying to prove and to whom was she trying to prove it? Finding no ready answer to her questions, Maggie flip-flopped her way to the kitchen, where she made herself a baloney, cheese, liverwurst, and raw onion sandwich. She munched as she dragged the Liberty House shopping bags out to the lanai.

She separated the mail into four categories. Bills, family, refinery business, and Valentine Mitchell. "Obviously," she muttered, "I am going to have to pay these bills or I won't have water or electricity." Her charge accounts were demanding payment in full. Insurance premiums were past the grace period, and she was being given ten days to come up with the premium or risk losing her valuable coverage. She snorted. God, she was hungry. She marched into the kitchen, trampling over the bills she tossed on the floor, for a box of Fig Newtons. She devoured one entire package as she moved on to the family mail. Pictures of baby Billie made her cry. Pictures of Sawyer's precocious twins made her mouth twitch. She really had to give some thought to whether she should put all the pictures in an album or frame them. It would be something to do on a rainy day.

Someday.

Everyone, according to the notes, was well. The Snoopy card from Susan said Cary was doing as well as could be expected, though he was depressed. Cary's doctor had placed him on a list for a donor transplant.

Maggie cringed at the scrawled P.S. at the bottom of the card. "I haven't heard from Vermont, nor has anyone else to my knowledge. Personally, I don't give a hoot if I don't hear anything until after it's a fact."

Maggie balled her hands into fists. "Susan, you are a first-class, unadulterated snot," she said aloud. "Someone should tie your tits in knots."

Maggie tossed Susan's card and envelope onto the pile of trash.

Eighteen letters addressed to her from the refinery glared up at her. She had nothing to do with the refinery. Chesney would have inherited Rand's half, and Cary owned the other half. She pushed them aside. One of these days she would send them on to Chesney in England.

One of these days.

Maggie puzzled over the thick stack of legal envelopes from Valentine Mitchell. For someone who no longer represented the family, she had sent much too much mail. Tying up loose ends, she supposed. Well, Val's loose ends, whatever they were, didn't have anything to do with her. Maggie ripped at one of the envelopes. She hated the crisp, crackling sound and wondered why all lawyers felt they had to use such stiff paper.

Rand's will. She threw it on top of Susan's card.

The deed to the house. She puzzled over that for a moment before she tossed it onto the pile of trash. She looked at the rest of the legal letters and decided she didn't want to know what messages they contained. Unopened, she pitched them in the general direction of Rand's will and the deed to the house.

Maggie trotted into the house for a trash bag. She smacked her hands together in satisfaction when she dumped it at the end of the driveway. *"Fini,"* she muttered.

The sun was gone, she noticed as she made her way back to the kitchen. Rain would be good, she decided while making a second sandwich, this time with two slices of Bermuda onion. She carried it with her to the dining room, where she wrote out the household checks. When she came to the insurance bills, she stared at them a moment before she ripped them up. "So bury me in a pine box."

Munching on the sandwich, her eyes watering from the onion, she walked out to the mailbox. She moved the red flag to indicate mail was to be picked up.

Her lights and water were secure.

The rest was history.

{{{{{{{{ CHAPTER TWELVE }}}}}}}}

Valentine Mitchell propped her bulging briefcase on top of the newsstand while she rummaged in her purse for money to pay for copies of *The Wall Street Journal* and *Business Week*. She counted her change, then tossed in a pack of Life Savers and a package of peanut butter and cheese crackers. Now she could nibble on her way to Los Angeles. She hated making the trip, but it was something she had to do. Make nice, do a little hand-holding, make promises on behalf of the new owners of her firm, give reassurances that if things didn't work out with the new partners, she would step in.

The last month had been so hectic, she had felt like pulling out her hair on more than one occasion. She'd gone to more parties hosted in her honor than she'd gone to in all the years she'd practiced law. Champagne breakfasts, catered luncheons, cheese and wine parties, cocktail parties, and elaborate dinners, all to honor her contribution to the legal profession.

It was all winding down now. Another day and she would be as free as the proverbial breeze. It hadn't been as easy as she anticipated, because no one was willing to put up the eleven million for the associates to buy her out. Even when she opened her books, the answer had been the same—no. She'd hated to do it, but she cut a deal with Riley and Cole. "You finance the associates' buyout, and I do the deal for Cary's inner city with ColeShad," was the way she'd presented it on a three-way conference call. They'd haggled, but she'd pulled it off and everyone got what they wanted.

Time to check in. She still had twenty minutes before boarding. She headed for the door marked LADIES. While she was washing her hands, she saw her. Maggie eyed her Scaasi suit. She eyed Maggie's Carolyn Roehm raspberry confection. Both women's eyes turned wary.

"Val," Maggie said quietly, by way of greeting, as she reached for a paper towel.

"Maggie," Val said, pushing the button of the hot air blower. She carried her greeting a step further. "I heard you were in town. Why haven't you answered any of my letters?" She asked a second question on top of the first. "Are you going to Los Angeles?"

Maggie adjusted the waistband of her skirt. She played with the collar of the silk blouse beneath the jacket. "Yes, I'm going to L.A. and on to Hawaii. You?"

"L.A. You didn't answer my first question," Val said, blotting her lipstick.

"I know." Maggie turned to walk away.

"We'll talk on the plane. I'm assuming you're taking the same flight I am."

"I have work to do," Maggie called over her shoulder.

"So do I. They serve subpoenas in Hawaii, you know. You can be forced back here. On the other hand, it will be relatively painless if we conduct business on the plane. Forty-five minutes and we're done."

"You can't force me to come back," Maggie said irritably. "Not for something so stupid as a will."

"Maybe I can't, but the IRS can. Inheritance tax and all that good stuff is a come-on for the IRS. Think about it. I have a bulkhead seat, so I can spread out. I just have to check in. Midsection," Val said, walking off.

Rand had been paranoid about the IRS. So was she. Never mess with them, Rand always told her. "Okay," Maggie said. People turned to look at her, but Val didn't turn around.

Maggie walked toward the gate where boarding was in progress.

When the pilot announced they were cruising at thirty thousand feet, Maggie unbuckled her seat belt and walked forward to the bulkhead seat where Val was sitting, her briefcase open in her lap. Maggie took the seat next to her.

"Plane's almost empty," Val said.

"I guess people don't like early morning flights. I prefer them myself," Maggie said.

"I do too. I hate to waste time. I'm taking the red-eye back tonight."

"That's a long day," Maggie said indifferently.

"If you'd read the mail I sent you, you'd know I'm trying to wind down all your family's business before I leave. I sold the firm to my associates. It's definite now. All I have to do is sign on the dotted line. Retirement sounds ominous now. It didn't when I made the decision."

"Why are you doing it, then?" Maggie asked coolly.

"I'm fifty-four. I've never had a life outside law. It's time. I'll find a house somewhere in a small town, grow some flowers, get a cat, go to pot-luck suppers, join the Grange, and learn to knit and cook. Not necessarily in that order."

"It sounds deadly." Maggie grimaced.

"Doesn't it, though? I might do some *pro bono* work. I'll decide that as I go along."

"You're a good lawyer, Val. It will be a shame to let all that go. *Pro bono* is good, but I rather thought you liked to sink your teeth into *really* big cases and walk off a winner."

"Are we communicating here?" Val smiled.

"We could really communicate if you'd tell me the truth," Maggie said coldly.

"I did tell you the truth." Their eyes met. Val was stunned to see the *nothingness* in Maggie's gaze. She was more certain than ever that she'd done the right thing by lying to the woman sitting next to her.

"Why don't I just sign a power of attorney for you in regard to Rand's estate? That will make it easy, won't it?"

"Easier than it's been. Thad and Billie were executors. They both signed over a power of attorney. Judge Freize okayed it. I did all the preliminary work, but I'll turn it all over to the firm. They'll be in touch with you. Can you deal with that, Maggie?"

Maggie nodded. She pulled up the arm tray and straightened it out, then signed her name on the form Val handed her without bothering to read what it said. After she had handed over the paper, she got up. "Good-bye, Val. I hope you enjoy your retirement."

"Maggie, wait. What are you going to do?"

She sounds, Maggie thought, as if she cares. "Take it one day at a time. I'm working on Billie Limited. I manage to use up my time. And I still don't believe you," she said with a catch in her voice.

"I know you don't. I'm sorry about that," Val said earnestly.

Maggie walked back to her seat. The seats next to hers were empty. She tucked the gored raspberry skirt tightly around her legs. She was asleep in minutes.

In the bulkhead section, Val replaced the tray table Maggie had been writing on. She moved the armrest and slid across to stare out the window at the carpet of marshmallow clouds below the plane. They look like *warm fuzzies*, she thought, something you could hug to yourself to garner comfort. All their lives the Colemans had warm fuzzies to comfort them. All *she'd* had was textbooks, a law library, briefs, trials, appeals, and lots of money in the bank. Not a warm fuzzy in the bunch. But it was by my own choice, Val thought.

What was going to happen to Maggie? What would happen to the Colemans when Billie was gone? Riley, Cole, and Sawyer would be all right. They had families, children, spouses. And they had all that *money*. Susan was as wired as a tomcat on diet pills. A wild card. There was no telling what Susan would do. Cary, according to their last conversation, was going to take it one day at a time, the way Maggie said she was doing. She'd felt sad when Cary said the memorial to Amelia was in a holding pattern. There would be no completion date and no ceremony in July the way he'd planned. Thad would crawl into a shell, and if she was any judge of love and devotion, he'd be gone inside of a year. Childishly, Val crossed her fingers and wished the best for Thad.

Val rummaged in her briefcase for the peanut butter and cheese crackers. She noticed her hands trembling when she ripped at the cellophane wrapper. Ivy. Steady on her feet Ivy. Rock solid Ivy. She understood perfectly why Billie had entrusted her living will to the young woman. She cringed, remembering how sick Billie looked on the video and how hard she'd tried to cover up her emaciated appearance. Hot tears pricked at Val's eyelids.

Now all the Colemans would have to stare at their own mortality. When Billie was gone, there would be no more buffer shielding them from the inevitable.

Below, the carpet of marshmallows parted, then moved together to form a giant cotton ball. Her eyelids pricked again.

Not for all the money in the world would she want to walk in Ivy Coleman's shoes. She wished now she hadn't given Ivy the advice she had, which was in direct opposition to Billie's wishes. She was clearheaded, impartial, and could see down the road to what was going to happen, which was why she'd told Ivy to tell Riley *now*. She'd also insisted Ivy turn the tape over to her for safekeeping. To her knowledge, Ivy hadn't followed her advice, for if she had, Riley would have demanded to see the tape.

Val finished the crackers, wished for more. She looked up to see the stewardess handing out salted peanuts. "Two," Val said. "And a glass of tomato juice, if you don't mind."

Val ripped at the vacuum-sealed bag. They certainly didn't give you many peanuts. It was a good thing she'd asked for two bags. If there was one thing she hated, it was to get her taste buds going and then be cut off just as she was starting to enjoy something. She wondered if there was such a thing as cholesterol-free, fat-free peanuts.

Why did she care what happened to the Colemans? They were clients. You represented your clients, you got paid, and that was supposed to be the end of it. Not so with the Colemans. Somewhere along the way she'd become attached to them, allowed the family to sneak into her heart, where they carved their own little niche, and now she was ... not stuck with them, that was unkind. No, it was more like she felt responsible for them. Even though she'd severed her relationship and returned the balance of their retainer, she hadn't been able to turn them away.

How was she supposed to walk away, go to Oxmoor and start her new life, with that family standing in the shadows?

There was really no *pending* business with the Colemans. Ivy's *problem* had been presented on a friend-to-friend basis. Was Ivy going to need an ally, someone in her corner? She supposed she could give Ivy her new address and swear her to secrecy. "This whole thing is just *shitful*," Val muttered. She'd broken the first rule of any good lawyer—she'd allowed herself to get involved. She ripped at the roll of tropical fruit Life Savers, separating the ones she didn't like from the ones she did. Coconut and lemon were wadded into a napkin. The tangerine and melon went into her mouth.

What was Maggie doing? What was she thinking? *What was she feeling?*

Life goes on. Val bit down on the candies in her mouth. She ground them between her teeth. Now what would she eat? "Miss," she called to the stewardess, her voice fierce, "do you have any more peanuts?"

Val followed the hordes of people heading for the baggage area, her eyes searching for the Carolyn Roehm suit. She half turned before she stepped onto the moving stair, but she didn't see what she was looking for. She shrugged. She and Maggie Nelson would never be friends, so why was she persisting in worrying about

her? Because, she answered herself, Maggie looked so
fragile, so vulnerable. What she *should* be doing, Val
told herself, was thinking about her upcoming meeting
and the whopping bill she was going to present for services rendered.

Time permitting, she might take a stroll down Rodeo
Drive to pick up gifts for the office staff. She'd meant
to do it earlier, but she hadn't gotten around to it.

Val stepped off the moving stair. There was still no
sign of Maggie. She could check out the United gates
for Hawaii, if she cared to, but she decided she didn't
care to. She kept on walking, her eyes alert for a limo
driver holding up a placard bearing her name. The moment she saw it, Val switched into her legal mode and
forgot everything but the business at hand.

LAX had to be one of the busiest airports in the
world, Val thought as she looked around at the weary
travelers, some lugging oversize suitcases, others carrying crying infants and children. Everyone looked tired.
She was tired too, but in a different kind of way. She
looked at the plates of deep fried onion rings, deep fried
cheese sticks, deep fried beer-batter shrimp. The odds of
her not dripping grease on the Scaasi suit had to be one
in a million, she thought irritably. She looked at the
greenery on the plates, wondering if it was scallion tips
or green weeds. She pushed the plates away and concentrated on her second glass of white wine.

The table next to hers was suddenly filled by a young
woman and three youngsters, the oldest no more than
six. She blinked when she saw a baby peeking over the
canvas sack attached to the young mother's shoulders.
The young woman looked so tired, Val's heart ached for
her.

The woman was pretty, with a wealth of red-gold hair trailing down her shoulders. The infant in the shoulder harness yanked at the hair, snapping the woman's head backward. Her voice was gentle, patient when she admonished the child. At the table the three children whispered among themselves. "Hamburgers, french fries, ice cream, Cokes."

"I told you," the woman whispered, "you can split some french fries. We only came in here to heat the baby's milk. If I don't have the money, I can't pay for it. Do you understand?"

Val watched from the corner of her eye as the children nodded solemnly.

Val waved down the waitress and asked for her check. She followed her to the cash register and said, "See that family over there? I want to pay for their order." She handed a fifty dollar bill to the waitress. "The change goes to the woman, okay?"

"Sure," the tired waitress said.

Val walked over to the newsstand, where she browsed through a copy of *Time*. She watched as the young mother shook her head, her eyes swiveling around the restaurant. Finally, she nodded. Val grinned from ear to ear when the children clapped their hands in glee. Val paid for a Tom Clancy novel, two packages of peanut butter and cheese crackers, two mint patties, three peanut butter cups, and two packages of tropical fruit Life Savers. She headed for the gate to wait for the boarding call, thinking about the check in her purse and how happy her accountant was going to be when she told him to put it into her retirement account.

Her future was secure and looking better with each passing day. Tomorrow would be her first day of unemployment in so many years ... she grew light-headed just thinking about it.

At noon the following day, Val snapped her briefcase shut, took a last look around the office that was no longer hers, and headed for the door. She knew the minute she opened it the staff was going to yell "Surprise!" At which point she would yell, "Surprise yourself!" and hand out the gifts that had arrived by Federal Express two hours earlier.

"Fog lights!" she squealed moments later. "Monogrammed floor mats! A down sleeping bag! Mud flaps! Don't tell me this is a tent!" Val shrieked with laughter.

The oldest member of the firm spoke. "You said you were going to get into a Range Rover and just drive until you came to a place that suits you. As we speak, the maintenance people are installing a brush guard on your vehicle. In case you run into a cow or something at a crossing."

Tears rolled down Val's cheeks. "I don't know what to say."

"My mother always told me if you don't know what to say, don't say anything. Just smile. Like *you're* smiling," Val's secretary said, hugging her. "Thanks for the Gucci watch," she whispered. "And the bonus."

"I'm really going to miss all of you," Val said in a choked voice.

"Hey, we have an eight hundred number, call us anytime," someone shouted.

"Don't think I won't either," Val shot back.

"We have one last present for you, Val," the seniormost man in the office said. "We talked about this and we all agreed we would worry ourselves sick with you driving wherever it is you're going alone, so we ...

ah, we decided to . . . hell, open the door," he said to one of the secretaries standing next to the kitchen.

Val's jaw dropped. More tears rolled down her cheeks.

"This is Samantha. She answers to Sam. Note the Gucci collar and the Gucci lead."

"Ohhhh," Val said, dropping to her knees to cradle the golden retriever's head. More tears rolled down her cheeks. "I don't know what to say."

"Whoof."

"Sounds good to me." Val grinned. "Is she housebroken?" She was remembering Isaac's contribution to her decor months before.

"Completely," the senior man said. "She was on a list to go to the Seeing Eye Farm, though at the bottom of the list, I admit. The owner seemed to think she was too playful, and he didn't want to take a chance. She's yours, Val."

"Okay. Listen, I'll be in touch. I'll call in. I'll be back from time to time. When I finally light in one place, I'll let you know. Thanks for everything."

In the parking lot, out of sight of her office staff, Val unhooked the leash from the dog's collar. All of a sudden she felt like the kid she never had a chance to be. She kicked one spike-heeled shoe in the air and then the other. She ran, feinting to the right and then to the left. Sam chased her, her tail wagging furiously. In and out among the cars they ran, spooking one another. Exhausted with her efforts, Val backed up against her new brush guard, her chest heaving. Sam stood on her hind legs, her front paws on Val's shoulders. She growled softly, her eyes wet and adoring.

"God, I just love you," Val said, rubbing her face against the dog's silky head. "Come on, let's get this show on the road. You can either have the front passenger seat or all of the back." She opened the door to let the dog leap in. Sam settled herself comfortably on the passenger seat. Val wiggled her butt on the seat before she swung her legs inside. Designer, skintight skirts were not conducive to four-wheel drives, she decided. She'd remedy that as soon as she drove to her condo to pick up her bags. Her jeans, endangered species sweatshirt, and L.A. Gear sneakers were all laid out, just waiting for her to arrive home.

Val backed the Range Rover from her parking space. She looked at her name on the metal marker and saluted smartly before she swung the four-by-four about. She drove carefully, mindful of the dog on the seat.

"We," Val said, "have one stop to make before we head for the open road. Not to worry, it's in my building. We can do our visiting while my bags are being loaded into the car. There's somebody I want you to meet." The dog looked at her expectantly. "Okay, two stops. Food for you. God, I hope you aren't going to need all that stuff Isaac needs. He's a sissy. He even has a toothbrush. I draw the line at that." She grinned and almost swerved off the road when one silky, shaggy paw stretched out to touch her arm. "I guess that means you like me," she chortled happily as she tooled down the road. She felt like singing, but she didn't know the words to any songs. Instead she switched on the radio, fumbling with the buttons. Lionel Ritchie's voice exploded into the confines of the truck. Val switched stations until she heard Carly Simon's voice. She turned down the volume and hummed along.

When they arrived at Assante Towers, Sam leaped out of the truck, as if she knew they were home. Home for another thirty minutes.

In the apartment, Val called down to the security station to ask for help in getting her bags to the car. She watched as Sam checked out her new surroundings, stopping twice at the dining room table leg Isaac had christened. Val looked at her watch. In thirty minutes, noon actually, the electricity and phone would be turned off. One week from today the new owner was moving in, a dentist who had his offices on the fifteenth floor. She hoped he would be happier here than she had been.

"I'm happy now," Val chortled as she punched out a new set of numbers. She was glad when Cary Assante answered the phone. "I'm coming up to say good-bye, and I'm bringing a friend, is that okay?"

"Sure," Cary said.

"Okay, see you in a bit."

Sam was at the door before the doorbell rang. She backed up, her tail between her legs, as she waited for Val to open the door. She gave one sharp warning bark before she growled softly. Val pointed to her four oversize French bags and the three boxes of personal papers and the few files she was taking with her. She handed the porter a ten dollar bill before she closed the door.

"We'll get some cheeseburgers when we hit the road," she said to the dog. She bent over to tie the laces in her sneakers. "I hate shoes," she said to the dog. "Come on, I want you to meet a friend of mine. Well, he's sort of a friend. Closest thing to a friend. I think so anyway," she muttered.

"Come in," Cary called. "Door's open. I'm on the terrace."

Val looked around. Nothing had been changed since Amelia's death. She just knew all of Amelia's clothes were still in the closets, her things still on the dresser, her robe still on the hook on the bathroom door. Cary was not a man to change.

Val bent over to kiss Cary's cheek. "This is Sam. My office staff gave her to me at my going-away party. She's a golden retriever." Val smiled when Sam plopped one of her paws on Cary's leg.

"He feels silky. Is his coat shiny?"

"She. Yep, you can almost see your reflection in her back. I never had a dog. I love her. How's it going, Cary?"

"It isn't. I pretty much hang out here on the terrace. I listen to the television; Susan reads to me. I have stacks of books on cassettes, though I never was much of a reader. I go to the doctor's twice a week. I'm on a donor list. Friends call. I've put the memorial on hold. My heart isn't into much of anything these days."

"It hasn't been all that long," Val said softly.

"Depends on who's doing the counting. This is July. The memorial was supposed to be finished by now."

"It's just a temporary setback, Cary. Is there anything I can do before I leave?"

"Like what?"

"Like I don't know. That's why I'm asking."

"I am a little worried about the payments on the mortgage," Cary said quietly.

"Well, don't be. I structured it with your condition in mind. Some people owed me some favors, and I called them in. You don't have a thing to worry about. By the time the first payment comes due, the plane will be ready for testing. Sawyer tells me it's going full-speed, and, to quote her, 'is lookin' good.' Don't frown, Cary. The year's interest is tacked on to the last balloon payment at the end. There really is no problem here. Trust me."

"If it was anyone but you, Val, I'd be chewing my toenails worrying if I bit off more than was wise. Tell me, what's your game plan?"

Val sighed. "I'm just going to drive. West. When I see something that pleases me, I'll stop, stay awhile and see if it's what I want. I'll let you know where I end up. I have all the files and records in the car. I plan to keep my eyes and ears on things."

"Have you heard anything about Billie or Maggie?"

"Not really. I saw Maggie on a flight out to L.A. yesterday, but I haven't heard a thing about Billie. I would think Susan would know. Doesn't she?"

"No," Cary said curtly. "She's refusing to deal with it. She's blaming her mother for dying. I don't know how to deal with *that*. She's starting to smother me, Val, and I don't know what to do about that either. I like Susan, I really do. Part of me wants her to leave and part of me—the part of me that's afraid to be alone—wants her to stay. Can you understand that?"

"Of course. Why don't you have a talk with her?"

"She's in a very shaky emotional state, but then so am I. I don't want her to get ... I'm afraid she's becoming too attached to me. How do you tell someone something like that?"

"Very carefully, I would think. Do you want me to talk to her before I leave? By the way, where is she?"

"She went to get her hair and nails done. What time is it?"

"Almost noon."

"She should be back by now. She may have stopped by the market. She likes to cook. She says I need to eat more. I probably would eat more if someone wasn't watching me slop my food all over myself. Jesus, Val, I don't know what to do."

"You didn't answer my question. Do you want me to talk to her? Believe it or not, I can be subtle. It will be up to you to follow through, though. Can you handle that?"

"No. Look, don't worry about me. I've pretty much come to terms with it all. I've been through the denial, the grief, the anger. I'm trying real hard to get to the acceptance part. I'm not ready to sell pencils yet. I'm not ready for anything."

"Life goes on, Cary. I've heard that term so many times lately, I feel it was created just for me. I don't think Amelia would approve of what you're doing. She'd tell you to get the lead out and put some grease on your sneakers. This is just my personal opinion, and I probably have no right even to voice it, but we've been friends for a long time. Stop wallowing. Boot Susan out of here and take responsibility for yourself. That's the end of my lecture. I don't *have* to leave today. I can stick around and set some things in motion for you."

"What kind of things?"

Val smiled at the curiosity in Cary's voice. Until now it had been resigned and pitiful.

"Things like Sam here. Man's best friend. I was told she was supposed to go into a Seeing Eye program, but the people that train the dogs said they felt Sam was too playful, and they didn't think she would outgrow her playfulness. With a Seeing Eye dog, you could get out and about on your own. There's a foundation in Austin that has trained people who will come here and mark off your stove, teach you to cook, and show you how to arrange your cabinets. And then, of course, there's Braille."

"That pretty much makes this a . . . hopeless condition. If I do that . . . it means I've given up." He started to shake, his body trembling uncontrollably. Sam whined deep in her throat as she pawed Cary's legs, trying to get to his face so she could lick at it.

"It doesn't mean any such thing, Cary," Val said gently. "It's *something* for you to do now. Something to get you through until things are more in your favor. You can't just vegetate. It's been five months."

He was calmer now. Sam nuzzled his hand to get her ears scratched. Cary obliged. "I'll think about it. I'll have to . . . psych myself up. I'm scared, Val. Piss-ass scared. I feel so helpless, and I'm so goddamn angry. Christ, I'm still trying to come to terms with Rand's death and . . . Billie. It's all closing in on me. If I don't stick my neck out and just sit here, nothing else can happen. I'll . . . I promise to think about everything you said. And, no, I don't want you to hang around. Get on with your life. Check in with me, let me know how you're doing."

Val bent over to hug him. "Thank you, Cary, for not asking."

"I've known you for a long time, Val, and it didn't compute. I've never been judgmental. I think you know that."

"Yes, yes, I know that. I think this might be a good time for me to take my friend here and leave before I start sobbing all over your carpet. Take care of yourself, Cary, and I'll be in touch. Say good-bye, Sam." The retriever woofed happily.

"Be happy, Val," Cary said huskily.

"You too."

Sam suddenly barreled to the front door, her huge paws slapping at the painted wood.

"Susan must be home," Cary said sourly.

Val's eyebrows shot upward. She called the dog, who immediately came to sit at her feet.

"I've always heard dogs are better judges of people than people themselves. Let's see what Sam thinks of Susan," Cary said sotto voce.

"I'm home," Susan trilled, closing the door behind her with her rump. She stopped in mid-stride when she saw Val and Sam. She set the grocery bag she'd been carrying on the end table. "What have we here?" She motioned to the dog, who was growling deep in her throat.

"Susan, this is Samantha, Sam for short. My new roommate. I came up to say good-bye. As a matter of fact I was just leaving. You look well, Susan," Val said with a bite in her voice.

"That's because I am well. I don't think I've ever been *more well* in my life." Her eyes slid from Cary to Val and back to Cary.

"For heaven's sake, I almost didn't recognize you in that *getup*." Susan looked down at her own pricey outfit, clearly a Billie original. "Are those *sneakers* I see on your feet?" She made the word sound obscene.

Val smirked. "I own stock in L.A. Gear. I'm wearing Jockey underwear. The jeans are Levi's, the shirt is Greenpeace. As you can see, Sam's collar and leash are Gucci. It's a question of priorities."

Cary chuckled and then guffawed. Sam ran to him, barking happily at the strange sound of his laughter. He tussled with the big dog, laughing as he did so. Val thought it a wonderful sound. Not so Susan.

"I don't like dogs. They breed germs, they shed, and they make messes, plus you have to walk them and feed them. They slobber all over the place."

"That's too bad, Susan, because I'm getting one,"

Cary said. "Val said she'd take care of it for me. I expect they'll deliver. . . . Do they deliver dogs, Val?"

"You bet. I'll take care of those other things we discussed too if you want."

"I do," Cary said.

"What other things?" Susan asked suspiciously. *"What other things?"*

"A live-in housekeeper, a male companion to help Cary over the rough spots until the foundation can set things up for him. And, of course, the dog."

"Cary doesn't need any of those things. I'm here. I cook for him, I take care of him. Everything is working out just fine. Cary, tell her you don't want or need other people. That's why I'm here, why I stayed on. Caryyyyy, tell her," Susan whined.

"Val's right, Susan. I have to start getting on with things," Cary said firmly. "I'm going to ... to learn Braille. I'm going to get out on my own. I'm going to learn to take care of myself."

"They're not going to care about you the way I do. They'll take advantage of you. You're *handicapped*, for heaven's sake," Susan said shakily.

"I don't like that word, Susan," Cary shouted.

Sam barked sharply, her ears flattening against her silky head. She continued to bark.

"Guess that answers our question," Cary said. "It was nice of you to stop by, Val. Stay in touch. I'm going to take a shower and go for a walk. See you around, lady," he said smoothly, ruffling Sam's sleek back.

"Wait a minute, I'll get you a towel and soap," Susan said. "We aren't scheduled for a walk until after dinner. Cary, you can't upset our routine like this."

"I know where the goddamn towels and soap are. I can open and close the shower door myself, and I want to go for a walk now," Cary said, feeling his way into the room.

"I'll lay out your clothes," Susan bleated.

"I can do that myself," Cary snorted.

"But they won't match," Susan whined.

"Who cares? When those people from the foundation come, they'll show me how to arrange my clothes so I do match. I read about that once. So long, Val. I keep saying that, don't I?"

Sam ran over to Cary, a whirlwind of motion, and nuzzled his leg. *"I love Paris in the spring,"* Cary bellowed. "That was Amelia's favorite song," he called over his shoulder.

"What are you trying to do?" Susan snarled at Val. "What *did* you do? You've spoiled everything. You ruined Maggie's life and now you want to ruin mine. You're jealous. You've always been jealous. I know all about Rand and Maggie. If it wasn't for you, Rand would still be alive."

"All you do, Susan, is breathe air other people need to live. It's not what I did, it's what you did. You took Cary's life and made it yours. You can't function on your own. You need to be an extension of someone else. You've been feeding off Cary. You need to grow up, Susan. I won't even bother to dignify your last statement."

"Bitch!" Susan seethed.

Sam tensed and growled, her teeth showing. Val never felt more protected in her life. From deep within the apartment she could hear the sounds of the shower. Val jerked her hand in the direction of the hallway. "Guess Cary was right. He can take a shower by himself. Bet he even found the soap and towel."

"Eat shit, Val," Susan spat.

Val laughed as she made her way out to the elevator. "I can't believe she said that. Miss Holier-Than-Thou. It just goes to prove, Sam, first instincts are usually right. I had Susan pegged from the first. It looks like we have more work to do," she said, fondling the dog's ears. "If the phone company is on schedule and the phone's been turned off, we'll have to fall back and regroup."

Back in her apartment, Val headed for the phone, praying for a dial tone. Dead. "Nuts," she muttered. "Okay, we'll go to the garage and call Ivy. Come on, girl, we're splitting this place."

She didn't look back and felt no regrets when she locked the door behind her. This part of her life was history now.

In the garage, Val settled Sam in the car and rolled down the window. "Stay," she said, her voice ringing with authority. Sam stayed. "Cheeseburgers within the hour," she promised.

Ivy answered the phone on the second ring. Val explained her visit to Cary's apartment and her encounter with Susan.

"You didn't!" Ivy squealed.

"I did. My phone's off, so will you make good on the promises I made to Cary? I'd really appreciate it."

"What are friends for? I'll get right on it. And Val, take care of yourself and call me once in a while, okay?"

"Of course. Right now I have to pick up some cheeseburgers. 'Bye, Ivy."

" 'Bye, Val."

"We're free as the breeze," Val said, climbing into the Range Rover. She studied the map and the route she'd marked with a felt-tipped pen. When she had it firmly in her mind, she started the engine, slid a Carly

Simon tape into the tape deck, ruffled the dog's ears, and drove down the ramp of the garage to the outside world.

"Six cheeseburgers coming up, complete with pickles, ketchup, and mustard. Helloooo world!"

Susan sat with her head in her hands, tears streaming down her cheeks. Damn Valentine Mitchell, damn her to hell, she thought. Always sticking her nose into my business. Cary was hers. She'd devoted so much time to him, done everything for him, anticipated his every need, put him ahead of herself. A sob escaped from her throat.

She saw him out of the corner of her eye, a brilliant cherry-red towel wrapped around his middle. She tried to square her shoulders, tried to gather her dignity, but it seemed a hopeless task. Then she remembered Cary couldn't see her. She stood, her knees wobbly.

"Guess I screwed up again," she said pitifully. "I just wanted to help."

"I know. I'm not blameless here," Cary said from the doorway. "It was easy for me to let you do everything. The plain truth is that I acted and you reacted, or vice versa. I appreciated everything you did, but Val is right and we both know it. I need to do for myself. Can we leave it that if I need you, I'll call you?"

Susan gulped. "Story of my life, Cary. Sure. Well, guess I'll be going. The groceries are on the table. Do you think you can put them away, or do you want me to do it?"

"Hey, I'll just dump them on the counter and work from there. If you brought cold cuts, I'll be fine. I've been making baloney sandwiches for years now. I can wash a piece of celery as good as the next guy. Apples are good. Cheese is okay. Finger foods. Don't worry about me, Susan. And I don't want to have to worry about you."

"Can I still call you?" Susan whimpered.

"Hell yes. Are you giving up Billie Limited? Maggie could probably use some sisterly intervention about now."

"Is that another way of saying hit the road?"

"It means whatever you want it to mean," Cary said quietly. "You need direction, Susan, and I'm not the right person for that. I have so many problems and hang-ups of my own, I can't give sound advice. Think about a therapist or a ... someone who can be impartial."

His voice was so kind, Susan started to cry all over again. "What you're saying without saying it is that you think I need a shrink, that I'm not stable."

Cary, holding on to the walls, made his way into the kitchen, where he fumbled around in the utility closet till he found the broom. Using it as a cane, he swept his way back to the living room and advanced to where Susan was sitting. "What I'm saying, Susan, is you need to talk to someone other than me. I've been a sounding board, nothing more."

"I was falling in love with you, Cary."

Cary shook his head. "No, you were feeling sorry for me, just the way you feel sorry for yourself. You saw in me an extension of yourself. We'd exist, flounder around, and be miserable. Amelia was and still is the only woman I'll ever love."

"You betrayed her, you had an affair with Thad's niece Julie. Don't stand there and tell me she's the only woman in the world for you!" Susan snarled.

"That was a low blow, Susan, but I guess I deserve

it. But knowing Amelia forgave me makes it a tad easier to live with.

"I've been wallowing, and Amelia *wouldn't* like that. She would approve of every single one of Val's suggestions. Amelia liked Val, just as I do. Val's real. She doesn't make excuses. And there isn't a mean bone in her body. You owe her a lot, Susan."

"She was paid," Susan said bitterly.

"There are some things money can't buy. Just look what she did for me in the space of fifteen minutes. Jesus, I feel alive, all charged up. I can't wait to get dressed and mess around in the kitchen. So what if I look like a nightmare, so what if I live in squalor until I get it down to a science? So what, Susan?"

When Susan let herself out the door, she could hear Cary singing "Pretty Woman" at the top of his lungs. She slammed the door so hard that one of the brass plaques fell to the floor. "So hang the damn thing up yourself. See if you can find the nail and the hammer. See if I care."

In the Coleman condo, Susan looked around. No one lived here. It was for visiting guests or for family to stay over when they didn't want to make the trek home. Spartan, hotel-suite decor. Susan flopped down on a long sofa that was covered in a scratchy nubby material the color of sand. The whole apartment was done in bland earth tones. It was depressing. She got up, jerked at the draperies to blot out the sun. She turned on the television, then turned it off. Tea. She looked at the box. Celestial Seasonings. It sounded, she thought, like something that would give you an orgasm. She pitched it in the general direction of the sink and was rewarded with fine bits of herbal tea showering all over the kitchen.

She was homeless. Literally homeless. Unless she wanted to go back to Minnesota and live in the house she'd once shared with Ferris. She could take it off the market. Or go to England. She hated England and its dreary weather. Homeless. At forty-eight.

In a fit of rage she grappled for the phone on the table next to the nubby couch. She dropped it twice before she managed to punch out her mother's telephone number. When Thad's voice came over the wire, Susan said, "I want to talk to my mother and I want to talk to her now. If you don't put her on the phone, I'm taking the next plane to Vermont. If you take her away, I swear to God I'll track you down. Now, get her!"

Thad's stinging voice hummed over the wire. "I will not allow you to upset your mother. Tell me what the problem is, and I'll decide if Billie is up to taking your call."

"You'll decide!" Susan screeched. "God is going to strike you dead for what you're doing. I told you I need to talk to her. This is all her fault. Everytime I need her, she's never around or she's too damn busy. She's so damn busy dying, she can't talk to me, is that it?" Susan heard the click. She stared at the phone in her hand. "You son of a bitch!" she dialed again and got a busy signal. "You bastard, you took the phone off the hook!"

Her rage was uncontrollable. She stomped about the apartment looking for a weapon of sorts, and found a cast-iron meat mallet in the kitchen drawer. She smashed everything in sight, all the mirrored walls, the sliding glass drawers, the porcelain sink in the bathroom, the tile on the wall. In the kitchen, she banged and pounded at the appliances until they were dented to her satisfaction. From the same drawer where she got the mallet, she picked up a huge carving knife. She ripped and gouged, sending fiberfill in all directions. Exhausted with the destruction she had caused, she slumped to the floor, but not before she threw a china vase at the television screen.

Almost at once she felt appalled at what she'd done. God, who was going to pay for this? She must be going crazy. At forty-eight, she was homeless *and* crazy. Ferris had said, among other things, that when you think you're crazy, you aren't. It was when you denied having problems that you did indeed have a problem. She wouldn't believe anything Ferris said if his tongue were notarized.

The sound of the phone ringing was louder than an explosion. Susan stared at it with glazed eyes. It was probably a wrong number, but at least it would be a human voice. She picked up the phone, her voice scratchy and gruff. "Hello."

She had to strain to hear the whispery words on the other end of the line. "Mam? Mam, is that you? Mam, I'm sorry for yelling at Thad. Mam, I need you. God, I'm homeless and I think I'm crazy. Do you think I'm crazy?" She rattled on, her voice shrill at times, dropping to a whisper and then turning shrill again. "I tried to help him, to be there for him. He said I need a goddamn shrink, so that's two people who think I'm crazy. Him and me." She finally wound down, her voice a whimper.

"Darling, you aren't crazy, but I do think you could do with some professional counseling. You need friends, Susan."

"I haven't had time to make friends, Mam."

"You have the time now, darling. There are so many

wonderful support groups out there. You need to get involved in things, to start a new life, and you can't do that
through someone else. I think, and I may be wrong, but
I think you tried to take Amelia's place with Cary. No
one, and we both know this, can ever do that. Things are
mixed up in your mind with regard to Amelia and myself, and that's why I think you need to go for counseling. I did not abandon you, Susan. I tried to do what was
best for you. If I was wrong, I'm sorry. Parents don't
always . . . We make mistakes too."

"I've disappointed you, haven't I? I'm sorry, Mam.
Tell me what to do, where to go. I can't seem to make
a decision."

On the other end of the phone she could hear Thad
saying, "One more minute, Billie, and then I'm cutting
off the phone." And then her mother's weak, gentle
voice. "Shush, Thad, my daughter needs to talk to me.
I'll rest when I hang up."

"Mam, it's okay. Thad's right. I'm just being selfish.
I'm sorry I bothered you."

"Darling, you aren't bothering me. I want to help, but
you have to be open and want to help yourself. What
can I do for you, Susan?"

"Just tell me what to do."

"If I do that, will you take my advice?"

"God yes. Do you think I like being like this?"

"Good, that's the first step. Do you have paper and
pen?"

"Yes, yes, right here by the phone. Mam, I destroyed
this apartment. I wrecked it with the meat mallet and
carving knife."

"Then you're going to have to pay to repair everything. If you did it, it's your responsibility. Now, write
this down."

Susan scribbled as her mother's weak, wan voice trailed off. "But that's what you said earlier," Susan complained.

"Yes, Susan, but now you have it in black and white. You can see it. Think of it as a road map to your . . . recovery. Will you promise me to act on it?"

"I'll do my best." As an afterthought she said, "How are you, Mam?"

"I'm not going to run the mile when we've hung up, but Thad is taking wonderful care of me. I'm comfortable."

"All right. Good-bye, Mam. Oh, Mam, will you tell me you love me?"

"My dearest Susan, of course I love you. I loved you the minute I saw you. I will love you into eternity."

Billie was crying. Susan realized she had made her mother cry. She wanted to say I love you too, but the words wouldn't slide past her tongue. She replaced the phone in the cradle. "Yeah, sure you love me. I had to ask you to say the words." She cried bitter, scalding tears.

Forty-eight. Homeless. Crazy. Unloved.

The lazy July sun cast its last shimmering light across the Pacific waters. The lanai was cloaked in its mystical glow. The air was redolent with the scent of plumeria. Scattered about were wet beach towels, chattering children, sand pails, shovels, vibrant, vinyl beach toys, and a set of parents ready to pull out their hair.

"You're sure you want to do this?" Sawyer demanded of her mother.

"Of course I'm sure. I think I'm capable of handling the twins. All you need is discipline. I can manage. You and Adam can go off to Japan without worrying. I know how to be a grandmother. I've been reading up on the matter. Like Adam says, all-day suckers and cookies mixed with discipline will do it. I'll teach them how to swim, and we'll build sand castles and all that good stuff."

"What about Billie Limited?" Sawyer asked anxiously.

"Hey, I'm Billie Limited, and I can take time off. Things are running smoothly since I decided on going American. I saw the labels two days ago. They gave me goose bumps. Made in the U.S.A. Next year's colors are in the running. Later, when the children are in bed, I'll show you the scarf. God, it's gorgeous. My first article, my first color. I can't wait to send it to Mam. Have you heard anything, Sawyer?"

"I called this morning before we left, but the machine was on. I left a message. At least you got to speak to her a few months back. Lord, I cannot believe it's the middle of July. Where is the time going?" Sawyer moaned.

"Don't think of time in the past, think of it as now, as in whose turn it is to give these children a bath," Adam grumbled.

"It's yours and you know it," Sawyer said sourly. "I gave them one this morning at home and this afternoon after they fell asleep on the beach. I washed their hair too. They're half asleep, so they won't fight you and drown. Please, Adam, I'm too tired to move."

When father and daughters were gone, Sawyer bustled about the lanai, popping cans of iced tea and setting out crackers and cheese. "So, tell me what's going on."

Maggie laughed with genuine mirth. "Absolutely nothing. You know I went back to Texas for a while. We spoke about that. Ivy called a few weeks ago to bring me up to date on Cary. She said he has a magnificent dog, which he absolutely adores. He's getting out and about on his own. He's got this nice older gentleman who works on a voluntary basis for the foundation. A part-time companion of sorts. He's doing just great. He told Ivy he owes it all to Val."

"What about Susan?"

"I haven't heard from her. Ivy said she's staying in the family condo, and when Cary can fit her into his schedule, she visits. Ivy said she thinks Suse will go back to England. It wouldn't surprise me. She's never called me, not once."

"And you, Maggie, how are you?" Sawyer asked softly.

"I'm here. It hasn't been easy. I have bad days and I have good days. Today is a good day. I'm so glad you decided to stop here and leave the girls with me. I hardly know them. It shouldn't be like this. I really would like the chance to be a grandmother. I can't wait to see Cole's daughter. He promised to bring Sumi and the baby here at the end of the month. He sounds so happy, Sawyer," Maggie said happily.

"That's because he is happy. I keep getting this vision of him and Riley *playing* with all that money. I'm going to tell you a secret, and you have to promise not to tell anyone."

Maggie nodded, her eyes dancing with interest.

"Cole and Riley think I don't know, but I overheard them talking back in the spring when we were all at Sunbridge. You'd just done *your number* and the family was in a turmoil. Anyway, those guys decided to finance Miranda through Valentine Mitchell. She set it all up. Cary thinks he got the financing from some English firm. It was Cole's way of securing Miranda in case anything goes awry with the plane. They're twits," Sawyer said fondly, "but as Adam says, they always come through when it counts. I just wanted to bust when I heard it. The only person I could tell was Adam, and he just said, 'I told you so.' You have reason to be proud of Cole."

"Val set it up?"

"Yes, she did. She was very good to this family, Maggie. I'm sorry she won't be representing us anymore. You could always count on Val. I don't think anyone has heard from her."

"In the beginning I was so certain she lied to me. Now I'm not sure. I don't know why that is, Sawyer."

"I don't know why either, Maggie. Does it really matter now?"

"I thought it did . . . does . . . maybe, I don't know. I try to block it all out, to keep busy. I got rid of all the furniture. At first I just got rid of the bedroom stuff, and Chesney's too. Then the office stuff and then the rest of everything. I would walk around here thinking I smelled Rand's after-shave, *him*. He never even told me he deeded this house to me. I had a real crying jag on the day Val sent the deed. It reminded me of the day I got the deed to Sunbridge. God, I was drunk as a skunk, but that sobered me up real quick. I never took another drink after that. I don't want to talk about this, Sawyer."

"That's fine with me. What do you want to talk about?"

"Mam, I guess. Your plane. Whatever."

"I'd rather not talk about Grandmam. I don't want to cry anymore. I'm so glad Adam agreed to this move. Sumi is looking for a little house for us to rent. I think it will be good for the girls. All those little cousins over there will be wonderful for them. I bet they learn Japanese with ease. The cousins will learn English. Sumi promised to get me a girl to watch the twins, and a housekeeper. Adam is going to be really busy. He's had an offer to do a book of his favorite cartoons for Random House. But don't think we're going to neglect the girls," Sawyer said hastily. "We'll have more quality time with them. They are a handful, Maggie."

"I don't doubt that for a minute. If things get wild, I'll call on Addie and have her get me some schoolgirls to help out. Take as long as you need. You said production is under way?"

"Yes, I made two fast trips over there. Things are under control. A year and it will fly. The switch over from Coleman Aviation to ColeShad Aeronautics throws me every so often. Cole thinks we should go public with CSA. I can't make up my mind. What do you think?"

Maggie shrugged. "I don't know much about it, but I don't think Cole would steer you wrong. Val can probably ... well, someone can ... talk to a lawyer." Maggie averted her eyes.

"Were ... *are* you jealous of Val?"

"That's as good a word as any. In many ways I admired her. She did everything on her own. It really doesn't matter how she did it, she did it. Ivy talks to me about her a lot. Ivy considers her a friend-friend, if you know what I mean. She said every club, organization, and legal firm in Miranda and Austin threw going-away parties for her. She said her picture was in the paper every day with glowing testimonials from judges, lawyers, and clients. She did it all on her own. I'm envious of that. Look at you, Sawyer, you did it. What have I done? Nothing. All I did was take. I was no mental match for Rand.

"I've had a lot of time to look back on things. The last year or so, Rand spent so much time away. He *said* he was going to Maui. He *said* he was going to Hilo. He *said* he was going to England. He *said* he was going to Hong Kong to see Chesney. He said a lot of things. I think I did to Rand what Ivy said Susan did to Cary. I made myself an extension of him. What was my contribution? I walked on the beach. I swam. I prepared food. I went to exercise class two or three times a week. I shopped. I read. My God, what kind of life is that? The worst part is, I didn't see ... didn't think I should do anything differently. Rand must have been bored out of his mind. When Chesney returned from one of her trips, he came *alive*."

"Don't do this to yourself . . . Mother," Sawyer said, taking Maggie in her arms. "Let it go. That's what you used to tell me. Take each new day as it comes."

"Easy for you to say," Adam said, flopping down on a beach chair. "The terrors are clean and asleep. They rise and shine around the time the sun comes up. Sometimes before the sun comes up."

"That's interesting to know. I'm an early riser myself," Maggie said.

"They're very demanding," Adam said.

"They are little shits," Sawyer said. "What one doesn't think of, the other one does. Then they both act on it. If you had told me twins run in your family, I never would have married you."

They argued back and forth good-naturedly, then heatedly, almost coming to blows. Maggie watched and listened. They were so passionate about everything. She couldn't ever remember having had such a discussion, such a fight, with Rand.

"I could punch your lights out with one hand behind my back," Sawyer blustered. "You were the one who forgot to buy the Fig Newtons. Don't lie, Adam!"

"While you're *trying* to do that, I'd be snatching you baldheaded," Adam stormed. "Jesus, I'm tired. Let's go to bed, honey."

The tempest was over, if that's what it was. Maybe this was the way young people *communicated*.

Sawyer leaned over to kiss her husband's cheek. "I'm kissing you now because when we get to bed I won't have the energy. You don't mind if we turn in, do you, Maggie?"

"Good heavens no. You both look exhausted. What time is your plane tomorrow?"

"Ten-thirty. We'll have to leave here at nine. 'Night, Maggie," Sawyer mumbled. Adam waved wearily.

"Sleep tight," Maggie said.

Maggie walked down to the ocean, the damp sand tickling her feet. She sat down, cross-legged, and stared out across the moonlit water. How beautiful. How peaceful. The waves' soft lapping was music to her ears. She hummed a few bars of a popular ditty until tears gathered in her eyes.

She was alone.

She thought about her family. Their lives seemed to be in order. No one needed her. Baby-sitting the twins for a week or so didn't really qualify as having someone. If Cary was on track, that left only her and Susan at odds with life. Maybe she should call Susan when she went back to the house. And say what? Ask her to come here? Not a good idea, Maggie. Make the offer anyway. You know she'll refuse.

Mam. Don't think about Mam. If you think about Mam, you'll set yourself back months. Maggie hugged her knees, her toes digging into the sand.

Sand castles.

Maggie leaped to her feet and ran back to the house and into the kitchen, where she rummaged in the cabinet for a bowl, a plastic glass, and a bucket from under the sink.

Grandmothers built sand castles.

Maggie worked diligently, lugging buckets of water to a spot high on the beach so it would stay intact until morning when the twins awoke. She molded and sculpted with the Tupperware bowl and Burger King plastic glass. When she finished at four o'clock, she rocked back on her heels to stare at the wonder she'd created. It had turrets, windows, a moat, and a drawbridge. The girls would love it. It was almost perfect. But every castle needed a flag. She raced to the garage, where she searched for a swatch of suitable material. She decided on one from the Pacific Jewels collection. She grimaced. What good was a flag without a flagpole? She bounded out of the garage and into the house. In the bathroom she found the perfect flagpole—a cuticle orange stick. She was back in the garage a moment later, dabbing Krazy Glue on the stick. When she had pressed the small flag around the cylinder, she reached for the pinking shears and snipped at the edges.

Perfecto.

Maggie ran back to the beach and positioned her flag to the right of her drawbridge—the shiny cardboard tray chicken cutlets came wrapped in. She felt pleased with herself, almost as pleased as the day her color swatches were made final.

In the shower, she remembered her intention to call Susan. She felt like singing and wasn't sure why.

Back on the lanai, dressed in a one-piece playsuit the color of the Hawaiian sky, Maggie reached for the portable phone. "Suse, it's Maggie."

"You're up early, aren't you?" Susan's voice accused. She sounds depressed, Maggie thought.

"Actually," Maggie said, and laughed. "I didn't go to bed last night. I stayed up and built this gorgeous sand castle for the girls. They're here, you know. I am going to baby-sit. Can you believe that? I don't know for how long. Adam and Sawyer are going to find a house in Japan. They're moving there temporarily, but then you know that, right?"

"No, I didn't know that," Susan snapped. "No one tells me anything."

"Sawyer said she spoke to you," Maggie said gently. "Is something wrong?" Of course there was something wrong. There was always something wrong in her sister's life. This conversation was already a downer. Think positive, she cautioned herself.

"She did call weeks ago, and she did say she was *thinking* about it. I'm out of sorts. What have you been doing since . . . are you all right?" Susan asked in an uninterested tone.

"I finished the dyes a few weeks ago. Look for Pacific Jewels and Egyptian Lights next spring. If you like, I can send you a scarf. I've been working on them. I want Mam to see them. Have you heard anything, Susan?"

"Hardly. Have you?"

"Not recently. How's Cary?"

"Cary's just fine. He's so fine, he's never home. He's so fine, he doesn't return calls. He's so damn fine, he told me to *do* something. I hate men, Maggie. I gave up my life for months for him, and I did everything humanly possible to make his life pleasant. I was there for him every hour of the day and night. Now he has this dog, and he has people over to his apartment all the time who are teaching him how to . . . how to cope. I *wanted* to do all that for him. He was so grateful until that bitch showed up and turned him against me. She did to me what she did to you, Maggie. She snatched Rand from you and . . . She just stirs up all this trouble in our family and then she takes off! She's a slut, a tramp, and a no-good bimbo!"

I will not let her ruin my day. I simply will not,

Maggie told herself. "I assume the bitch in question is Valentine Mitchell," Maggie said quietly.

"Of course. Who else do we know who does the things she does? She's always been jealous of us. Though we were good enough to pay her hundreds of thousands of dollars over the years."

"Maybe you should stop and think about what you just said, Susan. A few months ago you showed up on my doorstep with . . . what was it you said? Eighty dollars in your checking account? That's bread-line, pauper level. You're sitting on a velvet cushion now, thanks to Val. Give credit where credit is due. And don't forget that she was the one who bailed you out the first time around, when your first husband did the same thing to you your second husband did. Maybe you should take a long, hard look at yourself, Susan. You know, I called you to see how you were. We're sisters, and I care about you, but you are so bitter, Susan, so angry at everyone and at the world. You should be thrilled and delighted that Cary can do things for himself, that he isn't so traumatized that he sits and sucks his thumb. Instead, you're angry. Mentally, Cary is in a healthier place than you are right now. You think about *that* for a while, and if you want to call me back later with a smile in your voice, *maybe* I'll talk to you. Good-bye, Suse," Maggie said, slamming the phone down.

"*That* was a mistake," Maggie muttered as she filled the Mr. Coffee.

"Froot Loops," a tiny voice by her knees said. Maggie whirled about.

"Shoclit bears," a second tiny voice said.

"No. Scrambled eggs. Toast. Juice."

The tots shook their heads wildly.

"Oh, yes," Maggie said. "Sit!"

"No," the girls chorused in unison.

"Aha, well, then I'll eat by myself. You go pick some flowers for your mother." The twins watched, uncertain at the sternness in her voice. They continued to watch, thumbs in their mouths, as Maggie set one place at the table. "This is my plate," she said. "Shooo, go get the flowers. Pretty ones."

"Froot Loops," Katy said.

"Shoclit bears," Josie said.

"Eggs," Maggie said.

They cried, at the same time, both their lower lips trembling.

Maggie scooped some of the scrambled eggs onto her plate and sat down. She started to eat. The twins sobbed. Maggie ignored them. "Want some?"

"Popsicle," Josie said.

"Cookie," Katy wailed.

"Eggs," Maggie said.

"Sugar bread," Josie, the ringleader, pleaded.

"Gummi Bears," Katy hiccuped.

"Eggs," Maggie said.

The twins looked at one another. They stopped crying at the same moment their thumbs came out of their mouths. As one they scrambled onto their respective chairs. They wiggled until they were on their knees. "Eggs," they said.

"I thought you'd see it my way." Maggie smiled. The girls wolfed down their eggs and toast and finished their milk.

"Cookies?"

"Apples," Maggie said, wiping their faces with a wet paper towel. "Let's pick some flowers and make a lei for your mommy. That's a necklace of flowers. We'll have to work quickly before Mommy wakes up."

Darning needle and nylon thread in hand, Maggie led the twins out to the garden at the side of the house. "You pick them and I'll string them."

Chubby fingers piled the fragile blossoms at Maggie's feet. She worked quickly, stringing the sweet-smelling flowers on the thread. "For mommy."

"Daddy," they chorused.

"Okay, Daddy too." Maggie's needle worked furiously. "How about one for Josie and Katy?" Maggie kissed each of the girls as she placed the small leis around their necks. "Now take these to Mommy and Daddy and tell them to get up. Hurry." She smiled.

"Prize."

"When you get back I'll show you the surprise." She watched as they scampered off. What had she gotten herself into? Who cared? She was going to love every minute of it, if she survived.

"They smell wonderful," Sawyer said happily. "What a wonderful way to wake up. The girls said you made eggs for us. I'm starved."

"No. I made eggs for the twins. How do you like yours?"

"Over easy. *They ate them?*" Maggie pointed to the plates on the table. "Look, Adam, they ate eggs."

"I'm no authority on children, but did you two ever stop to think about how much sugar those children eat? That's probably one of the reasons they're so wired-up all the time."

"Pepsi," Josie said.

"Pepsi," Katy echoed.

"Juice," Maggie said.

Sawyer watched, her eyes round, as the girls drank their juice without a fuss.

"Prize?"

"Just as soon as I make breakfast for Mommy and Daddy. Pick some more flowers for me." Sawyer watched her children as they trotted off to do her mother's bidding without a fuss.

"Here you go," Maggie said, sliding the eggs onto Sawyer's plate. "I have to go now. Adam, you can push your own toast down, can't you?"

"Yeah, sure. What's your hurry?"

"I stayed up all night and built a sand castle for the girls. That's the *prize*. There's a lot of traffic Monday mornings, for some reason," she called over her shoulder. "Maybe you better leave fifteen minutes earlier."

"And you were worried?" Adam scoffed, dipping his toast into his wife's egg yolk. "When we come back for the terrors, they probably won't want to go with us. In which case we could board them out here and visit on holidays."

Sawyer threw her napkin at him.

"This is probably the best thing we could have done for your mother. Let's take a shower together," he said, leering at her, "wearing our leis."

"My dear, that is the best offer I've had since . . . God, since when?" Sawyer said, dashing off to the bedroom, her husband right behind.

The moment Sawyer and Adam drove off, Maggie took the girls by the hand and led them around the side of the house and down to the beach. Josie, the more verbal of the twins, had laid claim to the sand castle. Now it was time to build one for Katy.

It was almost noon when Maggie called a halt to the building. She had heard her name being called from the garage area. She never had visitors, and Addie was off today. She felt a flurry of panic and didn't know why.

It was probably the meter reader. She called out, "I'm down here."

He's huge, Maggie thought. He was six-two, at least, with a crown of thick dark hair mixed with silvery strands at the temples. He was dressed in creased navy chinos, with a crisp white shirt open at the throat and sleeves rolled to the middle of his arms. His tan, if it was a tan, was a glorious bronze color. Dock-Siders adorned his feet, along with white tennis socks. Obviously, Maggie thought, whoever he was, he wasn't trying to make a fashion statement. He looked comfortable in his clothes and with himself. From where she was standing, she thought him ugly, but as he approached with a smile on his face, she revised her opinion. She looked into warm, dark eyes the color of melted chocolate chips.

Maggie brushed the sand off her hands, her eyes wary.

"Mrs. Nelson?"

"Yes."

"I'm Henry Tanaka. Your stepdaughter's attorneys approached me in regard to selling her ten percent interest in the sugar refinery. I was wondering if you had any intention of selling your interest as well. I spoke personally to Mr. Assante yesterday, and he suggested I come up here to talk to you. He told me about his condition and expressed an interest in selling out, either to you or to me. I understand you'll want to verify all of this, but I would like to make an offer."

"I hadn't thought about it, Mr. Tanaka. As you can see, I more or less have my hands full right now. When would you want my answer?"

"I'm not in a hurry, but your stepdaughter seems to be. Take as long as you like. I haven't built one of those in years," he said, pointing to the sand castle. "My wife and I used to build them all the time for our grandchild. Then my son decided he wanted to work on the mainland and they moved. My wife died two years ago. For a while we would build them ourselves. . . ."

How sad he looks, Maggie thought. "We could use some help, if you have nothing to do. You see, I stayed up all night to build one, and I forgot how proprietary twins are, so we now have to build another. By the way, this is Josie and this is Katy. I'm baby-sitting. For a couple of weeks. I think."

"I'd like that. Would you mind if I change? I keep a swimsuit in the trunk of my car."

"Not at all. The bathroom is off the kitchen. You're sure you're an expert at this?" She twinkled.

"The best. We could have a contest. You take one of the girls to help you, and I'll take the other one."

"Before or after lunch?"

"If that's an offer, I accept. I'll just be a minute." He beamed.

The moment Henry Tanaka was out of her sight, Maggie started to worry. God, what if he was some kind of pervert? An ax murderer?

"Hims nice," Josie said.

"Yeah, hims nice," Katy agreed.

"I think you're right," Maggie said, "but I'm still going to call Cary."

"He's got a good reputation," Cary said. "Rich as sin, I hear. He more or less implied he'd pay cash if we want to sell. It's your call, Maggie. I won't be able to do much overseeing in my condition. Rand was the one who knew the refinery, not me. I'll go along with whatever you decide. Are you out on the lanai? A sand-castle building contest, huh?" he said wistfully. "Do you still have all those beautiful purple and pink flowers?"

Maggie looked around.

"Yeah. I'll call you back and let you know who wins, okay?"

"Promise?"

"I promise."

"Checking up on me?" Henry asked.

"Yes. Cary said you are who you say you are. He left the decision up to me. Grilled cheese and tomato soup for lunch," Maggie said, leading the way into the kitchen. "The bathroom is off the kitchen."

"Popcorn," Josie said.

"Jelly bread," Katy said.

"Grilled cheese and soup," Maggie said. She could hear Tanaka laughing in the bathroom.

"Hims nice," Josie said.

"Hims nice." Katy grinned.

"Let's wash up first," Maggie said. "While I fix lunch, you can pick some flowers for Mr. Tanaka. Maybe he'll help you."

Lord, he's big, Maggie marveled. She wondered if he was Hawaiian. She asked.

"My mother was a *hale*, so was my grandfather. It explains my height. I've lived here all my life. About two miles up the road. We've been neighbors for a long time. I knew your husband. Not well, of course. I'm sorry about his passing."

"Thank you."

"You must be very lonely here. I know I am. When my wife died, I went around the world. I thought I would never come back, but I did. Now I'll never leave. As a matter of fact, I couldn't wait to get back. One has to learn how to deal with memories. It isn't easy."

Josie tugged at his hand. "Flowers." Katy tugged at his other hand.

"They said, and this is a direct quote from both of them, 'Hims nice.' "

"I'm impressed."

"And well you should be." Maggie laughed.

The moment they were out of sight, Maggie ran to the bathroom to run a brush through her hair. She couldn't put on makeup now; it would be too obvious. She couldn't splash on perfume either. Thank God the playsuit was attractive. When she walked back to the kitchen she felt giddy. Hmmmmn. But her good mood soured almost immediately. Henry Tanaka wanted to buy the refinery, so naturally he would be nice and ingratiate himself with her. So what? she said to herself. For now, it's pleasant, and he's someone to talk to. She flipped the sandwiches onto a plate. She cut them up in little squares for the twins and poured their soup into small cups with thick handles.

"I think," Henry said thirty minutes later, "your charges are falling asleep in their soup."

He sounded so disappointed, Maggie said, "Let's carry them out to the lanai, and you and I can get a start on the castles. When they wake up, we'll finish them. Are you sure you can spare the time?"

"That's about all I have these days. Time."

"But you said you want to buy the refinery. Don't you work?" *That's about as blunt as you can get, Maggie.*

"I don't work. My daughter-in-law uses that term all the time. I acquire things."

"I see," Maggie said.

Tanaka laughed. "My wife used to say that all the time. Usually it meant she didn't fully approve. Ooops,

I think we better get these youngsters to someplace soft before they fall off their chairs."

"I don't understand. Sawyer said they never take naps. She said they don't sleep through the night and they don't eat anything," Maggie dithered. "God, you don't think there was anything wrong with the food, do you?"

"I think they're just tired. The sun and sand will do that to you. They do jabber a lot. You should have heard them when we were picking the flowers. This one," he said, indicating Josie, "is solid as a rock."

"So is this one." Maggie laughed. "Do you think I should cover them?"

"It's eighty degrees. Is this your first time with the girls?"

"I guess it shows, huh? I'm enjoying it, though. I promised I would teach them to swim. Now I don't think it's such a good idea. Josie is afraid of the waves."

"Come up to my place and use my pool. We have two ponies and three horses. Do you ride, Mrs. Nelson?"

"Call me Maggie." She told him about Sunbridge and the horses there. "I couldn't impose on you. Thank you for the offer, though."

"Tomorrow morning. I'll come down and get you and drive you up to my place. We have some new kittens in the barn."

"If you're sure we won't be taking you away from anything, then yes, okay, we'll accept."

"Have you given any thought to how you'll teach *two* children to swim at the same time? You need eyes in the back of your head when they're this age."

"Yes, I see what you mean. You'll teach one, and I'll teach one."

"Listen, I really don't care about the refinery. If you want to sell, that's fine. If you don't, that's fine too. I don't want you to think I'm buttering you up for the kill."

She believed him. "The thought did cross my mind."

"I like an honest woman. I like you, Maggie Nelson."

"Thank you," Maggie said, flustered. God, who could she call and tell?

They talked then, forgetting about the sand castles.

"You're Billie Limited," Henry said in amazement.

"You know about Billie Limited," Maggie said in surprise.

"My wife did. She wouldn't wear anything else. Now, there's a company I wouldn't mind acquiring."

"Too late. I'm running it now. Would you like to see my new line? I work out of the garage." She told him about that too.

They were as old friends, comfortable with one another, calling each other by their first names, when hours later Henry proclaimed himself the winner of the sand castle contest. "The winner gets to take the ladies out to dinner. Ice cream, soda pop, and hamburgers."

"Vegetables, chicken, fruit, and milk."

Henry looked at the girls. "She's the boss. I'll pick you up in an hour."

The twins clapped their hands in glee. Maggie did too. Now she could wear makeup and perfume. And a dress. Thank you, God.

"All right," Maggie said. "We'll be ready."

Maggie spent so much time pressing the girls' polka dot sunsuits and polishing their sandals, she had barely enough time to shower and change. She chose a gauze two-piece outfit with a straw belt riding low on her hips. She slipped her feet into matching sandals and was about to start on her makeup when she looked at the clock. No time for makeup, but time enough for a quick spritz of perfume.

She looked at the two cherubs sitting side by side on the bed. "We have a date." She laughed. "And," she said, dropping to her knees and lowering her voice, "I bet if we play our cards right, we can have even more. Dates, that is." The girls nodded solemnly.

They were off the bed in a flash when Henry blew the horn.

It was a date. Of sorts. A beginning.

{{{{{{ CHAPTER FOURTEEN }}}}}}

The trees rustled softly overhead in the weak, struggling breeze. Blue jays settled on the leafy branches, their eyes searching the water fountain and bird feeder in the middle of the yard. As they watched, their provider scooped out thick, fat worms from a Chinese-style container and placed them in the feeder along with sunflower seeds and crumbs from a strawberry Danish.

The oversize birdbath had been fashioned by Billie and himself in a pottery class they'd taken years ago. "Big enough for hundreds of birds, Thad," Billie said. "One that will take gallons of water." And that's what they had. Thad turned on the hose and tested the lukewarm water with his finger. When the bath was filled, he felt like jumping in himself, or at the very least, turning the hose to drench his perspiring body. It was a silly thought, and lately he hadn't had many silly thoughts. He sprayed his feet.

Today, according to the weatherman, was the hottest day of the year. The thermometer on the deck registered ninety-six degrees.

Thad dragged the hose over to a two-hundred-year-old maple tree, where he filled two buckets of water for any squirrel or chipmunk who cared to visit. He also filled the square wooden box at the base of the tree with acorns and the assorted animal food he purchased at the local feed store. His last chore was to fill the narrow metal tray with rabbit pellets, carrots, and lettuce for the family of rabbits that lived under the toolshed.

It was a job. Something to do. Something to take his mind off Billie. He knew that the minute he joined her on the deck, she was going to pick up the discussion they'd had before he'd come down to the yard to tend to the birds and animals. He dawdled to delay the moment of his return as long as possible. He knew he was going to do what his wife wanted, because he could deny her absolutely nothing. If she asked for a slice of the moon, he'd try to find a ladder big enough to climb to get it for her.

Thad coiled the hose and carried it back to hang it on the rack attached to the house. He noticed the lid to the barrel that held the acorns wasn't closing properly. Should he attempt to fix it and delay his return to the deck, or should he wait for another day?

He knew exactly what Billie was going to say. "Thad, why are you being so stubborn?" He felt like cursing. Suddenly he wanted to shout all the obscene four-letter words he'd ever heard during his stint in the Navy. Damn, he should be praying instead of cursing, but then he'd already tried both, and neither worked. What was going to be was going to be, and nothing he did or said was going to change a thing. He cursed then, every dirty, filthy word he knew, and when he ran out of words, he made up new ones. When he was finished he said, "I'm sorry, God, I had to do that."

Thad did his best to control his anger and to put a smile—even if it was a sickly smile—on his face when he flopped down in the lounge chair next to Billie. Here it comes, he thought. *Thad, why are you being so stubborn?*

"Why are you being so stubborn, Thad?" Billie asked quietly.

"Because you are in no physical condition to make a trip, any trip. What you want to do is make a pilgrimage. No."

Billie smiled wanly. "You've never refused me anything. I want to do this. I *need* to do it. I already spoke to Dr. Blake, and he said if I was up to it, to go ahead and do it. You're just being obstinate. I understand your concern and I truly appreciate it, but if you don't go with me, I'll hire someone to take me. Now, make your decision," Billie said. "I won't take no for an answer."

"Then I guess you have my answer," Thad grumbled. "When do you want to go?"

"What's wrong with right now? Our bags have been packed for the last ten days. That's how long you've been arguing with me, Thad. I gave in on the Hong Kong part because even I know the trip would be too much. But going to Philadelphia, Pennsylvania, is almost around the corner. We can stop every hour if need be."

Thad gaped at his wife. "You mean just get in the car and leave . . . now?"

Billie smiled. "Uh-huh. All we have to do is lock the door. Oh, Thad, let's do it!" Billie cajoled.

"You're whining, Billie." Thad smiled.

"No, this is my coaxing voice, my wheedling voice. Please, Thad."

"Oh, okay. Go to the bathroom. I'll get the car out. I can't believe I'm doing this," Thad pretended to grumble. "I suppose the *packed* bags are inside the closet."

"Thad, you are so astute, you amaze me," Billie said

as she got up to go to the bathroom. Thad watched her out of the corner of his eye. She was rail-thin now and wobbly on her legs. She reached for the pronged cane, waving him away. "I can do it," she said tightly.

"I just didn't want you to trip over my feet," Thad said, working his facial muscles into a smile.

"You're hovering, and you promised not to. Get a move on, Thad, time waits for no one."

Inside the bathroom, Billie leaned up against the door. Why was she doing this? Why was she insisting Thad take her to Philadelphia? Was the trip down memory lane for herself or for Thad? "For Thad," she muttered. He needed something to do, something to think about other than her. "I don't have much time left," she murmured.

She had to go to the bathroom, but did she have the strength to . . . Such a simple thing as going to the bathroom had become a major obstacle in her life. Give me the strength, she prayed.

"Hey, lady, what's taking you so long?" Thad called from the other side of the door.

"If you think I'm going to tell you, you have another thought coming," Billie shot back. She swayed dizzily. Her hands, she thought, looked like claws. She opened the door. "I think I need some help, Thad."

"That's what I'm here for." Thad scooped his wife into his arms. She couldn't weigh more than eighty pounds. More like seventy-five. "I'll come back for the cane. Do you think you'll be warm enough?" he dithered.

"Thad, it's over ninety degrees. I have my shawl on and a long-sleeved dress. It's August, remember?"

"I just want to be sure," Thad groused as he settled

Billie in the front seat of the car. "Put your seat belt on."

"It's on, Thad," Billie said, snapping the buckle into place.

"Okay, I'll get the bags. Want an apple?"

"Sure, bring all the fruit, and some crackers too. I know how you like to munch when you drive. Soda pop too, you get thirsty."

"That's going to take at least ten minutes."

"So I'll snooze while you do it."

"You had better be awake when I get back."

Billie nodded.

Satisfied that his wife would be all right, Thad went back to the house. He carried the two small bags to the front door. The trip to the kitchen for the fruit, soda, and crackers took all of a minute. He dropped the bags by the front door with the suitcases, then walked back to the kitchen and picked up the phone.

He thought this day would never come, that he would never have to make this call. He'd hoped, he'd prayed, he'd done everything humanly possible to ward off this moment. He squeezed his eyes shut and tapped out the numbers he wanted. He was in total control when he spoke to Ivy. It wasn't until he hung up that he thought he would completely fall apart.

Billie was wide awake when he settled the suitcases in the trunk. He handed her the bag of fruit and soda he knew he wasn't going to eat or drink.

"See what you think of this," Thad said, backing out of the driveway. He thought his heart would shatter when Billie looked back, her eyes drinking in the sight of the house and lawns. Almost as though she knew she wouldn't be coming back. My God, she does know that, Thad realized. She's doing this so she won't . . . so she won't die in the house and leave me that terrible memory. Oh God, oh God, oh God.

"Yes . . . ?" Billie drawled.

"Well, we'll drive through Connecticut, and if you aren't too tired, we can go through to New Jersey. Or we can stop in Connecticut at a five-star hotel and the following day head for New Jersey and Philly. Philly is only three hours from the Connecticut state line. I'm personally for the five stars, what about you?"

Billie giggled. "Okay, let's drive to Connecticut. Unless, of course, you get too tired." She was needling him, telling him in her own inimitable way that time was of the essence. He felt his heart skip a beat.

"I suppose you'll want to dine on greasy hamburgers and greasier french fries," he said.

"Absolutely. And one of those apple pie things that taste like cardboard."

"You got it. When was the last time we had one of those greasy killer meals?"

"Four days ago," Billie smiled. "It's un-American to take a trip and eat health food."

She was asleep a minute after she finished the sentence. From time to time Thad wiped at his eyes as he drove along. She would sleep for forty-five minutes and then awaken, unaware that she'd dozed off.

Thad glanced at the dashboard clock when Billie said, "Speaking of American, Maggie is going American. She said she isn't going to do business in Taiwan or Hong Kong. She asked my permission, and I gave it, to label our fabrics 'Made in the U.S.A.' I'm so pleased at the way she's taken over . . . under the circumstances. I can't wait to see the Cleopatra Gold scarf she said she's working on right now. She said those ten days she spent at Sunbridge staring at the sun were worth the blisters she got on her eyeballs. Those two lines are going to be all you see next year, mark my word, Thad. I'm so proud of her."

"I know you are, honey. I am too. I think turning over Billie Limited to her was the best thing that could have happened to Maggie."

"I'm just delighted. What was it you said you wanted to tell me? Or are my days mixed up again?" Billie said fretfully. "Can I have a pill, Thad?"

It was two hours ahead of schedule, but he didn't give a damn. "Sure, honey, wait till there's a break in traffic, and I'll pull over. Is the pain bad?" What a damn silly question that was.

"It's bearable. I thought with the trip and your driving, you just forgot. Take your time, darling, we don't want to have an accident."

"Here we go," Thad said, moving from the middle lane to the right and then off to the shoulder of the road. From his pocket he withdrew a bottle of capsules and shook one into the palm of his hand. "You'll have to take it with soda, is that okay with you?"

"That's fine. Now what was it you were going to tell me?"

Thad shifted his mental gears. "Sawyer sent me an article in the mail. I was going to read it to you this afternoon when we had our reading orgy, but I'll tell you instead. She also sent a note. She says she thinks Cole is into 'high-tech love hotels.' Rooms by the hour. The high-tech part is for discretion. They use state-of-the-art automation to choose a room, check in, eat and drink, pay the bill, and check out, and no one is the wiser. A guest checking in is greeted by tape-recorded check-in instructions and a floor plan showing room locations and availability. They even have frequent-customer cards, which go into a slot for payment. They have this oh-so-discreet-sounding bell that reminds guests when it's time to leave. Rooms go for thirty to ninety bucks for two hours. Two hours, can you believe that? It's twenty percent higher for an all-nighter. Repeat guests get a discount. Sawyer said she called Cole to ask him if he was involved, and he just laughed." Thad chuckled; Billie giggled.

"Would Cole really do that?"

"Wouldn't surprise me. Guess there's big money in sex."

"Good Lord, Thad, don't tell that to the family."

"I won't, but Sawyer loves to babble. I'm sure she's apprised everyone and sent them the same clipping. She does love to involve the family in all things that generate income. And she loves to one-up Cole, as you well know. How are you feeling, honey?"

"Almost normal," Billie said tiredly. "What was on our reading schedule today, Thad?"

"*Tokaido Road* by Lucia St. Clair Robson. It's that novel about feudal Japan you said we should read. That was your choice. My choice was *Under Siege* by Stephen Coonts. We can read them this evening when we stop." She was asleep again. Tears rolled down Thad's cheeks. God in heaven, what was he going to do without her at his side? How could he go on? Why go on? He blinked, dislodging the tears from his eyes. He continued to drive because it was what Billie wanted.

Fifteen minutes later Billie stirred, mumbled in her sleep, and said, "Is there really money in high-tech sex hotels?" Thad threw his head back and laughed uproariously. Billie slept, a smile on her face.

* * *

While Thad's Lincoln Town Car chewed up the miles and Billie slept, Ivy Coleman paced, her eyes those of a trapped animal. She shoved the VCR tape behind the cushion on the sofa. A second later she retrieved it and slid it under the couch, only to pull it out and hide it behind a book. She continued to pace, around the low-backed sofa with its oversize cushions, around the table with its yellow bowl of daisies, around the recliner and foot stool. Angrily, she walked back to the bookcase, where she yanked at the books. She snatched the tape and laid it on the coffee table. She shoved aside two copies of *Architectural Digest* and the August issue of *Better Homes and Gardens*. She slid the crystal ashtray to the far end of the table. The tape glared at her like a giant, square black eye. She started to shake. Her eyes turned to the clock on the bookshelf. Her mother would be walking through the door in less than twenty minutes to take Moss back to Florida with her. Riley would be home in a little over an hour.

Oh, God! She wished she'd followed Val's advice and told Riley about the tape. But she hadn't! She'd told Sumi, though. Sumi understood. Oh, God! She had agreed with Val's advice, and followed through by having an extra tape run off and left in Val's possession. Just in case, Val had said.

Five o'clock. By eight the family would be here. All of them. Riley didn't know that either. Would he forgive her for taking things into her own hands?

The calls had been so hard to make, but she'd done it. To spare Riley.

The moment Ivy heard her mother's voice, she calmed. She hugged her, her eyes brimming with tears. Her mother wiped at them with a tissue.

"You have to be strong," Tess said. "You're doing

what Billie wants, and if the family doesn't understand, then it's their problem. That goes for your husband too."

"What if they don't, Mama? What if they fight and carry on? What do I do then?"

"You just keep saying over and over it's what Billie wants. It's right there on that tape. Did that lady lawyer call you back?"

"Not yet, Mama."

"Honey, I don't have time to talk. I have to get right back or I'll miss the plane. Is Moss ready?"

Ivy pointed to the playpen and the pile of luggage by the door.

"Lord, Ivy, I'm not taking any of that. Coots is out buying everything we'll need." She held up her hand as Ivy was about to protest. "He feels important doing it. I just told him to get one of everything and to assemble it by the time I got back. He dropped me off at the airport, just *itching* to head for Burdine's. All I need for now is a diaper bag, Moss's bottles, and one change of clothes. That's all, honey."

"Okay, okay. Here, I wrote out—"

"Ivy, we'll manage. Where's his whuppie?"

"Right here," she said, handing it over.

"Ivy, if . . . if you need your daddy, you just call."

"I will, Mama. Give Daddy a kiss for me. Well, here he is, my bundle of joy," she said, giving Moss one last hug.

"We're going to spoil him, Ivy."

"I know that, Mama. Take care of him."

Tess nodded. "You stand up for yourself. Billie trusts you. Don't let her down. Not now. You tell the family I'm real sorry. I always liked Billie. I was jealous of her for a while, but I came to realize you can't be jealous of *good people*. You can only like good people. 'Bye, honey."

"Call me when you get home, okay?"

"Of course."

Ivy cried then, great, hard gulping sobs as she watched the airport limo until it was out of sight.

When Riley walked through the doorway at six-fifteen, Ivy was listening to Dan Rather on the news, her eyes on the VCR tape.

"Hey," Riley shouted, to be heard over the news, "are we going somewhere?"

Ivy took a deep breath as she lowered the volume on the television set. She was amazed at how steady her voice was when she said, "No, my mother came to pick up Moss. She took him back to Florida. I had his stuff all piled up, but she said Daddy wanted to go out and buy . . . what she said was, Daddy needs to feel important."

"Don't you think you should have told me?" Riley said quietly.

"Yes, I should have, but the circumstances . . . I just thought it would be better if Moss was away from here for a while. He'll be well taken care of."

"I don't doubt that for a minute, but what do you mean 'would be better,' and why didn't you tell me?"

"Because . . . because I gave my promise that I wouldn't. What that means is . . . sit down, Riley, I have something to show you. It will explain about . . . about Moss."

Riley watched his wife change the television channel to three and then turn on the VCR. He grew uneasy when he watched her walk over to the television set and insert the tape that had been lying on the table.

Ivy's eyes never left her husband as he watched the

tape. When it ended, she asked, "Do you want me to play it again?"

"Jesus Christ, no!" Riley exploded. "How long have you had this?"

"Since March."

"And you're just showing it to me now!" Riley sputtered.

"I promised your grandmother, Riley. She asked me not to tell you. She didn't want me to tell anyone. I told Val, who advised me to tell you. I wanted to, Riley, but your grandmother . . . how could I refuse to do what she asked? If it was wrong, I'm sorry. I have to tell you, though, I'd do it again."

"I'm sorry, honey. It's just that I thought this would never happen. It was . . . in my mind, I think, but . . . I wanted to think it wouldn't happen for . . . for a year, maybe longer," Riley said, his voice full of sorrow.

Ivy reached for his hand.

"The family?"

"I called them all. Cole is bringing Adam and Sawyer. Sumi, of course. Sumi's sisters are going to watch the children. They'll stop in Hawaii and pick up Maggie, who, by the way, is bringing a friend. Someone named Henry Tanaka. I said that was okay. Maggie needs a friend right now more than she needs family. I said I had no objection."

"What about Cary and Susan?"

"They'll be here around eight. Separately. I don't quite know what that means. Cary said his companion would drive him over, but he said he would have to spend the night, because the man has to pick up another . . . person early in the morning, to take . . . I don't know. I just said yes. Susan said she would leave for England in the morning. I'm sure she'll change her mind. She said, and this is a direct quote, 'These family get-togethers are getting to be a pain in the ass, and I can do without them.' End of quote."

"*She's* the pain in the ass," Riley said through clenched teeth.

Ivy pressed the rewind button on the VCR.

"Ivy, let's walk up the hill."

"Are you sure you want to?"

Riley nodded.

"Then I think we should take the shears and those clippers, along with a couple of trash bags. Your Aunt Maggie was very upset when she was here the last time. She said there was no excuse for the way you let the hill go."

"She's right. There is no excuse. Let's go, the stuff is in the barn."

It was something to do. Something that needed to be done. Something to pass the time until the family arrived.

While they worked, they talked: about Sawyer's revolutionary plane design; the prototype; Cole's progress in restructuring ColeShad; Maggie's new friend, Henry Tanaka; Cary's Seeing Eye dog; and about how similar the cherry blossom hill was to the spot on this hill. From time to time they both cried.

It was dark when they walked down the hill. Riley dragged three huge gun-metal-gray bags behind him; Ivy carried the basket of garden tools.

While they were washing their hands at the kitchen sink, Ivy whispered, "Riley, we didn't do that because ... because ..."

"We did it because it needed to be done. I want you to keep on top of me in regard to the hill. It's important that it be kept up. I'm ashamed I let it go so long. Do we have time for a quick shower?"

Ivy looked at the clock. "Sure."

Together they walked into the great room at ten minutes past eight. Cary arrived at almost the same moment, Susan soon afterward. The others arrived at twenty-five minutes to nine. Ivy had a moment to take Henry Tanaka aside and talk to him.

"I feel like I know all of you," Tanaka said, afterward, shaking hands all around. His eyes, Ivy noticed, turned wary when he reached for Susan's hand.

"Are you Hawaiian?" Susan asked.

"More or less."

"Does that mean you're like a half-breed?"

Tanaka laughed. "That about sums it up. Does it make a difference?"

"Not to me it doesn't," Susan snapped. "We could take a vote."

"Shut up, Susan," Sawyer ordered.

Riley watched tight-lipped. Susan was the instigator here, and she was going to cause more than one problem.

"Don't tell me what to do," Susan snarled.

"Somebody should tell you," Adam said quietly. "If you can't keep a civil tongue, then you should leave. I, for one, won't miss that smart mouth of yours."

"I've had a hell of a long day, crossing datelines and all," Cole said through clenched teeth. "None of us have had any sleep, and I'm not in the mood for a family harangue. I thought we left that behind us the last time we gathered here in this room."

They were in pairs, Ivy thought. Everyone had someone but Cary and Susan. God, here it comes, she thought as she visualized a nightmare scenario: Susan going berserk and killing all of them with a gun hidden in her purse.

"Well?" Riley said.

"Well what?" Susan demanded. "You called this get-together, so get on with it. I have things to do."

"I hope dropping dead is at the top of the list," Sawyer said.

"Enough!" Riley roared. "You all know Thad called yesterday. He called again this afternoon and spoke to Ivy. He said he's taking Grandmam to Philadelphia because she wants . . . to see it again, the place where she grew up. He told Ivy he thinks . . . she won't . . . she won't make it back home. He also said it's his opinion Grandmam didn't want to die at the farm. She didn't want that for him, for any of us."

" 'Ivy says,' " Susan put in. "Why did Thad call Ivy? Why not Maggie or me? We're Mam's daughters. Ivy is just a granddaughter-in-law."

"Well, I can tell you why Thad didn't call *you*, Susan," Sawyer shouted. "You're about as stable as a yo-yo. What that translates into in English is, you're nuts. Why does it matter who Thad called? We're all here. We all know. The question is, what are we to do? What does Thad want us to do?"

"Thad wants us all to be together so when it's . . . time," Riley said, "we'll be . . . we'll be a family. Grandmam entrusted Ivy with her living will. We're going to show it to all of you now. Thad hasn't seen this. According to Grandmam, he doesn't even know she made it. I don't think there will be any doubt in any of your minds when you . . . when you see with your own eyes what Grandmam wants."

Ivy pressed the play button on the VCR, then took her place next to Riley, who reached for her hand.

The family stared at the blank screen. The soft whirring of the machine was the only sound in the room. Billie's face flashed on the screen. She smiled a wan, weary smile before she clasped her thin hands in her lap. She was stick-thin, her eyes deep-set behind her tinted glasses. Ivy knew the preparations for this video must have taken a lot of time and effort on Billie's part. She was dressed in a meadow-green, flowing caftan with matching turban. Billie had designed the caftan, Ivy was certain, to hide her thinness.

The tinted glasses were new, a prop, Ivy felt, to hide the sunken hollows of her eyes and to draw less attention to her thin cheeks and sharp cheekbones.

A tear slid down Ivy's cheek. Riley leaned over and kissed it away. She snuggled deeper into the hollow beneath his arm.

Billie smiled and addressed each of them by name, then thanked them for leaving their lives to come to Sunbridge. Her smile was tired, but in place.

"As Thad always says, listen up, family. I had hoped to keep my condition a secret, but Cary's accident made that impossible. A secret to spare you. Perhaps I was wrong. If so, I apologize. You see, I love you all so much, so very much. When I first found out I was terminally ill, I wanted to run to each of you, to have you hug me, to hear you tell me things like 'It will go away, it's just one opinion, they're making medical advances every day.' I realized I just wanted to fool myself.

"I know you're all weeping now. It's very hard for me to sit here in front of this camera ... and not cry myself. But I promised myself that I'd be strong, that I couldn't go with any less dignity than my old friends who've gone before me. I ask myself over and over, how did Amelia leave us with such dignity, and yet with a sense of humor I still marvel at? I finally decided it was because she had all of us, was certain of our love. She told me ... she told me once near the end, that what bothered her most was what would happen to all of us. I assured her we were family and would always be there for one another. She ... please wait just a minute while I ... wipe my eyes. She said she knew I would keep us all together, and then she thanked me for being ... her friend ... all those years.

"Shadaharu, who was a wonderful friend, simply said to me before his passing, 'Life must go on.' And that's what I'm telling all of you now. I do not want any of you to grieve for me. What I want is for all of you to go on with your lives, remember me with love, and to visit me on the hill once in a while. I know there's a perch someplace in heaven, and ... and Amelia, Shad, and I will be sitting on it watching over all of you. If that sounds silly or unbelievable, allow me this last small indulgence. I am crying. I'm sorry, so very sorry. I think it's the medication, the steroids I'm taking.

"Bear with my ... roll call. I can't leave without one last word for all of you. Maggie darling, I remember you the day you were born. You were so pink and pretty and so very perfect. I was a mother for the first time. Some of our years weren't too easy, but then life is not always easy. You turned your life around against all odds. I am so very proud of you. I know I leave Billie Limited in good hands.

"Susan, darling, I also remember the day you were born. You were pink and blond and perfect too. I know you believe your father and I abandoned you.... We didn't. We did what we thought was best for you. And now, with all your efforts, you are one of the world's most renowned pianists. I don't know who was more proud of you, Amelia or me. I love you, Susan, with all my heart.

"Sawyer, sweetheart, Maggie and I shared our love for you. Like Susan, you had two mothers. I will always be grateful for the love you showered on me. Without you in my life during those bad years, I fear I wouldn't have made it. Love Adam and the twins with all your heart.

"Cole, Riley—I'm doing this in alphabetical order—you are the young blood who will keep this family together. You are both like bright, shining lights, taking the family out of the darkness and into the sun. East and West . . . West and East . . . No one could love you more than me except your wives.

"Ivy and Sumi—again in alphabetical order—I entrust to you these two fine young men who are my grandsons.

"Cary, my friend, I leave you my family, for they love you as much as I love you. Amelia asked me to look after you when she passed on, and I did my best. Now I ask that you look after my family. Thad . . . Thad won't be able to. . . . He's going to need you, Cary. Please, be there for him, all of you, help Thad through . . . the bad times.

"I want you all to pay close attention to what I'm going to say now. I do not want to be hooked up to any life-saving equipment. If there are any of . . . my body parts that are not eaten away by disease, I want them turned over to a donor bank. There will be no open casket. Thad won't be able to handle that. I want a one-day service, and I want to be buried on the hill. A private funeral. I don't want the state of Texas or Vermont to attend.

"I've anguished over who I should entrust with this

tape. As I sit here before you, I don't know who that person will be. You need only know the person who plays this tape has the final say in regard to my last wishes.

"I say good-bye now to all of you and ask only one thing. Please take care of Thad. Good-bye, dear ones. You were mine for such a little while, and now I must give you up. I love each and every one of you. I will carry my memories and my love for you into eternity, and share that love with Amelia and Shad. I truly believe they're chomping at the bit for me to get there. I'll give them both your regards."

When the tape ended, Riley turned the machine off. The silence in the room was so loud he shook his head to clear it.

Ivy stood to take her place beside her husband. "There is one last thing. Please, all of you, remember Billie chose me to be custodian of her living will. She believes you would all be too emotional to carry out her instructions. I gave her my promise to do what she wanted. At seven o'clock this evening, I discussed this with Riley for the first time. He's in agreement with me. But you need to know I spoke to Billie last week and she said . . . she trusted me to make sure her eyes went to a donor bank. The recipient of her eyes is to be Cary. There is no room for discussion. There is a plane waiting at the airport to take Cary to the hospital. I've spoken to Mr. Tanaka, and he has kindly agreed to go along to handle matters. It's what Billie wants, and as custodian of Billie's will, it's what I want too. Billie will . . . Billie will live on for all of us through Cary."

Cole and Riley jumped to their feet as one. Both of them offered to fly the plane.

"I'll fly the plane," Henry Tanaka said quietly.

"You're both too emotional, and I want Cary to arrive in one piece. It will be my pleasure to do this for your family."

"Wait," Cary said. "I don't know what to say. I want to say something wonderful and meaningful, but I don't know the words. I can't believe Billie would think of me during this time."

"Billie predicted you would say exactly that," Ivy said. "She said, and this is a direct quote, 'Tell him not to sweat the small stuff. I need to take a message to Amelia so I can see her smile. Knowing Cary is going to view the world the way Amelia and I viewed it is all the thanks I need.' End of quote. I'd get going if I were you, Cary."

Cary choked up, "She said that?"

Ivy smiled. "Word for word."

"Then I guess we'd better get going."

There were hugs and kisses, slaps on the back, handshakes, and more kisses. Susan stood to the side, her eyes full of bitter hatred, refusing to join the family.

"What a family" were Cary's last words as he was led from the room by Henry Tanaka.

{{{{{{{{ CHAPTER FIFTEEN }}}}}}}}

Thad's chest hurt. His head ached, and he had muscle cramps in both his legs. The lump in his throat was so large, he could barely swallow past it. Any minute now he was going to bawl, he could feel it building up in him. He risked a glance at Billie, who was peering out the window with such intensity he almost ran onto the curb.

"It's so pretty, just the way I remember it. The trees are bigger, of course, more leafy. They're elms, you know," she said in a voice he could barely hear.

How in the name of God was she doing it? She was hanging on by a thread, and they both knew it, but she wouldn't give in. Not yet. She belonged in a hospital. They both knew that too.

"There it is, Thad, Four seventy-nine Elm. Oh, they painted it. It used to be white. The shutters were black."

"It looks like baby-poop yellow," Thad said gruffly. "I guess the brown shutters go with it. I think I like black and white better. If I close my eyes, I can visualize it the way it was back in 1941."

"That was fifty years ago, Thad. Where did the time go? It seems like yesterday that I lived here. The day I met Moss was the day my mother rented out my room because we needed the money. I don't think I ever forgave her for that. Where are we staying tonight, Thad?"

"The Radisson." He wanted to say the hospital, but he didn't. Billie still had things to do.

"I'm ready now to go to the Navy Yard. It's not far. Not quite two miles. I walked that day with Tim Kelly and my friends. He was killed in the war. I can still see him clear as crystal."

"There's Loews Theatre," Billie said minutes later. "Moss took me to a movie there. I was supposed to go to a matinee with my friends the day I met him."

He didn't want to ask, but he did. "Do you ever regret . . . any of your life, Billie?"

"I wouldn't change a thing, Thad. I never came back. Why do you suppose that is? Fifty years is a very long time. I should have come back. I meant to. I wanted to, but I didn't. Now, now when it's too late, I . . . I guess this is where it began and where it has to end."

"I guess so," Thad mumbled heartbrokenly. "There's the USO building. Do you want to stop?"

"No. Seeing it is enough. I danced with you that first night. I remember that. I loved your New England twang. Moss kept calling you his Yankee friend. Moss loved you, Thad. You said I looked like an angel on top of a Christmas tree. I thought that was such a wonderful thing to say to someone you just met."

"And you said I reminded you of an Uncle Sam poster. I remember everything about you, Billie. I loved you the moment I met you, but you belonged to my best buddy."

"Well, here it is, the Navy Yard."

Thad bit down on his lower lip. He hated this kind of memory. Why was she doing this? So she could tell Moss when she saw him that she'd made this pilgrimage? The thought was so upsetting, Thad fought to get his breath. "You don't want to get out, do you?"

"No, darling. That first day there were so many ships here. Battleships, destroyers, camouflaged green and brown. Huge superstructures that seemed to reach for the sky. The chain-link fence was so awesome. Moss came up behind me and asked me how I liked it. He pointed out the aircraft carrier and told me about the *Enterprise*. Moss had summer-blue eyes. He absolutely mesmerized me that day. He took me home. Somehow he managed to borrow a 1938 Nash from someone. I felt so grown-up."

Thad choked up. "Anything else, Mrs. Kingsley?"

"No. I think I've seen enough. Thank you for bringing me, Thad. I'm sorry if this stroll down memory lane has upset you. I felt it was something I had to do."

"Hey, I'm the one who ended up with the girl."

"Thad, I love you so much. I think I loved you that night when I met you at the USO, and was too stupid to know it. Moss was so . . . he was bigger than life. He simply overwhelmed me. I did love him, though, for a very long time. How far is the hotel, Thad?"

"Not that far. Out by the airport. We can check into a hotel in town if you prefer. You're exhausted, aren't you? You're shivering."

"I am a little chilly," Billie whispered.

Sweat trickled down Thad's face. His shirt was soaked and clinging to his back. He rolled up the windows, praying he wouldn't pass out from the heat.

"How many puppies did Duchess have, Thad?"

"Eight, honey."

"Where's my green dress, the one I wore for you in Hong Kong?"

"At home in the closet. It's in a plastic bag," Thad lied.

"How could I forget something so important?" Billie murmured.

He knew exactly what she meant. He'd also seen it in the bottom of her bag, wrapped in tissue paper. She'd thought of everything. He wiped at the sweat and tears on his face.

"It's time to go, Thad. How far are we from New York City? I should know that, shouldn't I?"

"An hour and a half, two at the most." He knew exactly what that meant too. Sloan Kettering was in New York. He turned the car around, checked to get his bearings, and headed back the way they'd come.

It was dusk when Thad pulled up to the back of Sloan Kettering. He looked at the huge red letters that said EMERGENCY. He thought the color was the same as Maggie's Firecracker Red.

"We'll take over from here," an attendant said quietly. He looked at Billie, blinked, and said, "Park the car, sir." His voice was so kind, Thad cried.

"I won't be long, honey," Thad said, leaning over to kiss his wife. His tears mingled with hers. She tried to smile. The effort it cost her broke Thad's heart. A moment later she was gone from his sight.

He had to move the goddamn fucking car. He had to put it in reverse and back out and then put it in gear and park it. Climbing the Himalayas would have been easier.

The moment Thad had parked the car, at a crazy angle, he lost whatever sanity he had. Bellowing obscenities at the top of his lungs, he beat the wheel with his clenched fists until his hands were swollen and red.

An eternity later he found himself in a waiting room. All the necessary papers had been signed. He was wait-

ing now for word from Billie's doctor in Vermont. He
was also waiting for the oncologist who had treated Billie from the beginning to make an appearance. He
stared down at his swollen hands and the Styrofoam cup
of muddy-looking coffee he was holding.

He felt a thousand years old when he made his way
to the phone booth. He didn't have the energy to rummage in his pockets for the change he needed to make
the call. Somewhere in his wallet he had a phone card,
but he didn't have the energy to look for it either. He
pressed the button for the operator and placed a collect
call to Texas.

"Riley," was all he could say. He could see them all,
gathered in the great room, their eyes filled with tears,
dreading the moment the phone would ring. He wondered if the sound was different for this particular call.
How long would it take them to get here? Three hours
at most. He was a pilot, for God's sake, he should know
to the very minute how long it would take Cole to clear
a flight plan, get off the ground, get airborne and . . . he
should know, but he didn't. He couldn't think. He stared
at the muddy coffee. Billie made such wonderful coffee.
Ivy did too. The family was probably drinking it by the
gallon. "Riley."

"I'm here, Thad. We're all here. Well, Susan isn't
here, but the rest of us are. She left for England this
morning. Where are you?"

"New York. Sloan Kettering. I've been here a couple
of hours."

"We're on our way," Riley said quietly.

"Good. That's good, Riley. I'll wait for you. I'll be
right here. I mean I'll wait right here. Jesus, will you
hurry, Riley?"

"Hang up, Thad," Riley said in a strangled voice.

"You want me to hang up? Why is that, Riley? We need to talk. I . . . Billie packed the green dress. I didn't know it was in her bag until last night. She knew. That's why she packed the dress. I should have looked earlier. Do you think I should have looked earlier, Riley?"

"No, no, you did the right thing. Green is Grandmam's favorite color. I'm going to hang up now, Thad. You . . . you wait for us."

"I'll wait, Riley. Right here. I won't go away."

He waited.

Twice they let him see his wife for a total of ten minutes. He wanted to die when he saw the tubes and machines that monitored her progress. They said she was in a coma.

He questioned God and received no answer. He drank the muddy coffee.

The oversize clock in the waiting room read twelve-ten when the family walked into the waiting room.

"I can't bear to see her like this," Maggie said against Sawyer's shoulder.

"Mother of God," Sawyer whispered tearfully.

Sumi reached for Cole, who was leaning against Riley, his eyes filled with tears.

"Billie is hooked up to life support systems," Ivy whispered to Maggie. The break in her voice tore at Maggie's heart.

"Now, we have to do it now," Ivy said to Riley. "Billie said not one minute longer than necessary." Her voice was strong, firm, when she spoke.

"Can you do it, Ivy?"

"I can do it, Riley. I gave my word. Thad's down in the office."

"It's up to you, Cole, to see that things go forward for Cary. He's got to be ready. I'll do my job, you do yours."

The family was in the waiting room, each with a cup of the same cold, muddy coffee Thad had had earlier.

Riley spoke quietly to Thad, explaining about the tape.

"Don't do this, please, don't do this," Thad cried. "Don't take her from me. Riley, please, I'm begging you." He turned to Ivy, his eyes imploring her, pleading with her to change her mind. She shook her head, her eyes full of sorrow.

"If it's what Billie wants," Thad whispered, relenting. "It doesn't matter what we want. Not anymore."

"When?" Sawyer said.

"Now," Ivy said in a voice no one recognized, as she walked away. "I'll tell them."

"One at a time," the doctor said quietly.

The family looked at one another. Maggie stepped forward, her eyes swimming in tears. She walked over to the hospital bed. How gaunt, how emaciated she was. This wasn't her mother. Her mother was vibrant, always smiling, always warm and caring. Always loving. Her tears overflowed. She should have a pretty gown on, one of the Billie colors she loved so much. Maggie plucked at the cotton stocking cap on her mother's head, seeing the fine, thin baby hair that had grown back in wispy tufts. From her purse Maggie withdrew the Cleopatra Gold scarf wrapped in tissue paper. She looked down at the embroidered logo and the label she'd sewn herself: Made in the U.S.A. Her hands were steady when she raised her mother's head to wrap the scarf around it. She bunched the folds with care under her mother's chin. "You can't go to meet Aunt Amelia and Shad in that tacky stocking cap. You gotta go in style, Mam." She leaned over, the tears splashing on the scarf, to kiss her mother one last time. " 'Bye, Mam."

She ran from the room, straight into Ivy's arms. "I forgot to tell her about Susan. I wanted to explain. . . . When it's your turn, Ivy, will you tell her?"

"Yes, yes, I'll tell her."

"Do you think she'll come back for the funeral?" Maggie whimpered.

"No. Susan will never come back. I like your fella, Maggie."

"He's not my fella, Ivy. He's a wonderful friend, though. He insisted on coming with me. I'm glad he did. Everyone seems to like him. I know Mam would . . . would have liked him. This has been awful for you, hasn't it, Ivy?"

"Billie said she chose me because none of you would have been able to do it. I think she was wrong. Not that it matters."

"No, Ivy, she wasn't wrong. I know myself. I would have kept her hooked up to those damn machines forever. Sawyer too. Cole and Riley could have done it, maybe, but I doubt it. Thad never could have done it. How are we going to handle looking at Cary, knowing Mam's . . . oh, God, Ivy, how?"

"I don't know, Maggie. I have to go now, it's my turn."

The family sat together on the two ugly brown sofas that faced each other. All their eyes turned to follow Thad when he entered the room.

They waited.

Thad sat down on the chair next to Billie's bed. The tubes running into her nose and arms had been removed. He reached for her thin hand. He talked, his voice barely a whisper, telling her things she already knew, and then whispered things only the two of them knew. Once, he thought her eyelids fluttered. He talked faster, his voice more urgent. His voice cracked and then steadied. He thought he felt her thin hand squeeze his. "Nobody ever loved you the way I love you, my darling. Let go, Billie. They're all waiting for you: Amelia; Moss; your son, Riley; your mother; Shadaharu. They'll ... they'll take care of you until I get there. Let go, Billie," Thad said gently.

He knew the minute Billie slipped away. He took her in his arms and cradled her to his breast. "Rest, Billie," he whispered against her cheek. He laid her down gently and pulled the stark white sheet up to meet the folds of the scarf. How peaceful she looked.

"Shadaharu, Amelia, take care of her, you hear me?" Thad whispered. He watched as the flat line blipped to the top of the screen, did a crazy jig, then flat-lined again. "Thanks." He smiled wanly.

Outside, he nodded curtly to the doctors and nurses before he walked over to the family. "I left her in good hands." He told them about the blip and the jig. He was rewarded with smiles as tired as his own.

Billie Ames Coleman Kingsley's death was recorded at 5:55 A.M. At 6:45 A.M., Cary Assante was undergoing anesthesia while the family waited in the waiting room.

At noon Henry Tanaka ushered them all into a limousine waiting to take them to Kennedy Airport. There they boarded the ColeShad corporate jet that would transport them all back to Sunbridge. Billie's body was in the cargo hold.

Billie Kingsley was laid to rest next to Amelia Assante the following day.

On the walk down the hill, Cole inched close to Riley. "I smelled the cigar smoke, did you?" He sucked in his breath, waiting for his cousin's answer.

"Yeah, I did. I heard Aunt Maggie say she smelled Aunt Amelia's perfume. Guess they came to pay their respects," Riley said shakily.

"Wouldn't surprise me," Thad said airily. "Right now, I bet they're all lined up in a row watching us. If we believe that, I think we'll be okay." The others nodded.

"Stew for lunch?" Adam said to Ivy.

"Yep. Homemade bread too."

"I gotta get back home," Thad said. "I have a whole menagerie to take care of, and at least fifty letters I promised myself I'd write to different authors telling them how much pleasure they gave Billie."

"What a wonderful idea," Maggie said, squeezing Henry's arm.

"I miss the twins," Sawyer grumbled.

"My mother and father are bringing Moss home this evening." Ivy beamed. Riley grinned from ear to ear.

"Little Billie is getting a tooth." Cole laughed. "I can't wait to see it."

Sumi giggled. "Me too."

They were in the courtyard when the sun dimmed. When it crept from its cloud cover, it was brighter than ever.

"That's Mam telling us things are under control." Maggie smiled. "Either you believe or you don't."

The family, as one, chose to believe.

{{{{{{{{{ EPILOGUE }}}}}}}}}

In delicate, oversize script, the brass plate read: The Amelia Assante, Billie Kingsley Memorial.

Thad hefted the bottle of champagne in his hand. Cary did the same.

The gathering was small, family only.

Cary grinned as he stepped up to bat. "This one's for you, babe," he said, swinging wildly. The family clapped in approval.

Thad's swing was just as wild, connecting with the same cornerstone as Cary's.

"I have to sit down," Sawyer complained.

"Twins again," Adam said, his eyeballs bulging from their sockets.

Sumi sat down next to Sawyer. They compared their stomach sizes. Sumi was the winner. "Cole said it's going to be a boy this time. If it isn't a girl."

Ivy squeezed onto the bench. She patted her protruding stomach. "Riley says this one is going to be a girl. If it isn't a boy."

"I think it's wonderful!" Maggie chortled. "Oh, Henry, isn't it wonderful? Eight grandchildren!"

"I guess I have to get six more ponies and enlarge the swimming pool. But not till after I marry Maggie!"

Cole grinned. " 'Bout time."

"I get to be maid of honor!" Sawyer said sourly.

"Sumi and I are bridesmaids!" Ivy giggled. "Josie, Katy, and little Billie are the flower girls. Moss, the ring bearer."

"It's a deal," Henry said, his smile embracing the family.

"Well, I'm at loose ends now, how about you, Thad?" Cary grinned.

"Hey, my time is yours."

"Three months from today!" Henry said, getting into the spirit of things.

"To Maggie and Henry," Cary said, holding up an unopened bottle of champagne.

"To the best family a guy ever had," Thad and Cary said in unison.

"Hear! Hear!" the family chorused together.

ABOUT THE AUTHOR

FERN MICHAELS is the *New York Times* bestselling author of the sizzling quartet of contemporary novels *Texas Rich*, *Texas Heat*, *Texas Fury* and *Texas Sunrise*, as well as the steamy books in the Captive series: *Captive Passions*, *Captive Embraces*, *Captive Splendors*, *Captive Secrets*, and *Captive Innocence*. She is also the author of *Serendipity*, *Seasons of Her Life*, *To Have and To Hold*, the Kentucky trilogy and the Sisterhood series.

www.fernmichaels.com